this girl

Also by Colleen Hoover

Slammed
Point of Retreat
Hopeless

this girl

A novel

Colleen Hoover

ATRIA PAPERBACK

NEW YORK   LONDON   TORONTO   SYDNEY   NEW DELHI

ATRIA PAPERBACK
A Division of Simon & Schuster, Inc.
1230 Avenue of the Americas
New York, NY 10020

Copyright © 2013 by Colleen Hoover

A Very Long Poem by Marty Schoenleber III

First Atria Paperback edition August 2013

ATRIA PAPERBACK and colophon are trademarks of Simon & Schuster, Inc.

For information about special discounts for bulk purchases, please contact Simon & Schuster Special Sales at 1-866-506-1949 or business@simonandschuster.com.

The Simon & Schuster Speakers Bureau can bring authors to your live event. For more information or to book an event, contact the Simon & Schuster Speakers Bureau at 1-866-248-3049 or visit our website at www.simonspeakers.com.

Manufactured in China

10 9 8 7 6 5 4 3 2 1

Library of Congress Cataloging-in-Publication Data

Hoover, Colleen.
  This girl : a novel / by Colleen Hoover. — First ATRIA pbk ed.
    pages   cm
  1. Life change events—Fiction. I. Title.
  PS3608.O623T45 2013
  813'.6—dc23   2013014139

ISBN 978-1-4767-4653-1
ISBN 978-1-4767-4654-8 (ebook)

For my mother

this girl

1.

the honeymoon

IF I TOOK every romantic poem, every book, every song, and every movie I've ever read, heard, or seen and extracted the breathtaking moments, somehow bottling them up, they would pale in comparison to this moment.

This moment is incomparable.

She's lying on her side facing me, her elbow tucked under her head, her other hand stroking the back of mine that's lying between us on the bed. Her hair is spread out across the pillow, spilling down her shoulder and across her neck. She's staring at her fingers as they move in circles over my hand. I've known her almost two years now, and I've never seen her this content. She's no longer solely carrying the weight that's been her life for the last two years, and it shows. It's almost as if the moment we said "I do" yesterday, the hardships and heartaches we faced as individuals were meshed, making our pasts lighter and easier to carry. From this point on I'll be able to do that for her. Should there be any more burdens I'll be able to carry them *for* her. It's all I've ever wanted to do for this girl since the moment I first laid eyes on her.

She glances up at me and smiles, then laughs and buries her face in the pillow.

I lean over her and kiss her on the neck. "What's so funny?"

She lifts her face off the pillow—her cheeks a deeper shade of red. She shakes her head and laughs. "*Us*," she says. "It's only been twenty-four hours and I've already lost count."

I kiss her scarlet cheek and laugh. "I'm done with counting, Lake. I've had about all the countdowns I can handle for a lifetime." I wrap my arm around her waist and pull her on top of me. When she leans in to kiss me, her hair falls between us. I reach to the nightstand and grab her rubber band, then twist her hair into a knot behind her head and secure it. "There," I say, pulling her face back to mine. "Better."

She was adamant about having the robes, but we haven't once used them. Her ugly shirt has been on the floor since I threw it there last night. Needless to say, this has been the best twenty-four hours of my life.

She kisses down my jaw and traces a trail with her lips up to my ear. "You hungry?" she whispers.

"Not for food."

She pulls back and grins. "We've still got another twenty-four hours to go, you know. If you want to keep up with me you need to replenish your energy. Besides, we somehow missed lunch today." She rolls off me, reaches into the nightstand, and pulls out the room service menu.

"No burgers," I say.

She rolls her eyes and laughs. "You'll never get over that." She scrolls the menu and points at it with her finger, holding it up. "What about beef Wellington? I've always wanted to try that."

"Sounds good," I say, inching closer to her. She picks up the phone to dial room service. The whole time she's on the phone I kiss up and down her back, forcing her to stifle her laughs as she tries to maintain her composure while ordering. When she hangs up the phone, she slides underneath me and pulls the covers over us.

"You have twenty minutes," she whispers. "Think you can handle that?"

"I only need ten."

THE BEEF WELLINGTON did not disappoint. The only issue now is that we're too stuffed and too tired to move. We've turned the TV on for the first time since I walked her over the threshold, so I think it's safe to say we're due for at least a two-hour break.

Our legs are intertwined and her head is on my chest. I'm running my fingers through her hair with one hand and stroking her wrist with the other. Somehow trivial things like lying in bed watching TV have become euphoric when we're tangled together like this.

"Will?" She pulls herself up onto her elbow and looks at me. "Can I ask you something?" She runs her hand across my chest, then rests it on top of my heart.

"I do about twelve laps a day on the University track, plus one hundred sit-ups twice a day," I say. She arches an eyebrow, so I point to my stomach. "Weren't you asking about my abs?"

She laughs and playfully punches me. "No, I wasn't asking about your *abs*." She leans down and kisses me on the stomach. "They *are* nice, though."

I stroke her cheek and pull her gaze back to mine. "Ask me anything, babe."

She sighs and drops her elbow and lays her head back onto the pillow, staring up at the ceiling. "Do you ever feel guilty?" she says quietly. "For feeling this happy?"

I scoot closer to her and lay my arm across her stomach. "Lake. Don't ever feel guilty. This is exactly what they'd want for you."

She looks at me and forces a smile. "I know it's what they'd want for me. I just . . . I don't know. If I could take back everything that happened, I would do it in a heartbeat if it meant I could have them back. But doing that would mean I never would have met you. So sometimes I feel guilty because I . . ."

I press my fingers to her lips. "Shh," I say. "Don't think like that, Lake. Don't think about *what ifs*." I lean in and kiss her on the forehead. "But I do know what you mean if that helps. It's counterproductive thinking about it, though. It is what it is."

She takes her hand in mine and intertwines our fingers, then brings them to her mouth and kisses the back of my hand. "My dad would have loved you."

"My mom would have loved *you*," I say.

She smiles. "One more thing about the past, then I'll stop bringing it up." She looks at me with a slightly evil grin on her face. "I'm so glad that bitch Vaughn dumped you."

I laugh. "No doubt."

She smiles and releases her fingers from mine. She turns toward me on the bed and looks at me. I pull her hand to my mouth and kiss the inside of her palm.

"Do you think you would have married her?"

I laugh and roll my eyes. "Seriously, Lake? Do you really want to talk about this right now?"

She smiles sheepishly at me. "I'm just curious. We've never really talked about the past before. Now that I know you aren't going anywhere, I feel more comfortable talking about it. Besides, there are a lot of things I want to know about you," she says. "Like how it felt when she broke up with you like she did."

"That's an odd thing to want to hear about on your honey-moon."

She shrugs her shoulders. "I just want to know everything about you. I've already got your future, now I want to get to know your past. Besides," she grins. "We've got a couple of hours to kill before your energy is fully replenished. What else are we going to do?"

I'm too exhausted to move right now and as much as I can pretend I'm not keeping count, nine times in twenty-four hours must be some sort of record. I roll over onto my stomach and prop a pillow under my chin, and then begin to tell her my story.

the breakup

"GOODNIGHT, CAULDER." I flip off the light and hope he doesn't crawl out of bed again. It's our third night with it being just the two of us here. He was too scared to sleep by himself last night so I let him sleep with me. I'm hoping it doesn't become a habit, but I would completely understand if it did.

I still can't wrap my head around all that's happened in the last two weeks, much less the decisions I've made. I hope I'm doing the right thing. I know my parents want us to be together, I just don't think they approve of my dropping my scholarship to make it happen.

Why do I keep referring to them in the present tense?

This is really going to be an adjustment. I make my way into my bedroom and drop onto the bed. I'm too exhausted to even reach over and turn off the lamp. As soon as I close my eyes, there's a light tap on my bedroom door.

"Caulder, you'll be fine. Go back to sleep," I say, somehow dragging myself off the bed again to coax him back to his room. He has successfully slept alone for seven years; I know he's capable of doing it again.

"Will?" The door opens and Vaughn walks in. I had no idea she was coming over tonight, but I'm thankful she's here. She seems to know exactly when I need her the most. I walk to her and close the bedroom door, then wrap my arms around her.

"Hey," I say. "What are you doing here? I thought you were heading back to campus today."

She places her hands on my forearms and pushes back, giving me the most pitiful smile I've ever seen. She walks over to my bed and sits, avoiding eye contact the entire time. "We need to talk."

The look on her face sends a chill up the back of my neck. I've never seen her look so distraught before. I immediately sit on the bed beside her and bring her hand to my mouth and kiss it. "What's wrong? You okay?" I brush a loose strand of hair behind her ear just as the tears begin to fall. I wrap my arms around her and pull her to my chest. "Vaughn, what's wrong? Tell me."

She doesn't say anything. She continues to cry so I give her a moment. Sometimes girls just need to cry. When the tears finally begin to subside, she straightens back up and takes my hands, but still doesn't look me in the eyes.

"Will . . ." She pauses. The way she says my name, the tone of her voice . . . it sends panic straight to my heart. She looks up at me but can't hold her stare, so she turns away.

"Vaughn?" I say hesitantly, hoping I'm misreading her. I place my hand on her chin and pull her gaze back in my direction. The fear in my voice is clear when I speak. "What are you doing, Vaughn?"

She almost looks relieved that I seem to have caught on to her intentions. She shakes her head. "I'm sorry, Will. I'm so sorry. I just can't do this anymore."

Her words hit me like a ton of bricks. *This?* She can't do *this* anymore? When did we become a *this*? I don't respond. What the hell do I say to that?

She senses the shock in my demeanor, so she squeezes my hands and whispers it again. "I'm so sorry."

I pull away and stand up, turning away from her. I run my hands through my hair and take a deep breath. The anger building inside me is suddenly coupled by tears that I have no intention of letting her see.

"I just didn't expect any of this, Will. I'm too young to be a mom. I'm not ready for this kind of responsibility."

She's really doing this. She's really breaking up with me. Two weeks after my parents die and she's breaking my heart all over again? Who *does* that? She's not thinking straight. It's just shock . . . that's all. I turn around and face her, not caring that she can see how much this is affecting me.

"I didn't expect this either," I say. "It's okay, you're just scared." I sit back down on the bed beside her and pull her to me. "I'm not asking you to be his mom, Vaughn. I'm not asking you to be *anything* right now." I squeeze her tighter and press my lips against her forehead; an action that immediately causes her to start crying again. "Don't do this," I whisper into her hair. "Don't do this to me. Not right now."

She turns her head away from me. "If I don't do this now, I'll never be able to do it."

She stands up and tries to walk away, but I pull her back to me and wrap my arms around her waist, pressing my head against her stomach.

"Please."

She runs her hands over my hair and down my neck, then bends forward and kisses the top of my head. "I feel awful, Will," she whispers. *"Awful.* But I'm not about to live a life that I'm not ready for, just because I feel sorry for you."

I press my forehead against her shirt and close my eyes, soaking in her words.

She feels *sorry* for me?

I release my arms from around her and push against her

stomach. She drops her hands and takes a step back. I stand up and walk to the bedroom door, holding it open, indicating she needs to leave. "The last thing I want is your pity," I say, looking her in the eyes.

"Will, don't," she pleads. "Please don't be mad at me." She's looking up at me with tears in her eyes. When she cries, her eyes turn a glossy, deep shade of blue. I used to tell her they were the exact same color as the ocean. Looking into her eyes right now almost makes me *despise* the ocean.

I turn away from her and grip both sides of the door, pressing my head against the wood. I close my eyes and try to hold it in. It feels like the pressure, the stress, the emotions that have been building up for the last two weeks—it feels like I'm about to explode.

She gently places her hand on my shoulder in an attempt to console me. I shrug it off and turn around to face her again. "Two *weeks*, Vaughn!" I yell. I realize how loud I'm being, so I lower my voice and step closer to her. "They've been dead for *two weeks*! How could you possibly be thinking about *yourself* right now?"

She walks past me through the doorway, toward the living room. I follow her as she grabs her purse from the couch and walks to the front door. She opens the door and turns to face me before she leaves. "You'll thank me for this one day, Will. I know it doesn't seem like it right now, but someday you'll know I'm doing what's best for us."

She turns to leave and I yell after her, "What's best for *you*, Vaughn! You're doing what's best for *you*!"

As soon as the door closes behind her I break down. I rush back to my bedroom and slam the door, then turn around and punch it over and over, harder and harder. When I can't feel my hand anymore, I squeeze my eyes shut and press my forehead against the door. I've had so much to process these past two weeks—I don't know how to process this, too.

What the hell has happened to my *life*?

I eventually make my way back to the bed and sit with my elbows on my knees, head in my hands. My mom and dad are smiling at me from the confines of the glass frame on my nightstand, watching me unfold. Watching as the culmination of all that has happened these last two weeks slowly tears me apart.

Why weren't they better prepared for something like this? Why would they risk leaving me with all of this responsibility? Their ill-preparedness has cost me my scholarship, the love of my life, and now, quite possibly, my entire future. I snatch the picture up and place my thumbs over their photograph. With all my force, I squeeze until the glass cracks between my fingertips. Once it's successfully shattered—just like my life—I rare back and throw it as hard as I can against the wall in front of me. The frame breaks in two when it meets the wall and shards of glass sprinkle the carpet.

I'm reaching over to turn off my lamp when my bedroom door opens again.

"Just leave, Vaughn. *Please*."

I look up and see Caulder standing in the doorway, crying. He looks terrified. It's the same look I've seen so many times since the moment our parents died. It's the same look he had when I hugged him good-bye at the hospital and made him leave with my grandparents. It's the same look that rips my heart in two every time I see it.

It's a look that immediately brings me back down to earth.

I wipe my eyes and motion for him to come closer. When

he does, I wrap my arms around him and pull him onto my lap, then hug him while he quietly cries into my shirt. I rock him back and forth and stroke his hair. I kiss him on the forehead and pull him closer.

"Want to sleep with me again tonight, Buddy?"

2.

the honeymoon

"WOW," LAKE SAYS in disbelief. "What a selfish bitch."

"Yeah. Thank God for that," I say. I clasp my hands together behind my head and look up at the ceiling, mirroring Lake's position on the bed. "It's funny how history almost repeated itself."

"What do you mean?"

"Think about it. Vaughn broke up with me because she didn't want to be with me just because she felt sorry for me. *You* broke up with me because you thought I was with you because I felt sorry for *you*."

"I didn't break up with you," she says defensively.

I laugh and sit up on the bed. "The hell you didn't! Your exact words were, 'I don't care if it takes days, or weeks, or months.' That's a breakup."

"It was not. I was giving you time to think."

"Time I didn't need." I lie back down on my pillow and face her again. "It sure felt like a breakup."

"Well," she says, looking at me. "Sometimes two people need to fall apart to realize how much they need to fall back together."

I take her hand and rest it between us, then stroke the back of it with my thumb. "Let's not fall apart again," I whisper.

She looks me in the eyes. "Never."

There's vulnerability in the way she looks at me in silence. Her eyes scroll over my face and her mouth is curled up into a slight grin. She doesn't speak, but she doesn't have to. I know in these moments, when it's just her and me and nothing else, that she truly, soul-deep loves me.

"What was it like the first time you saw me?" she asks. "What was it about me that made you want to ask me out? And tell me everything, even the bad thoughts."

I laugh. "There weren't any bad thoughts. *Naughty* thoughts, maybe. But not bad."

She grins. "Well then tell me those, too."

the introduction

I HOLD THE phone to my ear with my shoulder and finish buttoning my shirt. "I promise, Grandma," I say into the phone. "I'm leaving straight from work on Friday. We'll be there by five but right now we're running late, I need to go. I'll call you tomorrow."

She says her good-byes and I hang up the phone. Caulder walks through the living room with his backpack slung across his shoulder and a green, plastic army helmet on his head. He's always trying to sneak random accessories to school. Last week when I dropped him off, he was out of the car before I even noticed he was wearing a holster.

I reach out and snatch the helmet off his head and toss it onto the couch. "Caulder, go get in the car. I've got to grab my stuff."

Caulder heads outside and I scramble to gather all the papers scattered across the bar. I was up past midnight grading. I've only been teaching eight weeks now, but I'm beginning to understand why there's a teacher shortage. I shove the stack of papers inside my binder, then shove it into my satchel and head outside.

"*Great*," I mutter as soon as I see the U-Haul backing up across the street. This is the third family to move into that house in less than a year. I'm not in the mood to help people move again, especially after only four hours of sleep. I hope they'll be finished unloading by the time I get home today, or I'll feel obligated to help. I turn around and lock the door behind me, then quickly head for the car. When I open the car door, Caulder isn't inside. I groan and throw my stuff in the seat. He always picks the worst times to play hide-and-seek; we're already ten minutes late.

I glance in the backseat, hoping he's hiding in the floorboard again, but I catch sight of him in the street. He's laughing and playing with another little boy who looks about his age. *This is a plus.* Maybe having a neighbor to play with will get him out of my hair more often.

I start to call his name when the U-Haul catches my eye again. The girl driving can't be any older than me, yet she's confidently backing up the U-Haul without any help. I lean against my car door and decide to watch her attempt to navigate that thing around those gnomes. This should be interesting.

I'm quickly proven wrong and she's parked in the driveway in no time flat. Rather than hop out to inspect her parking job, she kills the engine and rolls down her window, then props her leg up on the dash.

I don't know why these simple actions strike me as odd. *Intriguing*, even. She drums her fingers on the steering wheel, then reaches up and tugs at her hair, letting down her ponytail. Her hair spills down around her shoulders and she massages her scalp, shaking her hair out.

Holy hell.

Her gaze falls on the boys playing in the street between us, and I can't help but let my curiosity get the best of me. Is she his sister? His mom? She doesn't look old enough to have a child that age, but I'm also at a visual disadvantage being all the way across the street. And why is she just sitting in the U-Haul?

I realize I've been staring for several minutes when someone pulls up beside her in a Jeep.

"Please don't let it be a guy," I whisper aloud to myself, hoping it's not a boyfriend. Or worse, a *husband.*

Why would I even care? The last thing I need right now is a distraction. Especially someone who lives right across the street.

I breathe a surprising sigh of relief when the person who steps out of the Jeep isn't a man. She's an older woman, maybe her mother. The woman shuts her door and walks up to greet the landlord, who's standing in the entryway. Before I can talk myself out of it, I'm walking toward their house. I suddenly have the urge to help people move today, after all. I cross the street, unable to take my eyes off the girl in the U-Haul. She's watching Caulder and the other little boy play, and hasn't once glanced in my direction. I don't know what it is about her that's pulling me in. That look on her face . . . she looks sad. And for some reason, I don't like it.

I'm standing unnoticed on the passenger side of the U-Haul, staring at her through the window, practically in a trance. I'm not staring because of the fact that she's attractive, which she *is*. It's that look in her eyes. The *depth*. I want to know what she's thinking.

No, I *need* to know what she's thinking.

She diverts her attention out her window and says something to the boys, then opens the door to get out. I suddenly realize I'm about to look like an idiot just standing in her driveway, staring. I glance across the street at my house and contemplate how I can get back over there without her seeing me. Before I have a chance to make a move, Caulder and the other little boy run around the U-Haul and smash into me, laughing.

"She's a zombie!" Caulder yells after I grab hold of them by their shirts. The girl rounds the U-Haul and I can't help but laugh. She's got her head cocked to the side and she's walking stiff-legged after them.

"Get 'em!" I yell to her. They're trying to fight to get away so I strengthen my grip. I look back up at her and we lock eyes.

Wow. Those *eyes*. They're the most incredible shade of green

I've ever seen. I try to compare the color to something, but nothing comes to mind. It's so unique, it's like her eyes have just invented their own hue.

Studying her features, I conclude she can't be the boy's mom. She looks my age. At the least, maybe nineteen or twenty. I need to find out her name. If I know her name I can look up her Facebook page and at least see if she's single.

Christ. This is the last thing I need in my life right now. A *crush.*

I feel like she knows what I'm thinking, so I force myself to break our gaze. The boy takes my moment of distraction and uses it to his advantage. He breaks free and slices at me with an imaginary sword, so I look back up at the girl and mouth *"help."*

She yells *"brains"* again and lunges forward, pretending to bite Caulder on top of the head. She tickles them until they melt onto the concrete driveway, then she stands back up and laughs. Her cheeks flush when she meets my gaze again and she contorts her mouth into an uncomfortable grimace, like she's suddenly embarrassed. Her unease disappears just as fast as it appeared and is replaced by a smile that suddenly makes me want to know every single minute detail about her.

"Hey, I'm Will," I say, extending my hand out to her. "We live across the street." She places her hand in mine. It's soft and cold, and the moment I wrap my fingers around hers, the physical contact sends a shockwave straight through me. I don't remember the last time a girl has had this kind of immediate effect on me. It must be my lack of sleep last night.

"I'm Layken," she says, her uneasiness once again masking her smile. "I guess I live . . . *here.*" She glances at the house behind her, then back to me.

She doesn't look too pleased about the fact that she lives

"here." That same look she had while sitting in the U-Haul consumes her features again and her eyes suddenly grow sadder. Why does that look affect me so much?

"Well, welcome to Ypsilanti," I say, wanting desperately to make that look go away. She looks down and it occurs to me that I'm still awkwardly shaking her hand, so I quickly pull it away from hers and shove my hands in my jacket pockets. "Where are you guys moving here from?"

"Texas?" she says.

Why does she say it like a question? Did I just ask a stupid question? I did. I'm making stupid small talk.

"Texas, huh?" I say. She nods her head, but doesn't come back with a response. I suddenly feel like an intrusive neighbor. I don't know what else to say without making it even more awkward, so I figure my best move at this point is to retreat. I bend over and grab Caulder by the feet, throwing him over my shoulder, then tell her I've got to get him to school. "There's a cold front coming through tonight. You should try to get as much unloaded today as you can. It's supposed to last a few days, so if you guys need help unloading this afternoon, let me know. We'll be home around four."

She shrugs. "Sure, thanks."

Her words are laced with the slightest hint of a southern drawl. I didn't know how much I liked southern accents until now. I continue across the street and help Caulder into the car. While he's climbing inside, I glance back across the street. The little boy is stabbing her in the back and she lets out a fake cry and falls to her knees. Her playful interaction with him is just one more thing that intrigues me about her. After he jumps on her back, she glances up and catches me staring at her. I shut Caulder's door and walk to my side. Before I get in, I muster a smile and wave, then climb into the car with an overwhelming urge to punch myself.

AS SOON AS the bell for third period rings, I open the lid to my coffee and pour two extra packets of sugar in. I'm about to need it. There's something about some of the students in third period that rub me the wrong way. Especially Javier. That kid is such a jackass.

"Morning, Mr. Cooper," Eddie says, taking her seat. She's as bubbly as ever. I've never seen Eddie in a bad mood, come to think of it. I need to figure out her secret, since the coffee obviously isn't doing it for me today.

"Morning, Eddie."

She turns and kisses Gavin on the cheek, then settles into her desk. They've been dating since right after I graduated. They're probably the only two people that *don't* annoy the hell out of me in here. Well, them and maybe Nick. Nick seems okay.

After the students are all seated, I instruct them to get out their books. The entire time I'm giving my lecture on the elements of poetry, my mind keeps wandering to the new neighbor.

Layken.

I like that name.

AFTER SIX HOURS and only a few dozen thoughts of the new neighbor later, Caulder and I finally pull into the driveway. I shut my car door and open the back door to remove the box of papers. When I turn back around, Layken's little brother has appeared out of nowhere and he's standing right in front of me, staring silently. It seems as though he's waiting on an introduction. Several seconds pass without him moving a muscle or blinking. Are we in a standoff? I shift the box to my left arm and reach out my hand.

"I'm Will."

"Kel is name my," he says.

I stare at him blankly. *Was that even English?*

"I can talk backwards," he says, explaining the clutter of words that just came out of his mouth. "Like this. Backwards talk can I."

Interesting. Someone possibly weirder than Caulder? I didn't think it was possible.

"Kel . . . you meeting . . . nice . . . was . . . it well," I say, a little slower than when he does it. He grins, then runs across the street with Caulder. I glance at their house and see that the U-Haul is now parked in the street with the latch shut. I'm disappointed they've already unloaded it; I was actually looking forward to helping.

I spend the rest of the evening working overtime for free . . . another side effect of being a teacher. I decide after my shower to make a living room detour to glance across the street for about the tenth time, but I don't see her.

"Why do you keep looking out the window?" Caulder asks from behind me.

His voice startles me and I snatch the living room curtain shut. I didn't realize he was sitting on the couch. I walk over to him and pull on his hand, then shove him toward the hallway. "Go to bed," I say.

He spins around before he closes his bedroom door behind him. "You were looking out the window to see if you could see that girl, weren't you? Do you like Kel's sister?"

"Goodnight, Caulder," I say, ignoring his question.

He grins and closes the door to his room. Before I head to my own bedroom, I walk to the window one more time. When I open the curtain, someone is standing in the window across the street with the curtains partially open. They suddenly snatch shut and I can't help but smile, wondering if she's just as curious about me as I am about her.

"IT'S COLD, IT'S cold, it's cold, it's cold, it's cold," Caulder says, jogging in place while I unlock the car doors. I crank the engine and turn the heat up, then head back inside to get the rest of my things while Caulder waits in the car. When I open the door to head back outside, I stop in my tracks when I see Layken standing in her entryway. She bends down and gathers a handful of snow to inspect it, then quickly drops it. She stands up and steps outside, closing the door behind her. I shake my head, knowing exactly what's about to happen. It's snowing and she isn't even wearing a jacket over her pajama bottoms and shirt. I don't know what she's doing, but she won't last long out here. She's not in Texas anymore. She begins to make her way to the driveway when my gaze falls on her feet.

Is she wearing house shoes? Seriously? Before I can even yell a warning, she's flat on her back.

Southerners. They just don't *get* it.

She doesn't move at first. She lies still in the driveway, staring up at the sky. A rush of panic overcomes me, thinking she may be hurt, but then she begins to pull herself up. As much as I don't want to come off like a bumbling idiot again, I head across the street to make sure she doesn't need my help.

The look on her face when she pulls one of the gnomes out

from beneath her makes me laugh. It's almost like she's blaming the poor guy for her fall. She pulls her arm back to throw him when I stop her.

"That's not a good idea!" I yell, making my way up her driveway. She tilts her head up and looks at me with a death grip on the gnome. "Are you okay?" I ask, still laughing. I can't help but laugh, she looks so pissed!

Her cheeks redden and she glances away. "I'll feel a lot better after I bust this damn thing."

I take the gnome out of her hands when I reach her. "You don't want to do that, gnomes are good luck." I place the freshly injured gnome back in his spot before she destroys him completely.

"Yeah," she says, inspecting her shoulder. "Real good luck."

I immediately feel guilty when I see the blood on her shirt. "Oh, my god, I'm so sorry. I wouldn't have laughed if I knew you were hurt." I assist her up and get a better look at the amount of blood coming from her injury. "You need to get a bandage on that."

She looks back to her house and shakes her head. "I wouldn't have any clue where to find one at this point."

I glance at our house, knowing I have a full supply of bandages in the first-aid kit. I'm hesitant to offer them, though, since I'm already running late for work as it is.

I'm looking at my house, struggling with my indecision, when all five of my senses are suddenly flooded. The slightest smell of vanilla that permeates the air around me . . . the sound of her accent when she speaks . . . the way her close proximity wakes up something inside me that's long been dormant. *Holy hell.* I'm in trouble.

Work can wait.

"You'll have to walk with me. There are some in our kitchen." I take my jacket off and wrap it around her shoulders, then help her across the street. I'm sure she can walk on her own, but for some reason I don't want to let go of her arm. I like helping her. I like the way she feels leaning against me. It seems . . . *right*.

Once we're inside my house, she follows me through my living room as I head to the kitchen to find a bandage. I pull the first-aid kit out of the cabinet and remove a Band-Aid. When I glance back at her, she's looking at the pictures on our wall. The pictures of my mom and dad.

Please don't ask me about them. *Please*.

This is not a conversation I want to have right now. I quickly say something to deflect her attention away from the pictures. "It needs to be cleaned before you put the bandage on it." I roll up my sleeves and turn on the faucet, then wet the napkin. I catch myself taking my time when I know I should be in a hurry. For whatever reason, I just want to drag this time out with her. I don't know why I feel like my desire to know her better has suddenly turned into a *need* to know her better. I turn back around and she darts her eyes away from me when I look at her. I don't really understand her sudden embarrassed look, but it's cute as hell.

"It's fine," she says, reaching for the napkin. "I can get it."

I hand her the napkin and reach for the bandage. It's awkwardly quiet as I fidget with the wrapper. For some reason, her presence makes the house seem eerily empty and quiet. I never notice the silence when I'm alone, but the lack of conversation occurring right now is uncomfortably obvious. I think of something to say to fill the void.

"So, what were you doing outside in your pajamas at seven o'clock in the morning? Are you guys still unloading?"

She shakes her head and tosses the napkin into the trash can. "Coffee," she says, matter-of-fact.

"Oh. I guess you aren't a morning person." I'm secretly hoping that's the case. She seems sort of pissy. I'd like to blame it on her lack of caffeine, rather than on indifference toward me. I take a step closer to place the bandage on her shoulder. I briefly pause before touching her and take in a silent breath, preparing for the rush I seem to get every time I touch her. I put the bandage in place and pat it softly, securing the edges with pressure from my fingertips. Her skin prickles and she wraps her arms around herself, rubbing her forearms up and down.

I gave her chills. This is good.

"There," I say, giving it one last, unnecessary pat. "Good as new."

She clears her throat. "Thanks," she says, standing up. "And I *am* a morning person, *after* I get my coffee."

Coffee. She needs coffee. *I've* got coffee.

I quickly walk over to the counter where the remaining brew is still warm in the pot. I grab a cup out of the cabinet and fill it up for her, then set it on the counter in front of her. "You want cream or sugar?"

She shakes her head and smiles at me. "Black is fine. Thanks," she says. I lean across the bar and watch as she brings the coffee to her lips. She blows softly into the cup before pressing her lips to the brim and sips, never taking her eyes off mine.

I've never wanted to be a coffee cup so bad in my life.

Why do I have to go to *work*? I could stay here and watch her drink coffee all day. She's looking right at me, probably wondering what the hell I'm doing staring at her so much. I straighten back up and look down at my watch. "I need to go, my brother is waiting in the car and I've got to get to work. I'll walk you back. You can keep the cup."

She looks down at the cup and reads it. I didn't even notice I gave her my father's cup. She runs her fingers across the letters and smiles. "I'll be okay," she says as she stands to leave. "I think I've got the whole walking erect thing down now." She walks through the living room and is opening the front door when I spot my jacket lying across the back of my couch. I reach over and grab it.

"Layken, take this. It's cold out there." She tries to refuse but I shake my head and make her take my jacket. If she takes the jacket, she'll eventually have to bring it back, which is exactly what I'm hoping will happen. She smiles and pulls my jacket over her shoulders, then she heads across the street.

When I reach my car I turn to watch her make her way back to her house. I like the way she looks, engulfed by my jacket over her pajamas. Who knew pajamas and Darth Vader house shoes could be so damn sexy?

"Layken!" I yell. She turns around just before she reaches her front door. "May the force be with you!" I laugh and hop in the car before she can say anything.

"What took you so long? I'm f-f-f-freezing," Caulder says.

"Sorry," I say. "Layken hurt herself." I back the car up and pull out onto the street.

"What happened?" he asks.

"She tried to walk on the frozen concrete in Darth Vader house shoes. She busted it and cut herself."

Caulder giggles. "She has Darth Vader house shoes?"

I smile at him. "I know, right?"

3.

the honeymoon

"I LOVE HEARING this," she says, grinning next to me on the bed. "So you thought I was cute, huh?"

"No, I didn't think you were cute. I thought you were absolutely beautiful," I correct her. I brush the hair out of her face and she leans into my hand and kisses my palm. "What did you think about me?" I ask.

She smiles. "I tried *not* to. I was attracted to you, but I had so much going on and we'd been in Michigan all of five minutes when we met. Circumstances just kept bringing us back together, though. Every minute I was around you, I just fell harder and harder in crush with you."

"In *crush*?" I laugh.

She grins. "I was *so* in crush with you, Will. Especially after you helped me with the bandage. And after our trip to the grocery store."

"I'd have to say we were *both* in crush after that trip."

crush

I ATTEMPT TO go over my lesson plans for the next week but I can't even concentrate. I try to pinpoint exactly what it is about her that completely consumes my mind, but I can't figure it out. After the incident with the bandage this morning, she was all that went through my head at work. I wish she would just do or say something stupid so this hold she has on me would break. It's weird.

I've never been so consumed by the thought of someone in my entire life. This is the last thing I need right now, but somehow it's the only thing I *want*.

Caulder bursts through the front door, laughing. He slips his shoes off and walks across the living room shaking his head. "That Darth Vader girl asked me how to get to the grocery store," he says. "I don't know how to drive. She's so dumb." He walks to the refrigerator and opens it.

I stand up. "Is she still out there?" I rush to the front door and see her Jeep parked in the street. I quickly pull my shoes on, then run outside before she drives away. I'm relieved when I see her fiddling with the GPS. It'll buy me some time.

I wonder if she would care if I went with her to the store.

Of course she would. That would be awkward.

"That's not a good idea," I say as I approach her car, then lean through the window.

She glances up at me, a smile hiding in the corners of her mouth. "What's not a good idea?" She begins to insert the GPS into its holder.

Shit. What's not a good idea? I didn't think this through.

I say the first lie that pops into my head. "There's quite a bit of construction going on right now. That thing will get you lost."

Just as she opens her mouth to respond, a car pulls up beside her and a woman leans over the seat and speaks to Layken through the window. This has got to be her mother; they're practically identical. Same accent and everything.

I continue to lean through the window, using her distraction as an opportunity to study her. Her hair is a deep brown, but not as dark as her mother's. Her nail polish is chipped. It looks like she picks at it, which somehow makes me like her even more. Vaughn never left the house unless her hair and nails were perfect.

Kel jumps out of the other car and invites Caulder, who is now standing next to me, over. Caulder asks if he can go, so I grab the handle of Layken's car door without worrying about possible consequences. *The hell with it.*

"Sure," I reply to him. "I'll be back in a little while, Caulder. I'm riding with Layken to the store." I open her door and climb inside without second-guessing my actions. She shoots me a look, but it seems more like an amused one than an irritated one. I take this as another good sign. "I don't give very good verbal directions. Mind if I go with you?"

She laughs and puts the car into gear, glancing at the seat belt I've already fastened. "I guess not."

The closest grocery store is only two blocks away. That's not nearly enough time with her, so I decide to take her the long way. It'll give me more of a chance to get to know her.

"So, Caulder is your little brother's name?" she asks as she turns off our street. I like how she says Caulder's name, drawing out the *Caul* a little bit more than necessary.

"One and only. My parents tried to have another baby for years. They eventually had Caulder, when names like Will weren't that cool anymore."

"I like your name," she says. She smiles at me and her cheeks redden, then she quickly darts her eyes back to the road.

Her embarrassment makes me laugh. Was that a compliment? Did she just flirt with me? *God, I hope so.*

I instruct her to turn left. She flips the blinker on, then brings her hand up to her hair, running her fingers through it all the way down to the ends; an action that causes me to gulp. When both of her hands are on the steering wheel again, I reach over and brush her hair behind her shoulders, then pull back the collar of her shirt.

I look at her bandage, wanting her to believe this is the reason I'm touching her, when really I just needed to feel her hair. When my fingers graze her skin, she flinches. It seems like I make her nervous. I'm hoping it's in a good way. "You're going to need a new bandage soon," I say. I pull her shirt back up and pat it.

"Remind me to grab some at the store," she says. She grips the steering wheel tightly and keeps her eyes focused on the road. She's probably not used to driving in the snow. I should have offered to drive.

The next few moments are quiet. I catch myself staring at her, deep in thought. I wonder how old she is. She doesn't look older than me, but it would suck if she is. Sometimes girls don't date guys who are younger than them. I should really find out more about her.

"So, Layken," I say casually. I place my hand on her headrest and glance behind me at all the boxes still in the back of the Jeep. "Tell me about yourself."

She cocks an eyebrow at me, then turns her attention back to the road. "Um, no. That's so cliché."

Her unexpected response makes me laugh under my breath. She's *feisty*. I like that, but it still doesn't answer any of my questions. I glance to her CD player and lean forward. "Fine. I'll figure you out myself," I say as I hit eject. "You know, you can tell a lot about a person by their taste in music." I pull the CD out of the player and hold my breath as I prepare to read it. *Please don't let her be into Nickelback.* I would have to jump out of the car. When I read the handwritten label, I laugh. *"Layken's shit?* Is shit descriptive here, or possessive?"

She snatches the CD out of my hands and inserts it back into the player. "I don't like Kel touching my shit, okay?"

And that's when it happens . . . the most beautiful sound in the world. Sure, the *song* is beautiful. *All* Avett Brothers songs are beautiful. But the sound I'm hearing is the sound of commonality. The sound of similarity. The sound of my favorite band that I've been listening to nonstop for two years . . . coming from her speakers.

What are the chances?

She immediately leans forward and turns down the volume. I unconsciously grab her hand to stop her. "Turn it back up, I know this."

She smirks at me like there isn't a shred of truth to what I just said. "Oh, yeah? What's it called?" she challenges.

"It's the Avett Brothers," I say. She arches her eyebrow and looks at me inquisitively as I explain the song. The fact that she apparently loves this band as much as I do stimulates a feeling deep in the pit of my stomach that I haven't felt in years.

Good lord, I've got butterflies.

She glances down at my hand still clasped on top of hers.

I pull my hand back and run it down my pants, hoping it didn't make her uncomfortable. I'm almost positive she's blushing again, though. That's a good sign. That's a *really* good sign.

The entire rest of the way to the grocery store, she tells me all about her family. She mostly talks about the recent death of her father and her birthday gift from him. She continues talking about her father and everything her family has been through this year. It explains that distant look she gets in her eyes sometimes. I can't help but feel somewhat connected with her, knowing she can relate on some level with what I've been through the last few years. I tense up at the thought of having to tell her about my parents right now.

I can feel the conversation on her end coming to a close, so I point her in the actual direction of the grocery store, hoping it will deflect the parental subject before it becomes my turn to share. When we pull into the parking lot, I'm both relieved *and* anxious. Relieved that I didn't have to explain my situation with Caulder to her, but anxious at the thought that I know the conversation is inevitable. I just don't want to scare her off yet.

"Wow," she says. "Is that the quickest way to the store? That drive took twenty minutes."

I swing the door open and wink at her. "No, actually it's not." I step out of the car, impressed with myself. It's been so long since I've been into a girl, I wasn't sure if I still had any game. She's got to realize I'm flirting with her. I like her. She seems to like me, but she's not as forward as I am, so I'm not sure. I'm definitely not one to play games, so I decide to just go with it. I grab her hand, tell her to run, and pull her faster toward the entrance. I do this partly because we're getting soaked, but mostly because I just wanted an excuse to grab her hand again.

When we get inside she's soaking wet and laughing. It's the first time I've really heard her laugh. I like her laugh.

There's a strand of wet hair stuck to her cheek, so I reach up and wipe it away. As soon as my fingers touch her skin, her eyes lock with mine and she stops laughing.

Damn, those eyes. I continue to stare at her, unable to look away. She's beautiful. *So* damn *beautiful.*

She breaks our stare and clears her throat. Her reaction is somewhat guarded, like I may have made her feel uncomfortable. She hands me the grocery list and grabs a cart. "Does it always snow in September?" she asks.

We just had a seriously intense, slightly awkward moment . . . and she's asking me about the *weather*? I laugh.

"No, it won't last more than a few days, maybe a week. Most of the time the snow doesn't start until late October. You're lucky."

She looks at me. *"Lucky?"*

"Yeah. It's a pretty rare cold front. You got here right in time."

"Huh. I assumed most of y'all would hate the snow. Doesn't it snow here most of the year?"

It's official. The southern accent is my absolute favorite now. *"Y'all?"* I laugh.

"What?" she says defensively.

I shake my head and smile. "Nothing. I've just never heard anyone say 'y'all' in real life before. It's cute. So southern belle."

She laughs at my comment. "Oh, I'm sorry. From now on I'll do like you Yankees and waste my breath by saying 'all you guys.'"

"Don't," I say, nudging her shoulder. "I like your accent, it's perfect."

She blushes again, but doesn't look away. I look down at the grocery list and pretend to read it, but I can't help but notice she's staring at me. *Intensely* staring. Almost like she's trying to figure me out or something.

She eventually turns her head and I steer her in the direction of the foods on her list.

"Lucky Charms?" I say, eyeing her as she grabs three huge boxes of the cereal. "Is that Kel's favorite?"

She grins at me. "No, actually it's mine."

"I'm more of a Rice Krispies fan myself." I take the boxes of cereal from her and throw them into the cart.

"Rice Krispies are boring," she says.

"The hell they are! Rice Krispies make Rice Krispies treats. What can your cereal do?"

"Lucky Charms have shooting star marshmallows in them. You get to make a wish every time you eat one."

"Oh, yeah?" I laugh. "And what are you gonna wish for? You've got three boxes, that's a lot of wishes."

She folds her arms across the handle of the cart and leans forward while she pushes it. She gets that same distant look in her eyes again. "I'd wish I could be back in Texas," she says quietly.

The sadness in her answer makes me want to hug her. I don't know what it is about Michigan that makes her feel this way. I just have an overwhelming need to console her. "What do you miss so much about Texas?"

"Everything," she says. "The lack of snow, the lack of concrete, the lack of people, the lack of . . ." She pauses. "The lack of unfamiliarity."

"Boyfriend?"

I say it without even thinking. It's like I lose my filter when I'm around her. She shoots me a look of confusion, almost as though she doesn't want to misinterpret my question.

"You miss your boyfriend?" I clarify.

She smiles at me, erasing the troubled look that consumed her features just seconds ago. "No boyfriend," she says.

I smile back at her. *Nice.*

I DECIDE TO take her the quick route home. I would have taken her the long way again, just to spend more time with her, but I figure she actually needs to know how to get to the grocery store in the event I can't invite myself along on the next trip. When we pull into her driveway I hop out and make my way around to the rear of the Jeep. When she pops the hood, I pull it open and watch as she gathers her things together. It surprises me how disappointed I am that we're about to part ways again. I hate the thought that once these groceries are unloaded, I'm going to have to go back home. I want to spend more time with her.

When she meets me at the back of the Jeep, she smiles and places her hand over her heart. "Why! I never would have been able to find the store without your help. Thank you so much for your hospitality, kind sir."

Oh.

My.

God.

That is the hottest damn southern impression I've ever heard. And that *smile.* And that nervous *laughter.* Everything she does pierces my heart. It's all I can do to stop myself from grabbing her face and kissing the hell out of her right here and now. Looking down at her, watching her laugh . . . God, I've never wanted to kiss a girl so bad in my entire life.

"*What?*" she says nervously. She can obviously see the internal struggle behind my expression.

Don't do it, Will.

I ignore my better judgment and step forward. Her eyes remain locked on mine as I cup her chin with my free hand. My bold move causes a small gasp to pass between her lips, but she makes no move to pull away. Her skin is soft beneath my fingertips. I bet her lips are even softer.

My eyes scroll over her features, admiring their beautiful simplicity. She doesn't shy away. In fact, she looks a little bit hopeful, like she would welcome my lips on hers.

Don't kiss her. Don't do it. You'll screw this up, Will.

I attempt to silence the voice in my head, but it ultimately wins out. It's way too soon. *And* it's broad daylight. Her mother's home, for Christ's sake! *What am I thinking?*

I slide my hand around to the back of her neck, then kiss her on her forehead, instead. I take a step back and reluctantly drop my hand. I have to remind myself to breathe. Being this close to her is suffocating, but in the best way.

"You're so cute," I say, attempting to make light of the moment. I grab a few sacks out of the back of the Jeep and quickly head to the front door before she comes to her senses and punches me. I can't believe I just kissed her on the forehead! I've only known the girl for two days!

I set the bags down and head back to the Jeep just as her mother makes her way outside.

I feel nothing but relieved over my decision not to kiss her when I realize we would have been interrupted. A humiliating thought.

I reach my hand out to introduce myself. "You must be Layken and Kel's mom. I'm Will Cooper. We live across the street."

She smiles a welcoming smile. She seems nice; not intimidating at all. It's amazing how much Layken looks like her.

"Julia Cohen," she says. "You're Caulder's older brother?"

"Yes, Ma'am. Older by twelve years."

She stares at me for a moment. "So that makes you . . . twenty-one?"

I'm not sure, because it happens so fast, but I could swear she glances behind me and winks at Layken. She returns her focus back in my direction and smiles again.

"Well, I'm glad Kel and Lake were able to make friends so fast," she says.

"Me, too."

Julia releases my hand and turns toward the house, grabbing the sacks in the entryway.

Lake. She calls her *Lake.* I might like that even more than Layken. I reach in and grab the last two sacks out of the back of her Jeep.

"Lake, huh? I like that." I hand her the sacks and shut the back. "*So*, Lake," I say, leaning against her car. I fold my arms across my chest and take a deep breath. This part is always the hardest. The "asking out" part.

"Caulder and I are going to Detroit on Friday. We'll be gone until late Sunday, family stuff," I say. "I was wondering if you had any plans for tomorrow night, before I go?"

She grins at me, then makes a face like she's trying to stifle the grin. I wish she wouldn't do that. Her smile is breathtaking.

"Are you really going to make me admit that I have absolutely no life here?" she says.

That wasn't a no, so I take it as a yes. "Great. It's a date then. I'll pick you up at seven-thirty." I immediately turn and head back to my house before she can object. I didn't officially *ask* her out. In fact, it was more like I just *told* her. But . . . she sure didn't object. That's a good sign. That's a *really* good sign.

4.

the honeymoon

LAKE PULLS HERSELF up onto her elbows and rests her chin in her hands.

"You're really enjoying this," I say.

She's smiling. "I don't think I ever told you, but when you kissed me on the forehead that day it was the best kiss I'd ever had. Up to that point, anyway," she says, falling back against her pillow.

I lean in and replicate the forehead kiss, except this time I don't stop there. I plant tiny pecks all the way down to the tip of her nose, then I pull back. "Mine, too," I say, looking into the eyes that I get to wake up to every morning for the rest of my life. At the risk of sounding cheesy, I've got to be the luckiest man in the world.

"Now I want to know all about our date." She puts her hands behind her head and relaxes, waiting for me to spill it.

I lie back on my pillow and think back to that day. The day that I fell for my wife.

the first date

I HAVEN'T BEEN in this good a mood in over two years. I also haven't been this nervous about a girl in over two years. In fact, I haven't even been on a single *date* in two years. A double load, a full-time job and a child really interfere with the whole dating scene.

There's half an hour left before Caulder and I have to leave for school, so I decide to do a little cleaning since I'll be with Lake tonight. I'm hesitant to take her to Club N9NE on our first date. Slam poetry is so much a part of me; I don't know how I'd take it if she didn't connect with it. Or worse, if she hated it.

Vaughn was never into it. She loved Club N9NE on any other night, just not slam night. Thursdays were usually the one night of the week we didn't spend together. I realize this moment is the first moment Vaughn has even crossed my mind since the moment I met Lake.

"Caulder, go make sure your room's clean. Maya's watching you tonight," I say as he emerges from the hallway. He rolls his eyes and backtracks into the bedroom. "Clean *is* it," he mumbles.

He's been talking backward since he met Kel a few days ago. I just ignore him half the time. It's too much to keep up with.

I take the overloaded bag out of the kitchen trash can and begin to head outside with it, but I pause at the hallway. Something about the picture of Caulder and me with our dad in the front yard catches my eye. I take a step forward and get a closer look. I've never noticed it before this moment, probably because it actually has meaning now . . . but in the background right over my father's shoulder, you can see the gnome with the red hat from across the street. The same gnome Lake fell on and broke. The gnome is staring right at the camera with a smirk on his face, almost like he's posing.

I glance at the rest of the pictures on the wall, recalling the moments they were all captured. I used to hate looking at these pictures. I hated the way it would make me feel and how much I would miss them when I looked into their eyes. It doesn't hurt as much anymore. Now when I look at them, I mostly recall the good memories.

Seeing their pictures brings the realization back to the forefront of my mind that Lake has no idea of the responsibilities I have in my life. I need to tell her tonight. It's better to get it out now, that way if she can't handle it, I won't be too far gone. It'll be a lot easier to be rejected by her tonight, before whatever it is I'm feeling toward her becomes even more intense.

I close the lid to the trash can and pull it to the curb. When I near the end of the driveway, I see the back door to Lake's Jeep is open. She's leaning all the way across the seat, searching for something. When she finds what she's looking for, she climbs out of the backseat with a coffeepot in her hands. She's still wearing pajamas and her hair is piled on top of her head in a knot.

"That's not a good idea," I say, heading across the street toward her.

She jumps when she hears my voice, then spins around to face me and grins. "What am I doing wrong *this* time?" She shuts the door to the Jeep and walks toward me.

I point to the coffeepot. "If you drink too much coffee this early in the morning, you'll crash after lunch. Then you'll be too exhausted to go out with your hot date tonight."

She laughs. Her smile is fleeting, though. She looks down at her pajamas, then runs her hands over her hair with a slight look of panic in her eyes. She's silently freaking out about the way she looks, so I ease her mind. "You look great," I assure her. "Bed hair looks really good on you."

She smiles, then leans against her car. "I know," she says confidently, looking down at her pajamas. "This is what I'm wearing on our date tonight. You like?"

I slowly look her up and down, then shake my head no. "Not really," I say, eyeing her boots. "I'd prefer it if you wore the house shoes."

She laughs. "I'll do that, then. Seven-thirty, right?"

I nod and smile back at her. We're about four feet apart, but the way her eyes are piercing into mine makes it feel like she's just inches away. She smiles at me with an unfamiliar sparkle in her eye. Unlike the last two days, she actually looks *happy* right now.

We continue to stare at each other, neither of us speaking . . . or walking away. There's a long silence, but it's not awkward. The way she's watching me this time seems more confident. More at ease.

More hopeful.

I decide to give in before the awkwardness *does* set in, so I take a couple of steps backward toward my house. "I have to get to work," I say. "I'll see you tonight."

She lifts her hand and waves good-bye before turning toward her house. Not just a normal back-and-forth wave, either. It's a fingers up and down *flirty* wave.

Wow. Who knew a simple wave could be so damn *hot*?

"Lake?"

She glances back at me, the corners of her mouth hinting at a smile. "Yeah?"

I point to her pajamas. "I really am digging this unwashed,

straight-out-of-bed look. Just make sure you brush your teeth before I pick you up tonight, because I'm gonna kiss you." I wink at her and turn back toward my house before she can respond.

"GOOD MORNING, MRS. Alex," I say, careful not to sound too friendly. I have to watch every word that comes out of my mouth around this woman; she takes it all the wrong way. The *inappropriate* way. I walk past her desk and into the mailroom, then grab the contents from inside my box. When I exit the mailroom, she's already rushing toward me.

"Did you get my note? I left you a sticky note." She glances down at the stack of papers I'm holding.

I look at the papers in my hands and shrug. "I don't know yet. I just checked my box five seconds ago."

Mrs. Alex isn't known for her kind demeanor, except toward *me.* Her obvious favoritism has become a running joke among the staff. A joke that I'm the butt of. She's at least twenty years older than me, not to mention married. However, it doesn't stop her from blatantly displaying her affection, which is why I only come to the mailroom once a week now.

"Well, I wrote you a message. Your faculty advisor called and needs to schedule a meeting with you." She grabs the stack of papers out of my hands and spreads them out on her desk, looking for the note she wrote. "He said he needs to do your quarterly observation. I swear I put it right on top."

I reach forward and swipe the contents of my mailbox back into a stack. "Thank you. I'm running late, so I'll look through it later. I'll let you know if I don't find it."

She smiles and waves good-bye as I back away from her.

Oh, shit. It was a *flirty* wave. I've got to quit coming in here.

"Have a great day," I say, turning to leave as fast as I can. I'm relieved when the door to the administration office closes behind me. I'm really going to have to get someone else to check my mail from now on.

"You really need to stop leading her on like that," Gavin says. I look up and he's staring through the window at Mrs. Alex.

I roll my eyes. "Nothing has changed since high school, Gavin. It's even worse now that I'm a teacher here."

Gavin looks past me and waves at Mrs. Alex through the window and smiles at her. "She's still watching you. Maybe you should flex your muscles; give her a little gun show. Or at least give her a nice view while you're walking away."

The thought of Mrs. Alex admiring me from behind makes me a little too uncomfortable, so I change the subject and walk toward my first-period class. "You and Eddie going to Club N9NE tonight? I haven't seen you guys there in a couple of weeks."

"Maybe. Why? You doing one?"

I shake my head. "No, not tonight," I say. "We'll be there a little after eight, though. My sitter isn't available until seven-thirty, so we'll probably miss the sac."

He stops in his tracks just as we reach my classroom door. "*We?* Who's we? Does Will Cooper have a *date?*" He cocks an eyebrow and waits for my reply.

I don't usually hang out with students outside of work, but Gavin and Eddie have been showing up at Club N9NE every now and then for a few months. We sometimes sit together, so I've gotten to know them pretty well. When you're teaching at twenty-one years old, it's sort of difficult to completely cut off socialization with people who are practically your age.

"So? Who is she?" he says. "Who's the elusive girl that may just be the end to Will Cooper's dry spell?"

I open the door to the classroom and lose the smile as I switch on teacher-mode. "Get to class, Gavin."

He laughs and salutes me, then heads down the hallway.

"THANKS AGAIN, MAYA," I say as I head through the living room. "There's cash on the table. I ordered pizza about fifteen minutes ago." I grab my keys and shove my wallet into my pocket. "He's been talking backward a lot so just ignore it. He'll talk frontward if he has anything important to say."

"You paying me double?" she says, falling onto the sofa with the remote in hand. "I didn't agree to watch that other kid."

"He's just the neighbor," I say. "He'll go home soon. If he doesn't, then yeah . . . I guess I'll pay you extra." I've turned to head outside when the boys make their way back into the house. Kel stops in the doorway and puts his hands on his hips, looking up at me.

"Are you my sister's boyfriend?"

I'm thrown off by his directness. "Um, no. Just her friend."

"She told my mom you were taking her on a date. I thought only boyfriends took girls on dates."

"Well," I pause. "Sometimes boys take girls on dates to see if they *want* them to be their girlfriend."

I notice Caulder standing beside me, taking in the conversation as if he's just as curious. I wasn't prepared to have to explain the rules of dating right now.

"So it's like a test?" Caulder asks. "To see if you want Layken to be your girlfriend?"

I shrug and nod. "Yeah, I guess you could say that."

Kel laughs. "You aren't gonna like her. She burps a lot. And she's bossy. And she never lets me drink coffee, so she probably won't let you have any either. And she has really bad taste in music and sings way too loud and leaves her bras all over the house. It's gross."

I laugh. "Thanks for the warning. You think it's too late to back out now?"

Kel shakes his head, missing my sarcasm completely. "No, she's already dressed so you have to take her now."

I sigh, pretending to be annoyed. "Well, it's just a few hours. Hopefully she won't burp a lot and boss me around and steal my coffee and sing to her really bad music and leave her bra in my car."

Or hopefully she *will*.

Kel walks past me into the house. "Good luck," he says, his voice full of pity. I laugh and shut the door behind me. I'm half-way to my car when Lake opens her front door and walks to the driveway.

"You ready?" I yell to her.

"Yes," she yells back.

I wait for her to walk to my car, but she doesn't. She *looks* ready. Why is she just standing there?

"Well, come on then!" I yell.

She still doesn't move. She folds her arms across her chest and stands still. I throw my hand up in defeat and laugh. "What are you doing?"

"You said you would pick me up at seven-thirty," she yells. "I'm waiting for you to pick me up."

I grin and get in the car, then back up into her driveway. When I get out and open her door, I notice she's not wearing the house shoes. I was sort of hoping she was serious this morning. It's not quite dark yet, which is unfortunate since I can't stop staring at her. She curled her hair and put on just a touch of makeup. She's wearing jeans and a purple shirt that brings out the hue of her eyes, making them even harder to look away from. She looks . . . *perfect*.

Once we're both in the car, I reach behind me and grab the bag out of the backseat. "We don't have time to eat, so I made us grilled cheese." I hand her the sandwich and a drink. I'm hoping she's not too upset that we aren't going out to eat. We just don't have time. I almost went to her house earlier to let her know we weren't, in case she didn't eat, but I decided to throw something together at the last minute instead. I sort of wanted to see how she'd react to not being taken on a typical date. Maybe it's a little mean, but she's smiling, so she doesn't seem to mind.

"Wow. This is a first." She puts her sandwich on her knee and twists open her soda. "And where exactly are we going in such a hurry? It's obviously not a restaurant."

I take a bite of my sandwich and pull out of her driveway. "It's a surprise. I know a lot more about you than you know about me, so tonight I want to show you what *I'm* all about."

She grins at me. "Well, I'm intrigued," she says before she takes a bite of her sandwich.

I'm relieved she doesn't press me further about where we're going. It would be sort of hard to explain that I'm taking her to a club on a Thursday night to watch a bunch of people recite poetry. It doesn't sound near as appealing as it actually *is*. I'd rather let her experience it for the first time in person without having preconceived notions.

When we finish our sandwiches, she puts the trash in the

backseat and shifts in her seat so that she's facing me. She casually rests her head against the headrest. "What are your parents like?"

I glance out my window, not wanting her to see the reluctance in my expression. It's the exact thing I was hoping she wouldn't ask about until the drive home, at least. I'd hate for this to be the first thing we talk about. It would put a somber mood on the whole night. I take a deep breath and exhale, hoping I'm not appearing as uncomfortable on the outside as I'm feeling on the inside.

How the hell can I redirect this conversation?

I decide to play the game Caulder and I play sometimes on the drive to our grandparents. I hope she won't think it's too cheesy, but it'll pass the time and may even help me get to know her better.

"I'm not big on small talk, Lake. We can figure all that out later. Let's make this drive interesting." I adjust myself in the seat and prepare to explain the rules to her. When I turn to look at her, she's staring at me with a repulsed look on her face.

What the hell did I say? I replay my last sentence in my head and realize how it sounded. I laugh when it dawns on me that she completely misconstrued what I just said. "Lake, no! I just meant let's talk about something besides what we're *expected* to talk about."

She expels a breath and laughs. "Good," she says.

"I know a game we can play. It's called, *'would you rather.'* Have you played it before?"

She shakes her head. "No, but I would *rather* you go first."

I feel like if I use some of the ones Caulder and I have used it would be cheating, so I take a few seconds to think of a new one. "Okay," I say when I come up with one. I clear my throat. "Okay, would you rather spend the *rest* of your life with *no* arms; or would you rather spend the rest of your life with arms you couldn't *control*?"

I remember when Caulder and I tried to get Vaughn to play this game on our way to Detroit once; she rolled her eyes and told us to grow up. I watch Lake, hoping for a different reaction, and she just stares at me straight-faced like she's actually contemplating an answer.

"Well," she says. "I guess I would rather spend the rest of my life with arms I couldn't control?"

"What? Seriously?" I laugh, glancing over at her. "But you wouldn't be controlling them! They could be flailing around and you'd be constantly punching yourself in the face! Or worse, you might grab a knife and stab yourself!"

She laughs. *Damn, I love that laugh.*

"I didn't realize there were right and wrong answers," she says.

"You suck at this. Your turn."

She smiles at me, then furrows her brows, facing forward and leaning back into her seat. "Okay, let me think."

"You have to have one ready!"

"Jeez, Will! I heard of this game for the first time thirty barely seconds ago. Give me a second to think of one."

I reach over and squeeze her hand. "I'm teasing."

It wasn't my intention to keep holding on to her hand, but for some reason it feels right, so I don't let go. It's so natural, like we didn't even contemplate the move. I'm still staring at our interlocked fingers when she continues with her turn, unfazed. I like how much she seems to be enjoying the game. I like how she seemed to prefer the grilled cheese sandwiches to a restaurant. I like girls who don't mind the simple things every now and then. I like that we're holding hands.

We play a few more rounds and the bizarre things she comes up with could give Caulder a run for his money. The half-hour drive to the club seems like it takes five minutes. I decide to ask one final question as we're pulling into the parking lot. I pull into a space and reach over with my left hand to kill the engine so that I don't have to move my right hand from hers. I glance over at her. "Last one," I say. "Would you rather be back in Texas right now? Or here?"

She looks down at our fingers that are interlocked and grazes her thumb across my hand. Her reaction to my question isn't a negative one. In fact, it almost seems just the opposite when her lips crack a smile and she looks back up. Just when she opens her mouth to respond, her attention is pulled to the sign on the building behind me and her smile fades.

"Uh, Will?" she says hesitantly. "I don't dance." She pulls her hand from mine and begins to open her door, so I do the same.

"Uh, neither do *I*."

We both exit the vehicle, but the fact that she didn't answer that last question isn't lost on me. I grab her hand when we meet at the front of the car and I lead her inside. When we walk through the doors I make a quick scan of the room. I know a lot of the regulars here and I'm hoping I can at least find a secluded area in order for us to have some privacy. I spot an empty booth in the back of the room and lead her in that direction. I want her to be able to get the full experience without the constant interruption of conversation from other people.

"It's quieter back here," I say. She's looking around with curiosity in her eyes. She asks about the younger audience when she notices pretty quickly that this isn't a regular club-going crowd. She's observant.

"Well, tonight it's not a club," I say. She scoots into the booth first and I slide in right next to her. "It's slam night. Every Thursday they shut the club down and people come here to compete in the slam."

She breaks her gaze from the table of kids and looks at me, the curiosity still present in her eyes. "And what's a slam?"

I pause for a second and smile at her. "It's poetry," I say. "It's what I'm all about." I wait for the laughter, but it doesn't come. She looks directly at me, almost like she didn't understand what I said.

I start to repeat myself when she interrupts. "Poetry, huh?" She continues to smile at me, but in a very endearing way. Almost like she's impressed. "Do people write their own or do they get it from other authors?"

I lean back in my seat and look at the stage. "People get up there and pour their hearts out just using their words and the movement of their bodies. It's amazing. You aren't going to hear any Dickinson or Frost here."

When I look at her again, she actually looks intrigued. Poetry has always been such a huge part of my life; I was worried she wouldn't understand it. Not only does she understand it, she seems *excited* about it.

I explain the rules to her regarding the competition. She asks a lot of questions, which puts me even more at ease. When I've explained everything to her, I decide to grab us drinks before the sac comes on stage.

"You want something to drink?"

"Sure," she says. "I'll take some chocolate milk."

I expect her to laugh at her joke, but she doesn't.

"Chocolate milk? Really?"

"With ice," she says, matter-of-fact.

"Okay. One chocolate milk on the rocks coming right up."

I exit the booth and walk over to the bar to order our drinks, then turn around and lean against the bar and watch her. This feeling I get when I'm with her . . . I've missed it. I've missed that feeling of *feeling*. Somehow, she's the first person in the last two years of my life who gives me any sense of hope about the future.

I realize as I'm watching her that I've made a huge mistake. I've been comparing what her reaction to things might be based on what Vaughn's reactions were in the past. It's not fair to Lake to assume she would be turned off by the simplicity of the date or by the game we played on the drive here. It's not fair to Lake that I assume she wouldn't like poetry simply because Vaughn didn't. It's also unfair of me to assume she would push me away if she knew that I was Caulder's guardian.

This girl isn't anything *like* Vaughn.

This girl isn't anything like *any* girl I've known. This girl is . . .

"She's cute." Gavin's voice jerks me out of my thoughts. I look over at him and he's leaning against the bar next to me, watching me watch Lake. "What's her name?" He turns around and orders two drinks from the waitress.

"Layken," I say. "And yeah. She *is* cute."

"How long have you guys been dating?" he asks, turning back to me.

I look down at my watch. "Going on forty-five minutes."

He laughs. "*Shit.* The way you were looking at her I would have guessed a hell of a lot longer. Where'd you meet her?"

The bartender hands me my change and the receipt for our drinks. I glance down at the receipt and laugh. It actually says, "*Chocolate milk—rocks.*" I fold the receipt and put it in my wallet.

"Actually," I say as I turn back to Gavin, "she's my new neighbor. Just moved in three days ago."

He shakes his head and looks back in her direction. "You better hope it works out. That could get really awkward, you know."

I nod. "Yeah, I guess so. But I have a good feeling about her."

Before he walks away he points to the front of the room. "Eddie and I are over there. I'll try to keep her occupied so you two can have your privacy. If she sees you here with a girl, she'll be over there in a second trying to be her new best friend."

I laugh, because he's right. "Thanks." I grab our drinks and head back to the booth, relieved that I won't have to deal with introductions tonight. I don't know if I'm ready for that.

5.

the honeymoon

LAKE SITS UP on the bed and glares at me. "What the *hell*, Will? Gavin knew? He's known this whole time?"

I laugh. "Hey, you and Eddie weren't the only ones keeping secrets."

She shakes her head in disbelief. "Does Eddie know he knew?"

"I don't think so. Unlike some people, Gavin can keep a secret."

She narrows her eyes and rolls back onto her pillow, dumbfounded. "I can't believe he knew," she says. "What did he say when I showed up in your poetry class?"

"Well, I could go ahead and tell you all about that day, but that would mean I would be skipping over our first kiss. You don't want to hear about the rest of our date?"

She grins. "You know I do."

falling

"WHAT'S THE SAC?" she says when I return with the drinks.

"Sacrifice. It's what they use to prepare the judges." I slide back into the booth but make it a point to scoot in closer this time. "Someone performs something that isn't part of the competition so the judges can calibrate their scoring."

"So they can call on anyone? What if they had called on me?" she asks. She looks terrified at the thought.

"Well, I guess you should have had something ready," I tease.

She laughs, then puts one of her elbows on the table, turning toward me. She runs her hand through her hair, sending a slight scent of vanilla in my direction. She watches me for a moment, her smile spreading up to her eyes. I love this peaceful look about her right now.

We're sitting so close together I can feel the heat of her body against mine, parts of us touching. Our thighs, her hip against mine, our hands just inches apart. Her gaze shifts from my eyes down to my lips and, for the first time tonight, I feel the *first kiss* pressure. There's something about her lips that makes me want to kiss them when she's in such close proximity. I remind myself that even though I'm just "Will" tonight, I've got at least one student who is more than likely intermittently spying on us.

The quiet moment between us causes her to blush and she looks back to the stage, almost as if she could sense that I was struggling with the desire to kiss her. I reach over and take her hand in mine and bring it under the table, placing it on my leg. I look down at it as I slowly stroke her fingers. I stroke up her wrist and want so bad to keep trailing up her arm, straight to her lips . . . but I don't. I circle back down to her fingertips, wishing more than anything that we weren't in public right now. I don't know what it is about her that completely enthralls me. I also don't know what it is with her that gets me to spout things I would normally be more reserved about.

"Lake?" I continue tracing up and over her hand with my fingertips. "I don't know what it is about you . . . but I like you." I interlock her fingers with mine and turn my attention toward the stage so she doesn't think I expect a response from her. I smile when I see her grab for her glass and quickly down her chocolate milk. She definitely feels it, too.

When the sac walks up to the stage, Lake's whole demeanor changes. It's almost as if she forgets I'm even here. She leans forward attentively when the woman begins her piece and she doesn't remove her attention from the performer the entire time. I'm so drawn to the emotion in Lake's expression that I can't take my eyes off *her*. As I watch her, I attempt to decipher the reason behind the intense connection I feel with her. It's not like we've spent that much time together. Hell, I hardly even know her. I still don't even know what her major is, what her middle name is, much less her birthday. Deep down, I know none of it matters. The only thing that matters right now is this moment, and this moment is definitely my sweet for the day.

As soon as the sac is finished with her poem, Lake pulls her hand from mine and wipes tears from her eyes. I put my arm around her and pull her to me. She accepts my embrace and rests her head against my shoulder.

"Well?" I ask. I rest my chin on top of her head and stroke her hair, taking in another wave of vanilla. I'm beginning to love the smell of vanilla almost as much as southern accents.

"That was unbelievable," she whispers.

Unbelievable. That was the exact word I used to describe it to my father the first time I saw it.

I fight the urge to lift her chin and pull her lips to mine, knowing I should wait until we're in private. The need is so overwhelming, though; my heart is at war with my conscience. I lean forward and press my lips against her forehead and close my eyes. It'll have to do for now.

We sit in the same embrace as several more poets perform. She laughs, she cries, she sighs, she aches, and she *feels* every single piece performed. By the time the final poet for round one comes onto the stage, it's obvious that it's too late. I was hoping to put everything out in the open between us before things became more serious. Little did I know it would happen this fast. I'm too far gone. There's no way I can stop myself from falling for this girl now.

I keep my attention on the stage, but I can't help but watch Lake out of the corner of my eye as she watches the performer prepare at the microphone. She's holding her breath again as he steps up to the microphone.

"This poem is called *A Very Long Poem*," the performer says. Lake laughs and leans forward in her seat.

This poem is very long
So long, in fact, that your attention span
May be stretched to its very limits
But that's okay
It's what's so special about poetry
See, poetry takes time
We live in a time

Call it our culture or society
It doesn't matter to me 'cause neither one rhymes
A time where most people don't want to listen
Our throats wait like matchsticks waiting to catch fire
Waiting until we can speak
No patience to listen
But this poem is long
It's so long, in fact, that during the time of this poem
You could've done any number of other wonderful
things
You could've called your father
Call your father
You could be writing a postcard right now
Write a postcard
When was the last time you wrote a postcard?
You could be outside
You're probably not too far away from a sunrise or a
sunset
Watch the sun rise
Maybe you could've written your own poem
A better poem
You could have played a tune or sung a song
You could have met your neighbor
And memorized their name
Memorize the name of your neighbor
You could've drawn a picture (or, at least, colored one in)
You could've started a book
Or finished a prayer
You could've talked to God
Pray

When was the last time you prayed?

Really prayed?

This is a long poem

So long, in fact, that you've already spent a minute

with it

When was the last time you hugged a friend for a

minute?

Or told them that you love them?

Tell your friends you love them

. . . no, I mean it,

tell them

Say, *I love you*

Say, *you make life worth living*

Because that is what friends do

Of all of the wonderful things that you could've done

During this very, very long poem

You could have connected

Maybe you are connecting

Maybe we're connecting

See, I believe that the only things that really matter

In the grand scheme of life are

God and people

And if people are made in the image of God

Then when you spend your time with people

It's never wasted

And in this very long poem

I'm trying to let a poem do what a poem does:

Make things simpler

We don't need poems to make things more

complicated

We have each other for that
We need poems to remind ourselves of the things that
really matter
To take time
A long time
To be alive for the sake of someone else for a single
moment
Or for many moments
'Cause we need each other
To hold the hands of a broken person
All you have to do is meet a person
Shake their hand
Look in their eyes
They are you
We are all broken together
But these shattered pieces of our existence don't have
to be a mess
We just have to care enough to hold our tongues
sometimes
To sit and listen to a very long poem
A story of a life
The joy of a friend and the grief of a friend
To hold and be held
And be quiet
So, *pray*
Write a postcard
Call your parents and forgive them and then thank
them
Turn off the TV
Create art as best as you can

Share as much as possible, especially money
Tell someone about a very long poem you once heard
And how afterward it brought you to them

SHE WIPES ANOTHER tear from her eye when the performer steps away from the microphone. She begins clapping with the rest of the crowd, completely engrossed in the atmosphere. When she finally relaxes against me again, I take her hand in mine. We've been here close to two hours now and I'm sure she's tired, based on the week she's had. Besides, I never stay for all of the performances, since I have work on Fridays.

I begin to stand up to lead her out of the booth when the emcee makes one last appeal for performers. She turns to me and I can see her thoughts written clearly across her face.

"Will, you can't bring me here and not perform. Please do one? Please, please, please?"

I had no intention of doing a poem tonight. *At all.* But oh, my God—that look in her eyes. She's really going to make me do this, I can already tell. There's no *way* I can say no to those eyes. I lean my head against the back of the booth and laugh. "You're killing me, Lake. Like I said, I don't really have anything new."

"Do something old then," she suggests. "Or do all these people make you *nervous?*"

She has no idea how often I perform and how natural it feels to me now. It's almost as natural as breathing. I haven't been nervous about taking the stage since the first time I took it five years ago.

Until now, anyway.

I lean in closer and look her directly in the eyes. "Not all of them. Just *one* of them."

Our faces are so incredibly close right now; it would be so easy to do it. Just a couple more inches and I could taste her. Her smile fades and she bites her bottom lip as her gaze slowly drops to my mouth again. I can tell by the look in her eyes that she wants me to kiss her just as much. The unfamiliar nerves that have occupied my stomach have now multiplied and I'm quickly losing my self-control. As soon as I start to lean in, she clasps her hands under her chin and resumes her plea.

"Don't make me beg."

For a moment, I had forgotten she even asked me to perform. I pull back and laugh. "You already *are*."

She doesn't pull her hands away from her chin and she's looking up at me with the most adorable expression. An expression I already know I'll never be able to say no to. "All right, all right," I say, easily giving in. "But I'm warning you, you asked."

I pull my wallet out of my pocket and take the money out, holding it up in the air. "I'm in!"

When the emcee recognizes me, I slide out of the booth and begin making my way to the stage. I'm not prepared for this at all. Why did I not think she would ask me to perform? I should have written something new. I'll just do my "go-to" piece about teaching. It's easy enough. Besides, I don't even think I've discussed my profession with her; this might be a fun way to do it.

I reach the stage and adjust the microphone, then look out over the audience. When we lock eyes, she perches her elbows on the table and rests her chin in her hands. She waves her flirty wave at me as her smile spreads across her face. The way she looks at me sends a pang of guilt straight to my heart. She's looking at me right now in the same way that I've been looking at her.

With *hope*.

It hits me with that look that I shouldn't waste this opportunity on a poem about my profession. This is my opportunity to put it all out there . . . to use my performance as a way to let her know who I really am. If her feelings for me are half what mine already are for her, then she deserves to know what she may be getting herself into.

"What's the name of your piece tonight, Will?"

Without breaking our gaze, I look straight into her eyes from up on the stage and reply, *"Death."*

The emcee exits the stage and I take a deep breath, preparing to say the words that will either make or break the possibility of a future with her.

Death. The only thing inevitable in life.
People don't like to *talk* about death because
it makes them *sad.*
They don't want to ***imagine*** how life will go on
without them,
all the people they love will briefly grieve
but continue to *breathe.*
They don't ***want*** to imagine how life will go on
without ***them,***
Their children will still ***grow***
Get married
Get *old* . . .
They don't want to ***imagine*** how life will ***continue*** to
go on without them,
Their material things will be *sold*
Their medical files stamped *"closed"*
Their name becoming a *memory* to everyone they *know.*

They don't *want* to *imagine* how life will go on
without them, so *instead* of accepting it *head-on*, they
avoid the subject *altogether*,
hoping and *praying* it will *somehow* . . .
pass them by.
Forget about them,
moving on to the *next* one in line.
No, they didn't *want* to imagine how life would
continue to go on . . .
without them.
But death
didn't
forget.
Instead they were met *head-on* by death,
disguised as an *eighteen-wheeler*
behind a cloud of *fog*.
No.
Death didn't *forget* about *them*.
If they *only* had been *prepared*, *accepted* the
inevitable, laid out their *plans*, understood that it
wasn't just *their* lives at hand.
I may have legally been considered an adult at the age
of nineteen, but I still felt very much
all
of just nineteen.
Unprepared
and *overwhelmed*
to suddenly have the *entire life* of a seven-year-old
In my *realm*.
Death. The only thing inevitable in *life*.

• • •

I TAKE A step away from the microphone, feeling even more nervous than when I began. I completely laid it all out there. My whole life, condensed into a one-minute poem.

When I step off the stage and make my way to our booth, she's wiping tears from her eyes with the back of her hand. I'm not sure what she's thinking, so I walk slowly in order to give her a moment to absorb my words.

When I slide into the booth she looks sad, so I smile at her and try to break the tension. "I warned you," I say as I reach for my drink. She doesn't respond, so I'm not sure what to say at this point. I become uncomfortable, thinking maybe this wasn't the best way to go about telling her my life story. I guess I sort of put *her* on the spot, too. I certainly hope she doesn't feel like she has to tell me how sorry she feels for me. I hate pity more than anything.

Just when I start to regret my choice in performance, she reaches out and takes my free hand in hers. She touches me so gently—it's like she's telling me what she's thinking without even speaking. I set my drink down on the table and turn to face her. When I look into her eyes, it's not pity I see at all.

She's still looking at me with hope in her eyes.

This girl just became privy to everything I've been scared to tell her about my life. The death of my parents, the anger I held toward them, the amount of responsibility I now face, the fact that I'm all Caulder has—and she's still looking at me with hope in her tear-filled eyes. I reach to her face and wipe away a tear, then lightly trace my thumb across the wet trail running down her cheek. She places her hand on top of mine and slowly pulls it to her mouth. She presses her lips into the center of my palm without breaking her gaze from mine, causing my heart to catch in my throat. She just somehow managed to convey every single thought and emotion she's feeling through this one simple gesture.

I suddenly don't care where we are or who might be watching us. I have to kiss her. I *have* to.

I take her face in my hands and lean in closer, ignoring the part of my conscience that is screaming for me to wait. She closes her eyes, inviting me in. I hesitate, but as soon as I feel her breath fall on my lips, I can't hold back. I close the gap between us, lightly pressing my lips against her bottom lip. It's even softer than it looks. Somehow the background noise has completely faded and all I can hear is the sound of my own heartbeat, pulsating throughout my entire body. I slowly move my lips up to her top lip, but as soon as I feel her mouth begin to part, I reluctantly pull away. As much as I want to kiss her with everything I've got, I'm also vaguely aware that we're in public, and I've got at least two students here tonight. I decide to save the better kiss for later, because if we do this right now, I know I won't want to stop.

"Patience," I whisper, mustering up all the self-control I've got. I stroke her cheek with my thumb and she smiles at me in understanding. Still holding her face in my hands, I close my eyes again and press my lips against her cheek. She sucks in a breath as I release my hold and slide my hands down her arms, trying to remember how to breathe again. I'm unable to pull away from her, so I press my forehead against hers and open my eyes. It's in this moment that I know she's feeling exactly what I'm feeling. I can see it in her eyes.

"Wow," she exhales.

"Yeah," I agree. "Wow."

We hold each other's stare for a few more seconds. When

the emcee begins announcing the qualifiers for round two I'm quickly brought back to reality. There is no way I can sit here any longer without pulling her onto my lap and kissing the hell out of her. I figure in order to avoid that, my best course of action would be to just leave.

"Let's go," I whisper. I take her hand as we slide out of the booth and I lead her to the exit.

"You don't want to stay?" she says after we walk outside.

"Lake, you've been moving and unpacking for days. You need sleep."

As soon as I say it, she yawns. "Sleep does sound good."

When we reach the car I open the door for her, but before she gets in, I wrap my arms around her and pull her to me. It's a movement that occurs so quickly, I don't even think about it beforehand. Why does she have that effect on me? It's like my conscience just goes out the window when she's around.

As much as I know I should let go before it gets awkward, I can't. She returns my embrace, then rests her head against my chest and sighs. We stand there, neither one of us speaking or moving, for several minutes. There's not a single kiss passed between us, not a single graze of my hand across her skin, not a single word spoken . . . yet somehow, this is the most intimate moment I've ever shared with anyone.

Ever.

I don't want to let go, but as soon as I look up and see Gavin and Eddie exiting the club, I pull back and motion for her to climb inside. Now is not the time for an Eddie introduction.

As we're pulling out of the parking lot, she leans her head against the window and sighs.

"Will? Thank you for this."

I reach over and take her hand in mine. All I really want to do is thank *her*, but I don't respond. I had a lot of hope for tonight, but she far exceeded my expectations. She's exhausted and I can tell she's about to fall asleep. She closes her eyes and I drive home in silence and let her sleep.

When I pull into her driveway, I expect her to wake up, but she doesn't. I kill the engine and reach over to shake her awake, but the peacefulness in her features stops me. I watch her sleep as I try to sift through everything I've been feeling. How can I possibly feel like I care about someone after only knowing her a matter of days?

I loved Vaughn, but I can honestly say we never connected this way. On this sort of emotional level, anyway. I can't remember feeling this way since . . . well, *ever*. It's new. It's scary. It's exciting. It's nerve-racking. It's calming. It's every single emotion I've ever felt balled up into an intense urge to grab hold of her and never let go.

I lean closer and press my lips against her forehead while she sleeps. "Thank *you* for this," I whisper.

When I walk around and open her door, she wakes up. I help her out of the car and we're both silent as we make our way to her front door, hand in hand. Before she goes inside, I pull her to me again. She rests her head against my chest and we resume the same embrace from outside the club. I can't help but wonder if this feels as natural to her as it does to me.

"Just think," she says. "You'll be gone three whole days. That's the same length of time I've known you."

I laugh and squeeze her tighter. "This will be the longest three days of my life." We continue to hold on to each other, neither of us wanting to let go, because maybe we realize it really *will* be the longest three days of our lives.

I notice her glance toward the window like she's worried someone's watching us. As much as I want to give in to the insatiable need I have to kiss her, I give her a quick peck on the cheek, instead. I release her and slowly walk back to my car. When her fingers release from mine, her arm drops to her side and she smiles a smile that quickly causes me to regret not kissing her better. As soon as I'm in my car, I conclude that there is absolutely no way I'll be able to sleep tonight if I don't rectify this.

I roll down my window. "Lake, I've got a pretty long drive home. How about one for the road?"

She laughs, then walks to my car and leans through the window. I slip my hand behind her head and pull her to me. The second our lips meet, I'm a goner. She parts her lips and at first, our kiss is slow and sweet. She reaches through the window and runs her hands through my hair, pulling me closer, and it completely drives me insane. My mouth becomes more urgent against hers and for a brief second, I contemplate canceling my trip this weekend. Now that I've finally tasted her, I know I won't be able to go three days without it. Her lips are everything I've been imagining they would be. The door between us is pure torture. I want to pull her through the window and onto my lap.

We continue kissing until we get to a point where we both realize that either she needs to climb inside the car with me, or we need to come to a halt. We simultaneously slow down and eventually stop, but neither of us pulls away.

"Damn," I whisper against her lips. "It gets better every time."

She smiles and nods in agreement. "I'll see you in three days. You be careful driving home tonight." She presses her lips against mine again, then pulls away.

I regretfully back out of the driveway and into my own, wishing more than anything I wasn't about to leave town for the next three days. When I exit my car she's making her way back up her driveway. I watch as she gathers her hair and pulls it up in a knot, securing it with a band while she nears her front door. Her hair looks good like that. It looked great down, too. As I'm admiring the view, it dawns on me that I never even complimented her on how great she looked tonight.

"Lake!" I yell. She turns around and I jog back across the street to her. "I forgot to tell you something." I wrap my arms around her and whisper into her hair, "You look beautiful to-night." I kiss her on top of the head, then release her and walk back to my house. When I reach my door, I turn around and she's still standing in the same spot watching me. I smile at her and go inside, then immediately head straight for the window. When I pull back the curtain, I see her twirl back toward her house and practically skip inside.

"What are you looking at?" Maya says.

Her voice startles me and I snatch the curtain shut and turn around. "Nothing." I take my jacket off and step on the heel of my shoe to ease my foot out of it. "Thanks, Maya. You want to watch him again next Thursday?"

She stands up and heads to the front door. "Don't I always?" she says. "But I'm not watching that weird one again." She shuts the door behind her and I throw myself on the couch and sigh. This was by far the best date I've ever been on, and I have a feeling they're only going to get better.

6.

the honeymoon

LAKE SMILES, THINKING back on how blissfully happy we both were after that date. "I had never had a night like that in my life," she says. "Everything about it was perfect, from beginning to end. Even the grilled cheese."

"Everything except the fact that I failed to mention my occupation."

She frowns. "Well, yeah. That part sucked."

I laugh. "Sucked is an understatement for how I felt in that hallway," I say. "But, we got through it. As tough as it was, look at us now."

"Wait," she says, pressing her fingers to my lips. "Don't jump ahead. Start from where you left off. I want to know what you were thinking when you saw me in the hallway that day. My god, you were so pissed at me," she says.

"*Pissed* at you? Lake, you thought I was mad at *you*?"

She shrugs.

"*No*, babe. I was *anything* but pissed at you."

oh, shit

MY THREE-DAY WEEKEND. What can I say about my three-day weekend other than it was the longest, most treacherous three days of my entire life. I was distracted the entire time thinking about her. I could have kicked myself for not getting her phone number before I left; at least we could have texted. My grandfather apparently noticed the difference in my attention span during the course of the visit. Before we left their house last night, he pulled me aside and said, "So? Who is she?"

Of course I played dumb and denied having met someone. What would he think if he knew I went on one date with this girl, and she already had me in a stupor? He laughed when I denied it and he squeezed my shoulder. "Can't wait to meet her," he said.

I usually dread Monday mornings, but there's a different air about today. Probably because I know I'll get to see her after work today. I slide the note under the windshield wiper of her Jeep, then head back across the street to my car. As soon as I place my fingers on the door handle, I have second thoughts. I'm being way too forward. Who says, "I can't wait to see you" in a note after one date? The last thing I want to do is scare her off. I walk back to her Jeep and lift the wiper blade to remove the note from her windshield.

"Leave it."

I spin around and Julia is standing in their entryway, holding a cup of coffee between her hands. I look down at the note, then back at the Jeep, then back at Julia, not really knowing what to say.

"You should leave it," she says, pointing to the note in my hand. "She'll like it." She smiles and heads back into the house, leaving me completely and utterly embarrassed in her driveway. I place the note back under the windshield wiper and make my way back across the street, hoping Julia is right.

"I TOLD YOU last week he was coming," Mrs. Alex says in a defensive tone of voice.

"No, you said he *called* about coming. You never told me it was today."

She turns to her computer and begins typing. "Well, I'm telling you now. He'll be here at eleven o'clock to observe your fourth-period class." She reaches to her printer and removes a freshly printed form. "And you'll have a new student in your next class. I just registered her this morning. Here's her information." She hands me the form and smiles. I roll my eyes and shove the form into my satchel, suddenly dreading the remainder of the day.

I walk in a hurry to third period considering I'm already five minutes late. I look down at my watch and groan. *An eleven o'clock observation?* That's just an hour from now. All I have scheduled for my classes today are section tests. I wasn't prepared to lecture at all, much less in front of my faculty advisor. I'll just have to use this period to prepare something last-minute.

God, could this day get any worse?

When I round the corner to Hall D, the day somehow gets one hundred percent better as soon as I lay eyes on her.

"Lake?"

She's got her hands in her hair, pulling it up into a knot again. She spins around and her eyes widen when she sees me. She pulls a sheet of paper from between her lips and smiles, then immediately wraps her arms around my neck.

"Will! What are you doing here?"

I return her hug, but the sheet of paper that just flashed in front of my face has left my entire body feeling like an immobile solid block of concrete.

She's holding a schedule.

I suddenly can't breathe.

She's holding a *class* schedule.

This can't be good.

Mrs. Alex said something about enrolling a new student.

Oh, shit.

Holy shit.

I immediately begin to internally panic. I wrap my fingers around her wrists and pull her arms away from my neck before someone sees us. *Please let me be wrong. Please.*

"Lake," I say, shaking my head—trying to make sense of this. "Where . . . what are you doing here?"

She lets out a frustrated sigh and thrusts the schedule into my chest. "I'm trying to find this stupid elective but I'm lost," she whines. "Help me!"

Oh, shit. What the hell have I done?

I take a step back against the wall, attempting to give myself space to think. Space to *breathe.*

"Lake, no . . ." I say. I hand her back the schedule without even looking at it. There's no need to look at it. I know exactly where her "stupid elective" is. I can't seem to process a coherent thought while looking at her, so I turn around and clasp my hands behind my head.

She's a *student?*

I'm her *teacher?*

Oh, shit.

I close my eyes and think back to the past week. Who have I told? Who saw us together? Gavin. *Shit.* There's no telling who else may have been at Club N9NE. And Lake! She's about to figure this out any second. What if she thinks I was trying to hide this from her? She could go straight to administration and end my career.

As soon as the thought crosses my mind, she picks up her backpack and begins to storm off. I reach out and pull her to a stop. "Where are you going?" It's obvious she's pissed and I hope her intentions aren't to report me.

She rolls her eyes and sighs. "I get it, Will," she says. "I *get* it. I'll leave you alone before your girlfriend sees us." She pulls her arm out of my grasp and turns away from me.

"Girlfr—*no*. No, Lake. I don't think you *do* get it." I wait for her to process what's happening. I would just come out and say it, but I *can't.* I don't think I could say it out loud if I wanted to.

The sound of footsteps closing in on us diverts her attention away from me. Javier suddenly rounds the corner and comes to a quick stop when he sees me in the hallway.

"Oh, man, I thought I was late," he says.

If Lake hasn't figured it all out by now, she's about to.

"You *are* late, Javier," I reply. I open the door to my classroom and wave him inside. "Javi, I'll be there in a few minutes. Let the class know they have five minutes to review before the exam." I slowly close the door behind me and look down at the floor. I can't look at her. I don't think my heart can take what she's about to feel. There's a brief moment of silence before she quietly gasps. I raise my eyes to hers and the disappointment on her face tears my heart in two. She *gets it* now.

"Will," she whispers painfully. "Please don't tell me . . ."

Her voice is weak and she tilts her head slightly to the side, slowly shaking her head back and forth. She isn't angry. She's *hurt*. I'd almost rather her be pissed right now than feel the way she's feeling. I look up at the ceiling and rub my hands over my face in an attempt not to punch the damn wall. How could I be so stupid? Why wasn't my profession the first thing I thought to share with her? Why did I not see this as a possibility? I continue to pace, hoping beyond all hope that *I'm* the one not getting it. When I reach the lockers in front of me, I tap my head against them, silently cursing myself. I've really screwed it up this time. For both of us. I drop my hands and reluctantly roll around to face her.

"How did I not *see* this? You're still in *high school*?"

She backs up to the wall behind her and leans against it for support. *"Me?"* she says in defense. "How did the fact that you're a teacher not come up? *How* are you a teacher? You're only twenty-one."

I realize I'm going to have to answer a lot of her questions. My teaching situation isn't particularly normal, so I understand her confusion. But we can't do this here. Not right now.

"Layken, listen." I realize when her name falls off my tongue that I didn't call her "Lake." I guess that's probably best at this point. "There has apparently been a huge misunderstanding between the two of us." I look away from her when I finish my sentence. An overwhelming feeling of guilt overcomes me when I look into her eyes, so I just don't. "We need to talk about this, but now is definitely not the right time."

"I agree," she whispers. It sounds like she's attempting not to cry. I couldn't take it if she cried.

The door to my classroom opens and Eddie walks out into the hall, looking directly at Lake. "Layken, I was just coming to look for you," she says. "I saved you a seat." She looks at me, then back at Lake, leaving no traces or hint that she's put two and two together. *Good.* That just leaves Gavin to contend with. "Oh, sorry, Mr. Cooper. I didn't know you were out here."

I stand straight and walk toward the classroom door. "It's fine, Eddie. I was just going over Layken's schedule with her." I pull the door open wider and wait for Lake and Eddie to make their way into the room. I'm thankful it's a test day. There's no *way* I would be able to lecture right now.

"Who's the hottie?" Javier asks when Lake slides into her seat.

"Shut it, Javi!" I snap. I am so not in the mood for his smart-ass comments right now. I reach over and grab the stack of tests.

"Chill out, Mr. Cooper. I was paying her a compliment." He leans back in his chair and gives Lake a slow, full-body glance that makes my blood boil. "She's hot. Look at her."

I point to the classroom door. "Javi, get out!"

He snaps his focus back to me. "Mr. Cooper! Jeez! What's with the temp? Like I said, I was just . . ."

"Like *I* said, get out! You will not disrespect women in my classroom!"

He snatches his books off his desk. "Fine. I'll go disrespect them in the hallway!"

After the door shuts behind him, I cringe at my own behavior. I've never lost my temper in a classroom before. I look back at the students and everyone is watching Lake, waiting on some sort of reaction from her. Everyone except Gavin. His eyes are burrowing a hole right through me. I give him a slight nod, letting him know that I acknowledge the fact that we obviously have a lot to discuss. For right now, though, it's back to the task at hand.

"Class, we have a new student. This is Layken Cohen," I say, quickly wanting to brush what just happened under the rug. "Review is over. Put up your notes."

"You're not going to have her introduce herself?" Eddie asks.

"We'll get to that another time," I say, holding up the papers. "Tests."

I begin passing out the tests. When I reach Gavin's desk, he looks up at me inquisitively. "Lunch," I whisper, letting him know I'll explain everything then. He nods and takes his test, finally breaking eye contact.

When I pass out all but one of the tests, I reluctantly walk closer to her desk. "Lake," I say. I quickly clear my throat and correct myself. "Layken, if you have something else to work on, feel free. The class is completing a chapter test."

She straightens up in her desk and looks down at her hands. "I'd rather just take the test," she says quietly. I place the paper on her desk, then make my way back to my seat.

I spend the rest of the hour grading papers from the first two classes. I occasionally catch myself peeking in her direction, trying hard not to stare. She just keeps erasing and rewriting answers over and over. I don't know why she chose to take the test; she hasn't been here for any of the lectures. I break my gaze from her paper and look up. Gavin is glaring at me again, so I dart my eyes down at my watch right when the dismissal bell rings. Everyone quickly files to the front of the room and places their papers on my desk.

"Hey, did you get your lunch switched?" Eddie asks Lake.

I watch as Eddie and Lake converse about her schedule and I'm secretly relieved that Lake has already found a friend. I'm not so sure I like that it's Eddie, though. I don't have a problem with Eddie. It's just that Gavin knows way too much now and I'm not sure if he would tell Eddie or not. I hope not. I glance back down to my desk as soon as Eddie begins to walk away from Lake. Rather than exiting the classroom, she heads straight to my desk. I look up at her and she removes something from her purse. She shakes a few mints into her hand and lays them on my desk.

"Altoids," she says. "I'm just making assumptions here, but I've heard Altoids work wonders on hangovers." She pushes the mints toward me and walks away.

I stare at the mints, unnerved that she assumed I have a hangover. I must not be as good at hiding my emotions as I thought I was. I'm disappointed in myself. Disappointed I lost my temper, disappointed I didn't use my head when it came to the whole situation with Lake, disappointed that I now have this huge dilemma facing me. I'm still staring at the mints when Lake walks to the desk and places her paper on top of the pile.

"Is my mood that obvious?" I say rhetorically. She takes two of the mints and walks out of the room without saying a word. I sigh and lean back in the chair, kicking my feet up on the desk. This is by far the second-worst day of my life.

"I can't wait that long, man." Gavin walks back into the room and closes the door behind him. He throws his backpack on the desk in front of me, then scoots it closer and climbs into it. "What the *hell*, Will? What were you thinking?"

I shake my head and shrug my shoulders. I'm not ready to talk about this right now, but I do owe him an explanation. I bring my feet down from the desk and rest my head in my hands, rubbing my temples with my fingers. "We didn't know."

Gavin laughs incredulously. "Didn't know? How the hell could you not *know*?"

I close my eyes and sigh. He's right. How did we not know? "I don't know. It just . . . it never came up," I say. "I was out of town all weekend. We haven't spoken since our date Thursday. It just . . . somehow it never came up." I shake my head, sorting through my thoughts as they're flowing from my lips. I'm a jumbled mess.

"So you *just* found out she's a student? Like, *just* now?"

I nod.

"You didn't have sex with her, did you?"

His question takes a moment to register. He takes my silence as an admission of guilt and he leans forward and whispers, "You had sex with her, didn't you? You're gonna get fired, man."

"No, I didn't have sex with her!" I snap.

He continues to glare at me, attempting to analyze my demeanor. "Then why are you so upset? If you didn't have sex with her, you can't really get in trouble. I doubt she'll report it if all you did was kiss her. Is that what you're worried about? That she'll report you?"

I shake my head, because that's not at all what I'm worried about. I could see in Lake's demeanor that the thought of reporting me never even crossed her mind. She was upset, but not with me.

"No. No, I know she won't say anything. It's just . . ." I run my hand across my forehead and sigh. I have no idea how to handle this. No idea. "Shit," I say, exasperated. "I just need to think, Gavin."

I run my fingers through my hair and clasp my hands behind my head. I don't think I've ever been this confused and overwhelmed in my life. Everything I've worked for could possibly be going to hell today simply because of my stupidity. I've got three months left until graduation, and there's a good chance if this gets out, I've just ruined my entire career.

What confuses me though is the fact that it's not my career that has me in a jumbled mess right now. It's *her*. These emotions are a direct result of *her*. The main reason why I'm so upset right now is that it feels like I somehow just broke her heart.

"Oh," Gavin says quietly. "*Shit*."

I look up at him, confused by his reaction. "What?"

He stands up and points to me. "You *like* her," he says. "*That's* why you're so upset. You already fell for her, didn't you?" He grabs his backpack and starts walking backward toward the door, shaking his head. I don't even bother denying it. He saw the way I was looking at her the other night.

When the classroom door opens and several students begin to file in, he walks back to my desk and whispers, "Eddie doesn't know anything. I didn't recognize anyone else at the slam, so don't worry about that part of it. You just need to figure out what you need to do." He turns toward the classroom door and exits . . . just as my faculty advisor enters.

Shit!

IF THERE'S ONE thing I've learned how to do well in my life, it's adapt.

I somehow made it through the observation unscathed and somehow made it to the end of last period without bashing my fists into a wall. Whether or not I'll make it through the rest of the day just knowing I'm right across the street from her is still up in the air.

When Caulder and I pull into the driveway, she's sitting in her Jeep. She's got her arm over her eyes and it looks like she's crying.

"Can I go to Kel's?" Caulder asks when he climbs out of the car.

I nod. I leave my things in the car and shut my door, then slowly make my way across the street. When I reach the back of her car, I pause to gather my thoughts. I know what needs to be done, but knowing something and accepting it are two completely different things. I asked myself over and over today what my parents would have done in this situation. What would *most* people do in this situation? Of course, the answer is obviously to do the right thing. The responsible thing. I mean, we went on one date. Who would quit a job over *one* date?

This shouldn't be this hard. Why is this so hard?

I walk closer and lightly tap on her passenger window. She jerks up and flips the visor down and looks in the mirror, attempting to wipe away traces of her heartache. When the door unlocks, I open it and take a seat. I shut the door behind me and adjust the seat, then prop my foot on the dash. My gaze falls to the note that I left under her wiper this morning. It's unfolded, lying on her console. When I wrote the words, *see you at four o'clock*, this isn't how I envisioned four o'clock at all. I glance up at her and she's avoiding looking at me. Just seeing her causes my words to catch in my throat. I have no idea what to say. I have no idea where her head is right now.

"What are you thinking?" I finally ask.

She slowly turns toward me and pulls her leg up into the seat. She wraps her arms around it and rests her chin on top of her knee. I've never wanted to be a knee so bad in my entire life.

"I'm confused as hell, Will. I don't *know* what to think."

Honestly, I don't know what to think, either. *God, I'm such an asshole.* How could I have let this happen? I sigh and look out the passenger window. I can't for the life of me hold my composure if I keep looking into those eyes.

"I'm sorry," I say. "This is all my fault."

"It's nobody's fault," she says. "In order for there to be fault, there has to be some sort of conscious decision. You didn't know, Will."

I *didn't* know. But it's my own damn fault that I didn't know.

"That's just it, Lake," I say, turning to face her. "I should have known. I'm in an occupation that doesn't just require ethics inside the classroom; they apply to all aspects of my life. I wasn't aware because I wasn't doing my job. When you told me you were eighteen, I just assumed you were in college."

She looks away and whispers, "I've only been eighteen for two weeks."

That sentence. If that sentence could have just been spoken a few days ago, this entire situation would have been avoided. Why the *hell* didn't I just ask her when her birthday was? I close my eyes and rest my head against the seat, preparing to explain my unique situation to her. I want her to have a better understanding of why this can't work between us.

"I student teach," I say. "Sort of."

"Sort of?"

"After my parents died, I doubled up on all my classes. I have enough credits to graduate a semester early. Since the school was so shorthanded, they offered me a one-year contract. I have three months left of student teaching. After that I'm under contract through June of next year." I look over at her and her eyes are closed. She's shaking her head ever so slightly like she doesn't comprehend what I'm saying, or she just doesn't want to hear it.

"Lake, I need this job. It's what I've been working toward for three years. We're broke. My parents left me with a mound of debt and now college tuition. I can't quit now."

She darts her eyes toward me, almost like I've insulted her.

"Will, I understand. I'd never ask you to jeopardize your career. You've worked hard. It would be stupid if you threw that away for someone you've only known for a week."

Oh, but I would. If you would just ask me to . . . I would.

"I'm not saying you would ask me that. I just want you to understand where I'm coming from."

"I do understand," she says. "It's ridiculous to assume we even have anything worth risking."

She can deny it all she wants, but whatever it is that I'm feeling, I know she's feeling it, too. I can see it in her eyes. "We both know it's more than that."

As soon as the words leave my lips, I immediately regret them. This girl is my *student*. S-T-U-D-E-N-T! I've *got* to get this through my *head*.

We're both silent. The lack of conversation only invites the emotions we've been trying to suppress. She begins to cry, and despite the fact that my conscience is screaming at me, I can't help but console her. I pull her to me and she buries her face in my shirt. I want so bad to push the thought out of my head that this is the last time I'm going to hold her like this—but I know it's true. I know once we separate, it's over. There's no way I can continue to be around her with the way she consumes my every thought. I know, deep down, that this is good-bye.

"I'm so sorry," I whisper into her hair. "I wish there was something I could do to change things. I have to do this right for Caulder. I'm not sure where we go from here, or how we'll transition."

"Transition?" she says. She brings her eyes to meet mine and they're full of panic. "But—what if you talk to the school? Tell them we didn't know. Ask them what our options are."

She doesn't realize it, but that's all I've been trying to figure out for the last five hours. I've been thinking of any and all possible scenarios to change the outcome for us. There just *isn't* one.

"I can't, Lake. It won't work. It *can't* work."

She pulls apart from me when Kel and Caulder come out of her house. I reluctantly release my hold from around her, knowing it's the last time I'll hold her. This is more than likely the last time we'll have a conversation outside school. In order for me to do the right thing, I know that letting her go completely is the only way. I need to distance myself from her.

"Layken?" I say hesitantly. "There's one more thing I need to talk to you about."

She rolls her eyes like she knows it's something bad. She doesn't respond, though. She just waits for me to continue.

"I need you to go to administration tomorrow. I want you to withdraw from my class. I don't think we should be around each other anymore."

"Why?" she says, turning to face me. The hurt in her voice is exactly what I was afraid I would hear.

"I'm not asking you to do this because I want to avoid you. I'm asking you this because what we have isn't appropriate. We have to separate ourselves."

The hurt in her eyes is replaced by a look of incredulity. "Not appropriate?" she says, disbelievingly. "*Separate* ourselves? You live across the street from me!"

The hurt in her voice, the anger in her expression, the heartache in her eyes; it's too much. Seeing her hurt like this and not being able to console her is unbearable. If I don't get out of this car right now, my hands will be tangled in her hair and my lips will be meshed with hers in a matter of seconds. I swing open the door and get out.

I just need to breathe.

She opens her door, too, and looks at me over the hood of her car. "We're both mature enough to know what's appropriate, Will. You're the only person I know here. Please don't ask me to act like I don't even know you," she pleads.

"Come on, Lake. You aren't being fair. I can't do this. We can't *just* be friends. It's the only choice we have."

She has no idea how close I came to *not* being her friend just now. There's no possible way I can be around this girl and continue to do the right thing. I'm not that strong.

She opens her car door and reaches inside to grab her things. "So, you're saying it's either all or nothing, right? And since it *obviously* can't be *all*!" She slams the door and walks toward her house. She stops short and kicks over the gnome with the broken red hat. "You'll be rid of me by third period tomorrow!" She slams her front door, leaving me a heartbroken, emotional wreck in her driveway.

The last thing I wanted out of this was to upset her even more. I pound my fists against the top of her Jeep, pissed at myself for putting her in this situation to begin with. "Dammit!" I yell. I spin and turn to head home, but instead come face to face with Kel and Caulder. They're both staring at me, wide-eyed.

"Why are you so mad at Layken?" Kel asks. "Are you not gonna be her boyfriend?"

I glance back to Lake's house and clasp my hands behind my head. "I'm not mad at her, Kel. I'm just—I'm mad at myself." I drop my arms and turn back around to head home. They step apart as I pass between them. I hear them following me when I retrieve my things from my car. I'm still being followed when I walk inside and set the box down on the bar, so I turn around and look at the boys.

"What?" I say with a clear amount of annoyance. They both look at each other, then back at me.

"Um. We just wanted to ask you something," Caulder says nervously. He slides into one of the bar stools and rests his chin in his hand. "Maya said if Layken becomes your girlfriend and you marry her, me and Kel will be brothers of law."

Both boys are looking at me with hopeful expressions.

"It's brothers-*in*-law, and Layken's not going to be my girl-friend," I say. "We're just friends."

Kel steps around me and climbs into the other seat at the bar. "She burped too much, didn't she? Or did she leave her bra in your car? I bet she wouldn't let you have coffee, would she?"

I force a fake smile and step toward the stack of papers. "You nailed it," I say. "It was the coffee. She's so stingy."

Kel shakes his head. "I knew it."

"Well," Caulder says. "You could try going on another date to see if you like her better. Me and Kel want to be brothers."

"Layken and I aren't going on another date. We're just friends." I glance at both of them with a serious expression. "Drop it." I sit down and pull out my pen, then grab the test off the top and flip it over.

It's *her* test.

Of course it would be hers. I stare at it, wondering how in the hell this is going to get any easier. Just seeing her handwriting makes my pulse race. Makes my heart ache. I lightly trace her name with the tip of my finger. I'm pretty sure it's the most beautiful handwriting I've ever seen.

"Please?" Caulder says.

I flinch, having forgotten they were even standing here. I have *got* to stop thinking about her like this. She's a *student*. I slap her test facedown on the pile and stand up.

"Kel, do you like pizza?"

He shakes his head. "No. I *love* pizza."

"Go ask your mom if you can chill with us tonight. We need a boy's night."

Kel jumps out of his chair and they both run toward the front door. I take a seat at the bar again and drop my head into my hands.

This entire day is definitely my suck.

I REST MY hand on the door to the administration office, almost second-guessing my entrance. I'm not in the mood for Mrs. Alex today. Unfortunately, she sees me through the glass window and waves. Her *flirty* wave. I suck it up and reluctantly open the door.

"Good morning, Will," she says in her annoying singsong voice.

I know I was "Will" to her just a couple of years ago, but it wouldn't hurt her to extend me the courtesy that she extends to all the other teachers here. I don't bother arguing, though. "Morning." I shove a form across the desk toward her. "Can you have this signed by Mr. Murphy and fax it to my faculty advisor?"

She takes the form and places it in a tray. "Anything for you," she says and smiles. I give her a quick smile in return, then spin toward the exit, very conscious of my own ass this time.

"Oh, by the way," she calls after me. "That new student I registered yesterday just came by to drop your class. I guess she isn't a big fan of poetry. You'll need to sign the form I gave her before I can make it official. She's probably on her way to your classroom right now."

"Thanks," I mumble, exiting the office.

This is going to be impossible. It's not like I can just erase the fact that Lake exists. I'll more than likely see her at work on a daily basis, whether in passing . . . in the lunchroom . . . in the parking lot. I'll definitely see her at home every day considering her house is the first thing I see when I walk out my own front door. Or look out my window. Not that I'll be doing that.

Kel and Caulder are becoming inseparable, so I'll eventually have to interact with her regarding them. Trying to avoid her isn't going to work. Lake is absolutely right . . . it isn't going to work at all. I kept trying to tell myself over and over last night that what she said wasn't true, but it is. I wonder if the only other alternative would be to try and at least be her friend. We're obviously going to have to work through this situation somehow.

When I round the corner to my classroom, she's standing next to my door with the transfer form pressed against the wall, attempting to forge my name. My first instinct is to turn around and walk away, but I realize these are the exact types of situations we're going to have to learn to confront.

"That's not a good idea," I say, before she forges my name. If anyone could recognize my handwriting, it would be Mrs. Alex.

Lake spins around and looks at me. Her cheeks flush and she darts her eyes down to my shirt, embarrassed. I walk past her and unlock the door, then motion for her to enter the classroom. She walks to my desk and smacks her form down.

"Well, you weren't here yet, I thought I'd spare you the trouble," she says.

She must not have had her coffee today. I pick up the form and look it over. "Russian Lit? That's what you chose?"

She rolls her eyes. "It was either that or Botany."

I pull my chair out and take a seat, preparing to sign the form. As soon as the tip of my pen meets the paper, it occurs to me that in a way, I'm being incredibly selfish. She chose poetry as an elective before she even knew I would be teaching it. She chose poetry because she loves it. The fact that the thoughts I have about her make me uncomfortable is an extremely selfish reason to force her into Russian Literature for the rest of the year. I hesitate, then lay the pen back down on the paper.

"I thought a lot last night . . . about what you said yesterday. It's not fair of me to ask you to transfer just because it makes me uneasy. We live a hundred yards apart; our brothers are becoming best friends. If anything, this class will be good for us, help us figure out how to navigate when we're around each other." I reach into my satchel and pull out the test she somehow made a perfect score on. "Besides, you'll obviously breeze through."

She takes the test from my hands and looks down at it. "I don't mind switching," she says quietly. "I understand where you're coming from."

I put the lid back on the pen and scoot my chair back. "Thanks, but it can only get easier from here, right?"

She nods her head unconvincingly. "Right," she says.

I know I'm completely wrong. She could move back to Texas today and I would still feel too close to her. But once again, it's not my feelings that should matter at this point. It's hers. I've screwed her life up enough in the past week; the last thing I want to do is shove Russian Lit on top of that. I crumple up her transfer form and chuck it toward the trash can. When it misses, she walks over and picks it up, then throws it in.

"I guess I'll see you third period, Mr. Cooper," she says as she exits the room.

The way she refers to me as "Mr. Cooper" makes me scowl. I hate the fact that I'm her teacher.

I'd so much rather be her *Will*.

7.

the honeymoon

LAKE HASN'T MOVED a muscle in the last fifteen minutes. She's been soaking in every word I've said. Recalling the day we met and our first date was actually fun. Recalling the things that tore us apart is grueling.

"I don't like talking about this anymore," I say. "It looks like it's making you sad."

Her eyes widen and she turns her body toward me. "Will, no. I love hearing your thoughts on everything that happened. I actually feel like it helps me understand a lot of your actions better. I don't know why I felt like you sort of blamed me."

I kiss her softly on the lips. "How could I blame you, Lake? All I wanted was you."

She smiles and rests her head on my forearm. "I can't believe my mom told you to leave me that note," she says.

"God, Lake. That was so embarrassing. You have no idea."

She laughs. "She really liked you, you know. At first, I mean. She *loved* you in the end. It was the in-between where her feelings about you sort of waned."

I think about the day Julia found out, and how worried she must have been for Lake. To have everything going on in her life like she did, then have to watch your daughter deal with heartache? Unimaginable.

"Remember when she found out you were my teacher?" Lake says. "The look on your face when she was walking up the driveway toward you, it was awful. I was so afraid you would think I told her because I was mad at you."

"I was so scared of her that day, Lake. She could be really intimidating when she wanted to be. Of course after we talked again later that night, I saw a more vulnerable side to her, but still. I was scared to death of her."

Lake jerks up on the bed and looks at me. "What do you mean when y'all talked *again*?"

"Later that night when she came back to my house. Did I never tell you that?"

"No," she says abruptly, almost like I've deceived her. "Why did she come back? What did she say?"

"Wait, let me start from the beginning. I want to tell you about the night before she found out," I say. "I slammed a poem about you."

She perks up. "No way! How come you never told me?"

I shrug. "I was hurt. It wasn't a positive piece."

"I want to hear about it, anyway," she says.

this *girl*

I'M HOPING THIS situation is like dieting, where they say day three is when the cravings start to subside. I really hope that's the case. The fact that she sits two feet from me in class makes my mind feel like a damn hurricane. It takes everything in me not to look at her during third period. In fact, I spend the entire time in my class trying *not* to look at her. I've been fairly successful, which is good considering Gavin still watches me like a hawk. At least it felt like he was today, anyway. I've never so looked forward to a weekend off in my life.

One. More. Day.

"I might be a little late tonight, Maya. I'm performing so I may stay until it's over."

She plops down on the sofa with a carton of ice cream. "Whatever," she says.

I grab my keys and head out the front door. No matter how hard I try not to, I glance across the street during my short walk to the car. I could swear I see her living room curtain snap shut. I stop and stare for a minute, but it doesn't move again.

I'M ONE OF the first to arrive, so I take one of the seats toward the front of the room. I'm hoping the energy from the crowd will distract me long enough to get out of this funk. I'm almost embarrassed to admit it, but I feel more heartbroken over this entire situation with Lake than I did when Vaughn dumped me. I'm sure a lot of that heartache was lost in the heartache from losing my parents, so maybe it just seems different for that reason. How could ending things with a girl who wasn't even my girlfriend to begin with possibly cause this much distress?

"Hey, Mr. Cooper," Gavin says. He and Eddie pull out their chairs and sit at the table with me. Unlike last week, I actually welcome their distraction tonight.

"For the last time, Gavin, call me Will. It's weird hearing you say that when we're not in class."

"Hey, *Will*," Eddie says sarcastically. "You doing one tonight?"

I had planned on performing, but seeing Gavin has me second-guessing my choice. I know most of the pieces I perform are metaphorical, but he'll see right through this one. Not that it matters; he already knows how I feel.

"Yeah," I say to Eddie. "I'm doing a new one."

"Cool," she says. "Did you write it for that girl?" She turns around and scans the room. "Where is she? I thought I saw you leaving with someone last week." She returns her focus to me. "Was she your girlfriend?"

Gavin and I immediately look at each other. He makes a face that tells me he didn't say anything to Eddie. I try to steady my expression when I respond.

"Just a friend."

Eddie pushes her bottom lip out and pouts. "Friend, huh? That sucks. We really need to hook you up with someone." She leans forward onto the table and puts her chin in her hands while studying me. "Gavin, who can we hook Will up with?"

He rolls his eyes. "Why do you always think you have to hook everyone up? Not everyone feels the need to be in a relationship every second of their lives." He's obviously trying to squelch the subject and I appreciate him for that.

"I don't try to hook *everyone* up," she says. "Just the people who clearly need it." She looks back at me. "No offense, Will. It's just—you know. You never date. It might do you some good."

"Enough, Eddie," Gavin snaps.

"*What?* Two people, Gavin! I've mentioned finding dates for two people this week. That's not excessive. Besides, I think I may have figured out someone for Layken."

When Eddie says her name, I immediately shift in my chair. So does Gavin.

"I think I'm gonna try to get Nick to ask her out," she says, thinking aloud.

Before Gavin can respond, the sac is called to the stage. I'm relieved the subject is off the table now, but I can't deny the twinge of jealousy that just made its way into my stomach.

What did I expect would be the outcome of all this? Of course she's going to date other people. She's got her entire senior year of school left; it would be crazy if she *didn't* date. But still, it doesn't mean I'll be happy when she does.

"I'll be back," I say, excusing myself from the table. It's been five minutes and I already need a breather from Eddie.

When I return from the bathroom, the sac has already finished performing. As soon as I sit back down, the emcee calls me to the stage to perform first.

"Break a leg," Gavin says when I stand back up.

"That's theater, Gavin," Eddie says, hitting him on the arm.

I ascend the steps and take my place in front of the microphone. I've noticed in the past that if I concentrate and really put my emotions into writing, performing can actually be therapeutic. I really need to find some relief after all that's happened this week.

"My piece is called *This Girl*." I do my best to avoid Gavin's glare, but it's obvious by his expression that he knows the poem is about Lake as soon as the title passes my lips. I close my eyes and inhale a deep breath, then begin.

I dreamt about this girl last night.

Wow.

This *girl.*

In my *dream* I was standing on the edge of a *cliff*

Looking *down* over a *vast, barren valley below*

I wasn't wearing any *shoes* and the rocks were

crumbling beneath my *toes.*

It would have been so *easy* to take a step back,

To *move* away from the *ledge,*

Away from a *certain inevitable life* that had *somehow*

been *determined* for me

a life that had *somehow* become my only option.

It had been my life for *two years* and I *accepted* that.

I had not *embraced* it,

But I *had* accepted it.

It was where I belonged.

As much as it didn't *appeal* to me, as much as I *yearned*

for the *rivers* and *mountains* and *trees,*

As much as I *yearned* to hear their *songs . . .*

To hear their . . . *poetry?*

It was apparent that what *I* yearned for

wasn't *decided* by me . . .

it was decided *for* me.

So . . . I did the only thing I could do.

The only thing I *should* do.

I prepared myself to *embrace* this life.

I sucked it up and took a *deep* breath. I placed my

hands on the edge of the *cliff* and began to *lower*

myself onto the *rocks* protruding from the *edge.* I

burrowed my *fingers deep* into the *crevices* and *slowly*
began lowering myself *down*.

Down into the *vast*,

barren

valley

that had become

my

life.

But *then* . . .

Then this *girl* . . .

Holy *hell*, this *girl* . . .

She appeared out of *nowhere*, standing *directly* in front
of me on the edge of that *cliff*. She looked *down* at me
with her *sad eyes* that ran a *million* miles *deep* . . .

and she *smiled* at me.

This girl *smiled* at me.

A *look* that cut *straight* to my *core* and *pierced* through
my *heart* like a *million* of Cupid's arrows,

One right on top of the *other*, on top of the *other*, on

top of the *other*

Straight . . .

Into . . .

My *heart* . . .

Now *this* is the part of the dream where *most* girls
would bend down and grab my *hands*, telling me not
to *go* . . . not to *do* it. *This* is the part of the dream
where *most* girls would grab my *wrists* and *brace*
themselves with their *feet* as they *pulled* me *up* with
every ounce of strength in their *being*. *This* is the part

of the dream where *most* girls would *scream* at the top
of their *lungs* for help, doing *anything* and *everything*
they could to *save* me . . .

To *rescue* me

from that

vast,

barren

valley

below.

But *this* girl.

This girl wasn't most girls.

This girl . . .

This girl did something even *better.*

First, she sat down on the edge of the *cliff* and *kicked*
off her shoes and we both watched as they *fell* and *fell*
and *fell* and *continued* to *fall* until they landed in a
heap. One shoe right on top of the other in that *vast,*
barren valley below.

Then she *slid* a rubber *band* off her *wrist,*

Reached behind her . . .

And pulled her *hair*

into a *knot.*

And then this girl

This *girl* . . .

She *placed* her *hands* right next to *mine* on the *edge*
of that *cliff* and she *slowly* began to *lower* herself *off*
of it. She poked her *bare feet* into *whatever* crevice
she could *find* next to mine. She dug the *fingers* of her
right hand into the *cracks* between the *rocks,* then
placed her *left* hand

directly . . .

on *top* . . .

of *mine.*

She looked down at the **vast, barren valley below** us,

then she looked back up at me and she *smiled.*

She *smiled.*

She *looked* at me and *smiled* and said . . .

"Are you *ready?*"

And I *was.*

I *finally* was.

I had never been more *ready* in my *life.*

Yeah . . .

This *girl.*

My mother would have *loved* this girl.

Too bad she was just a *dream.*

I CLOSE MY eyes and tune out the noise of the crowd while I wait for my lungs to find their rhythm again. When I descend the stage and take a seat back at the table, Eddie stands up, wiping tears from her eyes. She looks down at me and frowns.

"Would it kill you to do something *funny* for once?" She storms toward the bathroom, I'm assuming to fix her makeup.

I look at Gavin and laugh, but he's staring back at me with his arms folded in front of him on the table. "Will, I think I've got an idea."

"Pertaining to . . ."

"You," he says. He gestures toward the stage, "and your . . . situation."

I lean forward. "What about my *situation?*"

"I know someone," he says. "She works with my mom. She's your age, cute, in *college*."

I immediately shake my head. "No. No chance," I say, leaning back into the booth.

"Will, you can't be with Layken. If your poem had anything to do with her, which I'm thinking it had *everything* to do with her, then you need to find a way to get over this. If you don't, you'll end up screwing up your entire career over *this girl*. A girl you went on *one* date with. One!"

I continue to shake my head at his reasoning. "I'm not looking for a girlfriend, Gavin. I wasn't even looking for anything when I met Lake. I'm fine with where I am right now; I definitely don't need to add even more female drama into the picture."

"You won't be adding more drama. You'll be filling an obvious void in your life. You need to date. Eddie was right."

"What was I right about?" Eddie says, returning to her seat.

Gavin gestures toward me. "About Will. He needs to date. Don't you think he and Taylor would hit it off?"

Eddie perks up. "I didn't even think about her! Yes! Will, you're gonna love her," she says excitedly.

"I'm not letting you guys set me up." I grab my jacket. "I've got to get back home. See you guys in class tomorrow."

Eddie and Gavin both stand. "I'll get her number tomorrow," Eddie says. "Is next Saturday night okay? You two could double date with us."

"I'm not going." I walk away without turning back or giving in.

8.

the honeymoon

"OKAY," LAKE SAYS. "Two things. One. That poem was . . . heart-breakingly *beautiful.*"

"Just like its subject," I say. I lean in to kiss her but she brings her hand up and pushes my face away.

"Two," she says, narrowing her eyes. "Gavin and Eddie tried to set you up with someone?" She huffs and sits up on the bed. "Good thing you didn't agree to it. I don't care how screwed up our situation was, there's no way I would have dated anyone else considering the way I felt about you."

I quickly change the subject before she realizes that, although I didn't *agree* to it, Eddie is pretty damn persistent.

"Okay, now for Friday night," I say, successfully taking her mind off the date. "Your mom."

"Yeah," she says, finding a comfortable spot next to me and throwing her leg over mine. "My mom."

secrets

"PASTA AGAIN?" CAULDER whines. He grabs his plate of food from the counter and takes it to the bar and sits.

"If you don't like it, learn how to cook."

"*I* like it," Kel says. "My mom cooks a lot of vegetables and chicken. That's probably why I'm so small, because I'm malnoure-dish."

I laugh and correct him. "It's mal*nourished*."

Kel rolls his eyes. "That's what I said."

I grab my own bowl and fill it with pasta . . . *again*. We do have pasta at least three times a week, but there are only two of us. I don't see the point in making expensive meals when it's just me and a nine-year-old most of the time. I take a seat at the bar across from the two boys and fill all of our glasses with tea.

"Suck and sweet time," Caulder says.

"What's suck and sweet?" Kel asks.

As soon as Caulder starts to explain, there's a knock at the front door. When I reach the door and open it, I'm surprised to find Julia standing in the entryway. Her presence has definitely become more intimidating since the first day I met her; especially after this afternoon when she found out about me being a teacher.

She looks up at me straight-faced, with her hands in the pockets of her scrub top.

"Oh. Hey," I say, trying not to appear as nervous as I am. "Kel just started eating. If you want, I'll send him home as soon as he's done."

"Actually," she says. She glances over my shoulder at the boys, then looks back at me and lowers her voice to a whisper. "I really wanted to talk to you if you have a few minutes."

She seems a little bit nervous, which just makes me ten times more nervous. "Sure." I step aside and motion for her to come in.

"You guys can eat in your room, Caulder. I need to talk to Julia."

"But we haven't said our suck and sweet for today," Caulder says.

"Do them in your room. I'll tell you mine later."

The boys pick up their bowls and drinks and head to Caulder's room, closing the door behind them. When I turn back to Julia her mouth is curled up in a smile.

"Suck and sweet?" she says. "Is that your way of getting him to tell you his good and bad for the day?"

I smile and nod. "We started it about six months ago." I take a seat on the same couch as her. "It was his therapist's idea. Although the original version wasn't called suck and sweet. I sort of ad-libbed that part to make it sound more appealing to him."

"That's sweet," she says. "I should start doing that with Kel."

I give her a slight smile but don't respond. I'm not really sure what she's doing here or what her intentions are, so I silently wait for her to continue. She takes a deep breath and focuses her gaze on the family picture hanging on the wall across from her.

"Your parents?" she says, pointing to the picture.

I relax into the couch and look up at the picture. "Yeah. My mom's name was Claire. My dad's name was Dimas. He was half Puerto Rican—named after his maternal grandfather."

Julia smiles. "That explains your natural tan."

It's obvious she's trying to deflect for some reason. She continues to stare at the picture. "Do you mind if I ask how they met?" she says.

Just a few hours ago she was ready to rip my head off after

finding out I'm Lake's teacher; now she's trying to get to know me? Whatever's going on with her, I'm in no position to question her, so I just go along with it.

"They met in college. Well, my mom was in college. My dad was actually a member of a band that played on her campus. He didn't go to college until a few years after they met. My mom was on a campus crew that would help set up their shows and they got to know each other. He asked her out and the rest is history. They married two years later."

"What'd they do for a living?"

"Mom was in human resources. Dad was a . . . he taught English." Just saying the word *teacher* in front of her makes me uncomfortable. "Not the best-paying jobs but they were happy."

She sighs. "That's what counts."

I nod in agreement. There's an awkward silence that follows while she slowly scans the pictures on the walls around us. I feel like she wants to bring up everything from earlier today, but maybe she doesn't know how.

"Listen, Julia." I turn toward her on the couch. "I really am sorry about what happened between Lake . . . between *Layken* and me. The position I've put her in isn't fair to her and I feel terrible. It's completely my fault."

She smiles and reaches across the couch, then pats the top of my hand. "I know it wasn't intentional, Will. What happened was an unfortunate misunderstanding; I know that. But . . ." She sighs and shakes her head. "As much as I like you and think you're a great guy . . . it's just not right. She's never been in love before and it scares me when I think about the way she looked when she walked through that front door last Thursday night. I know she wants to do the right thing, but I also know she would do anything to get back to that moment. It's the first time I've seen her that happy since before her father died."

Hearing her validate that Lake's feelings were just as intense as mine makes this whole thing even harder. I know she's only trying to make a point, but it's a point I'd rather not hear.

"What I'm trying to say is . . . this is in your hands, Will. I know she's not strong enough to deny her heart what it wants, so I need you to promise me that you *will*. You've got more at stake here than she does. This isn't a fairy tale. This is reality. If you two end up following your hearts and not your heads, it'll end in disaster."

I shift on the couch and attempt to think of a way to respond. Julia is obviously the type of person who can see through bullshit, so I know I need to be up front with her.

"I like her, Julia. And in some odd way, I care about her. I know I've only known her for a little over a week now, but . . . I do. I care about her. And that's exactly why you don't have anything to worry about. I want nothing more than to help Layken get past this—whatever it is she's feeling. I know the only way to do that is to keep our relationship strictly professional from now on. And I promise you, I will."

I hear the words coming from my mouth, and I would like to admit that I'm being one hundred percent honest with her. But if I'm being one hundred percent honest with *myself*, I know I'm not that strong. Which is why I have to keep my distance.

Julia rests her elbow against the back of the couch and lays her head on it. "You're a good person, Will. I hope one day she'll be lucky enough to find someone half as good as you. I just don't want her finding it yet, you know? And definitely not under these circumstances."

I nod. "I don't want that for her right now, either," I say quietly. And that response is for certain the truth. If there's anything I know for sure, it's that I don't want to burden Lake with all of my responsibilities. She's young and, unlike me, she still has a chance at an untainted future. I don't want to be the one to take that from her.

Julia leans back into the couch and looks at the picture of my parents again. I watch her while she stares at it. I can see now where Lake gets that distant gaze. I wonder if they were ever despondent before Lake's father passed away, or if it's a natural reaction after someone close to you dies. It makes me wonder if maybe I'm just as despondent when I think about my own parents.

Julia's hand goes up to her cheek and she wipes at newly formed tears in her eyes. I don't know why she's crying, but I instantly feel her sadness. It exudes from her.

"What was it like for you?" she whispers, still staring at the picture.

I face forward again and look at their picture. "What was *what* like?" I ask. "Their death?"

She nods, but doesn't look at me. I lean back and fold my arms across my chest, resting my head against the back of the couch again. "It was . . ." I realize I've never talked to anyone about what it was like for me. Other than the slam I've performed about their death, I've never spoken about it to a single person. "It was as if every single nightmare I've ever had throughout my entire life became reality in that single instant."

She squeezes her eyes shut and clamps her hand over her mouth, quickly turning away.

"Julia?"

She's unable to control her tears now. I scoot closer to her on the couch and put my arm around her and pull her to me. I know she isn't crying because of what I said. She's crying because of something else entirely. There's something bigger going on here than just me and Lake. Something much bigger. I pull back and look at her.

"Julia, tell me," I say. "What's wrong?"

She pulls away and stands up, heading toward the door. "I need to go," she says through her tears. She walks out the front door before I have a chance to stop her. When I make it outside, she's standing on my patio crying uncontrollably. I walk over to her, unsure of what to do. Unsure if I'm in the position to do anything, even if I wanted to.

"Look, Julia. Whatever this is, you need to talk about it. You don't have to tell me, but you need to talk about it. Do you want me to go get Layken?"

She darts her eyes up to mine. "No!" she says. "Don't. I don't want her to see me upset like this."

I place my hands on her shoulders. "Is everything okay? Are you okay?"

She breaks her gaze from mine, indicating I've hit the nail on the head. She's not okay. She steps away from me and wipes her tears away with her shirt. She inhales a few deep breaths, attempting to stop more tears from flowing.

"I'm not ready for them to know, Will. Not yet," she whispers. She hugs herself tightly and glances at her house. "I just want them to have a chance to settle in. They've been through so much already this year. I can't tell them yet. It'll break their souls."

She doesn't come out and say it, but I can hear it in her voice. She's sick.

I wrap my arms around her and hug her. I hug her for what she's going through, for what she's been through. I hug her for Lake, I hug her for Kel, and I hug her for Caulder and myself. I hug her because it's all I know to do.

"I won't say anything. I promise." I don't even know how to begin to put myself in her shoes in order to empathize. I can't imagine how hard this must be for her. To know that both of your children are possibly going to be left in the world without you? At least my parents didn't know what was about to happen to them before it happened. At least they didn't have to carry around the burden that Julia is carrying.

She finally pulls away and wipes at her eyes again. "Just send Kel home when he's finished eating. I need to get to work."

"Julia," I say. "If you ever feel like talking about it . . ."

She smiles, then turns and walks away. I'm left standing in front of my house with the emptiest feeling in the world. Knowing what's about to become of Lake's life—it makes me want to protect her even more. I've been in her shoes before and I wouldn't wish it on my worst enemy. I sure as hell don't wish it on the girl I'm falling in love with.

9.

the honeymoon

LAKE SLIDES OFF the bed and walks to the bathroom, wiping her eyes. This is such a bad idea. This is exactly why I don't like bringing up the past.

"Lake," I say, following after her. She's looking into the bathroom mirror, dabbing a tissue to her eyes. I stand behind her and wrap my arms around her waist, resting my head on her shoulder. "I'm sorry. We don't have to talk about it anymore."

She looks at my reflection in the mirror. "Will," she whispers. She turns around to face me and wraps her arms around my neck. "It's just that I had no idea. I didn't know you already knew she was sick."

I pull her to me. "I couldn't really come out and say it, you know. We weren't even speaking at that point. Besides, I would have never betrayed your mom."

She laughs into my shirt, causing me to pull back and look at her. *"What?"* I ask, confused about why she's laughing through her tears.

"Believe me," she says. "I know how your promises to my

mom work. We had to suffer the consequences of that last promise you made for an entire year." She throws her tissue into the trash can and grabs my hand, leading me back to the bed.

"I wouldn't call it suffering," I say, thinking back on last night. "In fact, I'm pretty sure it was worth all the waiting."

She places her hand between her cheek and the pillow and we turn toward each other. I run my fingers through her hair and tuck it behind her ears, then kiss her on the forehead.

"Speaking of suffering," she says. "You just wait until I see Gavin and Eddie again. I can't believe they tried to set you up."

I pull my hand away from her face and rest it on the bed between us. For some reason, I feel like I can't touch her when I'm withholding truth. I break eye contact and roll onto my back. If she's going to bring this up to Eddie, I might as well get it all out in the open now. Otherwise, we'll *all* suffer.

"Um . . . Lake?" I say hesitantly. As soon as her name comes out of my mouth, she shakes her head and scoffs at me.

"You didn't," she says, her words laced with disappointment. She's way too perceptive.

I don't respond.

My silence prompts her to jerk up and grab my jaw, forcing me to look at her.

"You went on a *DATE*?" she says in disbelief.

I place my hand on her cheek in a heartening gesture, hoping my touch will soothe the words about to come out of my mouth. She jerks her face away from my hand and sits up on her knees, placing her hands on them.

"Are you *serious*?"

I laugh a nervous laugh, attempting to make light of the situation. "Lake, you know how forceful Eddie can be. I didn't want to go. Besides, it was just one date."

"Just one date?" she says. "Are you saying you can't develop feelings for someone after just one date?" She spins around on the bed and stands up, dropping down into the desk chair beside the bed. She folds her arms across her chest, shaking her head again. "Please tell me you didn't kiss her."

I scoot toward her until I'm sitting on the edge of the bed. I reach forward and take her hands in mine and look her in the eyes. "I love you," I say. "And I'm here. With you. *Married* to you. Who cares what happened on one silly date more than two years ago?"

"You *KISSED* her?" she says, jerking her hands back. She places her foot on the bed between my legs and pushes against it, rolling her and the chair several feet away from me.

"She kissed *me*," I say defensively. "And it was . . . God, Lake. It was nothing like kissing you."

She glares at me.

"Okay," I say, wiping the smirk off my face. "Not funny. But seriously, you're making a big deal out of nothing. Besides, you agreed to go out with Nick that next week. Remember? What's the difference?"

"What's the *difference*?" she says, enunciating each word carefully. "I didn't *go* on a date with him. I didn't *kiss* him. That's a pretty damn big difference."

I lean forward and grab the arms of her chair and pull her back to me until she's flush against my legs. I place my hands on her cheeks and force her to look at me. "Layken Cooper, I love you. I've loved you since the second I laid eyes on you and I haven't stopped loving you for a second since. The entire time I was out with Taylor, all I was thinking about was *you*."

She crinkles up her nose. "*Taylor?* I didn't need to know her name, Will. Now I'll have a distaste for Taylors for the rest of my life."

"Like I have distaste for Javiers and Nicks?" I say. She grins, but quickly forces the smile away, still trying to punish me with her ineffective scowl.

"You're so cute when you're jealous, babe." I lean forward and softly press my lips to hers. She sighs a quiet, defeated sigh into my mouth and relents, parting her lips for me. I run my hands down her arms and to her waist, then pull her out of the chair and on top of me as I lean back onto the bed.

I place one hand on the small of her back, pressing her against me, and my other hand I run through her hair, grabbing the back of her head. I kiss her hard as I roll her onto her back, proving to her she has absolutely nothing to be jealous of. As soon as I'm on top of her, she places her hands on my cheeks and forces my face away from hers.

"So your lips touched someone else's lips? *After* our first kiss?"

I fall back onto the bed beside her. "Lake, *stop* it. Stop thinking about it."

"I can't, Will." She turns to me and makes that damn pouty face she knows I can't refuse. "I have to know details. In my head all I can picture is you taking some girl out on this perfect date and making her grilled cheese sandwiches and playing *"would you rather"* with her and sharing seriously intense moments with her, then kissing the hell out of her at the end of the night."

Her description of our first date makes me laugh. I lean over and press my lips to her ear and whisper, "Is that what I did to you? I kissed the *hell* out of you?"

She pulls her neck away and shoots me a glare, letting me know she isn't backing down until she gets her way. "Fine," I groan, pulling back. "If I tell you all about it will you promise to let me kiss the hell out of you again?"

"Promise," she says.

the *other* date

WHEN THE DISMISSAL bell rings, Lake is the first out of the classroom again. The tension in the air between us is so thick, it's like she has to run outside just to breathe. I walk to my desk and take a seat while the rest of the students file out.

"Saturday night. Seven o'clock good for you?" Gavin says. I look up at him and he's staring at me, waiting for a response.

"Good for *what?*"

"For Taylor. We're going on a double date and Eddie won't take no for an answer."

"No."

Gavin stares at me for a few seconds, finding it difficult to comprehend my answer. It was a pretty clear *no*, so I'm not sure what the problem is.

"Please?" he says.

"Puppy dog eyes only work on your girlfriend, Gavin."

He slumps his shoulders and lands in the desk in front of me. "She's not gonna let it go, Will. Once Eddie gets something in her head, it's way less painful to just go along with it."

I shake my head. "No. I'm not going," I say firmly. "Besides, you're the one who *put* this idea in her head. You should have to suffer the consequences, not me."

Gavin leans back in his chair and runs his hands over his face, defeated. As soon as I feel victorious, he shoots forward in his seat. "If you don't go, I'll tell."

I lean back in my chair and glare at him. "You'll tell *what?*"

He glances at the door, then back at me, ensuring our privacy. "I'll go to Principal Murphy and I'll tell him you went out with a student. I'm sorry it has to come to blackmail, Will, but you don't know Eddie when she gets an idea in her head. You *have* to do this for me."

Did he really just threaten to blackmail me?

I pick up my pen and pull my lesson plan in front of me, breaking eye contact with him. "Gavin, you won't tell," I say, laughing.

He groans at my response, because he knows he would never stoop that low. "You're right. I'd never tell. But don't you think you owe it to me for being so trustworthy?" he says. "It's just one date. One tiny favor. What difference can one date make?"

"Depending on who it's with, it can make a *huge* difference," I say. One date with Lake was enough to send my life into a tailspin.

"If it helps, you won't have to do much talking. Taylor and Eddie will completely monopolize the conversation. We can eat our steaks and grunt every few minutes and they'll be none the wiser. Then it'll be over. I swear."

I do owe him a favor. A *huge* favor. He's the only one who knows about my situation with Lake and he's never once given me flak about it. I don't know how Eddie can get her way when she's not even in the room, but I finally relent. I slap my pen down on the desk and sigh, giving him a stern look.

"Fine," I say. "Under one condition."

"Anything," he says.

"I don't want this to get back to Lake. Tell Eddie I'll go, but give her an excuse to keep her quiet. Tell her I'm not supposed to be hanging out with you two after hours or something."

Gavin stands and gathers his things. "Thank you, Will,"

he says. "You're a lifesaver. And hey, you might even like Taylor. Keep an open mind."

I WALK INTO the restaurant and spot the three of them in a booth in the far corner. I take a deep breath, then grudgingly walk toward them. I can't believe I'm going on a date. A date that's not with Lake, the only girl I *want* to be on a date with.

The girl I *can't* be on a date with.

Gavin's words, *"keep an open mind,"* linger in my head. I've been completely consumed by thoughts of Lake since I met her almost three weeks ago. I've made the right choice by not continuing something that could ruin my career, but now I just need to figure out how to accept that choice and get her out of my head. Maybe Gavin's right. Maybe I do need to try to move on. It could be better for both of us this way.

When Gavin spots me, he waves and stands up, prompting Taylor to turn around. She's . . . cute. *Really* cute. Her hair is darker than Lake's and shorter, but it fits her well. She's not as tall as Lake, either. She's got a great smile; one of those that seems to be permanently affixed.

I reach the table and smile back at her. Might as well give this a shot.

"Will, Taylor. Taylor, Will," Gavin says, gesturing between us. She smiles and stands up, then gives me a quick hug. General greetings pass around the table and we take our seats. It's odd sitting on the same side of the booth with her. I don't know if I should turn toward her or give my attention to Eddie and Gavin.

"So," she says. "Gavin says you're a teacher?"

I nod. "Student teacher. Until December graduation, anyway."

"You're graduating in December?" she asks, taking a sip of her soda. "How? Isn't that a semester early?"

The waitress walks up to the table and hands me a menu, interrupting the short conversation. "What can I get you to drink?"

"I'll have a sweet tea," I say. The waitress nods and walks away, then Eddie nudges Gavin and pushes his shoulder.

"Sorry, guys, but . . . something just came up," Eddie says. Gavin stands up and pulls his wallet out of his pocket, throwing some cash down on the table.

"This should cover our drinks. You can take Taylor home, right?" he says to me.

"Something came up, huh?" I ask, glaring at both of them. I can't believe they're doing this. I'm *so* going to fail them.

"Uh, yeah," Eddie says, taking Gavin's hand. "So sorry we can't stay. You two have fun."

And they're gone. Just like that.

Taylor laughs. "Wow. *That* wasn't obvious," she says.

I turn back to her and she's grinning, shaking her head. Now it *really* feels odd sitting in the same side of the booth with her. "Well," I say. "This is . . ."

We both say "awkward" at the same time, which causes us to laugh.

"Do you mind if . . ." I point to the other side of the booth and she shakes her head.

"No, please. I've never been a same-side-of-the-booth girl. It's weird."

"I agree," I say, scooting into the seat across from her. The waitress brings my drink and takes our order. It gives us about thirty seconds of distraction before she walks away again, leaving us to fend for ourselves.

Taylor lifts her glass up, motioning to mine. "To awkward first dates," she says. I pick my glass up and clink it against hers.

"So, before all that," she says, waving her hand in the air. "We were talking about how you were graduating a semester early?"

"Yeah . . ." I pause. I don't really feel like going into detail about the real reasons I'm graduating early. I lean back in the booth and shrug. "When I want something, I guess I just focus until I get it. Tunnel vision," I say.

She nods. "Impressive. I've still got a year left, but I'm going into teaching, too. Primary. I like kids."

Our conversation begins to flow better. We talk about college for a while, then when the food comes we talk about that. Then when we run out of things to talk about, she brings up her family. I let her talk about them, but I don't divulge. By the time the bill comes, the conversation is far from awkward. I've only thought about Lake ten times. Maybe fifteen.

Everything seems okay until we're in the car, backing out of the parking lot. Seeing her sitting in the passenger seat, staring out the window; it's reminiscent of just a few weeks ago when Lake was doing the exact same thing, in this exact same spot. But it doesn't feel anything like that. That night with Lake I couldn't keep my eyes off of her while we drove and she slept, her hand still locked with mine. I'm not one to believe that there is only one person right for me in the world. But the tug and pull Lake has on me, even when she isn't in my presence, it makes it feel like she's the *most* right for me. As much as I think Taylor and I would hit it off on a second date, I'm not so sure I'll ever be able to settle for anything less than what I feel for Lake.

We make more small talk and she directs me toward her house. When we pull up into the driveway, the awkwardness immediately sets in. I don't want to lead her on at all, but I also don't want her to think she did anything wrong to turn me off. She was great. The date was great. It's just that my date with Lake was so much more, and now I want nothing less.

I put the car in park and, as awkward as this is going to be, I offer to walk her to her door. When we reach the patio, she turns around and looks up at me with an inviting and welcoming look on her face. This is the point where I need to be honest with her. I don't want to get her hopes up.

"Taylor . . ." I say. "I had a really good ti—" Before I can finish my sentence, her lips are meshed with mine. She doesn't seem like the type to make such bold moves, so the kiss catches me completely off guard. She runs her hands through my hair and I'm suddenly faced with the realization that I don't know what to do with my *own* hands. Do I touch her? Do I push her away? To be honest, the kiss isn't half bad and I catch myself closing my eyes, bringing my hand to her cheek. I know I shouldn't be making comparisons but I can't help it. This kiss is reminiscent of kissing Vaughn. It's not bad . . . pleasant even. But there isn't any emotion in it. No passion. Nothing like what I felt when I kissed Lake.

Lake.

I prepare to pull myself away from her when she finally pulls back herself. I'm relieved I didn't have to be the one to push her away. She takes a step back and covers her mouth in embarrassment. "Wow," she says. "I'm so sorry. I'm not usually that forward."

I laugh. "It's fine. Really, Taylor. It was nice."

I'm not lying; it *was* nice.

"You're just really . . . I don't know," she says, still smiling uncomfortably. "I just wanted to kiss you," she shrugs.

I rub the back of my neck and glance at her front door, then back at her. *How am I going to say this?*

She follows my gaze to her front door, then back to me and smiles. "Oh. You uh . . . You want to come inside?"

Oh, god, oh, god. Why did I look at the door? She thinks I want to come inside now. *Do* I want to come inside? *Shit.* I don't want to come inside. I can't. I wouldn't be thinking about Taylor at all if I went inside.

"Taylor," I say. "I need to be honest with you. I think you're great. I had a great time. If we did this a few months ago, I'd be inside that house with you in a heartbeat."

She can see where I'm headed, so she just nods. "But . . ." she says.

"There's someone else. Someone recent that I can't seem to get past. I agreed to this date because I was hoping that maybe it would somehow help me get over her, but . . . it's too soon."

She looks up at the sky and drops her arms to her side. "Oh, god. I just kissed you. I thought you were feeling it, too, so I kissed you." She covers her face with her hands, embarrassed. "I'm an idiot."

"No," I say, taking a step closer. "No, don't say that. I know this is cliché and it's the last thing you want to hear, but . . . it's not you, it's me. It's completely me. Really. I think you're great and cute and I'm glad you kissed me. Honestly, the timing just really sucks. That's all."

She hugs herself with her arms and looks down at the ground. "If it's just timing," she says quietly, "will you keep my number? In case the timing thing ever gets better?"

"Yeah," I say. "Definitely."

She nods, then looks up at me. "Okay, then," she smiles. "To awkward first dates."

I laugh. "To awkward first dates," I say. She waves and heads inside. Once she's inside her house, I sigh and head back to my car. "Never again, Gavin," I mutter. "Never again."

10.

the honeymoon

"EXCUSE ME FOR a second," Lake says. She pushes herself up and walks to the bathroom, then slams the door behind her.

She's *mad*? *Seriously?* Oh, hell no. I jump up and try to open the bathroom door, but it's locked from the inside. I knock. After several seconds, she swings it open and spins back around toward the shower without looking at me. She turns the shower knob until the water comes to life, then she slips off her shirt.

"I just need a shower," she snaps.

I lean against the doorframe and cross my arms. "You're mad. Why are you mad? Nothing *happened*. I never went out with her again."

She shakes her head and closes the lid to the toilet, then takes a seat on top of it. She slips off her socks one at a time and tosses them to the floor with a jerk of her wrist. "I'm not mad," she says, still avoiding eye contact.

"Lake?" She doesn't look up at me. "Lake? Look at me," I demand.

She inhales a slow breath, then looks up at me through her lashes, her mouth puckered into a pout.

"Three days ago you made a promise to me," I say. "Do you remember what that promise was?"

She rolls her eyes and stands up, unbuttoning her pants. "Of course I remember, Will. It was three freaking days ago."

"What did you promise me you wouldn't do?"

She walks to the mirror and pulls at her ponytail, letting her hair down. She doesn't respond. I take a step closer to her. "What did you promise, Lake? What did we *both* promise each other the night before we got married?"

She grabs her brush off the counter and vigorously combs at her hair. "That we would never carve pumpkins with each other," she mumbles. "That we would talk everything out."

"And what are you doing right now?"

She slams the brush down on the counter and turns to me. "What the hell do you want me to say, Will? Do you want me to admit that I'm not perfect? That I'm jealous? I know you said it didn't mean anything to you, but that doesn't mean it didn't mean something to *me*!" She brushes past me and walks to my suitcase to grab her bottle of conditioner. I lean against the bathroom door again and watch her toss the contents of my suitcase onto the floor while she continues searching for more toiletries.

I don't give her a rebuttal; I have a feeling she isn't finished. Once she gets started like this, it's better if I don't interrupt her. She finds her razor and spins around, continuing her rant.

"And I know you didn't kiss her first, but you didn't *not* kiss her. And you admitted you thought she was cute! And you even admitted that if it weren't for me, you probably would have asked her out again! I hate her, Will. She sounded really, really nice and I hate her for it. It feels like she's been your backup plan in case the two of *us* didn't work out."

She marches toward me again, but this last comment of hers really gets to me. *My backup plan?* I block her way into the bathroom and look down at her, attempting to calm her down before she says something she'll regret.

"Lake, you *know* how I felt about you back then. I never even thought about that girl again. I knew exactly who I wanted to be with. It was just a matter of *when.*"

She drops her arms to her side. "Well, that's nice that you had that reassurance, because I sure as hell didn't. I lived every single day feeling like I was going through hell while you were across the street, choosing everything and everyone over *me.* Not to mention all the while going on dates and kissing other girls while I sat home, watching my own mother die right before my eyes."

I step forward and grab her face with both hands. "That's. Not. Fair," I say through clenched teeth. She darts her eyes away from mine, aware of the low blow she delivered. She pulls away from my grasp and walks around me, back into the bathroom. She pushes open the shower curtain and adjusts the water again, letting her pride and stubbornness win.

"That's it? You're leaving it at that?" I say loudly. She doesn't look up at me. I can sense when I need to step away from a situation, and this is one of those times. If I don't walk away, I'll say something I'll regret, too. I punch the door and storm out of the bathroom, then swing open the door to the hallway. I slam the hotel room door and pace back and forth, cursing under my breath. Each time I pass our hotel room, I pause and turn toward it, expecting her to open the door and apologize.

She never does.

She just got in the shower? How in the hell can she say something like that to me and just get in the damn shower without apologizing? God, she's so infuriating! I haven't been this mad at her since that night I thought she was kissing Javi.

I rest my back against our door and slide down to the floor, then take fistfuls of my hair into my hands. She can't seriously be mad about this. We weren't even dating! I try to justify her reasons for reacting the way she is, but I can't. She's acting like an immature high schooler.

"Will?" she says, her voice muffled by the door. She sounds close and I realize she's on the other side of the door at my level. The fact that she knew I was sitting on the floor in front of the door pisses me off even more. She knows me too well.

"What?" I say sharply.

It's silent for a moment, then she sighs. "I'm sorry I said that," she says softly.

I lean my head against the door and close my eyes, taking in a long, deep breath.

"It's just . . . I know we don't believe in soulmates," she says. "There are so many people in this world that can be right for each other. If there weren't, then cheating would never be an issue. Everyone would find their one true love and life would be great— relationships would be a piece of cake. But that's not how it is in reality, and I realize this. So . . . it just hurts, okay? It hurts me to know that there are other women out there in the world that could make you happy. I know it's immature and I was being petty and jealous, but . . . I just want to be your only one. I want to be your soulmate, even if I don't believe in them. I overreacted and I'm sorry," she says. "I'm really sorry, Will."

There's silence on both ends, then I hear the bathroom door shut. I close my eyes and contemplate everything she said. I know exactly how she feels; I've been prone to my own bouts of jealousy in the past when it comes to her. Back when I was her teacher and hearing her agree to that date with Nick, then later seeing Javi kiss her; I lost my mind both times. Hell, I beat the *shit* out of Javi, and Lake wasn't even my girlfriend at the time. Expecting her not to have a reaction when she finds out I kissed someone else in the midst of all our emotional turmoil makes me nothing but a hypocrite. She had a normal reaction just now, and I'm treating her like this is her fault. She's probably in the shower right now, crying. All because of me.

I'm such an *asshole*.

I jump up and slide the key card in, then open the door. I swing open the bathroom door and she's sitting on the edge of the shower, still in her pants and bra, crying into her hands. She looks up at me with the saddest eyes and guilt consumes me. I grab her hand and pull her up. She sucks in a breath like she's scared I'm about to yell at her again, which only makes me feel worse. I slide my hands through her hair and grip the nape of her neck, then look her in the eyes. She can see in my expression that I'm not here to fight.

I'm here to make up.

"Wife," I say, staring straight into her eyes. "Think what you want, but there isn't a single woman in this whole damn universe that I could ever love like I love you."

Our mouths collide so forcefully; she almost falls backward into the shower. I brace my hand against the shower wall with one arm, then pick her up around the waist with the other arm, lifting her over the lip of the tub. I shove her up against the wall, the water from the showerhead falling between us. We're both breathing heavily and I pull her as close against me as she can possibly get while her fingers tug and pull at my hair. My chest heaves with each breath I inhale as we frantically grab and pull and stroke every inch of each other within arm's reach.

I pull her bra up and over her head, then throw it behind me. My hand slides down to the small of her back, my fingers tracing a trail just inside the back of her jeans. She moans and arches her back, pressing herself harder against me. My fingers slowly slide around to the front of her jeans and I lower her zipper. Her pants are soaked, so it takes effort getting them off her, but I eventually do.

I slide my hand all the way up her thigh and I'm met with nothing but smooth skin. I grin against her lips. "Commando, huh?"

She doesn't waste any time pulling my mouth back to hers. I've been standing directly in the stream of water, so my clothes are soaked, making them more challenging to remove than hers were. Especially since she won't release me for a second longer than needed to pull off my shirt. Once my shirt is successfully gone, I lean back into her. She moans into my mouth when our bare skin collides, forcing me to immediately dispose of my pants as well. She grabs them out of my hand and tosses them over my shoulder, then pulls me against her. I reach down and grab her right leg behind the knee and I pull it up to my side.

She smiles. "Now *this* is how I pictured our first shower together," she says.

I take her bottom lip between my teeth, and I give her the best damn shower she's ever had.

"HOLY CRAP," SHE says, falling onto the bed. "That was intense."

Her arms are relaxed above her head, her robe open just far enough to keep my imagination in check. I sit down beside her and stroke her cheek, then run my hand down her neck. She shivers against my touch. I bend over and press my lips to her collarbone. "There's just something about this spot," I say, teasing her neck. "From here . . ." I kiss up her collarbone until I get to the curve in her neck. "To here." I kiss back down again. "It drives me insane."

She laughs. "I can tell. You can't keep your mouth off it. Most guys prefer the ass or the boobs. Will Cooper prefers the *neck*."

I shake my head, disagreeing with her while I continue running my lips across her incredibly smooth skin. "Nope," I say. "Will Cooper prefers the whole *Lake*."

I tug at the tie on her robe until it loosens between my fingertips. I slide my hand inside the robe and graze her stomach with my fingers. She squirms beneath my hand and laughs.

"Will, you can't be serious. It hasn't even been three minutes."

I ignore her and kiss the chills that are breaking out on her shoulder. "You remember the first time I couldn't resist kissing your neck?" I whisper against her skin.

the (first) mistake

IT'S BEEN THREE weeks since Julia told me she was sick, but from watching Lake and listening to Kel on a daily basis, I know she still hasn't told them. I've spoken to Julia a few times, but only in passing. She doesn't seem to want to bring it up again, so I give her that respect.

Having Lake in third period hasn't gotten any easier. I've learned how to adapt and focus more on what I'm teaching, but the fact that she's still just feet from me every day still has the same emotional impact. Every morning she comes to class, I try to watch for any hints or signs that Julia may have revealed everything to her, but every day is the same. She never raises her hand or speaks, and I make it a point never to call on her. I make it a point not to even look at her. It's been getting harder now that Nick seems to be marking his territory. I know it's none of my business, but I can't help but wonder if they're dating. I haven't seen him at her house but I've noticed they sit together at lunch. She always seems to be in a good mood around him. Gavin would know, but as far as he knows I've moved on, so I can't ask him. I really shouldn't even care . . . but I can't help it.

I'm running late when I get to class. When I walk in, the first thing I notice is Nick turned toward Lake. She's laughing again. She's always laughing at his stupid jokes. I like seeing her laugh, but I also hate that he's the reason she's laughing. It immediately puts me in a bad mood, so I decide to cancel the lecture I had planned and give a poetry writing assignment instead. After I lay out the rules and everyone begins on their assignment, I take a seat at my desk. I try to focus on completing a lesson plan, but I can't help but notice Lake hasn't written a single word. I know she doesn't have a problem with the material in class. In fact, she's had the best grades since the day she enrolled. Her lack of effort on this assignment makes me wonder if she has the same concentration problems during third period that I have.

I glance up from staring at the blank paper on her desk and she's staring right at me. My heart catches in my throat and the same emotional and physical responses I try so hard to squelch are suddenly consuming me again. It's the first eye contact we've had in three weeks. I try to look away, but I can't. She doesn't reveal any hint of emotion in her expression. I wait for her to look away, but instead she stares at me with the same intensity that I'm sure I'm returning in my own stare. This silent exchange between us causes my pulse to race just as fiercely as it did when I kissed her.

When the bell rings, I force myself out of my chair and walk to the door to hold it open. When everyone's gone, including Lake, I slam it shut.

What the hell am I thinking? That twenty seconds of whatever the hell that was negated my entire last three weeks of effort. I lean against the door and kick it out of frustration.

AS SOON AS I reach the parking lot after school, I see that the hood to Lake's Jeep is open. I look around, hoping someone else is around to assist her instead. I really don't need to be alone with her right now, especially after what happened in my classroom this morning. I'm finding it harder and harder to resist the thought of her, and this current predicament has trouble written all over it.

Unfortunately, I'm the only one around. I can't just leave her here stranded in a parking lot. I'm sure it would be just as easy to turn around and head inside before she notices me. Someone else will help her eventually. Despite my hesitation, I keep walking forward. When I near her vehicle, she's bludgeoning the battery with a crowbar.

"That's not a good idea," I say. I'm hoping she doesn't bust through the battery before I reach her. She spins around and looks at me, eyeing me up and down, then returns her focus back under the hood like she never even saw me.

"You've made it clear that you don't think a lot of what I do is a very good idea," she says firmly. She's obviously not happy to see me, which is just more confirmation that I should turn around and walk away.

But I don't.

I *can't.*

I reluctantly walk closer and peer under the hood. "What's wrong, it won't crank?" I check the connections on the battery and inspect the alternator.

"What are you doing, Will?" She has an edgy, almost annoyed tone to her voice. I lift my head out from under the hood and look at her. Her features are hard. It's obvious she's put up an invisible wall between us, which is probably a good thing. She seems offended that I'm even offering to help her.

"What does it look like I'm doing?" I break our stare and quickly turn my attention back to the battery cable. "I'm trying to figure out what's wrong with your Jeep," I say. I walk around to the door and attempt to turn the ignition. When it doesn't crank, I turn to exit the Jeep and she's standing right next to me. I'm quickly reminded what it feels like to be in such close proximity to her. I hold my breath and fight back the urge to grab her by the waist and pull her into the Jeep with me.

"I mean, *why* are you doing this? You've made it pretty clear you don't want me to speak to you," she says.

Her obvious annoyance at my presence almost makes me regret having decided to help her after all. "Layken, you're a student stranded in the parking lot. I'm not going to get in my car and just drive away." As soon as the words escape my lips, I regret them. She draws her chin in and glances away, shocked at my impersonal words.

I sigh and get out of the car. "Look, that's not how I meant it," I say as I reach back under the hood.

She steps closer to me and leans against the Jeep. I watch her out of the corner of my eye while I pretend to fidget with more wires. She tugs on her bottom lip with her teeth and stares at the ground, a saddened expression across her face. "It's just been really hard, Will," she says quietly. The softness in her voice now is even more painful to hear than the edginess. I inhale, afraid of what she's about to confess. She takes a deep breath like she's hesitating to finish her sentence, but continues anyway. "It was so easy for you to accept this and move past it. It hasn't been that easy for me. It's all I think about."

Her confession and the honesty in her voice cause me to wince. I grip the edge of the hood and turn toward her. She's looking down at her hands with a troubled expression on her face. "You think this is *easy* for me?" I whisper.

She glances at me and shrugs. "Well, that's how you make it seem," she says.

Now would be the opportune moment to walk away. Walk away, Will.

"Lake, nothing about this has been easy," I whisper. I know beyond a doubt that I shouldn't be saying any of the things I've been dying to say to her, but everything about her draws the truth out of me whether I want to share it or not. "It's a daily struggle for me to come to work, knowing this very job is what's keeping us apart." I turn away from the car and lean against it, next to her. "If it weren't for Caulder, I would have quit that first day I saw you in the hallway. I could have taken the year off . . . waited until you graduated to go back." I turn toward her and lower my voice. "Believe me, I've run every possible scenario through my mind. How do you think it makes me feel to know that I'm the reason you're hurting? That I'm the reason you're so sad?"

I just said way too much. *Way* too much.

"I . . . I'm sorry," she stutters. "I just thought—"

"Your battery is fine," I say as soon as I see Nick round the car next to us. "Looks like it might be your alternator."

"Car won't start?" Nick says.

Layken looks at me wide-eyed, then turns around to face Nick. "No, Mr. Cooper thinks I need a new alternator."

"That sucks," Nick says as he glances under the hood. He looks back up at Lake. "I'll give you a ride home if you need one."

As much as I'd rather punch him than let him take her home, I know it's her only option right now because *I* sure as hell don't need to take her home.

"That would be great, Nick," I say. I shut the hood of the Jeep and walk away before I add to my long list of stupid decisions.

I SHOULD JUST pull the list of stupid decisions back out, because I'm making another one right now.

We've spent the last fifteen minutes frantically searching for Kel and Caulder. I'd assumed they were at her house, she had assumed they were at mine. We finally found them passed out in the backseat of my car, where they still are.

Now, I'm rummaging through my satchel, searching for the keys to her Jeep. I had my mechanic put a new alternator on it this afternoon, then stupidly invited her inside to give her the keys back. I say *stupidly*, because every ounce of my being doesn't want her to leave. My heart is pounding against my chest just being in her presence. I locate the keys and turn around to hand them to her. "Your keys," I say, dropping them into her hand.

"Oh, thanks," she says, looking down at them. I'm not sure what she expected me to hand her, but she seems disappointed that it's just her keys.

"It's running fine now," I say. "You should be able to drive it home tomorrow." I'm hoping she'll be the strong one right now and just leave. I can't bring myself to walk her back to the door, so I make my way back into the living room and sit on the couch. The conversation at her Jeep this afternoon lingers silent and thick in the air between us.

"What? You fixed it?" she says, following me into the living room.

"Well, *I* didn't fix it. I know a guy who was able to put an alternator on it this afternoon."

"Will, you didn't have to do that," she says. Rather than leave like we both know she should, she sits on the couch beside me. When her elbow grazes mine, I bring my hands up and clasp them behind my head. We can't even graze elbows without my wanting to reach over and kiss the hell out of her.

"Thanks, though. I'll pay you back."

"Don't worry about it. You guys have helped me a lot with Caulder lately, it's the least I can do."

She looks down at her hand and twirls the keys around. She runs her thumb over the Texas-shaped keychain and I can't help but wonder if she'd still rather be there right now.

"So, can we finish our conversation from earlier?" she says, still staring down at the keychain.

I already regret having said what I said at her Jeep today. I confessed way too much. I can't believe I told her I would have quit my job if it weren't for Caulder. I mean, it's the truth. As crazy and desperate as it sounds, I would have quit in a heartbeat. I'm not so sure I still wouldn't if she would just ask me to.

"That depends," I say. "Did you come up with a solution?"

She shakes her head and looks up at me. "Well, no," she says. She tosses her keys onto the coffee table and pulls her knee up, turning to face me on the couch. She sighs, almost as if she's afraid to ask me something. She runs her fingers over the throw pillow between us and traces the pattern without looking up at me. "Suppose these feelings we have just get more . . . complex." She hesitates for a moment. "I wouldn't be opposed to the idea of getting a GED."

Her plan is so absurd I almost have to hold back a laugh. "That's ridiculous," I say, shooting a look in her direction. "Don't even think like that. There's no way you're quitting school, Lake."

She tosses the pillow aside. "It was just an idea," she says.

"Well, it was a dumb one."

Things grow quiet between us. The way she's turned toward me on the couch causes every muscle in my body to clench, even my jaw. I'm trying so hard not to turn toward her, to take her in my arms. This entire situation isn't fair. If we were in any other circumstances, a relationship between us would be absolutely fine. Accepted. Normal. The only thing keeping us apart is a damn job title.

It's so hard having to hide how I feel about her when it's just the two of us. It would be so easy to just say *"To hell with it,"* and do what I want to do. I know if I could just get past the moral aspect and the threat of getting caught, I'd do it in a heartbeat. I'd take her in my arms and kiss her just like I've been imagining for the past three weeks. I'd kiss her mouth, I'd kiss her cheek, I'd kiss that line from her ear down to her shoulder that I can't stop staring at. She'd let me, too. I know how hard this has been on her; I can see it in the way she carries herself now. She's depressed. I'm almost tempted to make all of this easier on her and just act on my feelings. If neither of us says anything, no one would know. We could do this secretly until she graduated. If we were careful, we could even keep it from Julia and the boys.

I pop my knuckles behind my head in order to distract myself from pulling her mouth to mine. My heart is erratic just thinking about the possibility of kissing her again. I inhale through my nose and out my mouth, trying to physically calm myself before I do something stupid. Or smart. I can't tell what's right or wrong when I'm around her because what's wrong feels so right and what's right feels so wrong.

Her finger grazes across my neck and the unexpected touch causes me to flinch. She defensively holds up her finger to show me the shaving cream she just wiped off my neck. Without even thinking, I grab her hand to wipe it onto my shirt.

Big mistake.

As soon as my fingers touch hers, whatever conscious thoughts remained get wiped away right along with the shaving cream. My hand remains clasped on top of hers and she relaxes it onto my chest.

I've reached the threshold of my willpower. My pulse is racing, my heart feels like it's about to explode. I can't let go of her hand and I can't stop looking into her eyes. In this moment, absolutely nothing is happening, but then again *everything* is happening. Every single second I silently look at her, holding on to her hand, erases days of willpower and determination I spent keeping my distance. Every ounce of energy I've put into doing the right thing has all been in vain.

"Will?" she whispers without breaking her gaze. The way my name flows from her lips makes my pulse go haywire. She strokes her thumb ever so slightly across my chest—a movement she may not have even been aware of, but one that I feel all the way to my core. "I'll wait for you," she says. "Until I graduate."

As soon as the words come from her lips, I exhale and close my eyes. She just said what I've wanted to hear from her for an entire month. I stroke my thumb across the back of her hand and sigh. "That's a long wait, Lake. A lot can happen in a year."

She scoots closer to me on the couch. She removes her hand from my chest and lightly touches my jaw with the tips of her fingers, pulling my gaze back to hers. I refuse to look into her eyes. I know if I do, I'll give in and kiss her. I slide my fingers down her hand with every intention of stopping at her wrist to pull her hand from my face. Instead, my fingers trail past her wrist and slowly graze up the length of her arm. I need to stop. I need to pull back, but my willpower and my heart are suddenly at war.

I pull my legs off the coffee table in front of me. I'm hoping she pushes me away from her—does what we both know one of us needs to do. When she doesn't, I find myself drawing in closer. I just want to put my arms around her and hold her. I want to hold her like I held her outside Club N9NE before all of this became out of our control. Before it became this overwhelming, convoluted mess.

Before I can stop myself or give myself time to think about it—my lips meet her neck, and all hell breaks loose inside me. She wraps her arms around me and inhales a breath deep enough for the both of us. The feel and taste of her skin against my lips is enough to completely wipe away the rest of my conscience.

To hell with it.

I kiss across her collarbone, up her neck and to her jaw, then take her face in my hands and pull back to look her in the eyes. I need to know we're on the same page. I need to know that she wants this as bad as I do. That she *needs* this as bad as I do.

The sadness in her eyes that has consumed her for the past three weeks is nonexistent right now. There's hope in her eyes again, and I want nothing more than to somehow help her maintain whatever it is she's feeling right now. I slowly lean in and press my lips against hers. The sensation from the kiss both kills me and brings me back to life in the same breath. She quietly gasps, then parts her lips for me, taking a fist of my shirt in her hands, gently pulling me closer.

I kiss her.

I kiss her like it's the first time I've ever kissed her.

I kiss her like it's the *last* time I'll ever kiss her.

Her hands are around my neck—my lips are caressing hers. Holding her in my arms right now feels like I'm taking the first breath I've taken since that moment I saw her standing in the hallway. Every moan from her mouth and every touch of her hands brings me back to life. Nothing and no one can come between us and this moment. Not Caulder, not my morals, not my job, not my school, not Julia.

Julia.

I clench my fists, fighting against the pull to release her when reality hits. The heaviness of the situation comes crashing back down on me like a ton of bricks, forcing itself into the forefront of my mind. Lake has no idea what's about to happen to her life, and I'm allowing myself to complicate it even *more*? With every movement of my mouth against hers, I'm pulling us further and further into a hole we aren't going to be able to crawl out of.

She runs her hands through my hair and begins to lower herself back onto the couch, pulling me with her. I know once our bodies are meshed together on this couch, neither one of us will be strong enough to stop.

I can't *do* this to her. There is so much more going on in her life than she's even aware of. What the hell am I thinking adding this kind of stress to that? I swore to Julia I wouldn't complicate Lake's life, and that's precisely what I'm doing. I somehow find the strength to tear my lips apart from hers and pull away. When I do, we both gasp for air.

"We've got to stop," I say, breathless. "We can't do this." I squeeze my eyes shut and cover them with my forearm, giving myself a minute to regroup. I feel her inching closer to me. She pulls herself onto my lap and forces her lips onto mine again in a desperate plea to keep going. The second our lips meet, I instinctively wrap my arms around her and pull her closer. My conscience is literally screaming at me so loud, I pull her face to mine even harder in an attempt to squelch the internal voice. My mind is telling me to do one thing; my heart and my hands are begging me to do another. She grasps my shirt and slips it over my head, then returns her lips to my mouth where they belong.

In my mind I'm pushing her away, but in reality I've got one hand on her lower back, pulling her against me, and my other hand gripping the nape of her neck. She runs her hands over my chest and I have a huge urge to do the same to her. Just as I grasp the hem of her shirt, I clench my fists and release it. I've already let it go way too far. I've got to put an end to this before I *can't*. It's entirely my responsibility to make sure she doesn't get hurt again, and right now I'm dropping the ball completely.

I push her off me and back onto the couch, then stand up. I've got one chance to prove to her that this is bad. As good as it feels, it's wrong. So wrong.

"Layken, get up!" I demand, taking her hand. I'm so incredibly flustered right now, I don't mean for my reaction to come off so harsh, but I don't know how else to react. I'm so pissed at myself I want to scream, but I struggle with the attempt to calm my nerves. She stands up with a look of embarrassment and confusion across her face.

"This—this can't happen!" I say. "I'm your teacher now. Everything has changed. We can't do this." I can hear the edge in my voice again. I'm trying my best not to come off as angry, but I *am* angry. Not at her, but how can she differentiate? Maybe she shouldn't. Maybe this would be easier for her if she were disappointed in me. Easier for her to let me go.

She sits back down on the couch and drops her face into her hands. "Will, I won't say anything," she whispers. "I swear." She looks back up at me and the sadness in her eyes has returned. All the hope is gone.

The hurt in her voice only solidifies the fact that I'm an asshole. I can't believe I just *did* this to her—led her on like this. She doesn't need this right now.

"I'm sorry, Layken, but it's not right," I say as I pace the floor. "This isn't good for either of us. This isn't good for *you*."

She glares at me. "You don't know what's good for me," she snaps.

I've really screwed this up. *Royally.* I need to fix it now. I need to *end* it now. For good. She can't leave here thinking this is going to happen again. I stop pacing and turn toward her.

"You won't wait for me. I won't let you give up what should be the best year of your life. I had to grow up way too fast; I'm not taking that away from you, too. It wouldn't be fair." I inhale a breath and tell the biggest lie I've ever told. "I don't want you to wait for me, Layken."

"I won't be giving *anything* up," she replies weakly.

The pain in her voice is too much, causing me to have an overwhelming urge to hug her again. I can't take these emotional swings anymore. One minute I'm wanting to kiss the living hell out of her and take her in my arms and protect her from every tear that's about to come her way, then the next minute my conscience kicks in and I want to kick her out of my house. I've hurt her so bad and she has no idea how much worse her life is about to get. Just knowing this makes me hate myself for what I just allowed to happen. *Despise* myself, even.

I grab my shirt and pull it over my head, then move across the living room to the back of the couch. I take a deep breath, feeling slightly more in control the farther away I am from her. I grip the back of the couch and prepare an attempt to rectify a nonrectifiable situation. If I could just get her to understand where I'm coming from, maybe she wouldn't take it so hard.

"My life is nothing but responsibilities. I'm raising a *child*, for Christ's sake. I wouldn't be able to put your needs first. Hell, I wouldn't even be able to put them *second*." I raise my head and meet her eyes. "You deserve better than third."

She stands up and crosses the living room, kneeling on the couch in front of me. "Your responsibilities *should* come before me, which is why I want to wait for you, Will. You're a good person. This thing about you that you think is your flaw—it's the reason I'm falling in love with you."

Whatever was left of my heart before those words left her mouth is in a million pieces now. I can't let her do this. I can't let her feel this way. The only thing I can do to make her stop loving me is to make her start hating me. I bring my hands up to meet her cheeks and I look her in the eyes, then I say the hardest words that I'll ever have to say. "You are *not* falling in love with me. You *cannot* fall in love with me." As soon as I see the tears welling in the corners of her eyes, I have to drop my hands and head toward the front door. I can't watch her cry. I don't want to see what I'm doing to her right now.

"What happened tonight—" I point to the couch. "That can't happen again. That *won't* happen again."

I open the front door and shut it behind me, then lean against the door and close my eyes. I rub my hands over my face and attempt to calm myself down. This is all my fault. I allowed her into my house, knowing how weak I am around her. I kissed her. *I* kissed *her*. I can't believe all of this just happened. Twenty minutes alone with her and I somehow screw her life up even more.

Seeing her sitting on the couch just now, dumbfounded and heartbroken because of my actions and my words . . . I *hate* myself. Pretty sure Lake hates me now, too. I hope it was worth it. Somehow doing the *right* thing in this situation seems completely and utterly *wrong*.

I walk to the car and pull Caulder out. He wraps his arms around my neck without even waking up. Kel opens his eyes and looks around, confused.

"You guys fell asleep in the car. Go home and go to bed, okay?"

He rubs his eyes and crawls out of the car, then makes his way across the street. When I walk back through the front door holding Caulder, Lake is still sitting on the couch, staring at the floor. As much as I want to grab her and tell her I'm so, so sorry for this entire night, I realize she needs this to get past whatever it is going on between us. She *needs* to be angry at me. And Julia needs her to be focused this year. She can't have Lake wrapped up in us when it might be the last year she ever gets to spend with her mom.

"Kel woke up, he's walking home now. You should go, too," I say.

She snatches the keys off the table in front of her and turns to face me. She looks me straight in the eyes; tears streaming down her face. "You're an *asshole*," she says, her words like a bullet of truth straight through my heart. She walks out and slams the door behind her.

I take Caulder to his room and tuck him in, then walk to my bedroom. When I close the door behind me, I lean against it and close my eyes, then slide down the length of the door until I meet the floor. I press the heels of my palms against my eyes, holding back the tears.

God, this *girl*. This girl is the only girl I care about, and I just gave her every reason in the world to hate me.

11.

the honeymoon

"I'm so, so sorry, Will," she whispers. She puts her hands over her face and covers her eyes. "I feel horrible. Terrible. And *selfish*. I didn't know how hard it was for you, too. I just thought you kicked me out because I wasn't worth the risk."

"Lake, you didn't know what all was going through my mind. For all you knew I was just some jerk who kissed you, then kicked you out of my house. I never blamed you. And you were absolutely worth the risk. If it weren't for knowing what I knew about Julia, I would have never let you go."

She pulls her hands away from her face and turns to me. "Oh, my god, and those *names*. I never did apologize for that." She rolls on top of me and brings her face inches from mine. "I'm so sorry I called you all those names the next day."

"Don't be," I shrug. "I sort of deserved it."

She shakes her head. "You can't sit here and tell me that didn't piss you off. I mean, I called you thirty different names in front of the entire class!"

"I didn't say it didn't piss me off. I just said I deserved it."

She laughs. "So you *were* mad at me." She lies back down on her pillow. "Let me hear it," she says.

regrets

I'VE GONE AS slowly as possible. I've called on each student, never rushed them, never even timed them. Usually they don't spit them out this fast. Of course, as soon as Gavin finishes his poem, there's still five minutes to spare. I have no choice but to call on her. I waited until last, hoping the bell would ring. I don't know if I'm trying to spare her from having to get up and speak after what happened between us last night, or if I'm scared to death about what she might say. Either way, it's her turn and I have no choice but to call her up.

I clear my throat and attempt to say her name, but it comes out all mangled. She walks to the front of the room and leaves her poem on her desk. I know for a fact she didn't write a single word yesterday in class. And considering the events that transpired in my living room last night, I doubt she was in the right mindset to even write one. However, she appears unwavering and confident and has apparently memorized whatever it is she's about to perform. It sort of terrifies me.

"I have a question," she says before she begins.

Shit. What the hell could she possibly need to ask? She left so angry last night, I wouldn't be surprised if she outs me right here and now. Hell, she's probably about to ask me if I kick *all* my students out of my house after I make out with them. I nod, giving her the go-ahead for her question . . . but all I really want to do is run to the bathroom and puke.

"Is there a time minimum?"

Jesus Christ. She's actually asking a normal question. I breathe a sigh of relief and clear my throat. "No, it's fine. Remember, there are no rules."

"Good," she says. "Okay, then. My poem is called *Mean.*"

The blood rushes from my head and pools in my heart as soon as the title flows from her mouth. She turns toward the room and begins.

> According to the thesaurus . . .
> *and* according to *me* . . .
> there are over thirty different meanings and
> substitutions for the word
> *mean.*

(SHE RAISES HER voice and yells the rest of the poem, causing me to flinch.)

> Jackass, jerk, cruel, dickhead, unkind, harsh, wicked,
> hateful, heartless, vicious, virulent, unrelenting,
> tyrannical, malevolent, atrocious, bastard, barbarous,
> bitter, brutal, callous, degenerate, brutish, depraved,
> evil, fierce, hard, implacable, rancorous, pernicious,
> inhumane, monstrous, merciless, inexorable.
> And *my* personal favorite—*asshole.*

MY PULSE IS pounding almost as fast as the insults are flying out of her mouth. When the bell rings, I sit stunned as most of the students make their way past my desk. *I can't believe she just did that!*

"The date," I hear Eddie saying to her. The word "date" snaps me back into the moment. "You said you'd have to ask your mom?" Eddie says. They're standing next to Lake's desk and Eddie has her back turned to me.

"Oh, that," Lake says. She looks over Eddie's shoulder and directly at me. "Yeah, sure," she says. "Tell Nick I'd love to."

I've never had a problem with my temper before, but it's almost as if the day I met Lake, every single emotion I had was multiplied by a thousand. Happiness, hurt, anger, bitterness, love, jealousy. I'm unable to control any of it when I'm around her. The fact that she apparently had been asked out by Nick *before* our little incident last night somehow pisses me off even more. I glare at her, open my drawer, and shove my grade book inside it, then slam it shut. When Eddie spins around, startled at the noise, I quickly stand up and begin wiping the board.

"Great," Eddie says, her attention back to Lake now. "Oh, and we decided on Thursday so after Getty's we can go to the slam. We've only got a few weeks, might as well get it out of the way. You want us to pick you up?"

"Uh, sure," Lake says.

Lake could have at least had the decency to agree to a date when she's not standing five feet from me. As much as I want her to be pissed at me, I never thought I'd be pissed at her. But she seems intent on ensuring that that happens. Once Eddie leaves the classroom, I drop the eraser and turn back toward Lake. I fold my arms across my chest and watch as she gathers her things and heads toward the door, not once looking in my direction. Before she exits, I say something I regret before I even say it.

"Layken."

She pauses when she gets to the door, but doesn't turn around to face me.

"Your mom works Thursday nights," I say. "I always get a sitter for Thursdays since I go to the slams. Just send Kel over before you leave. You know, before your *date*."

She doesn't turn around. She doesn't yell. She doesn't throw anything at me. She simply walks out the door, leaving me feeling as though I'm every single one of those names she just yelled in my classroom.

After fourth period, I sit at my desk and stare at nothing at all, wondering what the hell has gotten into me. I usually go to the teachers' lounge for lunch, but I know I can't eat right now. My stomach is in knots thinking about the last two hours. Actually, the last *twenty-four* hours.

Why would I say that to her? I know her poem stirred something in me unlike anything I've ever felt. It was a mixture of embarrassment, anger, hurt, and heartache. But that wasn't enough for her—she had to go and add *jealousy* on top of all that. If there's one thing I've learned about today, it's that I don't handle jealousy well. At all.

I know I thought the best way to help her get over me was to make sure she hated me, but I just can't do it. If I want to keep my own sanity, I can't let her hate me. I can't let her love me, though, either. *Shit!* This is so screwed up. *How the hell am I going to make this right?*

WHEN I REACH their table in the lunchroom, she's not even joined in on the conversation taking place around her. She's staring down at her tray, oblivious to the world. Oblivious to me. Eddie and I both try to get her attention. When she finally snaps out of her trance and looks up at me, the color runs from her face. She slowly rises from the table and follows me to the classroom. When we're safely inside I close the door and walk past her to my desk.

"We need to talk," I say. My head is spinning and I have no

idea what I even want to say to her. I know I want to apologize for the way I reacted earlier in class, but the words aren't coming. I'm a grown man acting like a blubbering fourteen-year-old boy.

"Then talk," she snaps. She's standing across the room glaring at me. Her current attitude coupled with the fact that she just agreed to go out on a date with another guy right in front of me infuriates me. I know everything about our situation is my fault, but she's not doing anything to help it.

"Dammit, Lake!" I spin away from her, frustrated. I run my hands through my hair and take a deep breath, then turn back to face her. "I'm not your enemy. Stop hating me."

I swear she chuckles under her breath right before her eyes fill with fury. "Stop *hating* you?" she says, rushing toward me. "Make up your freaking *mind*, Will! Last night, you told me to stop loving you, now you're telling me to stop *hating* you? You tell me you don't want me to wait on you, yet you act like an immature little boy when I agree to go out with Nick! You want me to act like I don't know you, but then you pull me out of the lunchroom in front of everyone! We've got this whole façade between us, like we're different people all the time, and it's exhausting! I never know when you're Will or Mr. Cooper and I *really* don't know when I'm supposed to be Layken or Lake."

She throws herself into a chair and folds her arms across her chest, letting out a rush of frustrated breath. She's eyeing me sharply, waiting for me to say or do something. There isn't anything to say. I can't refute a single word she just said, because it's the truth. The fact that I haven't been able to keep my own feelings in check have done more damage to her than I ever imagined.

I slowly walk around her desk and sit in the seat behind her. I'm exhausted. Emotionally, physically, mentally. I never imagined it would turn into this. If I had the slightest clue that the decision to keep my job over her would have this kind of effect on me, I would have picked her, despite whatever is going on with Julia. I *should* have picked her. I *still* should pick her.

I lean forward until I'm close to her ear. "I didn't think it would be this hard," I whisper. And that's the truth. Never in a million years did I think something as trivial as a first date could turn into something so incredibly *complicated*. "I'm sorry I said that to you earlier, about Thursday," I say. "I was being sincere—for the most part. I know you'll need someone to watch Kel and I did make the slam a required assignment. But I shouldn't have reacted like that. That's why I asked you to come here; I just needed to apologize. It won't happen again, I swear."

I hear her sniff, which only means she's crying. *Jesus.* I keep making this worse for her when all I want to do is fix it. I lift my hand to stroke the back of her hair in reassurance when the door to my classroom opens. I immediately pull my hand back and stand up, a hasty move that reeks of guilt. Eddie is standing in the doorway to the classroom holding Lake's backpack. She glances at me, then we both simultaneously look at Lake. Turning her head away from Eddie and toward me, I finally see the tears streaming down Lake's cheeks. The tears I put there.

Eddie sets the backpack in a desk and holds her palms up, backing out of the doorway. "My bad. Continue," she says.

As soon as the door is closed behind her, I begin to panic. Whatever Eddie just witnessed, it obviously wasn't a conversation between a teacher and his student. I've just added yet another shit-tastic thing to my list of screw-ups.

"That's just great," I mumble. How the hell do I even begin to fix all of this?

Lake rises out of her seat and begins walking toward the door. "Let it go, Will. If she asks me about it, I'll just tell her you were upset because I said asshole. And jackass. And dickhead. And bastar—"

"I get your point," I say, interrupting her before she can finish her stream of insults. She picks up her backpack and reaches the door.

"Layken?" I say cautiously. "I also want to say I'm sorry . . . about last night."

She slowly turns toward me. The tears have stopped but the residual effects of her mood are still written across her face. "Are you sorry it happened? Or sorry about the way you stopped it?"

I don't really understand what the difference is. I shrug my shoulders. "All of it. It never should have happened."

She turns her back to me and opens the door. "Bastard."

The insult cuts straight to my heart, right where she intended for it to hit.

As soon as the door closes behind her, I kick the desk over. "Shit!" I yell, squeezing the tension out of my neck with my hands. I let out a steady stream of cusswords as I pace the classroom. Not only have I screwed this up even worse with Lake, I've also screwed it up by making Eddie suspicious. I feel like I've somehow made this entire situation ten times worse. God, what I wouldn't give for my father's advice right now.

MRS. ALEX AND her pointless questions once again make me late for third period. I don't really mind being late today, though. After the interaction in my classroom yesterday with Lake, I'm still not ready to face her.

The hallways have cleared out and I'm nearing my classroom when I pass by the windows that look out over the courtyard. I stop in my tracks and step closer to the window and I see Lake. She's sitting on one of the benches, looking down at her hands. I'm a little confused, since she should be sitting in my classroom right now. She looks up at the sky and lets out a deep sigh, like she's trying not to cry. It's apparent that the last place she can be right now is two feet from me in a classroom. Seeing her out there, choosing the bitter Michigan air over my classroom, makes me hurt for her.

"She's something else, huh?"

I spin around and Eddie is standing behind me with her arms crossed, smiling.

"What?" I say, undoubtedly trying to recover from the fact that she just caught me staring at Lake.

"You heard me," she says, walking past me toward the courtyard entry. "And you agree with me, too." She walks out into the courtyard without turning back. When Lake looks up at her and smiles, I walk away.

It's not a big deal. Lake is a student skipping my class and I was looking at her. That's all. There wasn't anything happening there that Eddie could report. Despite my failed attempts at reassuring myself, I spend the rest of the day a nervous wreck.

12.

the honeymoon

"LET ME GET this straight," Lake says, glaring at me. "You were being an idiot, staring at me through the courtyard window. Eddie sees you staring at me, which only piques her curiosity at this point. But then the next weekend in your living room when Eddie figured it all out, you get mad at *me*?"

"I wasn't mad at you," I say.

"Will, you were pissed! You kicked me out of your house!"

I roll over and think back to that night. "I guess I did, huh?"

"Yes, you did," she says. "And on the worst day of my life at that." She rolls over on top of me and interlocks her fingers with mine, bringing them over my head. "I think you owe me an apology. After all, I did clean your entire house that day."

I look her in the eyes and she's grinning. I know she's not upset, but I actually do want to give her a sincere apology. The way I acted at the end of that day was purely selfish, and I've always regretted how I just kicked her out at one of the lowest points of her life. I bring my hands to her cheeks and pull her to the pillow next to me while we change positions. I lay her on her back and rest my head on my propped-up hand, stroking her face with my other hand. I run my fingers up her cheek, over her forehead, and down her nose until my fingers come to rest on her lips. "I'm sorry for the way I treated you that night," I whisper, bringing my lips to hers. I kiss her slowly at first, but the sincerity in my apology is apparently quite attractive to her, because she pushes my arm away and pulls me to her, then whispers, "You're forgiven."

"WHAT ARE YOU doing?" I ask, waking up from a nap induced by pure exhaustion. Lake has her shirt on and is pulling her jeans up.

"I need some fresh air. Wanna come?" she says. "They've got a really nice pool area and it doesn't close for another hour or so. We can sit on the patio and have coffee."

"Yeah, sure." I roll out of bed and search for my clothes.

Once we're outside, the courtyard is empty, as is the pool, even though it's heated. There are several lounge chairs, but Lake takes a seat at a table with bench-style chairs so we can sit together. She curls up next to me and rests her head against my arm, holding her coffee cup between her hands.

"I hope the boys are having fun," she says.

"You know they are. Grandpaul took them geocaching today."

"Good," she says. "Kel loves that." She brings her coffee cup to her lips and sips from it. We watch the moon's reflection on the surface of the water, listening to the sounds of the night. It's peaceful.

"We had a pool back in Texas," she says. "It wasn't as big as this one, but it was nice. It gets so hot there that the water in the pool would feel like it was heated, even when it wasn't. I bet Texas water on its coldest day is still hotter than this heated pool."

"Are you a good swimmer?" I ask her.

"Of course. I lived in that pool half the year."

I lean in and kiss her, distracting her from the fact that I'm taking the coffee cup out of her hands. I slowly lean over her, hooking my arm underneath her knees. She's used to my public displays of affection, so she's none the wiser. As soon as she runs her hands through my hair, I lift her onto my lap and stand up, heading for the water. She pulls her lips from mine and darts her eyes to the pool, then back at me.

"Don't you dare, Will Cooper!"

I laugh and keep walking toward the pool as she starts struggling to get out of my arms. When I reach the deep end of the pool, she's clinging to my neck for dear life.

"If I go, you go," she says.

I smile and kick off my shoes. "I wouldn't have it any other way."

As soon as I toss her into the water, I jump in after her. When she emerges, she swims toward me laughing. "These are my only clothes, you jerk!"

When she reaches me I wrap my arms around her and she pulls her legs up, wrapping them around my waist. She hooks her arms around my neck and I swim backward until my back meets the tile siding of the pool. I put one arm on the concrete ledge to hold us up and my other arm I secure around her waist, holding her against me.

"I'll have to throw this shirt away now. The chlorine probably just ruined it," she says.

I slide my hand underneath her shirt and up her back, then press my lips against the area of skin right below her ear. "If you throw this ugly shirt away, I'm divorcing you."

She throws her head back and laughs. "Finally! You love my ugly shirt!"

I pull her against me so close that even the water can't pass between us. I bring my forehead to hers. "I've *always* loved this shirt, Lake. This is the shirt you were wearing the night I finally admitted to myself that I was in love with you."

The corner of her lip curls up into a grin. "And what night was that?"

I tilt my head back until it rests against the concrete siding and look up to the sky. "Not a good one."

She kisses me at the base of my throat. "Tell me anyway," she whispers.

i *love* her

"CAULDER, ARE YOU sure Julia said it was okay for you to stay the night?" He's rummaging through his dresser looking for socks while Kel loads a bag with their toys.

"Yeah. She said I can't come over tomorrow night because they're having family night, so I should spend the night tonight."

Family night? I wonder if that means Julia is finally telling Lake she's sick. A knot forms in my stomach and I instantly become nervous for her. "I'll get your toothbrush, Caulder."

I'm in the bathroom packing a bag for Caulder when I hear yelling coming from outside. I immediately run to the living room window and see Lake storming out of her house toward Eddie's car. I can't hear what she's saying, but it's obvious she's pissed. Her face is almost the same shade of red as the shirt she has on. She swings open Eddie's back door and turns around, still yelling.

That's when I see Julia.

The look on her face makes my heart sink. Eddie's car pulls out of the driveway and Julia is left standing at the edge of the yard crying as she watches them pull away. As soon as the car is gone, I swing open the front door and run across the street.

"Is everything okay? Is she okay?" I say when I reach her. Julia looks up at me and shakes her head.

"Did you tell Lake that I'm sick?" she asks.

"No," I answer immediately. "No, I told you I wouldn't."

Julia stares down the street, still shaking her head. "I think she knows. I don't know how she found out but she knows. I should have told her sooner," she says, still crying.

The front door to my house slams shut and I spin around to see Kel and Caulder making their way out the front door. "Boys!

You guys are staying with me tonight instead. Go back inside," I yell. They roll their eyes and groan, and then head back into the house.

"Thank you, Will," Julia says. She turns to head back to her house and I follow after her.

"Do you want me to stay with you until she gets back?"

"No," she says quietly. "I just want to be alone for a while." She walks inside and closes the door behind her.

I spend the next two hours debating whether to text Gavin. It's killing me not knowing if Lake is okay or not. I wait on the couch with the living room curtains wide open, watching for her return. It's after eleven o'clock now, and I can't wait a second longer. I throw caution out the window and grab my phone to text Gavin.

Is Lake okay? Where are you guys? Is she spending the night with Eddie or coming home tonight?

I don't have to wait long before he replies.

Yes. Movies. No.

What the hell? Could he not elaborate a little?

How can she be okay? And why the hell would you guys take her to a movie when she's this upset?

Two minutes go by without a response, so I text him again.

Is she still crying? When are you guys bringing her home?

I wait a few more minutes without a response, then begin texting him again. Before I hit send, my phone rings.

"Hello?" I say, almost desperately.

"What the hell are you *doing*, Will?" Gavin yells into the phone. "You're acting like a psycho boyfriend."

"Is she with you right now?" I ask.

"The movie just let out, she's in the restroom with Eddie. I came outside to call you because I think you might need a reminder that you're her *teacher*."

I grip my cell phone and shake it out of frustration, then put it back to my ear.

"That doesn't matter right now. I saw her leaving after she found out about her mom's cancer. I just need to know that she's okay, Gavin. I'm worried about her."

I get nothing but silence. Gavin doesn't respond, but I can hear background noise so I know we're still connected. "Gavin?"

He clears his throat. "Her mom has cancer? Are you sure?"

"Yes, I'm sure. Has Lake not told you guys why she was crying when she got in your car? Julia doesn't know how, but Layken somehow figured it out."

Gavin is silent again for a few more seconds, then he sighs heavily into the phone. "Will," he says, his voice lower than before. "Layken thinks her mom has a new boyfriend. She has no idea she has cancer."

I fall onto the couch, but it feels like my heart falls straight through the floor.

"Will?" Gavin says.

"I'm here," I say. "Just get her home, Gavin. She needs to talk to her mom."

"Yeah. We're on our way."

I SPEND THE next several minutes debating whether to go across the street and let Julia know that Layken has misunderstood everything. Unfortunately, by the time I decide to go talk to her,

Eddie's car is pulling into their driveway. I watch as Lake gets out and walks to her front door. When she goes inside, I close my curtains and turn out the light. I wish more than anything I could be there for her right now. I know the heartache she's about to experience. The fact that I'm a hundred yards away and not able to do a damn thing about it is the hardest thing of all.

I walk to Caulder's room and check on the boys. They're both passed out, so I turn the TV off and shut their door, then head to my room. I can already tell it's going to be a sleepless night. I can just imagine Lake crying herself to sleep. God, what I wouldn't give to be able to hold her right now. If I could just take all of this away from her, I would.

I'm lying with my hands under my head, my eyes focused on nothing in particular. A tear rolls down to my temple and I wipe it away. I'm torn up over the sadness I feel for this girl.

IT'S HALF AN hour later when I hear a knock on the living room door. I immediately jump out of bed and run to the living room and swing the door open. She's standing on my patio, mascara streaked down her cheeks. She's wiping her eyes with her shirt and she looks up at me. All the things I've been willing myself to do for the entire past month get shoved aside by the sheer sadness in her eyes. I put my arm around her and pull her inside, then shut the door behind her. I'm positive she knows the truth about her mom at this point, but I still proceed with caution.

"Lake, what's wrong?"

She tries to catch her breath, sucking in gasps of air between sobs. I can feel her melting, so I wrap my arms around her as she sinks to the floor. I sink with her, then pull her to me and let her cry. I rest my chin on top of her head and stroke her hair while she continues to cry for several minutes. I grasp the back of her shirt and bury my head in the crevice of her neck, fully aware of the fact that she came to me. She needed someone, and she came to *me*.

"Tell me what happened," I finally whisper.

She begins to sob, so I pull her closer. Between breaths, she says the words that I know are the hardest words she'll ever have to say. "She's dying, Will. She has cancer."

I know from experience that there are no words comforting enough to follow that. I squeeze her and give her what she needs. Silent reassurance. I pick her up and take her to my bedroom, then lay her on the bed and pull the covers over her. My doorbell rings, so I bend forward and kiss her on the forehead, then head back to the living room.

I already know it's Julia before I open the door. When I see her, she looks in just as bad shape as Lake does. "Is she here?" she says through her tears.

I nudge my head toward my bedroom. "She's lying down," I say.

"Can you get her? She needs to come home so we can talk about this."

I glance back toward the hallway and sigh. I don't want her to go. I know how much she needs this time to absorb everything. I turn back to Julia and take the biggest risk I've ever taken in my life.

"Let her stay, Julia. She needs me right now."

Julia doesn't respond for a moment. The fact that I'm disagreeing with her seems to throw her off for a moment. She shakes her head. "I can't, Will. I can't let her stay the night here."

"I've been in her shoes before. She needs time to absorb this, trust me. Just give her the night to calm down."

Julia's shoulders fall and she looks down, unable to look at me. I don't know if it's because she's angry with me for wanting Lake to stay, or heartbroken because she knows I'm right. She nods, then turns and begins walking back toward her house. Her defeated demeanor makes me feel as though I just broke her heart. She thinks she's losing Lake to me and that couldn't be farther from the truth.

"Julia, wait," I say, calling after her. She pauses in my front yard and turns to face me. When we make eye contact, she immediately shifts her gaze to the ground again and puts her hands on her hips. When I reach her, she still doesn't look at me. I'm not sure what to say. I clear my throat, but have no idea what to say to her.

"Listen, Julia," I say. "I know how much your time with Lake means to you, I do. *Believe* me, I do. I want her to be there for you. The fact that she wants to be here right now instead doesn't mean anything. She just needs to process this. That's all. You won't lose her."

She runs her hands across her eyes, wiping away fresh tears. She kicks at the ground beneath her foot, giving herself a second to gather her thoughts. She eventually raises her head and looks me straight in the eyes. "You're in love with her, aren't you?"

I pause.

Am I?

I sigh and clasp my hands behind my head, not sure what to say. "I'm trying so hard *not* to be," I say quietly, admitting it to myself for the first time.

When she hears my confession, she looks up at me, her expression stoic. "Try *harder*, Will. I need her. I can't have her wrapped up in this whirlwind, forbidden romance. That's the last thing we need right now." Julia shakes her head then looks away again. Her disappointment stings. I've let her down.

I take a step closer to her and look her in the eyes, making another promise that I pray to God I'm strong enough to keep. "It doesn't matter how I feel about her, okay? I don't want her consumed by what's going on between us any more than you do. She just needs a friend right now, that's all this is."

She hugs herself and looks past me at my house. "I'll let her stay tonight," she finally says. "But only because I agree with you that she needs time to process everything." She shifts her gaze back to mine. The tears still fresh in her eyes, I can do nothing but nod in agreement. She returns my acknowledgment with her own nod, then turns to head home. "You better sleep on the couch," she says over her shoulder.

After Julia is back inside, I return to my own house and lock the front door. I walk into the bedroom but Lake doesn't acknowledge me. I slide into the bed behind her, placing one arm under her head and my other arm over her chest. I pull her to me and hold her while she cries herself to sleep.

13.

the honeymoon

WE REMAIN RELAXED in the water, holding on to each other. She's resting her head on my shoulder, quiet and still. She presses her lips against my shoulder, opening them slightly, and she kisses me. I inhale as she grazes my shoulder with her lips, softly kissing along my collarbone, then up to my neck. When she reaches my jaw, she pulls back and looks at me. "I love you, Will Cooper," she says with tears in her eyes. She leans in and presses her lips to mine. She tightens her grip around my waist with her legs and places her hands on the back of my head, filling me with slow, deep kisses. I don't think she's ever kissed me with such intensity and passion before. It's like she's somehow trying to show her gratitude through her kiss.

I let her. I let her thank me for a good five minutes.

When her lips finally separate from mine, she unwraps her legs from around me and grins. "That was for loving me like you do."

She kicks off the wall and floats on her back across the pool. When she reaches the other side, she props her elbows up behind her on the concrete ledge and smiles at me from across the pool. I'm left breathless, wishing we were back in the hotel room already.

"It's too bad you like my shirt now," she says, still grinning mischievously.

"Why is that?"

She releases her grip on the ledge and brings her hand to the top button of her shirt. "Because," she says in a sexy whisper. "I'm really tired of wearing it." She unbuttons the top button, revealing the outline of her bra. As many times as I've seen that bra in the last twenty-four hours, it's a whole hell of a lot sexier right now.

"Oh," I say. As much as I want that shirt off her, we're in the courtyard of a hotel. I look around nervously to make sure no one is out here. When I look back at her, the second button is unbuttoned and her fingers are already working on the third. She hasn't taken her eyes off mine.

"Lake."

"*What?*" she says innocently. The fourth button is undone now and she's working on the fifth.

I slowly shake my head. "That's not a good idea."

She slides the shirt halfway down her shoulders, revealing the entire bra now. "Why not?"

I try to think of why it's not a good idea, but I can't. I can't think. All I want to do is help her finish getting the damn shirt off. I swim across the water and ease closer to her until our faces are just inches apart. Without taking my eyes off hers, I grasp the sleeves of her shirt and pull it the rest of the way down her arms, then yank it off completely. I throw the shirt onto the concrete patio, then lower my hands to the button on her jeans. She gasps. I lean in and whisper in her ear as I slide her zipper down. "Why stop there?"

I thought I'd called her bluff, but I should know better than that. She wraps one arm around my neck and helps me pull her jeans off with her other hand. I grab her thighs and pull her flush against me, then spin us around until I'm against the ledge again. She braces her hands against the pool wall behind my head. I sink us both lower until our chins are barely above the surface of the water.

We're pressed firmly together; the only things separating us are my jeans and her underwear, and one of these items is about to go. I slide my thumb into her waistband at the hip and begin to inch her panties down. I pull them down just far enough. "What now?" I say, moving my hand farther down as I wait for her to call retreat.

She breathes heavily against my lips as her chin submerges and re-emerges against the waves of the water. Rather than call retreat, she closes her eyes, daring me to keep going.

She gasps when I unclasp her bra with my other hand and begin to slide it off her.

"Will," she says against my lips. "What if someone comes out here?" She covers herself with her arms when the bra is completely off.

I throw it on the concrete in the spot next to her shirt and I smile at her. "You started this. Don't tell me you're about to call retreat *now*." I kiss her on the chin and trail a line across her jaw with my lips. She uncovers her chest and sinks lower into the water, then pulls me against her.

"Retreat is no longer in my vocabulary," she says, finding the button on my pants.

"You two almost done here?" someone says from behind us, causing Lake to abandon her current mission. She throws her arms around me and buries her head against my neck. I glance to the left and see a hotel employee standing just inside the gated entry, his hands on his hips. "I've got to lock up," he says.

"Oh, my god, oh, my god, oh, my god," she whispers. "Where the hell are my clothes?"

I laugh. "Told you it wasn't a good idea," I say against her ear.

I keep my arms wrapped tightly around her and look over at the man, who appears a bit too amused at our plight. "Um. Could you throw me those?" I say, pointing to Lake's shirt and bra, which are several feet away. She's got a death grip on my neck.

The hotel employee looks down at the clothes and chuckles, then looks back at Lake and smiles, almost as if I'm not even here. He walks through the gate and over to the edge of the pool and tosses us the shirt, not taking his eyes off her the entire time. I wrap the shirt over her shoulders and he's still standing there, staring.

"Do you mind?" I say to him. The guy finally takes his eyes off Lake long enough to witness my glare. He clearly reads the expression on my face and turns around to head back inside.

Lake slips her shirt back on while I retrieve her pants and swim them back to her. "You're a bad influence Mrs. Cooper," I say.

"Hey, my plan was to stop at the shirt," she says. "You're the one who had other ideas."

I let her hold on to me while I help her struggle back into her jeans. "Well, if what just happened wasn't your intention, why did you lure me into the water to begin with?" I say.

She laughs and shakes her head. "I guess I just can't resist those abs."

I kiss her on the nose and swing her around onto my back, then carry her out of the pool. We leave a sopping wet trail the entire way back to our hotel room.

LAKE IS SPRAWLED across the bed on her stomach, wearing the robe I've fallen in love with. I'm stealing that robe before we leave here. She's flipping through the channels on the TV with the remote, so I crawl onto the bed next to her and take the remote from her hand.

"My turn," I say. I flip it to ESPN and she grabs the remote back from me.

"It's *my* honeymoon," she says. "I should get to watch what I want." She turns her attention back to the TV.

"*Your* honeymoon? What am I? An afterthought?"

She continues to stare at the TV without responding. She glances at me, then back to the TV. After a few seconds, she shifts her gaze in my direction again and I'm still staring at her. "What'd you say?" she teases. "Were you talking?"

I grab the remote from her and press the power button, then chuck it across the room. I grab her wrists and roll her onto her back, pinning her to the bed. "Maybe you need to be reminded who wears the pants in this family."

She laughs. "Oh, believe me, I know you wear the pants, Will. You even wear them in the bathtub, remember?"

I laugh and kiss her ear. "If I remember correctly, you wore clothes in the shower once, too."

"*Unwillingly!*" She laughs.

insanity

AFTER I FINISH cooking breakfast for the boys, I walk to my bedroom and slip inside, shutting the door behind me. The last thing I need is for them to know Lake spent the night here last night.

I sit on the edge of the bed by her feet. If I were to sit any closer, I wouldn't be able to prevent myself from reaching over and touching her or hugging her or stroking her hair. It was torture holding her last night while trying to hold back the urge to kiss away her pain. *Torture.* Not that I didn't give her a light peck after I was sure she was asleep. I might have also told her I loved her after I kissed her hair.

Torture.

"Lake," I whisper. She doesn't move so I repeat her name. She rustles slightly, but doesn't open her eyes. She looks so peaceful and serene right now. If I were to wake her up, reality would just hit her again. I stand up and decide to let her have a few more moments of peace. Before I leave the room, I walk to the head of the bed and lightly kiss her on the forehead.

"WHAT IF SHE loses weight?" Kel says.

"She doesn't need to lose weight," I say as I scoop a spoonful of eggs onto his plate. I walk back to the stove and set the pan down.

"Well, if you don't think she's fat and you like to kiss her, then why don't you want her to be your girlfriend?"

I spin around and face both of the boys. "I like *kissing* her?" I ask, afraid of his answer. He just nods and takes a bite of his food.

"You kissed her that night you took her on that test date.

Lake says you *didn't* kiss her, but I saw you. She says you can get in a lot of trouble for kissing her and that I didn't see what I thought I saw."

"She said that?" I ask.

Caulder nods. "That's what she told us. But Kel says he saw what he thought he saw and I believe him. Why would you get in trouble for kissing her, anyway?"

I wasn't expecting the third degree this early in the morning. I'm too tired to turn this into a life lesson, though. After everything that happened last night and having Lake next to me in my bed, I'm pretty sure I didn't even get an hour of sleep.

"Listen, boys," I say, walking back to them. I place my hands on the bar and come face-to-face with them. "Sometimes, there are things in life that are out of our control. I can't be Lake's boyfriend and she can't be my girlfriend. We're not going to get married, and the two of you aren't going to be brothers. Enjoy the fact that you get to be best friends and neighbors."

"Is it because you're a teacher?" Caulder asks pointedly.

I drop my head in my hands. They're relentless. And intuitive.

"Yes," I say, exasperated. "Yes. It's because I'm a teacher. Teachers cannot ask their students to be their girlfriends and vice versa. So Lake isn't going to be my girlfriend. I'm not going to be her boyfriend. We aren't going to get married. Ever. Now drop it." I walk back to the stove and place lids on all the pans to keep the food warm. I don't know when Lake will wake up, but I need to get these boys fed and out of this house before she walks out of my bedroom. How in the hell would I explain to them that teachers and students can't date, but they can sleep in the same bed?

• • •

AFTER BREAKFAST COMES and goes and she's still asleep, I walk the boys over to Julia's. Kel and Caulder rush in, but I feel inclined to knock on the door so I lag behind. When Julia opens the door, she shields her eyes from the sun and looks away.

"Sorry. Did I wake you up?"

She steps aside to let me in and shakes her head. "I don't think I've even slept," she says. She walks back into the living room, so I follow and sit on the sofa. "How is she?"

I shrug. "Still asleep. She hasn't come out of the bedroom since she got there last night."

Julia nods and leans back into the couch, then rubs her hands on her face. "She's scared, Will. She was so scared when I told her. I knew she would take it badly, but not like this. I wasn't expecting this reaction at all. I need her to be strong when we tell Kel, but I can't tell him when she's this emotional."

"It's only been seven months since her dad died, Julia. Losing a parent is hard, but the possibility of losing both of them at her age is incomprehensible."

"Yeah," she whispers. "I guess you would know."

She still doesn't seem convinced that Lake's reaction is normal. Everyone reacts differently to devastating news. I didn't even cry right away when I found out my parents died, but that's not to say it wasn't the worst moment of my life.

I was on my way to a game when I got the phone call. I was the emergency contact on their records. The person on the other line was telling me there was an accident and I needed to get to the hospital in Detroit. They wouldn't tell me anything, no matter how much I begged. I tried calling my parents' cell phones several times but never got an answer. I called my grandparents to tell them about the accident, since they were just minutes from the hospital. That was one of the hardest phone calls I've ever had to make.

I drove as fast as I could, holding my cell phone in my hand against the steering wheel, keeping a constant eye on it. All I could think of was Caulder. I just knew something terrible had happened and that my parents weren't answering their phones because they wanted to tell me in person.

When an hour passed and even my grandparents still hadn't called, I tried their phone for the fifth time. They weren't answering, either. I think it was after the sixth time I called them and they pushed it through to voicemail that I knew.

My parents. Caulder. All of them. They were all dead.

I pulled up to the emergency room and rushed inside. The first thing I saw was my grandmother doubled over in a chair, crying.

No, she wasn't crying. She was wailing. My grandfather had his back to me, but his shoulders were shaking. His entire body was shaking. I stood there and watched them for several minutes, wondering who these people were in front of me. These strong, independent people I had admired and respected and thought the world of. These people who could be broken by nothing.

Yet, here they were. Broken and weak. The only thing that can break the unbreakable is the unthinkable. I knew the moment I saw them alone in the waiting room that my worst fears were confirmed.

They were all dead.

I turned around and I walked out. I didn't want to be in there. I had to go outside. I couldn't breathe. When I reached the grass across from the parking lot, I fell to my knees. I didn't cry.

Instead, I became physically ill. Over and over, my stomach repelling the truth that I refused to believe. When there was nothing left in me, I fell backward onto the grass and stared up at the sky, the stars staring back at me. Millions of stars staring back at the whole world. A world where parents die and brothers die and nothing stops to respect that fact. The whole universe just goes and goes as if nothing has happened, even when one person's entire life is forced to a complete halt.

I closed my eyes and thought about him. It had been two weeks since I had spoken to him on the phone. I had promised him I'd come up the next weekend to take him to his football game. That was the same weekend Vaughn begged me not to go. She said midterms were in two weeks and we needed to spend time together before then. So, I called Caulder and canceled my trip. That was the last time I had talked to him.

The last time I would ever talk to him.

"Will?"

I looked up after hearing my grandfather's voice and he was standing over me, looking down. "Will, are you okay?" he asked, wiping fresh tears from his defeated eyes. I hated seeing that look in his eyes.

I didn't move. I just lay there in the grass, looking up at him, not wanting him to say anything else. I didn't want to hear it.

"Will . . . they . . ."

"I know," I said quickly, not wanting to hear the words come out of his mouth.

He nodded and looked away. "Your grandmother wants . . ."

"I *know*," I said louder.

"Maybe you should come . . ."

"I don't want to."

And I *didn't* want to. I didn't want to set foot back inside that hospital. Back inside the building that now housed the three of them. *Lifeless.*

"Will, you need to come . . ."

"I don't *want* to!" I screamed.

My grandfather—my poor grandfather just nodded and sighed. What else could he have done? What else could he have said? My entire life had just been ripped from me and I wasn't about to listen to reassurances from nurses or doctors or clergymen or even my grandparents. I didn't want to hear it.

My grandfather hesitantly took a few steps away from me, leaving me alone in the grass. Before heading back inside, he turned around one last time.

"It's just that Caulder has been asking for you. He's scared. So when you're ready . . ."

I immediately snapped my head in his direction. "Caulder?" I said. "Caulder's not . . ."

My grandfather immediately shook his head. "No, son. No. Caulder's fine."

It wasn't until those words came out of his mouth that everything hit me all at once. My chest swelled and the heat rose to my face, then my eyes. I pulled my hands to my forehead and I rolled onto my knees, my elbows buried in the grass, and I completely lost it. Sounds came from deep within me that I didn't even know I was capable of. I cried harder than I've ever cried before—harder than I've cried since. I sat on the lawn of that hospital and I cried tears of joy, because Caulder was okay.

"Are you okay?" Julia asks, breaking me out of my trance.

I nod, trying to push back the memories of that day. "I'm fine."

She readjusts her position on the couch and sighs. "I don't want her to have to raise Kel," she says. "Lake needs the chance to live her own life. I'd never burden her like that."

"Julia," I say, speaking confidently from experience, "it would burden her *not* to have him." Not having the choice to raise Kel would *kill* Lake. Just like it killed me when I thought I'd lost Caulder. It would absolutely devastate her.

Julia doesn't respond, indicating I may have crossed my boundaries with that comment. We both sit quietly on the couch for a while. I feel like neither of us has anything else to say, so I stand up.

"I'll take the boys somewhere this afternoon. I'll make sure Layken wakes up before I go so you guys will have time to talk."

"Thank you," she says, smiling a genuine smile at me. It feels good. I respect Julia's opinion and having her disappointed in me feels almost as bad as when Lake is disappointed in me.

I nod, then turn and leave. I make my way back inside the house and back into the bedroom where Lake is still sleeping. I ease onto the bed at her side and take a seat.

"Lake," I whisper, trying to wake her successfully this time.

She doesn't move, so I pull the covers off her head. She groans and pulls them back up.

"Lake, wake up."

She kicks her legs, then throws the covers off. It's well past lunchtime and she acts like she could sleep twelve more hours. She opens her eyes and squints, then finds me sitting next to her. She's got mascara smeared underneath her eyes, some of which is still on my pillowcase. Her hair is in disarray. Her ponytail holder is on the sheet beside her. She looks like hell. A *beautiful* hell.

"You really *aren't* a morning person," I say.

She sits up on the bed. "Bathroom. Where's your bathroom?"

I point to the bathroom across the hall and watch as she leaps off the bed and darts for the door. She's definitely awake now, but I can almost guarantee she needs coffee.

I go to the kitchen and make us both a cup. When she comes out of the bathroom I take a seat and place her coffee next to me.

"What time is it?"

"One-thirty."

"Oh," she says, shocked. "Well . . . your bed's really comfortable."

I smile and nudge her shoulder. "Apparently."

We drink our coffee and she doesn't say anything else. I have no idea where her head is at, so I remain silent, allowing her to think. When we finish our coffee, I put the cups in the sink and tell her I'm taking the boys to a matinee. "We're leaving in a few minutes. I'll probably take them to dinner afterward, so we'll be back around six. Should give you and your mom time to talk."

She frowns at me. "What if I don't want to talk? What if I want to go to a matinee?"

I lean forward across the bar. "You don't need to watch a movie. You need to talk to your mom. Let's go." I grab my keys and jacket and head toward the front door.

She kicks back in her chair and folds her arms across her chest. "I just woke up. The caffeine hasn't even kicked in yet. Can I stay here for a while?"

She's practically pouting, her bottom lip sticking out, pleading with me. I stare at her mouth a beat too long. I think she notices, because she pulls on her bottom lip with her teeth and her cheeks flush. I shake my head slightly, pulling my gaze away from her mouth.

"Fine," I say, snapping out of my trance. I walk over to her and kiss her on the forehead. "But not all day. You need to talk to her." I walk away, fully aware of the fact that the forehead kiss was probably crossing the line. However, the fact that she slept in my bed last night has already muddied the waters. The line isn't so black and white anymore. I'm pretty sure gray just became my new favorite color.

IT'S BEEN OVER five hours since I left with the boys, so Lake and Julia probably have had a chance to sort everything out. I tell Kel to stay the night with me to give them more time to adjust. I unlock the front door and follow the boys into the living room. We all come to a halt, not expecting to find Lake on my living room floor. There are dozens of white index cards sprawled out in front of her.

What the hell is she *doing*?

"What are you doing?" Caulder says, verbalizing my exact thoughts.

"Alphabetizing," she replies without looking up.

"Alphabetizing *what*?" I say.

"Everything. First I did the movies, then I did the CDs. Caulder, I did the books in your room. I did a few of your games, but some of those started with numbers so I put the numbers first, then the titles." I point to the piles in front of me. "These are recipes. I found them on top of the fridge. I'm alphabetizing them by category first; like beef, lamb, pork, poultry. Then behind the categories I'm alphabetizing them by—"

"Guys, go to Kel's. Let Julia know you're back," I say, without looking at them.

The boys don't move. They continue to stare at Lake. "Now!" I yell. They listen this time, opening the door and disappearing outside.

I slowly walk to the couch and sit down. I'm afraid to say anything. Something is off. She seems so . . . *chipper.*

"You're the teacher," she says. She looks at me and winks. "Should I put 'Baked Potato Soup' behind potato or soup?"

What the hell? She's in denial. *Intense* denial.

"Stop," I say. I'm not returning her smile. I don't know what happened with her mom today, but whatever is going on with her needs to stop. She needs to confront this.

"I can't stop, silly. I'm halfway finished. If I stop now you won't know where to find . . ." She picks up a random card off the floor. "Jerk Chicken?"

I glance around the living room and notice the DVDs have all been arranged next to my television. I stand and slowly walk to the kitchen, eyeing the surroundings. Did she clean the damn *baseboards*? I knew I shouldn't have left her today. Good God, I bet she cleaned the entire house and never even went to talk to her mother. I walk to my bedroom and my bed is made. Not only is it made; it's *perfect*. I hesitate before opening my closet door, afraid of what I might find. My shoes have all been rearranged. My shirts have all been moved to the right side of the closet and my pants are on the left. The way they're hung, their colors move from light to dark.

She color-coded my *closet*? I'm afraid to complete the inspection. There's no telling what all she did to this house. She probably left nothing untouched.

Shit. I rush to the bed and open the nightstand. I pull the book out and open it, but the receipt for her chocolate milk doesn't look like it's been touched. I breathe a sigh of relief, glad she didn't see it, then put the book back where it was. How embarrassing would that have been?

I walk back into the living room, more aware of the spotless condition of my house than before. She's been a little too busy, which can only mean one thing. She's still avoiding her mother.

"You color-coded my closet?" I say. I'm glaring at her from the hallway entrance. She shrugs and smiles, like this is any other day.

"Will, it wasn't that hard. You wear, like, three different color shirts." When she giggles, it makes me wince. She has to *stop* this. Her denial isn't good for her, and it certainly isn't going to be good for Kel when Julia tells him. I walk swiftly across the room and bend down to snatch up the cards. We're about to have a serious sit-down.

"Will! Stop! That took me a long time!" She begins to grab the cards as I pick them up. I realize we aren't getting anywhere, so I throw down the cards and try to pull her up off the floor. I need her to look me in the eyes and calm down.

That doesn't happen.

She actually starts kicking at me. She's literally *kicking* me. She's acting like a damn child.

"Let me go!" she yells. "I'm . . . not . . . done!"

I let go of her hands as she asked, and she falls back to the floor. I walk to the kitchen and grab an empty pitcher from under the sink and fill it up with water. I know I'll regret this, but she needs to snap out of it. I walk back to the living room and she doesn't even acknowledge me. I extend my arm and flip the pitcher upside down on top of her head.

"What the hell!" she screams. She throws her hands up in shock, then looks up at me with pure hatred. I realize once she lunges at me that perhaps this wasn't the best idea. Not enough water, maybe?

When she stands up and tries to hit me, I grab her arm and

wrap it behind her back, then move behind her while I push her toward the bathroom. Once we're inside, I wrap my arms around her and forcefully pick her up. There's no other way to do it. She's doing her best to attack me and she's almost succeeding. I hold her against the wall of the shower with one arm and turn the water on with the other. As soon as the water splashes across her face, she gasps.

"Jerk! Jackass! Asshole!"

I adjust the faucet and look her in the eyes. "Take a shower, Layken! Take a damn shower!" I release my hold and back away from her. When I shut the bathroom door, I hold the doorknob in case she tries to get out. Sure enough, she tries.

"Let me out, Will! Now!" She beats on the door and jiggles the knob.

"Layken, I'm not letting you out of the bathroom until you take off your clothes, get in the shower, wash your hair, and calm down."

I continue to hold the doorknob until I hear the shower curtain close a minute later. When I'm confident she isn't going to try to get out again, I put my shoes on and walk across the street to grab her some extra clothes.

"Is she okay?" Julia asks as soon as she opens the door. She motions behind her to let me know Kel and Caulder can hear our conversation.

"A little *too* okay," I whisper. "She's acting strange. Did you guys talk today?"

Julia nods, but doesn't elaborate. It's obvious she doesn't want to risk being overheard by Kel. "She's in the shower. I came to get her a change of clothes," I say, skirting the subject.

Julia nods and steps aside, then walks toward the kitchen.

"You can grab some out of her bedroom. Last door on the right," she says. "I'm in the middle of washing dishes." She returns to the sink and I hesitate, a little uncomfortable at the thought of going into Lake's bedroom.

I walk down the hallway and slowly open her door. When I do, it's not what I expect. I don't know if I thought it would be a typical teenager's bedroom, but I'm pleasantly surprised that there aren't posters on the walls and black lights on the ceiling. It's surprisingly mature for an eighteen-year-old. I walk to her dresser and pull the top drawer open, removing a tank top. When I open the next drawer to look for pants, I'm met with a drawer full of bras and panties. I feel somewhat guilty, knowing that she has no idea I'm in her room right now. I tell myself to just grab a pair and shut the drawer, but I begin scrolling through all of the contents, imaging what they would look like on her.

Dammit, Will! I grab a pair on top and slam the drawer shut, then search until I find some pajama bottoms. When I shut the last drawer, the tank top falls out of my hands and lands on the floor. I bend over to pick it up and a barrette catches my eye. It looks like a child's hair barrette. I pick it up and hold it between my fingers, curious why she would keep something so old.

"She used to think it was magic," Julia says from the door-way. I whip my head around, startled by her voice.

"This?" I say, holding up the barrette.

Julia nods, then walks into the bedroom and sits on the bed. "When she was a little girl her dad walked in right after she had cut a huge chunk of her bangs off. She was crying, scared I would be mad at her, so he brushed some hair over and snapped the clip in place. He told her it was magic and that as long as she kept that clip in her hair, I wouldn't notice."

I laugh, trying to imagine Lake with a chunk of her bangs missing. "I guess you noticed?"

Julia laughs. "Oh, it was so obvious. Horribly obvious. She cut a three-inch strip right out of the front of her hair. Her dad called to warn me and told me not to say anything. It was so hard. It took her hair months to grow back out and she looked ridiculous. But I couldn't say anything because every single day she woke up, the first thing she did was put that clip in her hair so I wouldn't know."

"Wow," I say. "She was strong-willed even then, huh?"

Julia smiles. "You have no idea. I've never met a person with a more indomitable will in my *life*."

I bend down and put the clip back where I found it, then turn back to Julia. She's looking down at her hands, picking at her nails. She looks just like Lake right now, but somehow even sadder.

"She hates me right now, Will. She doesn't understand where I'm coming from. She wants Kel, but I don't know if I can do that to her."

I don't even know if it's my place to be giving her advice, but she seems to be soliciting it. I just know I've been in Lake's shoes, and nothing could have stopped me from taking Caulder from my grandparents' house that night.

I tuck Lake's clothes underneath my arm and head to the door, then turn back toward Julia. "Maybe you should try to understand where she's coming from. Kel is the only thing she'll have left. The *only* thing. And right now, she feels like you're trying to take that away from her, too."

Julia looks up at me. "I'm not trying to take him away from her. I just want her to be happy."

Happy?

"Julia," I say. "Her father just died. You're about to die. She's eighteen and she's facing a lifetime without the two people she loves the most. Nothing you can do will make her happy. Her world is being ripped out from under her and she has absolutely no control over it. The least you could do is let her have a little bit of say-so over the only thing she'll have left. Because I can tell you from experience . . . Caulder is the *only* thing that kept me going. Your taking Kel away from her because you think it'll improve her situation? It's the absolute worst thing you could do to either of them."

Fearing I've overstepped my bounds again, I walk out of the bedroom and make my way back across the street.

I OPEN THE door to the bathroom and slip inside. I set the clothes and a towel down on the counter, then glance up to the mirror. It's mostly fogged over, but clear enough that I can see the shower in the reflection. There's a section a few inches wide where the wall should meet the shower curtain, but it's pulled slightly back. Lake's foot is propped up against the porcelain tub and she's shaving her legs. She's using my razor.

And my shower.

And her clothes are on the floor, next to my feet. Not on *her*. She's three feet from me without her clothes on.

It's one of the worst days of her life and I'm sitting here thinking about how she's not wearing anything. Ass-hole.

If I had any semblance of a decent conscience at all, I'd have never allowed her into my house last night to begin with. Now I'm watching the razor glide up her ankle, praying she's too upset to go home for at least one more night.

Just one more night. I'm not ready to let her go.

I quietly back out of the bathroom and shut the door behind me. I head straight to the kitchen sink and splash water on my face.

I grip the edge of the counter and take a deep breath, preparing my earth-shattering apology for when she comes storming out of the bathroom. She's so pissed at me right now for yelling at her and throwing her into the shower. I don't blame her. I'm sure there was an easier way I could have calmed her down.

"I need a towel!" she yells from the bathroom. I walk to the edge of the hallway.

"It's on the sink. So are your clothes." I go back to the living room and sit on the couch in a lame attempt to appear casual. Maybe if I don't seem so pissed anymore, she'll remain calm.

God, I can't stand the thought of her being mad at me for another day. The day she recited her poem in class was probably the hardest knock my heart has ever taken from a girl . . . and it happened in front of seventeen other students. I realize none of them knew I was her target, other than Gavin, but *still*. It felt like I'd taken over thirty bullets straight to the heart with each insult that came out of her mouth.

The door to the bathroom begins to open and my attempt at casual goes out the window. I jump over the back of the couch, wanting nothing more than to hold her and apologize for everything I did tonight.

When she sees me rushing toward her, her eyes grow big and she backs up to the wall. I wrap my arms around her and squeeze her tight. "I'm sorry, Lake. I'm so sorry I did that. You were just *losing* it," I say in my best attempt to excuse my actions. Rather than try to hit me, she wraps her arms around my neck, causing my chest to tighten as I attempt to hold on to my will-power before it slips away from me again.

"It's okay," she says softly. "I kinda sorta had a bad day."

I want nothing more than to stifle her words with my mouth right now. I want to tell her how much I need her. How much I love her. How, no matter how bad things get for her, I'll be by her through every second of it.

But I don't. Because of Julia, I don't. I reluctantly pull back and place my arms on her shoulders.

"So we're friends? You aren't gonna try to punch me again?"

"Friends," she says with a forced smile. I can tell she wants to be my friend about as much as I want to be hers. I have to turn away from her and head down the hallway before the words "I love you" fall helplessly from my mouth.

"How was the matinee?" she asks from behind me.

I can't make small talk. We need to get to the heart of why she's here, or I'm going to forget she's not here for me.

"Did you talk to your mom?" I ask.

"Jeez. Deflect much?"

"Did you talk to her? Please don't tell me you spent the entire day cleaning." I continue into the kitchen and grab two glasses. She takes a seat at the bar.

"No. Not the entire day. We talked."

"And?" I ask.

"And . . . she has cancer."

Damn that indomitable will.

I roll my eyes at her stubbornness and walk to the refrigerator, removing the milk. When I begin to pour it into her glass, she turns away from the bar and flips her head over, then pulls the towel off her head. Her hair falls around her and she brushes at the tangles with her fingers. She smoothes out the strands, working her fingers through them delicately. What I wouldn't give to touch—crap! I realize, just as she glances up, that I've poured way too much milk. It's trickling down my hand and onto the counter. I quickly wipe it up with a hand towel.

Please tell me she didn't see that.

I grab the powdered chocolate out of the cabinet and a spoon, then stir some chocolate into her cup. "Will she be okay?"

"No. Probably not."

I should know better than to ask close-ended questions with her. But I haven't asked Julia any details and I'm curious.

"But she's getting treatment?"

She rolls her eyes and looks incredibly annoyed. "She's dying, Will. *Dying.* She'll probably be dead within the year, maybe less than that. They're just doing chemo to keep her comfortable. While she dies. 'Cause she'll be dead. Because she's dying. There. Is that what you wanted to hear?"

Her response sends a surge of guilt through me. I'm doing the exact thing to her that I hated having done to me. Forcing her to talk about something she hasn't even accepted yet. I decide to drop it. She'll come to this on her own terms. I walk to the freezer and grab a handful of ice, then drop it into her cup, sliding it across the counter to her. "On the rocks."

She looks down at the chocolate milk and smiles. "Thanks," she says. She finishes her drink in silence.

When the glass is empty, she stands up from the bar and walks to the living room. She lies down on the floor and stretches her arms above her head.

"Turn the lights off," she says. "I just want to listen for a while."

I turn out the lights, then walk to where she is and lower myself onto the floor beside her. She's quiet, but the stress radiates from her.

"She doesn't want me to raise Kel," she whispers. "She wants to give him to Brenda."

I inhale a deep breath, understanding completely where her pain is coming from. I reach out across the floor until I find her hand and I hold it, wanting more than anything for her to know she's not alone in this.

MY EYES SNAP open at the sound of Eddie's voice. I sit up on the floor, shocked that I even fell asleep, and see Lake watching Eddie walk out the door.

Shit! Shit, shit, shit! What the hell was Eddie doing in my house? Why would Lake even let her *in*? I'm getting fired. That's it. I'm done.

After the door closes behind Eddie, Lake turns around and sees me sitting up on the floor. She purses her lips and tries to smile, but she knows I'm not happy.

"What the hell was she doing here?"

She shrugs. "Visiting," she mutters. "Checking on me."

She has no idea what kind of jeopardy she just put my entire career in!

"Dammit, Layken!" I push myself off the floor and throw my hands in the air, defeated. "Are you *trying* to get me fired? Are you that selfish that you don't give a crap about anyone *else's* problems? Do you know what would happen if she let it get out that you spent the night here?"

Lake's eyes dart down to the floor.

Oh, god. She knows. Eddie already knows.

I take a step closer to her and she glances up at me again. "Does she know you spent the night here?" I demand. She looks down at her lap. "Layken, what does she know?"

She doesn't look at me, which answers my question.

"Christ, Layken. Go home."

She nods, then walks to the door. She slips her shoes on and pauses before she leaves, looking at me apologetically. I'm standing in the middle of the living room with my hands clasped behind my head, watching her. As mad as I am right now, it hurts to let her go. I know she needs me, but there's so much we both need to process at this point. Besides, she needs to be home with her mother. Being here instead of at her own house isn't helping her confront her situation at all.

A tear rolls down her cheek and she quickly turns away.

"Lake," I say softly, dropping my hands to my sides. I can't let her leave with the added stress of my outburst lingering in her mind. I walk to the door where she's standing and reach down and touch her fingers, then take her hand in mine. She allows me to hold her hand, but she doesn't face me again. She keeps one hand on the front door and sniffs, her head still focused on the floor.

This girl. In love with the boy she can't have. Grieving the death of her father, only to find out she's about to grieve the death of the only adult left in her life? This girl who's being told she can't keep the only family member she has left? I squeeze her hand and rub my thumb over hers. She slowly turns to meet my eyes. Seeing the pain behind them and knowing that a lot of it is because of me reminds me of all the reasons I need to let her go.

Her mother.

My career.

Her reputation.

My and Caulder's future.

Her future.

Doing the right thing. The *responsible* thing.

Out of all the reasons I can come up with for her to go, there's only one reason I can come up with for her to stay. I love her. This one reason for her to stay is the *only* reason that derives from pure selfishness. If I continue whatever this is with her, it'll be completely selfish of me. I'll be putting everything I've worked for and everyone I love at risk, just to fulfill my own desires.

I drop her hand. "Go home, Layken. She needs you."

I turn around.

I walk away.

14.

the honeymoon

I'M HOLDING HER hand now and I have no intentions of letting her walk out of my life again.

Lake can see the regret I have over that night, so she takes my face in her hands and smiles reassuringly at me. "You do realize you are the most selfless person I know, right?"

I shake my head. "Lake, I'm not selfless. I put so much at risk every time I was around you, but I still couldn't control myself. It's like I couldn't breathe unless I was near you."

"You are *not* selfish. We were in love. *Really* in love. You warred with yourself to do the right thing and that says so much about your character. I respect you for that, Will Cooper."

I knew I married her for a reason. I grab the back of her neck and pull her forehead toward mine and kiss it.

She lays her head on my chest and wraps her arm around me. "Besides, there's no way you could have been perfect the *whole* time we were forced apart," she says. "It's just too hard to *not* love me, considering how irresistible I am."

I laugh and flip her off me and onto her back. "You got that right," I say, tickling her ribs. I try to straddle her and pin her down, but she squirms beneath me and somehow breaks free, scooting off the bed. I grab her wrist and she pulls back, yanking me forward. She turns and tries to break free but trips over the desk chair. I grab her waist just as she falls to the floor, then I slide on top of her and pin her wrists to the carpet.

"See how irresistible I am?" She laughs. "You won't even let me off the butterflying bed without you!"

My eyes drink in every inch of her from head to toe. "Maybe if you'd put on some clothes I'd feel less inclined to attack you."

She pulls one of her hands from mine and reaches to the chair above her head where her robe landed earlier. "Fine," she says, yanking it off the chair. "I'll wear this until we leave tomor-row."

I grab the robe from her hands and toss it behind me. "The *hell* you will. I told you what you were allowed to wear on this honeymoon, and that robe wasn't on the list."

"Well, everything that *was* on the list is sort of soaking wet, thanks to you."

I laugh. "That's only inconvenient for anyone who isn't *me*." As soon as I kiss her, she finds the one spot on my stomach that's ticklish and she attacks. I'm immediately off her, trying to get away from her hands. I hop back onto the bed and she jumps on top of me. Once I realize she has me pinned to the bed, I immedi-ately give up and let her win.

Who *wouldn't*?

"Fun should have been the fourth thing on my mom's list," she says, dropping herself beside me, breathless from the effort she spent trying to attack me. I cock my eyebrow, curious about what list she's referring to. She sees I'm not following, so she elaborates. "She said there were three things every woman should look for in a man. Having fun with him wasn't on the list, but I think it should be." She sits up and scoots back to the headboard. "Tell me about a fun time. A happy time. I need a break from all the sad memories for a while."

I think back to the months after we first met, and struggle to come up with a positive one. "It's hard, Lake. There were happy moments, but not really happy times. There was so much heart-ache under the surface of that entire year."

"Then tell me one of your happy moments."

carving pumpkins

IT'S ALMOST FIVE, so after I unload the groceries I walk across the street to get Caulder. Julia and Lake need to talk, so I think I'll offer to take Kel for a while, too. Before I knock, I take a deep breath and prepare for whatever reaction Lake might have. I gave her detention today so I could talk to her and Eddie, then I just left her and Eddie a blubbering mess in my classroom. I'm not sure if she's pissed at me right now but I felt like I needed to make a point, which is the only reason I did it. Whether or not Lake got my point, I guess I'm about to find out.

When the door opens, I'm shocked to see Caulder. "Hey, buddy. You answering doors here now?"

He smiles and grabs my hand, pulling me inside. "We're carving pumpkins for Halloween. Come on, Julia bought one for you, too."

"No, it's fine. I'll carve mine another time. I just wanted to bring you home so they can have some family time."

I look up to see the four of them sitting at the bar carving pumpkins. I know Lake hasn't had a chance to talk with Julia, since she had to have just gotten home, so I'm a little confused at the serene family appearing in front of me.

Julia pulls out a chair and pats it, indicating she wants me to stay. "Sit down, Will. We're just carving pumpkins tonight. That's *all* we're doing. Just carving pumpkins."

It's obvious from her tone that Lake must have told her she doesn't want to talk about it again. That doesn't surprise me. "Okay, then. I guess we're carving pumpkins." I sit in the chair Julia pulled out for me, directly across from Lake. We glance at each other as I take my seat. Her expression is soft but not very telling. I don't know how she feels about what I said during deten-tion today, but if her expression is any indication, she doesn't seem angry. She almost seems apologetic.

"Why were you so late getting home today, Layken?" Kel asks. I glance away just as Lake snaps her head in his direction. I focus my attention on the pumpkin in front of me.

"Eddie and I had detention," she says matter-of-factly.

"Detention? What were you in detention for?" Julia asks.

I can feel the blood pooling in my cheeks.

Lie to her, Lake.

"We skipped class last week, took a nap in the courtyard."

That's my girl. I silently let out a sigh of relief.

"Lake, why would you do something like that? What class did you skip?" Julia asks, obviously disappointed. Lake doesn't re-spond, which causes me to look up. She and Julia are both staring at me.

"She skipped my class!" I laugh. "What was I supposed to do?"

Julia laughs and pats me on the back. "I'm buying you sup-per for that."

I WALK TO the door with Julia when the pizza arrives and take it from the delivery guy while she pays him. I set it on the counter and make the boys a plate.

"I want to try this suck and sweet Kel keeps telling me about," Julia says after we all sit down. Lake looks up at her, con-fused about what "suck and sweet" is, but she doesn't ask for an explanation.

"Good idea, I'll go first. Show you guys how it's done," I say. I take a sip of my drink and start with my suck.

"Mrs. Alex was my suck today," I say.

"Who's Mrs. Alex and why was she your suck?" Julia asks.

"She's the secretary, and . . . let's just say she *favors* me. Today I had to go turn in my absentee reports. We always place them in our boxes before the end of the day and Mrs. Alex collects them all in order to enter them into the system. When I looked at my name on my box, there were two purple hearts doodled over the Os in my last name. Mrs. Alex is the only one who writes with purple ink."

Lake and Julia both burst out laughing. "Mrs. Alex has a *crush* on you?" Lake says, laughing. "She's . . . *old*. And *married!*"

I smile and nod, a little embarrassed. I try to turn my focus back to Julia, but seeing Lake finally laughing is captivating. It's amazing how one smile from her can shift the mood of my entire day. Lake sighs and leans back in her chair. "So are you supposed to say a 'sweet' now? Is that how this works?"

I nod, unable to look away from her. Her smile meets her eyes, and even though I know she has a lot to deal with in the coming days, I feel a sense of relief just seeing her happiness break through, if only for a moment. The fact that she can still find something positive in her current situation reassures me that she'll be okay.

"My sweet?" I say, staring directly at her. "My sweet is right now."

For a moment, it's just the two of us in the room. I don't hear or think about or acknowledge anyone else around us. She smiles at me and I smile back and neither of us breaks our stare. It's as if a silent truce occurs between us and all is suddenly right in our little two-person world.

Julia clears her throat and leans forward. "Okay, I think

we know how to play now," she says, interrupting our moment. I glance at Julia and she's looking at the boys. "Kel, you go next," Julia says, pretending not to have noticed my and Lake's little "moment." I watch Kel, forcing myself to avoid looking at Lake again. If I do, I won't be able to stop myself from jumping over the bar and kissing her.

"My suck is that I still can't think of what to be for Halloween," Kel says. "My sweet is that Will agreed to take us geocaching again this weekend."

"I'm taking you geocaching?" This is the first I've heard of it.

"You are?" Kel says sarcastically. "Aww, gee, Will. That sounds like fun! I'd *love* to go geocaching this weekend."

I laugh and look over at Caulder. "Your turn."

He nudges his head toward Kel. "Same thing," he says.

"That's a cop-out," Julia says to Caulder. "You have to be original."

Caulder rolls his eyes. "Fine," he groans, setting down his pizza. "My suck today is that my best friend's suck is that he can't think of what he wants to be for Halloween. My sweet is that my best friend's sweet is that Will agreed to take us geocaching this weekend."

"You're such a smart-ass," I say to Caulder.

"My turn," Julia says. "My sweet today is that we got to carve pumpkins together." She leans back in her chair and smiles at all of us. I glance at Lake and she's staring down at her hands, folded in front of her on the table. She's picking at her nail polish, something I noticed she does when she's stressed, just like Julia. I know she's thinking what I'm thinking. That this is more than likely Julia's last time to carve pumpkins. Lake brings her hand to her eyes and it looks like she's trying to stop a tear from falling. I quickly turn to Julia to remove any focus from Lake.

"What's your suck?" I ask.

Julia continues to watch Lake when she responds. "My suck is the same as my sweet," Julia says quietly. "We're still carving pumpkins."

I'm beginning to understand that "carving pumpkins" has taken on a whole new meaning. Lake immediately stands up and grabs empty plates off the bar, completely ignoring her mother's gaze.

"*My* suck is that it's my night to do dishes," Lake says. She walks to the sink and turns on the water. Kel and Caulder begin discussing Halloween costumes again, so Julia and I help throw out a few ideas.

No one ever asks Lake what her sweet is.

15.

the honeymoon

"I DID HAVE a sweet that night," she says. "Remember the conversation we had when we took the trash out? When you told me about the first time you saw me?"

I nod.

"That was my sweet. Having that moment with you. All the little moments I got with you were always my sweets." She kisses me on the forehead.

"That was my sweet, too," I say. "That and the intense stare you gave me while we were playing suck and sweet."

She laughs. "If you only knew what I was thinking."

I cock my eyebrow at her. "Naughty thoughts?"

"As soon as you said 'My sweet is right now,' I wanted to jump across the bar and ravish you," she says.

I laugh. I never would have thought we were both thinking the exact same thing. "I wonder what your mom would have done if we had both attacked each other, right there on the bar."

"She would have kicked your ass," she says. She rolls onto her side and faces the other direction. "Spoon me," she says. I scoot closer to her and slide my arm underneath her head, wrapping my other arm tightly around her. She yawns a deep yawn into her pillow. "Tell me about *The Lake*. I want to know why you wrote it."

I kiss her hair and rest my head on her pillow. "I wrote it the next night. After we had basagna with your mom," I say. "When we all sat around the table that night and discussed how things with the boys were going to be handled during her treatments, I realized that you had done it. You were doing exactly what I wished my parents had done before they died. You were taking responsibility. You were preparing for the inevitable. You were facing death head-on, and you were doing it without fear." I put my leg over her legs and tuck her in closer to me. "Every time I was around you, you inspired me to write. And I didn't want to write about anything but you."

She tilts her head back toward me. "That was on the list," she says.

"Your mom's list?"

"Yeah. *'Does he inspire you?'* is one of the questions."

"*Do* I inspire you?"

"Every single day," she whispers.

I kiss her forehead. "Well, like I said, you inspired me, too. I knew I already loved you long before then, but that night at dinner something just clicked inside me. It's like every time we were together, all was right with the world. I had assumed, just like your mom did, that staying apart would help you focus on her, but we were both wrong. I knew that the only way either of us could have been truly happy was if we were together. I wanted you to wait for me. I wanted you to wait for me so bad, but I didn't know how to tell you without crossing some sort of boundary.

"The next night at the slam when I saw you walk in, I couldn't stop myself from performing that piece so you would hear it. I knew it was wrong, but I wanted you to know how much I thought about you. How much I really did love you."

She rolls over and scowls at me. "What do you mean when you saw me walk in? You said you didn't know I was there until you saw me leaving."

I shrug. "I lied."

the lake

AS SOON AS I step up to the microphone, I see her. She walks through the doors and heads straight for a booth, never once looking up at the stage. My heart rate speeds up and beads of sweat form on my forehead, so I wipe them away with the palm of my hand. I'm not sure if it's from the heat of the spotlight or the onslaught of nerves that have just overcome me seeing her walk through the door. I can't perform this poem now. Not with her here. *Why is she here?* She said she wasn't coming tonight.

I take a step away from the microphone to gather my thoughts. Should I do it anyway? If I do it, she'll know exactly how I feel about her. That could be good. Maybe if I go ahead and do it I could gauge her reaction and know if asking her to wait for me is the right thing to do. I *want* her to wait for me. I want her to wait for me so bad. I don't want to think about her ever allowing anyone besides me to love her. She needs to know how I feel about her before I'm too late.

I shake the tension out of my shoulders. I step up to the microphone, brush away my doubt, and say the words that will strip away everything but the truth.

I used to *love* the ocean.
Everything about her.
Her coral *reefs*, her *whitecaps*, her roaring *waves*, the
rocks they *lap*, her *pirate* legends and *mermaid* tails,
Treasures *lost* and treasures *held* . . .
And *ALL*
Of her *fish*
In the *sea*.

Yes, I used to *love* the ocean,
Everything about her.
The way she would *sing* me to *sleep* as I *lay* in my *bed*
then *wake* me with a *force*
That I *soon* came to *dread.*
Her *fables,* her *lies,* her *misleading* eyes,
I'd drain her *dry*
If I *cared* enough to.
I used to *love* the ocean,
Everything about her.
Her coral *reefs,* her *whitecaps,* her roaring *waves,* the
rocks they *lap,* her *pirate* legends and *mermaid* tails,
treasures *lost* and treasures *held.*
And *ALL*
Of her *fish*
In the *sea.*
Well, if you've ever tried *navigating* your *sailboat*
through her stormy *seas,* you would *realize* that
her *whitecaps* are your *enemies.* If you've ever tried
swimming ashore when your *leg* gets a *cramp* and
you just had a *huge meal* of *In-n-Out* burgers that's
weighing you down, and her *roaring waves* are
knocking the *wind* out of you, filling your *lungs* with
water as you *flail* your arms, trying to get *someone's*
attention, but your friends
just
wave
back at you?
And if you've ever grown up with *dreams* in your *head*
about *life,* and how one of these days you would pirate

your *own* ship and have your *own* crew and that *all* of
the mermaids
would *love*
only
you?
Well, you would *realize* . . .
Like I eventually realized . . .
That all the *good* things about her?
All the *beautiful?*
It's not *real.*
It's *fake.*
So you *keep* your *ocean*,
I'll take the *Lake.*

I CLOSE MY eyes and exhale, not sure what to do next. Do I walk
to the booth where she's sitting? Do I wait and let her come find
me? I slowly back away from the microphone and walk toward the
side stairs, taking them one by one, afraid of what, if anything,
might happen next. I know I need to see her.

When I reach the back of the room, she isn't in the booth
anymore. I walk toward the front of the club, toward the stage, in
case she came to find me up here. She's nowhere. After looking
around for several minutes, I see Eddie and Gavin sliding into the
booth Lake was seated in just moments ago.

What are they doing here? Lake said none of them were
coming. Thank God they're late, I wouldn't have wanted Gavin
to hear that piece. I walk over to them and attempt to appear casual, but my entire body is nervous and tense.

"Hey, Will," Gavin says. "You want to sit with us?"

I shake my head. "Not yet. Have you guys . . ." I pause, not really wanting Gavin to give me one of his looks again when he finds out I'm looking for Lake. "Have you guys seen Layken?" Gavin leans back in the booth and cocks an eyebrow.

"Yeah," Eddie says with a grin on her face. "She said she was leaving. She was headed toward the back parking lot of the club, but I just found her purse right here," she says, holding up a purse. "She'll be back as soon as she realizes she doesn't have it."

She *left*? I immediately turn and head toward the door without saying another word to either of them. If she stayed for the whole poem and just up and left, I must have pissed her off. Why did I not switch poems? Why didn't I think about how it would make her feel? I swing the door open and immediately round the corner toward the back parking lot. Frantic to catch her before she drives away, I find myself switching from a brisk walk, to a jog, then to a desperate sprint. I spot her Jeep, but she isn't inside it. I spin around searching for her, but I don't see her. I turn to walk back and check the club again and I hear her voice, coupled with someone else's. It sounds like a guy. My fists immediately clench, worried for her safety. I don't like the thought of her being out here alone with someone else, so I follow the sound of the voices until I see her.

Until I see *them*.

She's backed up against Javi's truck, her hands on his chest, his hands on her cheeks. Seeing his lips meshed with hers pulls a reaction from deep within me that I didn't even know I was capable of. The only thing running through my head at this point is how the hell to get this asshole off her. Of all the guys she could choose to help her move on from me, it sure as hell isn't going to be Javi.

Before I can even contemplate a more sane decision, my hands have hold of his shirt and I'm pulling him away from her. When he trips and falls onto his back, I drop my knee onto his chest and punch him. As soon as my fist meets his jaw, I realize it took all of three seconds to throw away every single thing I've worked for. There is no way I'm getting out of this predicament with a job.

My split-second realization is enough distraction to allow Javi to regain his footing and deliver a punch right to my eye, sending me back to the ground before I can react. I press my hand against my eye and feel the warm blood seeping through my fingers. I hear Lake yelling for him to stop. Or she's yelling for me to stop. Or maybe both of us. I stand up and open my eyes just as Lake jumps in front of Javi. She's hurled forward when Javi hits her in the back with a blow that was obviously intended for me. She gasps and falls against me.

"Lake!" I yell, rolling her onto her back. As soon as I confirm she's conscious, I'm consumed by rage.

Vengeance.

Hatred.

I want to *kill* this asshole. I grab the door handle of the car nearest me and pull myself up. Javi is making his way toward Lake, apologizing. I don't give him time to make amends. I hit him with every ounce of force behind my fist and watch as he falls to the ground. I kneel and hit him again, this time for Lake. As soon as I pull my fist back to hit him again, Gavin jerks me off him, sending us both backward. Gavin has hold of both my arms from behind and is yelling for me to calm down. I yank my arms away from him and stand up, intent on getting Lake out of here, away from Javi. She's probably beyond pissed at me right now, but the feeling is pretty damn mutual.

She's sitting up, clutching her chest, attempting to take a breath. As much as I want to yell at her, I'm immediately overcome by worry when I realize she's hurting. I just want to get her away from everyone. I take her hand and pull her up, then wrap my arm around her waist to help her walk.

"I'm taking you home."

When we reach my car, I help her inside and shut her door, then walk around to my side of the car. Before I get in, I take several deep breaths in an attempt to calm myself down. I can't imagine what possessed her to allow him to kiss her after seeing me practically confess my love for her on stage. Does she not even *give* a shit anymore? I close my eyes and inhale through my nose, then open the door and climb in.

I pull out of the parking lot, unable to form a thought, much less a coherent sentence. My hands are shaking, my heart is about to beat out of my chest, I probably need stitches, and my career is now in jeopardy . . . but the only thing I can think about is the fact that she kissed him.

She *kissed* him.

The thought consumes me the entire drive. She hasn't said a single thing, so she has to be feeling pretty guilty right now. As soon as I feel the urge to turn to her and tell her exactly what I think of her actions tonight, I choose to get out of the car, instead. It's better for both of us if I get a breather. I can't keep this all in anymore. I pull the car over to the side of the road and punch the steering wheel. I can see her flinch out of the corner of my eye, but she says nothing. I swing the car door open and quickly get out before I say something I'll regret. I start walking in an attempt to clear my head. It doesn't help. When I'm at least fifty yards away from the car, I bend down and pick up a handful of gravel, then throw it at nothing.

"Shit!" I yell. "Shit, shit, shit!" I'm not sure at this point what or why or who I'm even mad at. Lake is in no way tied to me. She can date whomever she wants. She can kiss whomever she wants. The fact that I overreacted isn't her fault at all. I should never have performed that poem. I freaked her out. We were finally in a good spot and I went and screwed it all up.

Again.

I tilt my head up to the sky and close my eyes, allowing the cold flakes of snow to fall on my face. I can feel the tightness and pressure increasing near my eye. It hurts like hell. I hope Javi is hurting worse than I am.

Asshole.

I throw another rock, then walk back toward the car. We drive home with so much that needs to be said, but not a single word spoken.

WHEN WE GET to my house, I help her onto the couch, then walk to my kitchen and grab an ice pack out of the freezer. The tension between us has never been thicker, but I can't bring myself to talk to her about it. I don't want to know why she ran after I performed. I don't want to know why she ran to *Javi* of all people. I sure as hell don't want to know why she kissed him.

Her eyes are closed when I reach the couch again. She looks so peaceful just lying there. I watch her for a moment, wishing I knew what the hell was going through her head, but I refuse to ask. I can carve pumpkins just as well as she can.

I kneel beside her and her eyes flick open. She looks at me with horror and reaches up to my eye. "Will! Your eye!"

"It's fine. I'll be fine," I say, shaking it off. She pulls her hand back and I lean forward and grasp the bottom edge of her shirt. "Do you mind?" I say, asking permission to lift her shirt. She shakes her head, so I pull the shirt up over her back. She's already got a bruise from where that asswipe punched her. I lay the ice-pack over her injury, then pull her shirt back down on top of it.

I walk to the front door and leave her on the couch as I make my way across the street to inform Julia. When I knock on the door, it takes her a while to finally answer. When she sees me standing there with blood on my face, she immediately gasps Lake's name.

"She's okay," I quickly say. "There was a fight at the club and she was hit in the back. She's on my couch." Before I can say any-thing else, Julia shoves past me and runs across the street. When I finally make my way back into my living room, she's holding Lake in her arms. Julia takes her hand and helps her up. I hold the door open as they both walk out. Lake doesn't even make eye contact with me when she leaves. I shut the door behind them, then head to the bathroom and begin cleaning my injury. When I've got it bandaged up, I grab my phone and text Gavin.

If I come pick you up first thing in the morning, can you go
with me to get Lake's Jeep and drive it back to Ypsi?

I hit send and sit down on the couch. I can't even wrap my mind around everything that's happened tonight. I feel like I'm living someone else's dream. Someone else's *nightmare*.

How early?

Early. I have to be at the school by 7:30. Is 6:00 okay?

I'll do it under one condition. If you don't get fired tomorrow,

I'm exempt from every single assignment for the rest of the year.

See you at six.

HE OPENS THE passenger door and climbs inside. Before I've even backed out of his driveway, he lays into me.

"You realize you screwed up, right? Do you know who Javier's father is? If you even have a job to go back to today, you won't have it by this afternoon."

I nod, but don't respond.

"What the hell prompted you to kick a student's ass, Will?"

I sigh and pull onto the main road, keeping my eyes focused in front of me.

"I know whatever happened had to do with Layken. But what the hell did Javi do? You were pummeling him like he was your punching bag. Please tell me it was self-defense so you at least have a chance at keeping your job. Was it self-defense?" he asks, looking straight at me for an answer.

I shake my head no. He sighs, then leans forcefully back against his seat.

"And then you take her home! Why the hell would you let her in your car alone in front of him? That's enough to get you fired without even *kicking* his ass. Why the hell *did* you kick his ass?"

I look over at him. "Gavin, I screwed up. I realize this. You can shut the hell up now."

He nods and props his leg on the dash and doesn't say another word.

• • •

IT'S THE FIRST time I've ever made it into the office before Mrs. Alex. It's eerily quiet, and for a moment, I actually wish she were here. I walk around her desk toward Mr. Murphy's office. I glance inside and he's casually seated at his desk with the phone to his ear and his feet propped up. His face lights up when he sees me, but the illumination quickly fades when he sees the damage to my eye. He holds up a finger, so I take a few steps away from his door to give him some privacy.

I've thought about this moment so many times before. The moment I would walk into Mr. Murphy's office and resign. Of course, I always imagined the end result would be my walking out of his office and into Lake's life.

My fantasy is nothing like my current reality. Lake hates me right now and her feelings are warranted. I push her away every time she gets close to me, then every time she finally gets used to being without me, I do something to screw with her head even more. Why did I think performing that poem last night was a good idea? We were finally in a good spot. She was finally learning to balance all the negativity in her life, and I go and make it worse. *Again.*

That's all I do is make things worse for her. That's probably the reason she turned to Javi. I'd like to think she was just kissing him to make me jealous, but my biggest fear is that she was kissing him because she's completely moved on from me. It's my biggest fear, yet it's exactly what I know she needs.

"Mr. Cooper," Mr. Murphy says, walking past me. "Is this something that can wait until I get back? I've got an eight o'clock meeting."

"Uh," I stammer. "Well, actually it's pretty important."

He stops next to the wall of mailboxes and pulls the contents of his box out. "How important? So important it can't wait until ten?"

I shrug. "It can't wait," I say reluctantly. "I, um . . . sort of got in a fight last night. With a student."

Mr. Murphy stops sorting his mail and darts his head toward me. "Sort of? You did or you didn't, Mr. Cooper. Which is it?"

"Did," I reply. "Definitely did."

He turns to face me full on and leans his back against the row of mailboxes behind him. "Who?"

"Javier Cruz."

He shakes his head, then rubs the back of his neck while he thinks. "I'll have Mrs. Alex set up an appointment with his father at ten. In the meantime, I suggest you find someone to fill in for you," he says. "Be back here at ten." He walks over to Mrs. Alex's desk and writes something down. I nod, not at all surprised by his guarded reaction. I pick my satchel up and walk toward the office exit.

"Mr. Cooper?" he calls out.

"Yes, sir?"

"Were there any other students involved? Anyone who can give an accurate account of what happened?"

I sigh. I really don't want to get her involved, but it doesn't seem like I'm going to have a choice. "Yes. Layken Cohen," I say.

"Is this Javier's girlfriend?" he asks, writing down Layken's name.

The question causes me to wince, but from the looks of them last night I'd say it's a very legitimate question. "Yeah, I guess so." I exit the office, hoping they don't bring Lake and Javi in at ten. I don't know if I can keep it together in the same room with both of them.

• • •

I'M SEATED AT the table, waiting for the conference to begin. Luckily, Mr. Murphy met with Javier privately, not wanting us to have to interact. I'm supposed to meet with Mr. Murphy as soon as the conference with Javier's father is over. I'm not really that eager to share my version of events, since I'm obviously the one in the wrong here. The fact that Mr. Murphy brought in a member of campus police doesn't do anything to ease my apprehension. I'm not sure what the legal ramifications are of what occurred last night and if Javier is planning on pressing charges, but I guess I deserve whatever result my actions bring about.

The door opens and Lake walks into the room. I literally have to force myself not to look at her. I can't help the emotional reaction I have to her, and I'm afraid everyone in the room will see it. I keep my gaze focused on the table in front of me.

"Ms. Cohen, please take a seat," Mr. Murphy says. Lake takes a step forward and slides into the seat next to me. I clench my fists, fighting the tension between us that seems to have only increased since last night.

"This is Mr. Cruz, Javier's father," says Mr. Murphy. "This is Officer Venturelli," he says, motioning to both men. "I'm sure you know why you're here. It is our understanding that there was an incident involving Mr. Cooper that occurred off of school grounds," he says. "We would appreciate it if you could tell us your version of events."

I glance toward Lake just as she turns her head toward me. Her eyes search mine for guidance, so I nod, silently encouraging her to tell the truth. I could never let her lie for me. She turns back to Mr. Murphy. The exchange we just shared was no more than three seconds, but the look of concern for me in her eyes was undeniable.

She doesn't hate me. She's *worried* for me.

She clears her throat and adjusts herself in her seat. She places her hands on the table in front of her and begins picking at her nail polish when she speaks. "There was a misunderstanding between me and Javier," she says. "Mr. Cooper showed up and pulled him off me."

I can feel the heat in my face when the lies start coming out of her mouth. Why is she lying for me? Did I not make it clear that I wanted her to tell the truth about last night? I tap my knee against hers when she pauses. She glances up at me, but before I can tell her to tell the truth, Mr. Murphy interrupts.

"Can you start at the beginning, please, Ms. Cohen? We need to be clear on the entire sequence of events. Where were you and what were all of you doing there?"

"We were in Detroit at a poetry slam. It's part of a required assignment for Mr. Cooper's class. I arrived early before the other students. Something happened and I felt uncomfortable and had to leave, so I left just a few minutes after I arrived, which is when I ran into Javier outside."

"What happened that made you uncomfortable?" Officer Venturelli asks her. She flicks her gaze in my direction, but only for a moment. She looks back at Officer Venturelli and shrugs. "Maybe uncomfortable isn't the right word," she says quietly. "One of the performers . . ." She pauses and takes a deep breath. Before she continues, she touches her knee to mine and doesn't retract it, causing me to swallow a lump in my throat. The move is deliberate, and it confuses the hell out of me. "I was just really moved by one of the pieces performed last night. It meant a lot to me," she whispers. "So much that I just wanted to leave, before I got too emotional."

I lean forward and put my elbows on the table, then rest my face in the palms of my hands. I can't believe she just said those words, and she said them just for my benefit. Knowing that she's trying to tell me how my poem made her feel is making this too much to bear. I have the overwhelming urge to pull her up out of her chair and kiss her in front of everyone, then scream my resignation at the top of my lungs.

"My Jeep was parked behind the venue and on my way outside, I ran into Javier. He offered to walk me to my car. I needed to use his phone, so we were standing by his truck while it was charging. We were talking about the weather and . . ." Her voice grows quiet and she shifts uncomfortably in her seat.

"Ms. Cohen, is this something you would rather tell me in private?" Mr. Murphy asks.

She shakes her head. "No, it's fine," she says. "I was . . . I was asking him about the weather and he just started kissing me. I told him no and tried to push him away, but he wouldn't stop kissing me. I didn't know what to do. He had me pinned against his truck, and I guess that's when Mr. Cooper saw what was happening and he pulled him off me."

I have a grip on the edge of the table that is so tight, I don't even notice until Lake taps my leg and glances down at my hands. I release the table from my grasp and close my eyes, breathing slow and steady. Her confession should give me nothing but relief, knowing that my bout of jealousy will now be played off as if I were protecting her. However, I'm anything *but* relieved. I'm furious. Javier is lucky his ass isn't in here, because there would have been an extremely detailed reenactment of last night right in this office.

Lake continues sharing her version of the story, but I don't hear another word of it. I do my best to hold it together until everyone's dismissed, but it's the hardest five minutes I've ever had to contain myself. As soon as they dismiss her, Mr. Cruz and Officer Venturelli follow her out the door. I stand up in my seat and let out a breath. I pace back and forth under the intense gaze of Mr. Murphy. I'm not able to speak yet due to the rage coursing through me, so I continue to pace and he continues to silently watch me.

"Mr. Cooper," he says calmly, "do you have anything else to add or is her version accurate?"

I pause and look at him. "I wish it *wasn't* accurate," I say, "but unfortunately it is."

"Will," Mr. Murphy says. "You did the right thing. Quit being so hard on yourself. Javier was completely out of line and if you weren't there to stop him, there's no telling what would have happened to that girl."

"Is he being expelled?" I ask, stopping to grip the back of the chair.

Mr. Murphy stands and walks to the door where Officer Venturelli is outside speaking with Mr. Cruz. He closes the door and turns toward me. "We can't expel him. He's claiming it was a misunderstanding and he thought she wanted him to kiss her. We'll suspend him for a few days for the fight, but that's the extent of his punishment."

I nod, very aware that what I'm about to do is the only answer at this point. There's no way I can ever be in the same room with Javier again and not have it end badly.

"Then I'd like to resign," I say evenly.

16.

the honeymoon

"YOU *WILLINGLY* RESIGNED?" Lake asks, dumbfounded. "I thought it was a mutual agreement. They would have let you keep your job, Will. Why the hell did you *resign*?"

"Lake, there's no way I could have continued teaching there. I'd reached my breaking point. I was going to get fired one of two ways if I hadn't resigned that day."

"Why do you think that?"

"Because it's true. They would have fired me the first day Javier returned to school because I would have kicked his ass the moment I laid eyes on him. That, or they would have fired me because one more second in a room with you and I would have jumped *you*, but in a completely different way."

She laughs. "Yeah. The tension was intense. We would have lost control eventually."

"*Eventually?* We lost control that same day," I say, reminding her of our incident in the laundry room.

She frowns and closes her eyes, then sighs a deep sigh.

"What's wrong?" I ask her.

She shakes her head. "Nothing. It's just hard thinking about that night. It really hurt," she whispers.

I kiss her lightly on the forehead. "I know. I'm sorry."

laundry room

I SOMEHOW MADE it to the end of the workday without getting suspended, fired, or arrested. I'd say being transferred to Detroit to finish out my student teaching is one of the best outcomes I could have anticipated.

I pull into the driveway and the boys are helping Lake and Julia with groceries. I haven't even made it out of the car yet when Caulder meets me at the door, beaming with excitement.

"Will!" he says, grabbing my hand. "Wait till you see this!"

I walk across the street with him and grab the rest of the sacks and take them inside. When I set them down, I notice the contents aren't groceries. It looks like sewing supplies.

"Guess what we're going to be for Halloween?" Caulder says.

"Uh—"

"Julia's cancer!" he yells.

Did I just hear him right?

Julia walks into the room with her sewing machine and I give her a questioning look.

"You only live once, right?" She smiles and places the sewing machine on the bar.

"She's letting us make the tumors for the lungs," Kel says. "You want to make one? I'll let you make the big one."

I don't even know how to respond. "Uh—"

"Kel," Lake interrupts. "Will and Caulder can't help, they'll be out of town all weekend." Seeing the excitement on Caulder's face, there's nowhere I'd rather be than right here. "Actually, that was before I found out we were making lung cancer," I say. "I think we'll have to reschedule our trip."

• • •

"WHERE'S YOUR MEASURING tape?" Lake asks Julia.

"I don't know," she says. "I don't know if I have one, actually."

I have measuring tape, so I try to think of a way to get Lake to come with me to get it. I know she's dying to know what happened today and I owe her a huge apology for acting the way I did toward her last night. She had experienced what was more than likely a horrifying event alone with Javi, and I acted like a jerk the entire way home. I was trying to refrain from yelling at her last night, when I should have been consoling her.

"Will has one. We can use his," Lake says. "Will, do you mind getting it?"

I play dumb. "I have measuring tape?"

She rolls her eyes. "Yes, it's in your sewing kit."

"I have a sewing kit?"

"It's in your laundry room." She spreads the material out in front of her. "It's next to the sewing machine on the shelf behind your mother's patterns. I put them in chronological order according to pattern nu— Never mind," she says quickly. She shakes her head and stands. "I'll just show you."

Thank you.

I quickly jump up, maybe a little too eagerly.

"You put his patterns in chronological order?" Julia asks.

"I was having a bad day," Lake says over her shoulder.

I hold the door for Lake, then close it behind us. She turns around and completely loses her calm demeanor. "What happened? God, I've been worried sick all day," she says.

"I got a slap on the wrist," I say as we walk toward my house. "They told me since I was defending another student, they couldn't really hold it against me."

I jog a few steps and open my front door for her, stepping aside to let her in.

"That's good. What about your internship?" she asks.

"Well, it's a little tricky. The only available ones they had in Ypsilanti were all primary. My major is secondary, so I've been placed at a school in Detroit."

She looks up at me, her eyes full of concern. "What's that mean? Are y'all moving?"

I love the fact that the thought of our moving scares her so bad. I laugh. "No, Lake, we're not moving. It's just for eight weeks. I'll be doing a lot of driving, though. I was actually going to talk to you and your mom about it later. I'm not going to be able to take the boys to school, or pick them up either. I'll be gone a lot. I know this isn't a good time to ask for your help—"

"Stop it. You know we'll help." She grabs the tape measure and shuts the box, then walks the kit back to the laundry room. I follow her, but I'm not sure why I feel compelled to. I'm afraid she's about to head straight back to her house and I still have so much left I need to say to her. I walk into the laundry room be-hind her and pause in the doorway. She's staring quietly in front of her, running her fingers across my mother's patterns. She's got that distant look in her eyes again. I lean against the doorframe and watch her.

I still can't believe I thought she would willingly allow Javi to kiss her, especially after seeing my performance last night. I know her better than that, and she knows she deserves so much better than Javi.

Hell, she deserves so much better than *me*.

She reaches to the wall and flicks off the light, then turns toward me. She comes to a halt when she sees that I'm blocking the doorway. She quietly gasps and looks up at me, her beautiful green eyes full of hope again. She scrolls her eyes over my features, searching my face, waiting for me to either speak or move out of her way. I don't want to do either. All I want to do is take her in my arms and show her how I feel about her, but I can't. She stares up at me, slowly dropping her gaze to my mouth. She tugs on her bottom lip with her teeth and nervously darts her eyes to the floor.

I've never wanted to be teeth so bad in my entire life.

I take a deep breath and prepare to get out what I need to say, despite knowing I shouldn't say it. I just need her to know why I did what I did last night, and why I acted the way I acted. I fold my arms across my chest and prop my foot against the doorway, looking down at it. Avoiding eye contact with her is probably best right now, considering my lack of resolve at the moment. It's been a while since we've been alone in a situation like this. The way things have been going the past few weeks, I had myself convinced that I was stronger than I am, and that I've overcome the weakness I feel when I'm around her.

I was completely wrong.

My heart slams against my chest at record speed and I'm consumed by an insatiable desire to grab her by the waist and pull her to me. I hug myself tighter in an attempt to keep my hands to myself. I work my jaw back and forth, hell bent on finding a way to bury my urge to confess to her, but I can't. The words spill out of me before I can stop them.

"Last night," I say, my voice cracking the tension like a sledgehammer. "When I saw Javi kissing you . . . I thought you were kissing him back."

I swing my eyes to her, searching for a reaction. *Any* reaction. I know how she tries to hide what she's feeling more than any other person I've ever met.

Her eyes widen at the realization that I wasn't defending her at all last night. I was reacting like a possessive boyfriend, not her knight in shining armor.

"Oh," she says.

"I didn't know the whole story until this morning, when you told your version," I say. I don't know how I held myself together in the office this morning when I found out. All I wanted to do was lunge across the table and punch Javi's father across the jaw for raising such an asshole. Just thinking about it causes my blood to boil. I inhale a deep breath, filling my lungs to their maximum capacity before huffing out a sigh. I notice my hands are clenched into tight fists, so I relax them and run my hands through my hair, turning to face her.

"God, Lake. I can't tell you how pissed I was. I wanted to hurt him so bad. And now? Now that I know he really *was* hurting you? I want to *kill* him." I lean my head back against the door-frame and close my eyes. I have to get the thought of him out of my head. He hurt her, and I wasn't there in time to protect her. The image of him pressing his mouth to hers against her will is clear in my mind, as is the fact that his lips were the last to touch hers. She doesn't deserve to be kissed like that. She deserves to be kissed by someone who loves her. Someone who spends every waking moment trying to do everything right by her. Someone who would rather die than see her hurt. She doesn't deserve to be kissed by anyone other than me.

Her brows are furrowed and she's staring at me with a confused expression. "How did you"—she pauses—"How'd you know I was there?"

"I saw you. When I finished my piece, I saw you leaving."

She looks up at me and quietly sucks in a small breath with my admission. Her hand searches for support behind her and she takes a step back, steadying herself. Despite the darkness, I can see her eyes dance with hope. "Will, does this mean—"

I immediately take two steps forward, closing the gap between us. My chest heaves with each passing breath as I attempt to calm my desire to show her just how sincere my words were last night. I trail the back of my fingers against the smooth skin of her cheek, then hook my thumb under her chin, bringing her face closer to mine. The simple contact of her skin against my fingers reminds me of what her kiss is capable of doing to me. It hypnotizes me. Her touch completely, wholeheartedly shakes me to my core and I try to force myself to slow down.

She places her hand against my chest when I wrap my arms around her. I can feel her wanting to resist, but her need is just as strong as mine. I take a step forward until she finds solid backing and I quickly lean in and press my lips to hers before either of us has time to change our minds. When my tongue finds hers, she moans a soft moan and becomes putty in my hands, dropping her arms to her sides. I kiss her passionately, tenderly, and eagerly all at the same time.

I grip her by the waist and easily lift her up onto the dryer, taking a stance between her legs and never losing contact with her lips. She begins to pull at my shirt, wanting me closer, so I oblige by pulling her against me as she encircles me with her legs. Her nails lightly dig into the muscles of my forearms as her fingers search their way up my arms. When she reaches my neck, her hands glide through my hair, sending chills to places I didn't even know could *get* chills. She grabs tufts of my hair in her fists and pulls my head down, repositioning my mouth against the sweet skin of her neck. She takes the opportunity to catch her breath, panting and quietly moaning as my lips tease their way across her collarbone. I reach behind her and grab a handful of hair just as she did mine, then lightly tug until she leans her head back, giving me more access to the incredibly perfect skin against my lips. She does just as I'd hoped and arches her back, giving my lips silent permission to resume their pursuit as I make my way down her neck. I release her hair and slide my hand down her back, slipping my fingers between her skin and her jeans. My fingertips skim the top edge of her panties, and I groan under my breath.

Having her in my arms fills the constant void that has been in my heart since the first night I kissed her, but with every passing moment, every kiss, and every stroke of her hands, an even greater desire builds within me. I need more of her than these stolen moments of passion. I need so much more.

"Will," she breathes.

I mumble against her skin, unable to get out an audible response. I don't really feel like talking at the moment. I run my other hand up the back of her shirt until it meets her bra and I pull her against me as I work my way back up her neck toward her mouth.

"Does this mean . . ." she breathes heavily. "Does it mean we don't have to pretend . . . anymore? We can be . . . together? Since you're not . . . since you're not my teacher?"

My lips freeze against her neck with her breathless words. I want more than anything to cover her mouth with my own and make her stop talking about it. I just want to forget about it all for one night. Just for one night.

But I can't.

My incredibly irresponsible moment of weakness just gave her the wrong idea. I'm still a teacher. Maybe not *her* teacher, but I'm still a teacher. And she's still a student. And everything happening between us right now is still completely wrong, no matter how right I want it to be.

In the process of thinking about all of the potential complications of her question, I've somehow released her from my death grip and have taken a step away from her.

"Will?" she says, sliding off the dryer. She steps closer to me and the fear in her eyes makes my stomach drop. I did this to her. *Again.*

I can feel the regret and agony creep up to my face, and it's obvious she can see it, too.

"Will? Tell me. Do the rules still apply?" she says fearfully.

I don't know what to say that can make it any less painful. It's obvious I just made a huge mistake. "Lake," I whisper, my voice full of shame. "I had a weak moment. I'm sorry."

She steps forward and shoves her hands into my chest. "A weak *moment*? That's what you call this? A weak *moment*?" she yells. I flinch at her words, knowing I just said the wrong thing. "What were you gonna *do*, Will? When were you gonna stop making out with me and kick me out of your house *this* time?"

She spins on her heel and storms out of the laundry room. Seeing her walk away causes me to panic at the thought of not only upsetting her, but losing her for good. "Lake, don't," I plead, following after her. "I'm sorry. I'm so sorry. It won't happen again, I swear."

She turns to face me, tears already streaming down her cheeks. "You're damn right it won't! I finally accepted it, Will! After an entire month of torture, I was finally able to be *around* you again. Then you go and do *this*! I can't do it anymore," she says, throwing her arms up in defeat. "The way you consume my mind when we aren't together? I don't have time for it anymore. I've got more important things to think about now than your little *weak moments*."

Her words slam me. She's absolutely right. I've gone so long trying to get her to accept things and move on so she won't be burdened by my life, but I can't even resist her long enough not to cave in to my selfish desire for her. I *don't* deserve her. I don't deserve her forgiveness, let alone to be loved by her.

"Get me the measuring tape," she says, standing with her hand on the door.

"Wh—what?"

"It's on the damn floor! Get me the measuring tape!"

I walk back into the laundry room and retrieve the measuring tape, then take it back to her, placing it in her hand. She looks down at my hand clamped over hers. She wipes away falling tears with her other hand. She refuses to even look at me. The thought of her hating me for what just happened between us terrifies me. I love her so much and I want more than anything to be able to give it all up for her.

But I can't. Not yet.

She has to know how hard this is for me, too. "Don't make me the bad guy, Lake. *Please*."

She pulls her hand from mine and looks into my eyes. "Well you're certainly not the martyr, anymore." She walks out, slamming the door behind her.

The words "wait for me" pass my lips just as the door closes, but she doesn't hear me. "I want you to wait for me," I say again. I know she can't hear me, but the fact that I can say it out loud gives me the confidence I need to run after her and tell her to her face.

I love her. I know she loves me. And despite what Julia thinks is good for us, I want her to wait for me. We need to be together. We *have* to be together. If I don't stop her from walking away right now, I'll regret it for the rest of my life.

I swing open the door, prepared to run after her, but I pause when I see her. She's standing in her entryway, wiping away the tears that I'm responsible for. I watch as she takes a few deep breaths, trying to pull herself together before walking into her house. Seeing her effort to move past what just happened so that she can help her mother inside her own home brings it all back into perspective.

I'm the last thing she needs in her life right now. I have too much responsibility, and with how things are going for her right now, the last thing she needs is to put her life on hold for me. Everything I say or do just brings her more grief and heartache and I can't ask her to hold on to that while she waits for me. She doesn't need to focus on me. Julia's right. She needs to focus on her family.

I reluctantly walk back into my house and shut the door behind me. The realization that I need to let her go for good physically brings me to my knees.

17.

the honeymoon

"I WISH MORE than anything I had gone after you that night," I say. "I should have told you exactly what I wanted to say. It would have saved us both a world of heartache."

Lake sits up on the bed and hugs her knees, looking down at me. "Not me," she says. "I'm happy things worked out the way they did. I think we both needed that breather. And I definitely don't regret all the time I spent with my mother during those three months. It was good for us."

"Good." I smile. "That's the only reason I didn't run after you."

She releases her knees and falls back onto the bed. "But still. It was so hard living across the street from you. All I wanted to do was be with you, but I didn't want anyone to know that. It's like I spent the entire three months pretending to be happy when I was in front of other people. Eddie was the only one who knew how I really felt. I didn't want Mom to know because I felt like it would just burden her even more if she knew how sad I was."

I raise up and lean forward, crawling on top of her. "Thank God she knew how we both really felt, though. Do you think you would have showed up at the slam the night before my graduation if she didn't encourage you to go?"

"There's no way I would have shown up. If it weren't for her telling me about your conversation with her, I would have continued the rest of the year thinking you didn't love me like I loved you."

I press my forehead against hers. "I'm so glad you showed up," I whisper. "You changed my life forever that night."

schooled

I'VE SPOKEN TO Lake once in the last three months.

Once.

You would think it would get easier, but it hasn't. Especially today, since my last day of student teaching is finally over. I graduate tomorrow, which should be a day I'm looking forward to more than anything. Instead I'm dreading it, knowing Lake won't be waiting for me.

There are two emotions in this world I've learned I can handle. Love and hate. Lake has loved me at times and she's hated me at times. Love and hate, despite their polar opposites, are both feelings that are induced by passion. I can handle that.

It's the indifference I don't know how to process.

I went to her house a few weeks ago to talk to her about my new job at the junior high and she didn't seem to care one way or another. I would have taken it well if she had been happy for me and wished me good luck. I would have taken it even better if she had cried and begged me not to do it, which is what I was hoping would happen more than anything. It's the sole reason I even went to tell her about the job in the first place. I didn't want to accept it if I thought I still had a chance with her.

Instead, she didn't react either way. She congratulated me, but the indifference in her voice was clear. She was simply being polite. Her indifference finally sealed our fate, and I knew in that moment that I had messed with her heart one too many times. She was over me.

She *is* over me.

I have a two-week window in which I'll be nothing. I won't be a student. I won't be a teacher. I'll be a twenty-one-year-old college graduate. I've thought about walking straight over to Lake's house today to tell her how much I love her, even though I'm technically still a teacher, considering the contract I have with the junior high. Not even *that* would stop me if it weren't for the way she reacted to me last month with so much indifference. She seemed to have accepted our fate, and it was good to see her handling everything so well, as much as it hurt. The last thing I want to do, or *need* to do, is pull her back down with me.

God, this is going to be the hardest two weeks of my life. I need to keep my distance from her, that's a fact.

When the audience begins clapping, I snap back to reality. I'm supposed to be judging tonight, but I haven't heard a single word any of the performers have said. I hold up the standard 9.0 on my scorecard without even looking up at the stage. I don't even want to be here tonight. In fact, I don't want to be *anywhere* tonight.

When the scores are tallied, the emcee begins to announce the winners. I lean back in my seat and close my eyes, hoping the night goes fast. I just want to go home and get to bed so graduation will come and go tomorrow. I don't know why I'm dreading it. Probably because I'll be the only person there who couldn't find enough people to give my graduation tickets to. The average person never gets *enough* tickets for graduation. I have too many.

"I would like to perform a piece I wrote."

I jerk up in my seat at the sound of her voice, the sudden movement almost causing my chair to flip backward. She's standing on the stage, holding the microphone. The guy next to me laughs along with the rest of the crowd once they realize she's interrupting the night's schedule.

"Check this chick out," he says, nudging me with his elbow.

The sight of her paralyzes me. I'm pretty sure I forgot how to breathe. I'm pretty sure I'm about to die. *What the hell is she doing?* I watch intently as she brings the microphone back to her lips. "I know this isn't standard protocol, but it's an emergency," she says.

The laughter from the audience causes her eyes to widen and she spins around to look for the emcee. She's scared. Whatever she's doing, it's completely out of character for her. The emcee nudges her to face the front of the room again. I take a deep breath, silently willing her to keep calm.

She places the microphone back in its stand and lowers it to her height. She closes her eyes and inhales when the guy next to me yells, "Three dollars!"

I could punch him.

Her eyes flick open and she shoves her hand into her pocket, pulling out money to hand to the emcee. After he takes the money, she prepares herself again. "My piece is called—" The emcee interrupts her, tapping her on the shoulder. She shoots him an irritated glance. I expel a deep breath, becoming just as irritated by all the interruptions. She takes the change from him and shoves it back into her pocket, then hisses something at him that makes him retreat off the stage. She turns back toward the audience and her eyes scan the crowd.

She has to know I'm here. What the hell is she doing?

"My piece is called *Schooled*," she says into the microphone. I swallow the lump in my throat. If I wanted to move at this point, my body would fail me. I'm completely frozen as I watch her take several deep breaths, then begin her piece.

I got **schooled** this year.
By **everyone**.
By my little brother . . .

by The *Avett* Brothers . . .

by my *mother*, my *best friend*, my *teacher*, my *father*,

and

by

a

boy.

A boy that I'm *seriously, deeply, madly, incredibly,*

and undeniably in *love* with.

I got *so schooled* this year.

By a *nine*-year-old.

He taught me that it's *okay* to live *life*

a little *backward.*

And how to *laugh*

At what you would *think*

is *unlaughable.*

I got *schooled* this year

By a *band*

They taught me how to find that *feeling* of *feeling*

again.

They taught me how to *decide* what to *be*

And go *be* it.

I got *schooled* this year.

By a *cancer* patient.

She taught me *so* much. She's *still* teaching me so

much.

She taught me to *question.*

To *never* regret.

She taught me to *push* my boundaries,

Because *that's* what they're *there* for.

She told me to find a *balance* between *head* and *heart*

And then
she taught me how . . .
I got *schooled* this year
By a *foster kid*.
She taught me to *respect* the hand that I was *dealt*.
And to be *grateful* I was even dealt a *hand*.
She taught me that *family*
Doesn't have to be *blood*.
Sometimes your *family*
are your *friends*.
I got *schooled* this year
By my *teacher*
He taught me
That the *points* are not the *point*,
The *point* is *poetry* . . .
I got *schooled* this year
By my *father*.
He taught me that *heroes* aren't always *invincible*
And that the *magic*
is *within* me.
I got schooled this year
by
a
boy.
A boy that I'm *seriously, deeply, madly, incredibly,*
and undeniably in *love* with.
And he taught me the most important thing of *all*—
To put the *emphasis*
On *life*.

COMPLETELY.

Utterly.

Frozen.

My eyes drop to the table in front of me when she finishes. Her words are still sinking in.

A boy that I'm seriously, deeply, madly, incredibly, and undeniably in love with.

In *love* with?

That's what she said.

In love with. As in *present* tense.

She *loves* me. Layken Cohen *loves* me.

"Hold up your scores, man," the guy next to me says, forcing the scorecard into my hand. I look at it, then look up at the stage. She's not up there anymore. I spin around and see her making her way toward the exit in a hurry.

What the hell am I doing just sitting here? She's waiting on me to acknowledge everything she just said, and I'm sitting here frozen like an idiot.

I stand up when the judges to the right of me hold up their scorecards. Three of them gave her a nine, the other an 8.5. I round the front of the table and flip the scores on all of their cards to tens. The points may not be the point, but her poetry kicked ass. "She gets tens."

I turn around and jump onto the stage. I grab the microphone out of the emcee's hands and he rolls his eyes, throwing his hands up in the air.

"Not again," he says, defeated.

I spot her as soon as she swings the doors open to step outside. "That's not a good idea," I say into the microphone. She stops in her tracks, then slowly turns around to face the stage. "You shouldn't leave before you get your scores."

She looks at the judges' table, then back to me. When she makes eye contact, she smiles.

I grip the microphone, hell bent on performing the piece I wrote for her, but the magnetic pull to jump off the stage and take her in my arms is overwhelming. I stand firm, wanting her to hear what I have to say first. "I'd like to perform a piece," I say, looking at the emcee. "It's an *emergency*." He nods and takes a few steps back. I turn around to face Lake again. She's standing in the center of the room now, staring up at me.

"Three dollars," someone yells from the crowd.

Shit. I pat my pockets, realizing I left my wallet in my car. "I don't have any cash," I say to the emcee.

His eyes shift to Lake and mine follow. She pulls out the two dollars in change from her fee and walks to the stage, slapping it down in front of us.

"Still a dollar short," he says.

Jesus! It's one freaking *dollar*!

The silence in the room is interrupted as several chairs slide from under their tables. People from all over the floor walk toward the stage, surrounding Lake as they throw dollar bills onto the stage. Everyone quickly makes their way back to their seats and Lake eyes the money, dumbfounded.

"*Okay*," the emcee says, taking in the pile of cash at my feet. "I guess that covers it. What's the name of your piece, Will?"

I look down at Lake and smile right back at her. "*Better than third.*"

She takes a few steps back from the stage and waits for me

to begin. I take a deep breath and prepare to tell her everything I should have said to her three months ago.

I met a girl.
A *beautiful* girl
And I fell for her.
I fell *hard*.
Unfortunately, sometimes *life* gets in the *way*.
Life *definitely* got in *my* way.
It got *all up* in my damn way,
Life *blocked* the *door* with a stack of wooden *two-by-fours* nailed together and *attached* to a fifteen-inch *concrete wall* behind a *row* of solid steel *bars*, *bolted* to a *titanium frame* that *no matter* how *hard* I shoved
against it—
It
wouldn't
budge.
Sometimes *life* doesn't *budge*.
It just gets *all up* in your *damn* way.
It blocked my *plans*, my *dreams*, my *desires*, my *wishes*,
my *wants*, my *needs*.
It blocked out that *beautiful* girl
That I *fell* so *hard* for.
Life tries to tell you what's *best* for you.
What should be most *important* to you.
What should come *first*
Or *second*
Or *third*.
I tried *so hard* to keep it all *organized, alphabetized,*

stacked in **chronological order**, everything in its
perfect space, its **perfect place**.
I thought that's what life *wanted* me to do.
This is what life *needed* for me to do.
Right?
Keep it **all** in **sequence?**
Sometimes life gets in your *way*.
It gets all up in your damn *way*.
But it doesn't get all up in your damn way because it
wants you to just **give up** and let it **take control**. Life
doesn't get all up in your damn way because it just
wants you to **hand** it all **over** and be **carried along**.
Life wants you to *fight* it.
Learn how to make it your *own*.
It wants you to grab an **axe** and **hack** through the **wood**.
It wants you to get a **sledgehammer** and **break** through
the **concrete**.
It wants you to grab a **torch** and **burn** through the **metal**
and **steel** until you can reach through and **grab** it.
Life wants you to **grab** all the **organized**, the
alphabetized, the **chronological**, the **sequenced**. It
wants you to mix it all **together**,
stir it up,
blend it.
Life doesn't want you to let it **tell** you that your little
brother should be the **only** thing that comes **first**.
Life doesn't want you to let it **tell** you that your **career**
and your **education** should be the **only** thing that comes
in **second**.

And life *definitely* doesn't want *me*
To just let it *tell* me
that the *girl* I met—
The *beautiful, strong, amazing, resilient girl*
That I fell *so hard* for—
Should *only* come in *third*.
Life *knows*.
Life is trying to *tell* me
That the *girl* I *love?*
The girl I fell
So *hard* for?
There's room for her in *first*.
I'm putting *her* first.

AS SOON AS the last line escapes my lips, I set the microphone down on the stage and jump off. I walk directly to her and take her face in my hands. Tears are falling down her cheeks, so I wipe them away with my thumbs.

"I love you, Lake." I lean my forehead against hers. "You deserve to come first."

Telling her exactly how I feel about her is the easiest thing I've ever done. The honesty comes so naturally. It's the months of hiding my feelings that have been unbearable. I breathe a huge sigh of relief when the weight of holding everything back disappears.

She laughs through her tears and places her hands on top of mine, looking up at me with the most beautiful smile. "I love you, too. I love you so much."

I kiss her softly on the lips. My heart feels like it literally swells within my chest when she kisses me back. I wrap my arms around her and bury my face into her hair, pulling her tightly against me. I close my eyes, and it's suddenly just the two of us. Me and this girl. This girl is in my arms again . . . touching me, kissing me, breathing me in, loving me back.

She's not just a dream, anymore.

Lake moves her mouth to my ear and whispers, "We probably shouldn't be doing this here." I open my eyes and the concern on her face registers with me. She's still a student. I'm still technically a teacher. This probably doesn't look very good if anyone here knows us.

I reach down and take her hand, then pull her toward the exit. As soon as we're outside, I grab her by the waist and push her against the door. I've been waiting months to be with her like this. Two more seconds without touching her and I. Will. Die.

I lower my hand to the small of her back, then lean in and kiss her again. The feeling I get when my lips are on hers is something I've thought about, over and over, since the first time I kissed her. But actually being in the moment with her again, knowing my feelings for her are reciprocated, is nothing short of amazing.

She runs her hands inside my jacket and up my back, pulling me to her as she returns my kiss. I can't think of anything I'd rather do for the rest of my life than be wrapped up in her arms with her lips pressed to mine. But I know that despite what we've been through and despite how I feel about her, I've still got responsibilities. I don't know how much more waiting she's willing to do. The thought of it takes all of the excitement built up inside of me and crushes it.

I stop kissing her and wrap my hands in her hair, then pull her to my chest. I take a long, deep breath and she does the same, locking her hands together behind my back.

"Lake," I say, stroking her hair. "I don't know what will happen in the next few weeks. But I need you to know that if I can't back out of my contract . . ."

She immediately jerks her head up and looks at me with more fear in her eyes than I've ever seen. She thinks I'm telling her I might not choose her, and the fact that something so absurd is running through her mind right now makes me hurt for her. This is how I've made her feel for the past three months and she thinks I'm doing it to her all over again.

"Will, you can't do this to . . ."

I press my finger to her lips. "Shut up, babe. I'm not telling you we can't be together. You're stuck with me now whether you like it or not." I pull her back to my chest. "All I'm trying to say is, if I can't break out of my contract, it's only four months. I just need you to promise that you'll wait for me if it comes to that. We can't let anyone know we're together until I find out what I need to do."

She nods against my shirt. "I promise. I'll wait as long as you need me to."

I close my eyes and rest my cheek against her head, thankful that all the times I've pushed her away haven't made her lose faith in me completely.

"This probably means we shouldn't be standing out here like this," I say. "You want to come to my car?"

I don't wait for her to answer, because I need her to come to my car with me. I'm not ready to stop kissing her yet, but I can't keep doing it so carelessly and in public like this. I grab her hand and lead her to my car. I open the passenger door, but rather than let her get in first, I sit in the seat and pull her onto my lap, then shut the door. I pull my keys out of my pocket and reach over to crank the car so it'll warm up. She positions herself on my lap, straddling me. I acknowledge that our position is incredibly intimate, being as though I can count the number of times we've kissed on one hand, but it's the only comfortable way to make out in a car.

I take her hands and pull them up between us, then kiss them. "I love you, Lake."

She smiles. "Say it again. I love hearing you say that."

"Good, because I love saying it. I love you." I kiss her cheek, then her lips. "I love you," I whisper again.

"One more time," she says. "I can't tell you how many times I've imagined hearing you say it. I've been hoping this whole time that whatever I was feeling wasn't one-sided."

The fact that she had no idea how I felt about her makes my chest ache. "I love you, Lake. So much. I'm so sorry for putting you through everything I've put you through."

She shakes her head. "Will, you were doing the right thing. Or trying to, anyway. I get that. I just hope this is for real now, because you can't push me away again. I can't go through that again."

Her words are like a knife to my heart, but deservedly so. I don't know what I could do or say that could convince her that I'm here. I'm staying. I chose *her* this time.

Before I have the chance to convince her of that, she grabs my face and kisses me hard, causing me to groan under my breath. I slip my hands underneath her shirt and around to her back. The softness and warmth of her skin beneath my palms is a feeling I never want to forget.

As soon as my hands meet her skin, she takes my jacket in her fists and begins tugging it off me. I lean forward, still meshed to her mouth, and struggle to free myself from the jacket. Once it's off, I toss it behind me and place my hands back underneath her shirt.

Touching her, kissing her, being with her . . . it feels so natural. So right.

I move my lips to the spot on her neck that drives me crazy. She tilts her neck to the side and moans quietly. I move my hands to her waist and tighten my grip while I trail kisses along her collarbone. I slowly inch my hands up her waist until my thumbs meet her bra. I can feel her heart hammering against her chest, and it causes my own heart to try to outrace hers. As soon as I slip my right thumb underneath her bra, she pulls back, away from my lips. She gasps for air.

I immediately pull my hands out from underneath her shirt and place them on her shoulders, silently cursing myself for being so impatient. I push her shoulders back in order to give us space to breathe. I lean my head back against the seat and close my eyes.

"I'm sorry." I open my eyes and keep my head flush against the headrest. "I'm going too fast. I'm sorry. I've just imagined touching you so many times I feel like it's so natural. I'm sorry."

She shakes her head and pulls my hands away from her shoulders, holding them together between us. "It's okay," she says. "We're both going too fast. I just need a moment. But it feels right, doesn't it? It feels so right being with you."

"That's because it *is* right."

She stares at me silently, then out of nowhere, she crushes her lips to mine again. I groan and wrap my arms tightly around her, pulling her back against me. As soon as she's pressed against my chest, I place my hands on her shoulders and push her away. As soon as she's apart from me, I pull her back to me for another kiss. This happens several times and I keep having to remind myself to slow down. I eventually have to push her off my lap and onto the driver's seat. However, this doesn't help, because as soon as she leans her back against the driver's side door, I lean across the seat and kiss her again. Seeing how much I need her causes her to laugh, which makes me laugh at how pathetically desperate I'm acting right now. I somehow pull away and slump against the passenger door. I run my hand through my hair and grin at her.

"You're really making this hard," I laugh. "Pun intended."

She smiles and even in the dark I can see her blush.

"Ugh!" I run my palms over my face and groan. "God, I want you so bad." I lunge forward and kiss her, but place my hand on the doorknob. I yank it and the door opens up behind her. "Get out," I say against her lips. "Go get in your car where you're safe. I'll see you when we get home."

She nods and swings one of her legs out of the car, but I don't want her to go. I grab her thigh and pull her back in and kiss her again. "*Go*," I groan.

"I'm *trying*." She laughs, pulling away from me. She climbs out of the car and I slide across the seats, following her straight out the car door.

"Where'd you park?" I ask her. I wrap my arms around her and press my lips to her ear.

"A few cars over," she says, pointing behind her. I slide my hand into her back pocket and retrieve her keys, then walk her to her car. After I open the door for her and she climbs in, I lean in to kiss her one last time.

"Don't go inside when you get home. I'm not finished kissing you," I say.

She grins. "Yes, sir."

I shut her door and once her Jeep is cranked, I tap my knuckles against the window and she rolls it down. I place my hand on the nape of her neck and lean through her window. "This drive home is about to be the longest thirty minutes of my life." I kiss her on the temple and take a step back. "Love you."

She rolls up her window, then places her palm against the glass. I lift my hand up to mirror hers, matching our fingertips together. She mouths, "I love you, too," and begins backing away.

I wait until she's out of the parking lot, then I walk back to my car.

I don't understand it. I don't understand how I went so long without her and now I feel like she's such a vital part of me, I'll die if I'm not touching her.

I'M NOT EVEN in my car for a minute before I dial her number. I've never called her without the conversation being linked to Kel or Caulder before. It feels good calling her for her.

She's driving directly in front of me so I can see her reach for her phone when it rings. She tilts her head and holds the phone between her shoulder and her neck. "Hello?"

"You shouldn't talk on the phone while you're driving," I tell her.

She laughs. "Well, you shouldn't call me when you know I'm driving."

"But I missed you."

"I miss you, too," she says. "I've missed you for the whole sixty seconds we've been apart," she says sarcastically.

I laugh. "I want to talk to you while we drive, but I want you to put your phone on speaker and set it down."

"Why?"

"Because," I say, "it's not safe for you to drive with your head cocked to the side like that."

I can see her smile in her rearview mirror. She drops the phone and sits up straight. "Better?" she says.

"Better. Now listen, I'm about to play you an Avett Brothers song. Make sure the volume on your phone is turned all the way up." I turn on the song I've listened to on repeat since the night I fell for her and turn the volume up. When the chorus hits, I start singing along to the lyrics.

I lower my voice and continue to sing the rest of the song, then the song after that, and the song after that. She listens silently the entire drive back to Ypsilanti.

LAYKEN PULLS INTO her driveway right before I turn into mine. I rush to kill the engine and head across the street before she has a chance to open her car door. When I reach her, I swing the door open and reach in, pulling her out by her hand. I want to push her against the Jeep and kiss her crazy, but I know we've more than likely got at least three pairs of eyes on us. What I wouldn't give to have her alone in my house right now, rather than out here in the open. I kiss the top of her head and stroke her hair, accepting whatever time I can get with her right now.

"Do you have a curfew?"

She shrugs. "I'm eighteen. I don't know if she could give me one if she wanted to."

"We don't need to push our luck with her, Lake. I want to do this right." I'm lucky that Julia would even allow her to be with me at this point. The last thing I want to do is upset her.

"Do we have to talk about my mom right now, Will?"

I smile and shake my head. "No." I slip my hand behind her head and pull her mouth to mine, kissing her like I don't care *who* might be watching. Hell, I *don't* care. I kiss her crazy for several minutes until it gets to the point that my hands can't stay above her shoulders for much longer. I pull away just enough for us to catch our breath.

"Let's go to your house," she whispers.

The suggestion is so tempting. I close my eyes and pull her to my chest. "I need to talk to your mom first before I pull something like that. I need to know what our boundaries are."

She laughs. "Why? So we can push them?"

I lift her chin and pull her gaze to mine. "Exactly."

The entryway light flicks off, then back on. An indication that Julia is setting some boundaries.

"Dammit," I groan into her neck. "I guess this is goodnight."

"Yeah, I guess so," she says. "I'll see you tomorrow, though, right? What time do you have to leave for graduation?"

"Not until tomorrow afternoon. You want to come over for breakfast? I'll make you whatever you want."

She nods. "And lunch? What are you doing for lunch?"

"Cooking for you," I say.

"And dinner? I might want to have dinner with you, too."

She's so cute. "Actually, we have plans. My grandparents are coming to graduation and we're going out to dinner afterward. Will you come?"

A worried look crosses her face. "Do you think that's a good idea? What if someone sees us together? You're technically still a teacher, even though you're between jobs."

Dammit. I'm really starting to hate this new job and I haven't even started yet. "I guess I do need to figure that out tomorrow."

"I do want to come to your graduation, though. Is that okay?"

"You better," I say to her. I've wanted her there more than anyone, but until tonight I didn't think that was a possibility. "It'll be hard as hell keeping my hands off you, though."

I kiss her one last time, then back away from her. "I love you."

"I love you, too."

I turn and begin walking away. My emotions are contradicting themselves because I feel absolutely elated that we're finally together, but devastated that I have to leave her right now. I turn around to look at her one last time and when I catch sight of her watching me walk away, a satisfied smile spreads across my face.

"*What?*" she asks when she sees the look on my face.

Just seeing the smile on her face is enough to keep me satisfied for the rest of my life. Seeing her happy again is better than any feeling in the world. I never want to see her sad again. "This will be worth it, Lake. Everything we had to go through. I promise. Even if you have to wait for me, I'll make it worth it."

The smile fades from her eyes and she clutches her hand to her heart. "You already have, Will."

That. Right there. I don't deserve her.

I walk swiftly back to where she's standing and take her face in my hands. "I mean it," I say. "I love you so damn much, it hurts." I force my lips against hers, then pull away just as fast. "But it hurts in a really *good* way." I briefly kiss her again. "We thought it was hard being apart before? How the hell am I supposed to sleep after tonight? After actually getting to kiss you like this? After hearing you tell me you love me?" I kiss her again and walk her until she's against her Jeep.

I kiss her like I've wanted to kiss her since the moment I knew how perfect we were together. How much we made sense. I kiss her with abandon, knowing I'll never have to walk away from her again. I kiss her knowing that this won't be our last kiss. That it won't even be our best kiss. I kiss her knowing that this kiss is our beginning, not another good-bye.

I continue to kiss her, even when the light turns off and on several more times.

We both notice the light, but neither of us seems to care. It takes us several minutes to actually slow down and pull apart. I press my forehead to hers and look directly into her eyes when she opens them. "This is it, Lake," I say, pointing back and forth between us. "It's real now. I'm not walking away from you again. Ever."

Her eyes fill with tears. "Promise?" she whispers.

"I *swear*. I love you so much."

A tear rolls down her cheek. "Say it again," she whispers.

"I love you, Lake." My eyes scroll over every inch of her face, afraid I'll miss something if I don't take every last piece of her in before I go.

"One more time."

Before *I love you* can come out of my mouth again, the front door swings open and Julia walks outside. "We're going to have to set some ground rules," she says. There's more amusement in her voice than anger or annoyance.

"Sorry, Julia," I yell over my shoulder. I turn back to Lake and kiss her one last time, then take a step away from her. "It's just that I'm madly in love with your daughter!"

"Yeah." Julia laughs. "I can see that."

I mouth one last *I love you* before heading across the street.

18.

the honeymoon

"AND WE LIVED happily ever after," she says.

I laugh, because that couldn't be further from the truth.

"Yeah, for like two weeks," I say. "Until your mother put the brakes on things the night she walked in on us."

Lake groans. "Oh, my God, I forgot about that."

"Trust me, it's not something I wish I remembered."

point of retreat

"WHERE ARE WE going?"

I put my seat belt on and lower the volume on the radio. "It's a surprise."

It's the first night I've been able to take her out in public since we officially started dating two weeks ago. I was able to pull out of my contract with the job at the junior high when I was accepted into the Master's level teaching program. So technically, we're able to date. I'm not sure how it would look, since I was her teacher just a few weeks ago. But to be honest, I don't really care. Like I told her, she comes first now.

"Will. It's Thursday night. I have a feeling wherever you're taking me, it's not that much of a surprise. Are we going to Club N9NE?"

"Maybe."

She smiles. "Are you doing a slam for me?"

I wink at her. "Maybe." I reach over and take her hand in mine.

"We're leaving early, though. Are you actually taking me out to eat? No grilled cheese tonight?"

"Maybe," I say again.

She rolls her eyes. "Will, this date is going to be my suck for the day if you don't become a little more talkative."

I laugh. "Yes, we're going to Club N9NE. Yes, we're going to dinner first. Yes, I wrote a slam for you. Yes, we're leaving the club early so we can go back to my house and hardcore make out in the dark."

"You just became my sweet," she says.

• • •

"OUT OF ALL the restaurants in Detroit, you chose a burger joint," I say, shaking my head. I take her hand and lead her toward the club entrance. I like to give her a hard time, but I love that she chose a burger joint.

"Bite me. I like burgers."

I wrap my arms around her and nip at her neck. "I like *you.*" I keep my arms wrapped around her and my lips attached to her neck as we walk through the door. She pries my fingers from around her waist and presses her palm against my forehead, pushing me away from her neck. "You need to be a gentleman in public. No more kissing until we're back in your car."

I lead her back to the exit. "Well, in that case, we're done here. Let's go."

She yanks my hand back. "No way. If you plan on seducing me on your couch later, you have to seduce me with your words, first. You promised a performance tonight and we're not leaving until I see one." She walks me toward the booth that Eddie and Gavin saved us seats in. She scoots in beside Eddie and I scoot in beside her.

"Hey," Eddie says, eyeing us curiously.

"Hey," Lake and I say simultaneously. Eddie's expression grows even more curious.

"This is weird," Eddie finally says.

Gavin nods. "It *is* weird. It really is."

"What's so weird?" Lake asks.

"You two," Eddie says to Lake. "I know you've been dating for a couple of weeks now, but this is the first time I've actually seen you with him. Like this, anyway. You know, all in love and stuff. It's just weird."

"Oh, shut up," Lake says.

"It'll take some getting used to. It just seems like you're doing something wrong. Something illegal," Eddie says.

"I'm twenty-one," I say defensively. "I'm not even a teacher anymore. What's so weird about it?"

"I dunno," she says. "It's just weird."

"It *is* weird," Gavin says again. "It really is."

I can see their point, but I think they're overreacting. Especially Gavin. He's known how I've felt about Lake for months. "What exactly is so weird?" I put my arm around Lake's shoulders. "This?" I turn and kiss Lake hard on the mouth until she laughs and pushes me away. We both turn back to Eddie and Gavin and they're still staring at us like we're a freak show.

"Gross," Eddie says, crinkling up her nose.

I pick up a sugar packet and toss it in Eddie's direction. "Go sit somewhere else, then," I tease.

Gavin picks up the sugar packet and throws it back at me. "We were here first."

"Then deal with it," I say.

The table grows quiet and it's obvious Lake and Eddie have no idea Gavin and I are only kidding around.

"Personally," Gavin says, leaning forward. "I thought you and Mrs. Alex made a much better couple."

I shrug. "She shot me down. I had to go with my second choice," I say, nudging my head toward Lake.

Lake scoffs at the same time the emcee begins speaking into the microphone.

"The sac has been preselected tonight, due to time constraints by the performer. Everyone please welcome Will Cooper back to the stage."

The crowd starts clapping and I slide out of the seat. Lake arches her eyebrow. "Time constraints?" she says.

I bend down and press my lips to her ear. "I already told you we can't stay long. We'll be really, really, really busy after this." I kiss her on the cheek and walk to the stage. I don't even give myself time to prepare. I begin my poem as soon as I reach the microphone so that I don't waste another second. "My piece is called *The Gift.* . . ."

If my *dad* were alive, he'd be sitting right there
Watching me up here, with a *smile* on his face
He'd be *proud* of the man I've become
He'd be *proud* that I stepped up to take his *place*
If my *mother* were alive, she'd be at home
Teaching my *brother* all the things she taught *me*
She'd be *proud* of the man I've become
She'd be *proud* of who I grew up to *be*
But they *aren't* here. They *haven't* been for a *while*.
It takes *time*, but it's starting to make *sense*.
I *still miss* them every time I take a *breath*.
Their absence will *never* go unnoticed.
But every *smile* on your *face* seems to *replace*
A *memory* I'd rather not *hold*
Each time you *laugh*, it fills a *void*
Each *kiss* heals another *wound* in my *soul*
If my *dad* were here, he'd be sitting with you
He'd be *hugging* you . . . saying *thank you*.
Thank you for saving my *boy*.
Thank you for bringing *light* to his *world*.

If my *mother* were here, she'd be *so* happy
To *finally* have a *daughter* in her life
She'd *love* you as much as *I* love you
She'd make me *promise* to one day *make* you my *wife.*
But they *aren't* here. They haven't been for a *while.*
But I can feel their *pride.* I can feel their *smiles.*
I can hear them say, *"You're welcome, Will."*
When I *thank* them for sending you from *heaven.*

AS SOON AS I return to the booth she's trying to thank me with a hug, but instead I grab her hand and wave over my shoulder as I pull her to the exit. "See you guys later," I say to Gavin and Eddie. I don't even wait for them to say good-bye as we make our way to the door. I remain two steps in front of Lake the entire way back to the car, practically dragging her along behind me. I can't think of anything but being alone with her tonight. We're never alone and I need some uninterrupted, alone time with her before I go crazy.

When we reach the car, I practically shove her inside, then climb into the driver's seat. I crank the car, then turn toward her and grab her shirt and pull her mouth to mine while I back out of the parking spot.

"Will, do you realize your car is moving?" she says, attempting to pull away from my grip. I glance out the rear window and cut the steering wheel to the right, then turn back to her.

"Yep. We need to hurry. You've got a curfew and that only gives us two more hours together." I press my lips to hers again and she shoves my forehead back with the palm of her hand.

"Then stop kissing me and drive. It won't be much fun making out with you when you're dead."

• • •

"PULL OVER," SHE says, several houses down from my driveway.

"Why?"

"Just pull over. Trust me."

I pull over and park the car on the side of the street. She leans across the seat and kisses me, then pulls the keys from the ignition. "If my mom sees your car, she'll know we're back. She told me to bring you to my house if we came home early. She doesn't want us alone at your house. Let's sneak in through your back door and we can come get your car later."

I stare at her in awe. "I think I'm in love with your brain," I say.

We both exit the car and run toward the back of the house we parked in front of. We make our way behind the fence, then crouch down and run across three backyards until we reach mine. I take the keys out of her hands and unlock the back door. Why do I feel like I'm breaking in? It's my house.

"Don't turn on the lights. She'll know we're back," I say as I help her make her way through the darkened doorway.

"I can't see," she says.

I put my arm around her back and bend down, scooping her legs up with my other arm. "Allow me."

She throws her arms around my neck and squeals. I walk her until we've reached the couch and gently lay her down. I take off my jacket and slip off my shoes, then reach down until I find her. I slide my hand down the length of her legs until I reach her feet, then I remove her shoes while she slips off her jacket.

"Anything else you need me to remove?" I whisper.

"Uh-huh. Your shirt."

I immediately agree with that and pull my shirt over my head. "Why are we whispering?" I ask her.

"I don't know," she whispers.

The sound of her voice when she whispers . . . knowing she's on her back . . . on my couch.

The significance of the next two hours is almost more than I can handle, knowing the things that could occur between us. I recognize that, so rather than lower myself on top of her, I kneel on the floor next to the couch. As much as I want her, I want to take it at her pace tonight, not mine. I tend to be extremely impatient when it comes to her.

I find her cheek in the dark and turn her face toward mine. When I touch her, her breath hitches. I feel it, too. I've touched her face countless times before, but somehow in the dark with absolutely no interruptions, it seems a hell of a lot more intimate.

She moves her hand to the back of my neck and I press my lips lightly against hers. They're wet and cold and perfect, but as soon as I part her lips and taste her, perfect becomes the understatement of the year.

She responds to my kiss tentatively. We're both slowly exploring our limits and I want to be sure I'm not taking it too fast this time. My hand remains on her cheek while we kiss, then I begin to slowly move it down her neck, trailing over her shoulder and down to her hip. Each movement I make only seems to encourage her, so I slip my hand underneath her shirt and grip her waist. I wait for any indication that she wants me to stop.

Or go *further.*

She presses her hands into my back, pulling me forward, indicating she wants me on the couch with her.

"Lake," I say, pulling back several inches. "I can't. If I get on this couch with you . . ." I release a deep breath. "Just trust me. I can't get on this couch with you."

She reaches down to my hand that's still gripping her by the waist. She slides my hand up her stomach and doesn't stop until my hand is covering the cup of her bra.

Holy shit.

"I want you on the couch with me, Will."

I immediately pull my hand away, but only because I need her shirt off. I practically yank it over her head and immediately join her on the couch. As soon as I lower myself on top of her and feel her pressed against my chest, I kiss her again and return my hand right where she put it. She smiles and wraps her legs around me as I kiss my way down her chin, straight to her neck.

"I can feel your heartbeat right here," I say, kissing the base of her throat. "I like it."

She takes my hand and slips it *beneath* her bra this time. "You can feel it beating right here, too."

I bury my face in the couch and groan. "Oh, my god, Lake."

I want to touch her. I want to feel *all* of her. I don't know what's stopping me. Why the hell am I so nervous?

"Will?"

I pull my face away from the couch, very aware that my hand is still tucked safely beneath her bra. My hand has never been happier. "You want me to slow down? I will, Lake. Just tell me."

She shakes her head and runs her hands down my back. "No. I want you to speed up."

My hesitation immediately disappears with those words. I slide my hand around her back and unfasten her bra, then slide it down her shoulders. I drop my mouth to her skin and as soon as the softest moan escapes her lips, my hand finds its way back to where she planted it earlier. I lower my lips, then immediately freeze at the sound of a key turning in the front door.

"Shh." About that time, the front door swings open and my living room light flicks on. I lift my head far enough to peer over the back of the couch and see Julia walking toward the hallway. I drop my head to Lake's neck. "Shit. It's your mom."

"Shit," she whispers, frantically pulling her bra back up. "Shit, shit, shit."

I clamp my hand over her mouth. "She might not notice us. Be still."

Our hearts are pounding now faster than they've ever pounded before. I know this, because my palm is still firmly planted right on top of Lake's breast. Apparently she recognizes the awkwardness of the moment, too.

"Will, move your hand. This is weird."

I pull my hand away. "What is she doing here?"

Lake shakes her head. "I have no idea."

And that's when it happens. I've heard people can see their lives flash before their eyes in the moments before death.

It's true.

Julia walks back into the room and screams.

I jump off Lake.

Lake jumps off the couch and *there* it is. My entire life flashes before my eyes the moment Julia sees Lake standing in my living room, fastening her bra.

"It's just us," I blurt out. I don't know why I chose those words to be my possible last words. Julia is standing with her hand over her mouth, staring at us wide-eyed. "It's just us," I say again, as if she doesn't already know that.

"I was . . ." Julia holds up Caulder's pillow. "Caulder wanted his pillow," she says. She looks back and forth between us and in a split second, her expression turns from fear to anger. I imme-diately reach down and retrieve Lake's shirt, then hand it to her.

"Mom," Lake says. She doesn't follow it up with anything else because she has no idea what to say.

"Go home," Julia says to Lake.

"Julia," I say to Julia.

"Will?" Julia says to me, cutting a warning shot in my direc-tion. "I'll deal with you later."

As soon as the words come out of Julia's mouth, Lake's face turns from embarrassed to really, really angry. "Mom, we're adults! You can't talk to him like that!" Lake yells. "And you can't prevent us from making out! This is ridiculous."

I grab Lake's elbow in an attempt to calm her down. "Don't, babe," I say quietly.

She looks at me defensively. "She can't tell me what to do, Will. I'm an adult."

I calmly place my hand on her shoulder. "Lake, you're still in high school. You live under her roof. I shouldn't have brought you here, I'm sorry. She's right." I lean in and kiss her briefly to calm her, then I take her shirt and help her pull it over her head.

"Oh, my God!" Julia yells. "Are you kidding me, Will? Don't help her put her clothes back on! I'm standing right here!"

What the hell am I thinking?

I release the shirt and hold my palms up in the air, then back away from Lake. She looks at me apologetically and whispers, "I'm sorry," then heads toward the door.

The door doesn't even shut before Julia begins yelling at her. "You've been dating him for two weeks, Lake! What do you think you're doing going that far with him that fast?" The door finally closes and I sink back to the couch, feeling incredibly stupid. Incredibly guilty. Incredibly pathetic. Yet . . . somehow still incredibly happy.

I reach down and am picking my own shirt up when the front door swings open again. Julia has a grip on Lake's arm and marches her straight back into the living room, then positions her on the couch across from me.

"This can't wait," Julia says. "I don't even trust that y'all won't start this back up tonight as soon as I go to bed."

Lake is looking at me the same way I'm looking at her. Confused.

Julia turns to Lake. "Are y'all having sex already?"

Lake groans and covers her face with her hands.

"You *are*?"

"No!" Lake says defensively. "We haven't had sex yet, okay?"

I'm watching the conversation between them, hoping to hell I don't get involved in it.

"*Yet?*" Julia says. "So you're going to?"

Lake stands and throws her hands up in the air. "What do you want me to say, Mom? I'm eighteen! Do you want me to tell you I'll be celibate forever? Because that would be a lie."

Julia rolls her head back and looks up at the ceiling for several seconds. When she looks at me, I dart my eyes to the floor. I'm so embarrassed I can't even look at her.

"Where's your car?" she says flatly.

I glance at Lake, then to Julia. "At the end of the street," I reluctantly admit.

"Why?" she asks accusingly, and rightfully so.

"Mom, stop. This is ridiculous."

Julia turns her attention to Lake. "Ridiculous? Really, Lake?

What I find ridiculous is the fact that you two parked at the end of the street and snuck over here to have sex less than a hundred yards from your mother. You've only been dating him for two weeks! What I also find ridiculous is that you're acting like you did nothing wrong, when it's obvious you were trying to hide it by parking at the end of the damn street!"

We're all quiet for a moment. Lake leans her head against the back of the couch and closes her eyes. "What now, then? If you're going to ground me let's just get it over with so you can stop embarrassing me."

Julia sighs an extremely frustrated sigh. She walks over to the couch, taking a seat next to Lake. "I'm not trying to embarrass you, Lake. I just . . ."

Julia sighs again and drops her face into her hands.

Lake rolls her eyes again.

I groan.

Julia lifts her head from her hands and takes a deep breath. "Lake?" she says quietly. "I just . . ." She attempts to get out what she wants to say, but her eyes well up with tears. When Lake realizes Julia is crying, she sits up straight.

"Mom," Lake says, scooting closer to her. She puts her arms around Julia and hugs her. Seeing her care for her mom despite her frustration with her absolutely melts my heart. It makes me love her even more, somehow.

Julia separates from Lake and wipes at her eyes. "Ugh!" she says. "This is so hard for me. You have to understand that." She turns to Lake and takes her hands. "I don't want to play the sick card, but it's impossible not to. We're at this transition in our lives where you're becoming the grown-up. Sometime this year, as much as we don't want to admit it, you'll be raising my little boy. It breaks my heart to know that I'm responsible for you being forced to grow up so fast. I'm forcing you to become his guardian. I'm forcing you to become the head of a household at eighteen. It's not fair to you. All the other areas of your life like falling in love and enjoying high school and new boyfriends and . . . having sex? I just feel like these are the last things you have left before you're forced to grow up completely. I know I can't slow down the inevitable, but I'm taking away every other part of your youth by leaving you with all of this responsibility. Until that time comes, I guess I just want you to stop growing up. For my sake. Just stop growing up so fast."

As soon as she finishes speaking, Lake begins to cry. "I'm sorry," she says to Julia. "I get it, Mom. I'm sorry."

I feel like an ass. "I'm sorry, too," I say to Julia.

Julia smiles at me and wipes at her eyes. "I'm still mad at you, Will." She stands up and looks at both of us. "Okay. Now that we have that out of the way." She turns her attention to Lake. "I'm taking you to the doctor tomorrow. You're getting on the pill." She turns to face me. "And both of you need to think about this. There's no rush. You have the rest of your lives to be in a hurry. You both need to set good examples for these boys who look up to you. Sneaking around is not the kind of thing you want to be modeling. You think they don't notice, but they do. And you two are going to be the ones dealing with them as teenagers, so believe me. You don't want them throwing your own actions back in your faces."

She makes a terrifying, but excellent point.

"I want you both to promise me something," she says.

"Anything," I say.

"Wait one year. There's no rush. You're both still young, so young. You've been dating all of two weeks and believe me when I say this, the more you know about each other and the more in love you are, the better it'll be."

I do my best to pretend this is not coming out of my girl-friend's mother's mouth, but it doesn't help ease the awkwardness.

"Mom," Lake groans, sinking back into the couch.

"We promise," I say, standing up. I immediately regret making the promise to her, knowing what that will entail. An entire year of having to keep myself in check around Lake is like agreeing to infinity. Especially after being on that couch with her tonight.

"I'm sorry, Julia. Really. I respect Lake and I respect you and . . . I'm sorry. We'll wait. I love Lake and that's all I need from her right now. Just knowing I can love her is more than enough."

Lake sighs and I look over at her. She's smiling at me. She stands up and throws her arms around my neck. "God, I love you," she says. She pulls away from my neck and kisses me.

"Make sure that kiss is a good one, Lake, because you're grounded for two weeks."

Lake and I both snap our heads in Julia's direction.

"Grounded?" Lake says incredulously.

Julia nods. "Regardless of how much I love your boy-friend . . . you snuck over here knowing I told you I didn't want you alone at his house. So, yeah. You're grounded. I'll give you five minutes to say your good-byes and get home." Julia walks out and shuts the door behind her.

"Two *weeks*?" I say to Lake. I press my lips to hers and kiss her crazy for five solid minutes.

• • •

I MADE IT twenty-one years without her. After meeting her earlier this year, I somehow made it three months without her. Now, after finally being able to date her, I've had to go another two weeks without her. But these past two weeks have been the most unbearable two weeks without her of my entire twenty-one years.

I know it's not even eight in the morning and it might seem desperate if I show up at her door this early, but we've been waiting for these two weeks to pass for what feels like an eternity. I rush across the street and am lifting my hand to knock on the door when it swings open and she jumps into my arms, showering kisses all over my face.

"Way to play hard to get," I hear Julia say from behind Lake. I put Lake down and shake my head slightly, letting her know we need to tone it down. Lake rolls her eyes and pulls me inside.

"What are we doing today?" she asks.

"Whatever you want. I was thinking maybe we could take the boys somewhere."

"Really?" Julia says from the kitchen. "That would be great. I need a day of peace after being cooped up in this house with your mopey girlfriend for two weeks."

Lake laughs and pulls me toward the hallway. "Come to my room while I get ready." We disappear down the hallway and into her room. She shuts the door and pulls me to her bed. She falls back and I fall on top of her, our lips reconnecting after the torturous time they had to spend apart.

"I missed you so much," I whisper.

"Not as much as I missed you."

We kiss some more.

And some more.

And some more.

I wish we didn't have to leave this bedroom, because I could do this all day. She's already working her hands up the back of my shirt and I'm groaning into her neck, remembering how close I got to actually being with her two weeks ago. I want to run my hand up her shirt, or touch her waist, or pull her legs around me, but I have no idea what's safe with her now. Now that we have to wait a whole damn *year*.

Why did I agree to that? As much as I understand where Julia was coming from, I still don't know how in the hell we're going to wait an entire year. Especially considering how much it's already driving me insane.

"Babe," I say, pulling my lips away from hers. "We need to talk about this." I lift up and sit on the bed beside her.

"About what? Our plans today?"

I shake my head. "No." I lean forward and kiss her again. "*This*," I say, waving my hand up and down her body. "We need to talk about what's okay and what's not. I really want to respect the promise we made to your mother, but at the same time there's no way in hell I can keep my hands off you. I just need to know what my boundaries are before I slip up."

She smiles at me. "So you're saying we need to set limits to how far we can go?"

I nod. "Exactly. I need you to tell me when I've reached the point of retreat."

She grins mischievously. "Well, there's only one way to find out what our boundaries are. I guess we need to test them."

I smile and scoot back down beside her, slowly looking her up and down. "I like that idea." I brush away a strand of hair from her face and kiss her softly on the mouth. I run my nose across her jawline and kiss my way to her ear. "How's this? Should I retreat yet?"

She shakes her head. "Hell, no. Not even close."

I place my hand on her shoulder and slowly run my fingers down her arm, resting my hand on her waist. I lean in until my lips are barely touching hers again. "How about this?" I ask her. I part her lips with my tongue, sliding my hand beneath her shirt and across her stomach. The muscles in her stomach clench beneath my palm. "Is this your point of retreat?" I whisper.

She shakes her head slowly. "Nope. Keep going."

I lower my lips to her neck and my fingers crawl up her stomach and come to a stop where her bra usually is, if she were wearing one right now. I bury my head in her pillow and groan. "God, Lake. Seriously? Are you trying to kill me?"

She shakes her head again. "Not retreating yet. Keep going."

I raise my head away from her pillow and scroll over her lips with my eyes. My thumb grazes her breast and that's when we both lose it. Our lips crash together, and as soon as I cup her breast, she moans into my mouth and wraps a leg around my thigh. I immediately slide off her and stand up.

"I think we found my point of retreat," I say, breathing heavily. I run my hands through my hair and back up to the wall, putting a safe distance between us. "You need to get dressed so we can leave. I can't be alone in here with you right now."

She laughs and rolls off the bed, then heads to her closet. "And Lake? If you want to survive the day without being completely mauled by me, make sure you put on a bra." I wink at her and walk out of the room.

19.

the honeymoon

HER EYES ARE closed, but there's a smile spread across her lips. I lean forward and lightly kiss them. "You asleep?"

It's late and we have to drive home tomorrow. I'm not ready to go to sleep yet. I want to drag this night out as long as I can.

She shakes her head no, then opens her eyes. "Remember the first time we didn't call point of retreat?"

I laugh. "Well, considering it was just last night, then I'd say I remember it pretty damn well."

"I want you to tell me all about that," she says. She closes her eyes and cuddles up to me.

"You want me to tell you about last *night*?"

She nods against my chest. "Yeah. It was the best night of my life. I want you to tell me all about it."

I smile, more than willing to tell her what I thought about the sweetest sweet I've ever had.

honeymoon night

"THREE MORE MINUTES," she says. She reaches behind her and pulls down on the handle, swinging the door open. "Now carry me over the threshold, husband."

I bend down and grab her behind the knees and pick her up, throwing her over my shoulder. She squeals, and I push the door all the way open with her feet. I take a step over the threshold with my wife. The door slams behind us, and I ease her down onto the bed.

"I smell chocolate. And flowers," she says. "Good job, husband."

I lift her leg up and slide her boot off. "Thank you, wife." I lift her other leg up and slide that boot off, too. "I also remembered the fruit. And the robes."

She winks at me and rolls over, scooting up onto the bed. When she gets settled, she leans forward and grabs my hand, pulling me toward her. "Come here, husband," she whispers.

I start to make my way up the bed but pause when I come face to face with her shirt. "I wish you'd take this ugly thing off," I say.

"You're the one who hates it so much. You take it off."

So I do. I start from the bottom this time and press my lips against her skin where her stomach meets the top of her pants, causing her to squirm. She's ticklish there. Good to know. I unbutton the next button and slowly move my lips up another inch to her belly button. I kiss it. She lets out another moan, but it doesn't worry me this time. I continue kissing every inch of her until the ugly shirt is lying on the floor. When my lips find their way back to hers, I pause to ask her one last time. "Wife? Are you sure you're ready to not call retreat? Right now?"

She wraps her legs around me and pulls me closer. "I'm butterflying positive," she says.

I grin against her lips, hoping that this entire year of being frustratingly patient will be worth it to her. "Good," I whisper. I reach my hand beneath her and unclasp her bra, then help her slip it off. She slides her hands through my hair and pulls me against her.

By the time all of our clothes are off and we're wrapped together under the covers, I'm breathing too hard to hear the pounding in my chest anymore, but I can definitely feel it. I press my lips to her neck and inhale a deep breath.

"Lake?" My hands are exploring her and touching her and I can't decide if I ever want to stop long enough to actually consummate this marriage.

"What is it?" she says breathlessly.

I somehow find it in me to pull back and give myself enough space to look her in the eyes. I need her to know that she's not the only one experiencing something for the first time right now. "I want you to know something. I've never . . ." I pause and pull back a little bit farther and hold my weight up on my left arm. I reach up and slip my hand to the nape of her neck, then dip my head and kiss her softly on the mouth. I look her directly in the eyes and finish telling her what I need her to know. "Lake . . . I've never made love to a girl before. I didn't realize that until this very moment. You're the first girl I'll ever make love to." She smiles a heartbreakingly beautiful smile that completely swallows me up. "And you're the *last* girl I'll ever make love to," I add. I lower my head and press my forehead to hers. We keep our eyes locked together as I lift her thigh and brace myself against her.

"I love you, Will Cooper," she whispers.

"I love *you*, Layken Cooper."

I hold still against her, taking one final look at this amazing, beautiful girl beneath me. "You're the greatest thing that's ever happened to my life," I whisper. As soon as I push myself inside her, our lips collide, our tongues collide, our bodies collide, and our hearts collide. Then this girl completely shatters the window to my soul and crawls inside.

20.

the honeymoon

"I LIKE THAT version," she says.

She's wrapped up in my arms where she's been most of the weekend. I couldn't have imagined a better way to spend the last forty-eight hours. I think back on everything we've gone through . . . everything I just shared with her. Everything she learned about me and I learned about her and how, by some miracle, I'll leave this hotel room loving her just a little bit more than I did when we arrived. I kiss her on her forehead and close my eyes.

"Goodnight, wife."

"Goodnight, husband."

welcome home

I CAN'T COUNT how many times I've pulled into my own drive-way. At least once a day since I've lived here; sometimes twice. But I've never pulled into this driveway with my *wife* before. I've never pulled into the driveway of a house where I live with my own family—a family other than my mom and dad. I've never pulled into this driveway feeling so complete before.

"Are you gonna turn off the car?" Lake asks.

Her hand is on her door handle and she's waiting for me to put the car in park and turn it off, but I'm staring at the house, lost in thought. "Don't you just love this driveway? I'm pretty sure we have the best driveway in the whole world."

She lets go of the door handle and falls back against her seat. "I guess," she shrugs. "It's a driveway."

I put the car in park and reach over and grab her hands, then pull her onto my lap. "But it's *our* driveway now. That makes it the best. And it's *our* house." I slip her shirt over her head and she tries to cover herself, but I move her arms out of the way and kiss up her neck while I talk about all the things that are no longer just mine. "And the dishes in the kitchen are *our* dishes. And the couches are *our* couches. And the bed is *our* bed."

"Will, stop." She laughs and attempts to pull my hands away from her bra. "You can't take off my bra, we're in our driveway. What if they come outside?"

"It's dark," I whisper. "And it's not *your* bra. It's *our* bra and I want it off." I slip it off her, pulling her against me as I rub my hands down the length of her back, then around to the button on the front of her jeans. "And I want to take off *our* pants."

She grins against my lips and slowly nods. "Okay, but hurry," she whispers.

"I can be quick," I assure her. "But I'll *never* hurry."

AFTER CHRISTENING THE driveway, we make it inside to a completely empty, dark house. I flip on the light switch in the kitchen and there's a note on the table.

"My grandparents left a few hours ago. The boys are with Eddie and Gavin across the street."

Lake tosses her purse on the couch and makes her way into the kitchen. "Do we have to go get them right away? I sort of want to enjoy some quiet while we can. The second we tell them we're back, the honeymoon will officially be over. I'm having fun; I don't want it to end yet."

I pull her to me. "Who says it has to end? We still have rooms to christen. Where should we start?"

"Besides your driveway?"

"*Our* driveway," I correct her.

She squints her eyes, then they suddenly widen with excitement. "Your laundry room!" she says excitedly. "*Our* laundry room," she adds quickly, before I can correct her. She grabs the collar of my shirt and stands on her tiptoes, pressing her lips to mine. "Come on," she whispers, pulling me along with her while she continues to kiss me.

The front door swings open and someone runs through the living room. I squeeze my eyes shut and groan as Lake separates her mouth from mine.

"Don't mind me, we just need the ketchup," Caulder yells.

He runs past us and into the kitchen. He grabs the ketchup and glances at us as he makes his way back to the front door. "Gross," he mumbles before he pulls the door shut behind him.

Lake laughs and presses her head against my shoulder. "Welcome home," she says unenthusiastically.

I sigh. "I wonder what they're eating? You gave me a solid two-day workout and I'm hungry now."

Lake shrugs and pulls away from me. "I don't know but I'm hungry, too."

We both make our way across the street. When we reach the front door, she puts her hand on the doorknob, but pauses and turns to me before opening it.

"Should I knock? It feels weird knocking on my own door, but I don't live here anymore."

I ease past her and grip the doorknob. "Nobody else knocks, why should we?" I open the door and we make our way inside. The boys and Kiersten are seated at the table and Eddie and Gavin are both in the kitchen, filling plates with food.

"Look who's back!" Kiersten says when she spots us. "How was the honeymoon?"

Lake walks into the kitchen and as soon as Eddie sees her, she immediately takes her hand and pulls her down the hallway. "Yes, Layken. How was the honeymoon? I need details," Eddie says. They disappear into the bedroom.

I walk into the kitchen and take over the plates Eddie was working on. "The honeymoon was perfect," I tell Kiersten.

"What's a honeymoon?" Kel asks. "What do people do when they go on one?"

Gavin spits out his drink with his laugh. "Yes, Will," Gavin says, smirking at me. "I must know what people do on honeymoons so that I'm prepared for when I have mine. Enlighten us."

I pick the plates up and glare at Gavin, then walk to the table. "A honeymoon is what people have after they get married. It's when they spend a lot of time together . . . telling stories about their past. And eating. They tell stories and eat. That's it."

"Oh," Caulder says. "Like a campout?"

"Exactly," I say, taking my seat at the table across from Kiersten, who's rolling her eyes at me. She shakes her head.

"He's lying to both of you because he thinks you're still nine years old. A honeymoon is when newlyweds have sex, traditionally for the first time. But in *some* cases," she rolls her head toward Gavin, "people get ahead of themselves."

We're all staring at Kiersten with our mouths agape when Lake and Eddie return.

"Why is everyone so quiet?" Eddie asks.

Gavin clears his throat and glances at Eddie. "Suck and sweet time," he says. "Sit down, ladies."

"Me first," Caulder says. "My sweet is that me and Kel are finally brothers. My suck is that I now know what Will and Layken did during their honeymoon."

"I second that," Kel says.

Lake looks at me questioningly, so I nudge my head toward Kiersten. "Blame her."

Kiersten shoots me a glare that has become all too familiar from her. "*My* suck," she says, "is that I seem to be the only person in this room aware of the importance of sex education. My sweet is that a few months from now, thanks to Gavin's inability to wait for his honeymoon, I'll have a steady job babysitting."

Gavin spits his drink out for the second time in five minutes. "No. No *way* are you babysitting my daughter." He wipes his mouth and stands up, clinking his fork on the red plastic cup in his hand. "I'm going next because I can't wait another second to share my sweet." He turns to Eddie, seated next to him, and he clears his throat. Eddie smiles up at him and he presses his hand to his heart. "*My* sweet is that the woman I love, as of last night, has agreed to become my wife."

As soon as the word *wife* leaves his mouth, Kiersten and Lake are making high-pitched noises and hugging Eddie and jumping up and down. Eddie takes a ring out of her pocket and puts it on her finger to show the girls. Lake says something about this being her sweet and Eddie agrees, but Gavin has sat back down and all the boys are now eating while the girls are still squealing.

I look over at Lake and she's turning Eddie's hand back and forth in the light, admiring her ring. She's smiling. She looks so happy. Eddie is happy, too. The boys, aside from learning what you do during your honeymoon, are smiling. Gavin is watching Eddie and looks genuinely happy. I can't help but think back on these past two years and all we've been through. The heartache we had to endure to get here and the tears we've all shed in the process. I don't know how one minute, a person can think his life is nothing more than a barren valley with nothing left to look forward to. Then, in the blink of an eye, someone can come along and change it with a simple smile.

Lake looks at me and catches me smiling at her. She grins and leans against me as I wrap my arm around her. "You want to know my sweet?" I ask her.

She nods.

I kiss her on the forehead. "You. Always you."

The End.

epilogue

"GIVE HER SOME medicine!" Gavin yells at the nurse. He's pacing back and forth. Beads of sweat have pooled on his forehead and he lifts a hand to wipe them away. "Look at her! She's in pain, just look at her! Give her something!" His face is pale and he's gesturing toward the hospital bed. Eddie rolls her eyes and stands up, taking Gavin by the shoulders and shoving him toward the door.

"Sorry, Will. You would think he would take it better since I'm not the one in labor this time. If I don't get him out of here he'll pass out like he did when Katie was born."

I nod, but can't find it in me to laugh. Seeing Lake on that bed in as much pain as she's in has me feeling completely helpless. She's refusing medicine, but I'm about to go grab a damn needle and give her some myself.

I walk to the head of her bed and as soon as the contraction passes, the tension eases slightly from her face and she looks up at me. I take the wet rag and press it against her cheek to cool her off. "Water. I want water," she grumbles.

This is the tenth time she's asked for water in the past hour, and the tenth time I'll have to tell her no. I don't want to see the anger in her face again, so I just lie. "I'll go ask the nurse." I quickly walk out of the room and take a few steps past the doorway, then collapse against the wall with no intention of looking for a nurse. I slide to the floor and drop my face into my hands and try to focus on the fact that this is really happening. Any minute now, I'll become a dad.

I don't think I'm ready for this.

At least if Kel and Caulder turn out horrible, we can still blame my and Lake's parents. This is a completely different ball-game. This baby is our responsibility.

Oh, god.

"Hey." Kel drops down beside me and kicks his legs out in front of him. "How is she?"

"Mean," I answer truthfully.

He laughs.

It's been three years since Lake and I married, and three years since Kel moved in with me. I know that technically I'm becoming a dad for the first time today, and in so many ways it's so different, but I can't imagine loving Kel any more if he really were my own. I can honestly say when my parents died, I felt cursed that my life had to change course like it did. But now, looking back, I know I've been blessed. I couldn't imagine things any differently.

"So," Kel says. He pulls his leg up and ties his shoe, then straightens it back out again. "My mom? She left me something I'm supposed to give to you today."

I glance at him and, without having to ask, know immediately what it is. I hold out my hand and he reaches into his pocket and pulls out a star. "It was in one of the gifts she left me for my birthday last year, along with a note. In fact, she left eight of them. One for each kid y'all might have. Four blue ones and four pink ones."

I fist the star in my palm and laugh. "*Eight?*"

"Yeah, I know," he shrugs. "I guess she wanted to be covered, just in case. And they were all numbered, so that one goes with this kid."

I smile and look down at the star in my hand. "Is it for Lake too? I don't know if she's in the mood for this right now."

Kel shakes his head. "Nope. Just for you. Lake got her own." He pushes himself up off the floor. He pauses after taking a few steps back toward the waiting room, then he turns around and looks down at me. "My mom thought of everything, didn't she?"

I smile, thinking of all the advice I'm still somehow getting from Julia. "She sure did."

Kel smiles and turns away. I open the star; one of many that I incorrectly assumed would be the last.

> *Will,*
> *Thank you for taking on the role of father to my little boy.*
> *Thank you for loving my daughter as much as I love her.*
> *But most of all, thank you in advance for being the best father I could ever hope for a grandchild of mine to have. Because I know without a doubt that you will be.*
> *Congratulations,*
> *Julia*

I STARE AT the star in my hands, wondering how in the world she could be thanking *me* when they're the ones who changed *my* life. Her whole family changed my life.

I guess in a way, we all changed each *other's* lives.

"Will," Lake yells from inside the room. I quickly stand up and put the star in my pocket. I walk back into the room and over to the bed. Her jaw is clenched tight and she's gripping the handrail so hard, her knuckles are white. She reaches up with one hand and grabs my shirt, then pulls me to her. "Nurse. I need the nurse."

I nod and once again rush out of the room. This time to actually find a nurse.

WHEN THE WORDS "You're ready to push" come out of the doctor's mouth, I grip the rail of Lake's bed and have to hold myself upright. This is it. This is finally it and I'm not sure I'm ready. In the next few minutes I'm going to be a dad and the thought of it makes my head spin.

I am not Gavin.

I will not pass out.

The seconds turn into nanoseconds as the room fills with more nurses and they're doing things to the bed and to the equipment and to Lake and to the lights that are really, really, *really*, bright and then a nurse is standing over me, looking down at me.

Why is she looking down at me?

"You okay?" she asks.

I nod. *Why am I looking up at her?*

I've either shrunk six feet or I'm on the floor.

"Will." Lake's hand is reaching over the side of the bed for me. I grip the rail and pull myself up. "Don't do that again," she breathes heavily. "Please. I need you to suck it up right now because I'm freaking out." She's looking at me with fear in her eyes.

"I'm right here," I assure her. She smiles, but then her smile does this twisted thing where it flips upside down and turns into a mangled, demonic groan. My hand is being twisted worse than her voice, though.

I lean over the rail and wrap my arm around her shoulders,

helping her lean forward when the nurse tells her to push. I keep my eyes focused on hers and she keeps her eyes focused on mine. I help her count and I help her breathe and I do my best not to complain about the fact that I'll never be able to use my hand again. We're counting to ten for what feels like the thousandth time when the twisted sounds begin coming out of her mouth again. Except this time the noises are followed by another sound.

Crying.

I look away from Lake and at the doctor, who is now holding a baby in his hands.

My baby.

Everything begins moving in fast motion again, but I'm frozen. I want so bad to pick her up and hold her but I also want to be next to Lake and ensure she's okay. The nurse takes our baby out of the doctor's hands and turns around to wrap her in a blanket. I'm craning my neck, trying to look over the nurse's shoulder at her.

When the nurse finally has her wrapped up, she turns and walks to Lake, then lays her on her chest. I push the rail down on Lake's bed and climb in beside her, sliding my arm beneath her shoulders. I pull the blanket away from our baby's face so we can both see her better.

I wish I could explain how I feel, but nothing can explain this moment. Not a vase of stars. Not a book. Not a song. Not even a poem. Nothing can explain the moment when the woman you would give your life for sees her daughter for the very first time.

Tears are streaming down her face. She's stroking our baby girl's cheek, smiling.

Crying.

Laughing.

"I don't want to count her fingers or toes," Lake whispers. "I don't care if she has two toes or three fingers or fifty feet. I love her so much, Will. She's perfect."

She *is* perfect. So perfect. "Just like her mom," I say.

I lean my head against Lake's and we just stare. We stare at the daughter who is so much more than I could have asked for. The daughter who is so much more than I dreamt of. So much more than I ever thought I would have. This *girl*. This baby girl is my life. Her mother is my life. These girls are *both* my life.

I reach down and pick up her hand. Her tiny fingers reflexively wrap around my pinky and I can't choke back my tears any longer. "Hey, Julia. It's me. It's your daddy."

my final piece

We're born into the world
As just **one small piece** to the **puzzle**
That makes up an entire **life**.
It's up to us throughout our years,
to find **all** of our pieces that **fit**.
The pieces that connect **who** we are
To who we **were**
To who we'll one day **be**.
Sometimes pieces will **almost** fit.
They'll **feel** right.
We'll carry them around for a while,
Hoping they'll change **shape**.
Hoping they'll **conform** to our puzzle.
But they **won't**.
We'll eventually have to let them **go**.
To find the puzzle that is **their** home.
Sometimes pieces won't fit at **all**.
No **matter** how much we **want** them to.
We'll **shove** them.
We'll **bend** them.
We'll **break** them.
But what isn't **meant** to be,
won't be.
Those are the hardest pieces of **all** to accept.

The pieces of our puzzle

That just don't *belong*.

But *occasionally* . . .

Not very often at *all*,

If we're *lucky*,

If we pay enough *attention*,

We'll find a

perfect match.

The *pieces* of the *puzzle* that *slide* right *in*

The pieces that *hug* the *contours* of our *own* pieces.

The pieces that *lock* to us.

The pieces that *we* lock *to*.

The pieces that fit *so well*, we can't tell where *our* piece

begins

And that piece *ends*.

Those pieces we call

Friends.

True loves.

Dreams.

Passions.

Beliefs.

Talents.

They're *all the pieces* that complete our *puzzles*.

They *line* the *edges*,

Frame the *corners*,

Fill the *centers*.

Those pieces are the pieces that make us who we *are*.

Who we *were*.

Who we'll *one day be*.

Up until today,

When I looked at my *own* puzzle,

I would see a finished *piece.*

I had the *edges lined,*

The *corners framed,*

The *center filled.*

It *felt* like it was complete.

All the pieces were *there.*

I had everything I *wanted.*

Everything I *needed.*

Everything I *dreamt* of.

But up until today,

I realized I had collected *all*

but *one piece.*

The most *vital* piece.

The piece that completes the *picture.*

The piece that completes my *whole life.*

I held this girl in my arms

She *wrapped* her *tiny fingers* around *mine.*

It was *then* that I *realized*

She was the *fusion.*

The *glue.*

The *cement* that *bound* all my pieces *together.*

The piece that seals my *puzzle.*

The piece that completes my *life.*

The *element* that makes me who I *am.*

Who I *was.*

Who I'll *one day be.*

You, baby girl.

You're my *final piece.*

acknowledgments

I would like to thank my agent, Jane Dystel. Your work ethic is inspiring and you are doing exactly what you were born to do. Without your support, advice, and honesty, I know I wouldn't be where I am today. And to each and every person in the Dystel & Goderich offices, thank you for your constant support of the authors you represent. And a special thanks to Lauren Abramo. Thank you, gracias, dank u, merci, danke, grazie.

I would also like to thank my editor, Johanna Castillo. You have been an absolute joy to work with and I look forward to many more years together. Thank you for constantly being so positive and supportive.

It's bittersweet knowing that this is the final book in the Slammed series. On one hand, I'm happy to say goodbye to Will and Lake and the gang. They deserve their happy ending. But on the other hand, I'll miss these characters who completely changed my life. It might be a little odd to acknowledge the characters of a book, but I want to thank each and every one of them. After being inside their heads for a year and a half now, I feel like I'm saying goodbye to friends.

And the biggest thank-you of all I'm reserving for fans of this series. Those of you who read the books. Those of you who asked for a sequel. Those of you who took the time to email me and let me know how the books touched you. Those of you who were inspired to write your own books. Those of you who have supported me and have helped spread the word, simply because you want to. This has definitely been a whirlwind of a year, but each and every one of you have kept me sane. You've kept me inspired and you've kept me motivated. It's because of you that I am where I am today, and I'll never forget that.

Because of *you*.

about the author

Colleen Hoover is the *New York Times* bestselling author of three novels: *Slammed*, *Point of Retreat*, and *Hopeless*. She lives in Texas with her husband and their three boys. To read more about this author, visit her website at www.colleenhoover.com.

Don't miss the highly anticipated sequel to the
"**riveting**" (*Kirkus Reviews*, starred review)
#1 *New York Times* bestselling novel

IT ENDS WITH US

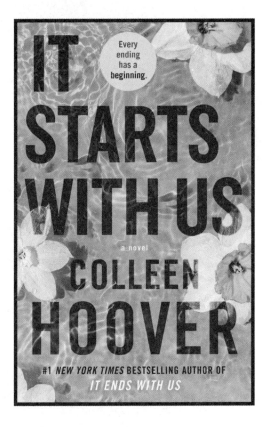

Available **October 2022** wherever books are sold or
at SimonandSchuster.com

point of retreat

Also by Colleen Hoover

Slammed

point of retreat

a novel

Colleen Hoover

ATRIA PAPERBACK

NEW YORK   LONDON   TORONTO   SYDNEY   NEW DELHI

ATRIA PAPERBACK
A Division of Simon & Schuster, Inc.
1230 Avenue of the Americas
New York, NY 10020

Copyright © 2012 by Colleen Hoover

First Atria Paperback edition September 2012

ATRIA PAPERBACK and colophon are trademarks of Simon & Schuster, Inc.

The author and publisher gratefully acknowledges permission from the following source to reprint material in their control: Poem, "Write Poorly." Reprint permission granted by Edmund Davis-Quinn.

For information about special discounts for bulk purchases, please contact Simon & Schuster Special Sales at 1-866-506-1949 or business@simonandschuster.com.

The Simon & Schuster Speakers Bureau can bring authors to your live event. For more information or to book an event contact the Simon & Schuster Speakers Bureau at 1-866-248-3049 or visit our website at www.simonspeakers.com.

Designed by Suet Y. Chong

Manufactured in China

10 9 8 7 6 5 4 3 2 1

Library of Congress Cataloging-in-Publication data is available.

ISBN 978-1-4767-1592-6
ISBN 978-1-4767-1593-3 (ebook)

This book is dedicated to everyone who read Slammed *and encouraged me to continue telling the story of Layken and Will.*

a note to the reader

Point of Retreat is the second novel in a two-book series. For the first novel, *Slammed,* visit the author's website: www.colleenhoover.com.

point of retreat

prologue

DECEMBER 31

"Resolutions"

I'm confident this will be our year. Lake's and my year.

The last few years have definitely not been in our favor. It was over three years ago when my parents both passed away unexpectedly, leaving me to raise my little brother all on my own. It didn't help that Vaughn decided to end our two-year relationship on the heels of their death. To top it off, I ended up having to drop my scholarship. Leaving the university and moving back to Ypsilanti to become Caulder's guardian was one of the hardest decisions I've ever made . . . but also one of the best decisions.

I spent every single day of the next year learning how to adjust. How to adjust to heartbreak, how to adjust to having no parents, how to adjust to essentially becoming a parent myself and the sole provider of a family. Looking back on it, I don't think I could have made it without Caulder. He's the only thing that kept me going.

I don't even remember the entire first half of last year. Last year didn't start for me until September 22, the day I first laid eyes on Lake. Of course, last year turned out to be just as difficult as the previous years, but in a completely different way. I'd never felt more alive than when I was with her—but considering our circumstances, I couldn't be with her. So I guess I didn't spend a lot of time feeling alive.

This year has been better, in its own way. A lot of falling in love, a lot of grief, a lot of healing, and even more adjusting. Julia passed away in September. I didn't expect her death to be as hard on me as it was. It was almost like losing my mother all over again.

I miss my mother. And I miss Julia. Thank God I have Lake.

Like me, my father loved to write. He always used to tell me that writing down his daily thoughts was therapeutic for his soul. Maybe one of the reasons I've had such a difficult time adjusting over the past three years is that I didn't take his advice. I assumed slamming a few times a year was enough "therapy" for me. Maybe I was wrong. I want the upcoming year to be everything I've planned for it to be: perfect. With all that said (or written), writing is my resolution. Even if it's just one word a day, I'm going to write it down . . . get it out of me.

part one

1.

I registered for classes today. Didn't get the days I wanted, but I only have two semesters left, so it's getting harder to be picky about my schedule. I'm thinking about applying to local schools for another teaching job after next semester. Hopefully, by this time next year, I'll be teaching again. For right now, though, I'm living off student loans. Luckily, my grandparents have been supportive while I work on my master's degree. I wouldn't be able to do it without them, that's for sure.

We're having dinner with Gavin and Eddie tonight. I think I'll make cheeseburgers. Cheeseburgers sound good. That's all I really have to say right now . . .

"IS LAYKEN OVER HERE OR OVER THERE?" EDDIE ASKS, peering in the front door.

"Over there," I say from the kitchen.

Is there a sign on my house instructing people *not* to

5

knock? Lake never knocks anymore, but her comfort here apparently extends to Eddie as well. Eddie heads across the street to Lake's house, and Gavin walks inside, tapping his knuckles against the front door. It's not an official knock, but at least he's making an attempt.

"What are we eating?" he asks. He slips his shoes off at the door and makes his way into the kitchen.

"Burgers." I hand him a spatula and point to the stove, instructing him to flip the burgers while I pull the fries out of the oven.

"Will, do you ever notice how we somehow always get stuck cooking?"

"It's probably not a bad thing," I say as I loosen the fries from the pan. "Remember Eddie's Alfredo?"

He grimaces when he remembers the Alfredo. "Good point," he says.

I call Kel and Caulder into the kitchen to have them set the table. For the past year, since Lake and I have been together, Gavin and Eddie have been eating with us at least twice a week. I finally had to invest in a dining room table because the bar was getting a little too crowded.

"Hey, Gavin," Kel says. He walks into the kitchen and grabs a stack of cups out of the cabinet.

"Hey," Gavin responds. "You decide where we're having your party next week?"

Kel shrugs. "I don't know. Maybe bowling. Or we could just do something here."

Caulder walks into the kitchen and starts setting

places at the table. I glance behind me and notice them setting an extra place. "We expecting company?" I ask.

"Kel invited Kiersten," Caulder says teasingly.

Kiersten moved into a house on our street about a month ago, and Kel seems to have developed a slight crush on her. He won't admit it. He's just now about to turn eleven, so Lake and I expected this to happen. Kiersten's a few months older than he is, and a lot taller. Girls hit puberty faster than boys, so maybe he'll eventually catch up.

"Next time you guys invite someone else, let me know. Now I need to make another burger." I walk to the refrigerator and take out one of the extra patties.

"She doesn't eat meat," Kel says. "She's a vegetarian."

Figures. I put the meat back in the fridge. "I don't have any fake meat. What's she gonna do? Eat bread?"

"Bread's fine," Kiersten says as she walks through the front door—without knocking. "I like bread. French fries, too. I just don't eat things that are a result of unjustified animal homicide." Kiersten walks to the table and grabs the roll of paper towels and starts tearing them off, laying one beside each plate. Her self-assurance reminds me a little of Eddie's.

"Who's she?" Gavin asks, watching Kiersten make herself at home. She's never eaten with us before, but you wouldn't know that by how she's taking command.

"She's the eleven-year-old neighbor I was telling you about. The one I think is an imposter based on the things that come out of her mouth. I'm beginning to suspect she's really a tiny adult posing as a little redheaded child."

"Oh, the one Kel's crushing on?" Gavin smiles, and I can see his wheels turning. He's already thinking of ways to embarrass Kel at dinner. Tonight should be interesting.

Gavin and I have become pretty close this past year. It's good, I guess, considering how close Eddie and Lake are. Kel and Caulder really like them, too. It's nice. I like the setup we all have. I hope it stays this way.

Eddie and Lake finally walk in as we're all sitting down at the table. Lake has her wet hair pulled up in a knot on top of her head. She's wearing house shoes, sweatpants, and a T-shirt. I love that about her, the fact that she's so comfortable here. She takes the seat next to mine and leans in and kisses me on the cheek.

"Thanks, babe. Sorry it took me so long. I was trying to register online for Statistics, but the class is full. Guess I'll have to go sweet-talk someone at the admin office tomorrow."

"Why are you taking Statistics?" Gavin asks. He grabs the ketchup and squirts it on his plate.

"I took Algebra Two in the winter mini-mester. I'm trying to knock out all my math in the first year, since I hate it so much." Lake grabs the ketchup out of Gavin's hands and squirts some on my plate, then on her own.

"What's your hurry? You've already got more credits than Eddie and I do, put together," he says. Eddie nods in agreement as she takes a bite of her burger.

Lake nudges her head toward Kel and Caulder. "I've already got more *kids* than you and Eddie put together. *That's* my hurry."

"What's your major?" Kiersten asks Lake.

Eddie glances toward Kiersten, finally noticing the extra person seated at the table. "Who are you?"

Kiersten looks at Eddie and smiles. "I'm Kiersten. I live diagonal to Will and Caulder, parallel to Layken and Kel. We moved here from Detroit right before Christmas. Mom says we needed to get out of the city before the city got out of us . . . whatever that means. I'm eleven. I've been eleven since eleven-eleven-eleven. It was a pretty big day, you know. Not many people can say they turned eleven on eleven-eleven-eleven. I'm a little bummed that I was born at three o'clock in the afternoon. If I would have been born at eleven-eleven, I'm pretty sure I could have got on the news or something. I could have recorded the segment and used it someday for my portfolio. I'm gonna be an actress when I grow up."

Eddie, along with the rest of us, stares at Kiersten without responding. Kiersten is oblivious, turning to Lake to repeat her question. "What's your major, Layken?"

Lake lays her burger down on her plate and clears her throat. I know how much she hates this question. She tries to answer confidently. "I haven't decided yet."

Kiersten looks at her with pity. "I see. The prover-bial undecided. My oldest brother has been a sophomore in college for three years. He's got enough credits to have five majors by now. I think he stays undecided because he'd rather sleep until noon every day, sit in class for three hours, and go out every night, than actually graduate and get a real job. Mom says that's not true—she says it's because he's trying to 'discover his full potential' by examining all of his interests. If you ask me, I think it's bullshit."

I cough when the sip I just swallowed tries to make its way back up with my laugh.

"You just said 'bullshit'!" Kel says.

"Kel, don't say 'bullshit'!" Lake says.

"But she said 'bullshit' first," Caulder says, defending Kel.

"Caulder, don't say 'bullshit'!" I yell.

"Sorry," Kiersten says to Lake and me. "Mom says the FCC is responsible for inventing cuss words just for media shock value. She says if everyone would just use them enough, they wouldn't be considered cuss words anymore, and no one would ever be offended by them."

This kid is hard to keep up with!

"Your mother *encourages* you to cuss?" Gavin says.

Kiersten nods. "I don't see it that way. It's more like she's encouraging us to undermine a system flawed through overuse of words that are made out to be harmful, when in fact they're just letters, mixed together like every other word. That's all they are, mixed-up letters. Like, take the word 'butterfly,' for example. What if someone decided one day that 'butterfly' is a cuss word? People would eventually start using the word 'butterfly' as an insult and to emphasize things in a negative way. The actual *word* doesn't mean anything. It's the negative association people give these words that make them cuss words. So, if we all just decided to keep saying 'butterfly' all the time, people would stop caring. The shock value would subside, and it would become just another word again. Same with every other so-called bad word. If we would all start saying them all the time, they wouldn't be bad anymore. That's what my mom says, anyway." She smiles and takes a french fry and dips it in ketchup.

I often wonder, when Kiersten's visiting, how she turned out the way she did. I have yet to meet her mother, but from what I've gathered, she's definitely not ordinary. Kiersten is obviously smarter than most kids her age, even if it is in a strange way. The things that come out of her mouth make Kel and Caulder seem somewhat normal.

"Kiersten?" Eddie says. "Will you be my new best friend?"

Lake grabs a french fry off her plate and throws it at Eddie, hitting her in the face with it. "That's bullshit," Lake says.

"Oh, go *butterfly* yourself," Eddie says. She returns a fry in Lake's direction.

I intercept the french fry, hoping it won't result in another food fight, like last week. I'm still finding broccoli everywhere. "Stop," I say, dropping the french fry on the table. "If you two have another food fight in my house, I'm kicking *both* of your butterflies!"

Lake can see I'm serious. She squeezes my leg under the table and changes the subject. "Suck-and-sweet time," she says.

"Suck-and-sweet time?" Kiersten asks, confused.

Kel fills her in. "It's where you have to say your suck and your sweet of the day. The good and the bad. The high and the low. We do it every night at supper."

Kiersten nods as though she understands.

"I'll go first," Eddie says. "My suck today was registration. I got stuck in Monday, Wednesday, Friday classes. Tuesday and Thursdays were full."

Everyone wants the Tuesday/Thursday schedules. The classes are longer, but it's a fair trade, having to go only twice a week rather than three times.

"My *sweet* is meeting Kiersten, my new best friend," Eddie says, glaring at Lake.

Lake grabs another french fry and throws it at Eddie. Eddie ducks, and the fry goes over her head. I take Lake's plate and scoot it to the other side of me, out of her reach.

Lake shrugs and smiles at me. "Sorry." She grabs a fry off my plate and puts it in her mouth.

"Your turn, Mr. Cooper," Eddie says. She still calls me that, usually when she's trying to point out that I'm being a "bore."

"My suck was definitely registration, too. I got Monday, Wednesday, Friday."

Lake turns to me, upset. "What? I thought we were both doing Tuesday/Thursday classes."

"I tried, babe. They don't offer my level of courses on those days. I texted you."

She pouts. "Man, that really is a suck," she says. "And I didn't get your text. I can't find my phone again."

She's always losing her phone.

"What's your sweet?" Eddie asks me.

That's easy. "My sweet is right now," I say as I kiss Lake on the forehead.

Kel and Caulder both groan. "Will, that's your sweet *every* night," Caulder says, annoyed.

"My turn," Lake says. "Registration was actually my sweet. I haven't figured out Statistics yet, but my other four classes were exactly what I wanted." She looks at Eddie and continues. "My suck was losing my best friend to an eleven-year-old."

Eddie laughs.

"I wanna go," Kiersten says. No one objects. "My suck was having bread for dinner," she says, eyeing her plate.

She's ballsy. I toss another slice of bread on her plate. "Maybe next time you show up uninvited to a carnivore's house, you should bring your own fake meat."

She ignores my comment. "My sweet was three o'clock."

"What happened at three o'clock?" Gavin asks.

Kiersten shrugs. "School let out. I butterflying *hate* school."

All three kids glance at one another, as if there's

an unspoken agreement. I make a mental note to talk to Caulder about it later. Lake nudges me with her elbow and shoots me a questioning glance, letting me know she's thinking the same thing.

"Your turn, whatever your name is," Kiersten says to Gavin.

"It's Gavin. And my suck would have to be the fact that an eleven-year-old has a larger vocabulary than me," he says, smiling at Kiersten. "My sweet today is sort of a surprise." He looks at Eddie and waits for her response.

"What?" Eddie says.

"Yeah, what?" Lake adds.

I'm curious, too. Gavin just leans back in his seat with a smile, waiting for us to guess.

Eddie gives him a shove. "Tell us!" she says.

He leans forward in his chair and slaps his hands on the table. "I got a job! At Getty's, delivering pizza!" He looks happy, for some reason.

"*That's* your sweet? You're a pizza delivery guy?" Eddie asks. "That's more like a suck."

"You know I've been looking for a job. And it's Getty's. We love Getty's!"

Eddie rolls her eyes. "Well, congratulations," she says unconvincingly.

"Do we get free pizza?" Kel asks.

"No, but we get a discount," Gavin replies.

"That's my sweet, then," Kel says. "Cheap pizza!"

Gavin looks pleased that someone is excited for him. "My suck today was Principal Brill," Kel says.

"Oh Lord, what'd she do?" Lake asks him. "Or better yet, what did *you* do?"

"It wasn't just me," Kel says.

Caulder puts his elbow on the table and tries to hide his face from my line of sight.

"What did you do, Caulder?" I ask him. He brings his hand down and looks up at Gavin. Gavin puts his elbow on the table and shields his face from my line of sight as well. He continues to eat as he ignores my glare. "Gavin? What prank did you tell them about this time?"

Gavin grabs two fries and throws them at Kel and Caulder. "No more! I'm not telling you any more stories. You two get me in trouble every time!" Kel and Caulder laugh and throw the fries back at him.

"I'll tell on them, I don't mind," Kiersten says. "They got in trouble at lunch. Mrs. Brill was on the other side of the cafeteria, and they were thinking of a way to get her to run. Everyone says she waddles like a duck when she runs, and we wanted to see it. So Kel pretended he was choking, and Caulder made a huge spectacle and got behind him and started beating on his back, pretending to give him the Heimlich maneuver. It freaked Mrs. Brill out! When she got to our table, Kel said he was all better. He told Mrs. Brill that Caulder saved his life. It would have been fine, but she had already told someone to call 911. Within minutes, two ambulances and a fire truck showed up at the school. One of the boys at the next table told Mrs. Brill they were faking the whole thing, so Kel got called to the office."

Lake leans forward and glares at Kel. "Please tell me this is a joke."

Kel looks up with an innocent expression. "It was a joke. I really didn't think anyone would call 911. Now I have to spend all next week in detention."

"Why didn't Mrs. Brill call me?" Lake asks him.

"I'm pretty sure she did," he says. "You can't find your phone, remember?"

"Ugh! If she calls me in for another conference, you're grounded!"

I look at Caulder, who's attempting to avoid my gaze. "Caulder, what about you? Why didn't Mrs. Brill try to call me?"

He turns toward me and gives me a mischievous grin. "Kel lied for me. He told her that I really thought he was choking and I was trying to save his life," he says. "Which brings me to my sweet for the day. I was rewarded for my heroic behavior. Mrs. Brill gave me two free study hall passes."

Only Caulder could find a way to avoid detention and get rewarded instead. "You two need to cut that crap out," I say to them. "And Gavin, no more prank stories."

"Yes, Mr. Cooper," Gavin says sarcastically. "But I have to know," he says, looking at the kids, "does she really waddle?"

"Yeah." Kiersten laughs. "She's a waddler, all right." She looks at Caulder. "What was your suck, Caulder?"

Caulder gets serious. "My best friend almost choked to death today. He could have *died*."

We all laugh. As much as Lake and I try to do the responsible thing, sometimes it's hard to draw the line between being the rule enforcer and being the sibling. We choose which battles to pick with the boys, and Lake says it's important that we don't choose very many. I look at her and see she's laughing, so I assume this isn't one she wants to fight.

"Can I finish my food now?" Lake says, pointing to her plate, still on the other side of me, out of her reach. I scoot the plate back in front of her. "Thank you, Mr. Cooper," she says.

I knee her under the table. She knows I hate it when she calls me that. I don't know why it bothers me so much. Probably because when I actually was her teacher, it was absolute torture. Our connection progressed so quickly that first night I took her out. I'd never met anyone I had so much fun just being myself with. I spent the entire weekend thinking about her. The moment I walked around the corner and saw her standing in the hallway in front of my classroom, I felt like my heart had been ripped right out of my chest. I knew immediately what she was doing there, even though it took her a little longer to figure it out. When she realized I was a teacher, the look in her eyes absolutely devastated me. She was hurt. Heartbroken. Just like me. One thing I know for sure, I never want to see that look in her eyes again.

Kiersten stands up and takes her plate to the sink. "I have to go. Thanks for the bread, Will," she says sarcastically. "It was delicious."

"I'm leaving, too. I'll walk you home," Kel says. He jumps out of his seat and follows her to the door. I look at Lake, and she rolls her eyes. It bothers her that Kel has developed his first crush. Lake doesn't like to think that we're about to have to deal with teenage hormones.

Caulder gets up from the table. "I'm gonna watch TV in my room," he says. "See you later, Kel. Bye, Kiersten." They both tell him goodbye as they leave.

"I really like that girl," Eddie says after Kiersten leaves. "I hope Kel asks her to be his girlfriend. I hope they grow up and get married and have lots of weird babies. I hope she's in our family forever."

"Shut up, Eddie," Lake says. "He's only ten. He's too young for a girlfriend."

"Not really, he'll be eleven in eight days," Gavin says. "Eleven is the prime age for first girlfriends."

Lake takes an entire handful of fries and throws them toward Gavin's face.

I just sigh. She's impossible to control. "You're cleaning up tonight," I say to her. "You, too," I say to Eddie. "Gavin, let's go watch some football, like real men, while the women do their job."

Gavin scoots his glass toward Eddie. "Refill this glass, woman. I'm watching some football."

While Eddie and Lake clean the kitchen, I take the opportunity to ask Gavin for a favor. Lake and I haven't had any alone time in weeks due to always having the boys. I really need alone time with her.

"Do you think you and Eddie could take Kel and Caulder to a movie tomorrow night?"

He doesn't answer right away, which makes me feel guilty for even asking. Maybe they had plans already.

"It depends," he finally responds. "Do we have to take Kiersten, too?"

I laugh. "That's up to your girl. She's her new best friend."

Gavin rolls his eyes at the thought. "It's fine; we had plans to watch a movie anyway. What time? How long do you want us to keep them?"

"Doesn't matter. We aren't going anywhere. I just need a couple of hours alone with Lake. There's something I need to give her."

"Oh . . . I see," he says. "Just text me when you're through 'giving it to her,' and we'll bring the boys home."

I shake my head at his assumption and laugh. I like Gavin. What I hate, however, is the fact that everything that happens between me and Lake, and Gavin and Eddie . . . we all seem to *know* about. That's the drawback of dating best friends: there are no secrets.

"Let's go," Eddie says as she pulls Gavin up off the couch. "Thanks for supper, Will. Joel wants you guys to come over next weekend. He said he'd make tamales."

I don't turn down tamales. "We're there," I say.

After Eddie and Gavin leave, Lake comes to the living room and sits on the couch, curling her legs under her as she snuggles against me. I put my arm around her and pull her closer.

"I'm bummed," she says. "I was hoping we'd at least get the same days this semester. We never get any alone time with all these butterflying kids running around."

You would think, with our living across the street from each other, that we would have all the time in the world together. That's not the case. Last semester she went to school Monday, Wednesday, and Friday, and I went all five days. Weekends we spent a lot of time doing homework but mostly stayed busy with Kel's and Caulder's sports. When Julia passed away in September, that put even more on Lake's plate. It's been an adjustment, to say the least. The only place we seem to be lacking is getting quality alone time. It's kind of awkward, if the boys are at one house, to go to the other house to be alone. They almost always seem to follow us whenever we do.

"We'll get through it," I say. "We always do."

She pulls my face toward hers and kisses me. I've been kissing her every day for over a year, and it somehow gets better every time.

"I better go," she says at last. "I have to get up early

and go to the college to finish registration. I also need to make sure Kel's not outside making out with Kiersten."

We laugh about it now, but in a matter of years it'll be our reality. We won't even be twenty-five, and we'll be raising teenagers. It's a scary thought.

"Hold on. Before you leave . . . what are your plans tomorrow night?"

She rolls her eyes. "What kind of question is that? You're my plan. You're always my only plan."

"Good. Eddie and Gavin are taking the boys. Meet me at seven?"

She perks up and smiles. "Are you asking me out on a real, live date?"

I nod.

"Well, you suck at it, you know. You always have. Sometimes girls like to be *asked* and not *told*."

She's trying to play hard to get, which is pointless, since I've already got her. I play her game anyway. I kneel on the floor in front of her and look into her eyes. "Lake, will you do me the honor of accompanying me on a date tomorrow night?"

She leans back into the couch and looks away. "I don't know, I'm sort of busy," she says. "I'll check my schedule and let you know." She tries to look put out, but a smile breaks out on her face. She leans forward and hugs me; I lose my balance, and we end up on the floor. I roll her onto her back, and she stares up at me and laughs. "Fine. Pick me up at seven."

I brush her hair out of her eyes and run my finger along the edge of her cheek. "I love you, Lake."

"Say it again," she says.

I kiss her forehead and repeat, "I love you, Lake."

"One more time."

"I." I kiss her lips. "And love." I kiss them again. "And you."

"I love you, too."

I ease my body on top of hers and interlock my fingers with hers. I bring our hands above her head and press them into the floor, then lean in as if I'm going to kiss her, but I don't. I like to tease her when we're in this position. I barely touch my lips to hers until she closes her eyes, then I slowly pull away. She opens her eyes, and I smile at her, then lean in again. As soon as her eyes are closed, I pull away again.

"Dammit, Will! Butterflying kiss me already!"

She grabs my face and pulls my mouth to hers. We continue kissing until we get to the "point of retreat," as Lake likes to call it. She climbs out from under me and sits up on her knees as I roll onto my back and remain on the floor. We don't like to get carried away when we aren't alone in the house. It's so easy to do. When we catch ourselves taking things too far, one of us always calls retreat.

Before Julia passed away, we made the mistake of taking things too far, too soon—a crucial mistake on my part. It was just two weeks after we started officially dating, and Caulder was spending the night at Kel's house. Lake and I came back to my place after a movie. We started making out on the couch, and one thing led to another, neither of us willing to stop it. We weren't having sex, but we would have eventually if Julia hadn't walked in when she did. She completely flipped out. We were mortified. She grounded Lake and wouldn't let me see her for two weeks. I apologized probably a million times in those two weeks.

Julia sat us down together and made us swear we would wait at least a year. She made Lake get on the pill and made me look her in the eyes and give her my word. She wasn't upset about the fact that her eighteen-year-old daughter almost had sex. Julia was fairly reasonable and knew it would happen at some point. What hurt her was that I was so willing to take that from Lake after only two weeks of dating. It made me feel incredibly guilty, so I agreed to the promise. She also wanted us to set a good example for Kel and Caulder; she asked us not to spend the night at each other's houses during that year, either. After Julia passed away, we've stuck to our word. More out of respect for Julia than anything. Lord knows it's difficult sometimes. A lot of times.

We haven't discussed it, but last week was exactly a year since we made that promise to Julia. I don't want to rush Lake into anything; I want it to be completely up to her, so I haven't brought it up. Neither has she. Then again, we haven't really been alone.

"Point of retreat," she says, and stands up. "I'll see you tomorrow night. Seven o'clock. Don't be late."

"Go find your phone and text me good night," I tell her.

She opens the door and faces me as she backs out of the house, slowly pulling the door shut. "One more time?" she says.

"I love you, Lake."

2.

FRIDAY, JANUARY 6

I'm giving Lake her present in a little while. I'm not even sure what it is, since it's not something I picked out. I can't write any more right now, my hands are shaking. How the hell do these dates still make me nervous? I'm so pathetic.

"BOYS, NO BACKWARD TONIGHT. YOU KNOW GAVIN CAN'T keep up when you guys talk backward." I wave goodbye and shut the door behind them.

It's almost seven. I go to the bathroom and brush my teeth, then grab my keys and jacket and head to my car. I can see Lake watching from the window. She probably doesn't realize it, but I could always see her watching from the window. Especially in the months before we were officially dating. Every day I would come home and see her shadow. It's what gave me hope that one day we would be able to be together: the fact that she still thought about me.

After our fight in the laundry room, though, she stopped watching from the window. I thought I'd screwed everything up for good.

I back out of the driveway and straight into hers. I leave the car running and walk around to open the door for her. When I get back inside the car, I get a whiff of her perfume. It's the vanilla one, my favorite.

"Where are we going?" she asks.

"You'll see. It's a surprise," I say as I pull out of her driveway. Rather than turn onto the street, I pull right into my own driveway. I kill the ignition and run around to her side of the car and open the door.

"What are you doing, Will?"

I take her hand and pull her out of the car. "We're here." I love the look of confusion on her face, so I spare the details.

"You asked me out on a date to your house? I got dressed up, Will! I want to go somewhere."

She's whining. I laugh and take her hand and walk her inside. "No, *you* made me ask you out on a date. I never said we were going anywhere. I just asked if you had plans."

I've already cooked pasta, so I walk into the kitchen and get our plates. Rather than setting the table, I take the plates to the coffee table in the living room. She pulls off her jacket, seeming a little disappointed. I continue to elude her while I make our drinks and then take a seat on the floor with her.

"I'm not trying to seem ungrateful," she says around

a mouthful of food. "It's just that we never get to go any-where anymore. I was looking forward to doing something different."

I take a drink and wipe my mouth. "Babe, I know what you mean. But tonight has sort of already been planned out for us." I toss another bread stick on her plate.

"What do you mean, *planned out* for us? I'm not fol-lowing," she says.

I don't respond. I just continue eating.

"Will, tell me what's going on, your evasiveness is making me nervous."

I grin at her and take a drink. "I'm not trying to make you nervous. I'm doing what I was told."

She can tell I'm enjoying this. She gives up trying to get anything out of me and takes another bite. "The pasta's good, at least," she says.

"So is the view."

She smiles and winks at me and continues to eat.

She's wearing her hair down tonight. I love it when she wears her hair down. I also love it when she wears it up. In fact, I don't think she's ever worn it in a way that made me not love it. She's so incredibly beautiful, espe-cially when she's not trying to be. I realize I've been star-ing at her, lost in thought. I've eaten barely half my food, and she's almost finished.

"Will?" She wipes her mouth with her napkin. "Does this have anything to do with my mom?" she asks quietly. "You know . . . with our promise to her?"

I know what she's asking me. I immediately feel guilty that I haven't considered what she would think my intentions were tonight. I don't want her to feel like I expect anything at all from her.

"Not in that way, babe." I reach across and take her hand. "That's not what tonight's about. I'm sorry if you thought that. That's for another time . . . when you're ready."

She smiles at me. "Well, I wasn't gonna object if it was."

Her comment catches me off guard. I've gotten so used to the fact that one of us always calls retreat; I haven't entertained the possibility of the alternative for tonight.

She looks embarrassed by her forwardness and diverts her attention back down to her plate. She tears off a piece of bread and dips it in the sauce. When she's finished chewing, she takes a drink and looks back up at me.

"Before," she whispers unsteadily, "when I asked if this had anything to do with my mom, you said, 'Not in that way.' What'd you mean by that? Are you saying tonight has something to do with her in a different way?"

I nod, then stand and take her hand and pull her up. I wrap my arms around her, and she leans against my chest and clasps her hands behind my back. "It does have to do with her." She pulls her face away from my chest and looks up at me while I explain, "She gave me something else . . . besides the letters."

Julia made me promise not to tell Lake about the letters and the gift until it was time. Lake and Kel have already opened the letters; the gift was meant for Lake and me. It was intended to be a Christmas gift for us to open together, but this is the first chance we've had to be alone.

"Come to my bedroom." I release my hold on her and grab her hand. She follows until we get to my room, where the box Julia gave me is sitting on the bed.

Lake walks over to it and runs her hand across the wrapping paper. She fingers the red velvet bow and sighs. "Is it really from her?" she asks quietly.

I sit on the bed and motion for her to sit with me. We pull our legs up and sit with the gift between us. There's a card taped to the top of it with our names on it, along with clear instructions not to read the card until after we open the gift.

"Will, why didn't you tell me there was something else? Is this the last one?" I can see the tears forming in her eyes. She always tries so hard to conceal them. I don't know why she hates it so much when she cries.

I run my finger across her cheek and wipe away a tear. "Last one, I swear," I say. "She wanted us to open it together."

She straightens up and does her best to regain her composure. "Do you want to do the honors, or should I?"

"That's a dumb question," I say.

"There's no such thing as a dumb question," she says. "You should know that, Mr. Cooper." She leans forward and kisses me, then pulls back and starts to loosen the edge of the package. I watch as she tears it open, revealing a cardboard box wrapped in duct tape.

"My God, there must be six layers of duct tape on here," she says sarcastically. "Kind of like your car." She looks up and gives me a sly grin.

"Funny," I say. I stroke her knee and watch her poke through the tape with her thumbnail. Just when she breaks through the final edge, she pauses.

"Thank you for doing this for her," she says. "For keeping the gift." She looks back down at it and holds it without opening it. "Do you know what it is?" she asks.

"No clue. I'm hoping it's not a puppy—it's been under my bed for four months."

She laughs. "I'm nervous," she says. "I really don't want to cry again." She hesitates before she opens the top of the box and folds the flaps back. She pulls the contents out as I pull the cardboard away. She tears the tissue off and reveals a clear glass vase, full to the brim with geometrical stars in a variety of colors. It looks like origami. Hundreds of thumbnail-sized 3-D paper stars.

"What is it?" I ask Lake.

"I don't know, but it's beautiful," she says. We continue to stare at the gift, trying to make sense of it. She opens the card and looks at it. "I can't read it, Will. You'll have to do it." She places it in my hands.

I open it and read aloud.

Will and Lake,

Love is the most beautiful thing in the world. Unfortunately, it's also one of the hardest things in the world to hold on to, and one of the easiest things to throw away.

Neither of you has a mother or a father to go to for relationship advice anymore. Neither of you has anyone to go to for a shoulder to cry on when things get tough, and they will get tough. Neither of you has someone to go to when you just want to share the funny, or the happy, or the heartache. You are both at a disadvantage when it comes to this aspect of love. You both only have each other, and because of this, you will have to work harder at building a strong foundation for your future together. You are not only each other's love; you are also each other's sole confidant.

I handwrote some things onto strips of paper and folded them into stars. It might be an inspirational quote, an inspiring lyric, or just some downright good parental advice. I don't want you to open one and read it until you feel you truly need it. If you have a bad day, if the two of you fight, or if you need something to lift your spirits . . . that's what these are for. You can open one together; you can open one alone. I just want there to be something both of you can go to if and when you ever need it.

Will . . . thank you. Thank you for coming into our lives. So much of the pain and worry I've been feeling has been alleviated by the mere fact that I know my daughter is loved by you.

Lake takes my hand when I pause. I wasn't expecting Julia to address me personally. Lake wipes away a tear. I do my best to fight back my own tears. I take a deep breath and clear my throat, then finish reading the letter.

You are a wonderful man, and you've been a wonderful friend to me. I thank you from the bottom of my heart for loving my daughter like you do. You respect her, you don't need to change for her, and you inspire her. You can never know how grateful I have been for you, and how much peace you have brought my soul.

And Lake, this is me nudging your shoulder, giving you my approval. You couldn't have picked anyone better to love if I'd hand-picked him myself. Also, thank you for being so determined to keep our family together. You were right about Kel needing to be with you. Thank you for helping me see that. And remember, when things get tough for him, please teach him how to stop carving pumpkins . . .

I love you both and wish you a lifetime of happiness together.
—Julia

"And all around my memories, you dance . . ."
   —*The Avett Brothers*

I put the card back in the envelope and watch as Lake runs her fingers along the rim of the vase, spinning it around to view it from all angles. "I saw her making these once. When I walked into her room, she was folding strips of paper, and she stopped and put them aside as we talked. I forgot about it. I forgot all about it. This must have taken her forever."

She stares at the stars, and I stare at her. She wipes more tears from her eyes with the back of her hand. She's holding it together well, all things considered.

"I want to read them all, but at the same time, I hope we never need to read them at *all*," she says.

I lean forward and give her a quick kiss. "You are as amazing as your mother." I take the vase and set it down on the dresser. Lake shoves the wrapping paper inside the box and sets it on the floor. She puts the card on the table, then lies back on the bed. I lie down beside her, turn toward her, and rest my arm over her waist. "You okay?" I ask. I can't tell whether she's sad.

She looks at me and smiles. "I thought it would hurt to hear her words again, but it didn't. It actually made me happy," she says.

"Me, too," I say. "I was really worried it was a puppy."

She laughs and lays her head on my arm. We lie there in silence, watching each other. I run my hand up her arm and trace her face and neck with my fingertips. I love watching her think.

She eventually lifts her head off my arm and slides on top of me, placing her hands on the back of my neck. She leans in and slowly parts my lips with hers. I become quickly consumed by the taste of her lips and the feel of her warm hands. I wrap my arms around her and run my fingers through her hair as I return her kiss. It's been so long since we've been alone together without the possibility of being interrupted. I hate being in this predicament, but I love being in this predicament. Her skin is so soft; her lips are perfect. It gets harder and harder to retreat.

She runs her hands underneath my shirt and lightly teases my neck with her mouth. She knows this drives me crazy, yet she's been doing it more and more lately. I think she likes pushing her boundaries. One of us needs to retreat, and I don't know if I can bring myself to do it. Apparently, neither can she.

"How much time do we have?" she whispers. She lifts up my shirt and kisses her way down my chest.

"Time?" I say weakly.

"Until the boys get home." She slowly kisses her way back up to my neck. "How long do we have until they get home?" She brings her face back to mine and looks at me. I can see by the look in her eyes that she's telling me she's not retreating.

I bring my arm over my face and cover my eyes. I try

to talk myself down. This isn't how I want it to be for her. Think about something else, Will. Think about college, homework, puppies in cardboard boxes . . . anything.

She pulls my arm away from my face so she can look me in the eyes. "Will . . . it's been a year. I want to."

I roll her onto her back and prop my head up on my elbow and lean in toward her, stroking her face with my other hand. "Lake, believe me, I'm ready, too. But not here. Not right now. You'll have to go home in an hour when the boys get back, and I don't think I could take it." I kiss her on the forehead. "In two weeks we get a three-day weekend. We'll go away together. Just the two of us. I'll see if my grandparents will watch the boys, and we can spend the whole weekend together."

She kicks her legs up and down on the bed, frustrated. "I can't wait two more weeks! We've been waiting fifty-seven weeks already!"

I laugh at her childishness and lean in, planting a kiss on her cheek. "If *I* can wait, you can *definitely* wait," I assure her.

She rolls her eyes. "God, you're such a bore," she teases.

"Oh, I'm a bore?" I say. "You want me to throw you in the shower again? Cool you off? I will if that's what you need."

"Only if you get in with me," she says. Her eyes grow wide, and she sits up and pushes me flat on my back, leaning over me. "Will!" she says excitedly as a realization dawns on her. "Does that mean we can take showers together? On our getaway?"

Her eagerness surprises me. Everything she does surprises me. "You aren't nervous?" I ask her.

"No, not at all." She smiles and leans in closer. "I know I'll be in good hands."

"You will definitely be in good hands," I say, pulling her to me. Just when I'm about to kiss her again, my phone vibrates. She reaches into my pocket and pulls it out.

"Gavin," she says. She hands the phone to me and rolls off.

I read the text. "Great, Kel threw up. They think he has a stomach bug, so they're bringing them home."

She groans and gets off the bed. "Ugh! I hate vomit! Caulder's probably gonna get it, too, the way they pass crap back and forth."

"I'll text him and tell him to take Kel to your house. You go home and wait; I'll run to the store and get him some medicine." I pull my shirt back on and grab the vase that Julia made us so I can put it on the bookshelf in the living room. We exit the bedroom in parent mode.

"Get some soup, too. For tomorrow. And some Sprite," she says.

When I set the vase down in the living room, she reaches her hand inside and grabs a star. She sees me eyeing her and grins. "There might be a good tip in here. For vomit," she says.

"We've got a long road ahead of us; you better not

waste those." When we walk outside, I grab her arm and pull her to me and hug her good night. "You want me to drive you home?"

She laughs and hugs me back. "Thanks for our date. It was one of my favorites."

"The best is yet to come," I say, hinting at our upcoming getaway.

"I'm holding you to that." She backs away and then turns and starts walking toward her house. I've opened the car door when she yells from across the street.

"Will! One more time?"

"I love you, Lake!"

3.

JANUARY 7

I butterflying hate cheeseburgers.

HELL. PURE HELL IS THE BEST WAY I CAN DESCRIBE THE last twenty-four hours. By the time Gavin and Eddie made it home with the boys, it was apparent that Kel didn't have a stomach bug after all. Gavin didn't knock when he ran through the front door and headed straight for the bathroom. Caulder was next, then Lake and Eddie. I was the last to feel the effects of the food poisoning. Caulder and I have done nothing but lie on the couch, taking turns in the bathroom since midnight last night.

I can't help but envy Kiersten. I should have just had bread, too. About the time that thought crosses my mind, there's a knock at the front door. I don't get up. I don't even speak. No one I know extends the courtesy of knocking, so

I don't know who could be at the door. I guess I won't find out, either, because I'm not moving.

I'm facing away from the door, but I hear it slowly open and can feel the cold air circulate as a female voice I don't recognize calls my name.

I still don't care who it is. At this point, I'm wishing it's someone here to finish me off, put me out of my misery. It takes all the energy I have to just raise my hand in the air to let whoever it is know that I'm here.

"Oh, you poor thing," she says. She shuts the door behind her and walks around to the front of the couch and stares down at me. I glance up at her and realize I have absolutely no idea who this woman is. She's probably in her forties; her short black hair is traced with gray. She's petite, shorter than Lake. I try to smile, but I don't think I do. She frowns and glances over to Caulder, who is passed out on the other couch. I notice a bottle in her hands when she passes through the living room into the kitchen. I hear her opening drawers, and she comes back with a spoon.

"This will help. Layken said you guys were sick, too." She pours some of the liquid into a spoon and bends down, handing it to me.

I take it. I'll take anything at this point. I swallow the medicine and cough when it burns my throat. I reach for a glass of water and take a sip. I don't want to drink too much; it's just been coming right back up. "What the hell is that?" I ask.

She looks disappointed at my reaction. "I made it. I make my own medicine. It'll help, I promise." She walks over to Caulder and shakes him awake. He accepts the medicine as I did, without question, then closes his eyes again.

"I'm Sherry, by the way. Kiersten's mother. She said you guys ate some rancid meat." She makes a face when she says the word "meat."

I don't want to think about it, so I close my eyes and try to put it out of my mind. I guess she sees the nausea building behind my expression, because she says, "Sorry. This is why we're vegetarian."

"Thanks, Sherry," I say, hoping she's finished. She's not.

"I started a load of laundry over at Layken's house. If you want, I'll wash some of yours, too." She doesn't wait for me to respond. She walks down the hallway and starts gathering clothes, then takes them into the laundry room. I hear the washer start, followed by noise in the kitchen. She's cleaning. This woman I don't know is cleaning my house. I'm too tired to object. I'm even too tired to be pleased about it.

"Will?" She walks back through the living room. I open my eyes, but barely. "I'll be back in an hour to put the clothes in the dryer. I'll bring some minestrone, too."

I just nod. Or at least I think I nod.

* * *

IT HASN'T BEEN an hour yet, but whatever Sherry gave me already has me feeling a little better. Caulder manages to make it to his room and passes out on his bed. I've gotten into the kitchen and poured myself a glass of Sprite when the front door opens. It's Lake. She looks as rough as I do, but still beautiful.

"Hey, babe." She shuffles into the kitchen and wraps her arms around me. She's in her pajamas and house shoes. They aren't the Darth Vader ones, but they're still sexy. "How's Caulder feeling?" she asks.

"Better, I guess. Whatever Sherry gave us worked."

"Yeah, it did." She rests her head against my chest and takes a deep breath. "I wish we had enough couches in one house so we could all be sick together."

We've brought up the subject of living together before. It makes economic sense; our bills would be cut in half. She's only nineteen, though, and she seems to like having her alone time. The thought of taking such a huge leap makes us both a little apprehensive, so we agreed to wait on that step until we're certain about it.

"I wish we did, too," I say. I naturally lean in to kiss her, but she shakes her head and backs away.

"Nuh-uh," she says. "We're not kissing for at least twenty-four more hours."

I laugh and kiss her on top of her head instead.

"I guess I'll go back now. I just wanted to check on you." She kisses me on the arm.

"You two are so cute!" Sherry says. She walks

through the dining room and places a container of soup in the fridge, then turns and heads into the laundry room. I never even heard her open the front door, much less knock.

"Thanks for the medicine, Sherry. It really helped," Lake says.

"No problem," Sherry says. "That concoction can knock the shit out of anything. You two let me know if you need more."

Lake looks at me and rolls her eyes. "See you later. Love you."

"Love you, too. Let me know when Kel feels better, and we'll come over."

Lake leaves, and I take a seat at the table and slowly sip my drink. I still don't trust ingesting anything.

Sherry pulls out the chair across the table from me and takes a seat. "So, what's your story?" she asks.

I'm not sure what story she's referring to, so I raise my eyebrows at her as I take another sip and wait for her to elaborate.

"With the two of you. And Kel and Caulder. It's a little strange, from a mother's point of view. I've got an eleven-year-old daughter who seems to enjoy spending time with all you guys, so I feel it's my duty as a mom to know your story. You and Lake are both practically children, raising children."

She's very blunt. However, the way she says it comes off as appropriate, somehow. She's easy to like. I see why Kiersten is the way she is.

I set my Sprite down on the table and wipe the condensation off the glass with my thumbs. "My parents died three years ago." I continue to stare at the glass, avoiding her gaze. I don't want to see the pity. "Lake's father died over a year ago, and her mother passed away in September. So . . . here we are, raising our brothers."

Sherry leans back in her chair and folds her arms across her chest. "I'll be damned."

I nod and give her a half smile. At least she didn't say how sorry she is for us. I hate pity more than anything.

"How long have the two of you been dating?"

"Officially? Since December eighteenth, a little over a year ago."

"What about *un*officially?" she says.

I shift in my seat. Why did I even specify "officially"?

"December eighteenth, a little over a year ago," I say again, and smile. I'm not getting any more detailed than that. "What's *your* story, Sherry?"

She laughs and stands up. "Will, has anyone ever told you it's rude to be nosy?" She makes her way to the front door. "Let me know if you need anything. You know where we live."

THE FOUR OF us spend the entire day Sunday watching movies and being sore. We're all a little queasy, so we skip the junk food. Monday it's back to reality. I drop Kel and Caulder off at their school and head to the college. Three of my four classes are in the same building: one of the benefits of being in grad school. Once your course of study is set, all the classes are similar and usually taught in the same area. The first of my four classes, however, is halfway across campus. It's a graduate-level elective called Death and Dying. I thought it would be interesting, since I'm more than experienced in the subject. I also didn't have a choice. There wasn't another graduate elective that I could take during the eight o'clock block, so I'm stuck with this one if I want all my credits to count.

When I walk in, students are seated sporadically around the room. It's an auditorium-style room set up with tables for two. I walk up the stairs and take a seat in the back of the room. It's different, being the student rather than the teacher. I got so used to being at the head of the classroom. The role reversal has taken some getting used to.

All twenty tables fill up fairly quickly, other than an empty seat next to me. It's the first day of the semester, so it will probably be the only day that people show up early. That's usually how it is; the newness wears off by day two. It's rare for a professor to have the entire roll show up after day two.

My phone vibrates inside my pocket. I take it out and slide my finger across the screen. It's a text from Lake.

> Finally found my phone. Hope you like your
> classes. I love you and I'll see you tonight.

The professor starts calling roll. I send Lake a quick reply text that states, "Thx. Love you, too," then put the phone back in my pocket.

"Will Cooper?" the professor says. I raise my hand, and he looks up at me and nods, then marks his form. I glance around the room to see if I recognize anyone. There were a couple of people from high school in my elective last semester, but I don't usually see many familiar faces. Most of my high school classmates graduated from college last May, and not many of them decided on grad school.

I notice a girl with blond hair in the front row turned completely around in her seat. When I meet her gaze, my heart sinks. She smiles and waves when she sees that I've recognized her. She gathers her things, then stands and makes her way up the stairs.

No. She's coming toward me. She's about to sit with me.

"Will! Oh my God, what are the chances? It's been so long," she says.

I do my best to smile at her, trying to figure out if what I'm feeling is anger or guilt. "Hey, Vaughn." I try to sound pleased to see her.

She takes the seat next to me and leans in and hugs me. "How are you?" she whispers. "How's Caulder?"

"He's good," I say. "Growing up. He'll be eleven in two months."

"Eleven? Wow," she says, shaking her head in disbelief.

We haven't seen each other in almost three years. We parted on bad terms, to put it mildly, yet she's acting genuinely excited to see me. I wish I could say the same.

"How's Ethan?" I ask her. Ethan is her older brother. He and I were pretty good friends while Vaughn and I dated, but we haven't spoken since the breakup.

"He's good. He's really good. He's married now, with a baby on the way."

"Good for him. Tell him I said so."

"I will," she says.

"Vaughn Gibson?" the professor calls.

She raises her hand. "Up here." She brings her attention back to me. "What about you? You married?"

I shake my head.

"Me, neither." She smiles.

I don't like how she's looking at me. We dated for over two years, so I know her pretty well. And right now her intentions aren't good for me.

"I'm not married, but I am dating someone," I clarify. I see the slight shift in her expression, though she attempts to mask it with a smile.

"Good for you," she says. "Is it serious?" She's digging for hints about my relationship, so I make it clear to her.

"Very."

When the professor starts explaining the semester requirements and going over the syllabus, we both face forward and don't speak much, other than occasional comments from her regarding the class. When the professor dismisses us, I quickly stand up.

"It's really good seeing you, Will," she says. "I'm excited about this class now. We have a lot of catching up to do."

I smile at her without agreeing. She gives me another quick hug and turns away. I gather my things and head to my second class as I think of a way to break this news to Lake.

Lake has never asked about my past relationships. She says there isn't anything good that can come from discussing them. I'm not sure she knows about Vaughn. She knows I had a pretty serious relationship in high school, and she knows I've had sex; we talked about that. I don't know how she'll take this. I'd hate to upset her, though I don't want to hide anything.

But what would I be hiding? Is it necessary to tell her about all the students in my classes? We've never discussed it before, so why do I feel the need to now? If I tell her, it will just cause her to worry unnecessarily. If I don't tell her, what harm is it doing? Lake's not in my class, she's not even in school on the same days I am. I've made it clear to Vaughn that I'm in a relationship. That should be good enough.

By the end of my last class, I've convinced myself that Lake doesn't need to know.

* * *

WHEN I PULL up at the elementary school, Kel and Caulder are seated outside on a bench, away from the rest of the students. Mrs. Brill is standing right behind them, waiting.

"Great," I mumble to myself. I've heard the horror stories about her, but I've never had to deal with her. I kill the engine and get out. It's obvious what she's expecting me to do.

"You must be Will," she says, extending her hand. "I don't believe we've met before."

"Good to meet you." I glance at the boys, who aren't making eye contact with me. When I look back at Mrs. Brill, she nods to the left, indicating that she would like to talk to me out of their earshot.

"There was an incident with Kel last week in the cafeteria," Mrs. Brill says as we walk down the sidewalk, away from the crowd. "I'm not sure what the relationship is between Kel and you, but I wasn't able to get in touch with his sister."

"We're aware of what happened," I say. "Layken misplaced her phone. Do I need to let her know to contact you?"

"No, that isn't why I want to talk to you," she says. "I just wanted to be sure both of you were aware of last week's incident and that it was handled appropriately."

"It was. We took care of it," I say. I don't know what she means by "handled appropriately," but I doubt she expects that the punishment was laughing about it at the dinner table. Oh well.

"I wanted to talk to you about a different matter. There's a new student here who seems to have taken to Kel and Caulder. Kiersten?" She waits for me to acknowledge that. I nod. "There was an incident today involving her and a few of the other students," she says.

I stop walking and turn toward her, becoming more vested in the conversation. If it has anything to do with how the kids acted at the dinner table the other night, I want to know about it.

"She's being picked on. Some of the other students find that her personality doesn't mesh well with theirs. Kel and Caulder found out about a couple of the older boys saying some things to her, so they decided to take matters into their own hands." She pauses and glances back at Kel and Caulder, who are still seated in the same positions.

"What'd they do?" I ask nervously.

"It's not what they did, really. It's what they said . . . in a note." She takes a piece of paper out of her pocket and hands it to me.

I unfold it and look at it. My mouth gapes open. It's a picture of a bloody knife with *"You will die, asswipe!"* written across the top.

"Kel and Caulder wrote this?" I ask, embarrassed.

She nods. "They've already admitted to it. You're a teacher, so you know the significance of this kind of threat on campus. It can't be taken lightly, Will. I hope you understand. They'll be suspended for the rest of the week."

"Suspended? For an entire week? But they were defending someone who was being bullied."

"I understand that, and those boys have been punished as well. But I can't condone bad behavior in the defense of more bad behavior."

I know where she's coming from. I look down at the note again and sigh. "I'll tell Lake. Is there anything else? They're free to come back on Monday?"

She nods. I thank her and walk back to the car and get in. The boys climb into the backseat, and we drive home in silence. I'm too pissed at them to say anything. Or at least I *think* I'm pissed. I'm supposed to be, right?

LAKE IS SEATED at the bar when I walk through her front door. Kel and Caulder follow behind me, and I sternly instruct them to take a seat. Lake shoots me a confused look when I walk through the living room and motion for her to follow me to her bedroom. I shut the door for privacy and explain everything that happened, showing her the note.

She stares at it for a while, then covers her mouth and tries to hide her laugh. She thinks it's funny. I feel relieved, because the more thought I gave it on the way home, the funnier I thought it was. When we make eye contact, we start laughing.

"I know, Lake! From a sibling standpoint, it's really funny," I say. "But what are we supposed to do from a *parent* standpoint?"

She shakes her head. "I don't know. I'm sort of proud of them for taking up for Kiersten." She sits down on her bed and throws the note aside. "Poor Kiersten."

I sit down beside her. "Well, we have to act mad. They really can't do crap like this."

Lake nods in agreement. "What do you think their punishment should be?"

I shrug. "I don't know. Being suspended seems kind of like a reward. What kid wouldn't want to get a week off from school?"

"I know, right?" she says. "I guess we could ground them from their video games while they're home," she suggests.

"If we do that, they'll just annoy us the entire time out of boredom," I say. She groans at the thought. I think back on my own punishments as a child and try to come up with a solution. "We could make them write 'I will not write threatening notes' a thousand times."

She shakes her head in disagreement. "Kel loves to write. He would consider that another reward, just like the suspension." We both think for a while, but neither of us comes up with any more ideas for punishment.

"I guess it's a good thing we have different schedules this semester," she says. "That way, every time they get suspended, at least one of us will be home."

I smile at her and hope she's wrong. This better be their first and last suspension. Lake doesn't know it, but she's made my life with Caulder so much easier. Before I met her, I agonized over every single parenting decision I had to make. Now that we make a lot of those choices together, I'm not as hard on myself. We seem to agree on most aspects of how the boys should be raised. It also doesn't hurt having her maternal instincts in the picture. It's in moments like these, when we're required to join forces, that it's almost unbearable for me to take things slowly. If I left my head out of it and followed my heart, I'd marry her today.

I push her back on the bed and kiss her. Due to the weekend from hell, I haven't been able to kiss her since Friday. I've missed kissing her. From the way she kisses me back, it's obvious she's missed kissing me, too.

"Have you talked to your grandparents about next weekend?" she asks.

My lips move from her mouth, down her cheek, and to her ear. "I'll call them tonight," I whisper. "Have you thought about where you want to go?" Goose bumps break out on her skin, so I continue kissing down her neck.

"We could stay here at my house, for all I care. I'm just looking forward to being with you for three whole days. And finally getting to spend the night together . . . in the same bed, at least."

I'm trying not to come off too eager, but next weekend is all I've been thinking about. She doesn't need to know that I've got an internal countdown going. Ten days and twenty-one more hours.

"Why don't we do that?" I stop kissing her neck and

look at her. "Let's just stay here. Kel and Caulder will be in Detroit. We can lie to Eddie and Gavin and tell them we're going away, so they won't stop by. We'll pull the shades down and lock the doors and hole up for three whole days, right here in this bed. And in the shower, too, of course."

"Sounds bemazing," she says. She likes to smoosh words together for emphasis. I'm pretty sure "bemazing" is "beautiful" and "amazing." I think it's cute.

"Now back to the punishment," she says. "What would our parents do?"

I honestly have no clue what my parents would do. If I did have a clue, it wouldn't be so hard to come up with solutions to all the problems that come along with raising kids.

"I know," I say. "Let's scare the butterfly out of them."

"How?" she says.

"Act like you're trying to calm me down, like I'm really pissed off. We can make them sit out there and sweat for a while."

She laughs. "You're so bad." She stands up and walks closer to the door. "Will! Calm down!" she yells.

I walk over to the door and hit it. "I will not calm down! I'm *pissed*!"

Lake throws herself onto the bed and pulls a pillow over her face to stifle her giggles before she continues. "No, stop it! You can't go out there yet! You need to calm down, Will! You might *kill* them!"

point of retreat | 53

I glare at her. *"Kill* them?" I whisper. *"Really?"* She laughs as I hop back on the bed with her. "Lake, you suck at this."

"Will, no! Not the belt!" she yells dramatically.

I clasp my hand over her mouth. "Shut up!" I say, laughing.

We give ourselves a few minutes to regain composure before we exit the bedroom. When we walk down the hallway, I do my best to look intimidating. The boys are watching us with fear in their eyes as we take our seats across the bar from them.

"I'll talk," Lake says to them. "Will is entirely too upset right now to speak to either of you."

I stare at them and don't speak, putting on my best display of anger. I wonder if this is how parenting is with real parents. A bunch of pretending to be responsible grown-ups.

"First of all," Lake says in a superbly faked motherly tone, "we would like to commend you for defending your friend. However, you went about it all wrong. You should have spoken to someone about it. Violence is never the answer to violence."

I couldn't have said it better if I'd been reading from a parenting handbook.

"You are both grounded for two weeks. And don't think your suspension will be fun, either. We're giving you each a list of chores to do every day. Including Saturday and Sunday."

I tap my knee against hers under the bar, letting her know that was a nice touch.

"Do either of you have anything to say?" she asks.

Kel raises his hand. "What about my birthday on Friday?"

Lake looks at me, and I shrug. She turns back to Kel. "You don't have to be grounded on your birthday. But you'll get an extra day of grounding at the end. Any more questions?"

Neither of them says anything.

"Good. Go to your room, Kel. No hanging out with Caulder or Kiersten while you're grounded. Caulder, same goes for you. Go to your house and to your room."

The boys get up from the bar and go to their respective bedrooms. When Kel has disappeared down the hallway and Caulder has disappeared out the front door, I give Lake a high five.

"Well played," I tell her. "You almost had me convinced."

"You, too. You really seemed pissed!" she says. She heads to the living room and sits down to fold a pile of laundry. "So? How were your classes?"

"Good," I reply. I spare her the details of first period. "I do have a lot of homework I need to get started on, though. Are we eating together tonight?"

She shakes her head. "I promised Eddie we could have some girl time tonight. Gavin started his job at Getty's. But tomorrow I'm all yours."

I kiss her on top of the head. "You two have fun. Text me good night," I say. "You do know where your phone is, right?"

She nods and pulls it out of her pocket to show me. "Love you," she says.

"Love you, too," I say as I leave.

When I shut the door behind me, I feel like I left a moment too soon. When I walk back in, she's facing the other way, folding a towel. I turn her around and take the towel out of her hands. I wrap my arms around her and kiss her again, but better this time. "I love you," I say again.

She sighs and leans in to me. "I can't wait until next weekend, Will. I wish it would just hurry up and get here."

"You and me both."

4.

If I were a carpenter, I would build you a window to my soul.
But I would leave that window shut and locked,
so that every time you tried to look through it . . . all you would
see is your own reflection.
You would see that my soul
is a reflection of you . . .

LAKE HAS ALREADY LEFT FOR SCHOOL BY THE TIME I WAKE up. Kel is asleep on the couch. She must have sent him over before she left. It's trash day, so I slip my shoes on and head outside to take the can to the curb. I have to knock almost a foot of snow off the lid before I can get it to budge. Lake forgot, so I walk to her house and pull hers to the curb as well.

"Hey, Will," Sherry says. She and Kiersten are making their way outside.

"Morning," I say to them.

"What happened with Kel and Caulder yesterday? Are they in lots of trouble?" Kiersten asks.

"Suspended. They can't go back until Monday."

"Suspended for what?" Sherry asks. I can tell by her tone that Kiersten must not have told her.

Kiersten turns toward her mother. "They threatened those boys the school called you about. They wrote them a note, threatening their life. Called them asswipes," she says matter-of-factly.

"Aww, how sweet," Sherry says. "They defended you." She turns to me before she gets in her car. "Will, tell them thank you. That's too sweet, defending my baby girl like that."

I laugh and shake my head as I watch them drive away. When I get back inside, Kel and Caulder are sitting on the couch watching TV. "Morning," I say to them.

"Are we allowed to watch TV, at least?" Caulder asks.

I shrug. "Whatever. Do what you want. Just don't threaten to kill anyone today." I should probably be stricter, but it's too early in the morning to care.

"They were really mean to her, Will," Kel says. "They've been being mean to her since she moved here. She hasn't done anything to them."

I sit down on the other couch and kick off my shoes. "Not everyone is gonna be nice, Kel. There are a lot of cruel people in the world, unfortunately. What kinds of things are they doing to her?"

Caulder answers me. "One of the sixth-grade boys asked her to be his girlfriend about a week after she moved here, but she told him no. He's kind of a bully. She said she was a vegetarian and couldn't date *meat*heads. It made him really mad, so he's been spreading rumors about her since then. A lot of kids are scared of him because he's a dickhead, so now other kids are being mean to her, too."

"Don't say 'dickhead,' Caulder. And I think you guys are doing the right thing by defending her. Lake and I aren't mad about that; we're actually a little proud. We just wish you would use your heads before you make some of the choices you do. This is two weeks in a row you guys have done something stupid at school. This time you got suspended because of it. We all have enough on our plates as it is . . . we don't need the added stress."

"Sorry," Kel says.

"Yeah. Sorry, Will," Caulder says.

"As for Kiersten, you two keep doing what you're doing, sticking by her. She's a good kid and doesn't deserve to be treated like that. Is anyone being nice to her other than you two? She doesn't have any other friends?"

"She's got Abby," Caulder says.

Kel smiles. "She's not the only one who has Abby."

"Shut up, Kel!" Caulder hits him on the arm.

"Whoa! What's this? Who's Abby? Caulder, do you have a girlfriend?" I tease.

"She's not my girlfriend," Caulder says defensively.

"Only because he's too shy to ask her," Kel says.

"You're one to talk," I say to Kel. "You've been crushing on Kiersten since the day she moved in. Why haven't you asked *her* to be your girlfriend?"

Kel blushes and tries to hide his smile. He reminds me of Lake when he does this. "I already asked her. She *is* my girlfriend," he says.

I'm impressed. He's got more nerve than I thought.

"You better not tell Layken!" he says. "She'll embarrass me."

"I won't say anything," I say. "But your birthday party is this Friday. Tell Kiersten not to be kissing you in front of Lake if you don't want her finding out."

"Shut up, Will! I'm not kissing her," Kel says with a disgusted look.

"Caulder, you should invite Abby to Kel's party," I say.

Caulder gets the same embarrassed look Kel had. "He already did," Kel says. Caulder hits him on the arm again.

I stand up. It's obvious my advice isn't needed here. "Well, you two have it all figured out. What do you need me for?"

"Someone has to pay for the pizza," Caulder says.

I walk to the front door and grab their jackets and toss them in their laps.

"Punishment time," I say. They groan and roll their eyes. "You guys get to shovel driveways today."

"Drive*ways*? As in plural? More than *one*?" Caulder asks.

"Yep," I say. "Do mine and Lake's, and when you're

done, do Sherry's, too. While you're at it, go ahead and do Bob and Melinda's."

Neither of them moves from the couch.

"Go!"

MY STOMACH IS in knots Wednesday morning. I really don't want to see Vaughn today. I try to leave a few minutes sooner, hoping I can make it to class early enough to pick a seat next to someone else. Unfortunately, I'm the first to arrive. I take a seat in the back again, hoping she won't want to make the trek to the back of the room.

She does. Arriving almost immediately after me, she smiles and runs up the steps, throwing her bag down on the table. "Morning," she says. "I brought you a coffee. Two sugars, no cream, just like you like it." She sets the coffee down in front of me.

"Thanks," I say. She's got her hair pulled back in a bun. I know exactly what she's doing. I told her once that I loved it when she wore her hair like that. It's no coincidence that she's wearing it like that today.

"So, I was thinking we should catch up. Maybe I could come by your house sometime. I miss Caulder; I'd like to see him."

Absolutely not! Hell no! That's what I really want to say. "Vaughn, I don't think that's a good idea," is what I actually say.

"Oh," she says quietly. "Okay."

I can tell I've offended her. "Look, I'm not trying to be rude. It's just . . . you know, we have a lot of history. It wouldn't be fair to Lake."

She cocks her head at me. "*Lake?* Your girlfriend's name is *Lake*?"

I don't like her tone. "Her name is Layken. I call her Lake."

She puts her hand on my arm. "Will, I'm not trying to cause trouble. If Layken is the jealous type, just say so. It's not a big deal."

She grazes her thumb across my arm, and I look down at her hand. I hate how she's trying to undermine my relationship with a snide comment. She always used to do this. She hasn't changed at all. I pull my arm away from her and face the front of the room. "Vaughn, stop. I know what you're doing, and it's not gonna happen."

She huffs and focuses her attention on the front of the room. She's pissed. Good, maybe she got the not so subtle hint.

I really don't understand where she's coming from. I never imagined I would see her again, much less have to practically fight her off. It's strange how I had so much love for her then but feel nothing for her now. I don't regret what I went through with her, though. We did have a pretty good relationship, and I honestly think I would have married her had my parents not passed away. But only because I was naive about what a relationship should be. What *love* should be.

We met when we were freshmen but didn't start dating until our junior year. We hung out at a party I went to with my best friend, Reece. Vaughn and I went out a few times, then agreed to make the relationship exclusive. We dated for about six months before we had sex for the first time. We both still lived at home with our parents, so it ended up being in the backseat of her car. It was awkward, to say the least. We were cramped, it was cold, and it was probably the most unromantic atmosphere a girl could want in that moment. Of course, it got much better over the next year and a half, but I'll always regret that being our first time. Maybe that's why I want Lake's first time to be perfect. Not just another spur-of-the-moment kind of thing like Vaughn and I had.

I was grieving and going through a lot of emotional issues after my relationship with Vaughn ended. Raising Caulder and doubling up on classes didn't leave me any time to date. Vaughn was the last relationship I had up until I met Lake. And after only one date with Lake, I knew the connection between us was something more than I'd had with Vaughn, more than I ever thought I could have with anyone.

At the time Vaughn broke up with me, I thought she was making a huge mistake, telling me she wasn't ready to be a mom to Caulder. She admitted she wasn't ready for that kind of responsibility and I resented her for it. I'm past the resentment now. Seeing how things may have turned out differently had she not made that decision, I'll be forever grateful to her for calling off our relationship when she did.

FRIDAY IS MUCH better. Vaughn doesn't show up to class, so it makes the rest of the day a lot easier. I stop by the store after my last class and grab Kel's birthday present, then head home to get ready for his party.

The only two people Kel and Caulder invited to the party were Kiersten and Abby. Sherry and Kiersten went to pick up Abby while Lake and Eddie left to go get the cake. Gavin showed up with pizza at the same time I pulled into the driveway. It's his night off, but I had him pick it up, since he gets a discount now.

"You nervous?" I ask Caulder as I unstack the pizzas on the counter. I know he's barely eleven, but I remember having my first crush.

"Stop it, Will. You're gonna make tonight my suck if you keep it up," he says.

"Fair enough, I'll drop it. But first I need to lay down some rules. No holding hands until you're at least eleven and a half. No kissing until you're thirteen. And no tongue until you're fourteen. I mean fifteen. Once you get to that point, we'll revisit the rules. Until then, you stick to those."

Caulder rolls his eyes and walks away.

That went well, I guess. Our first official "sex" talk. I think the one I really need to be having the talk with is Kel. He seems a little bit more girl-crazy than Caulder does.

"Who placed the order for this cake?" Lake asks as she walks through the front door carrying it. She doesn't look pleased.

"I let Kel and Caulder order it when we were grocery shopping the other day. Why? What's wrong with it?"

She walks over to the bar and sets the cake down. She opens the lid and stands back so I can see it. "Oh," I say.

The cake is covered in white buttercream frosting. The writing across the top is done in blue.

Happy Butterflying Birthday, Kel

"Well, it's not *really* a bad word," I say.

Lake sighs. "I hate that they're so damn funny," she says. "It's just gonna get harder, you know. We really need to start beating them now, before it's too late." She closes the lid and walks the cake to the refrigerator.

"Tomorrow," I say as I wrap my arms around her from behind. "We can't beat Kel on his birthday." I lean in and kiss her ear.

"Fine." She leans her head to the side, allowing me easier access. "But I get the first punch."

"Stop it!" Kel yells. "You guys can't do that crap tonight. It's my birthday, and I don't want to have to watch y'all make out!"

I let go of Lake and pick Kel up and throw him over my shoulder. "This is for the butterflying cake," I say. I turn his backside toward Layken. "Birthday beating, here's your chance."

Lake starts counting off birthday spankings while Kel fights to get out of my grasp. He's getting stronger. "Put me down, Will!" He's punching me in the back, trying to break free.

I put him down after Lake finishes with the beating. Kel laughs and tries to shove me, but I don't budge.

"I can't wait until I'm bigger than you! I'm gonna kick your butterfly!" He gives up and runs down the hallway to Caulder's room.

Lake is staring down the hallway with a serious expression. "Should we be letting them say that?"

I laugh. "Say what? Butterfly?"

She nods. "Yeah. I mean, it seems like it's already a bad word."

"Would you rather him say 'ass'?" Kiersten says, passing between Lake and me. Again, she's here, and I didn't even hear her knock.

"Hey, Kiersten," Lake says.

There's a young girl following closely behind Kiersten. She looks at Lake and smiles.

"You must be Abby," Lake says. "I'm Layken, this is Will."

Abby gives us a slight wave but doesn't say anything.

"Abby's shy. Give her time, she'll warm up to you,"

Kiersten says. They make their way to the table in the kitchen.

"Is Sherry coming?" Lake says.

"No, probably not. She wants me to bring her some cake, though."

Kel and Caulder run into the kitchen. "There they are," Kiersten says. "How was your week off school, lucky butts?"

"Abby, come here," Caulder says. "I want to show you my room."

After Abby follows Caulder out of the room, I look at Lake, a little concerned. She sees the worry in my eyes and laughs. "Relax, Will. They're only ten. I'm sure he just wants to show her his toys."

Regardless, I walk down the hallway and spy.

"I'm the guest, dork. I should get to be player one," I hear Abby say.

Sure enough, they're just being ten. I go back into the kitchen and wink at Lake.

AFTER THE PARTY is over, Eddie and Gavin agree to take Abby home. Kel and Caulder retreat to Caulder's room to play Kel's new video games. Lake and I are alone in the living room. She's lying on the couch with her feet in my lap. I rub her feet, massaging the tension away. She's been going nonstop all day, getting everything prepared for Kel's party. She's lying with her eyes closed, enjoying the relaxation.

"I have a confession to make," I say, still rubbing her feet.

She reluctantly opens her eyes. "What?"

"I've been counting down the hours in my head until next weekend."

She grins at me, relieved that this is my confession. "So have I. One hundred and sixty-three."

I lean back against the couch and smile at her. "Good, I don't feel so pathetic now."

"It doesn't make you any less pathetic," she says. "It just means we're both pathetic." She sits up and grabs my shirt, pulling me to her. Her lips brush against mine and she whispers, "What are your plans for the next hour or so?"

Her words cause my pulse to race and chills to run down my arms. She touches her cheek to mine and whispers in my ear. "Let's go to my house for a little while. I'll give you a little preview of next weekend."

She doesn't have to ask twice. I pull away from her and jump over the back of the couch and run to the front door. "Boys, we'll be back in a little while! Don't leave!" Lake is still sitting on the couch, so I go over and grab her hands, pulling her up. "Come on, we don't have much time!"

When we get to her house, she shuts the door behind us. I don't even wait until we get to the bedroom. I shove her against the front door and start kissing her. "One hundred and sixty-two," I say between kisses.

"Let's go to the bedroom," she says. "I'll lock the front door. That way, if they come over here, they'll have to knock first." She turns around and latches the dead bolt.

"Good idea," I say. We continue to kiss as we make our way down the hallway. We can't seem to make it very far without one of us ending up against a wall. By the time we get to the bedroom, my shirt's already off.

"Let's do that thing again where the first person to call retreat is the loser," she says. She's kicking off her shoes, so I do the same.

"You're about to lose, then, 'cause I'm not retreating," I say. She knows I'll lose. I always do.

"Neither am I," she says, shaking her head. She pulls her legs up and scoots back onto the bed. I stand at the edge of the bed and take in the view. Sometimes, when I watch her, it seems surreal that she's mine. That she really loves me back. She blows a strand of hair out of her face, then tucks her hair behind her ears and positions herself against the pillow. I slide on top of her and slip my hand behind her neck, gently pulling her lips to mine.

I move slowly as I kiss her, trying to savor every second. We hardly ever get to make out; I don't want to rush it. "I love you so much," I whisper.

She wraps her legs around my waist and tightens her arms around my back in an attempt to pull me in closer. "Spend the night with me, Will. Please? You can come over after the boys go to sleep. They'll never know."

"Lake, it's just one more week. We can make it."

"I don't mean for *that*. We can wait until next weekend. I just want you in my bed tonight. I miss you. Please?"

I continue kissing her neck without responding. I can't say no, so I don't respond at all.

"Don't make me beg, Will. You're so damn responsible sometimes, it makes me feel weak."

I laugh at the thought that she believes *she's* weak. I kiss my way down to the collar of her shirt. "If I spend the night . . . what are you gonna wear?" I slowly unbutton the top button of her shirt and press my lips to her skin.

"Oh my God," she breathes. "I'll wear whatever the hell you *want* me to wear."

I unbutton the next button and move my lips a little lower. "I don't like this shirt. I definitely don't want you to wear this shirt," I say. "In fact, it's a really ugly shirt. I think you should take it off and throw it away." I unbutton the third button, waiting for her to call retreat. I know I'm about to win.

When she doesn't, I continue kissing lower and lower as I unbutton the fourth button, then the fifth button, then the last button. She still doesn't call retreat. She's testing me. I slowly bring my lips back to her mouth, and she rolls me onto my back and straddles me, then slides her shirt off and tosses it aside.

I run my hands up her arms and over the curves of her chest. Her hair has gotten a lot longer since I met her.

It's hanging loosely around her face as she leans over me. I tuck it behind her ears so I can see her face better. It's dark in the room, but I can still make out her smile and the amazing emerald hue of her eyes. I slide my hands back up to her shoulders and trace the outline of her bra. "Wear this tonight." I slide my fingers under the straps. "I like this."

"So does that mean you're staying the night?" she asks. Her tone is more serious. Not so playful.

"If you wear this," I say, being just as serious. She presses her body against mine, our bare skin meeting for the first time in months. I'm definitely not calling retreat. I can't. I'm not usually so weak; I don't know what it is about her right now that's making me so weak.

"Lake." I break my lips apart from hers, though she continues kissing the edges as I speak, short of breath. "It's just a matter of hours until next weekend. It's coming up so fast, in fact, that this weekend can be considered part of the upcoming week. And the upcoming week is part of next weekend. So technically, next weekend is sort of occurring right now . . . this very second."

She grabs my face and positions me so that she can look straight in my eyes. "Will? You better not be saying this because you think I'm about to call retreat, because I'm not. Not this time."

She's serious. I gently roll her onto her back and ease myself on top of her. I stroke her cheek with my thumb.

"You're not? Are you positive you're ready to *not* call retreat? Right now?"

"Positive," she whispers. She wraps her legs tightly around my thighs, and we completely give in to our need for each other. I grab the back of her head and press her mouth into mine even harder. I can feel my pulse rushing through my entire body as we both begin to gasp for air between each kiss, as if we suddenly forgot how to breathe. We're both desperate, doing our best to get past the moment when one of us usually calls retreat. We pass that moment pretty quickly. I reach around to her back until I find the clasp on her bra, and I unhook it while she frantically tugs at the button on my pants. I've pulled the straps of her bra down over her arms to slide it off when the worst thing in the world happens. Someone knocks on the damn door.

"Christ!" I say. My head is spinning so fast, I have to take a moment to calm down. I press my forehead into the pillow next to her, and we try to catch our breath.

She slides out from under me and stands up. "Will, I can't find my shirt," she says with panic in her voice.

I roll onto my back and pull her shirt out from beneath me and toss it to her. "Here's your ugly shirt," I tease.

The boys are beating on the door now, so I hop out of the bed and go down the hallway to find my own shirt before opening the front door for them.

"What took you so long?" Kel asks as they shove their way past me.

"We were watching a movie," I lie. "We were at a really good part and didn't want to pause it."

"Yeah," Lake agrees, emerging from the hallway. "A *really* good part."

Kel and Caulder walk to the kitchen, and Kel flips the light on. "Can Caulder stay here tonight?" he asks.

"I don't know why you guys even bother asking anymore," Lake says.

"Because we're grounded. Remember?" Caulder says.

Lake looks to me for assistance.

"It's your birthday, Kel. The grounding can resume tomorrow night," I say. They go to the living room and turn on the TV.

I reach out to Lake. "Walk me home?" Lake grabs my hand, and we head out the front door.

"Are you coming back over later?" she asks.

Now that I've had the chance to cool off, I can see that coming back might not be a good idea. "Lake, maybe I shouldn't. We got really carried away just now. How do you expect me to sleep in the same bed with you after that?"

I expect her to object, but she doesn't.

"You're right, like always. It'd be weird, anyway, with our brothers in the house." She wraps her arms around me when we reach my front door. It's incredibly cold outside, but she doesn't seem to care as we stand there. "Or maybe you're wrong," she says. "Maybe you should come back in an hour. I'll wear the ugliest pajamas I can find, and I won't even brush my teeth. You won't want to touch me. All we'll do is sleep."

I laugh at her absurd plan. "You could go a week without brushing your teeth or changing clothes, and I still wouldn't be able to keep my hands off you."

"I'm serious, Will. Come back in an hour. I just want to cuddle with you. I'll make sure the boys are in their room, and you can sneak in like we're in high school."

She doesn't have to do much convincing. "Fine. I'll be back in an hour. But all we're doing is sleeping, okay? No tempting me."

"No tempting, I promise," she says with a grin.

I cup her chin in my hand and lower my voice. "Lake, I'm serious. I want this to be perfect for you, and I get really carried away when I'm with you. We only have a week left. I want to stay the night with you, but I need you to promise me you won't put me in that position again for at least a hundred and sixty-two more hours."

"One hundred sixty-one and a half," she says.

I shake my head and laugh. "Go put those boys to bed. I'll see you in a little while."

She kisses me goodbye, and I head into the house and take a shower. A *cold* shower.

When I get to her house an hour later, all the lights are off. I lock the door behind me and ease down the hallway and into her bedroom. She left the bedside lamp on for me. She's lying in bed with her back toward me, so I climb in behind her and slide my arm under her head. I expect her to respond, but she's out. She's actually snoring. I brush her hair behind her ear and kiss the back of her head as I pull the covers around us both and close my eyes.

5.

I love being with you so bad
When we aren't together, I miss you so bad
One of these days, I'm going to marry you so bad
And it'll be
so
so
good.

LAKE WAS UPSET WHEN SHE WOKE UP SATURDAY MORN-ing and I was already gone. She says it wasn't fair that she slept through our entire first sleepover. Regardless, I enjoyed it. I watched her sleep for a while before I went back home.

We didn't get into any more situations like the one in her bedroom Friday night. I think we were both surprised by how intense things got, so we're trying to keep it from happening again. Until this coming weekend, anyway. Saturday, we spent the evening at Joel's with Eddie and Gavin. Sunday, Lake and I did homework together. Pretty typical weekend.

Now I'm sitting here in Death and Dying, being stared down by the only person I've ever had sex with. It's awkward. The way Vaughn is acting, I feel like I really *am* hiding something from Lake. But telling her about Vaughn now would just prove that I wasn't being completely honest the first week of school. The last thing I want to do before this weekend is upset Lake, so I decide to wait another week before I bring it up.

"Vaughn, the professor is up there," I say, pointing to the front of the room.

Vaughn continues to stare at me. "Will, you're being a snob," she whispers. "I don't understand why you won't just talk to me. If you were really over what happened between us, it wouldn't bother you this much."

I can't believe she honestly thinks I'm not over us. I've been over us since the day I first laid eyes on Lake. "I'm over us, Vaughn. It's been three years. You're over us, too. You just always want what you can't have, and it's pissing you off. It's got nothing to do with me."

She folds her arms across her chest and sits back in her chair. "You think I *want* you?" She glares at me, then turns her attention to the front of the room. "Has anyone ever told you that you're an asshole?" she whispers.

I laugh. "As a matter of fact, yes. More than once."

* * *

TODAY HAS BEEN Kel and Caulder's first day back to school since their suspension. After school, they climb in the car with defeated expressions. I eye the books spilling out of their backpacks and realize it's going to be a night full of catching up on homework for the two of them. "I guess you guys learned your lesson," I say.

Lake is walking out of my house when the boys and I get out of the car. It doesn't bother me at all that she's at my house when I'm not home, but I'm a little curious about what she was doing. She sees the confusion on my face as she walks toward me. She holds out her hand and reveals one of the stars that her mother made, resting in her palm.

"Don't judge me," she says. She rolls the star around in her hand. "I just miss her today."

The look on her face makes me sad for her. I give her a quick hug, then watch her walk across the street and go back inside her house. She's in need of alone time, so I give it to her. "Kel, stay over here for a while. I'll help you guys with all your homework."

It takes us a couple of hours to finish the assignments that piled up while the boys were suspended. Gavin and Eddie are supposed to come over for dinner tonight, so I head to the kitchen to start cooking. We're not having burgers tonight. I'm sure we'll never have burgers again. I debate whether or not I want to make basagna but decide against it. Honestly, I don't feel like cooking. I go to the fridge and slide the Chinese menu out from under the magnet.

Half an hour later, Eddie and Gavin show up, followed a minute later by Lake, then the Chinese delivery guy. I set the containers in the middle of the table, and we all start filling our plates.

"We're in the middle of a game. Can we eat in my room tonight?" Caulder asks.

"Sure," I say.

"I thought they were grounded," Gavin says.

"They are," Lake replies.

Gavin takes a bite of his egg roll. "They're playing video games. What exactly are they grounded from, then?"

Lake looks to me for assistance. I don't know the answer, but I try anyway. "Gavin, are you questioning our parenting skills?" I ask.

"Nope," Gavin says. "Not at all."

There's a weird vibe tonight. Eddie is extremely quiet as she picks at her food. Gavin and I try to make small talk, but that doesn't last long. Lake seems to be in her own little world, not paying much attention to what's going on. I try to break the tension. "Suck-and-sweet time," I say. Almost simultaneously, all three of them object.

"What's going on?" I ask. "What's with all the depression tonight?" No one answers me. Eddie and Gavin look at each other. Eddie looks like she's about to cry, so Gavin kisses her on the forehead. I look over at Lake, who's just staring down at her plate, twirling her noodles around. "What about you, babe? What's wrong?" I say to her.

"Nothing. Really, it's nothing," she says, unsuccessfully trying to convince me she's fine. She smiles at me and grabs both of our glasses and goes to the kitchen to refill them.

"Sorry, Will," Gavin says. "Eddie and I aren't trying to be rude. We've just got a lot on our minds lately."

"No problem," I say. "Anything I can do to help?"

They shake their heads. "You going to the slam Thursday night?" Gavin asks, changing the subject.

We haven't been in a few weeks. Since before Christmas, I think. "I don't know, I guess we could." I turn to Lake. "You want to?"

She shrugs. "Sounds fun. We'll have to see if someone can watch Kel and Caulder, though."

Eddie clears the table while Gavin puts his jacket on. "We'll see you there, then. Thanks for supper. We won't suck so much next time."

"It's fine," I say. "Everyone's entitled to a bad day every now and then."

After they leave, I close the take-out containers and put them in the refrigerator while Lake washes our dishes. I walk over to her and hug her. "You sure you're okay?" I ask.

She turns around and hugs me back, laying her head against my chest. "I'm fine, Will. It's just . . ."

I lift her face to mine and see that she's trying to hold back tears. I place my hand on the back of her head and pull her to me. "What's wrong?"

She quietly cries into my shirt. I can tell she's trying to stop herself. I wish she wouldn't be so hard on herself when she gets sad.

"It's just today," she says. "It's their anniversary."

I realize she's talking about her mom and dad, so I don't say anything. I just hug her tighter and kiss the top of her head.

"I know it's silly that I'm upset. I'm mostly upset about the fact that it's making me so upset," she says.

I place my hands on her cheeks and pull her gaze to mine. "It's not silly, Lake. It's okay to cry sometimes."

She smiles and kisses me, then breaks away. "I'm going shopping with Eddie tomorrow night. Wednesday night I have a study group, so I won't see you until Thursday. Are you getting a sitter, or should I?"

"Do you really think they need one? Kel's eleven now, and Caulder will be eleven in two months. Don't you think they can stay home by themselves for a few hours?"

She nods. "I guess so. Maybe I'll ask Sherry if she'll at least feed them supper and check on them. I could give her some money."

"I like that idea," I say.

She calls for Kel after she gets her jacket and shoes on, then walks back to the kitchen and puts her arms around me. "Ninety-three more hours," she says, planting a kiss on my neck. "I love you."

"Listen to me," I say as I look her intently in the eyes. "It's okay to be sad, Lake. Quit trying to carve so many pumpkins. And I love you, too." I kiss her one last time and lock the door behind them when they leave.

Tonight was really strange. The whole vibe seemed off. Since we're going to the slam, I decide to try to put my thoughts down on paper. I'll surprise Lake and do one for her this week. Maybe it'll help her feel better.

FOR REASONS BEYOND my comprehension, Vaughn sits next to me again on Wednesday. You would think after our little tiff on Monday that she would have given up. I was hoping she would have, anyway.

She pulls out her notebook and opens her textbook to where we left off Monday. She doesn't stare at me this time. In fact, she doesn't speak at all during the entire class period. I'm happy she's not talking to me, but at the same time I feel a little guilty for being so rude to her. Not guilty enough to apologize about it. She did deserve it.

As we're packing up our things up, still not speaking, she slides something across the table to me, then walks out. I debate throwing the note in the trash without reading it, but my curiosity gets the better of me. I wait until I'm seated in my next class to open it.

Will,

You may not want to hear this, but I need to say it. I'm really sorry. Breaking up with you is one of my biggest regrets in life so far. Especially breaking up with you when I did. It wasn't fair to you, I realize that now—but I was young and I was scared.

You can't act like what we had between us was nothing. I loved you, and I know you loved me. You at least owe me the courtesy of talking to me. I just want the chance to apologize to you in person. I can't seem to let go of how things ended between us. Let me apologize.

Vaughn

I fold the note and put it in my pocket, then lay my head down on the desk and sigh. She's not going to let it go. I don't want to think about it right now, so I don't. I'll worry about it later.

THE NEXT NIGHT, I don't think about anything other than Lake.

I'm picking her up in an hour, so I rush through my homework and head to the shower. I walk past Caulder's bedroom on my way. He and Kel are playing video games.

"Why can't we go with you? You said yourself there wasn't an age limit," Kel says.

I pause and back-step to their doorway. "You guys actually want to go? You realize it's poetry, right?"

"I like poetry," Caulder says.

"Not me," Kel says. "I just want to go 'cause we never get to go anywhere."

"Fine, let me make sure it's okay with Lake first." I head out the front door and across the street. When I open the door to her house, she screams.

"Will! Turn around!" I turn around, but not before I see her. She must have just gotten out of the shower, because she's standing in the living room completely naked. "Oh my God, I thought I locked the door. Doesn't anyone knock?"

I laugh. "Welcome to my world."

"You can turn around now," she says.

When I turn around, she's wrapped in a towel. I wrap my arms around her waist, pick her up off the floor, and spin her around. "Twenty-four more hours," I say as her feet touch the floor again. "You nervous yet?"

"Nope, not at all. Like I said before, I'm in good hands."

I want to kiss her, but I don't. The towel is too much, so I back away and ask what I came here to ask her. "Kel and Caulder want to know if it's okay if they go with us tonight. They're curious."

"Really? That's weird . . . but I don't care if you don't care," she says.

"Okay, then. I'll tell them." I head toward the door. "And Lake? Thanks for giving me another preview."

She looks slightly embarrassed, so I wink at her and shut her front door behind me. This is about to be the longest twenty-four hours of my life.

WE TAKE A seat in the back of the club with Gavin and Eddie. It's the same booth where Lake and I sat on our first date. Kiersten wanted to come, too, so it's a tight fit.

Sherry must trust us a lot, although she did ask a lot of questions before she agreed to let Kiersten come. By the end of the question/answer session, Sherry was intrigued. She said it would be good for Kiersten to see a slam. Kiersten said doing a slam would be good for her portfolio, so she brought a pen and a notebook to take notes.

"All right, who's thirsty?" I take drink orders and head to the bar before the sacrifice is brought onstage to perform. I explained the rules to all the kids on the way here, so I think they have a pretty good understanding. I haven't told them I'm performing, though. I want it to be a surprise. Lake doesn't know, either, so before I take the drinks back to the table, I go pay my fee.

"This is so cool," Kiersten says when I get back to the booth. "You guys are the coolest parents ever."

"No, they aren't," Kel says. "They don't let us cuss."

Lake hushes them as the first performer steps up to

the microphone. I recognize the guy; I've seen him perform here a lot. He's really good. I put my arm around Lake, and he begins his poem.

"My name is Edmund Davis-Quinn, and this is a piece I wrote called 'Write Poorly.' "

Write poorly.

Suck

Write *awful*

Terribly

Frightfully

Don't *care*

Turn off the inner editor

Let yourself *write*

Let it *flow*

Let yourself *fail*

Do something *crazy*

Write fifty thousand words in the month of November.

I did it.

It was *fun,* it was *insane,* it was *one thousand six hundred and sixty-seven words a day.*

It was *possible.*

But you have to turn off your inner critic.

Off completely.

Just *write.*

Quickly.

In *bursts.*

With *joy.*

If you can't write, run away for a few.

Come *back.*

Write *again.*

Writing is like anything else.

You won't get good at it immediately.

It's a craft, you have to keep getting better.

You don't get to Juilliard unless you practice.

If you want to get to Carnegie Hall, *practice,*

practice, practice.

. . . Or give them a lot of money.

Like anything else, it takes ten thousand hours to

get to mastery.

Just like Malcolm Gladwell says.

So *write.*

Fail.

Get your *thoughts* down.

Let it *rest.*

Let it *marinate.*

Then edit.

But don't edit as you type,

that just slows the brain down.

Find a daily practice,

for me it's blogging every day.

And it's *fun.*

The *more* you write, the *easier* it gets. The more it is

a *flow,* the less a *worry.* It's not for *school,* it's not for a

grade, it's just to get your thoughts *out there.*

You *know* they want to come *out*.

So *keep at it*. Make it a practice. And write *poorly*,

write *awfully*, write with *abandon* and it may

end up being

really

really

good.

When the crowd starts cheering, I glance at Kiersten and the boys. They're just staring at the stage. "Holy shit," Kiersten says. "This is awesome. That was incredible."

"Why are you only now bringing us here, Will? This is so cool!" Caulder says.

I'm surprised they all seem to like it as much as they do. They're relatively quiet the rest of the night as they watch the performers. Kiersten keeps writing in her notebook. I'm not sure what kind of notes she's taking, but I can see she's really into it. I make a mental note to give her some of my older poems later.

"Next up, Will Cooper," the emcee says. Everyone at the table looks at me, surprised.

"Are you doing one?" Lake says. I smile at her and nod as I stand and walk away from the table.

I used to get nervous when I performed. A small part of me still does, but I think it's more the adrenaline rush than anything. The first time I ever came here was with my father. He was very into the arts. Music, poetry, painting, reading, writing, all of it. I saw him perform here the first time when I was fifteen. I've been hooked since. I hate that Caulder never got to know that side of him. I've kept as much of our dad's writings as I could find, even a couple of old paintings. Someday I'll give them all to Caulder. Someday when he's old enough to appreciate them.

I take the stage and adjust the microphone. My poem isn't going to make sense to anyone besides Lake. This one's just for her.

"My piece is called 'Point of Retreat,'" I say into the microphone. The spotlight is bright, so I can't see her from up here, but I have a pretty good idea that she's smiling. I don't rush the poem. I perform slowly so she can take in every word.

Twenty-two hours and our war *begins.*
Our war of *limbs*
and *lips*
and *hands* . . .
The point of *retreat*
Is no longer a *factor*
When both sides of the line
Agree to *surrender.*
I can't *tell* you how many times I've *lost* . . .
Or is it how many times you've *won*?
This game we've been playing for fifty-nine weeks
I'd say the score
is
none

to

none.

Twenty-two hours and our war ***begins***

Our war of ***limbs***

and ***lips***

and ***hands* . . .**

The best part of finally

Not calling retreat?

The ***showers*** above us

Raining down on our feet

Before the ***bombs explode*** and the ***guns*** fire their

rounds. Before the ***two*** of us ***collapse*** to the ***ground.***

Before the ***battle,*** before the ***war* . . .**

You need to ***know***

I'd go fifty-nine ***more.***

Whatever it ***takes*** to let you ***win.***

I'd retreat ***all over***

and ***all over***

and ***over***

again.

I back away from the microphone and find the stairs. I'm not even halfway back to the booth when Lake throws her arms around my neck and kisses me. "Thank you," she whispers in my ear.

When I slide into the booth, Caulder rolls his eyes. "You could have warned us, Will. We would have hidden in the bathroom."

"I thought it was beautiful," Kiersten says.

It's after nine when round two gets under way. "Come on, kids, you guys have school tomorrow. We need to go," I say. They whine as they slide out of the booth one by one.

ONCE WE GET home, the kids head into the houses, and Lake and I linger in the driveway, hugging. It's getting harder and harder to separate from her at night, knowing she's just yards away. It's become a nightly struggle not to text her and beg her to come crawl in bed with me. Now that our promise to Julia has been fulfilled, I have a feeling nothing will stop us after tomorrow night. Well, other than the fact that we're trying to set a good example for Kel and Caulder. But there are ways to sneak around that.

I slide my hands up the back of her shirt to warm them. She begins to squirm, trying to get out of my grasp. "Your hands are freezing!" she says, laughing.

I just squeeze her tighter. "I know. That's why you need to be still, so I can warm them up." I rub them against her skin, attempting to keep the images of tomorrow night from overtaking my thoughts. They're distracting, so I remove my hands from her shirt and wrap my arms around her.

"Do you want the good news or the bad news first?" I ask her.

She shoots me a dirty look. "Do you want me to punch you in the face or the nuts?"

I laugh but prepare to defend myself just in case. "My grandparents are worried the boys will get bored at their house, so they want to keep them at my house instead. The good news is, we can't stay at your house now, so I booked two nights at a hotel in Detroit."

"That's not bad news. Don't scare me like that," she says.

"I just thought you would be a little apprehensive about seeing my grandmother. I know how you feel about her."

She looks at me and frowns. "Don't, Will. You know good and well it's not how *I* feel about *her*. She hates me!"

"She doesn't hate you," I say. "She's just protective of me." I try to push the thought out of her mind by kissing her ear.

"It's your fault she hates me, anyway."

I pull back and look at her. "My fault? How is it my fault?"

She rolls her eyes. "Your graduation? You don't remember what you said the first night I met her?"

I don't remember. I don't know what she's talking about. Nothing comes to mind.

"Will, we were all *over* each other. After your graduation, when we all went out to eat, you could barely talk, you were kissing me so much. It was making your grandmother really uncomfortable. When she asked you how long we'd been dating, you told her eighteen hours! How do you think that made me look?"

I remember now. That dinner was really fun. It felt great not to be ethically bound from putting my hands all over her, so that was all I did all night long.

"But it's sort of true," I say. "We were only officially dating for eighteen hours."

Lake hits me on the arm. "She thinks I'm a slut, Will! It's embarrassing!"

I touch my lips against her ear again. "Not yet you're not," I tease.

She pushes me away and points to herself. "You aren't getting any more of this for twenty-four hours." She laughs and starts to walk backward up her driveway.

"Twenty-one," I correct her.

She reaches the front door and turns and goes inside without so much as a good-night kiss. What a tease! She's not getting the upper hand tonight. I run up the driveway and open her front door and pull her back outside. I push her against the brick wall of the entryway and look her in the eyes as I press my body against hers. She's trying to look mad, but I can see the corner of her mouth break into a smile. Our hands interlock, and I bring them over her head and press them against the wall. "Listen to me very carefully," I whisper. I continue to stare into her eyes. She listens. She likes it when I try to intimidate her. "I don't want you to pack a damn thing. I want you to wear exactly what you were wearing last Friday night. Do you still have that ugly shirt?"

She smiles and nods. I'm not sure she could speak right now if she wanted to.

"Good. What you're wearing when we leave tomorrow night is the only thing you're allowed to bring. No pajamas, no extra clothes. Nothing. I want you to meet me at my house at seven o'clock tomorrow night. Do you understand?"

She nods again. Her pulse is racing against my chest, and I can tell from the look in her eyes that she needs me to kiss her. My hands remain clasped with hers against the wall as I move my mouth closer to her lips. I hesitate at the last minute and decide not to kiss her. I slowly drop her hands and back away from her, then head to my house. When I reach the front door, I turn around. She's still leaning against the brick in the same position. Good. I got the upper hand this time.

6.

Lake will never read my journal, so I should say what's really on my mind, right? Even if she does read this, it'll be after I'm dead, when she's sorting through my things. So technically, maybe one day she will read this. But it won't matter by then, 'cause I'll be dead.

So, Lake . . . if you're reading this . . . I'm sorry I'm dead.

But for right now, in this moment, I am so alive. So very much alive. Tonight is the night. It's been worth the wait. All fifty-nine weeks of it. (Over seventy if you count from our first date.)

I'll just say what's on my mind, okay?

Sex.

Sex, sex, sex. I'm having sex tonight. Making love. Butterflying. Whatever you want to call it, we'll be doing it.

And I can't freaking wait.

I WANT TODAY TO BE PERFECT, SO I DECIDE TO SKIP school, clean the house, and finalize the plans before my grandparents arrive. I can't believe how nervous I am. Or maybe it's excitement; I don't know what it is. I just know I want the day to hurry the hell up.

On the way home from picking the boys up at school, we stop at the store to get a few things for dinner. Lake and I don't have plans to leave until seven, so I text my grandfather and tell them I'm making basagna. Julia said to wait for a good day to make it again, and it's definitely a good day. I'm running behind when I see their headlights through the living room window. I haven't even showered yet, and I still need to cook the bread sticks.

"Caulder, Grandma and Grandpa are here, go open the door!"

He doesn't need to—they open the door anyway. Without knocking, of course. My grandmother walks through the door first, so I go over and kiss her on the cheek.

"Hi, sweetie," she says. "What smells so good?"

"Basagna." I walk to my grandfather and give him a hug.

"*Basagna?*" she says.

I shake my head and laugh. "Lasagna, I mean."

My grandmother smiles, and it reminds me of my mom. She and my grandfather are both tall and thin, just like my mom. A lot of people find my grandmother intimidating, but I find it hard to be intimidated by her. I've spent so much time with her, I sometimes feel like she's my own mother.

My grandfather sets their bags down by the front door, and they follow me into the kitchen. "Will, have you heard of this *Twitter*?" He brings his glasses to the edge of his nose and looks down at his phone.

My grandmother looks at me and shakes her head. "He got one of those intelligent phones. Now he's trying to twit the president."

"Smart phones," I correct her. "And it's tweet, not twit."

"He follows me," my grandfather says defensively. "I'm not kidding, he really does! I got a message yesterday that said, 'The president is now following you.' "

"That's cool, Grandpa. But no, I don't tweet."

"Well, you should. A young man your age needs to stay ahead of the game when it comes to the social media."

"I'll be fine," I assure him. I put the bread sticks in the oven and start to grab plates out of the cabinet.

"Let me do that, Will," my grandmother says, pulling the plates out of my hands.

"Hey, Grandma, hey, Grandpa," Caulder says, running into the kitchen to hug them. "Grandpa, do you remember the game we played last time you were here?"

My grandfather nods. "You mean the one where I killed twenty-six enemy soldiers?"

"Yeah, that one. Kel got the newest one for his birthday. You want to play it with us?"

"You bet I do!" he says, following Caulder to his bedroom.

The funny thing is, my grandfather isn't being over-dramatic for Caulder's benefit. He genuinely wants to play.

My grandmother pulls a stack of glasses out of the cabinet and turns to me. "He's getting worse, you know," she says.

"How so?"

"He bought himself one of those game thingies. He's getting all into this technology stuff. Now he's on the Twitter!" She shakes her head. "He's always telling me things he twitted to people. I don't get it, Will. It's like some sort of midlife crisis, twenty years too late."

"It's tweeted. And I think it's cool. It gives him and Caulder a way to relate."

She fills the glasses with ice and walks back to the bar. "Should I set a place for Layken, too?" she says flatly. I can tell by her tone that she's hoping I'll say no.

"Yes, you should," I say sternly.

She darts a look in my direction. "Will, I'm just going to say it."

Oh boy, here we go.

"It's not appropriate, the two of you running off for the weekend like this. You aren't even engaged yet, much less married. I just think you two have rushed into things so quickly. It makes me nervous."

I put my hands on my grandmother's shoulders and smile reassuringly at her. "Grandma, we aren't rushing into things, believe me. And you need to give her a chance; she's amazing. Promise me you'll at least pretend to like her when she gets here. And be nice!"

She sighs. "It's not that I don't like her, Will. It just makes me uncomfortable, the way you two act together. It seems like you're . . . I don't know . . . too in love."

"If your only complaint is that we're too in love, I guess I'll take it."

She brings an extra place setting to the table for Lake.

"I still need to jump in the shower, it won't take long," I say. "The bread sticks should be done in a few minutes, if you'll take them out."

She agrees, and I head to my room to pack a few things before going to shower. I reach under the bed to grab my bag and set it on the comforter. When I zip it open, I notice my hands are shaking. Why the hell am I so nervous? It's not like I've never done this before. Then again, it's *Lake.* I realize as I'm shoving the last of my clothes into the bag that I'm grinning like a complete idiot.

I've grabbed my change of clothes and headed to the bathroom when I hear a knock on the front door. I smile. Lake is trying to impress my grandmother, so she's knocked this time. It's cute. She's making an effort.

"Oh my God! Look who it is!" I hear my grandmother squeal after she opens the front door. "Paul! Come look who's here!"

I roll my eyes. I know I asked her to be polite to Lake, but I didn't expect her to make a spectacle. I open the door and head for the living room. Lake will be pissed if I leave her to fend for herself while I shower.

Shit! Shit, shit, shit! What the hell is she doing here?

She's hugging my grandfather when she sees me standing in the hallway. "Hey, Will." She smiles.

I don't smile back.

"Vaughn, we haven't seen you in years," my grandmother says. "Stay for dinner, it's almost ready. I'll make you a plate."

"No!" I yell, probably a little too angrily.

My grandmother turns toward me and frowns. "Will, that's not very nice," she says.

I ignore her. "Vaughn? Can I talk to you, please?" I motion for her to join me in the bedroom. I need to get rid of her now. "What are you doing here?"

She sits down on the edge of the bed. "I told you, I just need to talk to you." She's got her blond hair pulled back in a bun again. She's looking at me all doe-eyed, trying to gain my sympathy.

"Vaughn, it's really not a good time."

She folds her arms over her chest and shakes her head. "I'm not leaving until you talk to me. All you've done is avoid me."

"I can't talk right now, I'm leaving in half an hour. I've got a lot I need to get done, and I won't be back until Monday. I'll talk to you after class on Wednesday. Just please *leave*."

She doesn't move. She looks down at her hands and

starts crying. Good God, she's crying! I throw my hands up in frustration and walk over to the bed and sit beside her. This is horrible. This is so bad.

We're in almost the same predicament that we were three years ago. We were sitting on this very bed when she broke up with me. She said she couldn't imagine being nineteen and raising a child and having such big responsibilities. I was so upset with her for leaving me during the lowest point in my life. I'm almost as upset with her now, but this time it's because she *won't* leave.

"Will, I miss you. I miss Caulder. Since I saw you the first day of class, I've done nothing but think about you and how we ended things. I was wrong. Please hear me out."

I sigh and throw myself back on the bed and cover my eyes with my arms. She could not have picked a worse time. Lake's going to be here in less than fifteen minutes. "Fine, talk. Make it quick," I say.

She clears her throat and wipes her eyes. It's odd how I don't care that she's crying. How can I love someone so much for so long, then have absolutely no sympathy for her whatsoever?

"I know you have a girlfriend. But I also know that you haven't been dating her nearly as long as you and I dated. And I know about her parents and that she's raising her brother. People talk, Will."

"What's your point?" I say.

"I think maybe you're with her for all the wrong

reasons. Maybe you feel sorry for her since she's going through what you went through with your family. It's not fair to her if that's why you're with her. I think you owe it to her to give you and me another shot. To see where your heart really is."

I sit up on the bed. I want to yell at her, but I take a deep breath and calm myself down. I feel sorry for her. "Vaughn, listen. You're right, I did love you. 'Did' being the key word here. I'm in love with Lake. I would never do anything to hurt her. And you being here, it would hurt her. That's why I want you to leave. I'm sorry, I know this isn't what you want to hear. But you made your choice, and I've moved on from that choice. Now you need to move on, too. Please do us both a favor and just go."

I stand beside the bedroom door and wait for her to do the same. She stands, but rather than following me to the door, she starts to cry again. I roll my head and walk over to her. "Vaughn, stop. Stop crying. I'm sorry," I say, putting my arms around her. Maybe I've been too hard on her. I know it took a lot for her to come here and apologize. If she does still love me, I shouldn't be acting like such a jerk due to her bad timing.

She pulls away. "It's fine, Will. I'm okay with it. I shouldn't be putting you in this predicament. I just hated how I hurt you, and I wanted to say I'm sorry in person. I'll go," she says. "And . . . I really do want you to be happy. You deserve to be happy."

I can tell by her tone of voice and the look in her eyes that she's being genuine. Finally. I know she's a good person; otherwise, I wouldn't have spent two years of my life with her. But I also know the selfish side of her, and I'm thankful that side didn't win tonight.

I brush the hair away from her face and wipe the tears from her cheeks. "Thank you, Vaughn."

She smiles and hugs me goodbye. I'll admit, it feels good having closure between us. I feel like I've had my own closure for a while, but maybe this is what she needs. Maybe being in class with her won't be so unbearable now. I give her a quick peck on the forehead when we separate, and I turn to the door.

And that's when it happens: My whole world comes crashing down around me.

Lake is standing in the doorway watching us, her mouth open as if she's about to say something but can't. Caulder brushes past her when he sees Vaughn standing behind me. "Vaughn!" he says excitedly, rushing to her and hugging her.

Lake looks into my eyes, and I see it—I see her heart breaking.

I can't find words. Lake slowly shakes her head, clearly trying to make sense of what she's seeing. She pulls her gaze away from mine and turns and leaves. I run after her, but she's already out the front door. I slip my shoes on and swing the door open.

"Lake!" I yell as soon as I'm outside. I reach her as she makes it to the street. I grab her arm and turn her to face me. I don't know what to say. What can I say?

She's crying. I try to pull her to me, but she fights. She shoves me backward and starts hitting me in the chest without saying a word. I grab her hands and pull her to me, but she continues to try to hit me. I keep holding her until she grows weaker in my arms and starts to fall to the ground. Rather than hold her up, I melt to the snow-covered street with her and hold her as she cries.

"Lake, it's nothing. I swear. It's nothing."

"I *saw* you, Will. I saw you hugging her. It wasn't nothing," she cries. "You kissed her on the forehead! Why would you *do* that?" She isn't trying to hold back her tears this time.

"I'm sorry, Lake. I'm so sorry. It didn't mean anything. I was asking her to leave."

She pulls away from me and stands and walks toward her house. I follow her. "Lake, let me explain. *Please.*"

She continues inside the house and slams the door in my face . . . and locks it. I place my hands on both sides of the doorframe and hang my head. I've screwed up again. I've really screwed up this time.

"Will, I'm so sorry," Vaughn says from behind me. "I didn't mean to cause problems."

I don't turn around when I respond. "Vaughn, just go. Please."

"Okay," she says. "One more thing, though. I know

you don't want to hear this right now, but you weren't in class today. He assigned our first test for Wednesday. I copied my notes for you and put them on your coffee table. I'll see you on Wednesday." I hear the crunch of the snow beneath her feet fading as she walks back to her car.

The lock unlatches, and Lake slowly opens her front door. She pulls it open just far enough so that I can see her face when she looks me in the eyes. "She's in your *class*?" she says quietly.

I don't respond. My whole body flinches when she slams the door in my face. She doesn't only lock it this time, she dead bolts it and turns off the outside light. I lean against the door and close my eyes, doing my best to hold back my own tears.

"HONEY, IT'S FINE. We're taking the box with us; that way they won't be bored. We don't mind, really," my grand-mother says as they pack their things in the car.

"It's not a box, Grandma, it's an Xbox," Caulder says. He and Kel climb into the backseat.

"Now, you go get some rest. You've had enough stress for one night," she says to me. She leans in and kisses me on the cheek. "You can pick them up on Monday."

My grandfather hugs me before he gets in the car. "If you need to talk, you can tweet me," he says.

I watch as they drive away. Rather than go inside and get some rest, I walk back to Lake's house and knock on the door, hoping she's ready to talk. I knock for five minutes, until I see her bedroom light turn off. I give up for the night and go back to my house. I leave the front light on and the door unlocked, in case she changes her mind and wants to talk. I also decide to sleep on the couch instead of in my bedroom. If she knocks, I want to be able to hear it. I lie there for half an hour, cussing myself. I can't believe this is happening right now. This isn't how I'd envisioned falling asleep tonight at all. I blame the damn basagna.

I jerk up when the front door opens and she walks in. She doesn't look at me as she continues across the living room. She stops at the bookshelf and reaches inside the vase and pulls out a star, then turns and goes back to the front door.

"Lake, wait," I plead. She slams the door behind her. I get off the couch and run outside after her. "Please let me come over. Let me explain everything." We cross the street. She keeps walking until she gets to her front door, then turns to face me.

"How are you going to explain it?" she says. Her cheeks are streaked with mascara. She's heartbroken, and it's all my fault. "The one girl you've had sex with has been sitting in class with you every day for over two weeks! Why haven't you explained *that*? And the very night I'm about to leave with you . . . to make *love* to you . . . I find you in your bedroom with her? And you're kissing her on the freaking forehead!"

She starts crying again, so I hug her. I have to; I can't

watch her cry and not hug her. She doesn't hug me back. She pulls away from me and looks up at me with pain in her eyes.

"That's the one kiss of yours that I love the most, and you gave it to her," she says. "You took that from me and gave it to *her*! Thank you for allowing me to see the *real* you before making the biggest mistake of my life!" She slams the door, then opens it again. "And where the *hell* is my brother?"

"In Detroit," I whisper. "He'll be back Monday."

She slams the door again.

I've turned to head back to my house when Sherry appears out of nowhere. "Is everything okay? I heard Layken yelling."

I pass her without responding and slam my own door. I don't do it hard enough, so I open it and slam it again. I do this two or three more times until I realize I'll have to pay for it when it breaks. I shut the door and punch it. I am an asshole. I'm an asshole, a jerk, a bastard, a dickhead . . . I give up and throw myself on the couch.

When Lake cries, it breaks my heart. But the fact that her tears are because of me? That my own actions are responsible for her heart breaking? That's a whole new emotion for me. One I don't know how to deal with. I don't know what to do. I don't know what I can say to her. If she would just let me explain. But that wouldn't help at this point. She's right. She didn't accuse me of anything I didn't actually do. God, I need my dad right now. I need his advice so bad.

Advice! I go to the vase and pull out one of the stars. I sit down on the couch and unfold it and read the words handwritten across it.

Sometimes two people have to fall apart to realize how much they need to fall back together.
—AUTHOR UNKNOWN

I fold the star and place it back inside the vase on the very top. I'm hoping Lake picks this one next.

7.

FML.

I DIDN'T GET ANY SLEEP AT ALL LAST NIGHT. EVERY SIN-gle noise I heard bolted me right off the couch in the hope that it was Lake. It never was.

I put on a pot of coffee and walk to the window. Her house is quiet; the shades are all drawn. Her car is in the driveway, so I know she's home. I'm so used to seeing the gnomes lining the driveway next to her car. They aren't there anymore. After her mother died, Lake gathered all the gnomes and threw them in the trash. She doesn't know it, but I dug one out and kept it. The one with the broken red hat.

I remember walking out of my house the morning after they moved here and seeing Lake dart out the front door with no jacket, in house shoes. I knew as soon as those shoes hit the pavement, she was going to bust her butt. Sure enough, she did. I couldn't help but laugh. Southerners seem to underestimate the power of cold weather.

I hated that she had cut herself when she landed on the gnome, but I was so happy to have the excuse to spend those few minutes with her. After I put the bandage on her and she left, I spent the entire day at work in a daze. I couldn't stop thinking about her. I was so nervous that my life and responsibilities would scare her off before I got the chance to know her. I didn't want to tell her everything right away, but the night of our first date, I knew I had to. There was something about her that was so much more than all the other girls I'd known. She had this resiliency and confidence.

I wanted to be sure Lake knew what my life was about that night. I wanted her to know about my parents, about Caulder, about my passion. I needed her to know the real me and understand who I was before we took it any further. When she watched her first performance that night, I couldn't take my eyes off her. I saw the passion and depth as she watched the stage, and I fell in love with her. I've loved her every second since.

Which is why I refuse to let her give up.

I'M ON MY fourth cup of coffee when Kiersten walks in. She doesn't check to see if Caulder is here, she just walks straight to the couch and plops down beside me. "Hey," she says flatly.

"Hey."

"What's going on with you and Layken?" she asks. She looks at me like she deserves an answer.

"Kiersten? Hasn't your mother ever told you it's rude to be nosy?"

She shakes her head. "No, she says the only way to get the facts is to ask the questions."

"Well, you can ask as many questions as you want. That doesn't mean I have to answer them."

"Fine," she says, standing up. "I'll go ask Layken."

"Good luck getting her to open the door."

Kiersten leaves, and I jump up and go to the window. She gets halfway down my driveway before she comes back. When she passes my window, she looks up with pity and slowly shakes her head. She opens the front door and comes back inside. "Is there anything in particular you want me to ask her? I can report back to you."

I love this kid. "Yeah, good idea, Kiersten." I think for a second. "I don't know, just gauge her mood. Is she crying? Is she mad? Act like you don't know we're fighting and ask her about me. See what she says."

Kiersten nods and starts to shut the front door.

"Wait—one more thing. I want to know what she's wearing."

Kiersten eyes me curiously.

"Just her shirt. I want to know which shirt she has on."

I wait by the window and watch as Kiersten walks across the street and knocks on the door. Why does she knock on Lake's door and not mine? The door opens almost immediately. Kiersten walks inside, and the door closes behind her.

I pace the living room and drink another cup of coffee, watching out the window, waiting for Kiersten to emerge. A half hour goes by before the front door opens. Kiersten heads to her house rather than coming back across the street.

I give her a while. Maybe she had to go home to eat lunch. After an hour passes, I can't wait any longer. I make a beeline to Kiersten's house and knock on the door.

"Hey, Will, come on in," Sherry says. She steps aside. Kiersten's watching TV in the living room.

Before bombarding Kiersten, I turn to Sherry. "Last night . . . I'm sorry. I wasn't trying to be rude."

"Oh, stop it. I was just being nosy," she says. "You want something to drink?"

"No, I'm good. I just need to talk to Kiersten."

Kiersten gives me a dirty look. "You're a jerk, Will," she says.

I guess Lake's not over it. I sit down on the couch and put my hands between my knees. "Will you at least tell me what she said?" This is so pathetic. I'm entrusting my relationship to an eleven-year-old.

"Are you sure you want to know? I should probably

warn you, I have an excellent memory. Mom says I've been able to quote entire conversations verbatim since I was three years old."

"Positive. I want to know everything she said."

Kiersten sighs and pulls her legs up on the couch. "She thinks you're a jerk. She said you were an asshole, a dickhead, a bas—"

"A bastard. I know, I get it. What else did she say?"

"She didn't tell me why she was mad at you, but she's *really* mad at you. I don't know what you did, but she's at her house right now, cleaning like a psycho. When she opened the door, she had hundreds of index cards all over the living room floor. It looked like recipes or something."

"Oh God, she's alphabetizing," I say. It's worse than I thought. "Kiersten, she won't answer the door if I go over there. Will you knock so she'll open the door and I can slip inside? I really need to talk to her."

Kiersten presses her lips together. "You're asking me to trick her? To basically *lie* to her?"

I shrug and nod.

"Let me get my coat."

Sherry comes from the kitchen and holds out her hand. I hold open my palm, and she puts something in it and folds my fingers over it. "If it doesn't go the way you're hoping, take these with some water. You look like shit." She can see my hesitation and smiles. "Don't worry, I made them. They're completely legal."

* * *

I DON'T HAVE a plan of attack. I'm hiding against the wall in front of Lake's house when Kiersten knocks. My heart is beating so fast, I feel like I'm about to commit a robbery. I take a deep breath when I hear the door open. Kiersten steps aside, and I brush past her and slip inside Lake's house faster than she can realize what happened.

"Get out, Will," she says as she holds the door open and points outside.

"I'm not leaving until you talk to me," I say. I back farther into the living room.

"Get out! Get out, get out, get out!"

I do what any sane male would do in this situation: I run down the hallway and lock myself in her bedroom. I realize I still don't have a plan. I don't know how I can talk to her if I'm locked in her bedroom. But at least she can't kick me out of her house. I'll stay here all day if I have to.

I hear the front door slam, and within seconds she's standing outside the bedroom door. I wait for her to say something or to yell at me, but she doesn't. I watch the shadow of her feet disappear as she walks away.

What now? If I open the door, she'll just try to kick me out again. Why didn't I formulate a better plan? I'm an idiot. I'm a freaking idiot! Think, Will. Think.

I see the shadow of her feet reappear in front of her bedroom door.

"Will? Open the door. I'll talk to you."

She doesn't sound angry. My idiotic plan actually worked? I unlock the door to her bedroom, and as soon as I open it all the way, I'm completely drenched in water. She just threw water on me! She threw an entire pitcher of water in my face!

"Oh," she says. "You look a little wet, Will. You better go home and change before you get sick." She calmly turns and walks away.

I'm an idiot, and she's not ready to give in. I make the walk of shame down her hallway, out the front door, and across the street to my house. It's freezing. She didn't even bother warming the water. I take off my clothes and get in the shower. A hot shower this time.

THE SHOWER DIDN'T help at all. I feel like complete crap. Five cups of coffee and no sleep on an empty stomach doesn't make for a great start to the day. It's almost two o'clock in the afternoon. I wonder what Lake and I would be doing right now if I weren't such an idiot. Who am I kidding? I know what we'd be doing right now. My reflection on the turn of events over the past twenty-four hours causes my head to hurt. I pick my pants up off the bedroom floor and reach inside the pocket, pulling out whatever it is that Sherry gave me. I walk to the kitchen and down the medicine with an entire glass of water before going to the couch.

* * *

IT'S DARK WHEN I wake up. I don't even remember lying down. I sit up on the couch and spot a note on the coffee table. I reach over and snatch it up and begin to read it. My heart sinks when I realize it's not from Lake.

> *Will,*
>
> *I was going to warn you not to drive after you take the medicine . . . but I see you already took it. So, never mind.*
>
> *—Sherry*
>
> *P.S. I had a talk with Layken today. You really should apologize, you know. That was kind of a dick move on your part. If you need any more medicine, you know where I live.*

I toss the letter back on the table. Was the smiley face really necessary? I wince as the cramps in my stomach intensify. When was the last time I ate? I honestly can't remember. I open the refrigerator and see the basagna. Unfortunately, it's the perfect night for basagna. I cut a piece and throw it on a plate and toss it in the microwave. As I'm filling a glass with soda, the front door swings open.

She's walking across the room, heading for the bookshelf. I dart into the living room just as she reaches it. She's ignoring me. Rather than reaching in for a single star this time, she grabs the vase off the bookshelf.

She is *not* taking this vase with her. If she takes it, she won't have a reason to come back. I grab the vase out of her hands, but she won't let go. We tug back and forth, but I'm not letting go. I'm not letting her take it. She finally releases her grasp and glares at me.

"Give it to me, Will. My mother made it, and I want to take it home with me."

I walk back to the kitchen with the vase. She follows me. I set it on the corner of the counter against the wall and turn around to face her, then place my arms on either side of it so she can't reach it. "Your mother made it for both of us. I know you, Lake. If you take this home, you'll open every single one of them tonight. You'll be opening stars all night just like you carve pumpkins."

She throws her hands up in the air and groans. "Stop saying that! Please! I don't carve pumpkins anymore!"

I can't believe she thinks she doesn't carve pumpkins anymore. "You don't? Really? You're carving them right now, Lake. It's been twenty-four hours, and you still won't let me talk to you about it."

She wads her hands into fists and stomps her feet in frustration. "Ugh!" she yells. She looks like she wants to hit something. Or some*one*. God, she's so beautiful.

"Stop looking at me like that!" she snaps.

"Like what?"

"You've got that look in your eyes again. Just stop!"

I have absolutely no idea what look she's talking about, but I divert my attention away from her. I don't want to do anything to piss her off even more.

"Have you eaten anything today?" I ask. I take my plate out of the microwave, but she doesn't answer me. She just stands in the kitchen with her arms folded over her chest. I pull the pan of basagna out of the refrigerator and fold back the tinfoil.

"You're eating basagna? How appropriate," she says.

It's not the conversation I was hoping we would have, but it's conversation nonetheless. I cut another square and put it in the microwave. Neither of us says anything while it cooks. She just stands there, staring at the floor. I just stand here, staring at the microwave. When it's finished, I put our plates on the bar and pour another glass of soda. We sit down and eat in silence. Very uncomfortable silence.

When we're finished, I clear off the bar and sit across from her so I can see her. I wait for her to speak first. She has her elbows resting on the bar while she stares down at her nails, picking at them, attempting to look uninterested.

"So, talk," she says evenly, without looking up at me.

I reach my hands across the bar to touch hers, but she pulls away and leans back in her chair. I don't like the barrier of the bar between us, so I get up and walk to the living room. "Come sit," I say to her. She comes to the living room and sits on the same couch, but at the opposite end. I rub my face with my hands, trying to sort out just how I'm going to make her forgive me. I pull my leg up on the couch and turn to face her. "Lake, I love you. The last thing in the world I want to do is hurt you. You know that."

"Well, congratulations," she says. "You just succeeded with accomplishing the last thing in the world you wanted to do."

I lean my head back into the couch. This is going to be harder than I thought. She's tough to crack. "I'm sorry I didn't tell you she was in my class. I didn't want you to worry."

"Worry about what, Will? Is her being in class with you something I should worry about? Because if it's nothing like you say it is, why would I need to worry?"

Jesus! Am I picking the worst ways in the world to apologize, or is she just that good? If she ever stops being mad at me, I'll tell her she's finally figured out her major: prelaw.

"Lake, I don't feel that way about Vaughn anymore. I was planning to tell you about her being in my class next week; I just didn't want to bring it up before our getaway."

"Oh. So you wanted to make sure you got laid *before* you pissed me off. Good plan," she says sarcastically.

I slap my forehead with my hand and close my eyes. There isn't a fight this girl couldn't win.

"Think about it, Will. Put yourself in my shoes. Let's say I had sex with a guy before I met you. Then right when you and I were about to have sex, you walk into my bedroom, and I'm hugging this guy. Then you see me kiss him on the *neck:* your *favorite* place to be kissed by me. Then you find out I've been seeing this guy every other day for weeks and I've kept it a secret. What would you do? Huh?"

She's not picking at her nails anymore. She's glaring right at me, waiting for my response.

"Well," I say. "I would allow you the chance to explain without interrupting you every five seconds."

She flips me off and jerks off the couch and starts toward the front door. I grab her arm and pull her back down on the couch. When she falls into the spot next to me, I wrap my arms around her and press her head into my chest. I try not to let her go. I don't want her to go. "Lake, please. Just give me a chance, I'll tell you everything. Don't leave again."

She doesn't struggle to pull away. She doesn't fight me, either. She relaxes into my chest and lets me hold her while I talk.

"I didn't know if you even knew about Vaughn. I know how much you hate talking about past relationships, so I thought it would be worse if I brought it up than if I didn't. Seeing her again meant nothing to me. I didn't want it to mean anything to you, either."

I run my fingers through her hair and she sighs, then starts crying into my shirt.

"I want to believe you, Will. I want to believe you so bad. But why was she here last night? If she doesn't still mean something to you, why were you holding her?"

I kiss her on top of the head. "Lake, I was asking her to leave. She was crying, so I hugged her."

She pulls her face away from my chest and looks up at me, frightened. "She was crying? Why was she crying? Will, does she still *love* you?"

How do I answer that without coming off like a jerk again? Nothing I'm saying right now is helping my cause. Nothing at all.

She sits up and scoots away from me so she can turn toward me as she speaks. "Will, you're the one who wanted to talk. I want you to tell me everything. I want to know why she was here, what you were doing in your bedroom with her, why you were hugging her, why she was crying— *everything*." I reach over and take her hand, but she pulls it back. "Tell me," she says.

I try to think of where to begin. I inhale a deep breath and exhale slowly, preparing to be interrupted a million more times.

"She wrote me a note in class the other day and asked if we could talk. She showed up last night out of the blue. I didn't let her in, Lake. I was in my bedroom when she got here. I never would have let her in." I look her in the eyes when I say that because it's the truth. "My grandmother wanted her to eat with us, and I told her no and said I needed to talk to her. I just wanted her to leave. She started crying and told me she hated how she ended things with me. She said she knew about you and our whole situation with our parents and us raising our brothers. She said I 'owed it to you' to find out where my heart really lies, and that maybe I was with you because I felt sorry for you. She wanted me to give her another chance, to see if I was with you for the right reasons. I told her no. I told her I loved *you*, Lake. I asked her to leave, and she started crying again, so I hugged her. I felt like I was being a jerk; that's the only reason I hugged her."

I watch for some sort of reaction, but Lake looks down at her lap so I'm unable to see her face. "Why did you kiss her on the forehead?" she asks softly.

I sigh and stroke her cheek with the back of my hand, pulling her focus back to me. "Lake, I don't know. You've got to understand that I dated her for over two years. There are some things that, no matter how long it's been, they're just habit. It didn't mean anything. I was just consoling her."

Lake lies back on the arm of the couch and stares up at the ceiling. All I can do is let her think. I've told her everything. I watch her as she lies there, not saying a word. I want so badly to lie down beside her and hold her. It's killing me that I can't.

"Do you think there's a chance that she's right?" she asks, still staring at the ceiling.

"Right about what? That she loves me? Maybe, I don't know. I don't care. It doesn't change anything."

"I don't mean about that. It's obvious she wants to be with you, she said it herself. I mean do you think there's a chance she could be right about the other thing? About the possibility of you being with me because of our situation? Because you feel sorry for me?"

I spring forward on the couch and climb on top of her and grasp her jaw, pulling her face to mine. "Don't, Lake. Don't you dare think that for a second!"

She squeezes her eyes shut, and tears slide down over her temples, into her hair. I kiss them. I kiss her face and her tears and her eyes and her cheeks and her lips. I need her to know that it's not true. I need her to know how much I love her.

"Will, stop," she says weakly. I can hear her tears being suppressed in her throat; I can see it in her face. She doubts me.

"Baby, no. Don't believe that. *Please* don't believe that." I press my head into the crevice between her shoulder and her neck. "I love you because of *you*."

I've never needed anyone to believe anything more in my entire life. When she starts to resist and push against me, I slip my arm underneath her neck and pull her closer. "Lake, stop this. Please don't go," I beg. I realize as I'm speaking that my voice is shaking. I've never been so scared of losing something in my entire life. I completely lose control. I start to cry.

"Will, don't you see it?" she says. "How do you *know*? How do you *really* know? You couldn't leave me now if you wanted to. Your heart is too good for that, you would never do that to me. So how do I know that you would really be here if our circumstances were different? If our parents were alive and we didn't have Kel and Caulder, how do you know you would even love me?"

I clasp my hand over her mouth. "No! Stop saying that, Lake. *Please.*" She closes her eyes, and her tears flow even faster. I kiss them again. I kiss her cheek and I kiss her forehead and I kiss her lips. I grasp the back of her head and I kiss her with more desperation than I've ever kissed her. She puts her hands on my neck and kisses me back.

She's kissing me back.

We're both crying, frantically trying to hold on to the last bit of sanity between us. She pushes against me. She's still kissing me, but she wants me to sit up, so I do. I lean back into the couch, and she slides onto my lap and strokes my face with her hands. We stop kissing briefly and look at each other. I wipe tears away from her face and she does the same for me. I can see the heartache in her eyes, but she squeezes them shut and brings her lips back to mine. I pull her in to me so close that it's hard to breathe. We're gasping for air as we try to find a constant rhythm amid our frantic struggle. I have never needed her with more intensity. She pulls at my shirt, so I lean forward, allowing her to slip it off over my head. When her lips separate from mine, she crosses her arms and grasps the hem of her shirt and pulls it over her head. I help her. When her shirt is on top of mine on the floor, I wrap my arms around her, placing my hands on the bare skin of her back, and I pull her in to me.

"I love you, Lake. I'm so sorry. I'm so, so sorry. I love you so much."

She pulls back and looks me in the eyes. "I want you to make love to me, Will."

I wrap my arms tightly around her back and stand up as she clings to my neck. She wraps her legs around my waist and I carry her to my bedroom and we collapse onto the bed. Her hands find the button of my jeans, and she unbuttons them as my mouth slowly moves from her lips to her chin and down her neck. I can't believe this is actually happening. I don't allow myself time to second-guess my own actions. I slide my fingers under the straps of her bra and pull them off her shoulders. She slides her arms out of the straps and I move my lips along the edge of her bra while she begins to struggle with the button on her own jeans. I lift up to assist her, then I guide her hands as we slide them off and toss them behind me onto the floor. She scoots farther up on the bed until her head meets the pillows. I pull the covers out from beneath her and slide on top of her, then pull the covers back on top of us. When our eyes meet, I see the heartache behind her expression and the tears still streaming down her face. She grasps at the waist of my jeans and begins to slide them down, but I pull her hands away. She's hurting so much. I can't let her do this. She still doesn't trust me.

"Lake, I can't." I roll off of her and try to catch my breath. "Not like this. You're upset. It shouldn't be like this."

She doesn't say anything, just continues to cry. We lie next to each other for several minutes without saying a single word. I reach over to put my hand on top of hers, but she pulls it away and slides off the bed. She picks her jeans up off the floor and walks back into the living room. I follow her and watch while she puts her shirt and pants back on. She sucks in a couple of breaths in an attempt to hold back her tears.

"Are you leaving?" I ask hesitantly. "I don't want you to go. Stay with me."

She doesn't respond. She goes to the door and slips her shoes on, then her jacket. I walk over to her and wrap my arms around her. "You can't be mad at me for this. You aren't thinking clearly, Lake. If we do this while you're angry, you'll regret it tomorrow. Then you'll be mad at yourself, too. You understand that, don't you?"

She wipes tears from her eyes and steps away from me. "You've had sex with her, Will. How do I get past that? How do I get past the fact that you've made love to Vaughn, but you won't make love to me? You don't know how it feels to be rejected. It feels like shit. You just made me feel like shit."

"Lake, that's absurd! I'm not about to have sex with you for the first time while you're crying. If we do this now, we'll *both* feel like shit."

She rubs her hands across her eyes again and looks at the floor, attempting not to cry. We stand in the living room, neither of us sure what happens next. I've said all I can say, and I just need her to believe me, so I give her time to think.

"Will?" She slowly brings her gaze back up to meet mine. It seems like it hurts her to even look at me. "I'm not sure I can do this," she says.

The look in her eyes makes my heart feel like it's come to a literal stop. I've seen this look in a girl before. She's about to break up with me.

"I mean . . . I'm not sure I can do *us*," she says. "I'm trying so hard, but I don't know how to get past this. How do I know this life is what you want? How do *you* know this is what you want? You need time, Will. We need time to think about it. We have to question everything."

I don't respond. I can't. Everything I say comes out wrong.

She's not crying anymore. "I'm going home now. I need you to let me go. Just let me go, okay?"

It's the clearheadedness behind her voice and the calm, reasonable expression in her eyes that rips my heart right out of my chest. She turns to leave, and all I can do is let her go. I just let her go.

AFTER AN HOUR of punching everything I can find to punch, cleaning everything I can find to clean, and screaming every cuss word I can think to scream, I knock on Sherry's door. When she opens it, she looks at me and doesn't say a word. She turns and comes back a moment later and holds out her fist. I open my palm, and she drops the pills in my hand and looks at me with pity. I hate pity.

When I'm back inside my house, I swallow the pills and lie on the couch, wishing it all away.

"WILL."

I try to open my eyes, to make sense of the voice I'm hearing. I try to move, but my entire body feels like concrete.

"Dude, wake up."

I'm discombobulated. I sit up on the couch and rub my eyes, attempting to open them, scared of the sunlight. When I finally do open them, it's not bright at all; it's dark. I look around the room and see Gavin sitting on the couch across from me.

"What time is it? What *day* is it?" I ask him.

"It's still today. Saturday. It's after ten, I think. How long have you been out?"

I think about that question. It was after seven when Lake and I had basagna. After eight when I let her go. When I just let her go. I lie back on the couch and don't answer Gavin as the scene from two hours before replays in my head.

"You want to talk about it?" Gavin asks.

I shake my head. I really don't want to talk about it.

"Eddie's over at Layken's house. She seemed pretty

upset. It was a little awkward, so I thought I'd come hide out here. You want me to leave?"

I shake my head again. "There's basagna in the fridge if you're hungry."

"I am, actually," he says. He stands up and walks to the kitchen. "You need something to drink?"

I do. I do need a drink. I go into the kitchen, pressing my hand against my forehead. My head is pounding. I reach above the refrigerator and move the boxes of cereal out of the way to get to the cabinet. I pull out the bottle of tequila and grab a shot glass and pour myself a drink.

"I was thinking more along the lines of a soda," Gavin says as he sits down at the bar and watches me down a shot.

"Good idea." I open the refrigerator and pull out a soda. I grab an even bigger glass and mix the soda with the tequila. Not the best mix, but it goes down smoother.

"Will? I've never seen you like this. You sure you're okay?"

I tilt my head back and finish the entire drink, then put the glass in the sink. I choose not to answer him. If I say yes, he'll know I'm lying. If I say no, he'll ask me why. So I sit down next to him while he eats, and I don't say a thing.

"Eddie and I wanted to talk to you and Layken together. I guess right now that's not going to happen, so . . ." Gavin's voice trails off, and he takes another bite.

"Talk to us about what?"

He wipes his mouth with a napkin and sighs. He brings his right arm down, gripping his fork with his hand so tightly that his knuckles turn white. "Eddie's pregnant."

I don't trust my own ears at this point. My head is still pounding, and the alcohol mixed with Sherry's homemade concoction is causing me to see two of Gavin.

"Pregnant? How pregnant?" I ask.

"Pretty damn pregnant," he says.

"Shit." I stand up and grab the tequila off the counter and refill the shot glass. I normally don't promote underage drinking, but there are occasionally times when even I push my boundaries. I place the shot in front of him, and he downs it.

"What's the plan?" I ask.

He walks to the living room and sits down on the third couch. When did I get a third couch? I swipe the bottle of tequila off the counter and rub my eyes as I make my way into the living room. When I open them, there are two couches again. I hurry up and sit down before I fall.

"We don't have a plan. The same plan, anyway. Eddie wants to keep it. That scares the shit out of me, Will. We're nineteen. We're not prepared for this at all."

Unfortunately, I know *exactly* how it feels to unexpectedly become a parent at nineteen.

"Do *you* want to keep it?" I ask.

8.

*. . . I think. It might still be Saturday night. Whatever.
WTF ever.*

*Lake . . . Lake, Lake, Lake, Lake. I'd take a mountain and
then I need another drink. But I love you so much. Yeah I think
I need more tequila . . . and more cow bell. I love you I'm so
sorry. I'm not thirsty. But I'm not hungry, just thirsty. But I'm
never drinking another cheeseburger again I love you so much.*

EDDIE'S PREGNANT. GAVIN'S SCARED. I LET LAKE GO.
That's all I remember about last night.

The sun is brighter than it's ever been. I throw the
covers off and head to the bathroom. When I make it
across the hall, I try to open the door, but it's locked. Why
the hell is my bathroom door locked? I knock, which feels
extremely odd—knocking on my own bathroom door
when I should be the only person in my house.

"Just a sec!" I hear someone yell. It's a guy. It's not Gavin. What the hell is going on? I walk to the living room and see a blanket and pillow on the couch. There are shoes by the front door, next to a suitcase. I'm scratching my head when the bathroom door opens, so I turn around.

"Reece?"

"Mornin'," he says.

"What are you doing here?" I ask him.

He shoots me a confused look as he sits on the couch. "Are you kidding?" he asks.

Why would I be kidding? What would I be kidding about? I haven't seen him in over a year.

"No. What are you doing here? When did you get here?"

He shakes his head with the same bewildered expression. "Will, do you not remember anything from last night?"

I sit down and try to remember. Eddie's pregnant. Gavin's scared. I let Lake go. That's all I remember. He can see from my struggle that I need a refresher.

"I got back last Friday. My mom kicked me out? I needed a place to stay last night, and you told me I could stay here. You really don't remember?"

I shake my head. "I'm sorry, Reece. I don't."

He laughs. "Dude, how much did you have to drink last night?"

I think back on the tequila, then remember the medicine Sherry gave me. "I don't think it was just the alcohol."

He stands up and looks awkwardly around the room. "Well, if you want me to leave . . ."

"No. No, I don't mind you staying here, you know that. I just don't remember. I've never blacked out before."

"You weren't making much sense when I got here, that's for sure. You kept saying something about a star . . . and a lake. I thought you were cracked out. You're not cracked out . . . are you?"

I laugh. "No, I'm not cracked out. I'm just having a really shitty weekend. The worst. And no, I don't feel like talking about it."

"Well, since you don't remember anything about last night . . . you kind of told me I could live here? For a month or two? Does that ring a bell?" Reece raises his eyebrows and waits for my reaction.

Now I know why I never drink. I always end up agreeing to things that I normally wouldn't agree to when I'm sober. I can't think of a reason not to let him stay here. We do have an extra bedroom. He practically lived here when we were growing up. Although I haven't seen him since his last break from deployment, I still consider him my best friend.

"Stay as long as you need to," I say. "Just don't expect me to be much fun. I'm not having a very good week."

"Obviously." He grabs his bags and shoes and takes them down the hallway to the spare bedroom. I walk to the window and look across the street at Lake's house. Her car is gone. Where would she be? She doesn't go anywhere on Sundays. They're her movies-and-junk-food days. I'm still looking out the window when Reece comes back.

"You don't have shit to eat," he says. "I'm hungry. You want me to grab you anything at the store?"

I shake my head. "I don't feel like eating," I say. "Just get whatever. I'll probably go later this afternoon, anyway. I need a few things before Caulder gets back tomorrow."

"Oh yeah, where is that little twerp?"

"Detroit."

Reece slides his shoes and his jacket on and slips out the front door. I walk to the kitchen to make coffee, but there's already a full pot. Nice.

AS SOON AS I step out of the shower, I hear the front door open. I don't know if it's Reece or Lake, so I rush to pull my pants on. When I emerge from the hallway, she's holding the vase in her hands, heading to the front door. When she sees me, she speeds up.

"Dammit, Lake!" I cut her off in the living room and don't let her by. "You aren't taking it. Don't make me hide it from you."

She tries to shove her way past me, but I block her again. "You have no right to keep them at your house, Will! It's just your excuse to make me keep coming over here!"

She's right. She's absolutely right, but I don't care. "No, I want them over here because I don't trust that you won't open them all."

She shoots me a dirty look. "While we're on the subject of trust, are you sabotaging these? Are you putting fake ones in here, trying to get me to forgive you?"

I laugh. She must be getting some great advice from her mom if she thinks I'm sabotaging the stars. "Maybe you should listen to your mother's advice, Lake."

She tries to brush past me again, so I grab the vase from her hands. She jerks it away harder than I expect, and the vase slips and lands on the floor, spilling out dozens of tiny stars onto the carpet. She bends down and starts scooping them up. Her hands are full, and I can see from her face that she doesn't know where to put them, since her pants don't have pockets. She pulls the collar of her shirt out and starts shoving them inside by the handful. She's determined.

I grab her hands and pull them away from her shirt. "Lake, stop it! You're acting like a ten-year-old!" I set the vase upright and start throwing the rest of them inside as fast as she's stuffing them inside her shirt. I do the only thing I can: I reach down her shirt and start grabbing them back. She slaps at my hands and tries to crawl backward, but I grab her shirt to stop her. She continues to back away as I continue holding her shirt until it slips over her head and is resting in my hands. She gathers more stars and stands and heads toward the front door with her hands clasped to her bra, trying to hold on to the stars.

"Lake, you aren't going outside without a shirt on," I say. She's relentless.

"Watch me!" she says. I jump up and wrap my arms around her waist and pick her up. Just as I'm about to release her onto the couch, the front door swings open. I look over my shoulder, and Reece walks in with groceries. He pauses and stares at us wide-eyed.

Lake is struggling to free herself from my grasp, ignoring the fact that someone she doesn't even know has a front-row seat to her tantrum. The only thing I can think of is that she's in her bra in front of another guy. I pick her up higher and toss her over the back of the couch. Just as fast as she's on the couch, she's back up, trying to make her way past me. She finally notices Reece standing in the doorway. "Who the *hell* are you?" she yells as she slaps at my arm.

He responds cautiously. "Reece? I live here?"

Lake stops struggling and folds her arms over her chest with an embarrassed look on her face. I take the opportunity to grab most of the stars out of her hands and toss them back toward the vase. I reach down and pick her shirt up and shove it at her. "Put your shirt on!"

"Ugh!" She throws the rest of the stars on the floor and turns her shirt right side out. "You're such a jerk, Will! You have no right to keep these here!" She pulls her shirt over her head and turns to Reece. "And when the *hell* did you get a roommate?"

Reece just stares at her. He clearly has no idea what to make of the scene. Lake goes back to the center of the room and grabs a small handful of stars, then rushes toward the front door. Reece steps aside as she goes outside. We watch as she crosses the street, stopping twice to pick up stars she drops in the snow. When she shuts her door behind her, Reece turns to me.

"Man, she's feisty. And *cute*," he says.

"And *mine*," I reply.

WHILE REECE IS cooking us lunch, I crawl around the living room and pick up all the stars that scattered, then I hide the vase in a kitchen cabinet. If she can't find it, she'll have to speak to me to ask me where it is.

"What are those, anyway?" Reece asks.

"They're from her mother," I say. "Long story."

Lake might find them too easily if I hide them in such an obvious spot. I move the cereal again and place the vase right behind the tequila.

"So is this chick your girlfriend?"

I'm not sure how to answer his question. I don't know how to label what's going on between us. "Yep," I say.

He cocks his head at me. "Doesn't seem like she likes you very much."

"She loves me. She just doesn't like me right now."

He laughs. "What's her name?"

"Layken. I call her Lake," I say as I pour myself a drink. A nonalcoholic drink this time.

He laughs. "That explains your incoherent rambling last night." He spoons some pasta into our bowls, and we sit at the table to eat. "So, what'd you do to piss her off so bad?"

I rest my elbows on the table and drop my fork into my bowl. I guess now is as good a time as any to fill him in on the last year. He's been my best friend since we were ten, minus the last couple of years or so, after he left for the army. I tell him everything. The entire story. From the day we met, to Lake's first day at school, to our fight about Vaughn, all the way up to last night. When I finish, he's on his second bowl of pasta, and I haven't even touched mine.

"So," he says, stirring his pasta around. "You think you're really over Vaughn?"

Out of all the things I just told him, *that's* what he focuses on? I laugh. "I'm absolutely over Vaughn."

He shifts in his chair and looks at me. "Just tell me if this isn't cool with you, but . . . would you care if I asked her out? If you say no, I won't, man. I swear."

He hasn't changed a bit. Of course this is the *one* thing he would pick up on. The *single* girl.

"Reece? I could honestly care less what you do with Vaughn. Honestly. Just don't bring her here. That's one rule you can't break. She's not allowed in this house."

He smiles. "I can live with that."

I SPEND THE next few hours finishing homework and studying the notes Vaughn left for me. I rewrite them and throw away her original notes. I hate looking at her handwriting.

I've cut down my spying to about once an hour. I don't want Reece to think I'm crazy, so I look out the window only when he leaves the room. I'm at the table studying, and he's watching TV, when Kiersten walks in—without knocking, of course.

"Who the hell are you?" she says to Reece as she walks across the living room.

"Are you even old enough to talk like that?" he asks.

She rolls her eyes and walks to the kitchen and takes a seat across from me. She puts her elbows on the table and rests her chin in her hands, watching me study.

"You see Lake today?" I ask without looking up from my notes.

"Yep."

"And?"

"Watching movies. And eating a lot of junk food."

"Did she say anything about me?"

Kiersten folds her arms on the table and leans in closer. "You know, Will, if I'm going to be working for you, I think it's a good time to negotiate fair compensation."

I look at her. "Are you agreeing to help me?"

"Are you agreeing to pay me?"

"I think we could work out a deal," I say. "Not with currency. But maybe I could help you build your portfolio."

She leans back in her seat and eyes me curiously. "Keep talking."

"I've got a lot of performance experience, you know.

I could give you some of my poetry . . . help you prepare for a slam."

I can see her thoughts churning behind her expression. "Take me to the slam. Every Thursday for at least a month. There's a talent show coming up at the school in a few weeks that I want to enter, so I need all the exposure I can get."

"An entire month? No way. This reconciliation between Lake and me better happen before four weeks! I can't go through this for a whole month."

"You really are an idiot, aren't you?" She stands up and pushes her chair in. "Without my help, you'll be lucky if she forgives you this *year*." She turns to walk away.

"Fine! I'll do it. I'll take you," I say.

She turns back and smiles at me. "Good choice," she says. "Now . . . is there anything you want me to plant in her head while I go to work?"

I stew on this for a moment. What's the best way to win Lake back? What in the world can I possibly say to get her to see how much I really love her? What can I have Kiersten do? I jump up when it hits me. "Yes! Kiersten, you need to ask her to take you to the slams. Tell her I refused to take you and that I said I'm never going back. Beg her to take you if you have to. If there's one way I can get her to believe me, it's while I'm on that stage."

She gives me an evil grin. "Devious. I love it!" she says on her way out.

"Who *is* she?" Reece says.

"*She* is my new best friend."

OTHER THAN THE fight we had over the stars today, I've given Lake all the alone time I possibly can. Kiersten reported back that Lake agreed to take her on Thursday, after an intense bout of begging on Kiersten's part. I rewarded her with one of my old poems.

It's after ten now. I know I shouldn't, but I can't seem to go to bed without trying to talk to Lake at least one more time. I can't decide whether leaving her alone or hounding her is the better choice. I figure it's time for another star. I hate that we're opening them so fast, but I consider this an emergency.

When I get to the kitchen, I'm shocked to see Lake peering in one of the cabinets. She's getting sneakier. When I pass by her, she jumps. I don't say anything as I reach into the cabinet and pull out the vase. I set it on the counter and take out one of the stars. She looks at me as though waiting for me to yell at her again. I hold the vase out to her, and she grabs her own star. We lean against opposite ends of the counter while we open them and read them silently to ourselves.

Adopt the pace of nature: her secret is patience.

—RALPH WALDO EMERSON

I do just that . . . I practice patience. I don't speak as Lake reads hers. As much as I want to run up to her and kiss her and make it all better, I decide to be patient instead. She scowls as she reads the paper in her hand. She wads it up and throws it on the counter, then walks away. Again I let her go.

When I know she's gone, I grab her slip of paper and unfold it.

> *So if you could find it in your heart*
> *To give a man a second start*
> *I promise things won't end the same.*
> —THE AVETT BROTHERS

I couldn't have said it better if I'd written it myself. "Thank you, Julia," I whisper.

9.

I'm not giving up
You're not giving in
This battle will turn into a war
Before I let it come to an end.

I KNOW LAKE DOESN'T LIKE ME RIGHT NOW, BUT I KNOW she doesn't hate me, either. I can't help but wonder if I should give her the space she's asking for. Part of me wants to respect where she's coming from, but part of me is scared that if I do back off, she may decide she likes the space. I'm terrified of that. So maybe I won't give her space. I wish I knew where to draw the line between desperation and suffocation.

Reece is in the kitchen drinking coffee. The fact that he actually makes coffee is a good enough reason alone to let him stay.

"What are your plans today?" he says.

"I have to go to Detroit to get the boys at some point. You want to go with me?"

He shakes his head. "Can't. I have plans with . . . I have plans today." He looks away nervously as he rinses out his coffee cup.

I laugh and take my own cup out of the cabinet. "You don't have to hide it. I already told you I was cool with it."

He places his cup upside down in the dish drainer and turns to face me. "It's still a little weird, though. I mean, I don't want you to think I was trying to get with her while you two were together. It wasn't like that."

"Stop worrying about it, Reece. Really. It's not weird for me at all. What is a little weird is that just a few days ago she was professing her love for me, and now she's about to spend the day with you. Does that not bother you just a little bit?"

He grins at me as he grabs his wallet and keys off the counter. "Believe me, Will, I've got skills. When Vaughn's with me, you'll be the last thing on her mind."

Reece has never been much for modesty. He puts on his jacket and heads out. As soon as the front door shuts, my phone vibrates. I pull it out of my pocket and smile. It's a text from Lake.

What time will Kel be home today? I have to go pick up a textbook on back order, and I won't be home for a while.

The text seems too impersonal. I read it a few times, trying to gain hints from any hidden meanings. Unfortunately, I'm pretty positive that it states exactly what she intended to say. I text her back, hoping to somehow talk her into going with me to pick the boys up.

Where are you going to pick up textbooks? Detroit?

I know which bookstore she's going to. It's a long shot, but I'm hoping I can trap her into riding with me instead of taking her own car. She replies almost immediately.

Yes. What time will Kel be home?

She's so hard to crack. I hate her short responses.

I'm going to Detroit to pick the boys up later. Why don't you just ride with me? I can take you to get your book.

Having the long drive to talk things over might give me a chance to convince her that things need to go back to the way they were.

I don't think that's a good idea. I'm sorry.

Or not. Why does she have to be so damn difficult? I throw my phone on the couch and don't bother texting her back. I walk to the window and pathetically stare at her house. I hate that her need for space is stronger than her need for me. I really need her to go to Detroit with me today.

I CAN'T BELIEVE I'm doing this. As I'm crossing the street, I double-check to make sure Lake isn't peeking out the window. She'll be so pissed if she catches me. I quickly open her car door and push the lever to pop the hood. I have to work fast. I decide the best way to disable her Jeep is to disconnect the battery. It's probably the most obvious, but she would never notice, considering her lack of mechanical knowledge. As soon as I succeed with my goal, I glance toward her window again, then make a mad dash back home. When I shut the door behind me, I almost regret what I just did. Almost.

I WAIT FOR her to come out that afternoon before I leave. I watch as she attempts to crank her vehicle. It doesn't start. She hits the steering wheel and swings open the car door. This is my opportunity. I grab my things and head out the front door to my car, pretending not to notice her. When I back up and pull onto the street, she has her hood up. I stop in front of her driveway and roll down my window. "What's wrong? Car won't start?"

She peers around the front of the hood and shakes her head. I pull my car over and get out to take a look. She steps aside and allows me by without speaking. I fidget with a few wires here and there and pretend to crank her car a couple of times. The whole time, she's just silently standing back.

"Looks like your battery is shot," I lie. "If you want, I can pick a new one up for you while I'm in Detroit. Or . . . you could ride with me, and I'll take you to get your book." I smile at her, hoping she'll cave.

She looks back at her house, then at me. She looks

torn. "No, I'll just ask Eddie. I don't think she has plans today."

That isn't what I need her to say. It isn't going how I planned. *Play it cool, Will.*

"I'm only offering you a ride. We both need to go to Detroit anyway. It's ridiculous to get Eddie involved just because you don't want to talk to me right now." I use the authoritative tone I've perfected on her. It usually works.

She hesitates.

"Lake, you can carve pumpkins the whole trip. Whatever you need. Just get in the car," I say.

She scowls at me, then turns and grabs her purse out of the Jeep. "Fine. But don't think this means anything." She walks down the driveway and toward my car.

I'm glad she's in front of me, because I can't hide my excitement as I punch at the air with my fists. An entire day together is exactly what we need.

AS SOON AS we pull away, she turns the Avett Brothers on, her way of letting me know she's carving pumpkins. The first few miles to Detroit are awkward. I keep wanting to bring everything up, but I don't know how. Kel and Caulder will be with us on the way home, so I know if I want to lay it all out, I need to do it now.

I reach over and turn the volume down. She's got her foot propped up on the dash, and she's staring out the window in an obvious attempt to avoid confrontation, like she always does. When she notices I've turned down the volume, she glances at me and sees me staring at her, then returns her attention to the window. "Don't, Will. I told you . . . we need time. I don't want to talk about it."

She is so damn *frustrating*. I sigh and shake my head, feeling another round of defeat coming on. "Could you at least give me an estimate of how long you'll be carving pumpkins? It'd be nice to know how long I have to suffer." I don't try to mask my aggravation.

I can tell by her scowl that I said the absolute wrong thing again.

"I knew this was a bad idea," she mumbles.

I grip the steering wheel even tighter. You would think after a year I would have found a way to get through to her or to manipulate her in some way. She's almost impenetrable. I have to remind myself that her indomitable will is one of the reasons I fell in love with her in the first place.

Neither of us says another word during the remainder of the drive. It doesn't help that neither of us turns the radio back up. The entire trip is incredibly awkward as I try my best to search for the right thing to say and she tries her best to pretend I don't exist. As soon as we arrive at the bookstore in Detroit and I pull into a parking spot, she swings open the car door and runs inside. I'd like to think she's running from the cold, but I know she's running from me. From confrontation.

While she's inside, I get a text from my grandfather

informing me that my grandmother is cooking us dinner. His text ended with the word "roast," preceded by a hash tag.

"Great," I mutter to myself. I know Lake has no intention of spending the evening with my grandparents. As soon as I text my grandfather letting him know we're almost there, Lake returns to the car.

"They're cooking dinner for us. We won't stay long," I say.

She sighs. "How convenient. Well, take me to get a new battery first so we can get it over with."

I don't respond as I head toward my grandparents' house. She's been to their house a couple of times, so she knows when we get closer that I have no intention of stopping at the store.

"You've passed like three stores that sell batteries," she says. "We need to get one now, in case it's too late on the way back."

"You don't need a battery. Your battery is fine," I say. I avoid looking at her, but out of the corner of my eye, I can see her watching me, waiting for explanation. I don't immediately respond. I flick the blinker on and turn onto my grandparents' street. When I pull into their driveway, I turn off the car and tell her the truth. What harm could it do at this point?

"I unhooked your battery cable before you tried to leave today." I don't wait for her reaction as I get out of the car and slam the door. I'm not sure why. I'm not mad at her, I'm just frustrated. Frustrated that she doubts me after all this time.

"You *what*?" she yells. When she gets out of the car, she slams her door, too.

I keep walking, shielding the wind and snow with my jacket until I reach the front door. She rushes after me. I almost walk inside without knocking but remember how it feels, so I knock.

"I said I unhooked your battery cable. How else was I going to convince you to ride with me?"

"That's real mature, Will." She huddles closer to the front door, farther away from the wind. I hear footsteps nearing the entryway when she turns to face me, opening her mouth as if to say something else. Then she rolls her eyes and turns away. The front door swings open, and my grandmother steps aside to let us in.

"Hi, Sara," Lake says with a fake smile as she hugs my grandmother. My grandmother returns her hug, and I walk in behind them.

"You two got here just in time. Kel and Caulder are setting the table," Grandma says. "Will, take your jackets and put them in the dryer so they won't be so wet when you leave."

My grandmother goes back to the kitchen, and I remove my jacket and head to the laundry room without offering to take Lake's. I smile when I hear her stomping angrily after me. Being the nice guy has not helped my case at all, so I guess I'll start being the jerk. I throw my jacket into the dryer and step aside so she can do the same. After she shoves her jacket inside, she slams the dryer door shut and turns it on. She spins around to exit the laundry room, but I'm blocking her way. She shoots me a dirty look and tries to ease past me, but I don't budge. She steps back and looks away. She's going to stand there until I move out of her way. I'm going to stand here until she talks to me. I guess we'll be here all night.

She tightens her ponytail and leans against the dryer, crossing one foot over the other. I lean against the laundry room door in the same position as I stare her down, waiting for something. I'm not sure what I'm trying to get out of her right now; I just want her to talk to me.

She wipes snow off the shoulder of her shirt. She's wearing the Avett shirt I bought her at the concert we went to a month ago. We had the best time that night; I never would have imagined then that we would be in this predicament.

I give in and speak first. "You know, you sure are quick to accuse me of being immature for someone giving me the silent treatment like a five-year-old."

She cocks her eyebrows at me and laughs. "Seriously? You have me trapped in a laundry room, Will! Who's being immature?"

She tries to move past me again, but I continue to block her way. She's flush against me, pathetically trying to shove against my chest. I have to fight the urge to wrap my arms around her. We're practically face-to-face when she finally stops pushing me. She's inches from me, staring at the floor. She may have doubts about my feelings for her, but there is no way she can doubt the sexual tension between us. I take her chin in my hand and gently pull her face toward mine.

"Lake," I whisper. "I'm not sorry about what I did to your car. I'm desperate. I'd do anything at this point just to be with you. I miss you."

She looks away, so I bring my other hand to her face and force her to look me in the eyes. She tries to pull my hands away, but I refuse to let go. The tension between us increases as we hold the stare. I can tell she wants to hate me so bad right now, but she loves me too much. There's a struggle of emotion in her eyes. She can't decide whether she wants to punch me or kiss me.

I take advantage of her moment of weakness and slowly lean in and touch my lips to hers. She presses her hands against my chest and halfheartedly tries to push me away, but she doesn't pull her mouth away from mine. Rather than honor her request for space, I lean in to her even farther and part her lips with mine. Her pressure against my chest weakens as her stubbornness finally dissolves and she lets me kiss her.

I place my hand on the back of her head and slowly move my lips in rhythm with hers. Our kiss is different this time. Rather than pushing it to the point of retreat, like we've been doing, we continue to slowly kiss, pausing every few seconds to look at each other. It's almost as if neither of us believes this is happening. I feel like this kiss is my last chance to remove any doubt from her mind, so I pour into it every single emotion I have. Now that I have her in my arms, I'm afraid to let her go. I take a step forward, and she takes a step back, until we end up against the dryer. The situation reminds me of the last time we were alone together in a laundry room, over a year ago.

It was the day after her kiss with Javi at Club N9NE. The moment I walked around his truck and saw his mouth on hers, I immediately felt jealousy coupled with intense hurt like nothing I'd ever experienced. I had never been in a physical fight. The fact that he was my student and I was his teacher was lost on me as soon as I began to pull him away from her. I don't know what would have happened if Gavin hadn't shown up when he did.

The day after the fight, when I heard Lake tell her version of events, I felt like such an idiot that I believed she'd kissed him back. I knew her better than that, and I hated myself for assuming the worst. As difficult as it was to allow her to believe I had chosen my career over her, I knew it was the right thing to do at the time. That night in my laundry room, though, I allowed my emotions to control my conscience, and I almost messed up the best thing that ever happened to me.

I push the fear of losing her again out of my mind. She moves her hands to my neck, sending chills down my entire body. Slow and steady loses out as we simultaneously pick up the pace. When she runs her hands through my hair, it sends me over the edge. I grab her by the waist and lift her up until she's seated on the dryer. Out of every single kiss we've ever shared, this is by far the best. I place my hands on the outside of her thighs and pull her to the edge of the dryer, and she wraps her legs around me. Just as my lips meet the spot directly below her ear, she gasps and shoves against my chest.

"Eh-hem," my grandmother says, rudely interrupting one of the best moments of my life.

Lake immediately jumps off the dryer, and I step back. My grandmother is standing in the doorway with her arms crossed, glaring at us. Lake straightens her shirt and looks down at her feet, embarrassed.

"Well, it's nice to see you two made up," my grandmother says, eyeing me disapprovingly. "Dinner is ready when you can find time to join us at the table." She turns and walks away.

As soon as she's gone, I turn back to Lake and wrap my arms around her again. "Babe, I've missed you so bad."

"Stop," she says, pulling away from me. "Just stop."

Her sudden hostility is unexpected and confusing. "What do you mean, *stop*? You were just kissing me back, Lake."

She looks up at me, agitated. She seems disappointed in herself. "I guess I had a *weak moment*," she says in a mocking tone.

I recognize the phrase, and more than likely, I deserve her reaction. "Lake, quit doing this to yourself. I know you love me."

She lets out a sigh as though she's unsuccessfully trying to get through to a child. "Will, I'm not struggling with whether or not I love *you*. It's whether or not you really love *me*." She heads into the dining room, leaving me behind in yet another laundry room.

I punch the wall, frustrated. I thought for a second I'd gotten through to her. I don't know how much longer I can take this. She's starting to piss me off.

"THIS ROAST IS delicious, Sara," Lake says to my grandmother. "You'll have to give me the recipe."

I snatch the bowl of potatoes off the table and silently seethe at the way Lake is so casually exchanging pleasantries with my grandmother. I have no appetite, but I'm piling on the food anyway. I know my grandmother: If I don't eat, she'll be offended. I scoop potatoes onto my plate, then take an exaggerated spoonful and drop them on Lake's plate, right on top of her roast. She's seated next to me, doing her best to pretend nothing is amiss as she eyes the massive mound of potatoes. I don't know whether she's putting on this fake display of happiness for my grandparents' sake or for Kel and Caulder's sake. Maybe for all of them.

"Layken, did you know Grandpaul used to be in a band?" Kel says.

"No, I didn't. And did you just call him Grandpaul?" Lake says.

"Yeah. That's my new name for him."

"I like it," my grandfather says. "Can I call you Grandkel?"

Kel smiles and nods at him.

"Will you call me Grandcaulder?" Caulder asks.

"Sure thing, Grandcaulder," he says.

"What was the name of your band, Grandpaul?" Lake asks.

It's almost scary how good she is at putting up a front. I make a mental note to retain this little detail about her for future reference.

"Well, I was in several, actually," he replies. "It was a hobby when I was younger. I played the guitar."

"That's neat," Lake says. She takes a bite and talks around the mouthful. "You know, Kel has always wanted to learn how to play the guitar. I've been thinking about putting him in lessons." She wipes her mouth and takes a sip of water.

"Why? You should just get Will to teach him," Grandpaul says.

Lake turns and looks at me. "I wasn't aware that Will knew how to play the guitar," she says in a somewhat accusatory tone.

I guess I've never shared that with her. It's not like I was trying to keep it from her; I just haven't played in a couple of years. I'm sure she thinks it's one more secret I've been keeping from her.

"You've never played for her?" my grandfather says to me.

I shrug. "I don't own a guitar."

Lake is still glaring at me. "This is really interesting, Will," she says sarcastically. "There sure is a lot about you that I don't know."

I look at her straight-faced. "Actually, sweetie . . . there isn't. You know pretty much everything about me."

She shakes her head and places her elbows on the table and squints at me, putting on that fake smile I'm growing to hate. "No, *sweetie*. I don't think I do know everything about you." She says this in a tone that only I could recognize as false enthusiasm. "I didn't know you played the guitar. I also didn't know you were getting a roommate. In fact, this Reece seems to have been a pretty big part of your life, and you've never even mentioned him—along with a few other 'old friends' who have popped up recently."

I set my fork down and wipe my mouth with the napkin. Everyone at the table is staring at me, waiting for me to speak. I smile at my grandmother, who seems oblivious to what's going on between Lake and me. She smiles back at me, interested in my response. I decide to raise the stakes, so I wrap my arm around Lake and pull her closer to me and kiss her on the forehead.

"You're right, *Layken*." I say her name with the same

feigned enthusiasm. I know how much it pisses her off. "I did fail to mention a few old friends from my past. I guess this means we'll just have to spend a lot more time together, getting to know every single aspect of each other's lives." I pinch her chin with my thumb and finger and smile as she narrows her eyes at me.

"Reece is back? He's living with us?" Caulder asks.

I nod. "He needed a place to crash for a month or so."

"Why isn't he staying with his mother?" my grand-mother asks.

"She got remarried while he was overseas. He doesn't get along with his new stepdad, so he's looking for his own place," I say.

Lake leans forward in an attempt to inconspicuously remove my arm from her shoulder. I squeeze her tighter and pull my chair closer to hers. "Lake sure made a good first impression on Reece," I say, referring to her shirtless tantrum in my living room. "Right, sweetie?"

She presses the heel of her boot into the top of my foot and smiles back at me. "Right," she says. She scoots her chair back and stands up. "Excuse me. I need to go to the restroom." She slaps her napkin down on the table and gives me the evil eye as she walks away.

Everyone else at the table is oblivious to her anger. "You two seem to have moved past your hump from last week," my grandfather says after she's disappeared down the hallway.

"Yep. Getting along great," I say. I shove a spoonful of potatoes in my mouth.

Lake remains in the bathroom for quite a while. When she returns, she doesn't speak much. Kel, Caulder, and Grandpaul talk video games while Lake and I finish eating in silence.

"Will, can you help me in the kitchen?" my grandmother says.

My grandmother is the last person who would ask for help in the kitchen. I'm about to either change a lightbulb or receive a lecture. I get up from the table and grab Lake's and my plates and follow her through the kitchen door.

"What's that all about?" she says as I scrape food off the plates and into the disposal.

"What's what all about?" I reply.

She wipes her hands on the dish towel and leans against the counter. "She's not very happy with you, Will. I may be old, but I know a woman's scorn when I see it. Do you want to talk about it?"

She's more observant than I give her credit for. "I guess it can't hurt at this point," I say, leaning against the kitchen counter next to her. "She's pissed at me. The whole thing with Vaughn last week left her doubting me. Now she thinks I'm with her just because I feel sorry for her and Kel."

"Why *are* you with her?" my grandmother asks.

"Because I'm in love with her," I say.

"I suggest you show her," she says. She takes the rag and begins wiping down the counter.

"I have. I can't tell you how many times I've told her. I can't get it through her head. Now she wants me to leave her alone so she can think. I'm getting so frustrated; I don't know what else I can do."

My grandmother rolls her eyes at my perceived ignorance. "A man can *tell* a woman he's in love with her until he's blue in the face. Words don't mean anything to her when her head is full of doubt. You have to *show* her."

"How? I disabled her car so she'd have to ride here with me today. Short of stalking her, I don't know what else I can do to show her."

My pathetic confession prompts a disapproving look. "That's a good way to get yourself put in jail, not win back the heart of the girl you're in love with," she says.

"I know. It was stupid. I was desperate. I'm out of ideas."

She walks to the refrigerator and pulls out a pie. She sets it on the counter next to me and starts cutting slices. "I think the first step is for you to take some time to question just why you're in love with her, then figure out a way to relay that to her. In the meantime, you need to give her the space she needs. I'm surprised your little spectacle at dinner didn't get you punched."

"The night is still young."

My grandmother laughs and places a slice of pie on

a plate, then turns around and hands it to me. "I like her, Will. You better not screw this up. She's good for Caulder."

My grandmother's comment surprises me. "Really? I didn't think you liked her very much."

She continues slicing the pie. "I know you think that, but I do like her. What I don't like is the way you're always all over her when you're around her. Some things are better left in private. And I'm referring to the bedroom, not the laundry room." She frowns at me.

I didn't realize how publicly I displayed my affection for Lake. Now that my grandmother and Lake have both brought it up, it's kind of embarrassing. I guess the laundry room incident from earlier didn't help to dispel what Lake believes my grandmother thinks of her.

"Grandma?" I ask. She never gave me a fork, so I tear off a piece of pie crust and pop it in my mouth.

"Hum?" She reaches into the drawer, pulls out a fork, and drops it on my plate.

"She's still a virgin, you know."

My grandmother's eyes grow wide, and she turns back to cut another slice. "Will, that's none of my business."

"I know," I say. "I just want you to know that. I don't want you thinking the opposite of her."

She hands me two more plates of dessert, then grabs two of her own and nods at the kitchen door. "You have a good heart, Will. She'll come around. You just need to give her time."

* * *

LAKE SITS IN the backseat with Kel on the way home, and Caulder rides in front with me. The three of them talk the entire way. Kel and Caulder are droning on to Lake about everything they did with Grandpaul. I don't say a word. I tune them out and drive in silence.

After I pull into my driveway and we all get out of the car, I follow Lake and Kel across the street. She heads inside without saying a word. I pop the hood on her Jeep and reconnect the battery, then head back to my house.

It's not even ten o'clock at night. I'm not tired at all. Caulder's in bed, and Reece is more than likely out with Vaughn. I'm sitting down on the couch to turn the TV on when someone knocks at the door.

Who would be coming over this late? Who would knock? I open the door, and my stomach flips when I see Lake shivering on the patio. She doesn't look angry, which is a good sign. She's pulling her jacket tightly around her neck and wearing her snow boots over her pajama bottoms. She looks ridiculous . . . and beautiful.

"Hey," I say a little too eagerly. "Here for another star?" I step aside and she walks in. "Why'd you knock?" I ask, shutting the door behind her. I hate that she knocked. She never knocks. That small gesture reveals some sort of change in our entire relationship that I can't pinpoint, but I know I don't like it.

She just shrugs. "Can I talk to you?"

"I wish you *would* talk to me," I say. We head to the couch. Normally, she would curl up next to me and sit on her feet. This time she makes sure there's plenty of space between us as she drops down on the opposite end of the couch. If I've learned anything at all this week, it's the fact that I hate space. Space sucks.

She looks at me and musters a smile, but it doesn't come off right. It looks more like she's trying not to pity me.

"Promise me you'll hear me out without arguing first," she says. "I'd like to have a mature conversation with you."

"Lake, you can't sit there and say I don't hear you out. It's impossible to hear you out when you're carving pumpkins all the damn time!"

"See? Right there. Don't do that," she says.

I grab the throw pillow next to me and cover my face with it to muffle a groan. She's impossible. I bring the pillow back down and rest my elbow on it as I prepare for her lecture. "I'm listening," I say.

"I don't think you understand where I'm coming from at all. You have no clue why I'm having doubts, do you?"

She's right. "Enlighten me," I say.

She takes her jacket off and throws it over the back of the couch and gets comfortable. I was wrong, she's not here to lecture; I can tell by the way she's speaking. She's here to have a serious conversation, so I decide to respectfully hear her out.

"I know you love me, Will. I was wrong to say that earlier. I know you do. And I love you, too."

It's obvious this confession is merely a preface to something else. Something I *don't* want to hear.

"But after I heard the things Vaughn said to you, it made me look at our relationship in a different way." She sits Indian-style, facing me. "Think about it. I started thinking back on that night at the slam last year, when I finally told you how I felt. What if I wouldn't have shown up that night? What if I hadn't come to you and told you how much I loved you? You never would have read me your slam. You would have taken the job at the junior high, and we probably wouldn't even be together. So you can see where my doubt comes into play, right? It seems like you wanted to sit back and let the chips fall where they may. You didn't fight for me. You were just going to let me go. You *did* let me go."

I did let her go, but not for the reasons she's telling herself. She knows that. Why does she doubt it now? I do my best to be patient when I respond, but my emotions are all jumbled up. I'm frustrated, I'm pissed, I'm happy she's here. It's exhausting. I hate fighting.

"You *know* why I had to let you go, Lake. There were bigger things going on last year than just us. Your mother needed you. She didn't know how much time she had. The way we felt about each other would have interfered with your time left with her, and you would have hated yourself for it later. That's the only reason why I gave up, and you *know* that."

She shakes her head in disagreement. "It's more than that, Will. We've both experienced more grief in the past couple of years than most people experience in a lifetime. Think about the effect that had on us. When we finally found each other, our grief was how we related. Then when we found out we couldn't be together, that made it even worse. Especially since Kel and Caulder were best friends by then. We had to interact constantly, which made it harder to shut off our feelings. Top it all off, my mom ended up having cancer, and I was about to become a guardian, just like you. That was how we related. There were all these external influences at play. Almost like life was forcing us together."

I let her continue without interrupting, as she requested, but I want to scream out of sheer frustration. I'm not sure what point she's getting at, but it seems to me she's been thinking way too hard.

"Remove all the external factors for a second," she says. "Imagine if things were like this: Your parents are alive. My mom is alive. Kel and Caulder aren't best friends. We aren't both guardians with huge responsibilities. We have no sense of obligation to help each other out. You were never my teacher, so we never had to experience those months of emotional torture. We're just a young couple with absolutely no responsibilities or life experiences tying us together. Now, tell me, if all that was our current reality, what is it about *me* that you love? Why would you want to be with me?"

"This is ridiculous," I mutter. "That's *not* our reality, Lake. Maybe some of those things are why we're in love. What's wrong with that? Why does it matter? Love is love."

She scoots closer to me on the couch and takes my hands in hers, looking me straight in the eyes. "It matters, Will. It matters because five or ten years from now, those external factors aren't going to be at play in our relationship. It'll just be you and me. My biggest fear is that you'll wake up one day and realize all the reasons you're in love with me are gone. Kel and Caulder won't be here to depend on us. Our parents will be a memory. We'll both have careers that could support us individually. If these are the reasons you love me, there won't be anything left to hold you to me other than your conscience. And knowing you, you would live with it internally because you're too good a person to break my heart. I don't want to be the reason you end up with regrets."

She stands up and puts her jacket back on. I start to protest, but as soon as I open my mouth, she interrupts me. "Don't," she says with a serious expression. "I want you to think before you object. I don't care if it takes you days or weeks or months. I don't want to hear from you again until you can be completely real with me and leave my feelings for you out of your decision. You owe it to me, Will. You owe it to me to make sure we aren't about to live a life together that someday you'll regret."

She walks out the door and calmly closes it behind her.

Months? Did she just say she didn't care if it takes *months?*

She did. She said months.

My God, everything she said makes sense. She's completely wrong, but it makes sense. I get it. I can see why she's questioning everything. I can see why she doubts me now.

Half an hour goes by before I so much as move a muscle. I'm completely lost in thought. When I finally break free from the trance, I come to one conclusion. My grandmother is right. Lake needs me to show her why I love her.

I decide to grab inspiration out of the jar. I unfold the star and read it.

> *Life's hard. It's even harder when you're stupid.*
> —JOHN WAYNE

I sigh. I miss Julia's sense of humor.

10.

The heart of a man
is no heart at all
If his heart isn't loved by a woman.
The heart of a woman
is no heart at all
If her heart isn't loving a man.
But the heart of a man and a woman in love
Can be worse than not having a heart
Because at least if you have no heart at all
It can't die when it breaks apart.

IT'S TUESDAY, AND SO FAR I'VE SPENT THE MAJORITY OF the day studying. I've spent only a portion of it being paranoid. Paranoid that someone's going to see me sneaking into Lake's house. Once I'm inside, I search around for everything I need and quickly head back out before everyone gets home from school. I throw my satchel over my shoulder and bend down to hide Lake's key under the pot.

"What are you doing?"

I jump back and nearly trip over the concrete patio rise. I control my balance on the support beam and look up. Sherry is standing in Lake's driveway with her hands on her hips.

"I . . . I was just . . ."

"I'm kidding." Sherry laughs, walking toward me.

I shoot her a dirty look for almost giving me a heart attack and turn back to push the pot into its original position. "I needed some things out of her house," I say without going into detail. "What's up?"

"Not much," she says. She has a shovel in her hands, and I glance behind her to see part of Lake's sidewalk cleared. "I'm just wasting time . . . waiting on my husband to get home. We've got errands to run."

I cock my head at her. "You have a husband?" I don't mean to sound surprised, but I am. I've never seen him.

She laughs at my response. "No, Will. My children are the result of immaculate conception."

I laugh. Her sense of humor reminds me of my mother's. *And* Julia's. *And* Lake's. How was I so lucky to be surrounded by such amazing women?

"Sorry," I say. "It's just that I've never seen him before."

"He works a lot. Mostly out of state . . . business trips

and the like. He's home for two weeks. I'd really like you to meet him."

I don't like that we're standing in front of Lake's house. She'll be home soon. I start walking away from the house as I respond. "Well, if Kel and Kiersten get married someday, we'll technically be in-laws, so I guess I should meet him."

"That's assuming you and Kel have a different type of relationship by then," she says. "Are you planning on popping the question?" She begins walking with me toward her house. I think she can sense I want to be off of Lake's property before they return home.

"I'd planned on it," I say. "I'm just not so sure now what Lake's answer would be."

Sherry tilts her head, then sighs. She's looking at me with pity again. "Come inside for a sec. I want to show you something."

I follow her into her house. "Sit down on the couch," she says. "Do you have a few minutes?"

"I've got more than a few."

She returns a moment later with a DVD. After she inserts it in the DVD player, she sits down on the couch beside me and turns the television on with the remote.

"What is it?" I ask.

"A close-up of me giving birth to Kiersten."

I jump up in protest, and she rolls her eyes and laughs. "Sit down, Will. I'm kidding."

I reluctantly sit back down. "That's not funny."

She presses play on the remote, and the screen shows a shot of a much younger Sherry. She looks about nineteen or twenty. She's sitting on a porch swing laughing, hiding her face with her hands. The person holding the camera is laughing, too. I assume it's her now-husband. When he walks up the porch steps, he angles the camera around and sits beside her, focusing the lens on both of them. Sherry uncovers her face and leans her head against his and smiles.

"Why are you filming us, Jim?" Sherry says to the camera.

"Because. I want you to remember this moment forever," he says.

The camera shuffles again and comes to a rest on what is probably a table. It's positioned on both of them as he kneels in front of her. It's obvious he's about to propose, but you can see Sherry attempting to suppress her excitement, in case that's not his intention. When he pulls a small box out of his pocket, she gasps and starts to cry. He brings a hand up to her face and wipes away her tears, then briefly leans forward and kisses her.

When he settles back onto his knees, he wipes a tear away from his own eyes. "Sherry, until I met you, I didn't know what life was. I had no clue that I wasn't even alive. It's like you came along and woke up my soul." He's looking straight at her as he talks. He doesn't sound nervous at all, as if he's determined to prove to her how serious he is. He takes a deep breath and then continues. "I'll never be able to give you everything you deserve, but I'll definitely spend the rest of my life trying." He pulls the ring out of the box and slides it on her finger. "I'm not asking you to marry me, Sherry. I'm *telling* you to marry me, because I can't live without you."

Sherry wraps her arms around his neck, and they hold on to each other and cry. "Okay," she says. When they begin to kiss, he reaches over and turns off the camera.

The television screen goes black.

Sherry presses the power button on the remote, and she's silent for a moment. I can tell the video brought back a lot of emotions for her. "What you saw in that video?" she says. "The connection Jim and I had? That's true love, Will. I've seen you and Layken together, and she loves you like that. She really does."

The front door to Sherry's house opens wide and a man enters, shaking the snow out of his hair. Sherry looks nervous as she hops up and hits eject on the DVD player and puts it back inside the case.

"Hey, sweetie," she says to him. She motions for me to stand up, so I do. "This is Will," she says. "He's Caulder's older brother from across the street."

The man walks across the living room, and I reach my hand out to him. As soon as we're eye to eye, Sherry's agitation is explained. This isn't Jim. This is a completely different man than whoever it was I just saw propose to Sherry on that DVD.

"I'm David. Nice to meet you. Heard a lot about you."

"Likewise," I say. I'm lying.

"I've been giving Will relationship advice," Sherry says.

"Oh yeah?" he says. He smiles at me. "Hopefully you take it with a grain of salt, Will. Sherry thinks she's a real guru." He leans in and kisses her on the cheek.

"Well, she is pretty smart," I say.

"That she is," he says as he takes a seat on the couch. "But take it from me . . . never accept any of her medicinal concoctions. You'll regret it."

Too late for that.

"I better get going," I say. "Nice meeting you, David."

"I'll walk you out," Sherry says.

Her smile fades after she shuts the door behind her. "Will, you need to know that I love my husband. But there are very few people in this world lucky enough to experience love on the same level that I've had in the past . . . on the same level that you and Layken have. I'm not getting into the details of why mine didn't work out, but take it from someone who's had it before . . . you don't want to let it slip away. Fight for her."

She steps back inside her house and shuts the door.

"That's what I'm trying to do," I whisper.

"CAN WE HAVE pizza tonight?" Caulder says as soon as he walks through the front door. "It's Tuesday. Gavin can get us the Tuesday special that comes with the dessert pizza."

"Whatever. I don't feel like cooking, anyway." I text

Gavin and offer to buy pizza if he'll bring it over when he gets off work.

By the time eight o'clock comes around, I've got a houseful. Kiersten and Kel showed up at some point. Gavin and Eddie walk in with the pizza, and we all sit down at the table to eat. The only one missing is Lake.

"Should you invite Lake?" I ask Eddie as I toss a pile of paper plates onto the table.

Eddie looks at me and shakes her head. "I just texted her. She said she's not hungry."

I sit down and grab one of the paper plates and toss a slice on it. I take a bite and drop the pizza back on the plate. I'm suddenly not hungry, either.

"Thanks for bringing a cheese pizza, Gavin," Kiersten says. "At least someone around here respects the fact that I don't eat meat."

I don't have anything to throw at her, or I would. I shoot her a dirty look instead.

"What's the plan of attack for Thursday?" Kiersten asks me.

I glance at Eddie, who's looking right at me. "What's Thursday?" she says.

"Nothing," I reply. I don't want Eddie ruining this. I'm afraid she'll go warn Lake.

"Will, if you think I'll tell her whatever it is you're planning to do, you're wrong. No one wants you two to work things out more than I do, believe me." She takes a bite of her pizza. She seems genuinely serious, although I'm not sure why.

"He's doing a slam for her," Kiersten blurts out.

Eddie looks back up at me. "Seriously? How? You aren't gonna be able to talk her into going."

"He didn't have to," Kiersten says. "I talked her into going."

Eddie grins at her. "You're a sly little thing. And just how are you planning to keep her there?" She looks back at me. "As soon as she sees you on that stage, she'll get pissed and leave."

"Not if I steal her purse and keys," Kel says.

"Good idea, Kel!" I say. As soon as I say it, the reality of the moment hits me. I'm sitting here praising eleven-year-olds for stealing and lying to my girlfriend. What kind of role model am I?

"And we can sit in the same booth we sat in last time," Caulder says. "We'll make sure Lake gets in first; that way we can trap her in. Once you start doing your slam, she won't be able to get up. She'll have to watch you."

"Great idea," I say. I may not be a role model, but at least I'm raising smart children.

"I want to go," Eddie says. She turns to Gavin. "Can we go? Aren't you off Thursday? I want to watch Will and Layken make up."

"Yeah, we can go. But how are we all getting there if she doesn't know you're going, Will? We can't all fit in

Layken's car, and I don't need to be driving all the way to Detroit in mine after all the deliveries I've been making."

"You can ride with me," I say. "Eddie can tell Lake you're working or something. Everyone else can ride with Lake."

We all seem to agree on the plans. The fact that everyone seems determined to help me win her back gives me a sense of hope. If everyone in this room can see how much we need to be together, surely Lake will see it, too.

I throw three slices of pizza on another plate, then take it to the kitchen. I glance over my shoulder to make sure no one is paying attention. I reach into the cabinet and pull out a star and set it under one of the slices of pizza before wrapping the plate.

"Eddie, will you take this to Lake? Make sure she eats something?"

Eddie grabs the plate, smiles at me, and goes.

"Kids, clean the table. Put the pizza in the fridge," I say.

Gavin and I go into the living room. He lies on the couch, pinches his forehead, and closes his eyes.

"Headache?" I say.

He shakes his head. "Stress."

"You guys decide on anything?"

He's quiet. He inhales a slow, deep breath, then exhales even slower. "I told her I was nervous about going through with it. Told her I think we need to weigh our options. She got really upset," he says. He sits up and puts his elbows on his knees. "She accused me of thinking she would make a bad mom. That's not what I think at all, Will. I think she would make a great mom. I just think she would make an even better mom if we wait until we're ready. Now she's pissed at me. We haven't talked about it since. We're both pretending like it's not happening. It's weird."

"So you're both carving pumpkins?" I say.

Gavin looks at me. "I still don't get that analogy."

I guess he wouldn't. I wish I had better advice for him.

Kiersten comes into the living room and sits down next to Gavin. "Know what I think?" she says.

Gavin looks at her, agitated. "You don't even know what we're talking about, Kiersten. Go play with your toys."

She glares at him. "I'm going to let that insult slide because I know you're in a bad mood. But for future reference, I don't *play*." She stares at him to make sure he doesn't have a response, then continues talking. "Anyway, I think you should quit feeling sorry for yourself. You're acting like a little bitch. You aren't even the one pregnant, Gavin. How do you think Eddie feels? I'm sorry, but as much as the guy likes to think he's got an equal part in these situations, he's wrong. You screwed up when you knocked her up. Now you need to shut your mouth and be there for her. For whatever she decides to do." She stands up and walks to the front door. "And Gavin? Sometimes things happen in life that you didn't plan for. All you can do now is suck it up and start mapping out a new plan."

She shuts the door behind her, leaving Gavin and me speechless.

"Did you tell her Eddie was pregnant?" I finally ask.

He shakes his head. "No." He continues to stare at the door, in deep thought. Then, "Dammit!" he yells. "I'm such an idiot! I'm a selfish idiot!" He jumps up from the couch and puts on his jacket. "I'll call you Thursday, Will. I've got to go figure out how to make this right."

"Good luck," I say. As soon as Gavin opens the front door, Reece walks in.

"Hi-Reece-bye-Reece," Gavin says.

Reece turns and watches Gavin run across the street. "You've got strange friends," he says.

I don't argue. "There's pizza in the fridge if you want some."

"Nah. I'm just here to grab some clothes. I already ate," he says as he heads down the hallway.

It's Tuesday. I'm pretty sure he and Vaughn went out for the first time yesterday. Not that it bothers me in the least, but things seem to be progressing a little fast. Reece comes back through the living room toward the front door. "You work things out with Layken yet?" He's shoving an extra pair of pants into his bag.

"Almost," I say, eyeing his overnight bag. "You and Vaughn seem to be hitting it off pretty well."

He grins and walks backward out the door. "Like I said, I've got skills."

I sit there on the couch and ponder my situation. I've got an old best friend who's dating the girl I spent two years of my life with. My new best friend is freaking out about becoming a dad. My girlfriend isn't speaking to me. I've got class in the morning with the very reason my girlfriend isn't speaking to me. My eleven-year-old neighbor gives better advice than I do. I'm feeling a tad bit defeated right now. I lie down on the couch and try to think of something going *right* in my life. Anything.

Kel and Caulder come in and sit on the other couch. "You with wrong what's?" Kel says backward.

"Wrong *not* what's?" I sigh.

"I'm too tired to talk backward," Caulder says. "I'm just gonna talk frontward. Will . . . can you come to school next Thursday and sit with me at lunch? It's supposed to be Dad Day, but Dad's dead, so that leaves you."

I close my eyes. I hate that he's so casual about not having a dad. Or maybe I'm glad he's so casual about it. Either way, I hate it for him. "Sure. Just let me know what time I need to be there."

"Eleven," he says as he stands up. "I'm going to bed now. See ya later, Kel."

Caulder goes toward his bedroom. Kel looks just as defeated as I feel as he heads toward the front door. When the door closes behind him, I slap myself in the forehead. You're such an idiot, Will!

I jump off the couch and follow Kel outside. "Kel!" I yell when I open the front door. He walks back toward me. We meet in my front yard.

"What about you?" I say. "Can I have lunch with you, too?"

Kel tries to suppress a smile, just like his sister. He shrugs. "If you want to," he says.

I ruffle his hair. "I'd be honored."

"Thanks, Will." He turns and walks back to his house. As I watch him close the front door behind him, it occurs to me that if things don't work out between Lake and me, it's not just *her* I'm afraid of losing.

I'M NOT SURE how today is going to go. When I get to my first class, all I can do is wait. I'm hoping she doesn't sit by me. Surely she knows that much. Most of the students arrive, and the professor walks in and hands out the tests. It's ten minutes after the start of class, and Vaughn still hasn't shown up. I've let out a sigh of relief and begun to focus on the test when she bursts through the door. She never has been much for subtlety. After she grabs her test, she comes straight up the stairs and sits right next to me. Of course she does.

"Hey," she whispers. She's smiling. She looks happy. I'm hoping it has everything to do with Reece and nothing to do with me. She rolls her eyes. "Don't worry. This is the last day I'm sitting by you," she says. I guess she could see the disappointment written across my face when she walked up. "I just wanted to say I was sorry about last week. I also wanted to say thanks for being so cool about Reece and me dating again." She picks her bag up from the table and starts sifting through it for a pen.

"Again?" I whisper.

"Yeah. I mean, I thought you'd be pissed that we started dating right after you and I broke up. Before he left for the military? Actually, it kind of upset me that it didn't piss you off," she says with a strange look in her eyes. "Anyway, we decided to give it another shot. But that's all I wanted to say." She turns her attention to the test in front of her.

Again? I want to ask her to repeat everything she just said, but that would mean I was inviting conversation, so I don't. But *again?* And I could swear she just said they dated before he left for the military. Reece left for the military two months after my parents died. If he and Vaughn dated before that . . . that means one thing . . . he was dating her right after she broke my heart. He was *dating* her? The entire time I was venting to him about her, he was *dating* her? What a *jackass.* Hopefully, he and Vaughn have gotten to know each other pretty well the whole three days they've been "back" together—because he's about to need a new place to live.

* * *

I EXPECT TO confront Reece about it when I get home, but he isn't here. The entire night is relatively quiet. Kel and Caulder are spending most of the evening at Lake's house. Kiersten is, too, I guess. It's just me and my thoughts. I use the rest of the evening to perfect what I want to say tomorrow night.

IT'S THURSDAY MORNING, the day Lake will forgive me. I hope. Caulder and Kel have already left with Lake. I hear Reece in the kitchen making coffee and decide that now would be a good time to have a talk with him. To thank him for being such a great friend all these years. Jackass.

When I walk into the kitchen, ready to confront him, it's not Reece making coffee. It's not Lake, either. Vaughn is standing in my kitchen with her back turned to me. In her *bra*. Making coffee in *my* kitchen. Using *my* coffeepot. In *my* house. In her *bra*.

Why the hell is this my life?

"What the hell are you doing here, Vaughn?"

She jumps and turns around. "I . . . I didn't know you were here," she stutters. "Reece said you weren't here last night."

"Ugh!" I yell, frustrated. I turn my back to her and rub my face, trying to sort out how the hell to fix this "roommate" situation. Just as I'm about to kick Vaughn out, Reece walks into the kitchen. "What the hell, Reece? I told you not to bring her here!"

"Chill out, Will. What's it matter? You were asleep. You didn't even know she was here."

He casually walks to the cabinet and grabs a coffee cup. He's wearing boxer shorts. She's in her bra. I can't imagine what Lake would think if she walked in and saw Vaughn in my kitchen in her bra. I'm *this close* to getting Lake to forgive me. This would derail my entire plan.

"Get out! Both of you, get out!" I yell.

Neither of them moves. Vaughn looks at Reece, waiting for him to say something or do something. Reece looks at me and rolls his eyes. "Let me give you a piece of advice, Will. Any girl who can make you as miserable as you've been this week isn't worth it. You're being an ass. You need to drop that chick. Move on."

This little piece of advice, coming from a man who could care less about anyone but himself, pushes me over the edge. I don't know what comes over me. I don't know if it's the comment about Lake not being worth it, or the fact that I'm now aware he lied to me for months. Either way, I lunge forward and punch the shit out of him. As soon as my fist meets his face, it's agony. Vaughn is screaming at me as I back away from him, holding my fist with my other hand.

Jesus! In the movies, it always looks like the one being hit is the only one hurt. They never show the damage it does to the hand *doing* the hitting.

"What the hell?" Reece yells, holding his jaw. I expect him to try to punch me back, but he doesn't. Maybe deep down, he knows he deserves it.

"Don't tell me she isn't worth it," I say, turning toward the refrigerator. I reach in and grab two ice packs. I throw one to Reece and put the other one on my fist. "And thanks, Reece. . . . for being such a *great* friend. After my parents died and she broke up with me . . ." I point to Vaughn. "You were the only one willing to stick around and help me through it. Too bad I didn't know you were helping *her* out, too."

Reece looks at Vaughn. "You told him?" he says.

Vaughn looks confused. "I thought he knew," she says defensively.

Reece becomes flustered. "Will, I'm sorry. I didn't mean for it to happen. It just did."

I shake my head. "Things like that don't just happen, Reece. We've been best friends since we were *ten*! My whole damn world collapsed around me. For an entire month, you acted like you were trying to help me get her back, but instead, you were *screwing* her!" Neither of them can look me in the eyes. "I know I said I'd let you stay here, but things are different now." I throw the ice pack on the counter and walk toward the hallway. "I want you both gone. Now."

I shut my bedroom door and collapse onto the bed. I can probably count the friends I have left on one hand. Actually, I can count them on one finger. I lie there for a while longer, wondering how I could have been so blind to his selfishness. I hear Reece go into the spare bedroom, then the bathroom, packing up his things. When I hear his car pull away, I go out to the kitchen and pour myself a cup of coffee. I guess I'll have to start making my own again.

This isn't a very good start to the day. I reach into the cabinet and grab a star out of the vase and unfold it.

I want to have friends that I can trust, who love me for the man I've become . . . not the man that I was.
—THE AVETT BROTHERS

As soon as I read it, I look over my shoulder, half expecting Julia to be there, smiling. It's eerie sometimes how fitting these quotes have been to the situation. Almost like she's writing them as life is happening.

11.

I can only hope that the next entry I write in this journal, after my performance tonight, will read something like this:

Now that I have you back, I'm never letting you go. That's a promise. I'm not letting you go again.

GAVIN WALKS THROUGH THE FRONT DOOR RIGHT AROUND seven o'clock. It's the first time he's walked in without knocking. It must be contagious.

He can tell I'm a nervous wreck as soon as he sees me. "They just left. We should let them get a head start," he says.

"Good idea," I say. I make another walk-through of the house, trying to find something to add to my satchel. I'm pretty sure I have it all. We give Lake and Eddie a good fifteen-minute head start before we leave. I warn Gavin that I'm not going to be much for conversation on the ride there. Luckily, he understands. He always understands. That's what best friends do, I guess.

During the drive, I recite everything I need to say over and over in my head. I've got the poem down. I already talked to the guys at Club N9NE, so everything is in place there. Unfortunately, I get only one shot with her. I've got to make it count.

When we arrive, Gavin goes inside first. He texts me a minute later to ensure that the plan is in place. I walk inside with my satchel across my shoulder and wait for my cue from the entryway. I don't want her to see me. If she sees me before it's time, she'll get angry and leave.

The seconds turn into minutes, and the minutes turn into eternity. I hate this. I've never been so nervous about performing. Normally, when I perform, there's nothing on the line. This performance could very well determine my path in life. I take a deep breath and focus on my nerves. Then the emcee takes the microphone. "We've got something special planned for open mike tonight. So without further ado . . ." He walks off the stage.

This is it. Now or never.

Everyone in the audience has their eyes glued to the stage, so I go unnoticed as I walk along the wall on the right of the room toward the front. Right before I walk onstage, I glance at the booth where they're all sitting. Lake is right in the middle with nowhere to go. She's looking down at her phone. She has no clue what's about to hit her. I've already prepared myself for her reaction . . . she's going to be pissed. I just need her to hear me out long enough to get through to her. She's hardheaded, but she's also reasonable.

The spotlight dims and focuses on a stool on the stage, just as I asked of the lighting tech. I don't like the bright lights hindering my view of the audience, so I made sure they would all be turned off. I want to see Lake's face the entire time. I need to be able to look her in the eyes, so she'll know just how serious I am.

Before I take the stairs, I stretch my neck and arms out to ease the apprehension building up inside of me. I exhale a few times, then take the stage.

I take a seat on the stool as I place my satchel on the floor. I remove the microphone from the stand and look straight at Lake, who looks up from her phone. As soon as she sees me, she frowns and shakes her head. She's pissed. She says something to Caulder, who's seated at the edge of the booth, and she points to the door. He shakes his head and doesn't move. I watch as she fidgets her hands around beside her, looking for her purse. She can't find it. She points to Kiersten, seated at the other end of the booth, and Kiersten shakes her head, too. Lake looks at Gavin and Eddie, then at Kiersten again, then she realizes they're all in on it. After accepting that they won't let her out of the booth, she folds her arms over her chest and returns her focus to the stage. To me.

"Are you finished trying to run away yet?" I say into

the microphone. "Because I have a few things I'd like to say to you."

The audience members turn, searching for the person I'm speaking to. When Lake notices everyone staring at her, she buries her face in her hands.

I bring the audience's attention back to me. "I'm breaking the rules tonight," I say. "I know that slams can't involve props, but I've got a few I need to use. It's an *emergency*."

I bend down and pick up the satchel, then stand and place it on the stool. I put the microphone back in the stand and position it at the right height.

"Lake? I know you told me you wanted me to think about everything you said the other night. I know it's only been two days, but honestly, I didn't even need two seconds. So instead of spending the last two days thinking about something I already know the answer to, I decided to do this. It's not a traditional slam, but I have a feeling you aren't that particular. My piece tonight is called 'Because of You.' "

I exhale and smile at her before I begin.

"There are moments in every relationship that define when two people start to fall in love.

"A first *glance*
A first *smile*
A first *kiss*
A first *fall* "

I remove the Darth Vader house shoes from my satchel and look down at them.

"You were wearing these during one of those
moments.
One of the moments I first started to fall in love
with you.
The way you made me feel that morning
had absolutely *nothing* to do with *anyone* else,
and *everything* to do with *you.*
I was falling in love with you that morning
because of you."

I take the next item out of the satchel. When I pull it out and look up, she brings her hands to her mouth in shock.

"This ugly little *gnome*
with his smug little *grin,*
He's the reason I had an excuse to invite you into
my house.
Into my life.
You took a lot of aggression out on him over those
next few months.
I would watch from my window as you kicked him
over every time you walked by him.
Poor little guy.
You were so *tenacious.*

That *feisty, aggressive, strong-willed* side of you . . .
the side of you that *refused* to take crap from this
concrete gnome?
The side of you that refused to take crap
from me?
I fell in love with that side of you
because of you."

I set the gnome down on the stage and grab the CD.

"This is your favorite CD.
'Layken's Shit.'
Although now I know you intended for 'shit' to be
possessive,
rather than *descriptive.*
The banjo started playing through the speakers of
your car
and I immediately recognized my favorite band.
Then when I realized it was *your* favorite band, *too*?
The fact that these *same lyrics* inspired *both* of us?
I fell in love with that about you.
That had absolutely *nothing* to do with *anyone* else.
I fell in love with that about you
because of you."

I take a slip of paper out of the satchel and hold it up.
When I look over, I notice Eddie sliding Lake a napkin. I
can't see from up here, but that can only mean she's crying.

"This is a receipt I kept.
Only because the item I purchased that night was
on the verge of *ridiculous.*
Chocolate milk on the rocks? *Who orders that?*
You were *different,* and you didn't *care.*
You were being *you.*
A piece of me fell in love with you at that moment,
because of you."

"This?" I hold up another sheet of paper.

"*This* I didn't really like so much.
It's the poem you wrote about me.
The one you titled 'Mean'?
I don't think I ever told you . . .
but you made a *zero.*
And then I *kept* it
to remind myself of all the things I *never* want to
be to you."

I pull her shirt from my bag. When I hold it up to the
light, I sigh into the microphone.

"This is that ugly shirt you wear.
It doesn't really have anything to do with why I fell
in love with you.
I just saw it at your house and thought I'd steal it."

I pull the second-to-last item out of my bag. Her purple hair clip. She told me once how much it meant to her and why she always kept it.

"This purple hair clip?
It really *is* magic . . . just like your dad told you it was.
It's magic because, no matter how many times it lets
you down, you keep having *hope* in it.
You keep *trusting* it.
No matter how many times it *fails* you,
You never fail *it*.
Just like you never fail *me*.
I love that about you,
because of you."

I set it down and pull out a strip of paper and unfold it.

"Your mother."

I sigh.

"Your mother was an amazing woman, Lake.
I'm blessed that I got to know her,
And that she was a part of my life, too.
I came to love her as my *own* mom . . . just as she
came to love Caulder and me as *her* own.

I didn't love her because of *you,* Lake.

I loved her because of *her.*

So, thank you for sharing her with us.

She had more advice about

life and *love* and *happiness* and *heartache* than

anyone I've ever known.

But the *best* advice she ever gave me?

The best advice she ever gave *us*?"

I read the quote in my hands. " 'Sometimes two people have to fall apart to realize how much they need to fall back together.' "

She's definitely crying now. I place the slip back in the satchel and take a step closer to the edge of the stage as I hold her gaze.

"The last item I have wouldn't fit, because you're

actually sitting in it.

That booth.

You're sitting in the exact same spot where you

sat when you watched your first performance on

this stage.

The way you watched this stage with passion in

your eyes . . . I'll *never* forget that moment.

It's the moment I knew it was too late.

I was too far gone by then.

I was in *love* with you.

I was in love with you because of *you.*"

I back up and sit down on the stool, still holding her gaze.

"I could go on all night, Lake.
I could go *on and on and on* about all the reasons
I'm in love with you.
And you know what? Some of them *are* the things
that life has thrown our way.
I *do* love you because you're the only other person I
know who understands my situation.
I *do* love you because both of us know what it's like
to lose your mom *and* your dad.
I *do* love you because you're raising your little
brother, just like I am.
I love you because of what you went through with
your *mother.*
I love you because of what *we* went through with
your mother.
I love the way you love *Kel.*
I love the way you love *Caulder.*
And I love the way *I* love Kel.
So I'm not about to apologize for loving all these
things about you, *no matter* the reasons or the
circumstances behind them.
And no, I don't need *days,* or *weeks,* or *months* to
think about *why* I love you.
It's an easy answer for me.
I love you because of *you.*

Because of

every

single

thing

about *you*."

I take a step back from the microphone when I'm finished. I keep my eyes locked on hers, and I'm not sure because she's pretty far away, but I think she mouths "I love
you." The stage lights come back up, and I'm blinded. I
can't see her anymore.

I gather the items and the satchel and jump off the
stage. I immediately head to the back of the room. When
I get there, she's gone. Kel and Caulder are both standing
up. They let her get out. They let her leave! Eddie sees the
confusion on my face, so she holds up Lake's purse and
shakes it. "No worries, Will. I've still got her keys. She just
walked outside, said she needed air."

I head to the exit and shove the door open. She's in
the parking lot, next to my car with her back to me, staring up at the sky. She's letting the snow fall on her face
as she stands there. I watch her for a minute, wondering
what she's thinking. My biggest fear is that I misread her
reaction from the stage and that everything I said meant
nothing to her. I slide my hands in my jacket pockets and
walk toward her. When she hears the snow crunch beneath
my feet, she turns around. The look in her eyes tells me

everything I need to know. Before I take another step, she rushes to me and throws her arms around my neck, almost knocking me backward.

"I'm so sorry, Will. I'm so, so sorry." She kisses me on the cheek, the neck, the lips, the nose, the chin. She keeps saying she's sorry, over and over between each kiss. I wrap my arms around her and pick her up, giving her the biggest hug I've ever given her. When I plant her feet back on the ground, she takes my face in her hands and looks into my eyes. I don't see it anymore . . . the heartache. She's not heartbroken anymore. I feel like the weight of the world has been lifted off my shoulders and I can finally breathe again.

"I can't believe you kept that damn gnome," she whispers.

"I can't believe you threw him away," I say.

We continue to stare at each other, neither of us fully trusting that the moment is real. Or that it will last.

"Lake?" I stroke her hair, then the side of her face. "I'm sorry it took me so long to get it. It's my fault you had doubts. I promise there won't be a day that goes by that I won't show you how much you mean to me."

A tear rolls down her cheek. "Me, too," she says.

My heart pounds against my chest. Not because I'm nervous. Not even because I want her worse than I've ever wanted her. It's pounding against my chest because I realize I've never been more sure about the rest of my life than

I am in this moment. This girl is the rest of my life. I lean in and kiss her. Neither of us closes our eyes; I don't think we want to miss a single second of the moment.

We're two feet from my car, so I walk her backward until she's up against it. "I love you," I somehow mutter while my lips are meshed with hers. "I love you so much," I say again. "God, I love you."

She pulls away from me and smiles. Her thumbs move to my cheeks, and she wipes at the tears that I didn't even realize were streaming down my face. "I love *you*," she says. "Now that we have that out of the way, will you just shut up and kiss me?"

And so I do.

After several minutes of making up for all the kisses we missed out on over the last week, the temperature begins to affect us. Lake's bottom lip starts shivering. "You're cold," I say. "Do you want to get in my car and make out with me, or should we go inside?" I'm hoping she chooses the car.

She smiles. "The car."

I've taken a step toward the car door when I realize I set my satchel on the booth where everyone's sitting. "Crap," I say as I step back to Lake and wrap my arms around her. "My keys are inside." Her whole body is trembling against me from the cold.

"Then break your butterflying window and unlock the door," she says.

"A broken window would defeat the purpose of trying to keep you warm," I say. I do my best to warm her by pressing my face against her neck.

"I guess you'll have to try and keep me warm in other ways."

Her suggestion tempts me to break the damn window. Instead, I take her hand in mine and pull her toward the entrance. As soon as we walk inside but before we pass through the entryway, I turn around to kiss her one more time before we head to our booth. I was just going in for a quick peck, but she pulls me in to her, and the kiss lingers.

"Thank you," she says when she pulls away. "For what you did up there tonight. And for trapping me in the booth so I couldn't leave. You know me too well."

"Thank you for listening."

We head back to the booth hand in hand. When Kiersten sees us walking in together, she starts clapping. "It worked!" she squeals. They all scoot toward the center so Lake and I can slide in. "Will, that means you owe me more poems," Kiersten says.

Lake looks at me and then at Kiersten. "Wait. You mean you two were conspiring this whole time?" she says. "Kiersten, did he put you up to begging me to bring you here tonight?"

Kiersten shoots me a look, and we both laugh.

"And last weekend!" Lake says. "Did you knock on my door just so he could get in my house?"

Kiersten doesn't answer as she looks back at me. "You

owe me an early return fee," she says. "I think twenty bucks should do it." She holds out her palm.

"We didn't agree to monetary compensation, if I remember correctly," I say, pulling twenty dollars from my wallet. "But I would have paid triple that."

She takes the money and puts it in her pocket with a satisfied expression. "I would have done it for free."

"I feel used," Lake says.

I put my arm around Lake and kiss her on top of the head. "Yeah, sorry about that. You're really hard to manipulate. I had to rally the forces."

She looks up at me, and I take the opportunity to give her a quick kiss on the mouth. I can't help it. Every time her lips come within a certain proximity to mine, it's impossible not to kiss them.

"I liked it better when you two weren't speaking," Caulder says.

"Same here," Kel says. "I forgot how gross it was."

"I think I'm gonna be sick," Eddie says.

I laugh because I think Eddie's making a joke about our public display of affection. She's not. She covers her mouth with her hand, and her eyes get big. Lake shoves against me, and I hop out of the booth, followed by Lake and Kiersten. Eddie scoots out of the booth with her hand still over her mouth and makes a mad dash for the bathroom. Lake runs after her.

"What's wrong with her?" Kiersten asks. "Is she having nausea?"

"Yep," Gavin says flatly. "Constantly."

"Well, you don't look very worried about her," Kiersten says.

Gavin rolls his eyes and doesn't respond. We're sitting quietly through another performance when I notice Gavin watching the hallway with concern. "Will, hop up. I need to go check on her," he says. Kiersten and I get back out of the booth, and Gavin exits. I grab Lake's purse and my satchel, and we all follow.

"Kiersten, go inside and see if she needs me," Gavin says.

Kiersten opens the door to the women's restroom. A minute later, she returns. "She said she'll be fine. Layken said for all you boys to go on and head home and us three will follow you in a few minutes. Layken needs her purse, though."

I hand Kiersten the purse. I'm a little bummed that Lake isn't riding with me, but I guess she did bring her own car. I'm anxious to get back to Ypsilanti. Back to our houses. I'm definitely sneaking into her room tonight.

We head outside to my car. I crank it and wipe the snow from the windows, then walk over to Lake's car and wipe the snow off her windows as well. When I get back to my car, the three of them are coming outside.

"You okay?" I ask Eddie. She just nods.

I walk over to Lake and give her a quick peck on the cheek as she unlocks her door. "I'll follow you guys in case she gets sick again and you have to pull over."

"Thanks, babe," she says, unlocking the doors for everyone else. She turns around and gives me a hug before climbing into her car.

"The boys are staying at my house tonight," I whisper in her ear. "After they fall asleep, I'm coming over. Wear your ugly shirt, okay?"

She smiles. "I can't. You stole it, remember?"

"Oh yeah," I whisper. "In that case . . . I guess you just shouldn't wear one at all." I wink at her and walk back to my car.

"She okay?" Gavin asks when I get in the car.

"I guess so," I say. "You want to go ride with them?"

Gavin shakes his head and sighs. "She doesn't want me to. She's still mad at me."

I feel bad. I hate that Lake and I just made up right in front of them. "She'll come around," I say as I pull out of the parking lot.

"Why do you two even bother with girls?" Kel asks. "Both of you have been miserable for days. It's pathetic."

"Someday you'll see, Kel," Gavin says. "You'll see."

He's right. Making up with Lake later tonight will make this entire week of hell worth every second. Deep down I know it'll happen tonight. We're both way beyond the point of retreat. I suddenly become nervous at the thought.

"Kel, you want to stay at my house tonight?" I try to act casual with my plan to corral the boys at my place. I feel like Kel can see right through me, even though I know he can't.

"Sure," he says. "But it's a school night, and Lake takes us to school on Fridays. Why doesn't Caulder just stay with me?"

I didn't think about that. I guess Lake could sneak over to my house after they fall asleep at her house. "Whichever," I say. "Doesn't really matter where."

Gavin laughs. "I see what you're up to," he whispers.

I just smile.

WE'RE ABOUT HALFWAY home when the snow begins to fall pretty heavily. Luckily, Lake is a pretty cautious driver. I'm following behind her even though I would normally drive about ten miles an hour faster. It's a good thing Eddie isn't driving; we'd all be in trouble.

"Gavin, you awake?" He's staring out the window and hasn't said much since we left Detroit. I can't tell whether he's lost in thought or passed out.

He grumbles a response, informing me that he's still awake.

"Have you and Eddie talked since you left my house the other night?"

He stretches in his seat and yawns, then puts his hands behind his head and leans back. "Not yet. I worked a double shift yesterday. We were both in school all day today and didn't even see each other until tonight. I pulled her aside and told her I wanted to talk to her later. I have a feeling she thinks it's bad. She hasn't said much to me since then."

"Well, she'll be—"

"Will!" Gavin yells. My first instinct is to slam on the brakes, but I'm not sure why I'm slamming on the brakes. I glance at Gavin, and his eyes are glued to the oncoming traffic in the lanes to the left of us. I turn my head and see it just as the truck crosses the median and hits the car in front of us.

Lake's car.

part
two

12.

I OPEN MY EYES BUT DON'T HEAR ANYTHING RIGHT AWAY. It's cold, though. I feel wind. And glass. Glass is on my shirt. Then I hear Caulder.

"Will!" he's screaming.

I turn around. Caulder and Kel both look fine, but they're panicking and trying to get out of their seat belts. Kel looks terrified. He's crying and yanking on the car door.

"Kel, don't get out of the car. Stay in the backseat." My hand goes up to my eye. I pull my fingers back, and there's blood on them.

I'm not sure what just happened. We must have been hit. Or we ran off the road. The back window is busted out, and there's glass all over the car. The boys don't look cut anywhere. Gavin is swinging his door open. He tries to jump out of the car, but he's stuck in his seat belt. He's frantic, trying to unlatch it. I reach over and push the button, releasing him. He trips as he lunges out of the car but catches himself with his hands and pushes himself back up and runs. What is he running from? My gaze follows as he runs around the car next to us. He's gone. I can't see him. I lean my head back into the headrest and close my eyes. *What the hell just happened?*

And then it hits me. "Lake!" I yell. I swing open the car door and get hung up in the seat belt just like Gavin did. After I free myself, I run. I don't know where I'm running. It's dark, it's snowing, and there are cars everywhere. Headlights everywhere.

"Sir, are you okay? You need to sit down, you're hurt." A man grabs my arm and tries to pull me aside, but I yank my arm away from him and keep running. There are pieces of glass and metal all over the highway. My eyes dart from one side of the road to the other, but I can't make anything out. I glance back to my car and to the space in front of us where Lake's car should be. My eyes follow the broken glass to the median on the right of the highway. I see it. Her car.

Gavin is on the passenger side. He's pulling Eddie out of the car, so I run around to help him. Her eyes are closed, but she winces when I pull on her arm. She's okay. I glance inside the car, but Lake's not there. Her door is wide open. A sense of relief washes over me when I realize she must be okay if she's able to walk away. My eyes dart to the backseat, and I see Kiersten. As soon as Eddie is safely on the ground, I climb into the backseat and shake Kiersten.

"Kiersten," I say. She doesn't respond. There's blood on her, but I'm not sure where it's coming from. "Kiersten!" I yell. She still doesn't respond. I take her wrist and hold it between my fingers. Gavin climbs into the backseat with me and sees me checking her pulse. He looks at me with terror in his eyes.

"She's got a pulse," I say. "Help me get her out." He unbuckles her seat belt as I put my hands underneath her arms and pull her over the front seat. Gavin climbs out and grabs her legs and helps me pull her out of the car. We lay her next to Eddie. Next to a growing crowd of concerned bystanders. I glance at all of them but don't see Lake.

"Where the hell did she go?" I stand up and look around. "Stay with them," I tell Gavin. "I need to find Lake. She's probably looking for Kel." Gavin nods.

I walk around several vehicles and pass the truck that hit them. What's left of the truck, anyway. There are several people surrounding it, talking to the driver inside, telling him to wait for help before he gets out. I'm in the middle of the highway, calling Lake's name. Where did she go? I run back to my car. Kel and Caulder are still inside.

"Is she okay?" Kel asks. "Is Layken okay?" He's crying.

"Yeah, I think so. She walked away . . . I can't find her. You guys stay here, I'll be right back."

I finally hear sirens as I'm making my way back to

Lake's car. When the emergency vehicles come closer, their flashing lights illuminate all the chaos, almost emphasizing it. I look at Gavin. He's hovering over Kiersten, checking her pulse again. The sirens fade as I watch everyone around me move in slow motion.

All I can hear is the sound of my own breath.

An ambulance pulls up beside me, and the lights slowly make their way in a circle, as if their job as lights is to display the perimeter of the damage. I follow along with my eyes as one of the red lights slowly illuminates my car, then the car next to mine, then over the top of Lake's car, then on top of the truck that hit them, then across Lake lying in the snow. *Lake!* As soon as the red light circles farther, it's dark, and I don't see her anymore. I run.

I try to scream her name, but nothing comes out. Though there are people in my way, I shove past them. I keep running and running, but it feels like the distance between us keeps growing.

"Will!" I hear Gavin yell. He's and running after me.

When I finally reach her, she's lying there in the snow with her eyes closed. There's blood on her head. So much blood. I tear off my jacket and throw it in the snow and remove my shirt. I begin wiping the blood off her face with it, trying desperately to find her injuries.

"Lake! No, no, no. Lake, no." I touch her face, trying to get some sort of reaction. It's cold. She's so cold. As soon as I put my hands under her shoulders to pull her into my lap, someone pulls me back. Paramedics swarm her. I can't see her anymore. I can't see her.

"Will!" Gavin yells. He's in my face. He's shaking me. "Will! We need to get to the hospital. They'll take her there. We need to go."

He's trying to push me away from her. I can't speak, so I shake my head and push him out of my way. I start to run back to them. Back to her. He pulls me back again. "Will, don't! Let them help her."

I turn around and shove him, then run back to her. They're moving her onto a gurney when I skid to a stop in the snow next to her. "Lake!"

One of the paramedics pushes me back as the others carry her to the ambulance. "I need in there!" I yell. "Let me in there!" The paramedic won't let me by as they shut the doors and tap on the glass. The ambulance pulls away. As soon as its lights fade into the distance, I fall to my knees.

I can't breathe.

I can't breathe.

I still can't breathe.

13.

WHEN I OPEN MY EYES, I IMMEDIATELY HAVE TO CLOSE them again. It's so bright. I'm shaking. My whole body is shaking. Actually, it's not my body that's shaking at all. It's whatever I'm lying on that's shaking.

"Will? Are you okay?"

I hear Caulder's voice. I open my eyes and see him sitting next to me. We're in an ambulance. He's crying. I try to sit up to hug him, but someone pushes me back down.

"Be still, sir. You've got a pretty bad gash I'm working on here."

I look at the person talking to me. It's the paramedic who was holding me back. "Is she okay?" I feel myself succumb to the panic again. "Where is she? Is she okay?"

He puts his hand on my shoulder to hold me still and places gauze over my eye. "I wish I knew something, but

I don't. I'm sorry. I just know I need to get this injury of yours closed. We'll find out more when we get there."

I look around the ambulance, but I don't see Kel. "Where's Kel?"

"They put him and Gavin in the other ambulance to check on them. They said we would see them at the hospital," Caulder says.

I lay my head back, close my eyes, and pray.

AS SOON AS the ambulance doors open and they pull me out, I unfasten the straps and jump off the gurney.

"Sir, get back here! You need stitches!"

I keep running. I glance back to make sure Caulder is following me. He is, so I keep running. When I get inside, Gavin and Kel are standing at the nurses' station. "Kel!" I yell. Kel runs up to me and hugs me. I pick him up, and he wraps his arms around my neck. "Where are they?" I say to Gavin. "Where'd they take them?"

"I can't find anyone," Gavin says. He looks as panicked as I do. He sees a nurse round the corner, and he runs up to her. "We're looking for three girls who were just brought here?"

She glances at all four of us, then walks around the desk to her computer. "Are you family?"

Gavin looks at me, then back at her. "Yes," he lies.

She eyes Gavin and picks up the phone. "The family is here . . . yes, sir." She hangs up the phone. "Follow me."

She leads us around the corner and into a room. "The doctor will be with you as soon as possible."

I set Kel down in a chair next to Caulder. Gavin takes off his jacket and hands it to me. I look down and realize for the first time since I took it off that I'm not wearing a shirt. Gavin and I pace the room. Several minutes pass with no word. I can't take it anymore. "I've got to find her," I say.

I start to walk out of the room, but Gavin pulls me back. "Just give it a minute, Will. If they need to find you, you won't be here. Just give it a minute."

I begin to pace again; it's all I can do. Kel is still crying, so I bend down and hug him again. He hasn't said anything. Not a single word.

She has to be okay. She *has* to.

I glance across the hall and see a restroom. I go inside, and as soon as I shut the door behind me, I get sick. I lean over the toilet and vomit. When I think I'm finished, I wash my hands in the sink and rinse my mouth. I grip the edges of the sink and take a deep breath, trying to calm down. I need to calm down for Kel. He doesn't need to see me like this.

When I look in the mirror, I don't even recognize myself. There's dried blood all over the side of my face. The bandage the paramedic placed above my eye is already saturated. I grab a napkin and try to wipe off some of the blood. As I'm wiping, I find myself wishing I had some of Sherry's medicine.

Sherry. "Sherry!" I yell. I throw open the bathroom door. "Gavin! We have to call Sherry! Where's your phone?"

Gavin pats his pockets. "I think it's in my jacket," he says. "I need to call Joel."

I reach into his jacket and pull out his phone. "Shit! I don't know her number, it's in my phone."

"Hand it to me, I'll dial," Kel says. He wipes his eyes and reaches for the phone, so I hand it to him. After he punches in the numbers and hands me the phone, I suddenly feel sick again.

Sherry picks up on the second ring. "Hello?"

I can't speak. What am I supposed to say?

"Hello?" she says again.

"Sherry," I say. My voice cracks.

"Will?" she says. "Will? What's wrong?"

"Sherry," I say again. "We're at the hospital . . . they . . ."

"Will! Is she okay? Is Kiersten okay?"

I can't respond. Gavin takes the phone from my hand, and I run back to the bathroom.

THERE'S A KNOCK on the bathroom door a few minutes later. I'm sitting on the floor against the wall with my eyes closed. I don't respond. When the door opens, I look up. It's the paramedic.

"We've still got to get you stitched up," he says.

"You've got a pretty bad cut." He offers his hand. I take it and he pulls me up. I follow him down the hall and into an exam room, where he instructs me to lie back on the table. "Your friend said you've had some nausea. You more than likely have a concussion. Stay here, the nurse will be by in a minute."

AFTER I'VE BEEN stitched up and given instructions on how to care for the apparent concussion, I'm told to go to the nurses' station to fill out paperwork. When I get there, the nurse grabs a clipboard and hands it to me. "Which patient is your wife?" she asks.

I just stare at her. "My wife?" Then it dawns on me that Gavin told her we were related. I guess it's better if they think that. I'll get more information that way. "Layken Cohen . . . Cooper. Layken Cohen Cooper."

"Fill out these forms and bring them back to me. And if you don't mind, take this clipboard to the other gentleman with you. What about the little girl? Is she related to you?"

I shake my head. "She's my neighbor. Her mother's on the way." I grab the paperwork and head back to the waiting room. "Any news?" I ask, handing Gavin his clipboard. He just shakes his head.

"We've been here almost an hour! Where is everybody?" I throw my clipboard in the chair and sit down.

Just as I land, a man in a white lab coat rounds the corner toward us, followed by a frantic Sherry. I jump back up.

"Will!" she yells. She's crying. "Where is she? Where's Kiersten? Is she hurt?"

I put my arms around her, then look to the doctor for answers, since I don't have any.

"You're looking for the little girl?" the doctor asks. Sherry nods. "She'll be okay. She's got a broken arm and got hit on the head pretty hard. We're still waiting on a few test results, but you're welcome to go see her. I've just put her in room 212. If you'll head to the nurses' station, they can direct you."

"Oh, thank God," I say. Sherry lets go of me and darts around the corner.

"Which one of you is with the other young lady?" he asks.

Gavin and I look at each other. The doctor's singular reference makes my heart stop. "There are two!" I'm frantic. "There are two of them!"

He looks puzzled as to why I'm yelling at him. "I'm sorry," he says. "I was only brought the girl and a young lady. Sometimes, depending on the injuries, they don't come to me first. I only have news on a young lady with blond hair."

"Eddie! Is she okay?" Gavin asks.

"She's stable. They're running tests, so you can't go back yet."

"What about the baby? Is the baby okay?"

"That's why they're running tests, sir. I'll be back as soon as I know more." He starts to walk away, so I cut him off in the hallway.

"Wait!" I say. "What about Lake? I haven't heard anything. Is she okay? Is she in surgery?"

He looks at me with pity. It makes me want to punch him.

"I'm sorry, sir. I only treated the other two. I'll do my best to find some answers and get back with you as soon as I can." He hurries away.

They're not telling me anything! They aren't telling me a damn thing! I lean against the wall and slide down to the floor. I pull up my knees and rest my elbows on them and bury my face in my hands.

"Will?"

I look up. Kel is looking down at me.

"Why won't they just tell us if she's okay or not?"

I grab his hand and pull him to the floor with me. I put my arm around him, and he hugs me back. I stroke his hair and kiss him on top of the head, because I know that's what Lake would do. "I don't know, Kel. I don't know." I hold him while he cries. As much as I want to scream, as much as I want to cry, as much as my world is crashing down around me, I have to hold it all in for this little boy. I can't even begin to imagine what he's feeling. How scared he must be. Lake is the only person he has in this world. I hold him and kiss his head until he cries himself to sleep.

* * *

"WILL?"

I look up and see Sherry standing over me. I start to get up, but she shakes her head and points at Kel, who has fallen asleep in my lap. She sits down on the floor next to me.

"How's Kiersten?" I ask.

"She'll be okay. She's asleep. They may not even keep her overnight." She reaches over and strokes Kel's hair. "Gavin said you guys haven't heard anything about Layken yet?"

I shake my head. "It's been well over an hour, Sherry. Why aren't they telling me anything? They won't even tell me if she's . . ." I can't finish the sentence. I take a deep breath, trying to maintain my composure.

"Will . . . if that were the case, they would have told you by now. That means they're doing everything they can."

I know she's trying to help, but her statement hits me hard. I pick Kel up and carry him back to the waiting room and lay him in the chair next to Gavin. He wakes up and looks at me. "I'll be back," I say. I run down the hallway to the nurses' station, but there isn't anyone there. The doors leading to the emergency rooms are locked. I look around for someone. There are a few people staring at me in the general waiting area, but no one offers to assist me. I walk behind the nurses' station and look around until I find the button that opens the emergency doors. I press the button, then jump over the desk and run through the doors just as they open.

"Can I help you?" a nurse asks when I pass her in the hallway. I round a corner and see a sign that says patient rooms are to the right and surgery is to the left. I turn left. As soon as I see the double doors to the operating rooms, I hit the button on the wall to open them. Before they're even open far enough, I try to squeeze myself through them, but a man pushes me back. "You can't be in here," he says.

"No! I need to be in there!" I try to shove past him.

He's a lot stronger than I am. He pushes me against the wall and lifts his leg, kicking the button with his foot. The doors close behind him. "You aren't allowed in there," he says calmly. "Now, who are you looking for?" He releases his grip on my arms and stands back.

"My girlfriend," I say. I'm out of breath. I lean forward and put my hands on my knees. "I need to know if she's okay."

"I've got a young woman who sustained injuries in a vehicle accident. Is that the person you're referring to?"

I nod. "Is she okay?"

He leans against the wall next to me. He slides his hands into the pockets of his white coat and pulls one of his knees up, settling his foot against the wall behind him. "She's hurt. She has an epidural hematoma that's going to require surgery."

"What is that? What does that mean? Will she be okay?"

"She experienced severe head trauma that has caused bleeding in her brain. It's too early to give you any more information at this point. Until we get her into surgery, we won't know the extent of her injuries. I was just coming to speak to the family. Do you need me to relay this information to her parents?"

I shake my head. "She doesn't have any. She doesn't have anyone. I'm all she's got."

He straightens up and walks back to the doors and presses the button. He turns just as they open. "What's your name?" he asks.

"Will."

He looks me in the eyes. "I'm Dr. Bradshaw," he says. "I'll do everything I can for her, Will. In the meantime, go back to the waiting room. I'll find you as soon as I know something." The doors close behind him.

I slide down to the floor in an attempt to regain my bearings.

She's alive.

WHEN I MAKE it back to the waiting room, Kel and Caulder are the only ones there.

"Where's Gavin?" I ask.

"Joel called. Gavin went outside to meet him," Caulder says.

"Did you hear anything?" Kel asks.

I nod. "She's in surgery."

"So she's alive? She's alive?" He jumps up and wraps his arms around me. I return his hug.

"She's alive," I whisper. I sit down and gently guide him back into his chair. "Kel, she's hurt pretty bad. It's too soon to know anything, but they'll keep us updated, okay?" I grab a tissue from one of the many boxes scattered around the room and hand it to him. He wipes his nose.

We all sit there in silence. I close my eyes and think back to the conversation I just had with the doctor. Were there any hints in his expression? In his voice? I know he knows more than he's telling me, which scares the hell out of me. What if something happens to her? I can't think about it. I don't think about. She'll be okay. She has to be.

"Anything?" Gavin asks as he and Joel walk into the waiting room. "I had Joel grab you a shirt," he says, handing it to me.

"Thanks." I give Gavin his jacket and pull the shirt on. "Lake's in surgery. She's got a head injury. They don't know anything yet. That's all I know. What about Eddie?" I ask. "Have you heard anything else? Is the baby okay?"

Gavin looks at me, wide-eyed.

Joel jumps up. "Baby?" he yells. "What the hell is he talking about, Gavin?"

Gavin stands up. "We were going to tell you, Joel. It's still so early . . . we . . . we haven't had a chance."

Joel storms out, and Gavin follows him. I'm such an idiot.

"Can we go see Kiersten?" Kel asks.

I nod. "Don't stay too long. She needs her rest."

Kel and Caulder leave.

I'm alone. I close my eyes and lean my head against the wall. I take several deep breaths, but the pressure in my chest keeps building and building and building. I try to keep holding it all in. I try to hold it in like Lake does. I can't. I bring my hands to my face and break down. I don't just cry; I *sob*. I *wail*. I *scream*.

14.

Now that I have you back, I'm never letting you go. That's a promise. I'm not letting you go again.

I'M IN THE BATHROOM SPLASHING WATER ON MY FACE when I hear someone talking outside the door. I swing it open to see if it's the doctor, but it's Gavin and Joel. I've started to shut the door when Gavin reaches in and stops me.

"Will, your grandparents are here. They're looking for you."

"My grandparents? Who called them?"

"I did," he says. "I thought maybe they could take Kel and Caulder for you."

I step out of the bathroom. "Where are they?"

"Around the corner," he says.

I see my grandparents standing in the hallway. My grandfather has his coat folded over his hands. He's saying something to my grandmother when he catches a glimpse of me. "Will!" They both run toward me.

"Are you okay?" my grandmother says, brushing her fingers against the bandages on my forehead.

I pull away from her. "I'm fine," I say.

She hugs me. "Have you heard anything?"

I shake my head. I'm getting really tired of this question.

"Where are the boys?"

"They're up in Kiersten's room," I say.

"Kiersten? She was involved, too?"

I nod.

"Will, the nurse is asking about paperwork. They need it. Have you finished filling it out yet?" my grandfather says.

"I haven't started it yet. I don't feel like doing paperwork right now." I begin walking back to the waiting room. I need to sit down.

Gavin and Joel are seated in the waiting room. Gavin looks awful. I didn't notice before, but his arm is in a sling.

"You okay?" I ask, nodding in the direction of the sling.

"Yeah."

I sit down and prop my legs up on the table in front of me and tilt my head against the back of the chair. My grandparents take seats opposite me. Everyone's staring at me. I feel like they're all waiting on me. I don't know why. Waiting for me to cry, maybe? To yell? To hit something?

"*What!*" I yell at all of them. My grandmother flinches. I immediately feel guilty, but I don't apologize. I close my eyes and inhale, trying to figure out the order of events. I remember talking to Gavin about Eddie, and I remember Gavin yelling. I even remember slamming on the brakes, but I can't remember why. I can't remember anything after that . . . up to opening my eyes in the car.

I bring my legs off the table and turn to Gavin. "What happened, Gavin? I don't remember."

He makes a face as if he's tired of explaining. He does it anyway, though. "A truck crossed the median and hit their car. You slammed on your brakes, so we weren't involved in that wreck. But when you slammed on your brakes, we were hit from behind. It knocked us into the ditch. As soon as I got out of the car, I ran to Layken's car. I saw her get out, so I thought she was okay . . . that's when I went to check on Eddie."

"So you saw her? She got out on her own? She wasn't thrown from the car?"

He shakes his head. "No, I think she was confused. She must have passed out. But I saw her walking."

I don't know if the fact that she got out on her own makes a difference, but it somehow eases my mind a little.

My grandfather leans forward in his chair and looks at me. "Will. I know you don't want to deal with it right now, but they need as much information as you can give them.

They don't even know her name. They need to know if she's allergic to anything. Does she have insurance? If you give them her social security number, they may be able to figure a lot of this out."

I sigh. "I don't know. I don't know if she has insurance. I don't know her social. I don't know if she's allergic to anything. She hasn't got anyone but me, and I don't know a damn thing!" I lay my head in my hands, ashamed that Lake and I have never discussed any of this before. Didn't we learn anything? From my parents' deaths? From Julia's death? Here I am, possibly facing my past head-on again . . . *unprepared* and *overwhelmed.*

My grandfather walks over to me and wraps his arms around me. "I'm sorry, Will. We'll figure it out."

ANOTHER HOUR PASSES with no word. Not even about Eddie. Joel goes with my grandparents and Kel and Caulder to the cafeteria for food. Gavin stays with me.

I guess he gets tired of sitting in the chairs because he gets up and lies down on the floor. It looks like a good idea, so I do the same thing. I put my hands under my head and raise my feet up in a chair.

"I'm trying not to think about it, Will. But if the baby isn't okay . . . Eddie . . ."

I hear the fear in his voice. "Gavin . . . stop. Stop thinking about it. Let's just think about something else for a while. We'll drive ourselves insane if we don't."

"Yeah . . ." he says.

We're silent, so I know we're both still thinking about it. I try to think about anything else.

"I kicked Reece out this morning," I say, doing my best to tear our minds away from reality.

"Why? I thought you guys were best friends," he says. He sounds relieved to be talking about something else.

"We used to be. Things change. People change. People get new best friends," I say.

"That they do."

We're quiet again for a while. My mind starts drifting back to Lake, so I reel myself back in. "I punched him," I say. "Right in the jaw. It was beautiful. I wish you could've seen it."

Gavin laughs. "Good. I never have liked him."

"I'm not so sure I did, either," I say. "It's just one of those things where you feel obligated to the friendship, I guess."

"Those are the worst kind," he says.

Every now and then, one of us will lift our head when we hear someone walk by. We eventually become too tired even to do that. I've begun to drift off to sleep when I'm sucked back into reality. "Sir?" someone says from the doorway. Gavin and I jump up.

"She's in a room now," the nurse says to Gavin. "You can go see her. Room 207."

"She's okay? Is the baby okay?"

The nurse nods at him and smiles.

And Gavin is gone. Just like that.

The nurse turns to me. "Dr. Bradshaw wanted me to let you know they're still in surgery. He doesn't have any updates yet, but we'll let you know as soon as we find something out."

"Thank you," I say.

MY GRANDPARENTS EVENTUALLY come back with Kel and Caulder. My grandfather and Kel are trying to fill out the paperwork for Lake. There aren't any questions I could answer that Kel doesn't already know the answers to. They leave most of the questions blank. My grandfather walks the forms to the nurses' station and returns with a box. "These are some of the personal items found in the vehicles," he says to me.

I lean forward and look inside the box. My satchel is on top, so I pull it out. Lake's purse is there. So are my cell phone and my jacket. I don't see her phone. Knowing Lake, she probably lost it *before* the wreck. I open her purse and pull out her wallet and hand it to my grandfather. "Look in there. She might have an insurance card or something."

He takes the wallet out of my hands and opens it. They must have already given Eddie's things to Gavin, because there's nothing left in the box.

"It's late," my grandmother says. "We'll take the boys

home with us so they can get some rest. Do you need anything before we go?"

"I don't want to go," Kel says.

"Kel, sweetie. You need some rest. There isn't anywhere you can sleep here," she says.

Kel looks at me and silently pleads.

"He can stay with me," I say.

My grandmother picks up her purse and coat. I follow them out and walk down the hall with them. When we get to the end of the hallway, I stop and give Caulder a hug. "I'll call you as soon as I find out anything," I say to him. My grandparents hug me goodbye, and they leave. My entire family leaves.

I'M ALMOST ASLEEP when I feel someone shaking my shoulder. I jerk up and look around, hoping someone's here with some news. It's just Kel.

"I'm thirsty," he says.

I look down at my watch. It's after one in the morning. Why haven't they told me anything? I reach into my pocket and take out my wallet. "Here," I say, handing him some cash. "Bring me a coffee." Kel takes the money and leaves just as Gavin walks back into the room. He looks at me for answers, but I shake my head. He sits down in the seat next to me.

"So Eddie's okay?" I ask.

"Yeah. She's bruised up but okay," he says.

I'm too tired to make small talk. Gavin fills the silent void.

"She's further along than we thought she was," he says. "She's about sixteen weeks. They let us see the baby on a monitor. They're pretty sure it's a girl."

"Oh yeah?" I say. I'm not sure how Gavin feels about the whole thing, so I refrain from congratulating him. Doesn't feel like a good situation for congratulations, anyway.

"I saw her heart beating," he says.

"Whose? Eddie's?"

He shakes his head and smiles at me. "No. My baby girl's." His eyes tear up and he looks away.

Now is the right time. I smile. "Congratulations."

Kel walks in with two coffees. He hands me one and plops down in the chair and takes a sip of the other.

"Are you drinking coffee?" I ask him.

He nods. "Don't try to take it from me, either. I'll run."

I laugh. "Okay, then." I bring the coffee up to my mouth, but before I take a sip, Dr. Bradshaw walks in. I jump up, and the coffee splashes on my shirt. Or Joel's shirt. Or Gavin's. Whoever the hell's shirt I have on, it's got coffee all over it now.

"Will? Walk with me?" Dr. Bradshaw tilts his head toward the hallway.

"Wait here, Kel, I'll be right back." I set the coffee down on the table.

We've gotten to the end of the hallway before he starts

to speak. When he does, I have to brace myself against the wall. I feel like I'm about to collapse.

"She made it through surgery, but we aren't close to being in the clear. She had a lot of bleeding. Some swelling. I did what I could without removing a portion of her parietal bone. Now all we can do is watch and wait."

My heart is pounding against my chest. It's hard to pay attention when I have a million questions on the tip of my tongue. "What is it we're waiting for? If she made it this far, what are the dangers?"

He leans against the wall next to me. We're staring at our feet, as if he's trying to avoid looking me in the eyes. He has to hate this part of his job. I hate this part of his job *for* him. That's why I don't look at him—I feel like maybe it takes the pressure off.

"The brain is the most delicate organ in the human body. Unfortunately, we aren't able to tell just by looking at scans what exactly a person's injuries are. It's more like a waiting game, so for right now we're keeping her under anesthesia. Hopefully, by morning we'll have more of an idea what we're dealing with."

"Can I see her?"

He sighs. "Not yet. She's in recovery throughout the night. I'll let you know as soon as they take her to ICU." He straightens up and puts his hands in the pockets of his lab coat. "Do you have any more questions, Will?"

Now I look him in the eyes. "A million," I reply.

He takes my response as it was rhetorically intended and he walks away.

WHEN I RETURN to the waiting room, Gavin is still sitting with Kel, who jumps up and rushes to me. "Is she okay?"

"She's out of surgery," I say. "But they won't know anything until tomorrow."

"Know anything about what?" Kel asks.

I sit and motion for him to sit down next to me. I pause so I can find the right words. I want to explain in a way that he'll understand. "When she hit her head, she hurt her brain, Kel. We won't know how badly she's hurt, when she'll wake up, or even if there's any damage until they take her off the anesthesia."

Gavin says, "I'll go tell Eddie. She's been hysterical," and he leaves the room.

I was hoping a weight would be lifted off my shoulders after finally speaking with the doctor, but it doesn't feel that way at all. It feels worse. I feel so much worse. I just want to see her.

"Will?" Kel says.

"Yeah?" I reply. I'm too tired to look at him. I can't even keep my eyes open.

"What'll happen to me? If . . . she can't take care of me? Where will I go?"

I manage to open my eyes and look at him. As soon

as we make eye contact, he starts crying. I wrap my arms around him and pull his head against my chest. "You aren't going anywhere, Kel. We're in this together. You and me." I pull back and look him in the eyes. "I mean it. No matter what happens."

15.

Kel,

I don't know what's about to happen in our lives. I wish I did. God, I wish I did.

I was lucky enough to be nineteen when I lost my parents; you were only nine. That's a lot of growing up left to do for a little boy without a dad.

But whatever happens . . . whichever road we have to take when we leave this hospital . . . we're taking it together.

I'll do my best to help you finish growing up with the closest thing to a dad you can have. I'll do my absolute best.

I don't know what's about to happen in our lives. I wish I did. God, I wish I did.

But whatever happens, I'll love you. I can promise you that.

"WILL."

I try to crack my eyes, but only one of them opens. I'm lying on the floor again. I close my eye before my entire head explodes.

"Will, wake up."

I sit up and run my hands along the chairs next to me, pulling myself into one by the arm. I still can't open my other eye. I shield my vision from the fluorescent lights and turn toward the voice.

"Will, I need you to listen to me."

I finally recognize the voice as Sherry's. "I'm listening," I whisper. It feels like if I spoke any louder, it would be too painful. My whole head hurts. I bring my hand to the bandage, then to my eye. It's swollen. No wonder I can't open it.

"I'm having the nurse bring you some medicine. You need to eat something. They aren't keeping Kiersten, so we're going home soon. I'll be back to wake up Kel after I get Kiersten into the car. I'll bring him back up here during the day; I just think he needs some rest. Is there anything you need from your house? Besides a change of clothes?"

I shake my head, which hurts less than speaking.

"Okay. Call me if you think of anything."

"Sherry," I say before she exits. Then I realize nothing audible came out of my mouth. "Sherry!" I say louder, and wince. Why does my head hurt so bad?

She comes back.

"There's a vase in my cabinet. Above the fridge. I need it."

She acknowledges that with a nod and leaves the room.

"Kel," I say, shaking him awake. "I'm going to get something to drink. Do you want anything?"

He nods. "Coffee."

He must not be a morning person: just like his sister. When I pass the nurses' station, one of the nurses calls my name. I back-step and she holds out her hand. "These will help your head," she says. "Your mother said you needed them."

I laugh. My mother. I pop the pills into my mouth and swallow them and head to find coffee. The double doors in the lobby open as I pass them, sending a swarm of cold air around me. I stop and look outside, then decide some fresh air might do me some good. I take a seat on a bench under the awning. Everything's so white. The snow is still falling. I wonder how deep our driveways will be by the time Lake and I get home.

I don't know how it happens, how the thought even creeps its way into my head, but for a second I wonder what would happen to everything in Lake's house if she died. She doesn't have family to finalize anything. To deal with her bank accounts, her bills, her insurance, her possessions. She and I aren't related, and Kel's only eleven. Would they even let me do those things? Am I even legally allowed to keep Kel? As soon as the thoughts register, I force them back. It's pointless thinking like this, because that isn't going to happen. I get pissed at myself for letting my mind get carried away, so I head back inside to get the coffee.

WHEN I RETURN to the waiting room, Dr. Bradshaw is sitting with Kel. They don't notice me right away. He's telling a story, and Kel's laughing, so I don't interrupt. It's nice to hear Kel laugh. I stand outside the door and listen.

"Then when my mother told me to go get the box to bury the cat, I told her there was no need. I'd already brought him back to life," Dr. Bradshaw says. "It was that moment, after I resuscitated that kitten, I knew I wanted to be a doctor when I grew up."

"So you saved the kitten?" Kel asks him.

Dr. Bradshaw laughs. "No. He died again a few minutes later. But I had already made up my mind by then," he says.

Kel laughs, too. "At least you didn't want to be a veterinarian."

"No, clearly, I'm not cut out for animals."

"Any news?" I walk into the room and hand Kel his coffee.

Dr. Bradshaw stands up. "We've still got her under anesthesia. We were able to run some tests. I'm waiting on the results, but you can see her for a few minutes."

"Now? We can see her? Right now?" I'm gathering up my things as I reply.

"Will . . . I can't let anyone else in," he says. He looks down at Kel, then back at me. "She hasn't been moved from recovery yet . . . I'm not even supposed to let you in. But I'm doing some rounds and thought I'd let you walk with me."

I want to beg Dr. Bradshaw to let me take Kel with us, but I know he's already doing me a huge favor. "Kel, if I'm not back before you leave with Sherry, I'll call you."

He nods. I expect him to argue, but I think he understands. The fact that he's being so reasonable fills me with a sense of pride. I bend over and hug him and kiss him on top of the head. "I'll call you. As soon as I hear anything, I'll call you." He nods once more. I reach over and grab her clip from my satchel, then turn back toward the door.

I follow Dr. Bradshaw past the nurses' station, through the doors, and down the hall to the double doors leading to surgery. Before we go any farther, he takes me into a room where we both wash our hands. When we get to the door, I can barely catch my breath. I'm so nervous. My heart is about to explode through my chest.

"Will, you need to know a few things first. She's on a ventilator to help her breathe, but only because we've got her in a medically induced coma. There's no chance of her waking up right now with the amount of medicine we're giving her. Most of her head is bandaged. She looks worse than she feels; we're keeping her comfortable. I'll allow you a few minutes with her, but that's all I can give you right now. Understand?"

I nod.

He pushes open the door and lets me in.

As soon as I see her, I struggle to breathe. The reality of the moment knocks the air from my lungs. The ventilator sucks in a rush of air and releases it. With each repetitive sound of the machine, it's as if hope is being pushed out of me.

I go to the bed and take her hand. It's cold. I kiss her forehead. I kiss it a million times. I just want to lie down with her, hug her. There are too many wires and tubes and cords running everywhere. I pull a chair up next to the bed and interlock her fingers with mine. It's getting hard to see her through my tears, so I have to wipe my eyes on my shirt. She looks so peaceful, like she's just taking a nap.

"I love you, Lake," I whisper. I kiss her hand. "I love you," I whisper again. "I love you."

The covers are pulled tightly around her, and she's got a hospital gown on. Her head is wrapped in a bandage, but most of her hair is hanging down around her neck. I'm relieved they didn't cut all of her hair. She'd be pissed. The ventilator tube is taped over her mouth, so I kiss her forehead again and her cheek. I know she can't hear me, but I talk to her anyway.

"Lake, you have to pull through this. You *have* to." I stroke her hand. "I can't live without you." I turn her hand over and kiss her palm, then press it against my cheek. The feel of her skin against mine is surreal. I wasn't sure if I'd ever feel it again. I close my eyes and kiss her palm again and again. I sit there and cry and kiss the only parts of her I can.

"Will," Dr. Bradshaw says. "We need to go now."

I stand up and kiss her on the forehead. I take a step back, then take a step forward and kiss her hand. I take two steps back, then walk two steps toward her and kiss her cheek.

Dr. Bradshaw takes my arm. "Will, we need to go."

I take a few steps toward the door. "Wait," I say. I put my hand in my pocket and pull out her purple hair clip. I open her hand and place it in her palm and close her fingers over it, then kiss her on the forehead again before we leave.

THE REST OF the morning drags by. Kel left with Sherry. Eddie was discharged. She wanted to stay with me, but Gavin and Joel wouldn't let her. All I can do now is wait. Wait and think. Think and wait. That's all I can do. That's all I do.

I wander the halls for a while. I can't keep sitting in that waiting room. I've spent way too much of my life in there, and in this hospital. I was here for six solid days after my parents died, when I stayed with Caulder. I don't remember much from those days. Caulder and I were both in a daze, not really believing what was happening. Caulder had hit his head in the wreck and broken his arm. I'm not sure his injuries were near extensive enough to warrant six days in the hospital, but the staff didn't seem to feel comfortable just letting us go. Two orphans, into the wild.

Caulder was seven at the time, so the hardest part was all the questions he had. I couldn't get through to him that we weren't going to see our parents again. I think that six-day hospital stay is why I hate pity so much. Every single person who spoke to me felt sorry for me, and I could see it in their eyes. I could hear it in their voices.

I was here with Lake for two months off and on when Julia was sick. When Kel and Caulder would stay at my grandparents' house, Lake and I would stay here with Julia. Lake stayed most nights, in fact. When Kel wasn't with me, he was here with them. By the end of Julia's first week here, Lake and I ended up bringing an air mattress. Hospital furniture is the worst. They asked us a few times to remove the mattress from the room. Instead, we would just deflate it every morning and then blow it up again every night. We noticed they weren't so quick to ask us to remove it when we were asleep on it.

Out of all the nights I've spent here, this time feels different. It feels worse. Maybe it's the absence of finality, the lack of knowledge. At least after my parents had died and Caulder was here, I didn't question anything. I knew they were dead. I knew Caulder was going to be okay. Even with Julia, we knew her death was inevitable. We weren't left with questions while we waited; we knew what was happening. But this time . . . this time is much harder. It's so hard not knowing.

AS SOON AS I begin to doze off, Dr. Bradshaw walks in. I sit up in my chair, and he takes a seat next to me.

"We've moved her to a room in ICU. You'll be able to see her in an hour, during visiting hours. The scans look good. We'll try easing her off the anesthesia over time and see what happens. It's still touch and go, Will. Anything can happen. Getting her to respond to us is our priority now."

The relief washes over me, but a new sense of worry creeps in just as fast. "Does . . ." It feels like my throat is squeezed shut when I try to speak. I grab my bottle of water off the table in front of me and take a drink, then try again to speak. "Does she have a chance? At full recovery?"

He sighs. "I can't answer that. Right now the scans show normal activity, but that may not mean anything when it comes to trying to wake her up. Then again, it could mean she'll be perfectly fine. Until that moment, we won't know." He stands up. "She's in room five in ICU. Wait until one o'clock before you head down there."

I nod. "Thank you."

As soon as I hear him round the corner, I grab my things and run as fast as I can in the opposite direction to

ICU. The nurse doesn't ask any questions when I walk in. I act like I know exactly what I'm doing and head straight to room five.

There aren't as many wires, though she's still hooked up to the ventilator, and she has an IV in her left wrist. I walk around to the right side of the bed and pull the rail down. I climb into bed with her and wrap my arm around her and lay my leg over her legs. I take her hand in mine and I close my eyes . . .

"WILL," SHERRY SAYS. I jerk my eyes open, and she's standing on the other side of Lake's bed.

I stretch my arms out above my head. "Hey," I whisper.

"I brought you some clothes. And your vase. Kel was still asleep, so I just let him stay. I hope that's okay. I'll bring him back when he wakes up."

"Yeah, that's fine. What time is it?"

She looks at her watch. "Almost five," she says. "The nurse said you've been asleep for a couple of hours."

I push my elbow into the bed and lift myself up. My arm is asleep. I slide off the bed and stand up and stretch again.

"You do realize visitors are only allowed fifteen minutes," she says. "They must like you."

I laugh. "I'd like to see them try to kick me out," I say. I walk over to the chair and sit. The worst thing about hospitals is the furniture. The beds are too small for two people. The chairs are too hard for any people. And there's never a recliner. If they would just have a recliner, I might not detest them so much.

"Have you eaten anything today?" she asks.

I shake my head.

"Come downstairs with me. I'll buy you something to eat."

"I can't. I don't want to leave her," I say. "They've been reducing her meds. She could wake up."

"Well, you need to eat. I'll grab you something and bring it back up."

"Thanks," I say.

"You should at least take a shower. You've got dried blood all over you. It's gross." She smiles at me and starts to head out the door.

"Sherry. Don't bring me a hamburger, okay?"

She laughs.

After she's gone, I get up, take out a star, and then crawl back in the bed with Lake. "This one's for you, babe." I unfold the star and read it.

Never, under any circumstances, take a sleeping pill and a laxative on the same night.

I roll my eyes. "Jesus, Julia! Now's not the time to be funny!" I reach over and grab another star, then lie back down. "Let's try this again, babe."

Strength does not come from physical capacity. It comes from an indomitable will.

—MAHATMA GANDHI

I lean over and whisper in her ear. "You hear that, Lake? Indomitable will. That's one of the things I love about you."

I MUST HAVE fallen asleep again. The nurse shakes me awake. "Sir, can you step outside for a moment?"

Dr. Bradshaw walks into the room. "Is she okay?" I ask him.

"We're removing the ventilator now. The anesthesia is wearing off, so she's not getting anything other than the pain medicine through her IV." He raises the bed rail. "Just step outside for a few minutes. I promise we'll let you back in." He smiles.

He's smiling. *This is good.* They're taking her off the ventilator. *This is good.* He's looking me in the eyes. *This is good.* I step outside and impatiently wait.

I pace the hallway for fifteen minutes before he emerges from the room. "Her vitals look fine. She's breathing on her own. Now we wait," he says. He pats me on the shoulder and turns to leave.

I go back in the room and crawl in the bed with her. I put my ear to her mouth and listen to her breathe. It's the most beautiful sound in the world. I kiss her. Of course I kiss her. I kiss her a million times.

SHERRY MADE ME take a shower when she got back with our food. Gavin and Eddie showed up around six o'clock and stayed for an hour. Eddie cried the whole time, so Gavin got worried and made her leave again. Sherry came back with Kel before visiting hours were over. He didn't cry, but I think he was upset seeing her like this, so they didn't stay long. I've been giving my grandmother hourly calls, although nothing has changed.

Now it's somewhere around midnight, and I'm just sitting here. Waiting. Thinking. Waiting and thinking. I keep imagining I see her toe move. Or her finger. It's driving me crazy, so I stop watching. I start thinking about everything that happened Thursday night. Our cars. Where *are* our cars? I should probably be calling the insurance company. What about school? I missed school today. Or was it yesterday? I don't know if it's Saturday yet. I probably won't be in school next week, either. I should figure out who Lake's professors are and let them know she won't be there. I should probably let my professors know, too. And the elementary school. What do I tell them? I don't know when the boys will go back. If Lake is still in the hospital next week, I know Kel won't want to go to school. But he just missed an entire week. He can't miss many more days. And what about Caulder? Where are Kel and Caulder going to stay while Lake and I are here? I'm not leaving the hospital without Lake. I may not even leave *with* Lake if I don't figure out what to do about a car. My car. Where *is* my car?

"Will."

I glance to the door. No one's there. Now I'm hearing things. Too many thoughts are jumbled up in my head right now. I wonder if Sherry left me any of her medicine. I bet she did. She probably sneaked it in my bag.

"Will."

I jerk up in my seat and look at Lake. Her eyes are closed. She isn't moving. I know I heard my name. I know I did! I rush to her and touch her face. "Lake?"

She flinches. She flinches! "Lake!"

Her lips part and she says it again. "Will?"

She squints. She's trying to open her eyes. I flick the light switch off, then pull the string to the overhead light until it clicks off. I know how much these fluorescent lights hurt.

"Lake," I whisper. I pull the rail down and climb into the bed with her. I kiss her on the lips, the cheek, the forehead. "Don't try to talk if it hurts. You're okay. I'm right here. You're okay." She moves her hand, so I take it in mine. "Can you feel my hand?"

She nods. It's not much of a nod, but it's a nod.

"You're okay," I say. I keep saying it over and over until I'm crying. "You're okay."

The door to her room opens, and a nurse walks in.

"She said my name!"

She looks up at me, then rushes out of the room and comes back with Dr. Bradshaw. "Get up, Will," he says. "Let us examine her. We'll let you back in soon."

"She said my name," I say as I slide off the bed. "She said my name!"

He smiles at me. "Go outside."

And so I do. For over half an hour. No one has left the room and no one has entered and it's been half a freakin' hour. I knock on the door, and the nurse cracks it. I try to peek past her, but she doesn't open the door far enough. "Just a few more minutes," she says.

I contemplate calling everyone, but I don't. I just need to make sure I wasn't hearing things, though I know she heard me. She spoke to me. She moved.

Dr. Bradshaw opens the door and steps outside. The nurses follow him out.

"I heard her, right? She's okay? She said my name!"

"Calm down, Will. You need to calm down. They won't let you stay in here if you keep freaking out like this."

Calm down? He has no idea how calm I'm being!

"She's responding," he says. "Her physical responses were all good. She doesn't remember what happened. She may not remember a lot of stuff right away. She needs rest, Will. I'll let you back inside, but you'll need to let her rest."

"Okay, I will. I promise. I swear."

"I know. Now go," he says.

When I open the door, she's facing me. She smiles a really pathetic, pained smile.

"Hey," I whisper.

"Hey," she whispers back.

"Hey." I walk to her bed and stroke her cheek.

"Hey," she says again.

"Hey."

"Stop it," she says. She tries to laugh, but it hurts her. She closes her eyes.

I take her hand in mine, and I bury my face in the crevice between her shoulder and her neck, and I cry.

FOR THE NEXT few hours, she goes in and out of consciousness, just like Dr. Bradshaw said she would. Every time she wakes up, she says my name. Every time she says my name, I tell her to close her eyes and get some rest. Every time I tell her to close her eyes and get some rest, she does.

Dr. Bradshaw comes in a few times to check on her. They lower the dose in the IV one more time so she can stay awake for longer periods. I decide again not to call anyone. It's still too early, and I don't want everyone bombarding her. I just want her to rest.

It's almost seven in the morning and I'm walking out of the bathroom when she finally says something besides my name. "What happened?" she asks.

I pull a chair up beside her bed. She's rolled over onto

her left side, so I rest my chin on the bed rail and stroke her arm. "We were in a wreck."

She looks confused, then terror washes over her face. "The kids—"

"Everyone's fine," I reassure her. "Everyone's okay."

She breathes a sigh of relief. "When? What day was it? What day *is* it?"

"It's Saturday. It happened Thursday night. What's the last thing you remember?"

She closes her eyes. I reach up and pull the string to the light above her bed, and it flicks off. I don't know why they keep turning it on. What hospital patient wants a fluorescent light three feet from her head?

"I remember going to the slam," she says. "I remember your poem . . . but that's all. That's all I can remember." She opens her eyes again and looks at me. "Did I forgive you?"

I laugh. "Yes, you forgave me. And you love me. A bunch."

She smiles. "Good."

"You were hurt. They had to take you into surgery."

"I know. The doctor told me that much."

I stroke her cheek with the back of my hand. "I'll tell you everything that happened later, okay? Right now you need to rest. I'm going outside to call everyone. Kel's worried sick. Eddie, too. I'll be back, okay?"

She nods and closes her eyes again. I lean forward

and kiss her on the forehead. "I love you, Lake." I grab my phone off the table and stand up.

"Again," she whispers.

"I love you."

VISITING HOURS ARE strictly enforced once everyone starts to arrive. They make me wait in the waiting room just like everyone else. Only one person is allowed in at a time. Eddie and Gavin got here first. Kel shows up with Sherry about the same time my grandparents show up with Caulder.

"Can I go see her?" Kel asks.

"Absolutely. She keeps asking for you. Eddie's with her right now. It's ICU, so Lake can only have visitors for fifteen minutes, but you're next."

"So she's talking? She's okay? She remembers me?"

"Yeah. She's perfect," I say.

Grandpaul walks over to Kel and puts a hand on his shoulder. "Come on, Grandkel, we'll get you some breakfast before you go see her."

My grandparents take Kel and Caulder to the cafeteria. I ask them to bring me something back. I finally have an appetite.

"Do you need me and Eddie to stay with the boys for a few days?" Gavin asks.

"No. Not now, anyway. My grandparents are keeping them for a couple of days. I don't want them to miss a lot of school, though."

"I'm sending Kiersten back to school on Wednesday," Sherry says. "If your grandparents have them home on Tuesday, they can stay with me until Layken is discharged."

"Thanks, guys," I say to both of them.

Eddie walks around the corner. She's wiping her eyes and sniffing. I sit up in my chair, and Gavin takes Eddie's arm and guides her to a seat. She rolls her eyes at him. "Gavin, I'm pregnant. Quit treating me like I'm an invalid."

Gavin sits next to her. "I'm sorry, babe. I just worry about you." He leans forward and kisses her stomach. "Both of you."

Eddie smiles and kisses him on the cheek.

It's good to see that he's accepted his upcoming role as a dad. I know they've got a lot of hurdles ahead of them, but I have faith that they'll make it. I guess Lake and I could start recycling our stars for them, just in case they need them."How's Lake feeling?" I ask.

Eddie shrugs. "Like shit," she says. "But she did just have her head cut open, so that's understandable. I told her all about the wreck. She felt kind of bad once she found out she was the one driving. I told her it wasn't her fault, but she still said she wishes you were driving. That way she could blame her injuries on you."

I laugh. "She can blame them on me anyway, if it makes her feel better."

"We're coming back this afternoon," Eddie says.

"She really needs some TLC in the makeup department. Is two o'clock okay? Does anyone have that time slot yet?"

I shake my head. "See you guys at two."

Before they leave, Eddie walks over and gives me a hug. An unusually long hug.

After she and Gavin walk out, I look down at my watch. Kel will see her next, then Sherry. My grandmother may want to see her. I guess I'll have to wait until after lunch before they'll let me back in.

"You've got great friends," Sherry says.

I raise my eyebrows at her. "You don't think they're weird? Most people think my friends are weird."

"Yeah, I do. That's why they're great," she says.

I smile and scoot down in my seat until my head is resting against the back of the chair. I close my eyes. "You're pretty weird yourself, Sherry."

She laughs. "You, too."

I can't get comfortable in the chair, so I resort to lying on the floor again. I stretch my arms out above my head and sigh. The floor actually feels comfortable. Now that I know Lake will be okay, I'm starting not to despise the hospital as much.

"Will?" Sherry says.

I open my eyes. She's not looking at me. She's got her legs crossed in the chair, and she's picking at the seam of her jeans.

"What's up?" I reply.

She looks at me and smiles. "You did a great job," she says quietly. "I know it was hard, calling me about Kiersten. And taking care of the boys during all of this. How you've handled everything with Layken. You're too young to have so much responsibility, but you're doing a good job. I hope you know that. Your mom and dad would be proud."

I close my eyes and inhale. I didn't know how much I needed to hear that until this very second. Sometimes it feels good to have your biggest fears discounted with a simple compliment. "Thank you."

She gets out of the chair and lies down next to me on the floor. Her eyes are closed, but I can tell from the set of her face that she's trying not to cry. I look away. Sometimes women just need to cry.

We're quiet for a little while. She blows out a deep breath. "He was killed a year later. A year after he proposed. In a car accident," she says.

I realize she's telling me the story about Jim. I roll over and face her, resting my head on my elbow. I don't really know what to say, so I don't say anything.

"I'm okay," she says. She smiles at me. This time it seems like she's trying not to pity herself. "It's been a long time. I love my family and wouldn't trade them for the world. But sometimes it's still hard. Times like these . . ." She pulls herself up and sits Indian-style on the floor. She begins to pick at the seam of her pants again. "I was so scared for you, Will. I was scared she wouldn't make it. Seeing you go through that brought back a lot of memories. That's why I haven't been up here very much."

I understand the expression in her eyes and the heartache in her voice. I understand it, and I hate it for her. "It's okay," I say. "I didn't expect you to stay. You had Kiersten to worry about."

"I know you didn't expect me to stay. I wouldn't have been any help. But I worry about you. I worry about all of you. Kel, Caulder, you, Layken. Now I even like your damn weird friends, and I'm gonna have to worry about them, too." She laughs.

I smile at her. "It's nice to be worried about, Sherry. Thank you."

16.

I've learned something about my heart.
It can break.
It can be ripped apart.
It can harden and freeze.
It can stop. Completely.
It can shatter into a million pieces.
It can explode.
It can die.
The only thing that made it start beating again?
The moment you opened your eyes.

ALL THE VISITS WEAR LAKE OUT, AND SHE SLEEPS THE majority of the afternoon. She slept through Eddie's second visit, which was probably good, for Lake's sake. I highly doubt she would feel like being pampered. The nurse brought her soup at dinnertime, and she sipped most of it. It was the first thing she's eaten since Thursday.

She asked more questions about the night of the wreck. She wanted to know all about her forgiving me and our making up. I told her everything that happened after I performed. For the most part, I was honest, but I may have thrown in a more climactic make-out scene for emphasis.

IT'S SUNDAY, AND the fact that she's in the hospital doesn't deter her from her routine. I walk into her hospital room and set the bags of movies and junk food down in the chair. Lake is sitting up on the side of the bed, and the nurse is working with the IV.

"Oh, good. You're right on time," the nurse says. "She doesn't want a sponge bath, she wants a standard bath. I was about to assist her in the bathroom, but if you'd rather do it, you can." She unhooks the IV and clamps it, then tapes the end of it to Lake's hand.

Lake and I look at each other. It's not like I've never seen her naked—just not for prolonged periods. And with the lights *on*.

"I . . . I don't know," I mutter. "Do you want me to help you?"

Lake shrugs. "It wouldn't be the first time you've put me in a shower. Although I hope you help me take my clothes *off* this time." She laughs at her own joke. She regrets the laugh, though. Her hand goes up to her head, and she winces.

The nurse can sense the slight awkwardness between us. "I'm sorry. I thought you guys were married. It said on her chart that you were her husband."

"Yeah . . . about that," I say. "Not quite yet."

"It's fine," the nurse says. "If you'll just go back to the waiting room, I'll let you know when we're finished."

"No," Lake says. "He'll help me." She looks up at me. "You'll help me." I nod at the nurse, who takes a few items off the tray next to Lake's bed and leaves the room.

"Have you walked any more today?" I take Lake's arm and help lift her off the bed.

She nods. "Yeah. They had me walk down the hall between visits. I feel better than yesterday, just dizzy."

The nurse comes back with a towel. "Just don't let her get her head wet. There's a handheld shower, or she can use the bathtub. The tub may be better for her, so she can lie down." The nurse leaves the towel in the chair and exits again.

Lake slowly stands up, and I assist her into the bathroom. Once we're inside, I close the door behind us.

"This is so embarrassing," she says.

"Lake, you asked me to stay. If you want, I'll go back and get the nurse."

"No. I just mean because I need to pee."

"Oh. Here." I walk around her and grab her other arm as she backs up.

She grabs hold of the metal bar attached to the wall and pauses. "Turn around," she says.

I face the opposite direction. "Babe, if you're already making me look away, it'll be kind of hard for me to help you in the shower. You aren't even naked yet."

"That's different. I just don't want you to watch me pee."

I laugh. And I wait. And I wait some more. Nothing happens.

"Maybe you need to leave for a minute," she says.

I shake my head and walk out of the bathroom. "Don't try to stand up without me." I leave the door open a few inches so I can hear her if she needs me. When she's finished, I go back in and help her stand up. "Shower or bath?" I ask.

"Bath. I don't think I can stand up long enough for a shower."

I make sure she's holding on to the bar before I let go of her arm. I adjust the tub faucet until the water turns warm. I grab the washcloth and get it wet, then set it on the side of the tub. It's a large tub, with two steps leading up to make it easier to walk down into. I take Lake's arm again and lead her to the bathtub. I stand behind her and brush her hair over her shoulder and untie the top of her gown. When it drapes open, I have to suppress a gasp. She's got bruises all over her back. There's one more tie on the gown, so I pull the string until it separates.

She slides the gown forward and down her arms. I

run my fingers under the stream of water to check the temperature, then help her up the steps and into the bathtub. Once she's seated, she pulls her knees up to her chest and wraps her arms around them, then rests her head on them. "Thank you," she says. "For not trying to put the moves on me just now."

I smile at her. "Don't thank me yet. We just got started." I dip the washcloth in the water and kneel beside the bathtub. The steps come out pretty far, so it's hard to reach her without hovering.

She takes the washcloth out of my hand and begins washing her arm. "It's weird how much energy everything takes. I feels like my arms weigh a hundred pounds each."

I open the bar of soap and hand it to her, but it slips out of her grasp. She feels around in the water until she finds it, then she rubs it in the washcloth.

"Do you know how long before they let me go home?" she asks.

"Hopefully by Wednesday. The doctor said recovery can take anywhere from a few days to two weeks depending on how the injury heals. You seem to be doing pretty well."

She frowns. "I don't feel like I'm doing well."

"You're doing great," I say.

She smiles and sets the washcloth back on the side of the tub and wraps her arms around her knees again. "I have to rest," she says. "I'll get to the other arm in a minute." She closes her eyes. She looks so tired.

I reach over and turn off the water, then stand up and take off my shoes and my shirt but leave my pants on. "Scoot up," I say to her.

She does, and I step into the bathtub and slide down into the water behind her. I put my legs on either side of her and gently lay her back on my chest. I grab the wash-cloth and run it up the arm she was too tired to get to.

"You're crazy," she says quietly.

I kiss her on top of the head. "So are you."

We're silent as I wash her. She rests against my chest until I tell her to lean forward so I can get her back. I put more soap on the washcloth and gently touch it to her skin. She's bruised so badly, I'm afraid I'll hurt her.

"You really got banged up. Does your back hurt?"

"Everything hurts."

I wash her back as softly as I can. I don't want to make it worse. When I've covered every inch, I lean forward and kiss her right on top of her bruise. I kiss her other bruise, and her other bruise, and her other bruise. I kiss every spot of her back that's hurt. When she leans back against my chest, I lift her arm and kiss the bruises on her arm, too. Then I do the same to the other arm. When I've kissed all the bruises I can find, I lay her arm back down in the water. "There. Good as new," I say. I wrap my arms around her and kiss her cheek. She closes her eyes, and we just sit there for a while.

"This isn't how I pictured our first bath together," she says.

I laugh. "Really? 'Cause this is exactly how I pictured it. Pants and all."

She takes a deep breath and exhales, then tilts her head back so she can look me in the eyes. "I love you, Will."

I kiss her on the forehead. "Say it again."

"I love you, Will."

"One more time."

"I love you."

LAKE IS DISCHARGED today after five days in the hospital. Luckily, since yesterday was a Monday, I was able to finalize reports with the insurance companies. Lake's Jeep was totaled. The damage to my car wasn't as bad, so I was given a rental until it's repaired.

Dr. Bradshaw is really pleased with Lake's progress. She has to go back to see him in two weeks. In the meantime, he's put her on bed rest. She's excited because that means she gets to sleep in my comfortable bed every night. I'm excited because that means I get to spend two solid weeks with her at my house.

I end up withdrawing her from all of her classes for the semester. She was upset, but she doesn't need the added stress of school right now. I told her she needs to focus on getting well. I'm taking the rest of the week off but plan on going back to school Monday, depending on how she's feeling. For now, we've got almost a whole week of nothing to do but watch movies and eat junk food.

*   *   *

KEL AND CAULDER bring their plates to the coffee table in
the living room and set them down next to mine. Lake's
lying on the couch, so we're eating in the living room
rather than at the table.

"Suck-and-sweet time," Caulder says. He crosses his
legs and scoots around to the opposite side of the coffee
table so we're seated in a semicircle that includes Lake.
"My suck is that I have to go back to school tomorrow. My
sweet is that Layken's finally home."

She smiles. "Awe, thanks Caulder. That *is* a sweet,"
she says.

"My turn," Kel says. "My suck is that I have to go
back to school tomorrow. My sweet is that Layken's finally
home."

She scrunches her nose up at Kel. "Copycat."

I laugh. "Well, my suck is that my girlfriend made me
rent six different Johnny Depp movies. My sweet is right
now." I lean over and kiss her on the forehead. Kel and
Caulder have no objection to my sweet tonight. I guess
they're getting used to it, or maybe they're just grateful
that she's home.

"My suck is obvious. I've got staples in my head,"
Lake says. She looks at me and smiles, then her eyes drift
to Kel and Caulder as she watches them eat.

"What's your sweet?" Caulder says with a mouthful
of food.

Lake stares at him for a moment. "You guys," she says. "All three of you."

It's quiet, then Kel picks up a french fry and throws it at her. "Quit being cheesy," he says. Lake grabs the french fry and throws it back at him.

"Hey," Kiersten says as she walks through the door. "Sorry I'm late." She heads to the kitchen. I didn't know she was coming over. Looks like she'll have to eat bread again.

"You need some help?" I ask her. She's only got one good arm, but she seems to be adjusting pretty well.

"Nope. I got it." She brings her plate into the living room and sits down on the floor. We all stare at her when she takes a huge bite of a chicken strip. "Oh my God, it's so gooood," she says. She shoves the rest of it in her mouth.

"Kiersten, that's meat. You're eating meat," I say.

She nods. "I know. It's the weirdest thing. I've been dying to come over here since you guys got home so I could try some." She takes another bite. "It's *heaven*," she says around her mouthful. She hops up and walks to the kitchen. "Is it good in ketchup?" She brings the bottle back and squirts some on her plate.

"Why the sudden change of heart?" Lake asks her.

Kiersten swallows. "Right when we were about to be hit by that truck . . . all I could think was how I was about to die and I'd never tasted meat. That was my only regret in life."

We all laugh. She grabs the chicken off of my plate and throws it on her own.

"Will, are you still coming to Dad Day on Thursday?" Caulder asks.

Lake looks at me. "Dad Day?"

"I don't know, Caulder. I'm not sure I feel comfortable leaving Lake alone yet," I say.

"Dad Day? What's Dad Day?" Lake asks again.

"It's Father Appreciation Day at our school," Kiersten says. "They're having a luncheon. Kids get to eat lunch with their dads in the gymnasium. Mom Day isn't until next month."

"But what about the kids who don't have dads? What are they supposed to do? That's not very fair."

"The kids who don't have dads just go with Will," Kel says.

Lake looks at me again. She doesn't like being out of the loop.

"I asked Kel if I could eat with him, too," I say.

"Will you eat with me, too?" Kiersten asks. "My dad won't be back until Saturday."

I nod. "If I go. I don't know if I should."

"Go," Lake says. "I'll be fine. You need to quit babying me so much."

I lean forward and kiss her. "But you *are* my baby," I say.

I'm not sure which direction it comes from, maybe all three, but I'm hit in the head with french fries.

* * *

I HELP LAKE into the bed and pull the covers over her. "You want something to drink?"

"I'm fine," she says.

I turn off the light and walk around to the other side of the bed and crawl in. I scoot closer to her and put my head on her pillow and wrap my arm around her. Her bandages come off at her next doctor's visit. She's so worried about how much hair they had to cut. I keep telling her not to worry about it. I'm sure they didn't cut much, and the incision is on the back of her head, so it won't be that noticeable.

It hurts her if she's not lying on her side, so she's facing me. Her lips are in close proximity to mine, so I have to kiss them. I lay my head back down on her pillow and brush her hair behind her ear with my fingers.

This entire past week has been hell. Mentally *and* physically. But especially mentally. I came so close to losing her. *So close.* Sometimes when it's quiet, my mind wanders to the possibility of having lost her and what I would have done. I have to keep reeling myself back in, reminding myself that she's okay. That everyone's okay.

I didn't think it was possible, but everything Lake and I have been through this past month has somehow made me love her even more. I can't begin to imagine my life without her in it. I think back to the video Sherry showed me and what Jim said to her: "It's like you came along and woke up my soul."

That's exactly what Lake did to me. She woke up my soul.

I lean in and kiss her again, longer this time. But not too long. I feel like she's so fragile.

"This sucks," she says. "Do you realize how hard it'll be sleeping in the same bed with you? Are you sure he specified an entire month? We have to retreat for a whole month?"

"Technically, he said four weeks," I say, stroking her arm. "I guess we could stick to four weeks, since it's a few days shy of a whole month."

"See? You should have taken me up on the offer when you had the chance. Now we have to wait four more weeks!" she says. "How many weeks is that, total?"

"It'll be sixty-five," I quickly respond. "Not that I'm counting. And four weeks from today is February twenty-eighth. Not that I'm counting that, either."

She laughs. "February twenty-eighth? But that'll be a Tuesday. Who wants to lose their virginity on a Tuesday? Let's make it the Friday before. February twenty-fourth. We'll get Kel and Caulder to stay with your grandparents again."

"Nope. Four weeks. Doctor's orders," I say. "We'll make a deal. I'll get my grandparents to watch the boys again if we can make it to March second. The Friday *after* it's been four weeks."

"March second is a Thursday."

"It's a leap year."

"Ugh! Fine. March second," she says. "But I want a suite this time. A big one."

"You got it."

"With chocolates. And flowers."

"You got it," I say. I lift my head off her pillow and kiss her, then roll over.

"And a fruit tray. With strawberries."

"You got it," I say again. I yawn and pull the covers up over my head.

"And I want those fluffy hotel robes. For both of us. That way we can wear them all weekend."

"Whatever you want, Lake. Now go to sleep. You need the rest."

She's done nothing but sleep for five days, so I'm not surprised she's wide awake. I, on the other hand, have had close to zero sleep for five days. I could barely keep my eyes open today. It feels so good to be back home, back in my bed. It especially feels good that Lake's right next to me.

"Will?" she whispers.

"Yeah?"

"I have to pee."

"ARE YOU SURE you'll be okay?" I ask Lake for the tenth time this morning.

"I'll be fine," she says. She holds the phone up to show me that she has it close by.

"Okay. Sherry's at home if you need her. I'll be back in an hour; the luncheon shouldn't last long."

"Babe, I'm fine. Promise."

I kiss her on the forehead. "I know."

And I do know she's fine. She's more than fine. She's been so focused and determined to get better that she's doing way too much on her own. Even things she shouldn't be doing on her own, which is why I worry. Her indomitable will that I fell in love with sometimes irritates the hell out of me, too.

WHEN I WALK into the gymnasium, I scan the area for the boys. Caulder is waving when I see him, so I head to his table.

"Where are Kel and Kiersten?" I say as I take a seat.

"Mrs. Brill wouldn't let them come," he says.

"Why?" I jerk my head around, looking for Mrs. Brill.

"She said they were just using this lunch as an excuse to get out of study hall. She made them go to regular lunch at ten-forty-five. Kel told her you'd be mad."

"Well, Kel's right," I say. "I'll be right back."

I exit the gymnasium and turn left for the cafeteria. When I walk inside, the noise penetrates my eardrums. I forgot how loud kids were. I also forgot how much my head still hurt. I glance at all the tables, but there are so many kids, I can't spot either of them. I walk over to a lady who looks like she's monitoring the cafeteria.

"Can you tell me where Kel Cohen is?" I ask.

"Who?" she says. "It's too loud, I didn't hear you."

I say it louder. "Kel Cohen!"

She points to a table at the other end of the cafeteria. Before I reach the table, Kel spots me and waves. Kiersten is seated next to him, wiping her shirt with a wad of wet napkins. They both stand up when I reach the table.

"What happened to your shirt?" I ask Kiersten.

She looks at Kel and shakes her head. "Stupid boys," she says. She points to the table across from theirs. There are three boys who look a little older than Kiersten and Kel. They're all laughing.

"Did they do something to you?" I ask her.

She rolls her eyes. "When do they *not*? If it's not chocolate milk, it's applesauce. Or pudding. Or Jell-O."

"Yeah, it's usually Jell-O," Kel says.

"Don't worry about it, Will. I'm used to it now. I always keep an extra change of clothes in my backpack just in case."

"Don't worry about it?" I ask. "Why the hell isn't something being done about it? Have you talked to a teacher?"

She nods. "They never see it when it happens. It's gotten worse since the suspension. Now kids just make sure they only throw things at me when the monitors aren't looking. But it's fine, Will. Really. I have Abby and Kel and Caulder. They're all the friends I need."

I'm pissed. I can't believe she has to go through this

every day! I look at Kel. "Who's the one Caulder was telling me about? The dickhead?" Kel points at the boy seated at the head of the table. "You guys wait here." I turn around and walk toward Dickhead's table. As I get closer, their laughter succumbs to confusion. I grab one of the empty chairs at their table and pull it around next to Dickhead and straddle the chair backward, facing him. "Hey," I say.

He just looks at me, then at his friends. "Can I help you?" he says sarcastically. His friends laugh.

"Yes. Actually, you can," I say. "What's your name?"

He laughs again. I can tell he's trying to play the part of the big, bad twelve-year-old that he is. He reminds me of Reece at that age. He can't hide the anxiety on his face, though.

"Mark," he says.

"Well, hi, Mark. I'm Will." I extend my hand, and he reluctantly shakes it. "Now that we've been formally introduced, I think it's safe to say that we can be frank with each other. Can we do that, Mark? Are you tough enough to take a little bit of honesty?"

He laughs nervously. "Yeah, I'm tough."

"Good. Because you see that girl over there?" I point back at Kiersten. Mark glances over my shoulder at her, then looks back at me and nods.

"Let me be candid with you. That girl is very important to me. *Very* important. When bad things happen to important people in my life, I don't take it very well. I guess you could say I have a bit of a temper." I scoot my chair closer to his and look him straight in the eyes. "Now, while we're being frank with each other, you should know that I used to be a teacher. You know why I'm not a teacher anymore, Mark?"

He's no longer smiling. He shakes his head.

"I don't teach anymore because one of my *dickhead* students decided to mess with one of my important people. It didn't end well."

All three of the boys are staring at me, wide-eyed.

"You can take that as a threat if you want to, Mark. But honestly, I have no intention of hurting you. After all, you're only twelve. When it comes to kicking someone's ass, I usually draw the line at fourteen-year-olds. But I will tell you this—the fact that you bully people? And *girls*, for that matter? Girls younger than you?" I shake my head in disgust. "It only goes to show what a pathetic human being you'll turn out to be. But that's not the worst of it." I look at his friends. "The worst of it is the people who follow you. Because anyone weak enough to let someone as pathetic as you be a leader is even *worse* than pathetic."

I look back at Mark and smile. "It was nice meeting you." I stand up and swing the chair under the table, then I place my hands on the table in front of him. "I'll be keeping in touch."

I look all three of them in the eyes as I back away from their table, then turn back to Kiersten and Kel. "Let's go. Caulder's waiting on us."

When the three of us get back to the gymnasium,

we go to Caulder's table and take a seat. We haven't been seated for two minutes when Mrs. Brill marches up with a scowl. Right before she opens her mouth, I stand up and reach a hand out to her. "Mrs. Brill," I say with a smile. "It's so good of you to let Kiersten and the boys eat with me today. It really means a lot that you recognize there are families in this world in nontraditional situations. I love these kids as if they're my own. The fact that you respect our relationship even though I'm not a typical father says a lot about your character. So I just wanted to say thank you."

Mrs. Brill lets go of my hand and steps back. She eyes Kiersten and Kel, then me. "You're welcome," she says. "Hope you all enjoy the luncheon." She turns and walks away without another word.

"Well," Kel says, "that was definitely my *sweet*."

17.

One more day . . .

"SO WHAT'S THE DAMAGE?" LAKE ASKS DR. BRADSHAW.

"To what? You?" He laughs as he slowly unwraps the bandage from her head.

"To my hair," she says. "How much did you chop off?"

"Well," he says, "we did have to cut through your skull, you know. We tried to save as much hair as we could, but we were faced with a pretty tough decision . . . it was either your hair or your life."

She laughs. "I guess I'll forgive you, then."

AS SOON AS we get home from the doctor, she heads straight for the shower to wash her hair. I'm pretty comfortable with

275

leaving her home now, so I go to pick up the boys. When I get there, I remember that the school talent show is tomorrow night, and the students who signed up to perform get to stay and practice. Kiersten and Caulder both signed up, but neither of them is giving hints as to what they're doing. I've given Kiersten copies of all my poems. She says she needed them for research. I didn't argue. There's just something about Kiersten that you don't argue with.

When the boys and I finally get home, Lake is still in the bathroom. I know she's tired of me babying her, but I check on her anyway. The fact that she's been in there so long worries me. When I knock on the door, she tells me to go away. She doesn't sound happy, which means I'm not going away.

"Lake, open the door," I say. I jiggle the doorknob, but it's locked.

"Will, I need a minute." She sniffs.

She's crying.

"Lake. Open the door!" I'm really worried now. I know how stubborn she is, and if she hurt herself, she's probably trying to hide it. I beat on the door and shake the knob again. She doesn't respond. "Lake!" I yell.

The doorknob turns, and the door slowly opens. She's staring down at the floor, crying. "I'm okay," she says. She wipes at her eyes with a wad of toilet paper. "You really need to quit freaking out, Will."

I step into the bathroom and hug her. "Why are you crying?"

She pulls away from me and shakes her head, then sits down on the seat in front of the bathroom mirror. "It's stupid," she says.

"Are you in pain? Does your head hurt?"

She shakes her head and wipes her eyes again. She brings her arm up and pulls the rubber band out of her hair, and it falls down over her shoulder. "It's my hair."

Her hair. She's crying about her damn hair! I breathe a sigh of relief. "It'll grow back, Lake. It's okay." I walk around behind her and pull her hair away from her shoulders to her back. She's got an area on the back of her head that's been shaved. It can't be covered up, because it's smack dab in the middle of her hair. I run my fingers over it. "I think you would look cute with short hair. Wait till it grows out some more, and you can get it cut."

She shakes her head. "That'll take forever. I'm not going anywhere like this. I'm not leaving the house for another month," she says.

I know she doesn't mean it, but I hate that she's so upset. "I think it's beautiful," I say, running my fingers over her scar. "It's what saved your life." I reach around her and open the cabinet doors underneath the sink.

"What are you doing? You aren't cutting the rest of my hair off, Will."

I reach inside and pull out the black box that contains my hair trimmer. "I'm not cutting your hair." I plug in the cord and take off the guard and turn it on. I reach behind my head and press it against the back of my hair and make a quick swipe. When I bring it back around, I pull the pieces of my hair out and toss them in the trash can. "There. Now we match," I say.

She swings around in her seat. "Will! What the hell? Why did you do that?"

"It's just hair, babe." I smile at her.

She brings the wad of toilet paper back up to her eyes and looks at our reflection in the mirror. She shakes her head and laughs. "You look ridiculous," she says.

"So do you."

OTHER THAN HER doctor's appointment yesterday, tonight is Lake's first time out of the house. Sherry is watching the boys for a few hours after the talent show so we can have a date. Of course, Lake got upset when I told her about our date. "You never ask me, you always tell me," she whined. So I had to get down on my knee and ask her out. I'm keeping her in the dark again. She has no clue what I have planned for tonight. No clue.

Eddie and Gavin are already in the school auditorium with Sherry and David when we arrive. I let Lake sit next to Eddie, and I take the seat next to Sherry. Lake was able to pull her hair back into a ponytail and hide most of her scar. I'm not so lucky.

"Ummm . . . Will? Is this some sort of new trend I'm not aware of?" Sherry asks when she sees my hair.

Lake laughs. "See? You look ridiculous."

Sherry leans in to me and whispers, "Can you give me a hint as to what Kiersten's doing tonight?"

I shrug. "I don't know what she's doing. I'm assuming it's a poem. She didn't read it to you guys?"

Sherry and David both shake their heads. "She's been pretty secretive about it," David says.

"So has Caulder," I say. "I have no idea what he's up to. I don't even think he has a talent."

The curtain opens, and Principal Brill walks up to the microphone and gives her introductions to kick off the evening. For every child who performs, there's a different parent holding a video camera at the front of the audience. Why didn't I bring my camera? I'm an idiot. A real parent would have brought a camera. When Kiersten is called to the stage, Lake reaches inside her purse and pulls out a camera. Of course she does.

Principal Brill introduces Kiersten, who doesn't look nervous at all. She really is a miniature version of Eddie. There's a small sack draped over her wrist with the cast. She lifts her good arm to lower the microphone.

"I'm doing something tonight called a slam. It's a type of poetry that I was introduced to this year by a friend of mine. Thank you, Will."

I smile.

Kiersten takes a deep breath and says, "My poem tonight is called 'Butterfly You.' "

Lake and I look at each other. I know she's thinking the same thing I'm thinking, which is: Oh, no.

"Butterfly.
What a beautiful word
What a delicate creature.
Delicate like the cruel *words* that flow right out of
your *mouths*
and the *food* that flies right out of your *hands* . . .
Does it make you feel *better*?
Does it make you feel *good*?
Does picking on a *girl* make you more of a *man*?
I'm standing *up* for myself
Like I *should* have done *before*
I'm not putting *up* with your
Butterfly anymore."

Kiersten slides the sack off her wrist and opens it, pulling out a fistful of handmade butterflies. She takes the microphone out of the stand and walks down the stairs as she continues speaking. "I'd like to extend to others what others have extended to me." She walks up to Mrs. Brill first and holds out a butterfly. "*Butterfly* you, Mrs. Brill."

Mrs. Brill smiles at her and takes the butterfly. Lake laughs out loud, and I have to nudge her to be quiet. Kiersten walks around the room, passing out butterflies to several of the students, including the three from the lunchroom.

"Butterfly *you*, Mark.

Butterfly *you*, Brendan.

Butterfly *you*, Colby."

When she's finished passing out the butterflies, she walks back on the stage and places the microphone in the stand.

"I have something to *say* to *you*

I'm not referring to the *bullies*

Or the ones they *pursue.*

I'm referring to those of you who just *stand by*

The ones who don't *take up* for those of us who cry

Those of you who just . . . turn a blind eye.

After all, it's not *you* it's happening to

You aren't the one being *bullied*

And *you* aren't the one being *rude*

It isn't *your* hand that's throwing the *food*

But . . . it is *your mouth* not *speaking up*

It is *your feet* not taking *a stand*

It is your *arm* not lending a *hand*

It is your *heart*

Not *giving* a damn.

So *take up* for yourself

Take up for your *friends*

I challenge you to be someone

Who doesn't give *in.*

Don't give in.

Don't let them *win.*"

As soon as "damn" comes out of Kiersten's mouth, Mrs. Brill is marching onto the stage. Luckily, Kiersten finishes her poem and rushes off the stage before Mrs. Brill reaches her. The audience is in shock. Well, most of the audience. Everyone in our row is giving her a standing ovation.

As we take our seats, Sherry whispers to me, "I didn't get the whole butterfly thing, but the rest of it was so good."

"Yeah, it was," I agree. "It was butterflying excellent."

When Caulder is called onto the stage, he looks nervous. I'm nervous for him. Lake's nervous, too. I wish I knew what he was doing so I could have given him some advice. Lake zooms the camera in and focuses it on Caulder. I take a deep breath, hoping he can get through it without cussing. Mrs. Brill already has her eye on us. Caulder walks to the microphone and says, "I'm Caulder. I'm also doing a slam tonight. It's called 'Suck and Sweet.' "

Here we go again.

"I've had a lot of sucks in life

A lot

My parents died almost four years ago, right after

I turned seven

With every day that goes by, I remember them *less*

and *less*

Like my mom . . .

I remember that she used to *sing*.

She was *always* happy,
always dancing.
Other than what I've seen of her in pictures, I don't
really remember what she looks like.
Or what she *smells* like
Or what she *sounds* like
And my *dad*
I remember *more* things about him, but only
because I thought he was the most amazing man in
the world.
He was *smart.*
He knew the answers to *everything.*
And he was *strong.*
And he played the *guitar.*
I used to *love* lying in bed at night, listening to the
music coming from the living room.
I miss that the *most.*
His *music.*
After they died, I went to live with my grandma
and grandpaul.
Don't get me wrong . . . I *love* my grandparents.
But I loved my *home* even more.
It *reminded* me of them.
Of my mom and dad.
My brother had just started college the year they died.
He knew how much I wanted to be home.
He knew how much it *meant* to me,
so he made it *happen.*

I was only seven at the time, so I let him do it.

I let him give up his *entire life* just so I could be home.

Just so I wouldn't be so *sad*.

If I could do it all over again, I would have *never* let

him take me.

He deserved a shot, too. A *shot* at being *young*.

But sometimes when you're seven, the world isn't

in *3-D*.

So,

I owe *a lot* to my brother.

A lot of *thank yous*

A lot of *I'm sorrys*

A lot of *I love yous*

I owe *a lot* to you, Will

For making the *sucks* in my life a little less *suckier*

And my *sweet?*

My *sweet* is right *now*."

I wonder if a person can cry too much. If so, I'm definitely reaching my quota this month. I stand up and make my way past Sherry and David and out into the aisle. When Caulder walks down the steps to the stage, I pick him up and give him the biggest damn hug I've ever given him.

"I love you, Caulder."

WE DON'T STAY for the awards. The kids are excited to be spending the evening with Sherry and David, so they're all in a hurry to leave. Kiersten and Caulder don't seem to care who won, which makes me a little proud. After all, I've been drilling Allan Wolf's quote into Kiersten's head every time I give her advice about poetry: *The points are not the point; the point is poetry.*

After David and Sherry drive away with the boys, Lake and I walk to the car, and I open the door for her.

"Where are we eating? I'm hungry," she says.

I don't answer. I shut her door and walk around to the driver's side. I reach into the backseat and grab two sacks off the floor and hand one to her. "We don't have time to stop and eat. I made us grilled cheese."

She grins when she opens her sack and pulls out her sandwich and soda. I can tell by the look on her face that she remembers. I was hoping she would.

"Do I actually have to eat it?" she says, crinkling up her nose. "How long has it been sitting in your car?"

I laugh. "Two hours, tops. It's more for show, bear with me." I take the sandwich out of her hands and drop it back into the sack. We have a pretty long drive," I say. "I know a game we can play; it's called Would You Rather. Have you ever played it before?"

She smiles at me and nods. "Just once, with this really hot guy. But it was a long time ago. Maybe you should go first, to refresh my memory."

"Okay. But there's something I need to do." I open the glove box and pull out the blindfold. "Our destination is sort of a surprise, so I need you to put this on."

"You're blindfolding me? Seriously?" She rolls her eyes and leans forward.

I wrap it around her head and adjust it over her eyes. "There. Don't peek." I put the car in drive and pull out of the parking lot, then ask the first question. "Okay. Would you rather I looked like Hugh Jackman or George Clooney?"

"Johnny Depp," she says.

That answer was a little too fast for my comfort. "What the *hell*, Lake? You're supposed to say Will! You're supposed to say you want me to look like me!"

"But you weren't one of the options," she says.

"Neither was Johnny Depp!"

She laughs. "My turn. Would you rather have constant, uncontrollable belching, or would you rather have to bark every time you heard the word 'the'?"

"Bark as in like a dog?"

"Yeah."

"Uncontrollable belching," I say.

"Oh, gross." She wrinkles up her nose. "I could live with your barking, but I don't know about the constant belching."

"In that case, I change my answer. My turn again. Would you rather be abducted by aliens or have to go on tour with Nickelback?"

"I'd rather be abducted by the Avett Brothers."

"Wasn't an option."

She laughs. "Fine, aliens. Would you rather be an old, rich man with only one year left to live? Or a young, poor, sad man with fifty years left to live?"

"I'd rather be Johnny Depp."

She laughs. "You suck at this," she teases.

I reach over and interlock fingers with her. She's leaning back in the seat, laughing, without a clue in the world where we're headed. She's about to be pissed—but hopefully only for a little while. I drive around a bit longer while we continue our game. I could honestly play this game all night with her, but we eventually pull up to our destination, and I hop out of the car. I open her door and help her stand up. "Hold my hands. I'll lead."

"You're making me nervous, Will. Why do you always have to be so secretive when it comes to our dates?"

"I'm not secretive, I just love surprising you. A little bit farther, and I'll let you take off your blindfold." We walk inside, and I position her exactly where I want her. I can't help but smile, knowing how she'll react once I take off her blindfold. "I'm about to take it off, but before I do, just remember how much you love me, okay?"

"I can't make any promises," she says.

I reach behind her and untie the blindfold. She opens her eyes and looks around. Yep, she's pissed. "What the *hell*, Will! You brought me on a date to your *house* again? Why do you always do this?"

I laugh. "I'm sorry." I throw the blindfold on the coffee table and put my arms around her. "It's just that some things don't need to be done on a stage. Some things need to be private. This is one of them."

"*What* is one of them?" She looks nervous.

I kiss her on the forehead. "Sit down, I'll be right back." I motion for her to sit on the couch. I go to my bedroom and reach into the closet and pull out her surprise. I stick it in my pocket and walk back to the living room. I turn on the stereo and set "I & Love & You" on repeat; it's her favorite song.

"You better tell me now, before I start crying again . . . does this have anything to do with my mom? Because you said the stars were the last thing."

"They *were* the last thing, I promise." I sit beside her on the couch and take her hand in mine, looking her straight in the eyes. "Lake, I have something to say, and I want you to hear me out without interrupting me, okay?"

"I'm not the one who interrupts," she says defensively.

"See? Right there. Don't do that."

She laughs. "Fine. Talk."

Something just doesn't feel right. I don't like how we're so formally seated. It's not us. I grab her leg and arm and pull her onto my lap. She straddles me, wrapping her legs around my back. She hangs her hands loosely around my neck and looks me in the eyes. I go to speak, but I'm cut off.

"Will?"

"You're interrupting me, Lake."

She gives me a half smile and brings her hands to my face. "I love you," she says. "Thank you for taking care of me."

She's sidetracking me, but it's nice. I slowly slide my hands up her arms and rest them on her shoulders. "You would do the same for me, Lake. It's what we do."

She smiles. A tear makes its way down her cheek, and she doesn't even try to hold it back. "Yep," she says. "It's what we do."

I take her hands in mine and bring her palms to my lips and kiss them. "Lake, you mean the world to me. You brought so much to my life . . . right when I needed it the most. I wish you could know how hopeless I was before I met you, so you would realize just how much you've changed me."

"I *do* know, Will. I was hopeless, too."

"You're interrupting again."

She grins and shakes her head. "I don't care."

I laugh and push her down onto the couch and climb on top of her, pressing my hands into the couch on either side of her head to hold myself up. "Do you have any idea how much you frustrate me sometimes?"

"Is that a rhetorical question? Because you just told me to stop interrupting you, so I'm not sure if you want me to answer it."

"Oh my God, you're *impossible*, Lake! I can't even get two sentences out!"

She laughs and grabs the collar of my shirt. "I'm listening," she whispers. "Promise."

I want to believe her, but as soon as I begin to speak again, she crushes her lips to mine. For a moment, I forget what my whole point is. I'm consumed by the taste of her mouth and the feel of her hands making their way up my back. I lower my body onto hers and let her sidetrack me some more. After several minutes of intense sidetracking, I'm somehow able to tear myself away from her grasp and sit back up on the couch.

"Dammit, Lake! Are you gonna let me do this or not?" I take her hands and pull her up to a sitting position, then I get off the couch and kneel on the floor in front of her.

Until this moment, I don't think she had any clue what tonight was about. She looks at me with a mixture of emotions in her expression. Fear, hope, excitement, apprehension. I'm sharing those exact same emotions. I hold her hands in mine and take a deep breath. "I told you the stars were the last gift from your mother, and technically, they were."

"Wait, *technically*?" she says. She realizes she's interrupting me again when I glare at her. "Oh yeah. Sorry." She puts her finger to her mouth, indicating she isn't going to say anything else.

"Yes, *technically*. I said the stars were the last thing she gave us, and they were. But she gave me one star that isn't in the vase. She wanted me to give it to you when I was ready. When you were ready. So . . . I hope you're ready."

I put my hand in my pocket and pull out the star. I place it in her hand for her to open. When she does, the ring slides out and into her palm. When she sees her mother's wedding ring, her hand goes up to her mouth, and she sucks in a deep breath. I take the ring and hold her left hand.

"I know we're young, Lake. We've got an entire lifetime ahead of us to do things like get married. But sometimes things in people's lives don't happen in chronological order, like they should. Especially in our lives. Our chronological order got mixed up a long time ago."

She holds out her ring finger. Her hand is shaking . . . but so are mine. I slide the ring onto her finger. It's a perfect fit. She wipes my tears away with her free hand and kisses me on the forehead. Her lips come a little too close to mine, so I have to pause and kiss them. She puts her hand on the back of my head and closes her lips over mine as she slides off the couch and into my lap. I lose my balance and we fall back. She doesn't let go of my head, and our lips never separate while she continues to give me the absolute best kiss she's ever given me.

"I love you, Will," she mutters into my mouth. "I love you, I love you, I love you."

I gently pull her face away from mine. "I'm not finished yet." I laugh. "Stop butterflying interrupting me!" I roll her over onto her back and prop myself up on my elbow beside her.

She starts kicking her legs up and down in a fit. "Hurry up and ask me already, I'm *dying* here!"

I shake my head and laugh. "That's just it, Lake. I'm not asking you to marry me . . ."

Before I can get the rest of my sentence out, a look of horror washes across her face. I immediately put my finger to her lips. "I know how you liked to be *asked* and not *told*. But I'm not asking you to marry me." I roll on top of her and lean in as close as I can while still looking her in the eyes. I lower my voice to a whisper. "I'm *telling* you to marry me, Lake . . . because I can't live without you."

She starts crying again . . . and laughing. She's laughing and crying and kissing me all at the same time. We both are.

"I was so wrong," she says between kisses. "Sometimes a girl *loves* to be told."

"ARE YOU KNOCKED up?" Eddie asks Lake.

"No, Eddie. That would be you."

We're all sitting in the living room. Lake couldn't wait to tell Eddie, so she called immediately to tell her the news. Eddie and Gavin were here within the hour.

"Don't get me wrong, I'm super excited for you. I just

don't get it. Why so sudden? March second is only two weeks away."

Lake looks at me and winks. She's snuggled up next to me, sitting on her feet. I lean in and kiss her lips. Like I said, I can't help it.

Lake turns back to Eddie and answers her. "Why would I want a traditional wedding, Eddie? Nothing about our lives is traditional. None of our parents would be there. You and Gavin would be our only guests. Will's grandparents probably wouldn't even show up . . . his grandmother hates me."

"Oh, I forgot to tell you," I say. "My grandmother actually likes you. A lot. It's me she wasn't happy with."

"Really?" Lake says. "How do you know?"

"She told me."

"Huh." She smiles. "That's nice to know."

"See?" Eddie says. "They'll show up. So will Sherry and David. That's nine people right there."

Lake rolls her eyes at Eddie. "Nine people? You expect us to pay for an entire wedding for nine people?"

Eddie sighs and falls onto Gavin's lap in a defeated slump. "I guess you're right. It's just that I was looking forward to planning a big wedding someday."

"You can still plan your own," Lake says. She looks at Gavin. "How many more minutes until you propose, Gavin?"

He doesn't skip a beat. "About three hundred thousand or so."

"See, Eddie? Besides, I need you to do my hair and makeup," Lake says. "We need witnesses, too. You and Gavin can come, and Kel and Caulder will be there."

Eddie smiles. She seems a little more excited now that she knows she's invited.

I was hesitant at first about Lake's plan, too. But after I heard her logic, and especially after I heard how much money it would save us not having a wedding, I was easily convinced. The date of the marriage was a given.

"What about the houses? Which one will you guys live in?" Gavin says.

We've been talking about it for two weeks, even before tonight's proposal. After she stayed here, we both knew it would be impossible to live in separate houses again. We came up with the plan about a week ago, but now seems like the perfect time to share it.

"That's one of the reasons we wanted you guys to come over," I say. "I had about three years left on my mortgage, and no less than two weeks after Julia passed away, the title came in the mail. She paid it off before she died. She paid the rent on Lake's house through September; that's when the lease is up. So now we'll have an empty house with six months of prepaid rent. We know you guys are looking for a place before the baby comes, so we're offering you Lake's. Until September, anyway . . . then you'll have to sign your own lease."

Neither one of them says anything. They just look at us in shock. Gavin shakes his head and starts to protest. Eddie slaps her hand over his mouth and turns to me. "We'll take it! We'll take it, we'll take it, we'll take it!" She starts clapping and jumps up and hugs Lake, then hugs me. "Oh my God, you guys are the best friends ever! Aren't they, Gavin?"

He smiles, obviously not wanting to appear desperate, but I know how much they need a place of their own. Eddie's excitement eventually outweighs Gavin's modesty, and he can no longer contain himself. He hugs Lake, then hugs me, then hugs Eddie, then hugs me again. When they finally calm down and sit back down on the couch, Gavin's smile fades.

"Do you know what this means?" he says to Eddie. "Kiersten's about to be *our* parallel neighbor."

18.

*It's worth all the **aches**,*
*All the **tears**,*
*the **mistakes** . . .*
The heart of a man and a woman in love?
*It's worth **all** the pain in the **world**.*

I'VE SPENT THE LAST TWO WEEKS GIVING HER EVERY OP-portunity to opt out of doing things this way. Lake insists she doesn't want a traditional wedding, but I don't want her to regret her decision someday. Most girls spend years planning out the exact details of their wedding. Then again, Lake's not most girls.

I take a deep breath, not really understanding why I'm so jittery. I'm sort of glad it's so informal. I couldn't imagine how shot my nerves would be if we had more of an audience. My hands won't stop sweating, so I wipe them on my jeans. Lake insisted I wear jeans, said she didn't want to see me in a tux. I'm not sure what dress she picked out, but she didn't want to wear a wedding dress. She didn't see the point in buying a dress to only wear once.

We aren't doing the traditional aisle walk, either. I'm pretty sure she and Eddie are down the hall in the courthouse public restroom doing her makeup right now. It all seems so surreal, marrying the love of your life in the same building where you register your car. But honestly, it wouldn't matter where we got married, I'd be just as excited . . . and just as nervous.

When the doors open, there isn't any music. No flower girls or ring bearers. Just Eddie, who comes in and sits in a chair next to Kel. The judge walks in right after Eddie and hands me a form and a pen. "You forgot to date this," he says.

I press the form down on the podium in front of me and date it. *March 2.* That's our day. Lake's and my day. I hand the paper back to him, and the door to the courtroom opens again. When I turn around, Lake's walking in, smiling. As soon as I lay eyes on her, a wave of relief washes over me, and I'm immediately calm. She has that effect on me.

She looks beautiful. She's wearing blue jeans, too. I laugh when I notice the shirt she has on. She's wearing that damn ugly shirt I love to hate. If I could have hand-picked what she would wear on our wedding day, it would be exactly this.

When she walks up to me, I wrap my arms around her, pick her up, and spin her around. When I plant her feet back on the floor, she whispers in my ear. "Two more hours."

She isn't referring to the marriage, she's referring to the honeymoon. I grab her face and kiss her. Everyone else in the room fades into the distance as we kiss . . . but only for a second.

"Eh-hem." The officiant is standing in front of us, unamused. "We haven't quite gotten to the kissing of the bride yet," he says.

I laugh and take Lake's hand as we position ourselves in front of him. When he begins reading his wedding service, Lake touches her hand to my cheek and pulls my gaze toward hers, away from the officiant. I take her hands in mine and pull them up between us. I'm pretty sure the officiant is still talking, and that I should be paying attention, but I can't think of anything else I'd rather be paying attention to. Lake smiles at me, and I can see she isn't paying attention to anything around us, either. It's just me and her right now. I know it isn't time yet, but I go ahead and kiss her anyway. I don't hear a single word of the wedding sermon as we continue to kiss. In less than a minute, this woman is about to become my wife. *My life.*

Lake laughs and says "I do" without pulling away from my mouth. I didn't even realize we had gotten to that part. She closes her eyes again and gets right back into rhythm with me. I know weddings are important to some people, but I have to fight back the urge to pick her up and carry her out of here before it's over. After a few more seconds, she starts giggling again and says, "He does."

I realize she just said my line, so I separate my lips from hers and look at the officiant. "She's right, I do." I turn back to her and resume where we left off.

"Well, then, congratulations. I now pronounce you husband and wife. You may *continue* kissing your bride."

And so I do.

"AFTER YOU, Mrs. Cooper," I say as we exit the elevator.

She smiles. "I like that. It has a nice ring to it."

"I'm glad you think so, because it's a little late to change your mind now."

When the elevator doors close behind us, I pull the key out of my pocket and check the room number again. "It's this way," I say, pointing to the right. I take her hand in mine and start down the hallway. I'm forced to an abrupt stop, however, when she jerks me back.

"Wait," she says. "You're supposed to carry me over the threshold. That's what husbands do."

Before I can bend down and take her in my arms the traditional way, she puts her arms on my shoulders and jumps up, wrapping her legs around my waist. I have to grab hold of her thighs before she slips. Her lips are right in proximity to mine, so they briefly get kissed. She grins and runs her hands through the back of my hair, forcing my mouth onto hers again. I try to grip her legs with one hand and her waist with the other, but I feel like she's slipping, so I take two quick steps until she's propped up against a hotel room door. It's not our door, but it'll do the job. As soon as her back hits the door, she moans. I remember the bruises from a few weeks ago. "Are you okay? Did I just hurt your back?"

She grins. "No. That was a good sound."

The intensity in her eyes is magnetic. I'm unable to break our stare as I stand there, holding her up against the door. I grab her under the thighs and hoist her even higher, pressing my body against hers for more leverage. "Five more minutes," I say.

I grin and lean in to kiss her again, but she's suddenly farther away. As soon as I realize that the door we're leaning against is opening up behind her, I do my best to catch her. Instead, I fall to the ground with her, and we both end up in a heap on the floor of someone's hotel room. She still has her arms around my neck, and she's laughing until she looks up and sees a man and two children staring down at us. The man doesn't look very pleased.

"Run," I whisper. Lake and I crawl out of the hotel room and pull ourselves up. I take her hand in mine, and we run down the hallway until we find our room. I slide the key into the reader, but before I open the door, she slips in front of me and faces me.

"Three more minutes," she says. She reaches behind

her and pulls down on the handle, swinging the door open. "Now carry me over the threshold, husband."

I bend down and grab her behind the knees and pick her up, throwing her over my shoulder. She squeals, and I push the door all the way open with her feet. I take a step over the threshold with my wife.

The door slams behind us, and I ease her down onto the bed.

"I smell chocolate. And flowers," she says. "Good job, husband."

I lift her leg up and slide her boot off. "Thank you, wife." I lift her other leg up and slide that boot off, too. "I also remembered the fruit. And the robes."

She winks at me and rolls over, scooting up onto the bed. When she gets settled, she leans forward and grabs my hand, pulling me toward her. "Come here, husband," she whispers.

I start to make my way up the bed but pause when I come face-to-face with her shirt. "I wish you'd take this ugly thing off," I say.

"You're the one who hates it so much. *You* take it off."

And so I do. I start from the bottom this time and press my lips against her skin where her stomach meets the top of her pants, causing her to squirm. She's ticklish there. Good to know. I unbutton the next button and slowly move my lips up another inch to her belly button. I kiss it. She lets out another moan, but it doesn't worry me this time. I continue kissing every inch of her until the ugly shirt is off and lying on the floor. When my lips find their way back to hers, I pause to ask her one last time. "Wife? Are you sure you're ready to *not* call retreat? Right now?"

She wraps her legs around me and pulls me closer. "I'm butterflying positive," she says.

And so we don't.

acknowledgments

To condense into a paragraph all of the people that deserve a thank you would be impossible. Therefore, I'm just going to have to write dozens of more books in order to fit you all in. For now, I want to recognize my girls of FP: my role models, my confidants, my sounding boards, my friends, my 21. I love each and every one of you and couldn't thank you enough for letting me slip through in that last second. You've changed my life.

about the author

Colleen Hoover is the *New York Times* bestselling author of two novels: *Slammed* and *Point of Retreat*. She lives in Texas with her husband and their three boys.

To read more about this author, visit her website at www.colleenhoover.com.

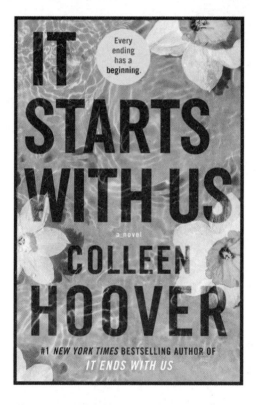

slammed

Also by Colleen Hoover

Point of Retreat

slammed

A Novel

Colleen Hoover

ATRIA PAPERBACK

NEW YORK   LONDON   TORONTO   SYDNEY   NEW DELHI

ATRIA PAPERBACK

A Division of Simon & Schuster, Inc.
1230 Avenue of the Americas
New York, NY 10020

First Atria Paperback edition September 2012

ATRIA PAPERBACK and colophon are trademarks of Simon & Schuster, Inc.

The author and publisher gratefully acknowledge permission from the following source to reprint material in their control: Portions of song lyrics from the Avett Brothers. Reprint permission granted by the Avett Brothers.

For information about special discounts for bulk purchases, please contact Simon & Schuster Special Sales at 1-866-506-1949 or business@simonandschuster.com.

The Simon & Schuster Speakers Bureau can bring authors to your live event. For more information or to book an event, contact the Simon & Schuster Speakers Bureau at 1-866-248-3049 or visit our website at www.simonspeakers.com.

Designed by Suet Y. Chong

Manufactured in China

10 9 8 7 6 5 4 3 2 1

Library of Congress Cataloging-in-Publication Data is available.

ISBN 978-1-4767-1590-2
ISBN 978-1-4767-1591-9 (ebook)

This book is dedicated to the Avett Brothers, for giving me the motivation to "decide what to be, and go be it."

part
one

1.

I'm as nowhere as I can be,
Could you add some somewhere to me?

—THE AVETT BROTHERS, "SALINA"

KEL AND I LOAD THE LAST TWO BOXES INTO THE U-HAUL. I slide the door down and pull the latch shut, locking up eighteen years of memories, all of which include my dad.

It's been six months since he passed away. Long enough that my nine-year-old brother, Kel, doesn't cry every time we talk about him, but recent enough that we're being forced to accept the financial aftermath that comes to a newly single-parented household. A household that can't afford to remain in Texas and in the only home I've ever known.

"Lake, stop being such a downer," my mom says, handing me the keys to the house. "I think you'll love Michigan."

3

She never calls me by the name she legally gave me. She and my dad argued for nine months over what I would be named. She loved the name Layla, after the Eric Clapton song. Dad loved the name Kennedy, after a Kennedy. "It doesn't matter which Kennedy," he would say. "I love them all!"

I was almost three days old before the hospital forced them to decide. They agreed to take the first three letters of both names and compromised on Layken, but neither of them has ever once referred to me as such.

I mimic my mother's tone, "Mom, stop being such an *upper*! I'm going to *hate* Michigan."

My mother has always had an ability to deliver an entire lecture with a single glance. I get the glance.

I walk up the porch steps and head inside the house to make a walk-through before the final turn of the key. All of the rooms are eerily empty. It doesn't seem as though I'm walking through the house where I've lived since the day I was born. These last six months have been a whirlwind of emotions, all of them bad. Moving out of this home was inevitable—I realize that. I just expected it to happen after the *end* of my senior year.

I'm standing in what is no longer our kitchen when I catch a glimpse of a purple plastic hair clip under the cabinet in the space where the refrigerator once stood. I pick it up, wipe the dust off of it, and run it back and forth between my fingers.

"It'll grow back," Dad said.

I was five years old, and my mother had left her trimming scissors on the bathroom counter. Apparently, I had done what most kids of that age do. I cut my own hair.

"Mommy's going to be so mad at me," I cried. I thought that if I cut my hair, it would immediately grow back, and no one would notice. I cut a pretty wide chunk out of my bangs and sat in front of the mirror for probably an hour, waiting for the hair to grow back. I picked the straight brown strands up off the floor and held them in my hand, contemplating how I could secure them back to my head, when I began to cry.

When Dad walked into the bathroom and saw what I had done, he just laughed and scooped me up, then positioned me on the countertop. "Mommy's not going to notice, Lake," he promised as he removed something out of the bathroom cabinet. "I just happen to have a piece of magic right here." He opened up his palm and revealed the purple clip. "As long as you have this in your hair, Mommy will never know." He brushed the remaining strands of hair across and secured the clip in place. He then turned me around to face the mirror. "See? Good as new!"

I looked at our reflection in the mirror and felt like the luckiest girl in the world. I didn't know of any other dad who had magic clips.

I wore that clip in my hair every day for two months, and my mother never once mentioned it. Now that I look back on it, I realize he probably told her what I had done. But when I was five, I believed in his magic.

I look more like my mother than like him. Mom and I are both of average height. After having two kids, she can't really fit into my jeans, but we're pretty good at sharing everything else. We both have brown hair that, depending on the weather, is either straight or wavy. Her eyes are a deeper emerald than mine, although it could be that the paleness of her skin just makes them more prominent.

I favor my dad in all the ways that count. We had the same dry sense of humor, the same personality, the same love of music, the same laugh. Kel is a different story. He takes after our dad physically with his dirty-blond hair and soft features. He's on the small side for nine years old, but his personality makes up for what he lacks in size.

I walk to the sink and turn it on, rubbing my thumb over the thirteen years of grime collected on the hair clip. Kel walks backward into the kitchen just as I'm drying my hands on my jeans. He's a strange kid, but I couldn't love him more. He has a game he likes to play that he calls "backward day," in which he spends most of the time walking everywhere backward, talking backward, and even requesting dessert first. I guess with such a big age difference between him and me and no other siblings, he has to find a way to entertain himself somehow.

"Hurry to says Mom Layken!" he says, backward.

I place the hair clip in the pocket of my jeans and head back out the door, locking up my home for the very last time.

* * *

OVER THE NEXT few days, my mother and I alternate driving my Jeep and the U-Haul, stopping only twice at hotels to sleep. Kel switches between Mom and me, riding the final day with me in the U-Haul. We complete the last exhausting nine-hour stretch through the night, only stopping once for a short break. As we close in on our new town of Ypsilanti, I take in my surroundings and the fact that it's September but my heater is on. I'll definitely need a new wardrobe.

As I make a final right-hand turn onto our street, my GPS informs me that I've "reached my destination."

"My destination," I laugh aloud to myself. My GPS doesn't know squat.

The cul-de-sac is not very long, lined with about eight single-story brick houses on each side of the street. There's a basketball goal in one of the driveways, which gives me hope that Kel might have someone to play with. Honestly, it looks like a decent neighborhood. The lawns are manicured, the sidewalks are clean, but there's too much concrete. Way too much concrete. I already miss home.

Our new landlord emailed us pictures of the house, so I immediately spot which one is ours. It's small. It's *really* small. We had a ranch-style home on several acres of land in Texas. The minuscule amount of land surrounding *this* home is almost nothing but concrete and garden gnomes. The front door is propped open, and I see an older man who I assume is our new landlord come outside and wave.

I drive about fifty yards past the house so that I can

back into the driveway, where the rear of the U-Haul will face the front door. Before I put the gearshift in reverse, I reach over and shake Kel awake. He's been passed out since Indiana.

"Kel, wake up," I whisper. "We've reached our *destination*."

He stretches his legs out and yawns, then leans his forehead against the window to get a look at our new house. "Hey, there's a kid in the yard!" Kel says. "Do you think he lives in our house, too?"

"He better not," I reply. "But he's probably a neighbor. Hop out and go introduce yourself while I back up."

When the U-Haul is successfully backed in, I put the gearshift in park, roll down the windows, and kill the engine. My mother pulls in beside me in my Jeep and I watch as she gets out and greets the landlord. I crouch down a few inches in the seat and prop my foot against the dash, watching Kel and his new friend sword fight with imaginary swords in the street. I'm jealous of him. Jealous of the fact that he can accept the move so easily, and I'm stuck being the angry, bitter child.

He was upset when Mom first decided on the move. Mostly because he was in the middle of his Little League season. He had friends he would miss, but at the age of nine your best friend is usually imaginary, and transatlantic. Mom subdued him pretty easily by promising he could sign up for hockey, something he wanted to do in Texas. It was a hard sport to come by in the rural south. After she agreed to that, he was pretty upbeat, if not stoked, about Michigan.

I understand why we had to move. Dad had made a respectable living managing a paint store. Mom worked PRN as a nurse when she needed to, but mostly tended to the house and to us. About a month after he died, she was able to find a full-time job. I could see the stress of my father's death taking its toll on her, along with being the new head of household.

One night over dinner, she explained to us that she wasn't left with enough income to continue paying all the bills and the mortgage. She said there was a job that could pay her more, but we would have to move. She was offered a job by her old high-school friend Brenda. They grew up together in my mother's hometown of Ypsilanti, right outside of Detroit. It paid more than anything she could find in Texas, so she had no choice but to accept. I don't blame her for the move. My grandparents are deceased, and she has no one to help her. I understand why we had to do it, but understanding a situation doesn't always make it easier.

"Layken, you're dead!" Kel shouts through the open window, thrusting his imaginary sword into my neck. He waits for me to slump over, but I just roll my eyes at him. "I stabbed you. You're supposed to die!" he says.

"Believe me, I'm already dead," I mumble as I open the door and climb out. Kel's shoulders are slumped forward and he's staring down at the concrete, his imaginary sword limp by his side. Kel's new friend stands behind him looking just as defeated, causing me immediately to regret the transference of my bad mood.

"I'm already dead," I say in my best monster voice, "because I'm a *zombie!*"

They start screaming as I stretch my arms out in front of me, cock my head to the side, and make a gurgling sound. "Brains!" I grumble, walking stiff-legged after them around the U-Haul. "Brains!"

I slowly round the front of the U-Haul, holding my arms out in front of me, when I notice someone grasping my brother and his new friend by the collars of their shirts.

"Get 'em!" The stranger yells as he holds the two screaming boys.

He looks a couple of years older than me and quite a bit taller. "Hot" would be how most girls would describe him, but I'm not most girls. The boys are flailing around, and his muscles flex under his shirt as he tries hard to maintain his grip on them.

Unlike Kel and me, these two are unmistakably siblings. Aside from the obvious age difference, they're identical. They both have the same smooth olive skin, the same jet-black hair, even the same cropped hairstyle. He's laughing as Kel breaks free and starts slicing at him with his "sword." He looks up at me and mouths "Help," when I realize I'm still frozen in my zombie pose.

My first instinct is to crawl back inside the U-Haul and hide on the floorboard for the remainder of my life.

Instead, I yell "Brains" once more and lunge forward, pretending to bite the younger boy on top of his head. I grab Kel and his new friend and start tickling them until they melt into heaps on the concrete driveway.

As I straighten up, the older brother extends his hand. "Hey, I'm Will. We live across the street," he says, pointing to the house directly across from ours.

I reciprocate his handshake. "I'm Layken. I guess I live here," I say as I glance toward the house behind me.

He smiles. Our handshake lingers as neither one of us says anything. I hate awkward moments.

"Well, welcome to Ypsilanti," he says. He pulls his hand from mine and puts it in his jacket pocket. "Where are you guys moving here from?"

"Texas?" I reply. I'm not sure why the tail end of my reply comes out like a question. I'm not sure why I'm even analyzing why it came out like a question. I'm not sure why I'm analyzing the reason why I'm analyzing—I'm flustered. It must be the lack of sleep I've gotten over the past three days.

"Texas, huh?" he says. He's rocking back and forth on his heels. The awkwardness intensifies when I fail to respond. He glances down at his brother and bends over, grabbing him by the ankles. "I've got to get this little guy to school," he says as he swings his brother up and over his shoulders. "There's a cold front coming through tonight. You should try to get as much unloaded today as you can. It's supposed to last a few days, so if you guys need help unloading this afternoon, let me know. We should be home around four."

"Sure, thanks," I say. They head across the street, and I'm still watching them when Kel stabs me in my lower back. I drop to my knees and clutch at my stomach, crouching forward as Kel climbs on top of me and finishes me off. I glance across the street again and see Will watching us. He shuts his brother's car door, walks around to the driver's-side door, and waves goodbye.

IT TAKES US most of the day to unload all of the boxes and furniture. Our landlord helps move the larger items that Mom and I can't lift on our own. We're too tired to get to the boxes inside the Jeep and agree to put it off until tomorrow. I'm a little disappointed when the U-Haul is finally empty; I no longer have an excuse to solicit Will's help.

As soon as my bed is put together, I start grabbing boxes with my name on them from the hallway. I get most of them unpacked and my bed made, when I notice the furniture in my bedroom casting shadows across the walls. I look out my window, and the sun is setting. Either the days are a lot shorter here, or I've lost track of time.

In the kitchen, I find Mom and Kel unloading dishes into the cabinets. I climb into one of the six tall chairs at the bar, which also doubles as the dining room table because of the lack of dining room. There isn't much to this house. When you walk through the front door, there's a small entryway followed by the living room. The living room is separated from the kitchen by nothing more than a hallway to the left and a window to the right. The living room's beige carpet is edged by hardwood that leads throughout the rest of the house.

"Everything is so clean here," my mother says as she continues putting away dishes. "I haven't seen a single insect."

Texas has more insects than blades of grass. If you aren't swatting flies, you're killing wasps.

"That's one good thing about Michigan, I guess," I reply. I open up a box of pizza in front of me and eye the selection.

"*One* good thing?" She winks at me as she leans across the bar, grabs a pepperoni, and pops it into her mouth. "I'd think that would be at least *two* good things."

I pretend I'm not following.

"I saw you talking to that boy this morning," she says with a smile.

"Oh, please, Mom," I reply as indifferently as I can get away with. "I'm pretty positive we'll find it no surprise that Texas isn't the only state inhabited by the male species." I walk to the refrigerator and grab a soda.

"What's anabited?" Kel asks.

"Inhabited," I correct him. "It means to occupy, dwell, reside, populate, squat, *live*." My SAT prep courses are paying off.

"Oh, kinda like how we anabited Ypsilanti?" he says.

"Inhabited," I correct him again. I finish my slice of pizza and take another sip of the soda. "I'm beat, guys. I'm going to bed."

"You mean you're going to *inhabit* your bedroom?" Kel says.

"You're a quick learner, young grasshopper." I bend and kiss the top of his head and retreat to my room.

It feels so good to crawl under the covers. At least my bed is familiar. I close my eyes and try to imagine that I'm in my old bedroom. My old, *warm* bedroom. My sheets and pillow are ice cold, so I pull the covers over my head to generate some heat. Note to self: Locate the thermostat first thing in the morning.

AND THAT'S EXACTLY what I set out to do as soon as I crawl out of bed and my bare feet meet the ice-cold floor beneath them. I grab a sweater out of my closet and throw it on over my pajamas while I search for socks. It's a futile attempt. I quietly tiptoe down the hallway, trying not to wake anyone while at the same time attempting to expose the least possible amount of foot to the coldness of the hardwood. As I pass Kel's room, I spot his Darth Vader house shoes on the floor. I sneak in and slip them on, finally finding some relief as I head into the kitchen.

I look around for the coffeepot but don't find it. I remember packing it in the Jeep, which is unfortunate since the Jeep is parked outside. Outside in this absurdly cold weather.

The jackets are nowhere to be found. Septembers in Texas rarely call for jackets. I grab the keys and decide I'll just have to make a mad dash to the Jeep. I open the front door and some sort of white substance is all over the yard. It takes me a second to realize what it is. Snow? In September? I bend down and scoop some up in my hands and examine it. It doesn't snow that often in Texas, but when it does it isn't *this* kind of snow. Texas snow is more like minuscule pieces of rock-hard hail. Michigan snow is just how I imagined real snow would be: fluffy, soft, and *cold*! I quickly drop the snow and dry my hands on my sweatshirt as I head toward the Jeep.

I don't make it far. The second those Darth Vader house shoes meet the snow-dusted concrete, I'm no longer looking at the Jeep in front of me. I'm flat on my back, staring up at the clear blue sky. I immediately feel the pain in my right shoulder and realize I've landed on something hard. I reach around and pull a concrete garden gnome out from beneath me, half of his red hat broken off and shattered into pieces. He's smirking at me. I groan and raise the gnome with my good arm and pull it back, preparing to chuck the thing, when someone stops me.

"That's not a good idea!"

I immediately recognize Will's voice. The sound of it is smooth and soothing like my father's was, but at the same time has an authoritative edge to it. I sit upright and see him walking up the driveway toward me.

"Are you okay?" he laughs.

"I'll feel a lot better after I bust this damn thing," I say, trying to pull myself up with no success.

"You don't want to do that: Gnomes are good luck," he says as he reaches me. He takes the gnome out of my hands and gently places it on the snow-covered grass.

"Yeah," I reply, taking in the gash on my shoulder that has now formed a bright red circle on my sweater sleeve. "*Real* good luck."

Will stops laughing when he sees the blood on my shirt. "Oh my god, I'm so sorry. I wouldn't have laughed if I knew you were hurt." He bends over and takes my un-injured arm and pulls me up. "You need to get a bandage on that."

"I wouldn't have a clue where to find one at this point," I reply, referring to the mounds of unopened boxes we have yet to unpack.

"You'll have to walk with me. There's some in our kitchen."

He removes his jacket and wraps it around my shoulders, holding on to my arm as he walks me across the street. I feel a little pathetic with him assisting me—I can walk on my own. I don't object though, and I feel like a hypocrite to the entire feminist movement. I've regressed to the damsel in distress.

I remove his jacket and lay it across the back of the

couch, then follow him into the kitchen. It's still dark inside, so I assume everyone is still asleep. His house is more spacious than ours. The open floor plans are similar, but the living room seems to be a few feet larger. A large bay window with a sitting bench and large pillows looks out over the backyard.

Several family pictures hang along the wall opposite the kitchen. Most of them are of Will and his little brother, with a few pictures that include his parents. I walk over to inspect the pictures while Will looks for a bandage. They must have gotten their genes from their dad. In one picture, which seems like the most recent but still looks a few years dated, his dad has his arms around the two boys, and he's squeezing them together for an impromptu photo. His jet-black hair is speckled with gray, and a thick black moustache outlines his huge smile. His features are identical to Will's. They both have eyes that smile when they laugh, exposing perfect white teeth.

Will's mother is breathtaking. She has long blond hair and, from the pictures at least, looks tall. I can't pick out any facial features of hers that were passed on to her boys. Maybe Will has her personality. All of the pictures on the wall prove one big difference between our houses— this one is a *home*.

I walk into the kitchen and take a seat at the bar.

"It needs to be cleaned before you put the bandage on it," he says as he rolls up his shirtsleeves and turns on the faucet. He's wearing a pale-yellow button-down collared shirt that is slightly transparent under the kitchen lights, revealing the outline of his undershirt. He has broad shoulders, and his sleeves are snug around the muscles in his arms. The top of his head meets the cabinet above him, and I estimate from the similarities in our kitchens that he stands about six inches taller than me. I'm staring at the pattern on his black tie, which is flipped over his shoulder to avoid getting it wet, when he turns the water off and walks back to the bar. I feel my face flush as I grab the wet napkin out of his hands, not proud of the amount of attention his physique is getting from me.

"It's fine," I say, pulling my sleeve down over my shoulder. "I can get it."

He opens a bandage as I wipe the blood off the wound. "So, what were you doing outside in your pajamas at seven o'clock in the morning?" he asks. "Are you guys still unloading?"

I shake my head and toss the napkin into the trash can. "Coffee."

"Oh. I guess you aren't a morning person." Will says this as more of a statement than a question.

As he moves in closer to place the bandage on my shoulder, I feel his breath on my neck. I rub my arms to hide the chills that are creeping up them. He adheres it to my shoulder and pats it.

"There. Good as new," he says.

"Thanks. And I *am* a morning person," I say. "*After* I get my coffee." I stand up and look over my shoulder, pretending to inspect the bandage as I plot my next move. I already thanked him. I could turn and walk out now, but that would seem rude after he just helped me. If I just stand here waiting on him to make more small talk, I might look stupid for *not* leaving. I don't understand why I'm even contemplating basic actions around him. He's just another inhabitant!

When I turn around, he's at the counter, pouring a cup of coffee. He walks toward me and sets it on the bar in front of me. "You want cream or sugar?"

I shake my head. "Black is fine. Thanks."

He's leaning across the bar watching me as I drink the coffee. His eyes are the exact same hue of deep green as his mother's are in the picture. I guess he did get a feature from her. He smiles and breaks our gaze by looking down at his watch. "I need to go: My brother's waiting in the car, and I've got to get to work," he says. "I'll walk you back. You can keep the cup."

I look at the cup before taking another sip and notice the big letters emblazoned on the side. World's Greatest Dad. It's exactly the same as the cup my father used to drink coffee from. "I'll be okay," I say as I head toward the front door. "I think I've got the whole walking-erect thing down now."

He follows me outside and shuts his front door behind him, insisting I take his jacket with me. I pull it on over my shoulders, thank him again, and head across the street.

"Layken!" he yells just as I'm about to walk back inside my house. I turn back toward him and he's standing in his driveway.

"May the force be with you!" He laughs and hops into his car as I stand there, staring down at the Darth Vader house shoes I'm still sporting. Classic.

THE COFFEE HELPS. I locate the thermostat, and by lunch the house has finally started to warm up. Mom and Kel have gone to the utility company to get everything switched into her name, and I'm left with the last of the boxes, if you don't count what's still in the Jeep. I get a few more things unpacked and decide it's high time for a shower. I'm pretty sure I'm closing in on day three of my granola-girl look.

I get out of the shower and wrap myself in a towel, flipping my hair forward as I brush it out and blow-dry it. When it's dry, I point the blow-dryer at the fogged up mirror, forming a clear circular area so that I can apply a little makeup. I notice my tan has started to fade. There won't be much lying-out here, so I might as well get used to a slightly paler complexion.

I brush my hair and pull it back into a ponytail and put on some lip gloss and mascara. I forgo the blush, since there no longer seems to be a need for it. Between the weather and my brief encounters with Will, my cheeks seem to stay red.

Mom and Kel have already returned and gone again while I was in the shower. There is a note from her informing me she and Kel are following her friend Brenda into the city to return the U-Haul. Three twenty-dollar bills are on the counter next to the car keys and a grocery list. I snatch them up and head to the Jeep, reaching it successfully this time.

I realize as I'm putting the car into reverse that I have absolutely no idea where I'm going. I know nothing about this town, much less whether I need to turn left or right off of my own street. Will's little brother is in their front yard, so I pull the car up parallel to their curb and roll down my passenger window.

"Hey, come here for a sec!" I yell at him.

He looks at me and hesitates. Maybe he thinks I'm going to bust out in zombie mode again. He walks toward the car, but stops three feet short of the window.

"How do I get to the closest grocery store?" I ask him.

He rolls his eyes. "Seriously? I'm nine."

Okay. So the resemblance to his brother is only skin deep.

"Well, thanks for nothing," I say. "What's your name anyway?"

He smiles at me mischievously and yells, "Darth Vader!" He's laughing as he runs in the opposite direction of the car.

Darth Vader? I realize the significance of his response. He's making a crack about the house shoes I had on this morning. Not a big deal. The big deal is that Will must have been talking about me to him. I can't help but try to imagine the conversation between them and what Will thinks about me. *If* he even thinks about me. For some reason, I've been thinking about him more than I'm comfortable with. I keep wondering how old he is, what his major is, whether he's *single*.

Luckily, I didn't leave any boyfriends behind in Texas. I haven't dated anyone in almost a year. Between high school, my part-time job, and helping out with Kel's sports, I hadn't had much time for boys. I realize it's going to be an adjustment, going from a person with absolutely no free time to a person with absolutely nothing to do.

I reach into the glove box to retrieve my GPS.

"That's not a good idea," Will says.

I look up to see him walking toward the car. I make my best attempt to stifle the smile that is trying to take over my face. "What's not a good idea?" I say as I insert the GPS into its holder and power it on.

He crosses his arms and leans in the window of the car. "There's quite a bit of construction going on right now. That thing will get you lost."

I'm about to respond when Brenda pulls up alongside me with my mother. Brenda rolls down her driver's-side window and my mother leans across the seat. "Don't forget laundry detergent—I can't remember if I put it on the list.

And cough syrup. I think I'm coming down with some-thing," she says through the window.

Kel jumps out of the backseat, runs to Will's brother, and invites him inside to look at our house.

"Can I?" Will's brother asks him.

"Sure," Will says as he opens my passenger door. "I'll be back in a little while, Caulder. I'm riding with Layken to the store."

He is? I shoot a look in his direction and he's buckling his seat belt.

"I don't give very good verbal directions. Mind if I go with you?"

"I guess not," I laugh.

I look back toward Brenda and my mother, but they have already pulled forward into the driveway. I put the car in drive and listen as Will gives me directions out of the neighborhood. "So, Caulder is your little brother's name?" I say, making a halfhearted attempt at small talk.

"One and only. My parents tried for years to have another baby after me. They eventually had Caulder when names like 'Will' weren't that cool anymore."

"I like your name," I say. I regret saying it as soon as it comes out of my mouth. It sounds like a lame attempt at flirting.

He laughs. I like his laugh. I hate that I like his laugh.

It startles me when I feel him brush the hair off my shoulder and touch my neck. His fingers slip under the collar of my shirt and he pulls it slightly down over my shoulder. "You're going to need a new bandage soon." He pulls my shirt back up and gives it a pat. His fingers leave a streak of heat across my neck.

"Remind me to grab some at the store," I say, trying to prove that his actions and his presence have no effect on me whatsoever.

"So, Layken." He pauses as he glances past me at the boxes still piled high in the backseat. "Tell me about yourself."

"Um, no. That's so cliché," I say.

He laughs. "Fine. I'll figure you out myself." He leans forward and hits eject on my CD player. His movements are so fluid, like he's been rehearsing them for years. I envy this about him. I've never been known for my grace.

"You know, you can tell a lot about a person by their taste in music." He pulls the CD out and examines the label. "'Layken's shit?'" he says aloud and laughs. "Is *shit* descriptive here, or possessive?"

"I don't like Kel touching my shit, okay?" I grab the CD out of his hands and insert it back into the player.

When the banjo pours out of the speakers at full volume, I'm immediately embarrassed. I'm from Texas, but I don't want him mistaking this for country music. If there's one thing I *don't* miss about Texas, it's the country music. I reach over and turn down the volume, when he grabs my hand in objection.

"Turn it back up, I know this," he says. His hand remains clasped on top of mine.

My fingers are still on the volume so I turn it back up. There's no *way* he knows this. I realize he's bluffing—his own lame attempt at flirting.

"Oh yeah?" I say. I'll call his bluff. "What's it called?"

"It's the Avett Brothers," he says. "I call it 'Gabriella,' but I think it's the end to one of their 'Pretty Girl' songs. I love the end of this one when they break out with the electric guitars."

His response to my question startles me. He really does know this. "You like the Avett Brothers?"

"I *love* them. They played in Detroit last year. Best live show I've ever seen."

A rush of adrenaline shoots through my body as I look down at his hand, still holding on to mine, still holding on to the volume button. I like it, but I'm mad at myself for liking it. Boys have given me the butterflies before, but I usually have more control over my susceptibility to such mundane movements.

He notices me noticing our hands and he lets go, rubbing his palms on his pant legs. It seems like a nervous gesture and I'm curious whether he shares my uneasiness.

I tend to listen to music that isn't mainstream. It's rare when I meet someone that has even heard of half the bands I love. The Avett Brothers are my all-time favorite.

My father and I would stay up at night and sing some of the songs together as he attempted to work out the chords on his guitar. He described them to me once. He said, "Lake, you know a band has true talent when their *imperfections* define *perfection*."

I eventually understood what he meant when I started really *listening* to them. Broken banjo strings, momentary passionate lapses of harmony, voices that go from smooth to gravelly to all-out screaming in a single verse. All these things add substance, character, and believability to their music.

After my father died, my mother gave me an early present he had intended to give me for my eighteenth birthday: a pair of Avett Brothers concert tickets. I cried when she gave them to me, thinking about how much my father was probably looking forward to giving me the gift himself. I knew he would have wanted me to use them, but I couldn't. The concert was just weeks after his death, and I knew I wouldn't be able to enjoy it. Not like I would have if he were with me.

"I love them, too," I say unsteadily.

"Have you ever seen them play live?" Will asks.

I'm not sure why, but as we talk, I tell him the entire story about my dad. He listens intently, interrupting only to instruct me when and where to turn. I tell him all about our passion for music. I tell him about how my father died suddenly and extremely unexpectedly of a heart attack. I tell him about my birthday present and the concert we never made it to. I don't know why I keep talking, but I can't seem to shut myself up. I never divulge information so freely, especially to people I barely know. Especially to *guys* I barely know. I'm still talking when I realize we've come to a stop in a grocery store parking lot.

"Wow," I say as I take in the time on the clock. "Is that the quickest way to the store? That drive took twenty minutes."

He winks at me and opens his door. "No, actually it's not."

That's *definitely* flirting. And I definitely have butter-flies.

The snow flurries start to mix with sleet as we're making our way through the parking lot. "Run," he says. He takes my hand in his and pulls me faster toward the entrance.

We're out of breath and laughing when we make it inside the store, shaking the wetness from our clothes. I take my jacket off and shake it out, when his hand brushes against my face, wiping away a strand of wet hair that's stuck to my cheek. His hand is cold, but the moment his fingers graze my skin, I forget about the frigid temperature as my face grows warm. His smile fades as we both stare at each other. I'm still trying to become accustomed to the reactions I have around him. The slightest touch and simplest gestures have such an intense effect on my senses.

I clear my throat and break our stare as I grab an available cart next to us. I hand him the grocery list. "Does it always snow in September?" I ask in an attempt to appear unfazed by his touch.

"No, it won't last more than a few days, maybe a week. Most of the time the snow doesn't start until late October," he says. "You're lucky."

"Lucky?"

"Yeah. It's a pretty rare cold front. You got here right in time."

"Huh. I assumed most of y'all would hate the snow. Doesn't it snow here most of the year?"

He laughs. "*Y'all?*"

"What?"

"Nothing," he says with a smile. "I've just never heard anyone say 'y'all' in real life before. It's cute. So southern belle."

"Oh, I'm sorry," I say. "From now on I'll do like you Yankees and waste my breath by saying 'all you guys.'"

He laughs and nudges my shoulder. "Don't. I like your accent; it's perfect."

I can't believe I've actually turned into a girl who swoons over a guy. I detest it so much; I start to inspect his features more intently, trying to find a flaw. I can't. Everything about him so far is perfect.

We get the items on our list and head to the checkout. He refuses to let me put anything on the conveyor belt, so I just stand back and watch as he unloads the items from the buggy. The last item he places on the line is a box of bandages. I never even saw him grab them.

When we pull out of the grocery store, Will tells me to turn in the direction opposite to the one from which we came. We drive maybe two whole blocks when he instructs me to turn left—onto our street. The drive that took us twenty minutes on the way there takes us less than a minute on the way back.

"Nice," I say when I pull in my driveway. I realize what he's done and that the flirtation on his end is blatantly obvious.

Will has already rounded to the back of the Jeep, so I press the trunk lever for him. I get out and walk to where he is, expecting him to have an armload of groceries. Instead, he's just standing there holding the trunk up, watching me.

With my best southern belle impression, I place my hand across my chest and say, "Why! I never would have been able to find the store without your help. Thank you *so* much for your hospitality, kind sir."

I sort of expect him to laugh, but he just stands there, staring at me.

"*What?*" I say nervously.

He takes a step toward me and softly cups my chin with his free hand. I'm shocked by my own reaction, the fact that I allow it. He studies my face for a few seconds as my heart races within my chest. I think he's about to kiss me.

I attempt to calm my breathing as I stare up at him. He steps in even closer and removes his hand from my chin and places it on the back of my neck, leaning my head in toward him. His lips press gently against my forehead, lingering a few seconds before he releases his hand and steps back.

"You're so cute," he says. He reaches into the trunk and grabs four sacks with one hefty swoop. He walks toward the house and sets them outside the door.

I'm frozen, attempting to absorb the last fifteen seconds of my life. Where did that come from? Why did I just stand there and let him do that? Despite my objections I realize, almost pathetically, that I have just experienced the most passionate kiss I've ever received from a guy— and it was on the freaking forehead!

AS WILL REACHES into the trunk for another handful of groceries, Kel and Caulder run out of the house, followed by my mother. The boys dart across the street to check out Caulder's bedroom. Will politely extends his hand out to my mother when she walks toward us.

"You must be Layken and Kel's mom. I'm Will Cooper. We live across the street."

"Julia Cohen," she says. "You're Caulder's older brother?"

"Yes, ma'am," he replies. "Older by twelve years."

"So that makes you . . . twenty-one?" She glances at me and gives me a quick wink. I'm standing behind Will at this point, so I take the opportunity to reciprocate one of her infamous glares. She just smiles and turns her attention back to Will.

"Well, I'm glad Kel and Lake were able to make friends so fast," she says.

"Me too," he replies.

She turns and heads inside but purposefully nudges me with her shoulder as she passes. She doesn't speak a word but I know what she's hinting at: She's giving me her approval.

Will reaches in for the last two sacks. "*Lake*, huh? I like that." He hands me the sacks and shuts the trunk.

"*So*, Lake." He leans back against the car and crosses his arms. "Caulder and I are going to Detroit on Friday. We'll be gone until late Sunday—family stuff," he says with a dismissing wave of his hand. "I was wondering if you had any plans for tomorrow night, before I go?"

It's the first time anyone has ever called me Lake, other than my mom and dad. I like it. I lean my shoulder against the car and face him. I try to keep my cool, but inside I'm screaming with excitement.

"Are you really going to make me admit that I have absolutely no life here?" I say.

"Great! It's a date then. I'll pick you up at seven thirty." He immediately turns and heads toward his house when I realize he never actually *asked*, and I never actually *agreed*.

2.

It won't take long for me
To tell you who I am.
Well you hear this voice right now
Well that's pretty much all I am.

—THE AVETT BROTHERS,

"GIMMEAKISS"

THE NEXT AFTERNOON, I'M PICKING OUT WHAT TO WEAR but can't seem to locate any clean, weather-appropriate clothing. I don't own many winter shirts besides what I've already worn this week. I choose a purple long-sleeved shirt and smell it, deciding it's clean enough. I spray some perfume, though, just in case it isn't. I brush my teeth, touch up my makeup, brush my teeth again, and let down my ponytail. I curl a few sections of my hair and pull some silver earrings out of my drawer, when I hear a knock on the bathroom door.

My mother enters with a handful of towels. She opens the cabinet next to the shower and places them inside.

"Going somewhere?" she says. She sits down on the edge of the bathtub while I continue to get ready.

"Yeah, somewhere." I try to hide my smile as I put in my earrings. "Honestly, I'm not sure what we're doing. I really never even agreed to the date."

She stands up and walks to the door, leaning up against the frame. She watches me in the mirror. She has aged so much in the short time since my dad's death. Her bright green eyes against her smooth porcelain skin used to be breathtaking. Now, her cheekbones stand out above the hollowed shadows in her cheeks. The dark circles under her eyes overpower their emerald hue. She looks tired. And sad.

"Well, you're eighteen now. You've had enough of my dating advice for a lifetime," she says. "But I'll provide you with a quick recap just in case. Don't order anything with onion or garlic, never leave your drink unattended, and *always* use protection."

"Ugh, Mom!" I roll my eyes. "You know I know the rules, and you *know* I don't have to worry about the last one. Please don't give Will a recap of your rules. Promise?" I make her promise.

"So . . . tell me about Will. Does he work? Is he in college? What's his major? Is he a serial killer?" She says this with such sincerity.

I walk the short distance from the bathroom to my

bedroom and bend down to search through my shoes. She follows me and sits on the bed.

"Honestly, Mom, I don't know anything about him. I didn't even know how old he was until he told you."

"That's good," she says.

"Good?" I glance back at her. "How is not knowing anything about him good? I'm about to be alone with him for hours. He could be a *serial killer.*" I grab my boots and walk over to the bed to slip them on.

"It'll give you plenty to talk about. That's what first dates are for."

"Good point," I say.

Growing up, my mother did give great advice. She always knew what I wanted to hear but would tell me what I *needed* to hear. My dad was her first boyfriend, so I have always wondered how she knows so much about dating, boys, and relationships. She's only been with one person, and it seems most knowledge would have to come from life experiences. She's the exception, I guess.

"Mom?" I say as I slip on my boots. "I know you were only eighteen when you met Dad. I mean, that's really young to meet the person you spend the rest of your life with. Do you ever regret it?"

She doesn't answer immediately. Instead, she lies back on my bed and clasps her hands behind her head, pondering my question.

"I've never regretted it. Questioned it? Sure. But never regretted."

"Is there a difference?" I ask.

"Absolutely. Regret is counterproductive. It's looking back on a past that you can't change. *Questioning* things as they occur can prevent regret in the future. I questioned a lot about my relationship with your father. People make spontaneous decisions based on their hearts all the time. There's *so* much more to relationships than just love."

"Is that why you always tell me to follow my head, not my heart?"

My mother sits up on the bed and takes my hands in hers. "Lake, do you want some real advice that doesn't include a list of foods you should avoid?"

Has she been holding out on me? "Of course," I reply.

She's lost the authoritative, parental edge to her voice, which makes me aware that this conversation is less mother-daughter and more woman to woman. She pulls her legs up Indian-style on the bed and faces me.

"There are three questions every woman should be able to answer yes to before she commits to a man. If you answer no to any of the three questions, run like hell."

"It's just a date," I laugh. "I doubt we'll be doing any committing."

"I know you're not, Lake. I'm serious. If you can't answer yes to these three questions, don't even waste your time on a relationship."

When I open my mouth, I feel like I'm just reinforcing the fact that I'm her child. I don't interrupt her again.

"Does he treat you with respect at all times? That's the first question. The second question is, if he is the exact same person twenty years from now that he is today, would you still want to marry him? And finally, does he inspire you to want to be a better person? You find someone you can answer yes about to all three, then you've found a good man."

I take a deep breath as I soak in even more sage advice from her. "Wow, those are some intense questions," I say. "Were you able to answer yes to all of them? When you were with Dad?"

"Absolutely," she says, without hesitation. "Every second I was with him."

A sadness enters her eyes as she finishes her sentence. She loved my dad. I immediately regret bringing it up. I put my arms around her and embrace her. It's been so long since I've hugged her, a twinge of guilt rises up inside me. She kisses my hair, then pulls away and smiles.

I stand up and run my hands down my shirt, smoothing out the folds.

"Well? How do I look?"

"Like a woman," she sighs.

It's seven thirty sharp, so I go to the living room, grab the jacket Will insisted I borrow the day before, and head to the window. He's coming out of his house, so I walk outside and stand in my driveway. He looks up and notices me as he's opening his car door.

"You ready?" he yells.

"Yes!"

"Well, come on then!"

I don't move. I just stand there and fold my arms across my chest.

"What are you doing?" He throws his hand up in defeat and laughs.

"You said you would pick me up at seven thirty! I'm waiting for you to pick me up!"

He grins and gets in the car. He backs straight out of his driveway and into mine so that the passenger door is closest to me. He hops out of the car and runs around to open it. Before I get in I give him the once-over. He's wearing loose-fitted jeans and a black long-sleeved shirt that outlines his arms. It's the defined arms that prompt me to return his jacket to him.

"That reminds me," I say, handing him his jacket. "I bought this for you."

He smiles when he takes it and slides his arms inside. "Wow, thanks," he says. "It even smells like me."

He waits until I've buckled up before he shuts the door. As he's walking around to his side, I notice the car smells like . . . cheese. Not old, stale cheese, but fresh cheese. Cheddar, maybe. My stomach growls. I'm curious where we're going to eat.

When Will gets in, he reaches into the backseat and grabs a sack. "We don't have time to eat, so I made us grilled cheese." He hands me a sandwich and a bottle of soda.

"Wow. This is a first," I say, staring at the items in my

hands. "And where exactly are we going in such a hurry?" I twist open the lid. "It's obviously not a restaurant."

He unwraps his sandwich and takes a bite. "It's a surprise," he says with a mouthful of bread. He navigates the steering wheel with his free hand as he simultaneously drives and eats. "I know a lot more about you than you know about me, so tonight I want to show you what *I'm* all about."

"Well, I'm intrigued," I say. I really *am* intrigued.

We both finish our sandwiches, and I put the trash back in the bag and place it in the backseat. I try to think of something to say to break the silence, so I ask him about his family.

"What are your parents like?"

He takes a deep breath and slowly exhales, almost like I've asked the wrong thing. "I'm not big on small talk, Lake. We can figure all that out later. Let's make this drive interesting." He winks at me and relaxes further into his seat.

Driving, no talking, keeping it interesting. I'm repeating what he said in my head and hope I'm misunderstanding his intent. He laughs when he sees the hesitation on my face and it dawns on him that I've misinterpreted what he said.

"Lake, no!" he says. "I just meant let's talk about something besides what we're *expected* to talk about."

I breathe a sigh of relief. I thought I had found his flaw. "Good."

"I know a game we can play," he says. "It's called 'would you rather.' Have you played it before?"

I shake my head. "No, but I know I would *rather* you go first."

"Okay." He clears his throat and pauses for a few seconds. "Okay, would you rather spend the *rest* of your life with *no* arms, or would you rather spend the rest of your life with arms you couldn't *control*?"

What the hell? I can honestly say this date is not going the way any of my previous dates have gone. It's pleasantly unexpected, though.

"Well . . ." I hesitate. "I guess I would rather spend the rest of my life with arms I couldn't control?"

"What? Seriously? But you wouldn't be controlling them!" he says, flapping his arms around in the car. "They could be flailing around and you'd be constantly punching yourself in the face! Or worse, you might grab a knife and stab yourself!"

I laugh. "I didn't realize there were right and wrong answers."

"You suck at this," he teases. "Your turn."

"Okay, let me think."

"You have to have one ready!" he says.

"Jeez, Will! I barely heard of this game for the first time thirty seconds ago. Give me a second to think of one."

He reaches over and squeezes my hand. "I'm teasing."

He repositions his hand underneath mine, and our fingers interlock. I like how easy the transition is, like we've been holding hands for years. So far, everything about this date has been easy. I like Will's sense of humor. I like that I find it so easy to laugh around him after having gone so many months without laughing. I like that we're holding hands. I *really* like that we're holding hands.

"Okay, I've got one," I say. "Would you rather pee on yourself once a day at random, unknown times? Or would you rather have to pee on someone *else*?"

"It depends on who I'd have to pee on. Can I pee on people I don't like? Or is it random people?"

"Random people."

"Pee on myself," he says, without hesitation. "My turn now. Would you rather be four feet tall or seven feet tall?"

"Seven feet tall," I reply.

"Why?"

"You aren't allowed to ask why," I say. "Okay, let's see. Would you rather drink an entire gallon of bacon grease for breakfast every day? Or would you rather have to eat five pounds of popcorn for supper every night?"

"Five pounds of popcorn."

I like the game we're playing. I like that he didn't worry about impressing me with dinner. I like that I have no idea where we're headed. I even like that he didn't compliment what I was wearing, which seems to be the standard opening line for dates. So far, I like everything about tonight. As far as I'm concerned, we could drive around for another two hours just playing "would you rather," and it would be the most fun I've ever had on a date.

But we don't. We eventually reach our destination, and I immediately tense up when I see the sign on the building.

Club N9NE

"Uh, Will? I don't dance." I'm hoping he'll be empathetic.

"Uh, neither do *I*."

We exit the vehicle and meet at the front of the car. I'm not sure who reaches out first, but once again our fingers find each other in the dark and he holds my hand and guides me toward the entrance. As we get closer, I notice a sign posted on the door.

Closed for Slam
Thursdays
8:00–Whenever
Admission: Free
Fee to slam: $3

Will opens the door without reading the sign. I start to inform him the club is closed, but he seems like he knows what he's doing. The silence is interrupted by the noise of a crowd as I follow him through the entryway and into the room. There is an empty stage to the right of us and tables and chairs set up all over the dance floor. The place is packed. I see what looks like a group of younger kids, around age fourteen or so, at a table toward the front.

Will turns to the left and heads to an empty booth in the back of the room.

"It's quieter back here," he says.

"How old do you have to be to get into clubs here?" I say, still observing the group of out-of-place children.

"Well, tonight it's not a club," he says as we scoot into the booth. It's a half-circle booth facing the stage, so I scoot all the way to the middle to get the best view. He moves in right beside me. "It's slam night," he says. "Every Thursday they shut the club down and people come here to compete in the slam."

"And what's a slam?" I ask.

"It's poetry." He smiles at me. "It's what I'm all about."

Is he for real? A hot guy who makes me laugh *and* loves poetry? Someone pinch me. Or not—I'd rather not wake up.

"Poetry, huh?" I say. "Do people write their own or do they recite it from other authors?"

He leans back in the booth and looks up at the stage. I see the passion in his eyes when he talks about it. "People get up there and pour their hearts out just using their words and the movement of their bodies," he says. "It's amazing. You aren't going to hear any Dickinson or Frost here."

"Is it like a competition?"

"It's complicated," he says. "It differs between every club. Normally during a slam, the judges are picked at random from the audience and they assign points to each performance. The one with the most points at the end of the night wins. That's how they do it here, anyway."

"So do you slam?"

"Sometimes. Sometimes I judge; sometimes I just watch."

"Are you performing tonight?"

"Nah. Just an observer tonight. I don't really have anything ready."

I'm disappointed. It would be amazing to see him perform onstage. I still have no idea what slam poetry is, but I'm really curious to see him do *anything* that requires a performance.

"Bummer," I say.

It's quiet for a moment while we both observe the crowd in front of us. Will nudges me with his elbow and I turn to look at him. "You want something to drink?" he says.

"Sure. I'll take some chocolate milk."

He cocks and eyebrow and grins. "Chocolate milk? *Really?*"

I nod. "With ice."

"*Okay,*" he says as he slides out of the booth. "One chocolate milk on the rocks coming right up."

While he's gone, the emcee comes to the stage and attempts to pump up the crowd. No one is in the back of the room where we're seated, so I feel a little silly when I yell "Yeah!" with the rest of the crowd. I sink further into my seat and decide to just be a spectator for the remainder of the night.

The emcee announces it's time to pick the judges and the entire crowd roars, almost everyone wanting to be chosen. They pick five people at random and move them to the judging table. As Will walks toward our booth with our drinks, the emcee announces it's time for the "sac" and chooses someone at random.

"What's the sac?" I ask him.

"Sacrifice. It's what they use to prepare the judges." He slides back into the booth. Somehow, he slides even closer this time. "Someone performs something that isn't part of the competition so the judges can calibrate their scoring."

"So they can call on anyone? What if they had called on me?" I ask, suddenly nervous.

He smiles at me. "Well, I guess you should have had something ready."

He takes a sip from his drink then leans back against the booth, finding my hand in the dark. Our fingers don't interlock this time, though. Instead, he places my hand on his leg and his fingertips start to trace the outline of my wrist. He gently traces each of my fingers, following the lines and curves of my entire hand. His fingertips feel like electric pulses penetrating my skin.

"Lake," he says quietly as he continues tracing up my wrist and back to my fingertips with a fluid motion. "I don't know what it is about you . . . but I like you."

His fingers slide between mine and he takes my hand in his, turning his attention back to the stage. I inhale and reach for my chocolate milk with my free hand, downing the entire glass. The ice feels good against my lips. It cools me off.

They call on a young woman who looks to be around twenty-five. She announces she is performing a piece she wrote titled "Blue Sweater." The lights are lowered as a spotlight is positioned on her. She raises the microphone and steps forward, staring down at the floor. A hush sweeps over the audience, and the only sound in the entire room is the sound of her breath, amplified through the speakers.

She raises her hand to the microphone, still staring down to the floor. She begins to tap her finger against it in a repetitive motion, resonating the sound of a heartbeat. I realize I'm holding my own breath as she begins her piece.

Bom Bom

Bom Bom

Bom Bom

Do you *hear* that?

(Her voice lingering on the word hear.)

That's the sound of my heart beating.

(She taps the microphone again.)

Bom Bom

Bom Bom

Bom Bom

Do you *hear* that?

That's the sound of *your* heart beating.

(She begins to speak faster, much louder than before.)

It was the *first* day of October. I was wearing my *blue*
sweater, you know the one I bought at **Dillard's?** The
one with a double-knitted *hem* and *holes* in the *ends*
of the *sleeves* that I could poke my *thumbs* through
when it was cold but I didn't feel like wearing *gloves?*
It was the *same* sweater you said made my **eyes** look
like reflections of the *stars* on the *ocean.*

You promised to love me *forever* that night . . .

and *boy*

did *you*

ever.

It was the *first* day of **December** this time. I was
wearing my *blue* sweater, you know the one I bought
at *Dillard's?* The one with a double-knitted *hem* and
holes in the *ends* of the *sleeves* that I could poke my
thumbs through when it was cold but I didn't feel like
wearing *gloves?* It was the *same* sweater you said made
my *eyes* look like reflections of the *stars* on the *ocean.*

I told you I was three weeks *late.*

You *said* it was *fate.*

You promised to love me forever that night . . .

and *boy*

did *you*

ever!

It was the first day of May. I was wearing my *blue*
sweater, although *this* time the double-stitched *hem*
was *worn* and the *strength* of each thread *tested* as
they were pulled *tight* against my *growing belly. You*
know the one. The same one I bought at *Dillard's*?
The one with *holes* in the *ends* of the *sleeves* that I
could poke my *thumbs* through when it was cold but I
didn't feel like wearing *gloves*? It was the *same* sweater
you said made my **eyes** look like reflections of the
stars on the *ocean*.

The *SAME* sweater you *RIPPED* off of my body as
you *shoved* me to the floor,

calling me a *<u>whore</u>*,

telling me

you didn't *love* me

anymore.

Bom Bom

Bom Bom

Bom Bom

Do you *hear* that? That's the sound of my heart
beating.

Bom Bom

Bom Bom

Bom Bom

Do you *hear* that? That's the sound of *your* heart
beating.

(There is a long silence as she clasps her hands to her stomach, tears streaming down her face.)

Do you *hear* that? Of course you don't. That's the
silence of my womb.
Because you
RIPPED
OFF
MY
SWEATER!

The lights come back up and the audience roars. I take a deep breath and wipe tears from my eyes. I'm mesmerized by her ability to hypnotize an entire audience with such powerfully portrayed words. Just *words*. I'm immediately addicted and want to hear more. Will puts his arm around my shoulders and leans back into the seat with me, bringing me back to reality.

"Well?" he says.

I accept his embrace and move my head to his shoulder as we both stare out over the crowd. He rests his chin on top of my head.

"That was unbelievable," I whisper. His hand touches the side of my face, and he brushes his lips against my forehead. I close my eyes and wonder how much more my emotions can be tested. Three days ago, I was devastated, bitter, hopeless. Today I woke up feeling happy for the first time in months. I feel vulnerable. I try to mask my emotions, but I feel like everyone knows what I'm thinking and feeling, and I don't like it. I don't like being an open book. I feel like I'm up on the stage, pouring my heart out to him, and it scares the hell out of me.

We sit in the same embrace as several more people perform their pieces. The poetry is as vast and electrifying as the audience. I have never laughed and cried so much. The way these poets are able to lure you into a whole new world, viewing things from a vantage point you've never seen before. Making you feel like you are the mother who lost her baby, or the boy who killed his father, or even the man who got high for the first time and ate *five plates* of bacon. I feel a connection with these poets and their stories. What's more, I feel a deeper connection to Will. I can't imagine that he's brave enough to get up on the stage and bare his soul like these people are doing. I have to see it. I *have* to see him do this.

The emcee makes one last appeal for performers.

I turn toward him. "Will, you can't bring me here and not *perform*. Please do one? Please, please, please?"

He leans his head back against the booth. "You're killing me, Lake. Like I said, I don't really have anything new."

"Do something old then," I suggest. "Or do all these people make you *nervous*?"

He tilts his head toward me and smiles. "Not all of them. Just *one* of them."

I suddenly have the urge to kiss him. I suppress the

urge for now, and continue to plead. I clasp my hands to-gether under my chin. "Don't make me beg," I say.

"You already *are!*" He pauses for a few seconds, then removes his arm from around my shoulders and leans for-ward. "All right, all right," he says. He grins at me as he reaches into his pocket. "But I'm warning you, you asked."

He pulls his wallet out just as the emcee announces the start of round two. Will stands up, holding his three dollars in the air. "I'm in!"

The emcee shields his eyes with his hand, squinting into the audience to see who spoke up. "Ladies and gentle-men, it's one of our very own, Mr. Will Cooper. So nice of you to finally join us," he teases into the microphone.

Will makes his way through the crowd and walks onto the stage and into the spotlight.

"What's the name of your piece tonight, Will?" the emcee asks.

" 'Death,' " Will replies, looking past the crowd and directly at me. The smile fades from his eyes and he begins his performance.

Death. The only thing inevitable in life.
People don't like to *talk* about death because
it makes them *sad.*
They don't want to ***imagine*** how life will go on
without them,
all the people they love will briefly grieve
but continue to *breathe.*

They don't *want* to imagine how life will go on
without *them*,
Their children will still *grow*
Get married
Get *old* . . .
They don't want to *imagine* how life will *continue* to
go on without them,
Their material things will be *sold*
Their medical files stamped *"closed"*
Their name becoming a *memory* to everyone they
know.
They don't *want* to *imagine* how life will go on
without them, so *instead* of accepting it head *on*, they
avoid the subject *altogether,*
hoping and *praying* it will *somehow* . . .
pass them by.
Forget about them,
moving on to the *next* one in line.
No, they didn't *want* to imagine how life would
continue to go on . . .
without them.
But death
didn't
forget.
Instead they were met *head-on* by death,
disguised as an **18-wheeler**
behind a cloud of *fog.*
No.

Death didn't *forget* about *them*.
If *only* they had been **prepared**, **accepted** the
inevitable, laid out their **plans**, understood that it
wasn't just **their** lives at hand.
I may have legally been considered an adult at the age
of nineteen, but I still felt very much

all

of just nineteen.
Unprepared
and *overwhelmed*
to suddenly have the **entire life** of a seven-year-old
In my *realm*.
Death. The only thing inevitable in **life**.

Will steps out of the spotlight and off of the stage before he even sees his scores. I find myself hoping he gets lost on his way back to our booth so that I have time to absorb this. I have no idea how to react. I had no idea that this was his life. That Caulder was his *whole life*. I'm amazed by his performance but devastated by his words. I wipe tears away with the back of my hand. I don't know if I'm crying for the loss of Will's parents, the responsibilities brought by that loss, or the simple fact that he spoke the truth. He spoke about a side of death and loss that never seems to be considered until it's too late. A side that I'm unfortunately all too familiar with. The Will I watched walk up to the stage is not the same Will I'm watching walk toward me. I'm conflicted, I'm confused, and most of all I'm taken aback. He was beautiful.

He notices me wiping tears from my eyes. "I warned you," he says, sliding back into the booth. He reaches for his drink and takes a sip, stirring the ice cubes with his straw. I have no idea what to say to him. He put it all out there, right in front of me.

My emotions take control over my actions. I reach forward and take his hand in mine and he sets his drink back down on the table. He turns toward me and gives me a half smile, like he's waiting for me to say something. When I don't say anything, he pulls his hand up to my face and wipes away a tear, then traces the side of my cheek with the back of his hand. I don't understand the connection I feel with him. It all seems so fast. I put my hand on top of his and pull it to my mouth, then gently kiss the inside of his palm as we hold each other's stare. We suddenly become the only two people in the entire room; all the external noise fades into the distance.

He brings his other hand to my cheek and slowly leans forward. I close my eyes and feel his breath draw closer as he pulls me toward him. His lips touch my lips, but barely. He slowly kisses my bottom lip, then my top lip. His lips are cold, still wet from his drink. I lean in further to return his kiss, but he pulls away when my mouth responds. I open my eyes and he's smiling at me, still holding my face in his hands.

"Patience," he whispers. He closes his eyes and leans in, kissing me softly on the cheek. I close my eyes and inhale, trying to calm the overwhelming impulse I have to wrap my arms around him and kiss him back. I don't know how he has so much self-control. He presses his forehead against mine and slides his hands down my arms. Our eyes lock when we open them. It's during this moment that I finally understand why my mother accepted her fate at the age of eighteen.

"Wow," I exhale.

"Yeah," he agrees. "Wow."

We hold each other's stare for a few more seconds until the audience starts to roar again. They are announcing the qualifiers for round two when Will grabs my hand and whispers, "Let's go."

As I make my way out of the booth, my entire body feels like it's about to give out on me. I've never experienced anything like what just happened. *Ever.*

We exit the booth and our hands remain locked as he navigates me through the ever-growing crowd and into the parking lot. I don't realize how warm I am until the cold Michigan air touches my skin. It feels exhilarating. Or I feel exhilarated. I can't tell which. All I know is that I wish the last two hours of my life could repeat for eternity.

"You don't want to stay?" I ask him.

"Lake, you've been moving and unpacking for days. You need sleep."

His mention of sleep induces an involuntary yawn from me. "Sleep does sound good," I say.

He opens my door, but before I get in, he wraps his

arms around me and pulls me to him in a tight embrace. Several minutes pass while we just stand there, holding on to the moment. I could get used to this, which is a completely foreign feeling. I've always been so guarded. This new side of me that Will brings out is a side of me I didn't know I had.

We eventually break apart and get into the car. As we drive away from the parking lot, I lean my head against the window and watch the club minimize in the rearview mirror.

"Will?" I whisper, without breaking my gaze from the building disappearing behind us. "Thank you for this."

He takes my hand into his, and I eventually fall asleep, smiling.

I wake up as he's opening my door and we're in my driveway. He reaches in and grabs my hand, helping me out of the car. I can't remember the last time I fell asleep in a moving vehicle. Will was right: I *am* tired. I rub my eyes and yawn again as he walks me to the front door. He wraps his arms around my waist, and I raise mine around his shoulders. Our bodies are a perfect fit. A chill runs down my body as his breath warms my neck. I can't believe we met only three days ago; it seems like we've been doing this for years.

"Just think," I say. "You'll be gone three whole days. That's the same length of time I've known you."

He laughs and pulls me even closer. "This will be the longest three days of my life," he says.

If I know my mother at all, then we've got an audience, so I'm relieved his final kiss is nothing more than a quick peck on the cheek. He slowly walks backward, his fingers sliding out of mine, eventually letting go. My arm falls limp to my side as I watch him get into his car. He cranks the engine and rolls down his window. "Lake, I've got a pretty long drive home," he says. "How about one for the road?"

I laugh, then walk to the car and lean through his window, expecting another peck. Instead, he slips his hand behind my neck and gently pulls me toward him, our lips opening when they meet. Neither of us holds back this time. I reach through the window and run my fingers through the back of his hair as we continue kissing. It takes all I have not to swing open the car door and crawl into his lap. The door between us feels more like a barricade.

We finally come to a stop. Our lips are still touching as we both hesitate to part.

"Damn," he whispers against my lips. "It gets better every time."

"I'll see you in three days," I say. "You be careful driving home tonight." I give him one final kiss and reluctantly pull away from the window.

He backs out of the driveway and again straight into his own. I'm tempted to run after him and kiss him again to prove his theory. Instead, I avoid temptation and turn to head inside.

"Lake!"

I turn around and he shuts his car door and jogs toward me. He smiles when he reaches me. "I forgot to tell you something," he says, wrapping his arms around me again. "You look beautiful tonight." He kisses me on top of my head, releases his hold, and turns back toward his house.

Maybe I was wrong earlier—about me liking the fact that he didn't compliment me. I was *definitely* wrong. When he gets to his front door, he turns around and smiles before he goes inside.

Just as I had imagined, my mother is sitting on the sofa with a book, attempting to appear uninterested when I walk through the front door. "Well, how'd it go? Is he a serial killer?" she says.

My smile is uncontrollable now. I walk to the sofa opposite her and throw myself on it like a rag doll and sigh. "You were right, Mom. I *love* Michigan."

3.

But I can tell by watching you
That there's no chance of pushing through
The odds are so against us
You know most young love, it ends like this.

—THE AVETT BROTHERS, "I WOULD BE SAD"

I'M MORE NERVOUS THAN I ANTICIPATED WHEN I WAKE UP Monday morning. My mind has been so preoccupied with all things Will I haven't had time to process my impending doom. Or rather, my first day at a brand-new school.

Mom and I finally had a chance to go shopping for weather-appropriate clothing over the weekend. I throw on what I picked out the evening before and slide on my new snow boots. I leave my hair down for the day but slide an extra band onto my wrist for when I want to pull it back, which I know I'll do.

After I finish up in the bathroom, I move to the

kitchen and grab my backpack and my class schedule off the counter. Mom began her new night shift at the hospital last night, so I agreed to take Kel to school. Back in Texas, Kel and I went to the same school. In fact, everyone in the vicinity of our town went to the same school. Here, there are so many schools I have to print out a district map just to be sure I'm taking him to the right place.

When we pull up to the elementary school, Kel immediately spots Caulder and jumps out of the car without even saying goodbye. He makes life look so easy.

Luckily, the elementary is only a few blocks from the high school. I'll have extra time to spare so that I can locate my first class. I pull into the parking lot of what I consider to be a massive high school and search for a spot. When I find one available, it's as far from the building as it could be, and there are dozens of students standing around their vehicles, chatting. I am hesitant to get out of my car, but realize when I do that no one even notices me. It's not like in the movies when the new girl steps out of her car onto the lawn of the new school, clutching her books, everyone stopping what they're doing to stare. It's not like that at all. I feel invisible and I like it.

I make it through first-period Math without being assigned homework, which is good. I plan on spending the entire evening with Will. When I went to leave this morning, there was a note on my Jeep from him. All it said was, "Can't wait to see you. I'll be back home by four."

Seven hours and three minutes to go.

History isn't any harder. The teacher is giving notes on the Punic Wars, something we had just covered in my previous school. I find it hard to focus as I literally count down the minutes. The teacher is very monotonous and mundane. If I don't find something to be interesting, my mind tends to wander. It keeps wandering to Will. I am methodically taking notes, trying my best to focus, when someone behind me pokes my back.

"Hey, let me see your schedule," the girl directs.

I inconspicuously reach for my schedule and fold it up tightly in my left hand. I raise my hand behind me and quickly drop the schedule on her desk.

"Oh, please!" she says louder. "Mr. Hanson is half blind and can barely hear. Don't worry about him."

I stifle a laugh and turn toward her while Mr. Hanson is facing the board. "I'm Layken."

"Eddie," she says.

I look at her questioningly and she rolls her eyes. "I *know*. It's a family name. But if you call me Eddie Spaghetti I'll kick your ass," she threatens mildly.

"I'll keep that in mind."

"Cool, we have the same third period," she says, inspecting my schedule. "It's a bitch to find. Stick with me after class and I'll show you where it is."

Eddie leans forward to write something down, and her slinky blond hair swings forward with her. It falls just below her chin in an asymmetrical style. Her nails are each painted a completely different color, and she has a variety of about fifteen bracelets on each of her wrists that rattle and clank every time she moves. She has a small, simple outline of a black heart tattooed on the inside of her left wrist.

When the bell rings, I stand up and Eddie passes me back the schedule. She reaches into my jacket pocket and pulls out my phone and starts punching numbers. I look at the schedule she has returned to me and it's now covered in websites and phone numbers in green ink. Eddie sees me looking and points to the first web address on the page.

"That's my Facebook page, but if you can't find me there, I'm also on Twitter. Don't ask me for my MySpace username because that shit's lame," she says, strangely serious.

She scrolls down the remaining numbers jotted on my schedule with her finger. "That's my cell phone number, that's my home phone number, and that's the number to Getty's Pizza," she says.

"Is that where you work?"

"No, they just have great pizza." She moves past me, and I start to follow her out the door, when she turns and hands me back my phone. "I just called myself so I have your number now, too. Oh, and you need to go to the office before next period."

"Why? I thought you wanted me to follow you?" I ask, feeling slightly overwhelmed by my new friend.

"They have you in B lunch. I'm in A lunch. Go switch yours to A lunch and meet me in third period."

And she's gone. Just like that.

THE ADMINISTRATION OFFICE is just two doors down. The secretary, Mrs. Alex, makes rolling her eyes a new form of art as she prints my *new* new schedule just as the second bell for third period rings.

"Do you know where this English elective is located?" I say before I leave.

She gives me somewhat lengthy and confusing directions, assuming that I know where Hall A is, and Hall D. I wait patiently until she's finished and walk out the door, more confused than before.

I wander across three different hallways, entering two wrong classrooms and one janitor's closet. I round the corner when I finally see Hall D and feel some relief. I set my backpack down on the floor and place the schedule between my lips, then pull the rubber band off my wrist. It's not even ten in the morning, and I'm already pulling my hair up. It's that kind of day already.

"Lake?"

My heart nearly jumps out of my chest when I hear his voice. I turn around and see Will standing next to me with a confused look on his face. I pull the schedule out of my mouth and smile, then instinctively wrap my arms around him. "Will! What are you doing here?"

He hugs me back, but only for a second before he wraps his hands around my wrists and removes my arms from around his neck.

"Lake," he says, shaking his head. "Where . . . what are you doing here?"

I sigh and thrust my schedule into his chest. "I'm trying to find this stupid elective but I'm lost," I whine. "Help me!"

He takes another step back against the wall. "Lake, no," he says, putting the schedule back into my hands without even looking at it.

I watch him react for a moment, and he seems almost horrified to see me. He turns away and clasps his hands behind his head. I don't understand his reaction. I stand still, waiting for some sort of explanation, when it dawns on me. He's here to see his girlfriend. The *girlfriend* that he failed to mention. I snatch my backpack up and immediately start to walk away, when he reaches out and pulls me to a stop.

"Where are you going?" he demands.

I roll my eyes and let out a short sigh. "I get it, Will. I *get* it. I'll leave you alone before your girlfriend sees us." I'm trying to hold back tears at this point, so I step out of his grasp and turn away from him.

"Girlfr—no. No, Lake. I don't think you do get it."

The faint sound of footsteps quickly becomes louder as they round the corner to Hall D. I turn to see another student barreling toward us.

"Oh man, I thought I was late," the student says when he spots us in the hallway. He comes to a stop in front of the classroom.

"You *are* late, Javier," Will replies, opening the door behind him, motioning for Javier to enter. "Javi, I'll be there in a few minutes. Let the class know they have five minutes to review before the exam."

Will closes the door behind him, and we're once again alone in the hallway. The air is all but gone from my lungs. I feel pressure building in my chest as this new realization sinks in. This can't be happening. This can't be possible. *How* is this possible?

"Will," I whisper, not able to get a full breath out. "Please don't tell me . . ."

His face is red and he has a pained look in his eyes as he bites his lower lip. He leans his head back and looks up at the ceiling, rubbing his palms on his face while he paces the length of the hallway between the lockers and the classroom door. With each step he takes, I catch a glimpse of his faculty badge as it sways back and forth from his neck.

He flattens his palms against the lockers, repeatedly tapping his forehead against the metal as I stand frozen, unable to speak. He slowly drops his hands and turns toward me. "How did I not *see* this? You're still in *high school*?"

4.

I am sick of wanting
And it's evil how it's got me
And every day is worse
Than the one before.

—THE AVETT BROTHERS, "ILL WITH WANT"

WILL LEANS WITH HIS BACK AGAINST THE LOCKERS. HIS legs are crossed at the feet and his arms are folded across his chest as he stares at the floor. The events unfolding have caught me so off guard I can barely stand. I go to the wall opposite him and lean against it for support.

"Me?" I reply. "How did the fact that you're a teacher not come up? How are you a teacher? You're only twenty-one."

"Layken, listen," he says, ignoring my questions.

He didn't call me Lake.

"There has apparently been a huge misunderstanding between the two of us." He doesn't make eye contact with me as he speaks. "We need to talk about this, but now is definitely not the right time."

"I agree," I say. I want to say more, but I can't. I'm afraid I'll cry.

The door to Will's classroom opens, and Eddie emerges. I selfishly pray that she, too, is lost. This cannot be my elective.

"Layken, I was just coming to look for you," she says. "I saved you a seat." She looks at Will, then back at me and realizes she's interrupted a conversation. "Oh, sorry, Mr. Cooper. I didn't know you were out here."

"It's fine, Eddie. I was just going over Layken's schedule with her." He says this as he walks toward the classroom and holds the door for both of us.

I reluctantly follow Eddie through the door, around Will, and to the only empty seat in the room—directly in front of the teacher's desk. I don't know how I am expected to sit through an entire hour in this classroom. The walls won't stop dancing when I try to focus, so I close my eyes. I need water.

"Who's the hottie?" asks the boy I now know as Javier.

"Shut it, Javi!" Will snaps as he walks toward his desk, picking up a stack of papers. Several students let out a small gasp at this reaction. I guess Will isn't his usual self right now, either.

"Chill out, Mr. Cooper! I was paying her a compliment. She's hot. Look at her." Javi says this as he leans back in his chair, watching me.

"Javi, get out!" Will says, pointing to the classroom door.

"Mr. Cooper! Jeez! What's with the temp? Like I said, I was just—"

"Like *I* said, get out! You will not disrespect women in my classroom!"

Javi grabs his books and snaps back. "Fine. I'll go disrespect them in the hallway!"

After the door shuts behind him, the only sound in the room is the distant second hand ticking on the clock above the blackboard. I don't turn around, but I can feel most of the eyes in the classroom on me, waiting for some sort of reaction. It's not so easy to blend in now.

"Class, we have a new student. This is Layken Cohen," Will says, attempting to break the tension. "Review is over. Put up your notes."

"You're not going to have her introduce herself?" Eddie asks.

"We'll get to that another time." Will holds up a stack of papers. "Tests."

I'm relieved Will has spared me from having to get in front of the class and speak. It's the last thing I would be able to do right now. It feels like there is a ball of cotton in my throat as I unsuccessfully try to swallow.

"Lake." Will hesitates, then clears his throat, realizing his slip. "Layken, if you have something else to work on, feel free. The class is completing a chapter test."

"I'd rather just take the test," I say. I have to focus on *something.*

Will hands me a test, and in the time it takes to complete it I do my best to focus entirely on the questions at hand, hoping I'll find momentary respite from my new reality. I finish fairly quickly, though, but keep erasing and rewriting answers just to avoid having to deal with the obvious: the fact that the boy I'm falling for is now my teacher.

When the dismissal bell rings, I watch as the rest of the class files toward Will's desk, laying their papers face down in a pile. Eddie lays hers down and walks to my desk.

"Hey, did you get your lunch switched?"

"Yeah, I did," I tell her.

"Sweet. I'll save you a seat," she says. She stops at Will's desk and he looks up at her. She removes a red tin from her purse and pulls out a small handful of mints and sets them on his desk. "Altoids," she says.

Will stares questioningly at the mints.

"I'm just making assumptions here," she whispers, loud enough that I hear her. "But I've heard Altoids work wonders on hangovers." She pushes the mints toward him.

And again, just like that, she's gone.

Will and I are the only ones left in the classroom at this point. I need to talk to him so bad. I have so many questions, but I know it's still not a good time. I grab my paper and walk over to his desk, placing it on top of the stack.

"Is my mood that obvious?" he asks. He continues to stare at the mints on his desk. I grab two of the Altoids and walk out of the room without responding.

As I navigate the halls, searching for my fourth-period class, I see a bathroom and quickly duck inside. I decide to spend the remainder of fourth period and my entire lunch in the bathroom stall. I feel guilty knowing Eddie is waiting for me, but I can't face anyone right now. Instead, I spend the entire time reading and rereading the writing on the walls of the stall, hoping to somehow make it through the rest of the day without bursting out in tears.

My last two classes are a blur. Luckily, neither of those teachers seem interested in my "about me," either. I don't speak to anyone, and no one speaks to me. I have no idea if I was ever even assigned homework. My mind is consumed by this whole situation.

I walk to my car as I search in my bag for my keys. I pull them out and fidget with the lock, but my hands are shaking so bad that I drop them. When I climb inside I don't give myself time to reflect as I throw the car in reverse and head home. The only thing I want to think about right now is my bed.

When I pull into my driveway I kill the engine and pause. I don't want to face Kel or my mother yet, so I kick my seat back and shield my eyes with my arms and begin to cry. I replay everything over and over in my head. How did I spend an entire evening with him and not know he was a teacher? How can something as big as an occupation not come up in conversation? Or better yet, how did I do so much talking and fail to mention the fact that I was still in high school? I told him so much about myself. I feel like it's what I deserve for finally letting down my walls.

I wipe at my eyes with my sleeve, trying hard to conceal my tears. I've been getting pretty good at it. Up until six months ago, I hardly had a reason to cry. My life back in Texas was simple. I had a routine, a great group of friends, a school I loved, and even a home I loved. I cried a lot in the weeks following my father's death until I realized Kel and my mother wouldn't be able to move on until I did. I started making a conscious effort to be more involved in Kel's life. Our father was also his best friend at the time, and I feel Kel lost more than any of us. I got involved in youth baseball, his karate lessons, and even Cub Scouts: all the things my dad used to do with him. It kept both Kel and me preoccupied, and the grieving eventually started to subside.

Until today.

A tap on the passenger window brings me back to reality. I don't want to acknowledge it. I don't want to see anyone, let alone speak to anyone. I look over and see someone standing there; the only thing visible is his torso . . . and faculty ID.

I flip the visor down and wipe the mascara from my eyes. I divert my gaze out the driver's-side window and press the automatic unlock button, focusing on the injured garden gnome, who is staring back at me with his smug little grin.

Will slides into the passenger seat and shuts the door. He lays the seat back a few inches and sighs, but says nothing. I don't think either of us knows what to say at this point. I glance over at him, and his foot is resting on the dash. He's stiff against the seat with his arms folded across his chest. He's staring directly at the note he wrote this morning that is still sitting on my console. I guess he made it by four o'clock after all.

"What are you thinking?" he asks.

I pull my right leg up into the seat and hug it with my arms. "I'm confused as hell, Will. I don't know what to think."

He sighs and turns to look out the passenger window. "I'm sorry. This is all my fault," he says.

"It's nobody's fault," I say. "In order for there to be fault, there has to be some sort of conscious decision. You didn't know, Will."

He sits up and turns to face me. The playful expression in his eyes that drew me to him is gone. "That's just it, Lake. I should have known. I'm in an occupation that doesn't just require ethics inside the classroom. They apply to all aspects of my life. I wasn't *aware* because I wasn't doing my job. When you told me you were eighteen, I assumed you were in college." His obvious frustration seems entirely directed toward himself.

"I've only been eighteen for two weeks," I reply.

I don't know why I felt the need to clarify that. After I say it, I realize it sounds like I'm placing blame on him. He's already blaming himself; he doesn't need me to be angry at him, too. This was an outcome that neither of us could possibly have predicted.

"I student teach," he says, in an attempt to explain. "Sort of."

"*Sort of?*"

"After my parents died, I doubled up on all my classes. I have enough credits to graduate a semester early. Since the school was so shorthanded, they offered me a one-year contract. I have three months left of student teaching. After that, I'm under contract through June of next year."

I listen and take in everything he says. Really, though, all I hear is, "*We can't be together . . . blah blah blah . . . we can't be together.*"

He looks me in the eyes. "Lake, I need this job. It's what I've been working toward for three years. We're broke. My parents left me with a mound of debt and now college tuition. I can't quit now." He breaks his gaze and leans back into the seat, running his hands through his hair.

"Will, I understand. I'd never ask you to jeopardize your career. It would be stupid if you threw that away for someone you've only known for a week."

He keeps his focus out the passenger window. "I'm not saying you *would* ask me that. I just want you to understand where I'm coming from."

"I do understand," I say. "It's ridiculous to assume we even have anything worth risking."

He glances at the note on my console again and quietly responds, "We both know it's more than that."

His words cause me to wince, because I know deep down he's right. Whatever was happening with us, it was more than just an infatuation. I can't possibly comprehend at this moment what it must be like to actually have a broken heart. If it hurts even one percent more than the pain I'm feeling now, I'll forgo love. It's not worth it.

I attempt to stop the tears from welling up again, but the effort is futile. He brings his leg off the dash and pulls me to him. I bury my face in his shirt, and he puts his arms around me and gently rubs my back.

"I'm so sorry," he says. "I wish there was something I could do to change things. I have to do this right . . . for Caulder." The physical grip he has on me seems less like a consoling hug and more like a goodbye. "I'm not sure where we go from here, or how we'll transition," he says.

" 'Transition'?" I suddenly start to panic at the thought of losing him. "But—what if you talk to the school? Tell them we didn't know. Ask them what our options are . . ." I realize as the words are coming out of my mouth that I'm grasping at straws. There is no way in which a relationship between us would be feasible at this point.

"I can't, Lake." His voice is small. "It won't work. It *can't* work."

A door slams, and Kel and Caulder come bounding down the driveway. We immediately pull apart and reposition our seats. I rest my head against the headrest and close my eyes, attempting to conjure up a loophole in our situation. There has to be one.

When the boys have crossed the street and are safely inside Will's house, he turns to me. "Layken?" he says, nervously. "There's one more thing I need to talk to you about."

Oh god, what else? What else could be relevant at this moment?

"I need you to go to administration tomorrow. I want you to withdraw from my class. I don't think we should be around each other anymore."

I feel the blood rushing from my face. My hands start to sweat, and the car is quickly becoming too small for the two of us. He really means it. Anything we had up to this point is over. He's going to shut me out of his life entirely.

"Why?" I make no effort to mask the hurt in my voice.

He clears his throat. "What we have isn't appropriate. We have to separate ourselves."

My hurt quickly succumbs to the anger building up inside of me. "Not appropriate? Separate ourselves? You live across the street from me, Will!"

He opens the door and gets out of the car. I do the same and slam my door. "We're both mature enough to know what's appropriate. You're the only person I know here. Please don't ask me to act like I don't even know you," I plead.

"Come on, Lake! You aren't being fair." He matches his tone to mine, and I know I've hit a nerve. "I can't do this. We can't *just* be friends. It's the only choice we have."

I can't help but feel like we're going through a horrible breakup, and we aren't even in a relationship. I'm angry at myself. I can't tell if I'm really just upset about what has happened today, or about my entire life this *year*.

The one thing I know for sure is that the only time I've been happy lately has been with Will. To hear him tell me that we can't even be friends hurts. It scares me that I'll go back to who I've been for the past six months, someone I'm not proud of.

I open the door to the car and grab my purse and keys. "So, you're saying it's either all or nothing, right? And since it *obviously* can't be *all*—" I slam the car door again and head toward the house, "you'll be rid of me by third period tomorrow!" I say as I purposely kick the gnome over with my boot.

I walk into the house and throw the keys toward the bar in the kitchen with such force that they glide completely across the surface and hit the floor. I step on the heel of my boot with my toe and kick it off in the entry, when my mother comes in.

"What was that all about?" she asks. "Were you just yelling?"

"Nothing," I say. "That's what it's about. Absolutely *nothing*!" I pick up my boots and walk to my room, slamming the door behind me.

I lock my bedroom door and head straight to the hamper of clothes. I pick it up and dump the contents out onto the floor, searching through them until I find what I'm looking for. My hand slides into the pocket of my jeans, and I remove the purple hair clip. I walk over to the bed, pull back the covers, and climb in. My fist tightens around the clip as I pull my hands to my face and cry myself to sleep.

When I wake up, it's midnight. I lie there a moment, hoping I'll come to the conclusion that this was all a bad dream, but the clarity never comes. When I pull back the covers, my hair clip falls from my hands and lands on the floor. This small piece of plastic, so old that it's probably covered in lead-ridden paint. I think about how I felt the day my father gave it to me, and how all the sadness and fears were eliminated as soon as he put it in my hair.

I lean forward and retrieve it from the floor, pressing down in the center so that it snaps open. I move a section of my bangs to the opposite side and secure it in place. I wait for the magic to take effect, but sure enough, everything still hurts. I pull the clip from my hair and throw it across the room and climb back into bed.

5.

I keep tellin' myself
That it'll be fine.
You can't make everybody happy
All of the time.

—THE AVETT BROTHERS,

"PARANOIA IN B-FLAT MAJOR"

MY PULSE IS POUNDING AGAINST MY TEMPLES AS I CLIMB out of bed. I'm in dire need of my own box of Altoids. My entire body is dragging from hours of alternating between crying and inadequate sleep.

I make a quick pot of coffee and sit down at the bar and drink it in silence, dreading the day that lies ahead of me. Kel eventually comes in, wearing his pajamas and Darth Vader house shoes. "Morning," he says groggily as he grabs a cup out of the dish strainer. He walks over to the coffeepot and proceeds to pour coffee into the World's Greatest Dad cup.

"What do you think you're doing?" I ask him.

"Hey, you aren't the only one who had a bad night." Kel climbs onto a stool on the opposite side of the bar. "Fourth grade is rough. I had two hours of homework," he says as he brings the cup to his mouth.

I take the coffee out of his hands and pour the contents into my own, then toss the mug into the trash can. I walk to the refrigerator, grab a juice, and place it in front of him.

Kel rolls his eyes and pokes through the hole at the top of the pouch, bringing it to his mouth. "Did you see they delivered the rest of our stuff yesterday? Mom's van finally got here. We had to unpack the whole thing by ourselves, you know," he says, obviously trying to guilt me.

"Go get dressed," I say. "We're leaving in half an hour."

IT BEGINS TO snow again after I drop Kel off at school. I hope Will is right about it being gone soon. I hate the snow. I hate *Michigan*.

When I arrive at the school, I go straight to the administration office. Mrs. Alex is powering on her computer when she notices me and shakes her head.

"Let me guess, you want C lunch now?"

I should have brought her Kel's coffee. "Actually,

I need a list of third-period electives. I want to switch classes."

She tucks her chin in and looks up at me through the top of her glasses. "Aren't you in the Poetry elective with Mr. Cooper? That's one of the more popular electives."

"That's the one," I confirm. "I'd like to withdraw."

"Well, you have until the end of the week before I submit your final schedule," she says as she grabs a sheet and hands it to me. "Which class do you prefer?"

I look over the short list of available electives.

Botany.

Russian Literature.

My options are limited.

"I'll take Russian Literature for two hundred, Alex."

She rolls her eyes and turns to enter the information into the computer. I guess she's heard that one before. She hands me yet another *new* new schedule and a yellow form.

"Have Mr. Cooper sign this, and bring it back to me before third period, and you'll be all set."

"Great," I mumble as I exit the office.

When I successfully navigate my way to Will's classroom, I'm relieved to find the door locked and the lights turned out. Seeing him again was not on my to-do list for the day, so I decide to take matters into my own hands. I reach into my backpack and retrieve a pen, press the yellow form up against the door to the classroom, and begin to forge Will's name.

"That's not a good idea."

I spin around and Will is standing behind me with a black satchel slung across his shoulder, keys in hand. My stomach flips when I look at him. He's wearing khaki slacks and a black shirt tucked in at the waist. The color of his tie matches his green eyes perfectly, making them hard to look away from. He looks so—*professional.*

I step back as he moves past me and inserts his key into the door. He enters the room and flips the light switch on, then places his satchel on the desk. I'm still standing in the doorway when he motions for me to come in.

I smack the form faceup on his desk. "Well, you weren't here yet, so I thought I'd spare you the trouble," I say, defending my actions with a defensive tone.

Will picks up the form and grimaces. "Russian Lit? *That's* what you chose?"

"It was either that or Botany," I reply evenly.

Will pulls his chair out and sits. He grabs a pen and lays the paper flat, pressing the tip of the pen on the line. He hesitates, though, and lays the pen down on the paper without signing his name.

"I thought a lot last night . . . about what you said yesterday," he says. "It's not fair of me to ask you to transfer just because it makes me uneasy. We live a hundred yards apart; our brothers are becoming best friends. If anything, this class will be good for us, help us figure out how to navigate when we're around each other. We're going to have to get used to this one way or another. Besides," he says as he pulls a paper from his satchel and shoves it forward on the desk. "You'll obviously breeze through."

I look at the test I had completed the day before, and it's marked with a 100.

"I don't mind switching," I say, even though I really *do* mind. "I understand where you're coming from."

"Thanks, but it can only get easier from here, right?"

I look up at him and nod. "Right," I lie.

He's completely wrong. Being around him every day is definitely not going to make it easier. I could move back to Texas today, and I'd still feel too close to him. However, my conscience still can't come up with a good enough argument to convince me to switch classes.

He crumples up my transfer form and chucks it toward the trash can. It misses by about two feet. I pick it up as I walk to the door and toss it in.

"I guess I'll see you third period, Mr. Cooper." I see him frown out of my peripheral vision as I exit.

I feel somewhat relieved. I hated how we had left things yesterday. Even though I would do whatever it took to rectify the awkward situation we're in, he still somehow finds a way to put me at ease.

"What happened to you yesterday?" Eddie says as we enter second period. "Get lost again?"

"Yeah, sorry about that. Issues with admin."

"You should have texted," she teases in a sarcastic tone. "I was worried about you."

"Oh, I'm sorry, dear."

" 'Dear'? You tryin' to steal my girl?" A guy I have yet to meet puts his arm around Eddie and kisses her on the cheek.

"Layken, this is Gavin," she says. "Gavin, this is Layken, your competition."

Gavin has blond hair almost identical to Eddie's except in length. They could pass for brother and sister, although his eyes are chestnut while hers are blue. He is wearing a black hoodie and jeans, and when he moves his arm from Eddie's shoulder to shake my hand, I notice a tattoo of a heart on his wrist . . . the same as Eddie's.

"I've heard a lot about you," he says, extending his hand out to mine.

I eye him curiously, wondering what he could have possibly heard.

"Not really," he admits, smiling. "I haven't heard anything at all about you. That's usually just what people say when they're introduced."

He turns toward Eddie and gives her another peck on the cheek. "I'll see you next period, babe. I've got to get to class."

I envy them.

Mr. Hanson enters the room and announces there's a chapter test. I don't object when he hands me a test, and we spend the rest of the class period in silence.

* * *

AS I FOLLOW Eddie through the crowd of students, my stomach is in knots. I'm already regretting not having switched to Russian Literature. How either of us thought this would help make things easier, I don't know.

We arrive in Will's class, and he's holding the door open, greeting the students as they arrive.

"Mr. Cooper, you look a little better today. Need a mint?" Eddie says as she walks to her seat.

Javi walks in and glares at Will as he slides into his seat.

"All right, everyone," Will says, shutting the door behind him. "Good efforts on the test yesterday. 'Elements of Poetry' is a pretty mundane section, so I know you're all glad to have it out of the way. I think you'll find the performance section more interesting, which is what we'll focus on the rest of this semester.

"Performance poetry resembles traditional poetry, but with an added element: the actual *performance*."

"Performance?" Javi asks, disdained. "You mean like in that movie about the dead poets? Where they had to read crap in front of the whole class?"

"Not exactly," Will says. "That's just poetry."

"He means slamming," Gavin adds. "Like they do down at Club N9NE on Thursdays."

"What's slamming?" a girl inquires from the back of the room.

Gavin turns toward her. "It's awesome! Eddie and

I go sometimes. You have to see it to really get it," he adds.

"That's one form of it," Will says. "Has anyone else ever been to a slam?"

A couple of other students raise their hands. I don't.

"Mr. Cooper, show them. Do one of yours," Gavin says.

I can see the hesitation in Will's eyes. I know from experience he doesn't like being put on the spot.

"I'll tell you what. We'll make a deal. If I do one of my pieces, everyone has to agree to go to at least one slam this semester at Club N9NE."

No one objects. I'd like to object, but that would require raising my hand and speaking. So I don't object.

"No objections? All right, then. I'll do a short one I wrote. Remember, slam poetry is about the poetry *and* the performance."

Will stands in the front of the room and faces the students. He shakes his arms out and stretches his neck left and right in an attempt to relax himself. When he clears his throat, it's not the kind of throat clearing people do when they're nervous; it's the kind they do right before they yell.

Expectations, evaluations, internal evasions
Fly out of me like *puddles* of *blood* from a *wound*
A fetus from the *womb* of a *corpse* in a *tomb*
Withered and *strewn* like red sheets on the bed
Of an immaculate **room.**

I can't *breathe*,

I can't *win*,

From this indelible *position* I'm in

It *controls* the only *piece* of my unfortunate soul

Left to *fend* for itself in this hollowed-out hole

That I *dug* from within, like a *prisoner* in

An *unlocked* cell sitting in the deepest *pits* of hell

Unencumbered he's *not* in his sweltering spot

He could open the door 'cause he don't *need*

a damn key

But then again,

Why *would* he?

Circumlocution is *his* revolution.

The silence in the room is deafening. No one speaks, no one moves, no one claps. We are in awe. *I* am in awe. How does he expect me to transition if he keeps doing things like this?

"There you go," he says matter-of-factly as he walks back to his seat. The rest of the class period is spent talking about slam poetry. I try hard to follow along as he goes into further explanation, but the entire time I'm simply focused on the fact that he hasn't made eye contact with me. Not even once.

I CLAIM MY seat next to Eddie at lunch. I notice a guy who sits a couple of rows behind me in Will's class walking toward us. He's balancing two trays with his left arm and his backpack and a bag of chips in his right. He positions himself in the seat across from me and proceeds to combine the food onto one tray. When that task is complete, he pulls a two-liter of Coke out of his backpack and places it in front of him. He unscrews the lid and drinks directly from it. As he is chugging the soda, he looks at me then places it back down on the table, wiping his mouth.

"You gonna drink that chocolate milk, new girl?"

I nod. "That's why I got it."

"What about that roll? You gonna eat that roll?"

"Got the roll for a reason, too."

He shrugs and reaches across to Gavin's tray and takes his roll just as Gavin turns around and swipes at his hand, a moment too late.

"Dude, Nick! There's no way you're gaining ten pounds by Friday. Give it up," Gavin says.

"Nine," Nick corrects him with a mouthful of bread.

Eddie takes her roll and throws it across the table. Nick catches it midair and gives her a wink. "Your girl has faith in me," Nick says to Gavin.

"He lifts weights." Eddie is directing her comment to me. "He's got to be nine pounds heavier by Friday to compete in his weight class, and it's not looking good."

With that, I grab my roll and toss it on Nick's tray. He winks at me and dips it in a mound of butter.

I'm thankful to Eddie for accepting me into her group of friends so easily. Not that I had a choice; it was done pretty forcibly. In Texas, there were twenty-one people in my entire senior class. I had friends, but with such a limited pool to choose from, I never really considered any of them to be my best friend. I mostly hung out with my friend Kerris, but I haven't even spoken to her since the move. From what I've seen of Eddie so far, she's intriguing enough that I can't help but hope we become closer.

"So, how long have you and Gavin been dating?" I ask her.

"Since sophomore year. I hit him with my car." She looks at him and smiles. "It was love at first swipe."

"What about you?" she asks. "You got a boyfriend?"

I wish I could tell her about Will. I want to tell her about how when we met, I immediately felt something I had never felt about a guy before. I want to tell her about our first date and how the entire night seemed like we had known each other for years. I want to tell her about his poetry, our kiss, everything. Most of all, though, I want to tell her about seeing him in the hallway, when we realized our fate was not our own to decide. But I know I can't. I can't tell anyone. So I don't. I simply reply, "No."

"Really? No boyfriend? Well, we can fix that," she says.

"No need. It's not broken."

Eddie laughs and turns to Gavin, discussing possible suitors for her new, lonely friend.

* * *

THE END OF the school week finally arrives and I have never felt more relieved to pull out of a parking lot in my entire life. Even though Will lives across the street from me, I feel less vulnerable when I'm inside my house than I do two feet from him in a classroom. He successfully achieved an entire week of absolutely no eye contact. Not saying I didn't do my best to catch even a glimpse in my direction: I practically stared him down.

During the drive home, I make a detour to better formulate my plan to spend the entire weekend indoors. It's called movies and junk food.

Mom is sitting at the bar in the kitchen when I walk through the front door. I can see by the stern look on her face that she isn't particularly happy to see me. I walk into the kitchen and lay the movies and bags of junk food on the counter in front of her.

"I'm spending the weekend with Johnny Depp," I say, attempting to appear oblivious to her demeanor.

She doesn't smile. "I took Caulder home from school today," she says. "He mentioned something very interesting."

"Oh, yeah? You sound sick, Mom. Do you have a cold?" I try to sound nonchalant, but I can tell by the tone in her voice that what she's really trying to say is, "*I found out something from your little brother's friend that I should have found out from you.*"

"Anything you want to tell me?" she asks, staring daggers through me.

I sip from a bottle of water and take a seat at the bar. I had planned on talking to her about everything tonight, but it looks like it's going to happen sooner rather than later.

"Mom. I was going to talk to you about it. I swear."

"He's a teacher at your school, Lake!" She starts coughing and grabs at a Kleenex, then gets up from the bar. After she regains her composure, she lowers her voice in an attempt to avoid attracting the attention of the nine-year-olds who are somewhere within our vicinity. "Don't you think that's something you should have mentioned before I allowed you out of the house with him?"

"I didn't know! *He* didn't know!" I say in an overly defensive tone.

She cocks her head to the side and rolls her eyes as though I've insulted her. "What are you doing, Lake? Don't you realize he's raising his little brother? This can ruin his—"

Both of our eyes dart to the front door when we hear Will's car pull into his driveway. I quickly head to the front door in an attempt to block it so she'll let me explain. She beats me to it so I follow her outside, pleading.

"Mom, please. Just let me explain everything. *Please.*"

She's walking up Will's driveway when he notices us bombarding him. He smiles when he first notices my mother, but his smile fades when he sees I'm right behind her. He has surmised that this is not a friendly visit.

"Julia, please," he says. "Can we go inside to talk about this?"

She doesn't respond. She just marches toward his front door and lets herself in.

Will looks at me questioningly.

"Your brother mentioned you were a teacher. I haven't had a chance to explain anything to her," I say.

He sighs, and we reluctantly make our way inside.

It's the first time I've been inside his home since I found out about the death of his parents. Nothing has changed, yet at the same time everything has changed. That first day when I sat at his bar, I assumed that everything in the house belonged to his parents, that Will's situation was not unlike my own. Now, when I take in my surroundings, it sheds a different light on him. A light of responsibility. Maturity.

My mother is sitting stiffly on the sofa. Will walks quietly across the room and sits on the edge of the couch across from her. He leans forward and clasps his hands in front of him, his elbows resting on his knees.

"I'll explain everything." He says this with a serious, respectful tone to his voice.

"I know you will," she replies evenly.

"Basically, I made a lot of assumptions. I thought she was older. She *seemed* older. Once she told me she was eighteen, I guess I assumed she was in college. It's only September; most students aren't eighteen when they start their senior year."

"Most of them. She's only been eighteen for two weeks."

"Yeah, I . . . I realize that now," he says, shooting a look in my direction.

"She wasn't attending school the first week you guys moved in, so I guess I just assumed. Somehow the topic never came up while we were together."

My mother starts to cough again. Will and I wait, but the coughing intensifies and she stands and takes a few deep breaths. I would think she's having a panic attack if I didn't already know she was coming down with something. Will goes to the kitchen and comes back with a glass of water. She takes a sip and turns toward the living-room window that faces the front yard. Caulder and Kel are outside now; I can hear them laughing. My mother walks to the front door and opens it.

"Kel, Caulder! Don't lie in the street!" She closes the door and turns toward us. "Tell me, when *did* the topic come up?" she asks, looking at both of us now.

I can't answer her. Somehow, in the presence of the two of them, I feel small. Two adults hashing it out in front of the children. That's what this feels like.

"We didn't find out until she showed up for my class," Will replies.

My mother looks at me, and her jaw gapes open. "You're in his *class*?" She looks at Will and repeats what she said. "She's in your *class*?"

God, it sounds really bad coming from her mouth.

She stands up and paces the length of the living room as both Will and I allow her time to process. "You're telling me that both of you deny having *any* knowledge of this prior to the first day of school?"

We both nod in agreement.

"Well, what the hell happens now?" she asks. She has both of her hands on her hips. Will and I are silent, hoping she can magically come up with the solution that we've both been searching for all week.

"Well," Will replies. "Lake and I are doing our best to work through this a day at a time."

She glares at him accusingly. "*Lake*? You call her *Lake*?"

Will looks down at the floor and clears his throat, unable to meet her stare.

My mother sighs and takes a seat next to Will on the sofa. "Both of you need to accept the severity of this situation. I know my daughter, and my daughter likes you, Will. *A lot*. If you share even a fraction of those feelings, you will do whatever you can to distance yourself from her. That includes ditching the nicknames. This will jeopardize your career *and* her reputation." She stands up and walks to the front door, holding it open for me to follow her out. She isn't allowing us the opportunity for any private time.

Kel and Caulder brush past us and run toward Caulder's bedroom. Mom watches as they disappear down the hallway. "Kel and Caulder don't need to be affected by this," she says, bringing her attention back to Will. "I suggest we work something out now so that the contact between you and Lake can be minimized."

"Absolutely. I completely agree," he says.

"I work nights and sleep in the mornings. If you want to take them to school, Lake or I will pick them up after school. Where they go from there can be up to them. They seem to do pretty well going back and forth."

"That sounds good. Thank you."

"He's a good kid, Will."

"Really, Julia. It's all fine with me. I haven't seen Caulder this happy in a . . ." Will's voice trails off, and he doesn't finish his sentence.

"Julia?" he asks. "Will you be talking to the school about this? I mean, I completely understand if that's what you need to do. I would just like to be prepared."

She looks at him, then at me, and holds her stare when she speaks. "There's nothing currently going on that I would *need* to inform them about, is there?"

"Not at all. I swear," I quickly reply. I want Will to look at me so he can see the apology in my eyes, but he doesn't. As soon as he shuts his front door behind us, I can't hold my tongue any longer.

"Why would you *do* that?" I yell. "You didn't even give me the opportunity to explain!" I dart across the street and don't look back. I run into the house and into the solitude of my bedroom, where I will remain until she's left for work.

* * *

"LAYKEN, DO WE have any packets of Kool-Aid?" Kel is standing in the entryway, covered in slush. It's not the oddest thing he's ever asked me for, so I don't question him as I grab a package of grape out of the kitchen cabinet and take it to him.

"Not purple, we need red," he says. I grab the purple package from his hands and return with a red one.

"Thanks!"

I close the door behind him and grab a towel and lay it down on the tile of the entryway. It's not even nine in the morning and already Kel and Caulder have been outside in the snow for over two hours.

I take a seat at the bar and finish my cup of coffee, staring at the pile of junk food that I'm no longer excited about eating. My mother got home around seven thirty this morning and climbed into bed, where she'll stay until around two o'clock. I'm still angry with her and don't feel like confronting the situation at all today, so it looks like I have about five more hours before I'll lock myself in my bedroom again. I grab a movie off the bar and, despite my lack of appetite, a bag of chocolate. If there is any man who can take my mind off of Will, it's definitely Johnny Depp.

Halfway through my movie, Kel comes bounding in the house, still covered in snow and slush as he grabs my hand and starts to pull me outside.

"Kel, stop! I'm not going outside!" I snap.

"Please? Just for a minute. You have to see the snow-man we made."

"Fine. Let me get some shoes on at least."

As soon as I pull the second boot on, Kel grabs my hand again and pulls me out the door. I continue to allow Kel to pull me along as I shield my eyes. It's taking them a moment to adjust to the sun's reflection on the snow.

"It's right over here," I hear Caulder saying, but not to me. I look up to see Caulder handling his brother in the same way that Kel is handling me. We are both led to the rear of the Jeep where they position us inches apart, directly in front of a casualty.

I now know the purpose behind the demand for red Kool-Aid. In front of us, lying flat on the ground beneath the rear of my Jeep, is a dead snowman. His eyes are small pieces of twig, shaped into a grim expression. His arms are two thin branches lying at his side, one of them broken in half under my rear tire. His head and neck are sprinkled with a trail of red Kool-Aid that leads to a pool of bright-red snow about a foot down from the snowman.

"He was in a terrible accident," Kel says seriously before he and Caulder break out into a fit of giggles.

Will and I look at one another, and for the first time in a week, he smiles at me. "Wow, I need my camera," he says.

"I'll grab mine," I say. I smile back at him and head

inside. So this is what it's going to be like from now on? Conversing under false pretenses in front of our brothers? Avoiding each other in public? I *hate* the transition.

When I return with the camera, the boys are still admiring the murder scene, so I snap a couple of pictures.

"Kel, let's kill a snowman with Will's car now," Caulder says before they dart across the street.

The tension is thick as Will and I stare excessively at the snowman in front of us, not knowing what else to look at. He eventually glances toward his house at our brothers.

"They're lucky to have each other you know," he says quietly.

I analyze this sentence and wonder if it has a deeper meaning, or if he was just making an observation.

"Yeah, they are," I agree.

We both stand there watching them gather more snow. Will takes a deep breath and stretches his arms out above his head. "Well, I better get back inside," he says. He turns away.

"Will, wait." He swings back around and puts his hands in his pockets, but doesn't say anything.

"I'm sorry about yesterday. About my mom," I say as I stare at the ground between us. I can't look him in the eye for two reasons. One—the snow is still blinding me. Two—it hurts when I look at him.

"It's fine, Layken."

And we're back to the official first name.

He stares at the ground where the "blood" has tinted the snow, and he kicks at it with his shoe. "She's just doing her job as a mom, you know." He pauses and lowers his voice even more. "Don't be so mad at her. You're lucky to have her."

He spins and walks back to his house. Guilt overcomes me as I think of what it's like for them to just have each other, and here I sit complaining about the only parent left among the four of us. I feel ashamed for bringing it up. I feel more ashamed of having been mad at my mother for what she did. It was my fault for not talking to her about it sooner. Will is right, as usual. I *am* lucky to have her.

THE SHOWER IN my mother's bedroom is running after lunch, so I heat up some leftovers and make her a glass of tea. I place them at her usual seat at the bar and wait for her. When she finally emerges from the hallway and sees the food, she gives me a slight smile and takes her seat.

"Is this a peace offering or did you poison my food?" she asks as she unfolds a napkin into her lap.

"I guess you'll have to eat it first to find out."

She eyes me cautiously and takes a bite of her food. She chews for a minute and takes another bite after she fails to keel over.

"I'm sorry, Mom. I should have talked to you about it sooner. I was just really upset."

She looks at me with pity in her eyes, so I turn away from her and busy my hands with the dishes.

"Lake, I know how much you like him, I do. I like him, too. But like I said yesterday, this can't happen. You have to promise me you won't do anything stupid."

"I swear, Mom. He's made it clear he wants nothing to do with me, so you don't have anything to worry about."

"I hope not," she says as she continues to eat.

I finish up the dishes and return to the living room to continue my affair with Johnny.

6.

Your heart says not again
What kind of mess have you got me in?
But when the feeling's there
It can lift you up and take you anywhere.

—THE AVETT BROTHERS, "LIVING OF LOVE"

THE NEXT FEW WEEKS FLY BY AS MY HOMEWORK GETS more intense, along with the isolation in Will's classroom. We haven't spoken since the day the snowman was murdered. We haven't had eye contact since then, either. He avoids me like the plague.

I haven't been adjusting very well to Michigan. Maybe everything that happened with Will ended up making the move even harder. All I ever feel like doing is sleeping. I guess because it doesn't hurt as bad when you're asleep.

Eddie keeps bringing up possible fillers for the obvious hole in my boyfriend department, but I've rejected them all. She has finally resorted to switching places in Will's class with Nick in the hopes that something will bloom there.

It won't.

"Hey, Layken," Nick smiles as he sits in his new spot nearest me. "Got another one for ya. Wanna hear it?"

In the past week alone, I've had to endure at least three Chuck Norris jokes a day from Nick. He incorrectly assumes that since I'm from Texas, I must be obsessed with *Walker, Texas Ranger*.

"Sure." I don't try to deny him this privilege anymore; it doesn't work.

"Chuck Norris got a Gmail account today. It's gmail@chucknorris.com."

It takes me a second to process. I'm normally quick with jokes, but my mind has been sluggish lately, and for good reason.

"Funny," I reply flatly in order to appease him.

"Chuck Norris counted to infinity. Twice."

As much as I didn't feel like laughing, I did. Nick did annoy me quite a bit, but his ignorance was endearing.

When Will walks into the classroom, his eyes dart to Nick. Although he still doesn't look at me, I like to imagine a twinge of jealousy building up inside of him. I've been making it a point recently to become more attentive toward Nick once Will comes into the room. I hate this new desire that has overcome me, the desire to make Will jealous. I know I need to stop before Nick starts to get the wrong idea, but I can't. I feel like this is the only aspect of this entire situation that I have any control over.

"Get out your notebooks, we're making poetry today," Will says as he takes a seat at his desk. Half the class groans. I hear Eddie clapping.

"Can we have partners?" Nick asks. He starts inching his desk toward mine.

Will glares at him. "No."

Nick shrugs and scoots his desk back into place.

"Each of you needs to write a short poem, which you will perform in front of the class tomorrow."

I start taking notes on the assignment, not willing to watch him as he speaks. Remaining in his class was a very bad idea. I can't focus on anything he's saying. I'm constantly wondering what's going on inside his head, whether he's thinking about us, what he does inside his house at night. Even at home he's been the only thing I can think about. I find myself stealing glances across the street any chance I get. Honestly, if I had switched classes it probably wouldn't have made a difference. I would just rush to get home first so I could watch from the window when he pulls up to the house. This game I'm playing with myself is so exhausting. I wish I could find a way to break the hold he has on me. He seems to have done a pretty good job of moving on.

"You just need to start out with about ten sentences for tomorrow's presentation. We can expand over the next couple of weeks, giving you something to prepare for the slam," Will says. "And don't think I've forgotten. So far no one in here has shown up at the slam. We made a deal."

The entire class starts to protest.

"That wasn't the deal! You said we just had to observe. Now we have to perform?" says Gavin.

"No. Well, technically not. Everyone in here is required to attend one slam. You aren't required to perform; I just want you to observe. However, there's a chance you could be chosen to be the sacrifice, so it wouldn't hurt to have something prepared."

Several students ask what the sacrifice is in unison. Will explains the term and how it can be anyone chosen at random. Therefore, he wants everyone to have a piece ready before the night they are to attend, just in case.

"What if we want to perform?" Eddie asks.

"I'll tell you what. We'll make one more deal. Whoever willingly slams will be exempt from the final."

"Sweet, I'm in," Eddie says.

"What if we don't go?" Javi asks.

"Then you're missing out on something amazing. *And* you get an F for participation," he replies.

Javi rolls his eyes and groans at Will's response.

"So, what kinds of things can we write about?" Eddie asks.

Will moves to the front of the desk and sits, only inches from me.

"There are no rules, you can write about anything.

You can write about love, food, your hobby, something significant that's happened in your life. You can write about how much you hate your Poetry teacher. Write about anything, as long as it's something you're passionate about. If the audience doesn't feel your passion, they won't feel you—and that's never fun, believe me." He says this as though he speaks from experience.

"What about sex? Can we write about that?" Javi asks. It's obvious he's trying to push Will's buttons. Will remains cool.

"Anything. As long as it doesn't get you in hot water with your parents."

"What if they don't let us go? I mean, it *is* a club," a student asks from the back of the room.

"I understand if they have hesitations. If there are any parents that don't feel comfortable, I'll talk to them about it. I also don't want transportation to be an issue. This club is somewhat of a drive, so if it's an issue, I'll take a school vehicle. Whatever the obstacle, we'll work through it. I'm very passionate about slam poetry and don't feel I'll be doing you justice as your teacher if I don't allow you the opportunity to experience this in person.

"I'll answer questions throughout the week regarding the semester requirement. But for now, let's get back to today's assignment. You have the entire class period to complete the poem. We'll start presenting them tomorrow. Get to it."

I open my notebook and lay it flat on my desk. I stare

at it, not having the first clue as to what to write about. The only thing that's been on my mind lately is Will, and there's no way I'm doing a poem about him.

By the end of the class period, the only thing that's written on my paper is my name. I glance up to Will, who is seated at his desk, biting the corner of his bottom lip. His eyes are focused on my desk, down on the poem that I've yet to write. He glances up and sees me watching him. It's the first eye contact we've had in three weeks. Surprisingly, he doesn't immediately look away. If he had any idea how this lip-biting quirk affects me, he'd stop. The intensity in his eyes causes me to flush, and the room suddenly becomes warm. His stare is unwavering until the class dismissal bell rings. He stands and walks to the door and holds it open for the students exiting. I immediately put away my notebook and throw my bag over my shoulder. I don't make eye contact when I leave the classroom, but I can feel him watching me.

Just when I think he's forgotten about me, he goes and does something like this. The entire rest of the day I'm extremely quiet as I attempt to analyze his actions. I eventually come up with just one conclusion: He's just as confused as I am.

I'M RELIEVED TO feel the warm sun beating down on my face as I walk toward my Jeep. The weather was insanely cold going into October. The predictions are that the next two weeks will be a nice respite from the snow before winter begins. I insert the key into the ignition and turn it.

Nothing happens.

Great, my Jeep is shot. I have no idea what I'm doing, but I pop the hood on the Jeep and take a look. There's a bunch of wires and metal; that's about all I can comprehend from a mechanical standpoint. I do know what the battery looks like, so I grab a crowbar from the trunk and tap it against the battery. After another failed attempt at getting the ignition to turn over, I resort to pounding a little harder until I'm pretty much bludgeoning the battery out of sheer frustration.

"That's not a good idea." Will walks up beside me, satchel across his chest, looking very much like a teacher and less like Will.

"You've made it clear that you don't think a lot of what I do is a very good idea," I say as I return my focus back under the hood.

"What's wrong, it won't crank?" He bends forward under the hood and starts to mess with wires.

I don't understand what he's doing. One minute he tells me he doesn't want to speak to me in public, the next minute he's staring me down in class, and now he's under my hood, trying to help me. I'm not a fan of inconsistency.

"What are you doing, Will?"

He rises out from under the hood and cocks his head at me. "What does it look like I'm doing? I'm trying to figure out what's wrong with your Jeep." He walks around to the driver's side and attempts to turn the ignition.

I follow him to the door. "I mean, *why* are you doing this? You've made it pretty clear you don't want me to speak to you."

"Layken, you're a student stranded in the parking lot. I'm not going to get in my car and just drive away."

I know his reference to me as a student isn't meant as an insult, but it sure feels like one. He realizes his poor choice of words and sighs as he gets out of the car and looks back under the hood. "Look, that's not how I meant it," he says, fidgeting with more wires.

I lean under the hood next to him in an attempt to look natural as I continue my point. "It's just been really hard, Will. It was so easy for you to accept this and move past it. It hasn't been that easy for me. It's all I think about."

Will grips the edge of the hood with his hands and turns his head toward me. "You think this is easy for me?" he whispers.

"Well, that's how you make it seem."

"Lake, nothing about this has been easy. It's a daily struggle for me to come to work, knowing this very job is what's keeping us apart." He turns away from the car and leans against it. "If it weren't for Caulder, I would have quit that first day I saw you in the hallway. I could have taken the year off . . . waited until you graduated to go back." He turns toward me, his voice lower than before.

"Believe me, I've run every possible scenario through my mind. How do you think it makes me feel to know that I'm the reason you're hurting? That I'm the reason you're so sad?"

The sincerity in his voice is surprising. I had no idea. "I . . . I'm sorry. I just thought—"

Will cuts me off midsentence and turns back toward the car. "Your battery is fine; looks like it might be your alternator."

"Car won't start?" Nick asks as he walks up beside us, explaining the reason behind Will's sudden guarded behavior.

"No, Mr. Cooper thinks I need a new alternator."

"That sucks," Nick says as he glances under the hood. "I'll give you a ride home if you need one."

I start to decline when Will interrupts.

"That would be great, Nick," Will says as he closes the hood of the Jeep.

I shoot Will a glance, and he ignores my silent protest. Will walks away and leaves me with Nick and no other option for a ride home.

"I'm parked over here," Nick says, heading to his car.

"Let me grab my stuff first." I reach for my bag and my hand goes up to find the ignition empty. Will must have accidentally taken my keys. I leave the door unlocked just in case he doesn't have them. I don't want to add a locksmith charge on top of our already mounting debt.

"Wow. Nice car," I say when we reach Nick's vehicle. It's a small black sports car. Not sure what kind, but there isn't a speck of dirt on it.

"It's not mine," he says as we climb inside. "It's my dad's. He lets me drive it when he's off work."

"Still, it's nice. Do you mind if we swing by Chapman Elementary? I'm supposed to pick up my little brother."

"No problem," he says, turning left out of the parking lot.

"So, new girl. You miss Texas yet?" Although it's been a month, he still calls me new girl.

"Yep," I reply shortly.

He attempts to make more small talk but I treat his questions as if they were rhetorical, even though they aren't. I can't stop thinking about the things Will said to me before Nick interrupted us. Nick finally grasps the idea that I'm not in a chatty mood, so he turns on the radio.

We pull up to Kel's school, and I get out of the car so Kel can spot me, since I'm not in my Jeep. When Kel notices me, he comes running up to me, followed by Caulder. "Hey, where's your Jeep?"

"Won't start. Hop in, Nick is giving us a ride home."

"Oh. Well, Caulder is supposed to go with us today."

I open the back door as the two climb in the small backseat. They immediately start oohing and aahing. The remainder of the short drive consists of transformer comparisons and Nick's car. When we arrive at the house, Kel and Caulder jump out of the car and run inside. I thank Nick and follow the boys toward the house when I hear Nick open his door.

"Layken, wait," Nick calls after me.

Ugh. Almost in the clear. I turn to see him standing in my driveway, looking nervous.

"Later this week, Eddie and Gavin and I are going to Getty's. You wanna come?"

I definitely should have laid off on the obvious flirtation with Nick. I feel guilty, knowing good and well I've sent him the wrong signals. "I don't know. I'd have to run it by my mom. I'll let you know tomorrow, okay?" I see the hope fill his eyes, and wish I had gone ahead and turned him down. I don't want to give him any more false hope than I already have.

"Yeah. Tomorrow. See ya," Nick says.

When I walk in the house, Kel and Caulder are both at the bar with their homework out. "Caulder, do you live with us now or what?"

He looks at me with his big green Will-looking eyes. "I can go home if you want me to."

"No. I was just kidding. I like you being here; it keeps this little creeper away from me." I squeeze Kel's shoulders, then walk into the kitchen and grab a drink.

"So is that Nick guy your boyfriend? I thought my brother was going to be your boyfriend."

Caulder catches me off guard with his observation, causing juice to spew from my mouth. "No, neither of them is my boyfriend. Your brother and I are just friends, Caulder."

"But Layken," Kel gives Caulder a mischievous grin. "I saw you kissing him that night y'all came home. In the driveway. I was watching from my bedroom window."

My heart jumps to my throat. I walk over to them and place my hands firmly on the bar in front of them. "Kel, don't ever repeat what you just said. Do you hear me?"

His eyes get big, and he and Caulder both lean back in their chairs as I lean forward across the bar.

"I'm serious. You did not see what you thought you saw. Will can get in a lot of trouble if you repeat what you said. I mean it."

They both nod as I back away and turn toward my room. I pull my notebook out of my bag and plop down on the bed next to it to start on my homework, but I can't. The thought of anything getting out about Will and me distracts me. As much as I hate the fact that we can't be together, I hate the thought of him getting fired even more. He needs this job. Will was only one year older than I am now when his parents died, and he essentially became a parent himself. The more I think about it, the guiltier I feel for being so hard on him and the decision he's made. The pain I'm feeling as a result of us not being together pales in comparison to what Will must be going through. I feel less like Will's peer every day and more like his student.

I decide to work on the poem I've yet to start, but

after half an hour I'm still staring at a blank page, when my mother walks in.

"Where's your Jeep?"

"Oh, I forgot to tell you. It won't crank—alternator or something. It's parked at school."

"How can you forget to mention that?" she says, obviously frustrated.

"I'm sorry. You were sleeping when I got home. I know you've been sick this week, so I didn't want to wake you up."

She sighs and sits on my bed. "I don't know when I'll be able to get it fixed. I work the next few days. Do you mind just keeping it at the school for a couple days until I can work it out?"

"I'll ask tomorrow. I doubt they would even notice it's there."

"Okay. Well, I've got to get to work." She stands up to leave.

"Wait. Your shift doesn't start for a few more hours."

"I need to run errands," she quickly replies. She shuts the door, leaving me to question the validity of her response.

I'M DRYING MY hair after my shower when I think I hear the doorbell. I turn the dryer off and listen for a moment, and it eventually rings again. "Kel, get the door!" I yell as I pull on my sweats. I pile my still-wet hair into a band and double it up on top of my head as I throw on a tank top. The doorbell rings again.

I make my way to the front door and check the peephole. Will is standing outside with his arms crossed, staring at the ground. My heart skips a beat at the sight of him, and I turn to check my reflection in the entryway mirror. Sure enough, I look like I just got out of the shower. At least I'm not wearing Kel's house shoes. Ugh! Why do I even care?

I open the door and motion for him to come inside. He steps in far enough for me to shut the door behind him but doesn't come any further inside.

"I just need Caulder. Bath time."

His arms are still crossed, and his speech is curt. I take this as a sign that I'm not getting any more confessions out of him right now, so I tell him to give me a sec as I go fetch Caulder. I check Kel's room, my mother's room, and eventually my room, when I run out of rooms to check.

"They aren't here, Will," I say as I walk back into the living room.

"Well, they have to be. They aren't at my house." He makes his way down the hallway and checks the rooms as he calls for them. I open the patio door, flick on the outdoor light, and make a quick scan of the small backyard.

"They aren't out back," I say when we meet back in the living room.

"I'll check my house again," he says.

Will makes his way across the street and I follow behind him. It's dark outside and the temperature has dropped since earlier in the day. I become increasingly concerned as we make our way to Will's house. I know Kel and Caulder wouldn't be outside this time of night. If they aren't in one of the houses, I don't know where they could be.

Will makes a quick run of his house. I don't feel comfortable walking through it, since I've never really been further than the hallway, so I stand in the doorway and wait.

"They aren't here," he says, unable to hide the uncertainty in his voice. My hands go to my mouth as I gasp, fully realizing the seriousness of the situation. Will can see the fear in my eyes, and he puts his arms around me.

"We'll find them. They're just off playing somewhere." His reassurance is brief as he lets go and heads back out the front door. "Check the backyard; I'll meet you out front," he says.

We're both calling the boys' names when the panic rises up in my chest. It reminds me of the time I was babysitting Kel when he was four, and I thought I had lost him. I searched the entire house for twenty minutes before finally breaking down and calling my mother. She immediately called the police, who arrived within minutes. They were still searching when she finally made it home—the panic in her eyes when she walked through the door cut through me and we both started to cry. After searching for over fifteen minutes, an officer found Kel passed out on the folded towels in the bathroom cabinet. Apparently he had been hiding from me when he fell asleep.

I'm hoping to find the same sense of relief when I look through Will's backyard, but they aren't here. I make my way around the side of his house and see Will standing in the driveway, staring inside his car. When he sees me running toward him, his finger goes up to his mouth, instructing me to be quiet. I peer into the backseat, where Kel and Caulder are both crouched on the floorboard, their fingers and hands clamped together in the shape of guns; they're both passed out.

I breathe a sigh of relief.

"They would make horrible guards," he whispers.

"Yeah, they sure would."

We both stand there, staring at our little brothers. Will's arm goes around me, and he gives my shoulders a quick squeeze. His hug doesn't linger at all though, so I know it's nothing more than a gesture expressing relief that our brothers are safe.

"Hey, before you wake them up, I've got something of yours inside." He walks toward his house, so I follow him inside and into the kitchen.

My heart is still pounding against my chest, although I can't distinguish if it's the aftermath of the search for our brothers, or if it's just being in Will's presence.

He pulls something out of his satchel and hands it to me. "Your keys," he says, dropping them into my hand.

"Oh, thanks," I say, somewhat disappointed. I don't know what I expected him to have, but I was fantasizing that maybe it was his resignation letter.

"It's running fine now. You should be able to drive it home tomorrow." He makes his way to his couch and sits.

"What? You fixed it?" I say.

"Well, *I* didn't fix it. I know a guy who was able to put an alternator on it this afternoon."

His reference in the parking lot comes back to mind. Somehow I doubt he would have an alternator put on any other student's vehicle.

"Will, you didn't have to do that," I say as I sit down beside him on the couch. "Thanks, though. I'll pay you back."

"Don't worry about it. You guys have helped me a lot with Caulder lately; it's the least I can do."

And yet again, I'm at a loss for what to say next. It feels like that first day I was standing in his kitchen, contemplating my next move after he helped me with my bandage. I know I should get up and leave, but I like being here next to him. Even if I am finding myself in his debt again. I somehow find the confidence to speak again.

"So, can we finish our conversation from earlier?" I say.

He adjusts himself on the couch and props his feet on the coffee table in front of us. "That depends," he says. "Did you come up with a solution?"

"Well, no," I reply, just as a possible solution comes

to mind. I lean my head against the back of the couch and meekly suggest my idea. "Suppose these feelings we have just get more . . . complex." I pause for a moment. I'm not sure how he's going to take this new suggestion of mine, so I tread lightly.

"I wouldn't be opposed to the idea of getting a GED."

"That's ridiculous," he says, eyeing me sharply. "Don't even think like that. There's no way you're quitting school, Lake."

I'm *Lake* again.

"It was just an idea," I say.

"Well, it was a dumb one."

We both think silently, neither of us coming up with any other solutions. My head is still resting against the back of the couch as I watch him. His hands are clasped behind his head, and he's staring up at the ceiling. His jaw is clenched tight, and he's absentmindedly popping his knuckles.

He's no longer wearing the clothes he wears as a teacher. Instead, he has a plain white fitted T-shirt on and gray jogging pants that are almost identical to the ones I'm wearing. For the first time tonight, I notice his hair is wet. I haven't been this close to him in weeks; I was beginning to forget what he smells like. I inhale and take in the scent of his aftershave. It smells like the air in Texas right before it starts to rain.

There's a small dab of shaving cream right below his left ear. My hand instinctively moves up to his neck and I wipe it away. He flinches and turns toward me, so I defensively hold up my finger as if to prove my reason for touching him. He pulls my hand toward him and rubs my finger across his shirt, wiping off the excess shaving cream.

Our hands come to rest on his chest and we continue to look at each other in silence. My palm is flat against his heart, and I can feel it rapidly beating against my hand. I know this exchange between us is wrong, but it feels incredibly right.

He allows my hand to remain on his chest as it moves up and down to the rhythm of his breath. The look in his eyes is the exact look he had when he was watching me in class today. But this time my physical response is more intense, and I struggle to control the powerful urge to lean in and kiss him. I've wanted to talk to him like this for over a month now. I still had so much to say before he started pretending I didn't exist. I'm afraid that as soon as I walk out of his house tonight, the isolation will return, so I decide to tell him what I've wanted to say to him for weeks.

"Will?" I whisper. "I'll wait for you—until I graduate."

He exhales and closes his eyes, stroking his thumb across the back of my hand. "That's a long wait, Lake. A lot can happen in a year." His pulse increases against my palm.

I don't know what comes over me, but I lean closer and turn his face toward mine. I just need him to look at me.

He doesn't meet my gaze. Instead, his eyes focus on his hand as he slowly moves it up my arm. All the same sensations that flowed through me the first night we kissed come flooding back. I've missed his touch so much.

He moves his hand to my shoulder and slides his fingers underneath the strap of my shirt, slowly tracing along the edges of it. His movements are slow and methodical as he pulls his legs off of the table in front of him and turns his body toward me. His expression seems full of conflict, but he slowly leans in and presses his lips against my shoulder. I place my hands on the back of his neck and inhale. His breath becomes heavier as his lips slowly move across my shoulder and onto my neck. The room starts to spin, so I close my eyes. His lips make their way to my jaw and closer to my mouth. When I feel him pull away, I open my eyes and he's watching me. There's a slight moment of hesitation in his eyes just before his lips close over mine.

In the past, his kisses have been very delicate and smooth. There's a different hunger behind him now. He slides his hands under my shirt and grasps at my waist. I return his kisses with the same feverish passion. I run my hands through his hair and pull him to me as I lie back on the couch. As soon as he begins to ease his body on top of mine, his lips break away and he sits back up.

"We've got to stop," he says. "We can't do this." He squeezes his eyes shut and rests his head against the couch.

I sit back up and ignore his protest, sliding my hands

up his neck and through his hair. I press my lips to his and pull myself onto his lap. His hands wrap around my waist again and he pulls me into him, returning my kiss with even more intensity than before.

He's right; they do get better every time.

My hands find the bottom edge of his shirt and I slide it up. Our lips separate for a brief moment when his shirt passes between us. I place my hands on his chest and run them over the contours of his muscles as we continue to kiss. He grips my arms and pushes me down onto the couch. I wait for him to find his way back to my mouth, but instead he pushes away from me and stands up.

"Layken, get up!" he demands. He grabs my hand and pulls me up from the couch.

I stand up, still caught up in the moment and unable to catch my breath.

"This—this can't happen!" He's attempting to catch his breath, too. "I'm your teacher now. Everything has changed—we can't do this."

His timing sucks. My knees are weak, so I sit back down on the couch for support. "Will, I won't say anything. I swear." I don't want him to regret what just happened between us. For a moment, it felt like we were back where we belonged. Now, seconds later, I'm confused again.

"I'm sorry, Layken, but it's not right," he says, pacing the floor. "This isn't good for either of us. This isn't good for *you*."

"You don't know what's good for me," I snap. I'm getting defensive again.

He stops pacing and turns toward me. "You won't wait for me. I won't let you give up what should be the best year of your life. I had to grow up way too fast; I'm not taking that away from you, too. It wouldn't be fair. I don't want you to wait for me, Layken."

The shift in his demeanor and the way my entire first name is flowing from his mouth is causing the oxygen to deplete from the room. I'm dizzy. "I won't be giving *anything* up," I reply weakly. I would have screamed it if I could muster enough energy.

He grabs his shirt and pulls it on over his head as he moves further away from me. He walks to the opposite side of the living room and around the back of the couch. He grips the back of it and lets his head fall between his shoulders, avoiding eye contact again. "My life is nothing but responsibilities. I'm raising a *child*, for Christ's sake. I wouldn't be able to put your needs first. Hell, I wouldn't even be able to put them *second*." He slowly raises his head and brings his gaze back to mine. "You deserve better than third."

I go to him and kneel on the couch in front of him, placing my hands on top of his. "Your responsibilities *should* come before me, which is why I want to wait for you, Will. You're a good person. This thing about you that you think is your flaw—it's the reason I'm falling in love with you."

My last few words trickle out as though I've lost what little control over myself I had left. I don't regret saying it, though.

He pulls his hands out from under mine and places them firmly on either side of my face. He looks me directly in the eyes. "You are *not* falling in love with me." He says this as if it's a command. "You *cannot* fall in love with me." His eyes are hard and he clenches his jaw again. I feel the tears begin to well in my eyes as he releases me and walks toward the front door.

"What happened tonight—" He's pointing to the couch as he speaks. "That can't happen again. That *won't* happen again." He says this as though he's trying to convince more than just me.

After he walks outside, he slams the door behind him, and I'm left alone in his living room. My hands clutch at my stomach; my nausea intensifies. I'm afraid if I don't regain my composure soon, I won't be able to stand long enough to make it out of the house. I inhale through my nose and exhale from my mouth, then count backward from ten.

It's a coping technique I learned from my father when I was younger. I used to have what my parents referred to as "emotional overloads." My dad would wrap his arms around me and squeeze me as tight as he could as we counted down. Sometimes I would fake the tantrums just so he would have to squeeze me. What I wouldn't give for my dad's embrace right now.

The front door opens, and Will reenters, carrying a sleeping Caulder in his arms. "Kel woke up; he's walking home now. You should go, too," he says quietly.

I feel completely embarrassed. Embarrassed by what just happened between us and the fact that he's making me feel desperate, *weaker* than him. I snatch my keys off the coffee table and turn toward the door, stopping in front of him.

"You're an *asshole*," I say. I turn and leave, slamming the door behind me.

As soon as I get to my bedroom, I collapse onto the bed and cry. Although it's negative, I finally have inspiration for my poem. I grab a pen and start writing as I wipe smudged tears off of the paper.

7.

ACCORDING TO ELISABETH KÜBLER-ROSS, THERE ARE FIVE stages of grief a person passes through after the death of a loved one: denial, anger, bargaining, depression, and acceptance.

I took a psychology class during the last semester of my junior year when we lived in Texas. We were discussing stage four when the principal walked into the room, pale as a ghost.

"Layken, can I see you in the hallway please?"

Principal Bass was a pleasant man. Plump in the belly, plump in the hands, plump in places you didn't know could be plump. It was an unusually cold spring day in Texas, but you wouldn't know it from the rings of sweat underneath his arms. He was the type of principal who hung out in his office rather than the halls. He never went looking for trouble, just waited for it to come to him. So why was he here?

I had a sinking feeling deep in the pit of my stomach as I stood up and walked as slowly as I could to the classroom door. He wouldn't make eye contact with me. I remember I looked right at him, and his eyes darted to the floor. He felt sorry for me. But why?

When I walked out into the hallway my mother was standing there, mascara streaked down her cheeks. The look in her eyes told me why she was there. Why *she* was there, and my father wasn't.

I shook my head, refusing to believe what I knew to be true. "No," I cried repeatedly. She threw her arms around me and started to collapse to the floor. Rather than hold her up, I simply melted with her. That day I experienced my first stage of grief in the hallway floor of my high school: denial.

GAVIN IS PREPARING to perform his poetry. He's standing in front of the class, his paper shaking between his fingers as he clears his throat and prepares to read from it.

I wonder, as I ignore Gavin's presence and focus on

Will, do the five stages of grief only apply to the death of a loved one? Could it not also apply to the death of an aspect of your life? If it does, then I'm definitely smack-dab in the center of stage two: anger.

"What's it called, Gavin?" Will asks. He's sitting at his desk, writing notes into his pad as students perform. It pisses me off—the way he's being so attentive, focused on everything except me. His ability to make me feel like this huge invisible void pisses me off. The way he pauses to chew on the tip of his pen pisses me off. Just last night, those same lips that are wrapped around the tip of his ugly red pen were making their way up my neck.

I push the thought of his kiss out of my mind as quickly as it crept in. I don't know how long it will take, but I'm determined to break from this hold he has on me.

"Um, I didn't really give it a title," Gavin responds. He's standing at the front of the classroom, second to last person to perform. "I guess you can call it 'Preproposal'?"

"'Preproposal'—go ahead then," Will states in a teacherish voice that also pisses me off.

"Ahem." Gavin clears his throat. His hands start trembling even more as he begins to read.

> One million fifty-one thousand and
> two hundred minutes.
> That's approximately how many minutes

I've loved you,

It's how many minutes I've *thought* about you,

How many minutes I've *worried* about you,

How many minutes I've thanked *God* for you,

How many minutes I've thanked *every deity* in the

Universe for you.

One million

Fifty-one thousand

And

Two

Hundred

Minutes . . .

One million fifty-one thousand and

two hundred times.

It's how many times you've made me *smile*,

How many times you've made me *dream*,

How many times you've made me *believe*,

How many times you've made me *discover*,

How many times you've made me *adore*,

How many times you've made me *cherish*,

My life.

(Gavin walks toward the back of the room, where Eddie is sitting. He bends down on one knee in front of her as he reads the last line of his poem.)

And exactly *one million fifty-one thousand and two*

hundred minutes from now, I'm going to *propose* to you, and ask that you share *all* the rest of the minutes of your *life* with me.

Eddie is beaming as she leans down and hugs him. The classroom is divided as the boys groan and the girls swoon. I simply squirm in my seat, anticipating the last poet of the day: me.

"Thanks, Gavin, you can take your seat. Good job." Will doesn't look up from his notes when he calls me to read my poem. His voice is soft, full of trepidation when he says my name. "Layken, it's your turn."

I'm ready. I feel good about my piece. It's short but to the point. I already have it memorized so I leave the poem on my desk and walk to the front of the classroom.

"I have a question." My heart races when I realize this is the first time I've spoken out loud to Will in his classroom since I entered it a month ago. He hesitates as though he can't decide if he should acknowledge that I even have a question. He gives me a slight nod.

"Is there a time minimum?" I say.

I'm not sure what he thought I was about to ask, but he looks relieved that this was my question.

"No, it's fine as long as you get your point across. Remember, there are no rules." His voice cracks slightly when he replies. I can see on his face that what happened between us last night is fresh on his mind. All the better.

"Good. Okay then," I stammer. "My poem is called 'Mean.'" I face the front of the classroom and proudly recite my poem by heart.

According to the thesaurus . . .
and according to *me* . . .
there are over thirty different meanings and
substitutions for the word
mean.

(I quickly yell the following words; the entire class flinches—including Will.)

Jackass, jerk, cruel, dickhead, unkind, harsh, wicked,
hateful, heartless, vicious, virulent, unrelenting,
tyrannical, malevolent, atrocious, bastard,
barbarous, bitter, brutal, callous, degenerate,
brutish, depraved, evil, fierce, hard, implacable,
rancorous, pernicious, inhumane, monstrous,
merciless, inexorable.
And *my* personal favorite—*asshole.*

I glance at Will as I return to my seat and his face is red, his teeth clenched. Eddie is the first to clap, followed by the rest of the girls in the class. I fold my arms across my chest and focus my eyes solely on my desk.

"Man," Javi says. "Who pissed you off?"

The bell rings and the students begin to file out. Will

never utters a word. I begin to pack my things into my bag, when Eddie runs up to me.

"Have you talked to your mom yet?" she asks.

"My mom? About what?" I have no clue what she's referring to.

"The date. Nick asked you out yesterday? You said you'd have to ask your mom?"

"Oh, that," I respond.

That was yesterday? It seems like a lifetime ago. I shoot a quick glance in Will's direction and see that he's watching me, waiting for my response to Eddie. His expression is stone cold. I wish at this moment he were easier to read. I assume his internal expression is jealousy, so I go with it.

"Yeah, sure. Tell Nick I'd love to," I lie as I keep my eyes locked on Will. He grabs his pen and paper and opens one of the desk drawers and drops them in, slamming it shut. The action startles Eddie and she jumps, spinning around to look at him. He's aware of the attention he brought upon himself, so he stands up and acts oblivious to us as he erases chalk off the board. Eddie turns back toward me.

"Great! Oh, and we decided on Thursday, so after Getty's we can go to the slam. We've only got a few weeks—might as well get it out of the way. You want us to pick you up?"

"Uh, sure."

Eddie claps excitedly and bounces out of the room.

Will continues to erase away nothing as I start toward the exit.

"Layken," he says with a hardness to his voice.

I pause at the door but don't turn toward him.

"Your mom works Thursday nights. I always get a sitter for Thursdays since I go to the slams. Just send Kel over before you leave. You know, before your *date*."

I don't respond. I simply walk out.

Lunch is awkward. Eddie has already informed Nick that I've agreed to go out with them, so everyone is extremely chatty about our new plans. Everyone except me. Other than the occasional nod and mutters of agreement, I don't speak. I have no appetite, so Nick eats the majority of my food. I stir the rice pudding around on my tray with my spoon, dribbling in traces of ketchup here and there. It reminds me of the remnants of the murdered snowman in my driveway. For days, every time I backed out, my tire would glide over his ice-hard body. I wonder if that's how quiet my Jeep would be if I were to run over Will? Just accidentally back up over him, then put my car in drive and continue on.

"Layken, are you just going to ignore him?" Eddie says.

I look up to see Will standing behind Nick, staring down at the mess I've made of my tray.

"What?" I say to Eddie.

"Mr. Cooper needs to see you," she says, nudging her head in Will's direction.

"I bet you're in trouble for saying 'asshole,'" Nick says.

I put my hand against my throat, afraid it's about to explode. What is he *doing*? Why is he asking me to go with him in front of everyone? Has he lost his mind?

I slide my chair back and leave my tray on the table as I eye him cautiously. He walks out of the cafeteria toward his classroom and I follow him. It's a long walk. A long, awkward, tension-filled, quiet walk.

"We need to talk," he says as he shuts his door behind us. "Now."

I don't know if he's being "Will" right now. I don't understand the angle he's coming at me from. I don't know whether to obey him—or punch him. I don't walk very far into his room. I fold my arms across my chest and attempt to look annoyed.

"Then talk!" I say.

"Dammit, Lake! I'm not your enemy. Stop hating me."

He's being Will.

I rush toward him and throw my hands up in the air in frustration. "Stop *hating* you? Make up your freaking mind, Will! Last night you told me to stop loving you, now you're telling me to stop *hating* you? You tell me you don't want me to wait for you, yet you act like an immature little boy when I agree to go out with Nick! You want me to act like I don't know you, but then you pull me out of the lunchroom in front of everyone! We've got this whole facade between us, like we're different people all the time, and it's exhausting! I never know when you're Will or Mr. Cooper and I *really* don't know when I'm supposed to be Layken or Lake."

I'm tired of playing his head games. I'm so tired. I throw myself into the seat I occupy during his class. He's hard to read as he stands motionless. Expressionless. He slowly walks around me and takes a seat in the desk behind me. I continue facing forward when he leans forward over the desk, close enough to whisper. My body tenses and my chest tightens when he speaks.

"I didn't think it would be this hard," he says.

I don't want to give him the gratification of seeing the tears that are making their way down my cheeks.

"I'm sorry I said that to you earlier, about Thursday," he says. "I was being sincere for the most part. I know you'll need someone to watch Kel, and I did make the slam a required assignment. But I shouldn't have reacted like that. That's why I asked you to come here: I just needed to apologize. It won't happen again, I swear."

The door to the classroom swings open, and Will hops up out of the seat. His sudden movement startles Eddie, and she eyes us curiously from the doorway. She's holding the backpack that I left in the cafeteria. I can't conceal the tears that are still flowing from my eyes, so I turn away from her. There's nothing Will or I could do at this point to mask the tension between us.

Eddie holds her palms up and gently lays my backpack on the desk closest to the door. She backs out of the room and whispers, "My bad . . . continue." She closes the door behind her.

Will runs his hands through his hair and paces the floor. "That's just great," he mutters.

"Let it go, Will," I say as I stand up and walk to my backpack. "If she asks me about it, I'll just tell her you were upset because I said 'asshole.' And jackass. And dickhead. And bastar—"

"I get your point!"

My hand is on the doorknob when he calls my name again so I pause.

"I also want to say I'm sorry . . . about last night," he says.

I turn toward him when I speak. "Are you sorry it happened? Or sorry about the way you stopped it?"

He cocks his head and shrugs his shoulders as if he doesn't understand my question. "All of it. It never should have happened."

"Bastard," I finish.

THE ENGINE OF my Jeep purrs its familiar sound when I crank it, and that pisses me off, too. I slam my fist against the steering wheel, wishing so many things. I wish I hadn't met Will the first week I was here. It would have been so much easier if I'd met him in class first. Or better yet, I wish we had never even moved to Ypsilanti. I wish my dad were alive. I wish my mother weren't being so vague about

her *errands*. I wish Caulder weren't at our house every day. Seeing him just makes me think of Will. I wish Will had never fixed my Jeep. I hate that he does considerate things like that. It would make it so much easier to hate him if he really *were* all those things I called him. Oh my god, I can't believe I called him all those names. Wait, no regrets.

I PICK THE boys up from school and drive home. I beat Will home today, but I won't be waiting at the window. I'm done waiting at the window.

"We'll be at Caulder's," Kel yells as they slam the Jeep door.

Good.

When I walk down the hallway, I hear my mother talking to someone in her bedroom, so I pause outside her door. It's a one-sided conversation, so she must be on the phone. Normally, I would never eavesdrop on one of her conversations. However, her behavior lately warrants a little nosiness. Or maybe *my* behavior warrants a little rebellion. Either way, I cup my ear to the door.

"I know. I *know*. I'll tell them soon," she says.

"No, I think it will go over better if I tell them alone . . ."

"Of course I will. I love you too, babe."

She's signing off. I quietly tiptoe to my bedroom and

slip inside. I shut the door behind me and slide to the floor.

Seven months. It took her all of seven months to move on. She can't be seeing someone else already, but her words on the phone couldn't have been more clear. I'm in stage one again: denial.

How could she? And whoever he is, he already wants her to introduce us to him? I already don't like him. And her nerve! How could she accost Will like she did, when what she's doing is just as deplorable, if not worse? Stage one is extremely brief. I'm back in stage two again: anger.

I decide not to bring it up right away. I want to find out more before I confront her about it. I want the upper hand in this situation, and it's going to take some thought.

"Lake? Are you back?" She's knocking on my door. I have to roll forward and hop up to get out of the way when she opens it. She sees me jump up and she eyes me curiously.

"What are you doing?" she asks.

"Stretching. My back hurts."

She doesn't buy it, so I clasp my hands behind me and stretch my arms upward, bending forward.

"Take some aspirin," she says.

"Okay."

"I'm off tonight, but I have a lot of sleep to catch up on. I didn't get any at all today so I'm going to lie down. Can you make sure Kel gets a bath before he goes to bed?"

"Sure."

We both start down the hallway. "Wait—Mom?"

She turns back to me, her lids dragging over her blood-shot eyes.

"I'm going out Thursday night. Is that okay?"

She eyes me suspiciously. "With who?"

"Eddie, Gavin, and Nick."

"Three guys? You aren't going anywhere with three guys."

"No. Eddie's a girl. She's my friend. Her boyfriend is Gavin, and we're double-dating. I'm going with Nick."

Her eyes brighten a little. "Oh. Well, good." She smiles and opens the door to her bedroom. "Wait," she says. "I work Thursday. What about Kel?"

"Will has a sitter on Thursdays. He already said Kel could stay there."

She looks pleased, but only for a second. "Will agreed to pay a sitter? To watch Kel? So you could go on a *date*?"

Crap. I didn't realize how this would look. "Mom, it's been weeks. We went on one date; we're over it."

She stares at me for several seconds. "Hmm." She returns to her room, still unappeased.

Her suspicion brings me a small sense of gratification. She thinks I'm lying about something. Now we're even.

"I'M NOT GOING to third period," I say to Eddie as we exit history.

"Why not?"

"I just don't feel like it. Headache. I think I'll go sit in the courtyard and get some fresh air."

I turn and start to head to the courtyard when she grabs my arm.

"Layken? Does this have anything to do with what happened at lunch yesterday with Mr. Cooper? Is everything okay?"

I smile at her reassuringly. "No, it's fine. He just wants me to refrain from my colorful choice of words in his class."

She purses her lips together and walks away with the same unappeased look my mother had last night.

The courtyard is empty. I guess none of the other students needs a breather from the teacher they're secretly in love with. I sit at a bench and pull my phone out of my pocket. Nothing. I've only spoken to Kerris once since I moved. She was the friend in Texas I was closest to, but *she* was actually best friends with *another* girl. It's odd when your best friend has an even better best friend. I chalked it up to the fact that I was too busy for best friends, but maybe it was more than that. Maybe I'm not a good listener. Maybe I'm not a good *sharer*.

"Mind if I join you?"

I look up and Eddie is taking a seat on the bench across from me. "Misery loves company," I say.

"Misery? And why are we miserable? You have a date

to look forward to tomorrow night. And your best friend is me," she says.

Best friend. Maybe. Hopefully.

"You don't think Will is going to come looking for us?" I say.

She cocks her head at me. "*Will?* You mean Mr. Cooper?"

Oh god, I just called him Will. She's already suspicious. I smile and come up with the first excuse that pops into my head.

"Yeah, Mr. Cooper. We called teachers by their first names at my last school."

She doesn't respond. She's picking at the paint on the bench with her blue fingernail. Nine of her fingernails are green; just the one is blue. "I'm just going to say something here," she says. Her voice is calm. "Maybe I'm way off base, maybe I'm not. But whatever I say, I don't want you to interject."

I nod.

"I think what was happening at lunch yesterday was more than just a slap on the wrist for inappropriate verbal usage. I don't know how *much* more, and honestly it's none of my business. I just want you to know you can talk to me. If you need to. I'd never repeat anything; I don't have anyone besides Gavin to repeat stuff to."

"No one? Best friends? Siblings?" I hope this changes the subject.

"Nope. He's all I have," she says. "Well, technically,

if you want to know the truth, I've had seventeen sisters, twelve brothers, six moms, and seven dads."

I can't tell if she's making a joke, so I don't laugh in case she isn't.

"Foster care," she says. "I'm on my seventh home in nine years."

"Oh. I'm sorry." I don't know what else to say.

"Don't be. I've been with Joel for four of those nine years. He's my foster dad. It works. I'm content. He gets his check."

"Were any of your twenty-nine siblings blood related?"

She laughs. "Man, you pay attention. And no, I'm an only child. Born to a mother with a yen for cheap crack and pricey babies."

She can see I'm not following.

"She tried to sell me. Don't worry, nobody wanted me. Or she was just asking too much. When I was nine she offered me to a lady in a Walmart parking lot. She gave her a sob story about how she couldn't take care of me, yada yada, offered the lady a deal. A hundred bucks was my going rate. It wasn't the first time she tried this right in front of me. I was getting bored with it, so I looked right at the lady and said, 'You got a husband? I bet he's hot!' My mother backhanded me for ruining the sale. Left me in the parking lot. The lady took me to the police station and dropped me off. That's the last time I ever saw my mom."

"God, Eddie. That's unreal."

"Yeah, it is. But it's my real."

I lie down on the bench and look up at the sky. She does the same.

"You said Eddie was a family name," I say. "Which family?"

"Don't laugh."

"But what if I think it's funny?"

She rolls her eyes. "There was a comedy DVD my first foster family owned. Eddie Izzard. I thought I had his nose. I watched that DVD a million times, pretending he was my dad. I had people refer to me as Eddie after that. I tried Izzard for a while, but it never stuck."

We both laugh. I pull my jacket off and pull it on top of me, sliding my arms through it backward so that it warms the parts of me that have been exposed to the cold for too long. I close my eyes.

"I had amazing parents," I sigh.

"Had?"

"My dad died seven months ago. My mother moved us up here, claimed it was for financial reasons, but now I'm not so sure she was being honest. She's seeing someone else already. So yes, amazing is past tense at the moment."

"Suck."

We both lie there pondering the hands we were dealt. Mine pales in comparison to hers. The things she must have seen. Kel is the same age now that Eddie was when she was put into foster care. I don't know how she walks around so happy, so full of life. We're quiet. Everything is comfortably quiet. I silently wonder if this is what it feels like to have a best friend.

She sits up on her bench after a while, hands stretched out in front of her as she yawns. "Earlier, the thing I said about Joel—and me being a check to him? It's not like that. He's really been a great guy. Sometimes when things get too real, my sarcasm takes over."

I smile at her in understanding. "Thanks for skipping with me, I really needed it."

"Thanks for needing it. Apparently I did, too. And about Nick—he's a good guy, just not for you. I'll drop it. But you still have to go with us tomorrow."

"I know I do. If I don't, Chuck Norris will hunt me down and kick my ass." I flip my jacket around and ease my arms in as we walk through the door and back into the hallway.

"So if Eddie is something you made up, what's your real name?" I ask her before we part ways. She smiles and shrugs her shoulders.

"Right now, it's Eddie."

8.

I wanna have friends
that will let me be
All alone when being alone
is all that I need.

—THE AVETT BROTHERS,
"THE PERFECT SPACE"

"WHERE'S MOM?" I ASK KEL. HE'S SITTING AT THE BAR with his homework out.

"She just dropped me and Caulder off. Said she would be back in a couple of hours. She wants you to order pizza."

If I'd been home a few minutes sooner, I would have followed her. "Did she say where she was going?" I ask him.

"Can you ask them to put the pepperonis under the sauce this time?"

"Where'd she say she was going?"

"No, wait. Tell them to put the pepperonis on first, then the cheese, then the sauce on top."

"Dammit, Kel! Where did she go?"

His eyes grow wide as he climbs off the stool and walks backward toward the front door. He slumps his shoulders and slips his shoes on. I've never cussed at him before.

"Know don't I. Caulder's to going I'm."

"Be back by six, I'll have your pizza."

I decide to knock my homework out first. Mr. Hanson may be half deaf and half blind, but he makes up for that in the sheer volume of homework he assigns. I finish within an hour. It's just four thirty.

I take this opportunity to play detective. Whatever she's up to and whomever she's with, I'm determined to find out. I rummage through kitchen drawers, cabinets, hallway closets. Nothing. I've never snooped in my parents' room before. Ever. This is definitely a year of firsts, though, so I let myself in and close the door behind me.

Everything is the same as it was in their old bedroom. Same furniture, same beige carpet. If it weren't for the lack of space, I would hardly be able to tell the difference between this room and the one she shared with my father. I check the obvious first: the underwear drawer. I don't find anything. I move to the edge of the bed and slide open the drawer to her nightstand. Eye mask, pen, lotion, book, note—

Note.

I slip it out of the drawer and open it. It's written in black ink, centered down the page. It's a poem.

Julia,
I'll paint you a world one day
A world where smiles don't fade
A world where laughter is played
In the background
Like a PSA
I'll paint it when the sun goes down
While you're lying there in your gown
The moment your smile turns around
I'll paint right over your frown
I'll be finished when the sun breaks in
You'll wake with a still-wet grin
You'll see that I finish what I begin
The world I've painted on your chin . . .

It's pathetic. The world I've painted on your chin? Like a PSA? What is that, anyway? Public service announcement? Who rhymes with acronyms? Whoever he is, I don't like him. I hate him. I fold the note up and put it back in its place.

I call Getty's and order two pizzas. Mom is pulling up in the driveway when I hang up the phone. Perfect opportunity for a shower. I lock myself in the bathroom before she makes it inside. I don't want to see the look on her face. That look of "falling in love."

* * *

"WHAT THE HELL?" my mother says when she opens up the box of pizza.

"That's Kel's. It's backward," I tell her. She rolls her eyes as she pulls the second box toward her. It makes me cringe how her eyes scroll over all the slices of pizza like she's trying to find the one that tastes the best. They're all slices from the same pizza!

"Just pick one!" I snap.

She flinches. "Jeez, Lake. Have you eaten today? Quite the crab, are we?" She picks up a slice and thrusts it toward me. I throw it on my plate and plop down at the bar, when Kel comes running in backward.

"Here pizza the is?" he asks, right before he trips over the rug and lands on his butt.

"God, Kel, grow up!" I snap.

My mother shoots me a look. "Lake! What is your problem? Is there something you need to talk about?"

I push my pizza across the table and get up from the bar. I can't pretend anymore.

"No, Mother! There's nothing I need to talk about. *I* don't *keep* secrets!"

She sucks in a small gasp of air. This is it—she knows I know.

I expect her to defend herself, yell at me, put up a fight, send me to my room. *Something.* Isn't that what happens when things come to fruition? The climax?

148 | colleen hoover

Instead, she simply looks away and grabs a plate for Kel, filling it with slices of backward pizza.

I march to my room and slam the door. Again. Who knows how many doors I've slammed since we moved here? I'm constantly leaving or entering rooms, pissed off at someone. Will slams poems; I slam doors.

THE ALARM CLOCK is flashing red when I wake up. The power must have gone out overnight. The sun is unusually bright for this early in the morning, so I grab my phone to check the time, and sure enough, we overslept. I jump out of bed and throw on my clothes, brush my teeth, and pull my hair on top of my head. No time for makeup. I wake Kel up and rush him to get dressed while I gather my homework. No time for coffee, either.

"But I ride to school with Caulder in the mornings," Kel whines as we pull our jackets on.

"Not today. We overslept."

It's apparent we aren't the only ones who overslept when I see Will's car still in his driveway. *Great!* I can't just leave and not wake them up.

"Kel, go knock on their door and wake them up."

Kel runs across the street and beats on the door as I climb inside my Jeep and crank it. I turn the heater up full blast and grab the scraper and start wiping the frost away from the windows. I get the final window cleared when Kel returns.

"No one answered the door. I think they're still asleep."

Ugh! I hand the scraper to Kel and tell him to get inside the Jeep; then I walk to Will's house. Kel already tried the front door, so I walk to the side of the house that the bedrooms are on. I don't know which one is Will's, so I knock on all three windows just to be sure I wake someone up.

As I round the front of the house, the front door swings open and Will is standing there, shielding his eyes from the sun, *shirtless*. My hands have touched those abs before. I force myself to look away.

"Power went out. We overslept," I tell him. "We" feels odd. It's like I'm insinuating we're a team.

"What?" he says groggily, rubbing his face. "What time is it?"

"Almost eight."

He immediately perks up.

"Shit!" he says, remembering something. "I've got a conference at eight!"

He turns back inside but leaves the door open. I peek my head further inside but don't dare step over the threshold.

"Do you need me to take Caulder to school?" I yell after him.

He reappears from the hallway.

"Would you? Can you? You don't mind?" He's really

frantic. He's got a tie around his neck, but still no shirt.

"I don't mind. Which one is his room? I'll get him ready."

"Oh. Yeah. That would be great. Thanks. First one on the left. Thank you." He disappears down the hallway again.

I go to Caulder's room and shake him awake. "Caulder, I'm taking you to school. You need to get dressed."

I assist Caulder while he gets ready, catching glimpses of Will running back and forth. The front door eventually shuts, followed by a car door. He's gone. I'm in his house. Awkward.

"Ready, buddy?"

"I'm hungry."

"Oh, yeah. Food. Let me see." I rummage through cabinets in Will's kitchen. The canned goods are stacked according to their labels. There's an abundance of pasta. It's easy enough to cook, I guess. Everything's so clean. Not like most twenty-one-year-old guys' kitchens. I locate some Pop-Tarts above the fridge and grab one for Kel and one for Caulder.

I'M HALF AN hour late for first period, so I decide to sit it out in my Jeep. That's two classes in two days. I'm becoming a real rebel.

I take my seat in history and Eddie swings in behind me.

"You skip Math, and you don't take me with you?" she whispers from behind me.

I turn around, and she draws her neck in and pouts.

"Oh. You overslept."

Makeup. I forgot to bring my makeup. Eddie reaches into her purse and pulls out a cosmetic bag. She can read my mind. Isn't that what best friends do?

"My hero," I say as I take it from her and turn around. I pull lipstick and mascara out, along with a mirror. I apply it quickly and hand her back the bag.

When we walk into third period, Will makes eye contact with me and mouths, "Thank you." I smile and shrug my shoulders, letting him know it wasn't a big deal. Eddie pinches my arm when she walks past me, letting *me* know she saw our exchange.

You wouldn't know by looking at him that Will got ready in less than three minutes. His black pants are wrinkle free, his white shirt tucked in at the waist. His tie . . . oh my god, his tie. I let out a laugh and he glances in my direction. He must not have noticed he put his tie on first this morning; it's barely visible underneath his white shirt. I tug at the collar of my shirt and point to him. He glances down and pats his chest where his tie should be. He laughs as he turns and faces the chalkboard and corrects his wardrobe malfunction. The other students were still taking their seats and chatting, but I know Eddie saw what just happened. I can feel her staring a hole into my back.

NICK THROWS HIMSELF into the seat next to me at lunch. Eddie is sitting right across from me. I expect her to give me the eye but she doesn't. She's just as exuberant as ever. She already knows too much. I'm afraid she may assume it's more than it is. I was late for school today; Will obviously got dressed in a hurry. She has every right to bombard me with questions, but she doesn't. I respect her for that—for respecting me.

"New girl, what time we leavin'?" Nick asks as he piles his food together.

"I don't know. Who's driving?"

"I'll drive," Gavin says.

Nick looks up at Gavin. "No way, man. We're taking my dad's car. No way I'm riding in Monte Car-no."

"Monte Car-no?" I look at Gavin.

"My car," Gavin replies.

"What's your address, Layken?" Eddie asks. I'm shocked she failed to obtain it the first time we met.

"Oh, I know where she lives," Nick says. "I gave her a ride home. Same street as Mr. Cooper. We'll pick her up last."

How does Nick know that? I glance down to my tray and stir my mashed potatoes, attempting to seem oblivious to Eddie's stare.

* * *

NICK AND GAVIN are both sitting in the front seat, so I take the backseat with Eddie. When I climb in she smiles a friendly smile. She's not going to press me. I breathe a sigh of relief.

"Layken, we need your help," Gavin says. "Settle something for us, will ya?"

"I like disputes. Shoot," I say as I put on my seat belt.

"Nick here thinks Texas is nothing but tornadoes. He says they don't have hurricanes because there's no beach. School him."

"Well, he's wrong on both counts," I say.

"I can't be," Nick says.

"There *are* hurricanes," I say. "You forgot about the little area known as the *Gulf of Mexico*. But there aren't any tornadoes."

They both pause.

"There's definitely tornadoes," Gavin says.

"No," I say. "There's no such thing as tornadoes, Gavin. Chuck Norris just hates trailer parks."

There's a moment of silence before they break out in laughter. Eddie scoots closer to me in the backseat and cups her hand to my ear.

"He knows."

I hold my breath, thinking back on conversations that might give me a clue who she's talking about.

"*Who* knows? And what does he know?" I finally ask.

"Nick. He knows you aren't interested. He's fine

with it. There's no pressure. We're just friends tonight, all of us."

I'm relieved. *So* relieved. I was already planning out how I would let him down.

I NEVER DID get to taste the pizza from Getty's that I had delivered the night before. It's heaven. We had to order two, since Nick is eating a whole one by himself. I haven't thought about being mad at my mother so far. I haven't even thought about Will (that much). I'm having fun. It's nice.

"Gavin, what's the stupidest thing you've ever done?" Nick asks.

We all quiet down at this question.

"I can only pick one?" Gavin asks.

"*The* one. The *stupidest* one," Nick replies.

"Hmm. I guess it would have to be the time I was visiting my grandparents on their ranch right outside of Laramie, Wyoming. I had to use the bathroom so bad. It's not a big deal: I'm a guy. We can whip it out anywhere. The big deal was that it was *my* turn."

"For what?" I ask.

"To complete the dare. My brothers used to dare me to do stuff all the time. They would do it first, and then I'd have to do it. The only problem was, I was younger by several years, so they always outsmarted me somehow. This particular day, they told me my rubber boots were too wet to wear so I had to throw on my hiking boots. They, of course, wore their rubber boots. Well, they came up with the dare to see who would pee on the electric fence."

"You didn't," Eddie laughs.

"Oh, just wait, babe. It gets better. They went first, and I realize now that rubber blocks electricity, so they didn't feel anything. I, on the other hand, was not so lucky. It knocked me on my back, and I was crying, trying to get up, when I tripped. I fell forward and met the fence with my mouth. Saliva and electricity don't mix well either. It shocked me so bad my tongue started to swell and my brothers freaked out. Both of them ran home to get my parents while I lay there, unable to move, with my dick hanging out of my pants."

Eddie, Nick, and I are all laughing so hard we get glares from the other customers. Eddie wipes away a tear when Gavin tells her it's her turn.

"I guess when I ran over you with my car," Eddie says.

"Try again," Gavin says.

"What? That's it! That's the stupidest thing I've ever done."

"What about *after* you ran over me? Tell them about that," he laughs.

"We fell in love. The end." She's obviously embarrassed by the aftermath of the swipe.

"You have to tell us now," I say.

"Fine. It was the second day after I got my license. Joel let me drive his car to school so I was being supercareful. I was focused. When Joel was teaching me to drive, he paid careful attention to how I parked. He hates people who double-park. In fact, I knew he was going to have someone drive him through the parking lot just to double-check my parking job, so I really wanted to be perfect. So that's what I was focused on. I didn't like how I parked the first time—"

"Or the second, third, or fourth time," Gavin says.

Eddie smirks at him. "So on the *fifth* time, I was determined to get it right. I backed out extra far to get a better angle, and that's when it happened. The thud. I turned around and didn't see anyone, so I panicked, thinking I had hit the car next to me or something. I continued to back out of the spot and threw the car in drive and was looking for a better spot so that I could inspect the car for damage. I pulled over in the next lot and got out. That's when I saw him."

"You . . . *dragged* him?" I ask. I'm trying to hold back the laughter.

"Over two hundred yards. After I hit him the first time, I kept backing up, and his pant leg got hung up in the bumper. I broke his leg. Joel was so worried they were going to sue, he made me take food to him at the hospital every day for a week. That's when we fell in love."

"You're lucky you didn't kill him," Nick says. "You'd be locked up on a hit-and-run charge *and* involuntary manslaughter. Poor Gavin would be ten feet under."

"*Six* feet under!" I laugh.

"I'd love to hear your stupid story, Layken, but it's gonna have to wait. We're gonna be late," Eddie says as she scoots out of the booth.

ON OUR DRIVE to the slam, Eddie pulls a folded up sheet of paper out of her back pocket.

"What's that?" I ask her.

"It's my poem. I'm going to slam tonight."

"Seriously? God, you're brave."

"I'm not, really. The first time Gavin and I went, I promised myself I would do one before I turned eighteen. My birthday is next week. When Mr. Cooper told us we could skip the final if we performed, I took it as a sign."

"I would just say I did one. Mr. Cooper won't know. I doubt he'll be there," Nick says.

"No," Gavin says. "He'll be there. He's always there."

The empty feeling in my stomach returns, despite its being full from supper. I slide my hands across my pants and fix my eyes on a star outside the window. I'll wait to join back in the conversation until the subject changes.

"Man, Vaughn really did a number on him," Nick says.

I cock my head in Nick's direction. Eddie sees the interest perk in me, and she folds up her paper and puts it back in her pocket.

"His ex," she says. "They dated their last two years of

high school. They were *the* couple. Homecoming queen, football star . . ."

"Football? He played football?" I'm shocked. This doesn't sound like Will.

"Oh yeah, star quarterback three years running," Nick says. "We were freshmen when he was a senior. He was a nice guy, I guess."

"Can't say the same about Vaughn," Gavin says.

"Why? Was she a bitch?" I ask.

"Honestly, she wasn't that bad in high school. It's what she did to him after they graduated. After his parents . . ." Eddie's voice trails off.

"What'd she do?" I sound too interested, I know.

"She dumped him. Two weeks after his parents were killed in a car wreck. He had a football scholarship but lost it when he had to move back home to take care of his little brother. Vaughn told everyone she wasn't marrying a college dropout with a kid. So that's it. He lost his parents, his girlfriend, and his scholarship *and* became a guardian all in the same two-week time frame."

I return my gaze out the window. I don't want Eddie to see the tears welling up in my eyes. This explains so much. It explains why he's scared to take everything away from me, like it was taken from him. I fade out of the conversation as we drive toward Detroit.

"Here," Eddie whispers, laying something in my lap. A tissue. I squeeze her hand to thank her, then wipe the tears from my eyes.

9.

A slight figure of speech
I cut my chest wide open
They come and watch us bleed
Is it art like I was hoping now?

—THE AVETT BROTHERS,

"SLIGHT FIGURE OF SPEECH"

WHEN WE ENTER THE BUILDING, I IMMEDIATELY SEARCH for Will. Nick and Gavin lead us to a table on the floor, so much more exposed than the booth Will and I sat in. The sac has already performed and they are well into round one. Eddie goes to the judges' table and pays her money and comes back.

"Layken, come to the bathroom with me," she says as she pulls me out of my chair.

When we get in the bathroom, she backs me up to

the sink and stands in front of me with her hands on my shoulders.

"Snap out of it, girl! We're here to have fun." She reaches into her purse and pulls out her makeup bag. She wets her thumbs under the faucet and wipes mascara from underneath my eyes. She meticulously applies my makeup, extremely focused on the task. No one's ever done my makeup before besides me. She pulls a brush out of her purse and pushes me forward, brushing my hair upside down over my head. I feel like a rag doll. She pulls me back up and does some fancy handiwork as her fingers twist and pull at my hair. She steps back and smiles as though she's admiring her accomplishment.

"There."

She turns me to the mirror and my jaw drops to the floor. I can't believe it. I look . . . *pretty*. My bangs are pulled into a French braid that hangs loose down my shoulder. The soft amber hue of eye shadow brings out my eyes. My lips are defined but not too colorful. I look just like my mother.

"Wow. You have a gift, Eddie."

"I know. Twenty-nine brothers and sisters in nine years, you're bound to learn a few tricks."

She pulls me out of the bathroom, and we head back. As we approach our seats, I stop. Eddie stops, too, since she has hold of my hand and is suddenly being jerked back. She follows my gaze to our table and sees Javi . . . and Will.

"Looks like we have company," she says. She winks at

me and pulls me forward, but I pull her hand back. My feet are weighted to the floor beneath me.

"Eddie, it's not like that. I don't want you thinking it's like that."

She faces me and takes my hands in hers. "I don't think *anything*, Layken. But if it really *is* like that, it would explain the obvious tension between you two," she says.

"It's only obvious to you."

"And that's how it shall remain," she says, pulling me forward.

When we reach the table, all eight eyes are focused on me. I want to run.

"Damn, girl, you look good," Javi says.

Gavin glares at Javi and then smiles back at me. "Eddie got hold of you, did she?" He wraps his arm around Eddie's waist and pulls her to him, leaving me to fend for myself. Nick pulls a chair out for me and I take it. I glance up at Will, and he gives me a half smile. I know what it means. He thinks I look pretty.

"All right, we've got four more performers for round one. Next one goes by the name of Eddie. Where is he?"

Eddie rolls her eyes and stands. "I'm a *she*!"

"Oh, my bad. There she is. Come on up, Ms. Eddie."

Eddie gives Gavin a quick peck on the lips and bounces to the stage, her confidence pouring from her smile. Everyone but Will takes a seat. Javi takes the seat to my left, and the only available seat at the table is to my right. Will hesitates before he takes a step and finally sits.

"What are you performing Eddie?" the emcee asks her.

She leans into the microphone and says, "'Pink Balloon.'"

As soon as the emcee is off the stage, Eddie loses her smile and goes into her zone.

My name is Olivia King

I am five years old.

My mother bought me a *balloon*. I remember the day she walked through the front door with it. The curly hot-pink ribbon *trickling* down her arm, *wrapped* around her *wrist*. She was *smiling* at me as she *untied* the ribbon and wrapped it around my hand.

"Here, Livie, I bought this for you."

She called me *Livie*.

I was so *happy*. I'd *never* had a *balloon* before. I mean, I always saw balloons wrapped around *other* kids' wrists in the parking lot of *Walmart*, but I never *dreamed* I would have my very *own*.

My *very own* pink balloon.

I was so *excited*! So *ecstatic*! So *thrilled*! I couldn't *believe* my mother bought me something! She'd *never* bought me *anything* before! I played with it for *hours*. It was full of *helium*, and it *danced* and *swayed* and *floated* as I *pulled* it around from *room* to *room* with me, thinking of places to take it. Thinking of places the balloon had *never* been before. I took it into the *bathroom*, the *closet*, the *laundry room*, the *kitchen*, the *living room*. I wanted my new best friend to see *everything* I saw! I took it to my mother's *bedroom*!

My mother's

Bedroom?

Where I wasn't supposed to *be?*

With my pink

balloon . . .

I *covered* my *ears* as she *screamed* at me, *wiping* the *evidence* off of her *nose*. She *slapped* me across the face and reminded me of how *bad* I was! How much I *misbehaved*! How I never *listened*! She *shoved* me into the hallway and *slammed* the door, locking my pink balloon inside with her. I wanted him *back*! He was *my* best friend! *Not hers*! The pink ribbon was *still* tied around my *wrist* so I *pulled* and *pulled*, trying to get my new best friend *away* from her.

And

it

popped.

My name is Eddie.

I'm seventeen years old.

My *birthday* is next week. I'll be the big *One-Eight*. My foster dad is buying me these boots I've been wanting.

I'm sure my friends will take me out to eat. My boyfriend will buy me a *gift*, maybe even take me to a *movie*. I'll even get a nice little card from my foster-care worker, wishing me a happy eighteenth birthday, informing me I've aged out of the *system*.

I'll have a good time. I know I will.

But there's *one* thing I know

for *sure*.

I better not get any

shitty-ass pink balloons!

When the crowd cheers for her, Eddie eats it up. She's bouncing up and down on the stage and clapping along with the crowd, forgetting all about the somber poem she just performed. She's a natural. We give her a standing ovation when she comes back to the table.

"That felt so awesome," she squeals. Gavin throws his arms around her and picks her up off the ground and kisses her cheek.

"That's my girl," he says as they sit back down in their seats.

"That was great, Eddie—guess you're exempt," Will says.

"That was so easy! Layken, you really need to do one next week. You've never had one of Mr. Cooper's finals before. They aren't fun, believe me."

"I'll think about it," I say. She did make it look easy.

Will laughs and leans forward. "Eddie, you haven't had one of my finals *either*. I've only been teaching two months."

"Well, I'm sure they suck," she laughs.

They call another performer to the stage and the table grows quiet. Javi's leg keeps brushing against mine.

Something about him gives me the creeps. Maybe it's the obvious creep factor. Throughout the performance, I keep drawing myself in more and more until I have nowhere else to go, but he somehow keeps getting closer. Just when I'm on the verge of punching him, Will moves in and whispers in my ear.

"Trade me seats."

I hop up, and he slides over as I take his seat. I silently thank him with a look. Javi straightens back up and glares at Will. It's obvious there is no love lost between the two of them.

By the start of the second round, everyone at our table is dispersing among the crowd. I spot Nick at the bar chatting up a girl. Javi eventually sulks off, leaving just Will and me at the table with Gavin and Eddie.

"Mr. Cooper, did you see—"

"Gavin," Will interrupts. "You don't have to call me Mr. Cooper here. We went to high school together."

A mischievous grin crosses Gavin's face. He nudges Eddie, and they both smile at Will. "Can we call you—"

"No! You can't!" Will interrupts again. He's blushing.

"I'm missing something here," I say, looking from Will to Gavin.

Gavin leans forward in his chair and puts his elbows on his knees. "You see, Layken, about three years ago—"

"Gavin, I'll fail you. I'll fail your little girlfriend, too," Will says.

Everyone's laughing now, but I'm still lost.

"Three years ago, Duckie here decided to start a prank war with the freshmen."

"Duckie?" I say. I look at Will and his face is buried in his hands.

"It became apparent that Will—I mean Duckie—was the one behind all the pranks. We suffered at the hands of this man." Gavin laughs as he gestures toward Will.

"So, we decided we'd had enough. We came up with a little plan of our own, now known as Revenge on Duckie."

"Dammit, Gavin. I knew it was you! I *knew* it," Will says.

Gavin laughs. "Will was known for his daily naps in his car. Particularly during Mr. Hanson's History class. So, we followed him to the parking lot one day and waited until he was off in la-la land. We got about twenty-five rolls of duct tape and wrapped him inside the car. There had to be six layers of duct tape around his car already before he finally woke up. We could hear him screaming and kicking at the door all the way back to the school."

"Oh my god. How long were you in there?" I ask Will. I don't even hesitate when I speak to him. I like that we're interacting again, even if it is just as friends. This is good.

He cocks an eyebrow at me when he responds. "Now that's the kicker. Mr. Hanson's History class was second period. I wasn't cut out of the car until my dad called the school trying to find me. I don't remember what time it was, but it was dark."

"You were in there almost twelve hours?"

He nods.

"How'd you use the bathroom?" Eddie asks.

"I'll never tell," he laughs.

We can do this. I watch Will as he interacts with Eddie and Gavin; they're all laughing. I didn't think it would be possible before—a friendship between us. But here, right now, I do.

Nick walks back up to the table with a sour look on his face. "I don't feel so hot. Can we go?"

"How much did you eat, Nick?" Gavin says, standing.

Eddie looks at me and tilts her head to the front door, insinuating it's time to go. "See you tomorrow, Mr. Cooper," she says.

"Are you sure about that, Eddie?" Will asks her. "You and your friend here aren't taking another courtyard nap tomorrow?"

Eddie looks back at me and clasps her hand to her mouth, exaggerating a gasp. Will and I stand up as they all file out.

"Just leave Kel at my house tonight," he says after everyone is out of earshot. "I'll get him to school tomorrow. They're probably asleep by now anyway."

"You sure?"

"Yeah, it's fine."

"Okay, thanks."

We both stand there, not certain how to part. He steps out of my way. "See ya tomorrow," he says. I smile and shuffle my way past him, then catch up to Eddie.

"PLEASE, MOM? PLEASE?" Kel says.

"Kel, y'all spent the night with each other *last* night. I'm sure his brother wants some time with him."

"No, he doesn't," Caulder says.

"See? We'll stay in our room. I swear," Kel says.

"Fine. But Caulder, I'll need you to be at your house tomorrow night. I'm taking Lake and Kel to dinner."

"Yes, ma'am. I'll go tell my brother and get my clothes."

Kel and Caulder run out the front door. I squirm in my seat on the couch as I unzip my boots. This dinner she's referring to must be it; the big *introduction*. I decide to press her a little further.

"Where are we going to dinner?" I ask.

She comes to the couch and sits, grabbing the remote to flip on the TV.

"Wherever. Maybe we'll just eat here. I don't know. I just want some alone time, just the three of us."

I pull my boots off and snatch them up. "The three of us," I mumble as I walk to my room. I think about that as I throw my boots in my closet and lie on the bed. It used to be "the four of us." Then it became "the three of us." Now, in less than seven months, she's making it "the four of us" again.

Whoever he is, he will never be included in a count with Kel and me. She doesn't know I know about him. She doesn't even know I've already labeled him and her as "the two of them," and Kel and me as "the two of us." Divide and conquer. That's my new family motto.

We've been living in Ypsilanti for a month now, and I've spent every single Friday night in my room. I grab my phone and text Eddie, hoping she and Gavin won't mind a third wheel tonight on their movie date. She texts me back in a matter of seconds, giving me thirty minutes to get ready. It isn't enough time to thoroughly enjoy a shower, so I go to the bathroom and touch up my makeup. The mail is in a pile on the bathroom counter next to the sink, so I pick it up and look at it. All three envelopes have a big red post office stamp across them. Forward to New Address is stamped over our old Texas address.

Eight more months. Eight more months and I'm moving back home. I contemplate hanging a calendar on my wall so I can start marking down the days. I toss the envelopes back on the counter, when the contents of one of them fall to the floor. When I pick it up, I notice the numbers printed in the top right-hand corner.

$178,343.00.

It's a bank statement. It's an account balance. I snatch up the rest of the mail and run to my room and shut the door.

I look at the dates on the bank statement and then sort through the other envelopes. One of them is from a mortgage company so I tear it open. It's an insurance invoice. An invoice for our house back in Texas that I was told we sold. Oh my god, I want to *kill* her. We aren't broke! We didn't even sell our house! She tore my brother and me from the only home we've ever known for some guy? I hate her. I have to get out of this house before I explode. I grab my phone and throw the envelopes in my purse.

"I'm going out," I say when I walk through the living room toward the front door.

"With who?" she asks.

"Eddie. Going to a movie." I keep my replies short and sweet so she won't hear the fury behind my voice. My whole body is shaking I'm so angry. I just want to get out of the house and process things before I confront her.

She walks over to me and grabs my cell phone out of my hand and starts pressing buttons.

"What the hell are you doing?" I yell as I grab it back out of her grasp.

"I know what you're up to, Lake! Don't pretend with me."

"What am I up to? I'd really like to know!"

"Last night you and Will were *both* gone. He conveniently had a babysitter. Tonight, his brother says he's spending the night, and half an hour later you're *going out?* You aren't going anywhere!"

I throw my phone in my purse and wrap my purse across my shoulder as I head to the front door.

"As a matter of fact, I am going out. With *Eddie*. You can watch me leave with *Eddie*. You can watch me *return* with Eddie." I walk out the front door and she follows me. Luckily, Eddie is pulling up in the driveway.

"Lake? Get back here! We need to talk," she yells from the doorway.

I open the door to Eddie's car and I turn to face her. "You're right, Mom, but I think you're the one that needs to do the talking. I know why we're having dinner tomorrow! I know why we moved to Michigan! I know about everything! So don't you dare talk to *me* about hiding stuff!"

I don't wait for her to respond as I get in the backseat and slam the door.

"Get me out of here. Hurry," I say to Eddie.

I start crying as we drive away. I never want to go back.

"HERE, DRINK THIS." Eddie shoves another soda across the table as she and Gavin watch me drink—and cry. We stopped at Getty's because Eddie said their pizza was the only thing that could help me right now. I couldn't eat.

"I'm sorry I ruined your date," I say to both of them.

"You didn't ruin it. Did she, babe?" Eddie says as she turns to Gavin.

"Not at all. It's a nice change of routine," he says, shoving his pizza into a takeout box.

My phone is vibrating again. It's the sixth time my mother has called, so I hold down the power button and throw it back into my purse.

"Can we still make it to the movie?" I ask.

Gavin looks at his watch and nods. "Sure, if you really feel like going."

"I do. I need to stop thinking about this for a little while."

We pay our bill and head to the theater. It's not Johnny Depp, but any actor will do right now.

10.

She puts her hands against
the life she had.
Living with ignorance,
Blissful and sad.
But nobody knows what lies behind
The days before the day we die.

—THE AVETT BROTHERS, "DIE DIE DIE"

WE PULL UP TO MY HOUSE A FEW HOURS LATER. I DON'T immediately get out of the car as I take a few deep breaths, preparing for the fight that's about to go down.

"Layken, call me later. I wanna know everything. Good luck," Eddie says.

"Thanks, I will." I get out of the car and walk up to the door as they drive away. When I enter, my mother is lying on the couch. She hears the door close and jumps up.

I expect her to continue yelling, but she runs to me and throws her arms around my neck. I stand stiff.

"Lake, I'm so sorry, I should have told you. I'm so sorry." She's crying.

I back away from her and go sit on the couch. There are tissues all over both end tables. She's been crying a lot. Good, she should feel bad. *Awful*, even.

"Dad and I were going to tell you before he—"

"Dad? You were seeing him before Dad even *died*?" I stand up and pace the floor. "Mom! How long has this been going on?" I'm yelling now. And crying again.

I look at her, waiting for her to defend her repulsive behavior, but she's just staring at the table in front of her.

She leans forward and cocks her head at me. "Seeing *who*? What do you think's going on?"

"I don't *know* who! Whoever wrote you that poem in your nightstand! Whoever you've been going to see every time you run errands. Whoever you've been saying 'I love you' to on the phone. I don't know *who* and I really don't care *who*."

She stands up and places her hands on my shoulders. "Lake, I'm not seeing *anyone*. You've misunderstood everything. All of it."

I can tell she's being honest, but I still don't have any answers.

"What about the note? And the bank statements? We aren't broke, Mom. And you never even sold the house!

You lied to us to drag us up here. If it wasn't for some guy, then why? Why are we here?"

She removes her hands from my shoulders and looks down at the floor, shaking her head. "Oh god, Lake. I thought you knew. I thought you figured it out." She takes a seat on the couch again and looks down at her hands.

"Apparently not," I say. This is so frustrating. I don't understand what could possibly be so important about Michigan that she would drag us away from our entire lives. "So tell me."

She looks up at me and places her hand on the couch cushion beside her. "Sit down. Please, sit down."

I sit back down on the couch and wait for her to explain everything. She pauses for a long time as she gathers her thoughts.

"The note, it's just something your dad wrote. He was being silly. He drew on my face one night and left the note on my pillow. I kept it. I loved your dad, Lake. I miss him *so* much. I would never do anything like that to him. There's no one else."

She's being sincere.

"Then why did we move here, Mom? Why did you make us move here?"

She takes a deep breath and turns to face me, placing her hands on top of mine. The look in her eyes makes my heart sink. It's the same look she had in the hallway earlier this year when she came to tell me the news about my dad. She takes another deep breath and squeezes my hands.

"Lake, I have cancer."

DENIAL. I'M DEFINITELY in denial. And anger. Bargaining? Yes, that too. I'm in all three. All five, maybe. I can't breathe.

"Your father and I were going to tell you. After he died, y'all were so devastated. I couldn't bring myself to talk to you about it. When I started getting worse, I wanted to move back here. Brenda begged me to, said she'd help take care of me. She's the one I've been talking to on the phone. There's a doctor in Detroit that specializes in lung cancer. That's where I've been going."

Lung cancer. It has a name. That makes it even more real.

"I was planning to tell you and Kel tomorrow. It's time you guys know, so we can all prepare."

I pull my hands away from her. "Prepare . . . for *what*, Mom?"

She wraps her arms around me and starts crying again. I push her back.

"Prepare for *what*, Mom?"

Just like plump Principal Bass, she can't look me in the eyes. She feels *sorry* for me.

I don't remember walking out of the house, and I don't remember going across the street. The only thing I know is that it's midnight and I'm beating on Will's door.

When he opens it, he doesn't ask any questions. He can see on my face that I just need him to be Will. Just for a little while. He puts his arm around my shoulders and ushers me inside as he shuts the door behind him.

"Lake, what's wrong?"

I can't respond. I can't breathe. He wraps his arms around me just as I start to collapse to the floor and cry. And just like in the school hallway with my mother, he melts to the floor with me. He puts my head under his chin and rubs my hair and just lets me cry.

"Tell me what happened," he finally whispers.

I don't want to say it. If I say it out loud, that means it's real. It *is* real.

"She's dying, Will," I say between sobs. "She has cancer."

He squeezes me tighter, then picks me up and carries me to his bedroom. He lays me on the bed and pulls the covers over me when the doorbell rings. He kisses me on the forehead, then leaves the room.

I can hear her speak when he answers the door, but I can't hear what she says. Will's voice is low, but I'm able to make out what he says.

"Let her stay, Julia. She needs me right now."

A few more things are spoken that I can't make out. I hear him eventually shut the door, and he comes back to the bedroom. He crawls into the bed, puts his arms around me, and holds me while I cry.

part
two

11.

Who cares about tomorrow?

What more is tomorrow,

Than another Day?

—THE AVETT BROTHERS, "SWEPT AWAY"

THE WINDOW IS ON THE WRONG SIDE OF THE ROOM. WHAT time is it? I throw my arm across the bed and reach for the phone on my nightstand. My phone's not there. Neither is the nightstand. I sit up in the bed and rub my eyes. This isn't my room. When it all comes flooding back to me, I lie back down and pull the blanket over my head, wishing it all away.

"LAKE."

I wake up again. The sun isn't as bright, but it's still not my room. I pull the covers tighter over my head.

"Lake, wake up."

Someone is pulling the covers back off my head. I groan and grip them even tighter. I try to wish it all away again, but my bladder is screaming at me. I throw the covers off and see Will sitting on the edge of the bed.

"You really *aren't* a morning person," he says.

"Bathroom. Where's your bathroom?"

He points across the hall. I jump out of the bed and hope I can make it. I run to the toilet and sit, but nearly fall in. The seat's up.

"Boys," I mutter as I let the seat down.

When I emerge from the bathroom, Will is at the bar in the kitchen. He smiles and scoots a cup of coffee to the empty seat next to him. I take the seat and the coffee.

"What time is it?" I say.

"One thirty."

"Oh. Well, your bed's really comfortable."

He smiles and nudges my shoulder. "Apparently," he says.

We drink our coffee in silence. *Comfortable* silence.

Will takes my empty cup to the sink and rinses it out before putting it in the dishwasher. "I'm taking Kel and Caulder to a matinee," he says. He turns on the dishwasher and wipes his hands on a rag. "We're leaving in a few minutes. I'll probably take them to dinner afterward, so we'll be back around six. Should give you and your mom time to talk."

I don't like how he throws that last sentence in there,

like I'm susceptible to his manipulation. "What if I don't want to talk? What if I want to go to a matinee?"

He lays his elbows on the bar and leans toward me. "You don't need to watch a movie. You need to talk to your mom. Let's go." He grabs his keys and jacket and starts walking toward the door.

I lean back in my chair and fold my arms across my chest. "I just woke up. The caffeine hasn't even kicked in yet. Can I stay here for a while?"

I'm lying. I just want him to leave so I can crawl back into his comfortable bed.

"Fine." He walks toward me and kisses me on top of my head. "But not all day. You need to talk to her."

He puts his jacket on and walks out, shutting the door behind him. I walk to the window and watch as Kel and Caulder climb into the car, and they all drive away. I look across the street at my house. My house that's not a home. I know my mom is inside, just yards away. I have no idea what I would begin to say to her if I walked over there right now. I decide not to go right away. I don't like that I'm so mad at her. I know this isn't her fault, but I don't know whom else to blame.

My gaze falls on the gnome with the broken red hat, perched upright in the driveway. He's staring right at me, grinning. It's like he knows. He knows I'm over here, too scared to go over there. He's taunting me. Just as I'm about to shut the curtain and let him win, Eddie pulls up in our driveway.

I open the front door to Will's house and wave when she gets out of her car. "Eddie, I'm over here!" She looks at me, back toward my house, then back at me with a confused look on her face before she crosses the street.

Great. Why did I just do that? How am I going to explain this?

I step aside and hold the door open for her when she enters, eyeing the living room curiously. "Are you okay? I've called you a hundred times!" she says. She plops down on the sofa and puts her foot on the coffee table and starts removing her boots. "Whose house is this?"

I don't have to answer her. The family portrait hanging on the wall in front of her answers for me.

"Oh," she says. That's *all* she says about it, though. "Well? What happened? Did she tell you who he is? Do you know him?"

I walk to the couch, step over her legs and take the seat next to her. "Eddie? Are you ready to hear my version of the stupidest thing I've ever done?"

She raises her eyebrows and waits for me to spill it.

"I was wrong. She's not seeing anyone, she's sick. She has cancer."

Eddie places her boots beside her and brings her feet back up to the coffee table as she leans back against the couch. Her socks are mismatched.

"Man, that's unreal," she says.

"Yeah, it is. But it's my real."

She sits there for a moment, picking at her black fingernails. I can tell she doesn't really know what to say. Instead of saying anything, she just leans across the couch and hugs me right before she bounces up.

"So, what's Mr. Cooper got to drink around here?" She walks to the kitchen and opens the refrigerator and removes a soda. She grabs two glasses and fills them with ice and brings them back to the living room, where she fills them with the soda.

"Couldn't find any wine. He's such a bore," she says. She hands me my drink and pulls her legs up onto the couch. "So, what's her prognosis?"

I shrug. "I don't know. It doesn't sound good, though. I left right after she told me last night. I haven't been able to face her." I turn my head toward the window and look at our house again. I know it's inevitable. I know I'll have to face her; I just want one more day of normalcy.

"Layken, you need to go talk to her."

I roll my eyes. "God, you sound just like Will."

She takes a sip of her drink and returns it to the coffee table. "Speaking of *Will*."

Here we go.

"Layken, I'm trying so hard to mind my business. I really am. But you're in his house! You're wearing the same clothes I dropped you off in last night. If you don't at least *deny* there's something going on, then I'll have to assume you're *admitting* it."

I sigh. She's right. From her standpoint, it seems like more is going on than there really is. I don't have a choice but to be honest with her, or she'll assume the worst of him.

"Fine. But Eddie, you have to—"

"I swear. Not even to Gavin."

"Okay. Well, I met him the first day we moved here. There was something there, between both of us. He asked me out, we went out. We had a great time. We kissed. It was probably the best night of my life. It *was* the best night of my life."

She's smiling now. I hesitate before I continue. She can tell by my body language that it's not a happy ending, and her smile fades.

"We didn't know. Until my first day of school, I didn't know he was a teacher. He didn't know I was in high school."

She stands up. "The hallway! That's what was going on in the hallway!"

I nod.

"Oh my god. So he ended it?"

I nod again. She falls back onto the couch.

"Shit. That sucks."

I nod again.

"But you're here. You spent the night," she grins. "He couldn't hold back, could he?"

I shake my head. "It's not like that. I was upset so he let me stay here. Nothing happened. He's just being a friend."

She slumps her shoulders and pouts, making it obvious she was hoping we caved.

"Just one more question. Your poem. It was about him, wasn't it?"

I nod.

"Nice," she laughs. She's quiet again, but not for long. "Last question. I swear. For real."

I look at her, letting her know it's okay to continue.

"Is he a good kisser?"

I smile. I can't help but smile. "Oh my god, he's so freakin' hot!"

"I know!" She claps her hands and bounces on the couch.

Our laughter fades as the reality of the moment returns. I turn and look out the window again and gaze at our house across the street while she takes our glasses to the sink. When she walks back through the living room, she grabs my hand and pulls me off the couch.

"Come on, we're going to talk to your mom."

We? I don't object. There's something about Eddie that you just don't object to.

12.

With paranoia on my heels
Will you love me still
When we awake and you see that
The sanity has gone from my eyes?

—THE AVETT BROTHERS,

"PARANOIA IN B-FLAT MAJOR"

EDDIE HAS NEVER BEEN INSIDE MY HOUSE BEFORE. YOU wouldn't know that by watching her bounce through the front door. She's still pulling me along behind her when we walk inside. My mother is sitting on the sofa, watching this stranger scamper toward her with a smile on her face, dragging her angry daughter behind her. I have to admit, the surprise on my mom's face is gratifying.

Eddie pulls me to the couch and pushes my shoulders down until I'm seated next to my mother. Eddie proceeds to take a seat on the coffee table directly in front of us, posture straight, head held high. She is in charge.

"I'm Eddie, your daughter's best friend," she says to my mother. "There. Now that we all know each other, let's get down to the nitty-gritty."

My mother looks at me, then back at Eddie, and doesn't respond. I actually have nothing to say either. I don't know where Eddie is taking this, so all I can do is allow her to continue.

"Julia, right? That's your name?"

My mother nods.

"Julia, Layken has questions. Lots of questions. You have answers." Eddie looks at me. "Layken, you ask questions, and your mother will answer them." She looks at both of us simultaneously. "That's how you do it. Any questions? For me, I mean?"

My mother and I both shake our heads. Eddie stands up. "All right, then. My work here is done. Call me later."

Eddie steps over the coffee table and heads for the front door, but spins on her feet and comes back to us. She wraps her arms around my mother's neck. My mother looks at me wide-eyed before she returns the hug. Eddie continues to squeeze my mother's neck for an unusually long time before she finally lets go. She smiles at us, hops over the coffee table, and walks out the front door. And she's gone. Just like that.

We both sit in silence, staring at the front door. I'm

confused as to where exactly things went wrong with Eddie. Or where exactly they went *right*. It's hard to tell. I glance back at my mother and we both laugh.

"Wow, Lake. You sure know how to pick 'em."

"I know. She's great, huh?"

We both settle into the couch, and my mother reaches over and pats the top of my hand. "We better do what she says. Ask me a question; I'll answer it best I can."

I cut right to the chase. "Are you dying?"

"Aren't we all?" she replies.

"That's a *question*. You're supposed to just *answer*."

She sighs like she's hesitating, not really wanting to answer.

"Possibly. Probably," she admits.

"How long? How bad is it?"

"Lake, maybe I should explain it first. It'll give you a better idea of what we're dealing with." She stands and moves to the kitchen and takes a seat at the bar. She motions for me to sit with her as she grabs a pen and a sheet of paper and starts to write something down. "There are two types of lung cancer. Non–small cell and small cell. Unfortunately, I have small cell, which spreads faster."

She's drawing a diagram. "Small cell can either be limited or extensive." She points to an area on a sketched pair of lungs. "Mine was limited. Which means it was contained into this area." She circles an area of the lungs and makes a pinpoint. "This is where they found a tumor.

I was having some symptoms a few months before your father died. He had me go in for a biopsy, and that's when we found out it was malignant. We researched doctors for a few days and finally decided our best course of action would be a doctor we found here in Michigan—in Detroit. He specializes in SCLC. We decided on the move before your father even died. We—"

"Mom, slow down."

She lays down the pen.

"I need a minute," I say. "God, it feels like I'm in science class." I rest my head in my hands. She's had months to think about this. She talks about it like she's teaching me how to bake a cake!

She patiently waits as I get up and go to the bathroom. I splash water on my face and stare at my reflection in the mirror. I look like complete crap. I haven't even glanced in a mirror since before I went out with Gavin and Eddie last night. My mascara is smudged under my eyes. My eyes are puffy. My hair is wild. I wipe the makeup off and brush out my hair before I go back to the kitchen and listen to her tell me how she's going to die.

She looks up at me when I walk back into the kitchen, and I nod, giving her the go-ahead. I take a seat across from her.

"A week after we decided we were moving to Michigan to be closer to the doctor, your father died. I was so consumed with it, with his death and the arrangements and everything. I just tried to push what was going on with me out of my mind. I didn't go back to the doctor for three months." Her voice grows softer. "By that time, it had spread. It was no longer limited small cell; it was extensive."

She looks away, wiping a tear from her eye. "I blamed myself—for your dad's heart attack. I knew it was the stress of the diagnosis that caused it." She stands and walks back into the living room. She leans against the window frame and stares outside.

"Why didn't you tell me? I could have helped you, Mom. You didn't need to deal with all of it on your own."

She rolls her back against the wall and faces me. "I know that now. I was in denial. I was angry. I was hoping for a miracle, I guess. I don't know. The days turned into weeks, then months. Now we're here. I started chemotherapy again three weeks ago."

I scoot my chair back and stand up. "That's good, right? If they're giving you chemo then there's a chance it'll go away."

She shakes her head. "It's not to fight it, Lake. It's to manage my pain. It's all they can do now."

Her words cause me to lose whatever strength I had left in my legs. I fall onto the couch and drop my head in my hands and cry. It's amazing how many tears one person can have. One night after my father died, I had cried so much I started to become paranoid I was doing damage to my eyes, so I googled it. I googled "Can a person cry too much?" Apparently, everyone eventually falls asleep and stops crying in order for their bodies to process normal periods of rest. So no, you can't cry too much.

I grab a tissue and take a few deep breaths in an attempt to hold back the rest of my tears. I'm really sick of crying.

My mother sits next to me and I feel her arms encircle me, so I turn into her and hug her. My heart aches for her. For *us.* I tighten my grip on her, afraid to let her go. I can't let her go.

She eventually starts coughing and has to turn away. I watch her as she stands and continues to cough, gasping for breath. She's so sick. How did I not notice? Her cheeks are even hollower than before. Her hair is thinner. I hardly recognize her. I've been so focused on my own misery that I haven't even noticed my own mother being swept away right before my eyes.

The coughing spell passes and my mother returns to her seat at the bar. "We'll tell Kel tonight. Brenda will be here at seven. She wants to be here, since she'll be his guardian."

I laugh. Because she's joking. *Right?* "What do you mean his *guardian?*"

She looks me in the eyes like *I'm* the one being unreasonable. "Lake. You're still in high school; soon you'll be in college. I don't expect you to give everything up. I don't *want* you to. Brenda has raised children before. She *wants* to do it. Kel likes her."

Of all the things I have been through this year.

This moment, these words that have just come out of her mouth—I have never been more enraged.

I stand up and grip the back of the chair and throw it to the floor with such force that the seat comes loose from the base. She flinches as I sprint toward her, pointing my finger into her chest.

"She is *not* getting Kel! You are not giving her *my* brother!" I scream so loud my throat burns.

She attempts to subdue me by putting her hands on my shoulders, but I spin away from her. "Lake, stop it! Stop this! You're still in high school! You haven't even started college yet. What do you expect me to do? We've got no one else." She walks after me as I head for the front door. "I've got no one else, Lake," she cries.

I open the door and swing around to her, ignoring her tears as I continue to scream. "You aren't telling him tonight! He doesn't need to know yet. You better not tell him!"

"We have to tell him. He needs to know," she says.

She's following me down the driveway now. I keep walking. "Go home, Mother! Just go home! I'm done talking about it! And if you ever want to see me again, you will *not* tell him!"

Her sobs fade as I slam the door to Will's house behind me. I run to his bedroom and throw myself on the bed. I don't just cry; I sob, I wail, I scream.

* * *

I've never used drugs before. If you don't count the sip of my mother's wine when I was fourteen, I've never even willingly had alcohol. It's not that I was too afraid, or too straitlaced. Honestly, I'd just never been offered anything. I never went to parties in Texas. I never spent the night with anyone who ever tried to coerce me into doing something illegal. I have frankly just never been in a situation where I could succumb to peer pressure. I spent my Friday nights at football games. Saturday nights, my dad usually took us out to a movie and to dinner. Sunday, I did homework. That was my life.

There was one exception, when Kerris's cousin had a wedding, and she invited me to go. I was sixteen, she had just gotten her license, and the reception had just ended. We stayed late to help clean up. We were having the best time. We drank punch, ate leftover cake, danced, drank more punch. We realized that someone had laced the punch when we both noticed how much fun we were having. I don't know how much of it we drank. So much that we were already too drunk to stop when we noticed we were drunk. We never even thought twice when we got into the car to go home. We got a mile down the road before she swerved and hit a tree. I got a laceration above my eye, and she broke her arm. We both ended up being okay. In fact, the car was still drivable. Rather than do the smart thing and wait for help, we turned the car around and drove back to the reception to call my dad. The trouble we got into the next day is a different story.

But there was a moment, right before she hit the tree. We were laughing at the way she said "bubble." We just kept saying it over and over until the car started to glide off the road. I saw the tree, and I knew we were about to hit it. But it was as if time slowed down. The tree could have been five million feet away. That's how long it took for the car to hit the tree. The only thing I thought about in that moment was Kel. The *only* thing. I didn't think about school, the boys, the college I would miss out on if I died. I thought about Kel, and how he was the only thing that was important to me. The only thing that mattered in the seconds when I thought I was about to die.

I SOMEHOW FELL asleep in Will's bed again. I know this because when I open my eyes, I'm no longer crying. See? People can't cry forever. Everyone eventually falls asleep.

I expect the tears to return once the fog clears from my mind, but instead I feel motivated, renewed. Like I'm on some sort of mission. I get out of bed and have an odd urge to clean. And sing. I need music. I head to the living room and immediately find what I'm looking for. The stereo. I don't even have to search for music when I turn it on: there's already an Avett Brothers CD inside. I crank up the volume on one of my favorites and get busy.

Unfortunately, Will's house is surprisingly clean for one with two male inhabitants, so I have to search hard for something to keep me busy. I hit the bathroom first, which is good. I know nine-year-olds don't have very good aim, so I start scrubbing. I scrub the toilet, the floor, the shower, the sink. It's clean.

I move on to the bedrooms where I organize, make beds, remake beds. Next I hit the living room, where I dust and vacuum. I mop the bathroom floors and wipe down every surface I can find. I end up at the kitchen sink, where I wash the only two dirty dishes in the house: Eddie's and my glasses.

It's almost seven when I hear Will's car pull up. He and the two boys walk into the house and come to a halt when they see me sitting on his living room floor.

"What are you doing?" Caulder asks.

"Alphabetizing," I reply.

"Alphabetizing what?" Will says.

"Everything. First I did the movies, then I did the CDs. Caulder, I did the books in your room. I did a few of your games, but some of those started with numbers so I put the numbers first, then the titles." I point to the piles in front of me. "These are recipes. I found them on top of the fridge. I'm alphabetizing them by category first; like beef, lamb, pork, poultry. Then behind the categories I'm alphabetizing them by—"

"Guys, go to Kel's. Let Julia know you're back," Will says as he continues to watch me.

The boys don't move. They just stare at the recipe cards in front of me.

"Now!" Will yells. They both jerk their eyes away and start back toward the door.

"Your sister's weird," I hear Caulder say as they leave.

Will sits down on the couch in front of me and watches as I continue to alphabetize the recipes.

"You're the teacher," I say. "Should I put 'Baked Potato Soup' behind potato or soup?"

"Stop," he says. He seems moody.

"I can't stop, silly. I'm halfway finished. If I stop now you won't know where to find . . ." I grab a random card off the floor. "Jerk Chicken?" It *would* be that one. I throw the card back in the pile and continue sorting.

Will eyes the living room, then stands and walks into the kitchen. I see him run his finger along the baseboards. Good thing I thought about those. He walks down the hallway and returns a couple of minutes later.

"You color coded my closet?" He's not smiling. I thought he would be happy.

"Will, it wasn't that hard. You wear like, three different color shirts."

He glides across the living room and bends down, snatching up the recipe cards I've organized into piles.

"Will! Stop! That took me a long time!" I snatch them back out of his hands as fast as he's picking them up.

He finally throws them back on the floor and grabs my wrists and tries to pull me up, but I start kicking at his legs. "Let me go! I'm . . . not . . . done!"

He lets go of my hands and I fall back to the floor. I pick up the recipe cards and start reorganizing them back into piles. He completely took me back to square one! I can't even find the Beef card. I flip over two cards that are upside down but—

"What the hell!" I scream. I'm suddenly drenched in water.

I look up and Will is standing over me with an empty pitcher in his hand and an angry look on his face. I lunge forward and start punching at his legs. He backs away when I start hitting at him, trying to get off the floor.

Why the hell did he just do that? I'm gonna punch him in the face! I stand up and try to hit him, but he steps aside and grabs my arm and twists it behind my back. I flail my other arm at him, and he pushes me toward the hallway and into the bathroom. Before I know it, his arms are around me and he lifts me up. He pulls the shower curtain back and shoves me in. I try to punch him, but his arms are longer than mine. He holds me against the wall with one arm and turns the faucet on with the other. A stream of ice-cold water splashes across my face. I gasp.

"Jerk! Jackass! Asshole!"

He continues to hold me back as he turns the other faucet on and the water gets warmer.

"Take a shower, Layken! Take a damn shower!" He lets go of me and walks out of the bathroom, slamming the door behind him.

I jump out of the shower; my clothes are drenched.

I try to open the bathroom door, but I can't, because he's holding the doorknob from the other side.

"Let me out, Will! Now!" I beat on the door and try to turn the knob, but it doesn't budge.

"Layken," he calmly responds from the other side of the door. "I'm not letting you out of the bathroom until you take off your clothes, get in the shower, wash your hair, and calm down."

I flip him off. He can't see me of course, but it still feels good. I take off my wet clothes and throw them on the floor, hoping I get something dirty. I climb into the shower. The warm water feels good against my skin. I close my eyes and let the water trickle through my hair and down my face.

Dammit. Will is right *again*.

"I NEED A towel!" I yell. I've been in the shower well over half an hour. Will has a showerhead with a jet setting. I turned it on and focused it on the back of my neck for most of the time. It really does relieve tension.

"It's on the sink. So are your clothes," he says from outside the bathroom.

I pull the curtain back and there is definitely a towel there. And clothes. *My* clothes. Clothes he obviously just got out of my house and somehow put in the bathroom. *While* I was in the shower.

I turn the water off and step out of the shower and

dry off. I twist the towel around my head and put on my clothes. He brought me pajamas. Maybe that means I'm sleeping in his comfortable bed again. I hesitate as I turn the doorknob, assuming I still won't be able to open it, but it swings open.

When he hears me open the bathroom door, he jumps over the back of the couch and runs toward me. I back up to the wall, afraid he's about to shove me back in the bathroom, when his arms go around me, and he hugs me.

"I'm sorry, Lake. I'm sorry I did that. You were just *losing* it."

I hug him back. *Of course* I hug him back. "It's okay. I kinda sorta had a bad day," I say.

He pulls away from me and places his hands on my shoulders. "So we're friends? You aren't gonna try to punch me again?"

"Friends," I say reluctantly. That's the last thing I want to be to him right now. His *friend*.

"How was the matinee?" I ask as we walk down the hallway.

"Did you talk to your mom?" He ignores my question.

"Jeez. Deflect much?"

"Did you talk to her? Please don't tell me you spent the entire day cleaning." He walks into the kitchen and takes two glasses out of the cabinet.

"No. Not the *entire* day. We talked."

"And?"

"And . . . she has cancer," I reply frankly.

He looks at me and scowls. I roll my eyes at him and put my elbows on the table, gripping my forehead with my hands. My fingers brush against the towel that's on my head. I bend away from the bar and pull the towel off and flip my head forward, brushing the tangled strands with my fingers to smooth them out.

After I remove all the tangles, I raise my head back up just as Will darts his eyes away from me and to the cup in his hand that's now overflowing with milk. I pretend not to notice the spill and continue to mess with my hair as he wipes up the milk with a rag.

He pulls something out of the cabinet and gets a spoon out of the drawer. He's making me *chocolate* milk.

"Will she be okay?" he asks.

I sigh. He's relentless.

"No. Probably not."

"But she's getting treatment?"

I've been able to go the entire day without thinking about it. I've been comfortably numb since I woke up from my nap. I know this is his house, but I'm beginning to wish he would leave again.

"She's dying, Will. *Dying.* She'll probably be dead within the year, maybe less than that. They're just doing chemo to keep her comfortable. While she *dies.* 'Cause she'll be *dead.* Because she's *dying.* There. Is that what you wanted to hear?"

His expression softens when he sets the milk in front

of me. He grabs a handful of ice out of the refrigerator and drops it into my cup. "On the rocks," he says.

He's good at deflecting and even better at ignoring my snide remarks. "Thanks," I say. I drink my chocolate milk and shut up. It feels like he somehow just won our fight.

THE AVETT BROTHERS are still strumming away in the background when I finish my chocolate milk. I walk to the living room and put the song on repeat. I lie on the floor and stare up at the ceiling with my hands stretched out above my head. It's relaxing.

"Turn the lights off," I tell him. "I just want to listen for a while."

He turns the lights off and I sense him lie down beside me on the floor. A dancing green glow from the stereo illuminates the walls as the Avett Brothers put on a color show. My thoughts drift with the music as we lie there motionless. After the song ends and loops around again, I tell him what's really on my mind.

"She doesn't want me to raise Kel. She wants to give him to Brenda."

He finds my hand in the dark and holds it. He holds it, and I let him just be my friend.

THE LIGHTS FLICK on and I immediately cover my eyes. I sit up and see Will next to me, sound asleep.

"Hey," Eddie whispers. "I knocked, nobody answered." She walks through the front door and sits on the couch. She watches Will as he snores, sprawled out on the living room floor.

"It's Saturday night," she says, rolling her eyes. "Told you he was a bore."

I laugh. "What are you doing here?"

"Checking on you. You haven't answered your phone or texted me back at all today. Your mom has cancer so you decide to swear off technology? Doesn't make sense."

"I don't know where my phone is."

We both stare at Will for a moment. He's snoring really loud. The boys must have worn him out today.

"So, I assume things didn't go well with your mom? Since you're here, sleeping on the damn floor." She looks annoyed that we weren't doing anything more than just sleeping.

"No, we talked."

"And?"

I get up and stretch before I sit on the sofa beside her. She's already got her boots off. I guess going so long without a permanent home makes you feel like you're at home anywhere you go. I pull my feet up and lay back on the arm of the couch, facing her.

"Last week in the courtyard when you were telling me about your mom and what happened when you were nine?"

"What about it?" she says, still watching Will snore.

"Well, I was grateful. I was so grateful that nothing like that would ever happen to Kel. I was grateful that he was able to live a normal nine-year-old life. But now—it's like God has it out for us. Why both of them? Wasn't my dad enough? It's like death came and punched us square in the face."

Eddie turns her gaze away from Will and looks at me.

"It wasn't death that punched you, Layken. It was *life*. Life happens. Shit happens. And it happens *a lot*. To *a lot* of people."

I don't even bother with the worst of the details. I'm too embarrassed to admit to her that my own mother doesn't even want me raising her child.

Will rustles on the floor. Eddie leans over and gives me a squeeze and grabs her boots. "Teacher's waking up, I better get outta here. I just wanted to check on you. Oh, and go find your phone," she says as she walks toward the door.

I watch her as she walks out the front door. She's in a room for three minutes, and her energy is infectious. When I turn back around, Will is sitting up on the floor. He's looking at me like he's about to give me detention. I smile at him as innocently as I can.

"What the hell was she doing here?" he says. He can be really intimidating when he wants to be.

"Visiting," I mutter. "Checking on me." If I don't make it sound like a big deal, maybe he won't either.

"Dammit, Layken!"

Nope. He thinks it's a big deal.

He pushes himself up off the floor and throws his hands up in the air. "Are you *trying* to get me fired? Are you that *selfish* that you don't give a crap about anyone *else's* problems? Do you know what would happen if she let it get out that you spent the night here?" A light bulb goes off in his head, and he takes a step toward me. "Does she know you spent the night here?"

I press my lips into a tight, thin line and look down at my lap, avoiding his eyes.

"Layken, what does she know?" he says, his voice lower. He can see by my body language that I've told her everything.

"Christ, Layken. Go home."

MY MOTHER IS already in bed. Kel and Caulder are sitting on the couch, watching TV. "Caulder, your brother wants you to go home. Kel and I have plans tomorrow, so we won't be home all day."

Caulder grabs his jacket and heads toward the front door. "See ya, Kel." He slips his shoes on and leaves.

I walk to the living room and throw myself into the seat beside Kel. I grab the remote and start flipping through channels, attempting to put the fact that I just pissed Will off out of my mind.

"Where were you?" Kel asks.

"With Eddie."

"What were y'all doing?"

"Driving around."

"Why were you at Caulder's house when we got home from the movies?"

"Will paid me to clean his house."

"Why is Mom sad?"

"Because. She doesn't have enough money to pay me to clean *her* house."

"Why? Our house isn't dirty."

"Do you want to go ice-skating tomorrow?"

"Yes!"

"Then stop asking so many questions."

I press the power button on the remote and send Kel to bed. When I climb into my own bed, I set the alarm for six o'clock. I want to be out of this house before my mother wakes up.

KEL AND I spend the entire day Sunday blowing every cent of my savings account. I take him to breakfast, where we order two meals each off of the menu. We go ice-skating, and we both suck at it, so we don't stay long. I take him to lunch at a concession stand inside an arcade, where we stay for four hours. After the arcade, I take him to an afternoon movie, where we have dinner that consists of even more concession-stand food. I would take him for dessert, but he's now complaining that his stomach hurts.

My mother is at work by the time we get home. My timing isn't accidental by any means. I take a shower, pick out our clothes for school, and put away a load of laundry. I'm so tired that I'm able to fall asleep without confronting anything at all.

13.

Shooting off vicious
collections of words
The losers make facts
by the things they have heard
And I find myself
trying hard to defend them.

—THE AVETT BROTHERS, "ALL MY MISTAKES"

"GOT ANOTHER ONE FOR YA," NICK SAYS AS HE TAKES HIS seat Monday morning.

If I have to hear another Chuck Norris joke, I'm going to explode. "Not today; my head hurts," I reply.

"You know what Chuck Norris does to a headache?"

"Nick, I'm serious. Shut up!"

Nick withdraws and turns to the unfortunate student to his right.

Will's not here. The class waits a few minutes, not

really knowing what to do. Apparently this is uncharacteristic of him.

Javi stands up and gets his books. "Five-minute rule," he says. He walks out the door but walks right back in, followed by Will.

Will shuts the door behind him and goes to his desk and sets a stack of papers down. He's on edge today, and it's obvious to everyone. He hands the first student of each row a smaller stack of the papers to pass back, including me. I look down at my paper and there are about ten sheets stapled together. I start flipping through them and recognize one page as Eddie's poem about the pink balloon. They must all be poems written by students. I don't recognize any of the others.

"Some of you in here have performed at the slam this semester. I appreciate it. I know it takes a lot of courage." He holds up his own copy of the collection of poems.

"These are your poems. Some were written by students in my other classes, some by students in here. I want you to read them. Once you've read them, I want you to score them. Write a number between zero and ten, ten being the best. Be honest. If you don't like it, give it a low score. We're trying to find the best and worst. Write the score in the bottom right of each page. Go ahead." He sits at his desk and watches the class.

I don't like this assignment. It doesn't seem fair. I'm raising my hand. Why am I raising my hand? He looks at me and nods.

"What's the point of this assignment?" I ask.

His eyes slowly make their way around the classroom. "Layken, ask that question again after everyone's finished."

He's acting strange.

I start reading the first poem, when Will grabs two slips of paper off of his desk and walks past me. I glance back just as he lays a slip on Eddie's desk. She picks it up and frowns. He walks back to the front, dropping the other slip on my desk. I pick it up and look it over. It's a detention slip.

I glance back at Eddie, and she just shrugs her shoulders. I wad my slip into a ball and throw it across the room to the trashcan by the door. I make it.

Over the next half hour, students begin to finish their scoring. Will is taking the stacks as they are finished and he's adding up the totals with his calculator. Once the last of the points have been added up, Will writes the totals on a sheet of paper and walks to the front of his desk and sits.

He holds the paper up in the air and shakes it. "Is everyone ready to hear which poems sucked? Which ones got the most points?" He's smiling as he waits on a response.

No one says anything. Except Eddie.

"Some of us who wrote those poems may not *want* to know how many points we got. I know I don't."

Will takes a few steps toward Eddie. "If you don't care how many points it's worth, then why did you write it?"

Eddie is quiet for a moment as she thinks about Will's question.

"Aside from wanting to be exempt from your final?" she asks.

Will nods.

"I guess because I had something to say."

Will looks at me. "Layken, ask your question again."

My question. I try to remember what my question was. Oh yeah, what's his point?

"What's the point of this assignment?" I ask cautiously.

Will holds the paper up in front of him that contains the tallied scores, and he rips it right down the middle. He reaches behind him and picks the stack of poems up that everyone scored and he throws them in the trash. He walks to the chalkboard and begins to write something on the board. When he's finished, he steps aside.

"The *points* are not the *point*; the *point* is *poetry*."
—Allan Wolf

The class is quiet as we take in the words sprawled across the board. Will allows a moment of silence before he continues.

"It shouldn't matter what anyone else thinks about your words. When you're on that stage—you share a piece of your soul. You can't assign points to that."

The bell rings. On any other day, students would be filing out the door. No one has moved; we're all just staring at the writing on the board.

"Tomorrow, be prepared to learn *why* it's important for you to write poetry," he says.

There was a moment, in the midst of all the distraction in my head, when I forgot he was *Will*. I listened to him like he was my *teacher*.

Javi is the first to get up, soon followed by the rest of the students. Will is facing the desk with his back to me when Eddie walks up, detention slip in hand. I had already forgotten he gave us detention. She gives me a wink as she passes me and stops at his desk.

"Mr. Cooper?" She's being respectful, but dramatically so. "It is my understanding that detention commences upon the conclusion of the final class period at approximately three thirty. It is my desire, as I'm sure it is Layken's desire as well, to be punctual, so that we may serve our fairly deserved sentences with due diligence. Would you be so kind as to share with us the location in which this sentence shall be carried out?"

Will never looks at her as he walks toward the door. "Here. Just you two. Three thirty."

And he's gone. Just like that.

Eddie bursts out laughing. "What did you do to him?"

I stand up and walk to the door with her. "Oh, it wasn't just me, Eddie. It was both of us."

She spins around wide-eyed. "Oh my god, he knows I know? What's he going to say about it?"

I shrug my shoulders. "I guess we'll find out at three thirty."

"DETENTION? DUCKIE GAVE you detention?" Gavin laughs.

"Man, he really needs to get laid," Nick says.

Nick's comment causes Eddie to laugh and spew milk out of her mouth. I shoot her a cease-and-desist look.

"I can't believe he gave you detention," Gavin says. "But you aren't positive that's what it's for, right? For skipping? I mean, he already mentioned that at the slam last week, and he didn't seem too mad."

I know what the detention is for. Will wants to make sure he can trust Eddie, but I'm not telling this to Gavin. "He said it's for not turning in the assignment we were supposed to do the day we skipped."

Gavin turns to Eddie. "But you did that one—I remember."

Eddie looks at me and replies to Gavin. "I guess I lost it," she says with a shrug.

EDDIE AND I meet outside the door to Will's classroom at approximately three thirty.

"You know, the more I think about it, this really sucks," Eddie says. "Why couldn't he just call me or something if he wanted to talk about what I know? I had plans today."

"Maybe we won't have to stay long," I say.

"I hate detention. It's boring. I'd rather lay on Will's floor with you than sit in detention," she says.

"Maybe we can try and make it fun."

She turns to open the door but hesitates, then spins around and faces me. "You know, you're right. Let's make it fun. I'm pretty sure detention is an hour long. Do you realize how many Chuck Norris jokes we can make in a whole hour?"

I smile at her. "Not as many as Chuck Norris could."

She opens the door to detention.

"Afternoon, Mr. Cooper," Eddie says as she flurries inside.

"Take a seat," he says, wiping the point of poetry off the board.

"Mr. Cooper, did you know that seats actually *stand up* when Chuck Norris walks into a room?" she says.

I laugh and follow Eddie to our seats. Rather than taking the two front seats, she keeps walking until she's in the very back of the room, where she scoots two desks together. We sit as far from the teacher as possible.

Will doesn't laugh. He doesn't even smile. He sits in his chair and glares at us while we giggle—like high school girls.

"Listen," he says. He stands back up and walks toward us, then leans against the window and folds his arms across his chest. He stares at the floor like he's trying to think of a delicate way to broach the subject. "Eddie, I need to know where your head's at. I know you were at my house. I know you know Layken spent the night. I know she told you about our date. I just need to know what you plan to do about it, if you plan to do *anything* about it."

"Will," I say. "She's not saying anything. There's nothing to say."

He doesn't look at me. He continues to look at Eddie, waiting for her response. I guess mine wasn't good enough. I don't know if it's nerves or the fact that I've had the strangest last three days of my life, but I start laughing. Eddie shoots me a questioning glance, but she can't hold it in. She starts laughing, too.

Will throws his hands up in the air, exasperated. "What? What the *hell* is so *funny*?" he says.

"Nothing," I say. "It's just weird. You gave us *detention*, Will." I inhale as I try to control my laughter. "Couldn't you just, like, come over tonight or something? Talk to us about it then? Why'd you give us detention?"

He waits until our laughter subsides before he continues. When we're finally silent, he straightens up and walks closer to us. "This is the first chance I've had to talk to either of you. I didn't sleep all night. I wasn't sure if I even had a job to come back to today." He looks at Eddie. "If anything gets out . . . if anyone finds out that a student slept in my bed with me, I'd get fired. I'd get kicked out of college."

Eddie stiffens in her seat and turns to me, smiling. "You slept in his *bed* with him? You're holding back vital information. You didn't tell me *that*," she laughs.

Will shakes his head and walks back to the front of the room and throws himself into his chair. He leans onto his desk and sets his face in his hands. It's apparent this isn't going how he had planned.

"You slept in his *bed*?" Eddie whispers, low enough so Will doesn't hear her.

"Nothing happened," I say. "Like you said, he's such a *bore*."

Eddie laughs again, causing me to lose my composure.

"Is this funny?" Will says from his desk. "Is this a joke to you two?"

I can see in his eyes that we're enjoying detention way more than we're supposed to. Eddie isn't fazed, however.

"Did you know Chuck Norris doesn't have a funny bone? It tried to make him laugh once, so he ripped it out," she says.

Will lays his head on his desk in defeat. Eddie and I look at each other and our laughter ceases as we respect that he's attempting to have a serious conversation with us. Eddie sighs and straightens up in her desk. "Mr. Cooper?" she says. "I won't say anything. Swear. It's not that big of a deal anyway."

He looks up at her. "It *is* a big deal, Eddie. That's what I'm trying to *tell* both of you. If you don't treat this as a big deal, you'll get careless. Something might slip. I've got too much at stake."

We both sigh. The energy in the room is nonexistent now. It's like a black hole just sucked all the fun out of detention. Eddie feels it too, so she attempts to rectify it.

"Did you know Chuck Norris likes his steaks med—" Eddie doesn't finish her sentence as Will reaches his limit. He slams his fist against the desk and stands up. Neither Eddie nor I are laughing at this point. I look at her wide-eyed and shake my head, letting her know that Chuck Norris needs to retreat.

"This isn't a *joke*," he says. "This is a *big deal*." He reaches over and takes something out of his drawer and swiftly walks to where we're sitting in the back of the room. He smacks a picture down on the crack where the edges of our desks meet and flips it over. It's a picture of Caulder.

He places his finger on the picture and says, "This boy. This boy is a *big* deal." He backs up a step and grabs a desk and turns it around to face us, then sits down.

"I don't think we're following you, Will," I say. I look at Eddie and she shakes her head in agreement. "What's Caulder got to do with what Eddie knows?"

He takes a deep breath as he leans across his desk and picks the picture back up. I can tell by the look in his eyes that his recollection is unpleasant. He stares at the picture for a while, then lays it down on the desk and leans back in the chair, folding his arms across his chest. He continues to stare at the picture, avoiding our eyes. "He was with them . . . when it happened. He watched them die."

I suck in a breath. Eddie and I give him respectful silence and wait for him to continue. I'm beginning to feel very small.

"They said it was a miracle he survived. The car was totaled. When the first person came on the scene, Caulder was still buckled up in what was left of the backseat. He was screaming for my mom, trying to get her to turn around. For five minutes he had to sit there alone and watch as they died."

Will clears his throat. Eddie reaches under the table and grabs my hand and squeezes it. Neither of us says a word.

"I sat in the hospital with him for six days while he recovered. Never left his side—not even for their funeral. When my grandparents came to pick him up and take him home with them, he cried. He didn't want to go. He wanted to stay with me. He begged me to take him back to campus with me. I didn't have a job. I didn't have insurance. I was nineteen. I didn't know the first thing about raising a kid . . . so I let them take him."

Will stands up and walks to the window. He doesn't say anything for a while as he watches the parking lot slowly empty. His hand goes to his face and it looks like he's wiping at his eyes. If Eddie weren't in here right now, I would hug him.

He eventually turns to face us again. "Caulder hated

me. He was so mad at me he wouldn't return my calls for days. It was in the middle of a football game when I started to question the choice I made. I was studying the football in my hands, running my fingers over the pigskin, across the letters of the brand name printed on the side. This elongated spheroid that didn't even weigh a whole pound. I was choosing this ridiculous ball of leather in my hands over my own flesh and blood. I was putting myself, my girlfriend, my scholarship—I was putting everything before this little boy that I loved more than anything in the world.

"I dropped the football and walked right off the field. I got to my grandparents' house at two in the morning and grabbed Caulder right out of bed. I brought him home that night. They begged me not to do it. Said it would be too hard on me and that I wouldn't be able to give him what he needed. I knew they were wrong. I knew all Caulder really needed—was *me*."

He slowly walks back to the desk in front of us and places his hands on the back of it. He looks at both of us, tears streaming down our faces.

"I've spent the last two years of my life trying to convince myself that I made the right decision for him. So my *job*? My *career*? This life I'm trying to build for this little boy? I take it very seriously. It *is* a big deal. It's a *very* big deal to me."

He calmly returns the desk to its place in the aisle and walks back to the front of the room, grabs his things, and leaves.

Eddie gets up and walks to Will's desk and grabs a box of tissues. She brings the box and slumps back down in her seat. I pull out a tissue and we both wipe at our eyes.

"God, Layken. How do you do it?" she says. She blows her nose and grabs another tissue out of the box.

"How do I do what?" I sniff as I continue to wipe the tears from my eyes.

"How do you not fall in *love* with him?"

The tears begin flowing just as quickly as they had ceased. I grab yet another tissue. "I *don't* not fall in love with him. I don't not fall in love with him *a lot*!"

She laughs and squeezes my hand. We spend the next hour alone, willingly sitting out our much-deserved detentions.

14.

And I know you need me in the next room over
But I am stuck in here all paralyzed.

—THE AVETT BROTHERS, "TEN THOUSAND WORDS"

I'VE NEVER HAD SEX. I CAME REALLY CLOSE ONCE BUT chickened out at the last minute. My longest relationship was with a boy I met through Kerris right before I turned seventeen.

Kerris had a brother who was in college, and he brought a friend home with him during spring break two summers ago. His name was Seth, and he was eighteen. I thought I loved him. I think I really just loved having a boyfriend.

He attended the University of Texas, which was a good four-hour drive away. We talked on the phone and online a lot. By the time we had been together for about six months, we had discussed it plenty, so I decided I was ready to have sex with him. I had a midnight curfew that night, so he rented a hotel room, and we told my mother we were going to the movie theater.

When we got to the hotel, my hands were shaking. I knew I had changed my mind, but was too scared to tell him. He had put so much effort into everything. He even brought his own sheets and blankets from home so it would feel more intimate. We had been kissing for a while on the bed when he took off my shirt. His hands were making their way to my pants when I started crying. He immediately stopped. Never pressured me, never made me feel guilty for changing my mind. He just kissed me and told me it was okay. We stayed in bed and rented a movie instead.

It was seven hours later and daytime when we finally woke up. We were both frantic. No one knew where we were; both of our phones had been turned off all night. I knew my parents were worried sick. He was too scared to face them with me, so he dropped me off at my driveway and left. I remember staring at my house, wanting to be anywhere else but there. I knew they were going to make me talk to them, tell them about where I had been. I hated confrontation.

I'M STANDING IN front of my Jeep now, staring at the gnome-filled yard of our house that's not our home. That same feeling of trepidation deep within the pit of my stomach is back. I know my mother is going to want to talk about it all. The cancer. Kel. She'll want to confront it, and I'll want to hide.

I slowly make my way to the front door and turn the knob, wishing someone were holding it shut from the other side. She, Kel, and Caulder are all seated at the bar.

They're carving pumpkins. She can't talk now. This is good.

"Hey," I say to no one in particular when I walk through the front door. She doesn't acknowledge me.

"Hey, Layken. Check out my pumpkin!" Kel says. He swings it around to face me. Its eyes and mouth are three big Xs, and he's taped a bag of candy to the side of the pumpkin's face.

"He's making a sour face. 'Cause he ate some Sour Skittles," he says.

"Creative," I say.

"Look at mine," Caulder says as he turns his around. There's just a bunch of huge holes where the pumpkin's face should be.

"Oh . . . what is it?" I ask him.

"It's God."

I cock my head at him, confused. "God?"

Caulder laughs. "Yeah, God." He looks at Kel, and in unison they both say, "Because he's *holy*."

I roll my eyes and laugh. "I don't know how you two found each other."

I look at my mom and she's watching me, trying to gauge my mood.

"Hey," I say, specifically to her this time.

"Hey," she smiles.

"So," I say, hoping she'll grasp the double meaning behind what I'm about to say. "Do you mind if we *just* carve pumpkins tonight? Is it okay if that's *all* we do? Just carve pumpkins?"

She smiles and turns her attention back to the pumpkin in front of her.

"Sure. But we can't carve pumpkins every night, Lake. One of these nights we'll eventually have to stop carving pumpkins."

I grab one of the available pumpkins off the floor and set it on the bar and take a seat, when someone knocks at the door.

"I'll get it," Caulder yells as he jumps down.

My mother and I both turn to the front door when he opens it. It's Will.

"Hey, Buddy. You answering doors here now?" Will says to him.

Caulder grabs his hand and pulls him inside. "We're carving pumpkins for Halloween. Come on, Julia bought one for you, too." He's pulling Will through the living room and toward the kitchen.

"No, it's fine. I'll carve mine another time. I just wanted to bring you home so they can have some family time."

My mother pulls out the available chair on the other side of her. "Sit down, Will. We're just carving pumpkins tonight. That's *all* we're doing. Just carving pumpkins."

Caulder already has a pumpkin and is placing it at the table in front of Will's chair.

"Okay, then. I guess we're carving pumpkins," Will says.

Caulder hands him a knife and we all sit at the bar—and just carve pumpkins.

Kel creates the first awkward moment when he asks why I'm so late getting home from school. Mom eyes me, waiting for my response, while Will just cuts away at his pumpkin and doesn't look up.

"Eddie and I had detention," I say.

"Detention? What were you in detention for?" my mom asks.

"We skipped class last week, took a nap in the courtyard."

She brings her scooper down to the table and looks at me, obviously disappointed.

"Lake, why would you do something like that? What class did you skip?"

I don't reply. I purse my lips together and nudge my head toward Will. My mother looks at Will just as he looks up from his pumpkin.

He shrugs his shoulders and laughs. "She skipped my class! What was I supposed to do?"

My mother stands up and pats him on the back as she picks up the phone book. "I'm buying you supper for that."

* * *

THE WHOLE EVENING is surreal. Everyone's eating pizza, talking, laughing, including my mother. It's good to hear her laugh. I can see a difference in her tonight. I think simply being able to tell me she was sick has helped relieve some of her stress. I can see it in her eyes, she's more at ease.

We listen as Kel and Caulder talk about what they want to be for Halloween. Caulder keeps switching back and forth between a Transformer and an Angry Bird. Kel still hasn't come up with anything.

I wipe up pumpkin remnants off the floor and take the rag to the sink and rinse it out. I put my elbows on the counter and rest my chin in my hands as I watch them. This is more than likely my mother's last time to carve pumpkins. Next month will be the last time she sees Thanksgiving. After that, she'll have her last Christmas. But she's just sitting here, talking to Will about Halloween plans, laughing. I wish I could freeze this moment. I wish we could just carve pumpkins forever.

WILL AND CAULDER leave after my mom goes to her room to get ready for her shift. I finish cleaning the kitchen and gather the sacks of pumpkin discards and combine them all into a large trash bag. I take the bag to the curb at the end of the driveway, when Will comes outside with his own bag of trash. He walks to the end of his driveway before he realizes I'm even there. He smiles at me and lifts the lid, throwing the bag inside.

"Hey," he says. He puts his hands in his jacket pockets and walks toward me.

"Hey," I reply.

"Hey," he says again. He walks past me and sits against the bumper of my Jeep.

"Hey," I reply as I lean against the Jeep next to him.

"Hey."

"Stop it," I laugh.

We both wait for the other to talk again, but instead there's just an awkward silence. I hate awkward silences, so I break it.

"I'm sorry I told Eddie. She's just so smart. She figured it out and thought there was more going on between us than there is, so I had to tell her the truth. I didn't want her to think badly of you."

He leans his head back and stares up at the sky. "I trust your judgment, Lake. I even trust Eddie. I just need her to know why this job is so important to me. Or maybe I said all that so *you* would know why it's so important to me."

My brain is too tired to even analyze his comment. "Either way," I say. "I know it was hard for you . . . telling us everything like that. Thank you."

We watch as a car passes by and pulls into the driveway next to us. A woman gets out, followed by two girls. They're all carrying pumpkins.

"You know, I don't know a single person on this whole street other than you and Caulder," I say.

He directs his gaze to the house that the three people just entered. "That's Erica. She's been married to her husband, Gus, for about twenty years, I think. They have two daughters, both teenagers. The older one is who babysits Caulder sometimes.

"The couple to the right of Caulder and me have been here the longest, Bob and Melinda. Their son just joined the military. They were great after my parents died. Melinda cooked for us every day for months. She still brings something over about once a week.

"The house over there?" He points down the street. "He's the one renting your house to you. His name is Scott. He owns six of the houses on this street alone. He's a good guy, but his renters come and go a lot. Those are about the only people I know anymore."

I look at all the houses along the street. They're all so similar, and I can't help trying to imagine the differences of all the families inside the homes. I wonder if any of *them* are hiding secrets? If any of them are falling in love. Or out of love. Are they happy? Sad? Scared? Broke? Lonely? Do they appreciate what they have? Do Gus and Erica appreciate their health? Does Scott appreciate his supplemental rental income? Because every bit of it, every last bit of it, is fleeting. Nothing is permanent. The only thing any of us have in common is the inevitable. We'll all eventually die.

"There was this one girl," Will says. "She moved into a house on the street a while back. I still remember the moment I saw her pull up in the U-Haul. She was so confident in that thing. It was a hundred times bigger than her, yet she backed it right up without even asking for help. I watched as she put it in park and propped her leg up on the dash, like driving a U-Haul was something she did every day. Piece of cake.

"I had to leave for work but Caulder had already run across the street. He was imaginary sword-fighting with the little boy that had been in the U-Haul. I was just going to yell at him to come get in the car, but there was something about that girl. I just had to meet her. I walked across the street, but she never even noticed me. She was watching her brother play with Caulder with this distant look on her face.

"I stood beside the U-Haul, and I just watched her. I stared at her while she looked on with the saddest look in her eyes. I wanted to know what she was thinking about, what was going on in her head. What had made her so sad? I wanted to hug her so bad. When she finally got out of the U-Haul and I introduced myself to her, it took all I had to let go of her hand. I wanted to hold on to it forever. I wanted to let her know that she wasn't alone. Whatever burden it was that she was carrying around, I wanted to carry it *for* her."

I lean my head on his shoulder, and he puts his arm around me.

"I wish I could, Lake. I wish I could take it all away. Unfortunately, that's not how it works. It doesn't just go away. That's what your mom is trying to tell you. She needs you to accept it, and she needs for Kel to know, too. You need to give that to her."

"I know, Will. I just can't. Not yet. I'm not ready to deal with it yet."

He pulls me to him and hugs me. "You'll never be ready for it, Lake. No one ever is." He lets go of me and walks away. And he's right again, but I don't care this time.

"LAKE? CAN I come in?" Mom says from outside the bedroom door.

"It's open," I say.

She walks in and shuts my door behind her. She's got her scrubs on now. She sits on the bed next to me as I continue to write in my notebook.

"What are you writing?" she asks.

"A poem."

"For school?"

"No, for me."

"I didn't know you wrote poetry." She tries to peek over my shoulder at it.

"I don't, really. If we read our poetry at Club N9NE we're exempt from the final. I'm thinking about doing one, but I don't know. The thought of getting up there in front of all those people makes me nervous."

"Push your boundaries, Lake. That's what they're there for."

I flip the poem upside down and sit up. "So, what's up?"

She smiles at me and reaches to my face and tucks my hair behind my ear.

"Not much," she says. "I just had a few minutes before I had to leave for work and thought we could talk. I wanted to let you know that it's my last night. I'm not working anymore after tonight."

I break our stare and lean forward and grab my pen. I put the cap back on it and close my notebook, tucking both the items inside my backpack.

"I'm still carving pumpkins, Mom."

She slowly inhales and stands up, hesitates, then walks back out the door.

15.

Forever I will move like the world that turns
beneath me
And when I lose my direction, I'll look up to the
sky
And when the black cloak drags upon the ground
I'll be ready to surrender, and remember
Well we're all in this together
If I live the life I'm given, I won't be scared to
die.

—THE AVETT BROTHERS,
"ONCE AND FUTURE CARPENTER"

WILL WALKS INTO THE CLASSROOM CARRYING A SMALL projector. He sets it on the desk and begins hooking it up to his laptop.

"What are we doing today, Mr. Cooper?" Gavin asks.

Will continues to prepare the projector as he responds to Gavin. "I want to show you why you should write poetry." He swings the plug around his desk and inserts it into the outlet on the wall.

"I know why people write poetry," Javi says. "Because they're a bunch of emotional saps with nothin' better to do than whine about ex-girlfriends and dead dogs."

"You're wrong, Javi," I say. "That's called country music."

Everyone laughs, including Will. He sits at his desk and turns the laptop on and glances at Javi. "So what? If it makes someone feel better to write a poem about their dead dog, then great. Let them. What if some girl broke your heart, Javi, and you decided to vent with a pen and paper? That's your business."

"That's fair," Javi says. "People are free to write what they want to write about. But the thing that bothers me is, what if the person who writes it doesn't want to relive it? What if a dude performs a slam about a bad breakup, but then he gets over it and moves on? He falls in love with some other chick, but now there's probably this YouTube video floating around on the Internet of him talking all sad about how his heart got broke. That sucks. If you perform it, or even write it down, someday you'll have to relive it."

Will stops fidgeting with the projector and stands up and turns to the board. He grabs a piece of chalk, writes something, and then steps aside.

The Avett Brothers

Will points to the name on the board. "Has anyone heard of them?" He looks at me and gives his head a slight shake, indicating he doesn't want me to speak up.

"Sounds familiar," someone says from the back of the room.

"Well," he says as he paces the room. "They're famous philosophers who speak and write extremely wise, thought-provoking words of wisdom."

I try to stifle my laugh. He's mostly right, though.

"They were asked about this once. I believe they were doing a *reading*. Someone asked them a question about their *poetry*, and whether it was hard having to relive their words each time they performed. Their reply was that although they had ideally moved *beyond* that—from the person or event that inspired their words at that point in time—it doesn't mean someone listening to them wasn't *in* that.

"So? So *what* if the heartache you wrote last year isn't what you're feeling today. It may be exactly what the person in the front row is feeling. What you're feeling now, and the person you may reach with your words five years from now—that's why you write poetry."

He flips on the overhead projector and I immediately recognize the words projected onto the wall. It's the piece he performed at the slam on our date. His piece about death.

"See this? I wrote this piece two years ago, after my parents died. I was angry. I was hurt. I wrote down *exactly* what I was feeling. When I read it now, I don't share those same feelings. Do I regret writing it? No. Because there's a chance that someone in this very room may relate to this. It might mean something to them."

He moves his mouse and the projector zooms in, highlighting one of the lines of his poem.

People don't like to **talk** about death because
it makes them *sad*.

"You never know, someone in this very room might relate to this. Does talking about death make you sad? Of course it does. Death sucks. It's not a fun thing to talk about. But sometimes, you *need* to talk about it."

I know what he's doing. I fold my arms across my chest and glare at him as he looks directly at me. He glances back to his computer, highlighting another line.

If *only* they had been *prepared*, *accepted* the
inevitable, laid out their *plans*,

"What about this one? My parents weren't prepared to *die*. I was *angry* at them for this. I was left with bills, debt, and a *child*. But what if they'd had warning? A chance to discuss it, to lay out their plans? If talking about death wasn't so easy to avoid while they were alive, then maybe I wouldn't have had such a hard time dealing with it after they died."

He's looking directly at me as he zooms in on another line.

understood that it **wasn't** just **their** lives at hand.

"Everyone assumes they have at least one more day. If my parents had any clue what was about to happen to them before it happened, they would have done everything in their *power* to prepare us. *Everything.* It's not that they weren't thinking about *us*, it's that they weren't thinking about *death.*"

He highlights the last line of his poem.

Death. The only thing inevitable in *life*.

I look at the phrase and I read it. I read it again. I read it again, and again, and again. I read it until the end of the class period, after everyone around me has left. Everyone but Will.

He's sitting at his desk, watching me. Waiting for me to understand.

"I get it, Will," I finally whisper. "I get it. In the first line, when you said that death was the only thing inevitable in life . . . you emphasized the word *death*. But when you said it again at the end of the poem, you didn't emphasize the word death, you emphasized the word *life*. You put the *emphasis* on *life* at the end. I get it, Will. You're right.

She's not trying to prepare us for her *death*. She's trying to prepare us for her *life*. For what she has left of it."

He leans forward and turns the projector off. I grab my stuff, and I go home.

I SIT ON the edge of my mother's bed. She's asleep in the center of it. She doesn't have a side anymore, now that she sleeps in it alone.

She's still wearing her scrubs. When she wakes up and takes them off, it'll be the last time she takes off a pair of scrubs. I wonder if that's why she's still wearing them: because she realizes this too.

I watch the rhythm of her body as she breathes. With every breath that she inhales, I can hear the struggle of her lungs within her chest. The struggle of lungs that failed her.

I reach over and stroke her hair. When I do, a few of the strands fall off in my fingers. I pull my hand back and slowly wrap them around my finger as I walk to my room and pick my purple hair clip up off the floor. I open the clip and place the strands of hair inside and snap it shut. I place the clip under my bedroom pillow and I go back to my mother's room. I slide into the bed beside her and wrap my arms around her. She finds my hand and we interlock fingers as we talk without saying a single word.

16.

" "

—THE AVETT BROTHERS,

"COMPLAINTE D'UN MATELOT MOURANT"

AFTER MY MOTHER FALLS BACK TO SLEEP, I GO TO THE grocery store. Kel's favorite food is basagna. It's how he used to say lasagna, so we still call it basagna. I gather everything I need for the meal and I go back home and start cooking.

"Smells like basagna," Mom says as she comes out of her bedroom. She's in regular clothes now. She must have taken her scrubs off for the last time.

"Yep. I figured we could make Kel his favorite tonight. He'll need it."

She walks to the sink and washes her hands before she starts helping me layer the noodles. "So, I guess we finally stopped carving pumpkins?" she asks.

"Yep," I reply. "The pumpkins have all been carved."

She laughs.

"Mom? Before he gets here, we need to talk. About what's going to happen to him."

"I *want* to, Lake. I *want* to talk about it."

"Why don't you want him to be with me? Do you not think I'm capable? That I wouldn't make a good mom?"

She layers the last of the noodles as I cover them with sauce.

"Lake, I don't think that at all. I just want you to be able to live your life. I've spent the entire last eighteen years raising you, teaching you everything I know. It's supposed to be time for you to go screw up. Make mistakes. Not raise a child."

"But sometimes life doesn't happen in chronological order," I say. "You're a prime example of that. If it did, you wouldn't die until you were supposed to. Until you were seventy-seven or so, I think. That's the average age of death."

She laughs and shakes her head.

"Seriously, Mom. I want him. I *want* to raise him. He'll want to stay with me—you know he will. You have to give us the choice. We haven't had a choice in any of this. You have to give us this one."

"Okay," she says.

"Okay? Okay you'll think about it? Or *okay*, okay?"

"*Okay*, okay."

I hug her. I hug her tighter than I've ever hugged her before.

"Lake?" she says. "You're getting basagna sauce all over me."

I pull away and realize I'm still holding the spatula and it's dripping all over her back.

"WHY CAN'T HE come over?" Kel asks after I pull in the driveway and send Caulder home.

"I told you already. Mom needs to talk to us."

We walk inside the house and Mom is putting the basagna in the oven.

"Mom, guess what?" Kel says as he runs to the kitchen.

"What, sweetie?"

"Our school is having a costume contest on Halloween. The winner gets fifty bucks!"

"Fifty bucks? Wow. Have you decided what you want to be yet?"

"Not yet." He walks over to the bar and throws his backpack down.

"Did your sister tell you we're all having a talk tonight?"

"Yeah. She didn't have to, though. We're having basagna."

My mother and I both look at him.

"Every time we have basagna it's bad news. Y'all

cooked basagna when Grandpa died. Y'all cooked basagna when y'all told me Dad was dead. Y'all cooked basagna when y'all told me we were moving to Michigan. Y'all are cooking basagna right now. Either someone's dying or we're moving back to Texas."

My mom looks at me wide-eyed, questioning our timing. He seems to have opened it up for an even earlier discussion. She walks over to him and sits down. I follow suit.

"You're very observant, that's for sure," she says.

"So, which one is it?" he asks, looking up at her.

She places her hand on the side of his face and strokes it. "I have lung cancer, Kel."

He immediately throws his arms around her and hugs her. She strokes the back of his head, but he doesn't cry. They are both silent for a while as she waits for him to speak.

"Are you gonna die?" he finally asks. His voice is muffled because his head is buried in her shirt.

"I am, sweetie. But I don't know when. Until then, though, we're going to spend a lot of time together. I quit my job today so that I can spend more time with you."

I wasn't sure how he would react. At only nine years old, he probably won't grasp the true reality of it until after she actually passes away. My father's death was sudden and unexpected, which naturally prompted a more dramatic reaction from him.

"But what about after you die? Who are we gonna go live with?"

"Your sister is an adult now. You're going to live with her."

"But I wanna stay here, by Caulder," he says as he lifts his head from her shirt and looks at me. "Layken, are you gonna make me move back to Texas with you?"

Up until this very second, I had every intention of moving back to Texas.

"No, Kel. We're staying right here."

Kel sighs, soaking in everything he's just been told. "Are you scared, Mom?" he asks her.

"Not anymore," she says. "I've had a lot of time to accept it. In fact, I feel lucky. Unlike your dad, at least I've got warning. Now I get to spend more time with the two of you here at home."

He lets go of my mother and puts his elbows on the bar.

"You have to promise me something, Layken."

"Okay," I respond.

"Don't ever make basagna again."

We all laugh. We all *laugh*. This was the hardest thing my mother and I have ever had to do, and we're *laughing*. Kel is amazing.

AN HOUR LATER, we have a huge spread of basagna, bread sticks, and salad. There's no way we're eating all of this.

"Kel, why don't you go see if Caulder and Will have

eaten yet," my mother says as she eyes the food with me. Kel darts out the door.

She sets two more places at the table while I fill drinks with tea.

"We need to talk to Will about helping out with Kel," I tell her.

"Will? Why?"

"Because I want to take you to your treatments from now on. It's too much for Brenda. I can miss a day of school every now and then, or we can go when I get out."

"Okay." She looks at me and smiles.

Kel and Caulder come running through the front door, followed by Will a moment later.

"Kel said we're having basagna?" Will asks, hesitantly.

"Yes, sir," my mother says as she scoops basagna onto plates.

"What *is* basagna? Bologna lasagna?"

He looks scared.

"It's basagna. And it's the last time we'll ever have it, so you better enjoy it," she says.

Will walks to the table and waits for Mom and I to sit before he takes his seat.

We pass around bread sticks and salad until everyone's plates are filled. And just like last night, Kel is the first one to make it awkward.

"My mom's dying, Caulder."

Will glances at me and I give him a half smile, letting him know we talked.

"When she dies, I'm gonna live with Layken. Just like you live with Will. It's like we'll be the same. All of our parents will be dead, and we'll live with our brother and sister."

"Cool. That's crazy," Caulder says.

"Caulder!" Will yells.

"It's fine, Will," my mom says. "It is kind of crazy if you think about it from the perspective of a nine-year-old."

"Mom," Kel says. "What about your bedroom? Can I have it? It's bigger than mine."

"No," I say. "It's got a bathroom in it. I get her bedroom."

Kel looks defeated. I don't budge, though. I'm getting the bedroom with the bathroom.

"Kel, you can have my computer," my mother says.

"Sweet!"

I look at Will, hoping this conversation isn't weirding him out, but he's laughing. This is exactly what he was hoping would happen. *Acceptance.*

Over dinner, we all discuss what will happen over the next few months and make arrangements for Caulder and Kel while Mom receives her treatments. Will agreed to let Kel come over whenever he needed to and said he'll continue to take them to school. I'll be picking them up on the way home every day, unless I'm at a treatment with

Mom. She made Will agree to let her cook them supper most nights in return for his help. The entire night was a success. I feel like together, we all just punched death square in the face.

"I'm exhausted," my mom says. "I need to take a shower and get to bed."

She walks into the kitchen where Will is washing dishes at the sink. She puts her arms around him and hugs him from behind. "Thanks, Will. For everything."

He turns around and hugs her back.

When she walks past me on her way to her bedroom, she purposefully nudges me with her shoulder. She doesn't speak a word but I know what she's hinting at—she's giving me her approval. Again. Too bad it doesn't count.

I wipe the table off and walk to the sink to rinse out the rag.

"Eddie's birthday is Thursday. I don't know what I should get her."

"Well, I know what you *shouldn't* get her," he says.

"Believe me, I know," I laugh. "I think Gavin's taking her out Thursday night. Maybe I'll do something for her on Friday."

"Oh, speaking of Friday. Do you guys need me to watch Kel? I forgot Caulder and I go to Detroit this weekend."

"No, you're fine. Family stuff?"

"Yeah. We stay with our grandparents one weekend a

month. Kind of a truce we worked out for me stealing him away in the middle of the night."

"That's fair enough," I say. I reach over to the sink and unplug the drain.

"So you won't be at the slam Thursday?" he asks.

"No. We'll watch Caulder that night, though. Just send him over after school."

He puts the last dish in the strainer and dries his hands on the towel. "It's pretty weird, isn't it? How everything worked out? You guys moving here when you did? Kel and Caulder finding each other, right when Kel probably needed a best friend the most? Him taking your mother's news so well? It just all worked out."

He turns toward me and smiles. "I'm proud of you, Lake. You did good today." He plants one of his lingering kisses on my forehead, then walks to the living room.

"Caulder still needs to take a shower; I guess we need to go. I'll see you tomorrow," he says.

"Yeah. See ya."

I sigh as I think about the one thing that *isn't* on his mind. The one incredibly huge thing that *didn't* work out: us.

I'm starting to accept it. That we won't be together. That we *can't* be together. Especially the last two nights he's been here. It really feels like we've finally transitioned. There are definitely still moments, but none we're not able to overcome. It's only October, and he'll be my teacher until June. That's still eight long months. When I look at the shift my life has made in the past eight months, I can't fathom what my life will be eight months from now. When I lie down and close my eyes, I make a resolution. Will is not going to be my first priority anymore. I'm putting my mother first, Kel second, and *life* third.

Finally. He no longer has a hold on me.

"EDDIE, WILL YOU go grab me a chocolate milk, babe? I forgot to get one." Gavin is giving Eddie puppy-dog eyes. Eddie rolls her eyes and gets up. As soon as she leaves the table, he turns toward us and starts whispering.

"Tomorrow night. Getty's. Six o'clock. Bring a pink balloon. And we're going to the slam afterward."

"Gavin, are you crazy? That's not funny; she'll be pissed," I whisper.

"Just trust me."

She's back at the table with the chocolate milk. "Here. You owe me fifty cents."

"I owe you my heart," Gavin says as he takes the milk.

She slaps him lightly across the head. "Oh, grow a pair! You're such a sap," she says, right before she kisses his cheek.

I RELUCTANTLY WALK into Getty's Pizza with a pink balloon in my hand. Gavin and Nick are gathered in the back of the room at a booth. He motions for me to join them. There are so many pink balloons. She's going to be pissed.

Gavin grabs my balloon and writes something on it with a big marker. "Here," Gavin says as he hands me the fistful of balloons. "Take all these and go to the back by the bathrooms. I'll come get you when it's time; she'll be here soon."

He shoves me toward the bathroom before I have a chance to object. I stand in a corner in the hallway between the men's room and the janitor's closet. I look up at all the balloons, and that's when I notice there are names written on each one of them.

Moments later, an older gentleman walks down the hall toward me.

"Are you Layken?" he asks.

"Yes," I reply.

"I'm Joel, Eddie's foster dad."

"Oh, hey."

"Gavin wants you out front; I'll take the balloons now. Eddie's out there. She thinks I went to the bathroom, so don't say anything about the balloons."

"Uh, okay." I hand him the balloons and walk back to the table.

"Layken! You came! Guys, this is so sweet," Eddie says. She starts to sit at the booth, when Gavin pulls her back up.

"We're not eating yet. We need to go outside."

"Outside? But it's cold out there."

"Come on," he says, pulling her toward the door.

We all follow Gavin outside and stand next to Eddie. I look at Nick but he shrugs, implying he doesn't know what's going on, either. Gavin pulls a piece of paper out of his pocket and stands in front of Eddie.

"I didn't write this letter, Eddie. But I was told to read it."

Eddie looks at us and smiles, trying to gain hints from our expressions. We can't give her any, because we don't know.

It was July 4th when you came to me. Independence Day. You were fourteen. You burst in the door and went straight to the refrigerator, telling me you needed a Sprite. I didn't have any Sprite. You told me it was okay, and you grabbed a Dr Pepper instead. You freaked me out. I told the caseworker there was no way I could keep you. I'd never fostered a teenager before. She told me she would find you somewhere to go the next day, that she just needed me to keep you for the night.

I was so nervous. I didn't know what to say to a fourteen-year-old girl. I didn't know what kinds of things they liked, what shows they watched. I was clueless. But you made it so easy. You were so worried about making me feel comfortable.

Later that night, when it was dark outside—we

heard fireworks. You grabbed my hand and pulled
me off the couch and dragged me outside. We lay
on the grass in the front yard, and we watched the
sky. You didn't shut up. You told me all about the
family you just came from, the family before that,
and the family before that. The whole time you were
talking, I was listening. Listening to this little girl,
so full of life. So full and enthralled with a life that
tried so hard to knock her down.

Eddie gasps when she sees Joel in the window of the restaurant with dozens of pink balloons. He walks outside and stands beside Gavin. Gavin continues reading the letter.

I've never been able to give you much. Other
than eventually teaching you how to park, I've
never even taught you very much. But you've
taught me more than you will ever know. And on
this very special birthday, your eighteenth birthday,
you no longer belong to the state of Michigan. And
as of right now, you legally no longer belong to me.
You no longer belong to any of the following people
that once held claim to you and your past.

Joel starts reading names out loud as he releases balloons one by one. Eddie is crying as we all watch the balloons slowly disappear into the darkness. He continues releasing them, until all twenty-nine siblings' and all thirteen parents' names have been read and released.

He still has one pink balloon remaining in his hand. Across the front of it, in big black letters, it says DAD.

Gavin folds the paper up and takes a step back as Joel walks toward Eddie.

"I hope for your birthday you'll accept this gift," Joel says as he hands her the pink balloon. "I want to be your dad, Eddie. I want to be your family for the rest of your life."

Eddie hugs him and they cry. The rest of us slowly walk back inside Getty's so they can have their moment.

"Oh my god, I need a napkin," I sniff as I search for something to wipe my eyes. I grab some napkins off the counter when I look at Nick and Gavin. They're both crying. I grab a few more napkins for them and we walk back to our booth.

17.

If I get murdered in the city
don't go revengin' in my name
One person dead from such is plenty
No need to go get locked away.

—THE AVETT BROTHERS,

"MURDER IN THE CITY"

I CAN HONESTLY SAY I FEEL LIKE I'VE MOVED THROUGH the five stages of grief in every aspect of my life.

I have accepted my father's death. I accepted his death months before we even moved to Michigan. I've accepted my mother's fate. I realize she hasn't died yet, and that the stages of grief will recommence when she does. But I know it won't be as hard.

I've accepted living in Michigan. The song I listened to on repeat at Will's house was called "Weight of Lies." A portion of the lyrics say,

The weight of lies will bring you down, follow you to every town 'cause

nothing happens here that doesn't happen there.

Every time the song looped, all I heard was the part about the lies—and how they weigh you down. Tonight, as I drive toward Detroit in my Jeep, I know what those words really mean. It's not just *lies* they're referring to. It's *life*. You can't run to another town, another place, another state. Whatever it is you're running from—it goes with you. It stays with you until you find out how to confront it.

Whatever it is I was hoping to run back to Texas from, it would eventually make its way back to me. So here I am in Ypsilanti, Michigan—where I'll stay. And I'm okay with that.

I've accepted the situation with Will. I don't blame him at all for what he chose. Sure, I had fantasies of him sweeping me off my feet, telling me he doesn't need a *career* when he has *love*. The reality of it is, if he had put his feelings for me first, it would've been hard to accept that he could so easily throw away the things that are the most important to him. It would have said a lot less for his character. So I don't blame him, I respect him. And someday, when I'm ready, I'll thank him.

I PULL UP to the club a little after eight o'clock. Gavin had a surprise for Eddie, so they took a detour, said they'd be here late. The parking lot is unusually crowded, so I have to take a spot in the back of the building. When I get out of the car, I take a deep breath and prepare myself. I'm not sure when it was that I decided I was going to perform tonight, but I'm having second thoughts.

My mother's words linger in my head as I make my way to the front door. *"Push your boundaries, Lake, that's what they're there for."*

I can do this. They're just words. Repeat them and you're done. It's that simple.

I walk in the door a few minutes late. I can tell the sac is about to perform, because you could hear a pin drop. I sneak in and quietly make my way to the back of the room. I don't want to draw attention to myself, so I slide into an empty booth. I take my phone out to turn the volume down and text Eddie letting her know where I'm sitting. That's when it happens; I hear him.

Will is standing in front of the microphone on the stage, performing a piece as the sacrifice.

I used to *love* the ocean.
Everything about her.
Her coral *reefs*, her white *caps*, her roaring *waves*, the
rocks they *lap*, her *pirate* legends and *mermaid* tails,
Treasures *lost* and treasures *held* . . .
And *ALL*
Of her *fish*
In the *sea*.
Yes, I used to *love* the ocean,

Everything about her.

The way she would *sing* me to *sleep* as I *lay* in my *bed*

then *wake* me with a *force*

That I *soon* came to *dread*.

Her *fables*, her *lies*, her *misleading* eyes,

I'd drain her *dry*

If I *cared* enough to.

I used to *love* the ocean,

Everything about her.

Her coral *reefs*, her *whitecaps*, her roaring *waves*, the

rocks they *lap*, her *pirate* legends and *mermaid* tails,

treasures *lost* and treasures *held*.

And *ALL*

Of her *fish*

In the *sea*.

Well, if you've ever tried *navigating* your *sailboat*

through her stormy *seas*, you would *realize* that

her *whitecaps* are your *enemies*. If you've ever tried

swimming ashore when your *leg* gets a *cramp* and

you just had a *huge meal* of *In-N-Out* burgers that's

weighing you down, and her *roaring waves* are

knocking the *wind* out of you, filling your *lungs* with

water as you *flail* your arms, trying to get *someone's*

attention, but your friends

just

wave

back at you?

And if you've ever grown up with *dreams* in your *head*

about *life*, and how one of these days you would pirate

your *own* ship and have your *own* crew and that *all* of

the mermaids

would *love*

only

you?

Well, you would *realize* . . .

As I eventually realized . . .

That all the *good* things about her?

All the *beautiful?*

It's not *real.*

It's *fake.*

So you *keep* your *ocean,*

I'll take the *Lake.*

Air. Or water. I don't know which one I need. I slide out of the booth and head toward the front door but make a beeline for the bathroom. I just need silence.

When I open the door to the bathroom, the stalls are empty. There's a girl washing her hands at the only available sink, so I decide to wait on the water. I pick the big stall. I lock it behind me and lean up against the door.

Did that just really happen? Does he know I'm even here? No, he doesn't. I told him I wasn't coming. He didn't intend for me to hear it. Even so, he *wrote* it. He said himself that he writes what he's feeling. Oh my god, he *loves* me. Will Cooper is *in love* with me.

I've known all along how he feels about me. I can see it in the way he looks at me. But to hear his words and the emotions behind them—how he said my name. How am I supposed to face him? I'm not. He still doesn't know I'm here. I just have to leave. I need to leave before he sees me.

I open the bathroom door and scan the area, but I don't see him. Luckily, another performer is onstage, so most of the eyes are glued to the front of the room. I slip through the entryway and out the front door.

"Layken! Look what Gavin got me!" Eddie is making her way inside, holding her hair back, wanting me to look at her ears.

"Eddie, I've got to go."

Her smile fades.

"I'll call you later." I brush past her without looking at the earrings. "You didn't see me!" I yell behind me as I go.

I make my way around the building and smash into Javi as he's rounding the corner. *Good grief!* Is the whole class here? Someone's going to let it slip that I was here. I don't want Will to know I saw him.

"Hey, what's the hurry?" he asks as I slip between him and the wall.

"I gotta go. I'll see you tomorrow." I quickly walk away. I don't have time for chitchat. I just want to get in my Jeep and pull out of this parking lot as soon as I can.

"Wait, I'll walk you to your car," he says as he catches up to me.

"I'm fine, Javi. Go ahead and go inside, they've already started."

"Layken, we're in Detroit. You're parked behind a club. I'm walking you to your car."

"Fine. But walk fast."

"What's your hurry?" he asks as we make our way to the rear of the building.

"I'm just tired. I need sleep." I slow down, feeling confident that Will didn't see me.

"There's a café down the road. Want to go grab some coffee?" he asks.

"No, thanks. I don't need caffeine, I need my bed."

When we get to my Jeep, I reach down to grab my keys out of my—shit! My purse. I left my purse in the booth.

"Shit!" I say. I kick at the gravel in front of me. My shoe loosens a piece of rock and it flicks against the door of my Jeep.

"What's wrong?" he asks.

"My purse. I left my keys and my purse inside." I fold my arms across my chest and lean against the Jeep.

"It's not that big a deal. We'll go back inside and get them."

"No, I don't want to. Would you mind getting them for me?" I smile at him, hoping it will be enough.

"Layken, you don't need to stay back here by yourself."

"Fine. I'll just text Eddie to bring it out. Do you have your phone?"

He pats his pockets. "No, it's in my truck. Come on, you can use it." Javi says this as he reaches down and takes my hand, leading me toward his truck. He unlocks his door and reaches inside for his phone. "It's dead." He plugs it into the charger. "Give it a couple minutes to get a charge, then you can call her."

"Thanks," I say as I lean against his truck and wait.

He stands next to me while we wait for the phone to charge. "It's snowing again," Javi says as he wipes something off my arm.

I look up and see the falling flakes contrasted against the black sky. I guess we're finally about to see what a Michigan winter really looks like.

I turn to face Javi. I was about to ask him something about snow tires, or plows, but it slips my mind as soon as his hands grasp my face and his tongue makes its way into my mouth. I turn my face and push against his chest with my hands. When he feels my resistance, his face backs away from mine, but his body is still pressed against me, pushing me against the cold metal of his truck.

"What?" he says. "I thought you wanted me to kiss you."

"No, Javi!" I'm still pushing against him with my hands but he doesn't budge.

"Come on," he says with a smug grin on his face. "You didn't leave your *keys* inside. You *want* this." His mouth encircles mine again, and my pulse starts to race in my chest. It's not the same reaction I get when Will makes my pulse race. This time it's more like fight-or-flight mode. I try to scream at him, but his hands are pulling my face into his so hard that I can't catch a breath. I try to move, but he's using his body to pin me against his truck, making it impossible for me to break free.

I close my eyes. *Think*, Layken. *Think*.

Just as I'm about to bite down on his lip, Javi pulls away from me. But he keeps going backward. Someone is dragging him away from me. He falls to the ground, and Will straddles him, grabs hold of his shirt, and sends a blow straight to Javi's jaw. Javi falls back to the ground but turns over and pushes off against it, causing Will to stumble backward.

"Stop!" I scream.

Will is knocked to the ground when Javi returns the punch. I'm afraid Javi is going to hit him a second time, so I throw myself between them just as Javi swings a punch intended for Will—straight into my back. I fall forward and land on Will. I try to catch a breath, but I have none. I can't inhale.

"Lake," Will says, rolling me onto the ground next to him. His worry is fleeting, however, and rage fills his eyes. He grabs the door handle of the car next to us and starts to pull himself up.

"I didn't mean to hit you, Layken," Javi says, walking toward me.

I'm on the ground so I don't see what happens next, but I hear a smack, and I can see Javi's feet are no longer planted on the ground. I look up just as Will leans over Javi and delivers another punch.

"Will, get off him!" Gavin yells. Gavin is pulling Will back and they both fall to the ground.

Eddie rushes to my side and pulls me upright. "Layken, what happened?" She has her arms around me, and I'm clutching my chest. I know I was hit in the back, but it feels like my lungs are concrete. I'm gasping for air, and I can't answer her.

Will rustles out of Gavin's grip and stands up. He walks to me and takes my hand as Eddie scoots out of his way. He pulls me up and puts my arm around his shoulder, wraps his other arm around my waist, and starts walking me forward.

"I'm taking you home," is all he says.

"Wait," Eddie yells as she circles to the front of us. "I found your purse."

I reach out and take it from her and attempt to smile. Her hand goes up to her ear in the shape of a phone and she mouths, "Call me."

Will assists me into his car and I lean back against the seat. My lungs have refilled with air, but every breath I take feels like I've got a knife protruding from my back. I close my eyes and focus on inhaling and exhaling through my nose as we drive away.

Neither one of us speaks. Me, because I can't. Will

because—I don't know why. We drive in silence until we're almost to the Ypsilanti city limits.

Will jerks the car to the side of the road and throws it in Park. He punches the steering wheel before he gets out of the car and slams the door. His figure is illuminated by the headlights of the car as he walks away from the vehicle, sporadically kicking at the ground and cursing obscenities. He finally stops and stands with his hands on his hips. His head is leaned back and he's looking up at the sky, letting the snow fall on his face. He stands like this for a while until he finally makes his way back to the car, sits down, and calmly shuts his door. He puts the car in gear, and we continue to drive in silence.

I'm able to walk, my breathing has returned to normal, and the knife in my back feels more like a lump now. Regardless, he still assists me into his house.

"Lie down on the couch, I'll get some ice," he says.

I do as he says. I ease myself stomach first onto the couch and close my eyes, wondering what in the world just happened to tonight.

I feel his hand on the couch when he kneels down next to me. "Will!" I gasp when I open my eyes and actually see his face. "Your eye." There's a trail of blood running down his neck from a gash above his eye.

"It's fine. I'll be fine," he says, leaning over me. "Do you mind?" His hands grasp the bottom edge of my shirt.

I shake my head.

He pulls my shirt up over my back and I feel something cold compress against my skin. He positions the ice pack on top of the injury, then stands and opens the front door, shutting it behind him when he leaves.

He *left*. He just left without saying a word. I lie there for a few more minutes, expecting him to return right away, but he doesn't. I roll onto my side and let the pack of ice fall onto the couch. I ease my shirt back down and prepare myself to stand up just as the door bursts open and my mother runs in.

"Lake? Sweetie, are you okay?" She throws her arms around me. Will walks in behind her.

"Mom," I say weakly. I return her hug and cry.

"IT'S FINE, MOM, really." She's tucking me into my bed, asking me how my back feels for the one hundredth time in the ten minutes that I've been home. She smiles and strokes my hair. That's what I'm going to miss the most about her. The way she strokes my hair and looks at me with so much love in her eyes.

"Will says you got hit in the back. Who hit you?"

I wince as I push myself up against my pillow. "Javi. He's in my class. He was trying to punch Will, but I got in the way."

"Why was he trying to punch Will?"

"Because Will punched *him*. Javi walked me to my Jeep when I left the club. He thought I wanted him to kiss me. I was trying to push him off of me—I couldn't get him to stop. The next thing I know Will's on top of him, punching him."

"That's awful, Lake. I'm so sorry." She leans forward and kisses my forehead.

"It's fine, Mom. I'm fine. I just need some sleep."

She strokes my head again before she stands up and flicks the lights off. "What about Will? What's he going to do?" she asks before she closes the door.

"I don't know," I reply. Because at first I think her question is referring to what he's going to do about Javi. But after she shuts the door, I realize she's asking what he's going to do about his *job*.

I lie awake for hours after that, dissecting the situation. We weren't on school grounds. He was defending me. Maybe Javi won't say anything. Will *did* throw the first punch, though. And the third. And the fourth. And probably would have thrown the fifth if Gavin hadn't walked up when he did. I try to recall every small detail of the entire night, in case I'm asked to defend his actions tomorrow.

THE NEXT DAY, I wake up to find Caulder eating cereal in my kitchen with Kel.

"Hey. My brother can't take us today. Says he has something he has to do."

"What does he have to do?"

Caulder shrugs. "I dunno. He brought your Jeep

home this morning. Then he left again." A spoonful of Froot Loops goes into his mouth.

I CAN BARELY sit through my first two classes. Eddie and I spend second period writing notes back and forth. I told her everything that happened last night. Everything except for Will's poem.

I feel like I'm floating when we walk to third period. Almost like in my dreams when I'm hovering above myself, watching myself walk. I feel like I'm not in control of my actions, I'm just observing them as they are carried out. Eddie opens the door and walks in first. I follow slowly behind her and make my way through the classroom. Will isn't here yet. Neither is Javi. I inhale and I take my seat. The bustling of the conversation among the other classmates is briefly interrupted by a crackling over the intercom.

"Layken Cohen, please report to administration."

I immediately swing around and look at Eddie. She gives me a half-hearted smile and a thumbs-up. She's just as nervous as I am.

There are several people in the office when I walk in. I recognize the principal, Mr. Murphy, speaking with two men I don't recognize. When he notices me walk in, he nods and motions for me to follow him through the door. When I enter the room, Will is seated with his arms folded at the table. He doesn't look up at me. This doesn't look good.

"Ms. Cohen, please take a seat," Mr. Murphy says. He seats himself at the head, opposite Will.

I choose the chair closest to me.

"This is Mr. Cruz, Javier's father," says Mr. Murphy, motioning toward one of the men I didn't recognize.

Mr. Cruz is sitting across from me. He stands slightly and reaches across the table and shakes my hand.

"This is Officer Venturelli," he says of the other man.

He follows suit and leans across the table, shaking my hand.

"I'm sure you know why you're here. It is our understanding that there was an incident involving Mr. Cooper that occurred off of school grounds," he says, pausing in case I need to object. I don't.

"We would appreciate it if you could tell us your version of events."

I glance toward Will and he gives me an ever so slight nod, letting me know he wants me to tell the truth. So I do. For ten minutes I explain in honest detail everything that happened last night. Everything except for Will's poem.

When I'm finished with the details, and the questions have all been asked, I'm released to return to class. As I get up to leave, Mr. Cruz calls after me.

"Ms. Cohen?"

I turn and look at him.

"I just want to say I'm sorry. I apologize for my son's behavior."

"Thank you," I say. I turn and make my way back to the classroom.

A substitute is filling in for Will. She's an older lady whom I've seen in the halls before, so she must also be a teacher here. I quietly take my seat. I can't think about anything other than Will, and if I'm about to be the reason he loses his job.

When the bell rings, the class begins to file out, and I turn to Eddie.

"What happened?" she says.

I tell her what happened, and that I still don't know anything. I linger outside the classroom door for a while, waiting for Will to return, but he never does. During fourth period, I realize I'm not in the state of mind to learn anything, so I give myself the rest of the day off.

When I turn onto our street, Will's car is in his driveway. I pull my Jeep up to the curb and don't even bother pulling into the driveway. I throw it in park and quickly run across the street. As soon as I'm about to knock on the door, it swings open and Will is standing there with his satchel slung across his shoulder and his jacket on.

"What are you doing here?" he says with a surprised look on his face.

"I saw your car. What happened?"

He doesn't invite me in. Instead, he walks outside and locks the door behind him. "I resigned. They withdrew my contract." He continues walking toward his car.

"But you only have eight weeks left of student teaching. It wasn't your fault, Will. They can't do that!"

He shakes his head. "No, it's not like that. I wasn't fired. We just all thought it was best if I finished my student teaching at a different school, away from Javier. I've got a meeting with my faculty advisor in half an hour; that's where I'm headed." He opens his door and removes his jacket and satchel, throwing them into the passenger seat.

"But what about your job?" I ask as I hold on to the door, not wanting him to shut it. I have so many questions. "So you're saying you don't have an income now? What are you going to do?"

He smiles at me and emerges back out of the car and places his hands on my shoulders. "Layken, calm down. I'll figure it out. But right now, I've got to go." He gets back inside, shuts his door, and rolls down his window.

"If I'm not home in time, can Caulder stay with you guys after school?"

"Sure," I say.

"We're leaving pretty early to go to my grandparents' tomorrow. Can you make sure he doesn't eat any sugar? He needs to get to bed early," he says as he slowly backs out of the driveway.

"Sure," I say.

"And Layken? Calm down."

"Sure," I say again.

And he's gone. Just like that.

18.

Close the laundry door
Tiptoe across the floor
Keep your clothes on
I got all that I can take
Teach me how to use
The love that people say you made.

—THE AVETT BROTHERS, "LAUNDRY ROOM"

I SPEND THE REST OF THE AFTERNOON HELPING MY
mother clean. It keeps my mind occupied. She never once
asks why I'm not at school. I guess she's leaving the mundane things up to me now. When it's time to pick Caulder
and Kel up, Will still isn't home. I bring both of the boys
back to the house, and we begin another discussion of Halloween costumes.

"I know what I want to be now," Kel says to my
mother.

She is folding clothes in the living room. She lays a towel on the back of the couch and looks at Kel, "What are you going to be, sweetie?"

He smiles at her. "Your lung cancer," he says.

She is so used to the things that come out of Kel's mouth, she doesn't skip a beat. "Oh yeah? Do they sell those at Walmart?"

"I don't think so," he says, grabbing a drink out of the refrigerator. "Maybe you could make it. I want to be a lung."

"Hey," Caulder says. "Can I be the other lung?"

My mom laughs as she grabs a pen and paper off the bar and sits down. "Well, I guess we better figure out how to sew a pair of cancerous lungs."

Kel and Caulder flock to her and start spitting out ideas.

"Mom," I say flatly. "You're not."

She looks up from her sketch at me and smiles. "Lake, if my baby boy wants to be a cancerous lung for Halloween, then I'm going to make sure he's the best cancerous, tumor-ridden lung there is."

I roll my eyes and join them at the bar, writing down a list of the supplies we'll need.

AFTER WE RETURN from the store with the supplies and materials needed for the cancerous lung costumes, Will pulls up in his driveway.

"Will!" Caulder runs across the street and grabs his hand, pulling him toward our house. "Wait till you see this!"

Will helps my mother and me grab the supplies out of the trunk, and we all head inside.

"Guess what we're going to be? For Halloween?" Caulder is beaming as he stands in the kitchen, pointing at the supplies on the floor.

"Uh—"

"Julia's cancer!" Caulder says, excitedly.

Will raises his eyebrows and glances at my mother, who has just returned from her bedroom with a sewing machine. "You only live once, right?" She places the sewing machine on the bar.

"She's letting us make the tumors for the lungs," Kel says. "You wanna make one? I'll let you make the big one."

"Uh—"

"Kel," I say. "Will and Caulder can't help, they'll be out of town all weekend." I carry two of the sacks to the bar and start unpacking them.

"Actually," Will replies as he grabs the other sacks off the floor, "that was before I found out we were making lung cancer. I think we'll have to reschedule our trip."

Caulder runs over to Will and hugs him. "Thanks, Will. They're gonna need to measure me while they're making it anyway. I've been growing a lot."

And once again, for the third time this week, we're one big happy family.

* * *

WE HAVE MOST of the design worked out and need to take measurements for the pattern. "Where's your measuring tape?" I ask my mother.

"I don't know," she says. "I don't know if I have one, actually."

"Will has one; we can use his," I say. "Will, do you mind getting it?"

"I have measuring tape?" he asks.

"Yes, it's in your sewing kit," I say.

"I have a sewing kit?"

"It's in your laundry room." I can't believe he doesn't know this. I clean his house once, and I can tell him where everything is better than he can? "It's next to the sewing machine on the shelf behind your mother's patterns. I put them in chronological order according to pattern nu— never mind," I say as I stand up. "I'll just show you."

"You put his patterns in chronological order?" my mother asks, perplexed.

I turn back to her as we're headed to the door. "I was having a bad day."

Will and I head across the street and I use the opportunity to ask him about what happened with his internship. I didn't want to ask him in front of Caulder, because I wasn't sure if he had said anything to him.

"I got a slap on the wrist," he says as we walk inside.

"They told me since I was defending another student, they couldn't really hold it against me."

"That's good. What about your internship?" I say as I walk through the kitchen and into the laundry room, where I grab the sewing kit.

"Well, it's a little tricky. The only available ones they had are here in Ypsilanti, but they were all primary. My major is secondary, so I've been placed at a school in Detroit."

I pause what I'm doing and look at him.

"What's that mean? Are y'all moving?"

He sees the worry cross my face, and he laughs. "No, Lake, we're not moving. It's just for eight weeks. I'll be doing a lot of driving, though. I was actually going to talk to you and your mom about it later. I'm not going to be able to take the boys to school, or pick them up, either. I'll be gone a lot. I know this isn't a good time to ask for your help—"

"Stop it." I grab the tape measure and return the contents into the box. "You know we'll help."

Will follows me as I walk back to the laundry room and replace the sewing kit next to the sewing machine. My hand brushes against the patterns that are neatly stacked in chronological order as I recall all the cleaning and alphabetizing I did the previous weekend. Is it possible that I had a momentary lapse of sanity? I shake my head and reach over and flick off the light switch, when I run into

Will. He's leaning against the door frame with his head resting against the wall, watching me. It's dark now, but his face is slightly illuminated by the glow from the kitchen behind him.

A warm sensation flows through me, and I try not to get my hopes up. He's got that look in his eyes again.

"Last night," he whispers. "When I saw Javi kissing you—" His voice trails off, and he's silent for a moment. "I thought you were kissing him back."

It's hard when he's in such close proximity, but I do my best to focus and process his confession. If he thought I was allowing it to happen, then why did he pull Javi off of me? Why did he punch him? Then it hits me. Will wasn't *defending* me last night. He was *jealous*.

"Oh," is all I can say.

"I didn't know the whole story until this morning, when you told your version," he says as he continues to block my way, making me stand in the dark. He runs his hands through his hair and sighs.

"God, Lake. I can't tell you how pissed I was. I wanted to hurt him so bad. And now? Now that I know he really *was* hurting you? I want to *kill* him." He turns away from me and rests his back against the door frame.

I think back on last night and the emotions Will must have been experiencing. To be professing his love for me onstage one minute and then thinking I was making out with Javi the next? No wonder he was so pissed on the drive home.

He's still blocking my way. Not that I plan on running anywhere. My entire body becomes tense, not knowing what he's about to say or do. I slowly exhale and try to calm my nerves. My breathing has increased so rapidly in the last minute, my lungs are starting to ache again as the knot in my back reminds me of its presence.

"How did you—" I stammer. "How'd you know I was there?"

He turns and faces me, placing both hands on either side of the door frame. His height and the way he has me blocked in are intimidating, but in a very good way.

"I saw you. When I finished my piece, I saw you leaving."

My knees start to fail me, so I place my hand on the dryer behind me for support. He knows I saw him perform? Why is he telling me this? I do my best not to get my hopes up, but maybe since he's no longer my teacher, we can finally be together. Maybe that's what he's trying to tell me.

"Will, does this mean—"

He takes a step toward me, leaving no space between us. His fingers brush against my cheek, and he studies my face with his eyes. I place my hands against his chest, and he wraps his arms around me, pulling me to him. I try to take a step away from him so I can finish my question, but his body presses me against the dryer.

Just as I try to ask him again, he brings his lips to mine, rendering me speechless. I immediately stop resisting, and I let him kiss me. *Of course* I let him kiss me. My entire body becomes weak. My arms fall to my side, and I drop the measuring tape on the floor.

He grabs me by the waist and lifts me up, setting me down on top of the dryer. Our faces are at the same height now. He kisses me like he's making up for an entire month of stolen kisses. I can't tell where my hands end and his begin as we both frantically pull at each other. I wrap my legs around him and pull his mouth to my neck so I can catch my breath. All the feelings I have for him come rushing back. I try to hold back tears as I realize just how much I really do love him. Oh my god, I *love* him. I'm in love with Will Cooper.

I no longer try to control my breathing; it would be pointless.

"Will," I whisper. He continues exploring my neck with his lips. "Does this mean . . . does it mean we don't have to pretend . . . anymore?" I'm breathing so heavily I can barely form a cohesive sentence. "We can be . . . together? Since you're not . . . since you're not my teacher?"

His hands soften their hold on my back, and his lips slowly close and pull away from my neck. I try to pull him back into me, but he resists. He puts his hands on my calves and unlocks my legs from around his waist as he backs up and leans against the wall behind him, avoiding my eyes.

My hands grip the edges of the dryer and I slide off with a jerk. "Will?" I say as I take a step toward him.

The light from the kitchen casts a shadow across his

face, but I can see his jaw—it's clenched. His eyes are full of shame as he looks at me apologetically.

"Will? Tell me. Do the rules still apply?"

He doesn't have to answer me—I can tell by his reaction that they do.

"Lake," he says quietly. "I had a weak moment. I'm sorry."

I shove my hands into his chest. "A weak *moment*? That's what you call this? A weak *moment*?" I yell. "What were you gonna *do*, Will? When were you gonna stop making out with me and kick me out of your house *this* time?" I spin and turn out of the laundry room and make my way through the kitchen.

"Lake, don't. I'm sorry. I'm so sorry. It won't happen again, I swear."

I stop and turn toward him. "You're damn right it won't! I finally accepted it, Will! After an entire month of torture, I was finally able to be *around* you again. Then you go and do *this*! I can't do it anymore," I cry. "The way you consume my mind when we aren't together? I don't have time for it anymore. I've got more important things to think about now than your little *weak moments*."

I cross the living room and open the front door and pause. "Get me the measuring tape," I say calmly.

"Wh—what?" he says.

"It's on the damn floor! Get me the measuring tape!"

His footsteps fade as he walks to the laundry room. He retrieves the measuring tape and brings it back to me.

When he places it in my grasp, he squeezes my hand and looks me intently in the eyes.

"Don't make me the bad guy, Lake. *Please*."

I pull my hand away from his. "Well, you're certainly not the martyr anymore." I turn and walk out, slamming the door behind me. I cross the street and don't look back to see if he's watching me. I don't care anymore.

I pause at our entryway and take a deep breath as I wipe my eyes. I open the front door to our *home*, put a smile across my face, and help my mother make her very last Halloween costumes.

19.

WILL AND CAULDER END UP GOING OUT OF TOWN AFTER all. Mom and I spend most of Saturday and Sunday putting the finishing touches on the costumes. I let my mother know about Will's schedule and how we'll be helping them out more. As pissed as I am, I don't want Caulder and Kel to have to suffer. Sunday night, when Will gets home, I don't even notice because I don't even care.

* * *

"KEL, CALL CAULDER and tell him he can come over and put his costume on," I say as I drag Kel out of bed. "Will has to leave early anyway. Caulder can get ready over here."

It's Halloween, day of the cancerous lungs. Kel runs to the kitchen and grabs the phone.

I take a shower and finish getting ready, then wake my mother up so she can see the results. After she's dressed, Kel and Caulder instruct her to close her eyes. I walk her into the living room and position her in front of the two boys.

"Wait!" Caulder says. "What about Will? He needs to see us, too."

I usher my mother back into the hallway and I run to the front door, throw on my boots, and go outside. Will is pulling out of his driveway so I flag him down. I can see by the look on his face that he's hoping I've forgiven him. I immediately cease any false hope.

"You're still an asshole, but your brother wants you to see his costume. Come in for a second." I return to the house.

When Will walks in, I position him and my mother in front of the boys, and tell them to open their eyes.

Kel is the right lung; Caulder is the left. The stuffed material is shaped so that their arms and head fit through small openings, and the bottom is open to their waist and legs. We dyed the material so that it would reflect dead spots here and there. There are larger lumps protruding from the lungs in various places—the tumors. There is a long pause before Will and my mother react.

"It's disgusting," Will says.

"Repulsive," my mother adds.

"Hideous," I say.

The boys high-five. Or rather, the lungs high-five. After we take pictures, I load them up in the Jeep, and I drop the pair of lungs off at school.

I'M NOT EVEN halfway through second period when my phone starts vibrating. I pull it out of my pocket and look at the number. It's Will. Will *never* calls me. I assume he's trying to apologize, so I put the phone back in my jacket. It vibrates again. I turn and look at Eddie.

"Will keeps calling me—should I answer?" I say. I don't know why I'm asking her. Maybe she's got some great advice.

"I dunno," she says.

Maybe not.

On his third attempt, I press the Accept button and put the phone to my ear. "Hello?" I whisper.

"Layken, it's me. Look, you've got to get to the elementary school. There's been an incident, and I can't get through to your mom. I'm in Detroit—I can't go."

"What? With who?" I whisper.

"Both of them, I guess. They aren't hurt; they just need someone to pick them up. Go! Call me back."

I quietly excuse myself from the classroom. Eddie follows me.

"What is it?" she says as we walk into the hallway.

"I don't know. Something with Kel and Caulder," I say.

"I'm going with you," she says.

WHEN WE ARRIVE at the school, I sprint inside. I'm out of breath and on the verge of hysteria when we find the office. Kel and Caulder are both sitting in the lobby.

My feet won't move fast enough as I run to them and hug them.

"Are y'all okay? What happened?"

They both shrug.

"We don't know," Kel says. "They just told us we had to sit here until our parents came."

"Ms. Cohen?" someone says from behind me. I turn around and am face-to-face with a tall, slender redhead. She's wearing a black pencil skirt that meets her knees and a white dress shirt tucked in at the waist. Observing her, I can't help but hope she isn't as uptight as her wardrobe portrays her to be. She gestures toward her office, and Eddie and I follow her.

She takes a seat at her desk, nodding to the chairs in front of her. Eddie and I both sit.

"I'm Mrs. Brill. I'm the principal here at Chapman Elementary. Principal Brill."

The curt way she's speaking to me and her hoity-toity posture have immediately turned me off. I already don't like her.

"Are Caulder's parents joining us?" she asks.

"Caulder's parents are dead," I reply.

She gasps, then attempts to control her reaction by sitting up even straighter. "Oh, that's right. I'm sorry," she says. "Is it his brother? He lives with his brother, right?"

I nod. "He's in Detroit; he can't make it. I'm Kel's sister. What's the problem?"

She laughs. "Well, isn't it obvious?" She gestures out her office window to them.

I look at the boys. They're playing rock-paper-scissors and laughing. I know she's referring to their costumes, but she's already lost my respect with her attitude, so I continue to act oblivious.

"Is rock-paper-scissors against school policy?" I ask.

Eddie laughs.

"Ms. Cohen," Principal Brill says. "They're dressed as cancerous lungs!" She shakes her head in disbelief.

"I thought they were rotten kidney beans," Eddie says.

We both laugh.

"I don't think this is funny," Principal Brill says. "They're causing a distraction among the students! Those are very offensive and crude costumes! Not to mention disgusting. I don't know who thought it was a good idea, but you need to take them home and change their clothes."

My focus returns to Principal Brill. I lean forward and place my arms on her desk.

"Principal Brill," I say calmly. "Those costumes were made by my mother. My mother, who has stage-four small-cell lung cancer. My mother, who will never watch her little boy celebrate another Halloween again. My mother, who will more than likely experience a year of 'lasts.' Last Christmas. Last birthday. Last Easter. And if God is willing, her last Mother's Day. My mother, who when asked by her nine-year-old son if he could be her cancer for Halloween, had no choice but to make him the best cancerous-tumor-ridden-lung costume she could. So if you think it's so offensive, I suggest you drive them home yourself, and tell my mother to her face. Do you need my address?"

Principal Brill's mouth gapes open and she shakes her head. She fidgets in her seat, but doesn't respond. I stand up, and Eddie follows me out the door. I stop short and spin around and walk back into her office.

"And one more thing. The costume contest? I hope it's *fairly* judged."

Eddie laughs as I shut the door behind us.

"What's going on?" Kel asks.

"Nothing," I say. "Y'all can go back to class. She just wanted to know where we got the materials for your costume so she can be a hemorrhoid next year."

Eddie and I try to contain our laughter after the boys

make their way back to class. We head outside, and as soon as we open the doors, we explode. We laugh so hard, we cry.

When we get back in the Jeep, I have six missed calls from my mother and two from Will. I return their calls and assure them, without sparing any details, that the situation has been resolved.

Later that afternoon, when I pick the boys up from school, they sprint to the car.

"We won!" Caulder yells when he climbs into the backseat. "We both won! Fifty dollars each!"

20.

Well I've been locking myself up in my house for some
time now
Reading and writing and reading and thinking
and searching for reasons and missing the seasons
The Autumn, the Spring, the Summer, the snow
The record will stop and the record will go
Latches latched the windows down,
the dog coming in and the dog going out
Up with caffeine and down with the shot
Constantly worried about what I've got
Distracted by work but I can't make it stop
and my confidence on and my confidence off
And I sink to the bottom I rise to the top
and I think to myself that I do this a lot
World outside just goes it goes it goes it goes it goes

. . .

—THE AVETT BROTHERS, "TALK ON INDOLENCE"

THE NEXT FEW WEEKS COME AND GO. EDDIE HELPS OUT with watching the boys until Will gets home on the days I take my mother to her treatments. Will leaves every morning at six thirty and doesn't return home until after five thirty. We don't see each other. I make sure we don't see each other. We've resorted to texting and phone calls when it comes to Kel and Caulder. My mother has been pressing me for information, wanting to know why he doesn't come around anymore. I lie and tell her he's just busy with his new internship.

He's only been to the house once in the past two months. It was the only time we've really spoken since the incident in the laundry room. He came to tell me he was offered a job at a junior high that starts in January, just over two weeks from now.

I'm happy for him, but it's bittersweet. I know how much the job means for him and Caulder, but I know what it means for Will and me, too. Deep down there was a part of me silently counting down the days until his last day of the internship. It's finally here, and he's already signed another contract. It solidifies things for us, really. Solidifies that they're over.

We finally put the house in Texas up for sale. Mom has managed to save almost $180,000 from life insurance Dad actually *had*. The house isn't paid off yet, but we should get another check from the sale. Mom and I spent most of November focusing on our finances. We set aside more for our college funds, and she opened a savings account for Kel. She paid off all the outstanding credit cards and charge cards that are in her name, and instructed me to never open any in my own name. Said she would *haunt* me if I did.

TODAY IS THURSDAY. It's the final day of school for all the districts, including Will's. We have early release today, so I bring Caulder home with us. He usually spends the night on Thursdays, while Will goes to the slam.

I haven't been back to Club N9NE since the night Will read his poem. I understand what Javi meant in class now—about having to relive heartache. That's why I don't go. I've relived it enough for a lifetime.

I feed the boys and send them to their bedroom and then head to my mother's room for what has become our nightly chat.

"Shut the door; these are Kel's," she whispers.

She's wrapping Christmas gifts. I shut the door behind me and sit on the bed with her and help her wrap.

"What are your plans for Christmas break?" she asks.

She's lost all of her hair now. She chose not to go with a wig—said it felt like a ferret was taking a nap on her head. She's still beautiful, nonetheless.

I shrug. "Whatever yours are, I guess."

She frowns. "Are you going to Will's graduation with us tomorrow?"

He sent us an invite two weeks ago. I think each graduate gets a certain number of guests, and his grandparents are the only other people he invited besides us.

"I don't know; I haven't decided yet," I say.

She secures a box with a bow and sets it aside. "You should go. Whatever happened between the two of you, you should still go. He's been there for us, Lake."

I don't want to admit to her that I don't want to go because I don't know how to be around him anymore. That night in his laundry room when I thought for a brief moment that we could finally be together, I had never felt so elated. It was the most amazing feeling I've ever experienced, to finally be free to love him. But it wasn't real. That one minute of pure happiness I felt and the heartache that came moments later is something I never want to experience again. I'm tired of grieving.

My mother moves the wrapping paper from her lap and reaches out and hugs me. I didn't realize I was wearing my emotions on my sleeve.

"I'm sorry, but I think I may have given you some terrible advice," she says.

I pull away from her and laugh. "That's impossible, Mom. You don't know how to do terrible." I take a box from the floor and pull it onto my lap as I grab a sheet of cut paper and begin to wrap it.

"I did, though. Your whole life, I've been telling you to think with your head, not your heart," she says.

I meticulously fold the edges up and grab the roll of tape. "That's not good advice, Mom. That's *great* advice.

That same advice is what has gotten me through these past few months." I tear a piece of tape and secure the edge of the package.

My mother grabs the box out of my hand before I'm finished wrapping it and sets it beside her. She takes my hands and turns me toward her.

"I'm serious, Lake. You've been doing so much thinking with your head that you're ignoring your heart completely. There has to be a balance. The fact that both of you are letting other things consume you is about to ruin any chance you'll ever have at being happy."

I shake my head in confusion. "Nothing is consuming me, Mom."

She shakes my hands like I'm not getting it. "*I* am, Lake. *I'm* consuming you. You've got to stop worrying so much about *me*. Go live your life. I'm not dead yet, you know."

I stare down at our hands as her words soak in. I *have* been focusing on her a lot. But that's what she needs. It's what we both need. She doesn't have that much time left, and I want to be there for every second of it.

"Mom, you need me. You need me more than I need Will. Besides, Will has made his choice."

She darts her eyes away and lets go of my hands. "No he hasn't, Lake. He made what he *thought* was the best choice, but he's wrong. You're both wrong."

I know she wants to see me happy. I don't have the heart to tell her that it's over between us. He made his choice that night in the laundry room when he let me go. He has his priorities, and right now I'm not one of them.

She takes the box I was wrapping and returns it in front of her and starts wrapping it again. "That night I told you I had cancer, and you ran to Will's house?" Her voice softens. She clears her throat, still avoiding my eyes. "I need to tell you what he said to me . . . at the door."

I remember the conversation she's referring to, but I couldn't hear what they were saying.

"When he answered the door I told him you needed to come home. That we needed to talk about it. He looked at me with heartache in his eyes. He said, 'Let her stay, Julia. She needs me right now.'

"Lake, you broke my heart. It broke my heart that you needed *him* more than you needed *me*. As soon as the words came out of his mouth, I realized that you were grown up . . . that I wasn't your whole life anymore. Will could see that. He saw how bad his words hurt me. When I turned away to walk back to the house, he followed me into the yard and hugged me. He told me he would never take you from me. He said he was going to let you go . . . let you focus on me and on the time I had left."

She places the wrapped gift on the bed. She scoots toward me and takes my hands in hers again. "Lake, he didn't move on. He didn't choose this new job over you . . . he chose *us* over you. He wanted you to have more time with *me*."

I take a deep breath as I absorb everything my mother

just revealed. Is she right? Does he love me enough that he would be willing to let me go?

"Mom?" My voice is weak. "What if you're wrong?"

"What if I'm *not* wrong, Lake? Question *everything*. What if he *wants* to choose you? You'll never know if you don't tell him how you feel. You've completely shut him out. You haven't given him the *chance* to pick you."

She's right, I haven't. I've been completely closed off since that night in the laundry room.

"It's seven thirty, Lake. You know where he is. Go tell him how you feel."

I don't move. My legs feel like Jell-O.

"Go!" she laughs.

I jump off the bed and run to my room. My hands are shaking and my thoughts are all jumbled together while I change my pants. I put on the purple shirt that I wore on our first and only date. I go to the bathroom and inspect my reflection.

There's something missing. I run to my room and reach under my pillow and pull out the purple clip. I snap it open and remove my mother's strands of hair and place them in my jewelry box. I go back to the bathroom and brush my bangs to the side of my head and snap the clip in place.

21.

Don't say it's over
'Cause that's the worst news I
could hear I swear that I will
Do my best to be here
just the way you like it
Even though it's hard to hide
Push my feelings all aside
I will rearrange my plans and
change for you.

—THE AVETT BROTHERS,
"IF IT'S THE BEACHES"

WHEN I WALK INTO THE CLUB, I DON'T STOP TO LOOK FOR him. I know he's here. I don't give myself time to second-guess myself as I walk with false confidence toward the front of the room. The emcee is announcing scores for the previous performer when I walk onto the stage. He's apprehensive as I grab the microphone from him and turn toward the audience. The lights are so bright, I can't see anyone's faces. I can't see Will.

"I would like to perform a piece I wrote," I say into the microphone. My voice is steady, but my heart is about to jump out of my chest. I can't turn back now. I have to do this. "I know this isn't standard protocol, but it's an emergency," I say.

Laughter overcomes the audience. The rumble of the crowd is loud, causing me to freeze at the thought of what I'm about to do. I start to have second thoughts and turn around to the emcee, but he nudges me back and gives me the go-ahead.

I place the microphone in the stand and lower it to my height. I close my eyes and take a deep breath before I begin.

"Three dollars!" someone yells from the audience.

I open my eyes and realize I haven't paid my fee yet. I frantically dig my hands in my pockets and pull out a five-dollar bill and walk it over to the emcee.

I return to the microphone and close my eyes.

"My piece is called—"

Someone's tapping me on the shoulder. I open my eyes and turn around to see the emcee holding up two one-dollar bills.

"Your change," he says.

I take the money and put it back in my pocket. He's still standing there.

"Go!" I whisper through clenched teeth.

He stammers and walks off the stage.

Once again, I turn toward the microphone and begin to speak. "My piece is called 'Schooled,'" I say into the microphone. My voice is shaking, so I take a few deep breaths. I just hope I can remember it: I rewrote a few lines on the way here. I inhale one last time and begin.

I got *schooled* this year.

By *everyone*.

By my little brother . . .

by the *Avett* Brothers . . .

by my *mother*, my *best friend*, my *teacher*, my *father*,

and

by

a

boy.

A boy that I'm *seriously, deeply, madly, incredibly,*

and undeniably in *love* with.

I got *so schooled* this year.

By a *nine*-year-old.

He taught me that it's *okay* to live *life*

a little *backward*.

And how to *laugh*

At what you would *think*

is *unlaughable*.

I got *schooled* this year

By a *band*!

They taught me how to find that *feeling* of *feeling*
again.
They taught me how to *decide* what to *be*
And go *be* it.
I got *schooled* this year.
By a *cancer* patient.
She taught me *so* much. She's *still* teaching me so
much.
She taught me to *question*.
To *never* regret.
She taught me to *push* my boundaries,
Because *that's* what they're *there* for.
She told me to find a *balance* between *head* and *heart*
And then
she taught me **how** . . .
I got *schooled* this year
By a *foster kid*.
She taught me to *respect* the hand that I was *dealt*.
And to be *grateful* I was even dealt a *hand*.
She taught me that *family*
Doesn't have to be *blood*.
Sometimes your *family*
are your *friends*.
I got *schooled* this year
By my *teacher*
He taught me
That the *points* are not the *point*,

The *point* is *poetry* . . .
I got *schooled* this year
By my *father.*
He taught me that *heroes* aren't always *invincible*
And that the *magic*
is *within* me.
I got schooled this year
by
a
boy.
A boy that I'm *seriously, deeply, madly, incredibly,*
and undeniably in *love* with.
And he taught me the most important thing of *all*—
To put the *emphasis*
On *life.*

The feeling that comes over you, when you're in front of an audience? All those people craving for your words, yearning to see a glimpse into your soul . . . it's exhilarating. I thrust the microphone back into the emcee's hands and run off the stage. I look around but don't see him anywhere. I look at the booth we sat in on our first date, but it's empty. I realize, after standing there, waiting to be swept off of my feet—that he's not even here. I spin around in a circle, scanning the room a second time. A third time. He's not here.

The same glorious feeling I had on that stage . . . on

his dryer . . . in the booth in the back of the room—it's gone. I can't do it again. I want to run. I need air. I need to feel the Michigan air against my face.

I throw open the door and take a step outside when a voice, amplified through the speakers, stops me in my tracks.

"That's not a good idea," it says. I recognize that voice *and* that phrase. I slowly turn around and face the stage. Will is standing there, holding the microphone between his hands, looking directly at me.

"You shouldn't leave before you get your scores," he says, motioning to the judges' table. I follow his gaze to the judges, who are all turned around in their seats. All four of them have their eyes locked on me; the fifth seat is empty. I gasp when I realize *Will* was the fifth judge.

I sense that I'm floating again as I make my way to the center of the room. Everyone is quiet. I look around, and all eyes are on me. No one understands what's happening. I'm not sure even *I* understand what's happening.

Will looks at the emcee standing next to him. "I'd like to perform a piece. It's an *emergency*," he says.

The emcee backs away and gives Will the go-ahead. Will turns back to face me.

"Three dollars," someone yells from the crowd.

Will darts a look at the emcee. "I don't have any cash," he says.

I immediately pull the two dollars out of my pocket

and run to the stage, smacking them down in front of the emcee's feet. He inspects the money I lay before him.

"Still a dollar short," he says.

The silence in the room is interrupted as several chairs slide from under their tables. There is a faint rumble as people walk toward me. I'm surrounded, being pushed and shoved in different directions as the crowd grows thicker. It begins to disperse just as fast and the silence slowly returns as everyone makes their way back to their seats. I return my gaze to the stage, where dozens of dollar bills are haphazardly thrown at the emcee's feet. My eyes follow along as a quarter rolls off the edge of the stage and falls onto the floor. It wiggles and spins as it comes to rest at my foot.

The emcee is focused on the pile of money before him. "*Okay*," he says. "I guess that covers it. What's the name of your piece, Will?"

Will brings the microphone to his mouth and smiles at me. " 'Better Than Third,' " he says. I take a few steps back from the stage and he begins.

I met a girl.
A *beautiful* girl
And I fell for her.
I fell *hard*.
Unfortunately, sometimes *life* gets in the *way*.
Life *definitely* got in *my* way.

It got *all up* in my damn way,
Life *blocked* the *door* with a stack of wooden *two-by-*
fours nailed together and *attached* to a fifteen inch
concrete wall behind a *row* of solid steel *bars*, *bolted* to
a *titanium frame* that *no matter* how *hard* I shoved
against it—
It
wouldn't
budge.
Sometimes *life* doesn't *budge.*
It just gets *all up* in your *damn* way.
It blocked my *plans*, my *dreams*, my *desires*, my
wishes, my *wants*, my *needs.*
It blocked out that *beautiful* girl
That I *fell* so *hard* for.
Life tries to tell you what's *best* for you.
What should be most *important* to you.
What should come *first*
Or *second*
Or *third.*
I tried *so hard* to keep it all *organized*, *alphabetized*,
stacked in *chronological order*, everything in its
perfect space, its *perfect place.*
I thought that's what life *wanted* me to do.
This is what life *needed* for me to do.
Right?
Keep it *all* in *sequence*?
Sometimes life gets in your *way.*

It gets all up in your damn *way*.

But it doesn't get all up in your damn way because it
wants you to just *give up* and let it *take control*. Life
doesn't get all up in your damn way because it just
wants you to *hand* it all *over* and be *carried along*.

Life wants you to *fight* it.

Learn how to make it your *own*.

It wants you to grab an *ax* and *hack* through the *wood*.

It wants you to get a *sledgehammer* and *break*
through the *concrete*.

It wants you to grab a *torch* and *burn* through the
metal and *steel* until you can reach through and
grab it.

Life wants you to *grab* all the *organized*, the
alphabetized, the *chronological*, the *sequenced*. It
wants you to mix it all *together*,

stir it up,

blend it.

Life doesn't want you to let it *tell* you that your little
brother should be the *only* thing that comes *first*.

Life doesn't want you to let it *tell* you that your *career*
and your *education* should be the *only* thing that
comes in *second*.

And life *definitely* doesn't want *me*

To just let it *tell* me

that the *girl* I met—

The *beautiful, strong, amazing, resilient girl*

That I fell *so hard* for—

Should *only* come in *third*.

Life *knows*.

Life is trying to *tell* me

That the *girl* I *love*?

The girl I fell

So *hard* for?

There's room for her in *first*.

I'm putting *her* first.

Will sets the microphone down and jumps off the stage. I've gone so long teaching myself how to let go of him, to break the hold he has on me. It hasn't worked. It hasn't worked a damn bit.

He takes my face in his hands and wipes my tears away with his thumbs. "I love you, Lake." He smiles and presses his forehead against mine. "You deserve to come first."

Everyone and everything else in the entire room fades; the only sound I hear is the crash of the walls I've built up around me as they crumble to the ground.

"I love you, too. I love you so much."

He brings his lips to mine, and I throw my arms around him and kiss him back. *Of course* I kiss him back.

epilogue

My parents taught me to learn
When I miss
Just do your best
Just do your best.

—THE AVETT BROTHERS, "WHEN I DRINK"

I WALK AROUND THE LIVING ROOM, TAKING LONG LEAPS over mounds of toys as I gather wrapping paper and stuff it into the sack. "Did y'all like your presents?" I ask.

"Yes!" Kel and Caulder yell in unison. I gather the last of the wrapping paper and tie the ends of the trash bag together and head outside to throw it away.

As I'm walking to the curb, Will emerges from his house and jogs toward me.

"Let me get that, babe," he says as he takes the bag out of my hands and carries it to the curb. He walks back to where I'm standing and puts his arms around me, nuzzling his face in my neck.

"Merry Christmas," he says.

"Merry Christmas," I reply.

It's our second Christmas together. The first without my mother. She passed away in September this year, almost a year to the day after we moved to Michigan. It was hard. It was *extremely* hard.

When someone close to you dies, the memories of them are painful. It isn't until the fifth stage of grief that the memories of them stop hurting as much—when the recollections become positive. When you stop thinking about the person's death and remember all of the wonderful things about their *life*.

Having Will by my side has made it bearable. After graduation, he applied to get his master's in education. He didn't take the job at the junior high after all. Instead, he lived off of student loans for another semester, until I graduated.

Will takes my hand as we walk back inside the house. The number of toys that are piled in my living room floor is astonishing.

"I'll be back—last load," Will says as he takes a stack of Caulder's things and walks back out the front door. This is his third trip across the street, transferring all of Caulder's new toys to their house.

"Kel, these can't all be yours," I say, scanning the living room. "Y'all start gathering them up and take them to the spare bedroom. I need to vacuum." There are small remnants of gift chaos all over the living-room floor. After I finish vacuuming, I wrap up the cord and return the vacuum to the hallway closet. Will walks in the front door with two gift sacks in hand.

"Uh-oh. How'd we forget those?" I ask, just before I call the boys into the living room.

"These aren't for the boys. These are for you and Kel." He walks to the couch and motions for Kel and me to take a seat.

"Will, you didn't have to do this. You already got me concert tickets," I say as I settle into the sofa.

He hands the sacks to us and kisses me on the forehead. "I didn't. They aren't *from* me." He takes Caulder's hand, and they quietly slip out the front door. I look at Kel, and he just shrugs.

We simultaneously rip the tissue out of the sacks and pull out envelopes. "Lake" is sprawled across the front in my mother's handwriting. My hands are weak as I slide the paper out of the envelope. I run my arm across my eyes and wipe away my tears as I unfold my letter.

> *To my babies,*
>
> *Merry Christmas. I'm sorry if these letters have caught you both by surprise. There is just so much more I have to say. I know you thought I was done giving advice, but I couldn't leave without reiterating a few things in writing. You may not relate to these things now, but someday you will. I wasn't able to be around forever, but I hope that my words* can *be.*
>
> *—Don't stop making basagna. Basagna is good. Wait until a day when there is no bad news, and bake a damn basagna.*

—Find a balance between head and heart. Hopefully you've found that, Lake, and you can help Kel sort it out when he gets to that point.

—Push your boundaries, that's what they're there for.

—I'm stealing this snippet from your favorite band, Lake. "Always remember there is nothing worth sharing like the love that let us share our name."

—Don't take life too seriously. Punch it in the face when it needs a good hit. Laugh at it.

—And laugh a lot. Never go a day without laughing at least once.

—Never judge others. You both know good and well how unexpected events can change who a person is. Always keep that in mind. You never know what someone else is experiencing within their own life.

—Question everything. Your love, your religion, your passions. If you don't have questions, you'll never find answers.

—Be accepting. Of everything. People's differences, their similarities, their choices, their personalities. Sometimes it takes a variety to make a good collection. The same goes for people.

—Choose your battles, but don't choose very many.

—Keep an open mind; it's the only way new things can get in.

—And last but not least, not the tiniest *bit least.* Never *regret.*

Thank you both for giving me the best *years of my life.*

Especially *the last one.*

Love,

Mom

acknowledgments

To Abigail Ehn with *Poetry Slam, Inc.* for answering all of my questions with lightning speed. To my sisters, Lin and Murphy, for equally sharing all of the awesome components of our father's DNA. To my mother, Vannoy, for loving "Mystery Bob" and encouraging my passion. To my amazing husband and children for not complaining about four weeks' worth of laundry and dishes that piled up while I locked myself in my bedroom. To Jessica Benson Sparks for her kind heart and willingness to help me succeed. And last but certainly not least, to my "life coach" Stephanie Cohen for being so butterflying bemazing!

about the author

Colleen Hoover is the *New York Times* bestselling author of two novels: *Slammed* and *Point of Retreat*. She lives in Texas with her husband and their three boys.

To read more about this author, visit her website at www.colleenhoover.com.

In the second book in the Slammed series by *New York Times* bestselling author Colleen Hoover, Layken and Will's relationship has endured through hardships, heartache, and a cruel twist of fate, further solidifying the fact that they belong together. But the two lovers could not have expected that the things that brought them together may ultimately be the things that tear them apart. Their connection is on the brink of being destroyed forever and it will take an extraordinary amount of willpower to keep their love afloat.

Layken is left questioning the very foundation on which her relationship with Will was built. Will is left questioning how he can prove his love for a girl who can't seem to stop "carving pumpkins." Upon finding the answers that may bring peace back into their relationship, the couple comes across an even greater challenge—one that could change not only their lives but the lives of everyone who depend on them.

Read on for a look at Colleen Hoover's
Point of Retreat.

1.

I registered for classes today. Didn't get the days I wanted, but I only have two semesters left, so it's getting harder to be picky about my schedule. I'm thinking about applying to local schools for another teaching job after next semester. Hopefully, by this time next year, I'll be teaching again. For right now, though, I'm living off student loans. Luckily, my grandparents have been supportive while I work on my master's degree. I wouldn't be able to do it without them, that's for sure.

We're having dinner with Gavin and Eddie tonight. I think I'll make cheeseburgers. Cheeseburgers sound good. That's all I really have to say right now . . .

"IS LAYKEN OVER HERE OR OVER THERE?" EDDIE ASKS, peering in the front door.

"Over there," I say from the kitchen.

Is there a sign on my house instructing people *not* to

knock? Lake never knocks anymore, but her comfort here apparently extends to Eddie as well. Eddie heads across the street to Lake's house, and Gavin walks inside, tapping his knuckles against the front door. It's not an official knock, but at least he's making an attempt.

"What are we eating?" he asks. He slips his shoes off at the door and makes his way into the kitchen.

"Burgers." I hand him a spatula and point to the stove, instructing him to flip the burgers while I pull the fries out of the oven.

"Will, do you ever notice how we somehow always get stuck cooking?"

"It's probably not a bad thing," I say as I loosen the fries from the pan. "Remember Eddie's Alfredo?"

He grimaces when he remembers the Alfredo. "Good point," he says.

I call Kel and Caulder into the kitchen to have them set the table. For the past year, since Lake and I have been together, Gavin and Eddie have been eating with us at least twice a week. I finally had to invest in a dining room table because the bar was getting a little too crowded.

"Hey, Gavin," Kel says. He walks into the kitchen and grabs a stack of cups out of the cabinet.

"Hey," Gavin responds. "You decide where we're having your party next week?"

Kel shrugs. "I don't know. Maybe bowling. Or we could just do something here."

Caulder walks into the kitchen and starts setting

places at the table. I glance behind me and notice them setting an extra place. "We expecting company?" I ask.

"Kel invited Kiersten," Caulder says teasingly.

Kiersten moved into a house on our street about a month ago, and Kel seems to have developed a slight crush on her. He won't admit it. He's just now about to turn eleven, so Lake and I expected this to happen. Kiersten's a few months older than he is, and a lot taller. Girls hit puberty faster than boys, so maybe he'll eventually catch up.

"Next time you guys invite someone else, let me know. Now I need to make another burger." I walk to the refrigerator and take out one of the extra patties.

"She doesn't eat meat," Kel says. "She's a vegetarian."

Figures. I put the meat back in the fridge. "I don't have any fake meat. What's she gonna do? Eat bread?"

"Bread's fine," Kiersten says as she walks through the front door—without knocking. "I like bread. French fries, too. I just don't eat things that are a result of unjustified animal homicide." Kiersten walks to the table and grabs the roll of paper towels and starts tearing them off, laying one beside each plate. Her self-assurance reminds me a little of Eddie's.

"Who's she?" Gavin asks, watching Kiersten make herself at home. She's never eaten with us before, but you wouldn't know that by how she's taking command.

"She's the eleven-year-old neighbor I was telling you about. The one I think is an imposter based on the things that come out of her mouth. I'm beginning to suspect she's really a tiny adult posing as a little redheaded child."

"Oh, the one Kel's crushing on?" Gavin smiles, and I can see his wheels turning. He's already thinking of ways to embarrass Kel at dinner. Tonight should be interesting.

Gavin and I have become pretty close this past year. It's good, I guess, considering how close Eddie and Lake are. Kel and Caulder really like them, too. It's nice. I like the setup we all have. I hope it stays this way.

Eddie and Lake finally walk in as we're all sitting down at the table. Lake has her wet hair pulled up in a knot on top of her head. She's wearing house shoes, sweatpants, and a T-shirt. I love that about her, the fact that she's so comfortable here. She takes the seat next to mine and leans in and kisses me on the cheek.

"Thanks, babe. Sorry it took me so long. I was trying to register online for Statistics, but the class is full. Guess I'll have to go sweet-talk someone at the admin office to-morrow."

"Why are you taking Statistics?" Gavin asks. He grabs the ketchup and squirts it on his plate.

"I took Algebra Two in the winter mini-mester. I'm trying to knock out all my math in the first year, since I hate it so much." Lake grabs the ketchup out of Gavin's hands and squirts some on my plate, then on her own.

"What's your hurry? You've already got more credits than Eddie and I do, put together," he says. Eddie nods in agreement as she takes a bite of her burger.

Lake nudges her head toward Kel and Caulder. "I've already got more *kids* than you and Eddie put together. *That's* my hurry."

"What's your major?" Kiersten asks Lake.

Eddie glances toward Kiersten, finally noticing the extra person seated at the table. "Who are you?"

Kiersten looks at Eddie and smiles. "I'm Kiersten. I live diagonal to Will and Caulder, parallel to Layken and Kel. We moved here from Detroit right before Christmas. Mom says we needed to get out of the city before the city got out of us . . . whatever that means. I'm eleven. I've been eleven since eleven-eleven-eleven. It was a pretty big day, you know. Not many people can say they turned eleven on eleven-eleven-eleven. I'm a little bummed that I was born at three o'clock in the afternoon. If I would have been born at eleven-eleven, I'm pretty sure I could have got on the news or something. I could have recorded the segment and used it someday for my portfolio. I'm gonna be an actress when I grow up."

Eddie, along with the rest of us, stares at Kiersten without responding. Kiersten is oblivious, turning to Lake to repeat her question. "What's your major, Layken?"

Lake lays her burger down on her plate and clears her throat. I know how much she hates this question. She tries to answer confidently. "I haven't decided yet."

Kiersten looks at her with pity. "I see. The prover-bial undecided. My oldest brother has been a sophomore in college for three years. He's got enough credits to have five majors by now. I think he stays undecided because he'd rather sleep until noon every day, sit in class for three hours, and go out every night, than actually graduate and get a real job. Mom says that's not true—she says it's because he's trying to 'discover his full potential' by examining all of his interests. If you ask me, I think it's bullshit."

I cough when the sip I just swallowed tries to make its way back up with my laugh.

"You just said 'bullshit'!" Kel says.

"Kel, don't say 'bullshit'!" Lake says.

"But she said 'bullshit' first," Caulder says, defending Kel.

"Caulder, don't say 'bullshit'!" I yell.

"Sorry," Kiersten says to Lake and me. "Mom says the FCC is responsible for inventing cuss words just for media shock value. She says if everyone would just use them enough, they wouldn't be considered cuss words anymore, and no one would ever be offended by them."

This kid is hard to keep up with!

"Your mother *encourages* you to cuss?" Gavin says.

Kiersten nods. "I don't see it that way. It's more like she's encouraging us to undermine a system flawed through overuse of words that are made out to be harmful, when in fact they're just letters, mixed together like every other word. That's all they are, mixed-up letters. Like, take the word 'butterfly,' for example. What if someone decided one day that 'butterfly' is a cuss word? People would eventually start using the word 'butterfly' as an insult and to emphasize things in a negative way. The actual *word* doesn't mean anything. It's the negative association people give these words that make them cuss words. So, if we all just decided to keep saying 'butterfly' all the time, people would stop caring. The shock value would subside, and it would become just another word again. Same with every other so-called bad word. If we would all start saying them all the time, they wouldn't be bad anymore. That's what my mom says, anyway." She smiles and takes a french fry and dips it in ketchup.

I often wonder, when Kiersten's visiting, how she turned out the way she did. I have yet to meet her mother, but from what I've gathered, she's definitely not ordinary. Kiersten is obviously smarter than most kids her age, even if it is in a strange way. The things that come out of her mouth make Kel and Caulder seem somewhat normal.

"Kiersten?" Eddie says. "Will you be my new best friend?"

Lake grabs a french fry off her plate and throws it at Eddie, hitting her in the face with it. "That's bullshit," Lake says.

"Oh, go *butterfly* yourself," Eddie says. She returns a fry in Lake's direction.

I intercept the french fry, hoping it won't result in another food fight, like last week. I'm still finding broccoli everywhere. "Stop," I say, dropping the french fry on the table. "If you two have another food fight in my house, I'm kicking *both* of your butterflies!"

Lake can see I'm serious. She squeezes my leg under the table and changes the subject. "Suck-and-sweet time," she says.

"Suck-and-sweet time?" Kiersten asks, confused.

Kel fills her in. "It's where you have to say your suck and your sweet of the day. The good and the bad. The high and the low. We do it every night at supper."

Kiersten nods as though she understands.

"I'll go first," Eddie says. "My suck today was registration. I got stuck in Monday, Wednesday, Friday classes. Tuesday and Thursdays were full."

Everyone wants the Tuesday/Thursday schedules. The classes are longer, but it's a fair trade, having to go only twice a week rather than three times.

"My *sweet* is meeting Kiersten, my new best friend," Eddie says, glaring at Lake.

Lake grabs another french fry and throws it at Eddie. Eddie ducks, and the fry goes over her head. I take Lake's plate and scoot it to the other side of me, out of her reach.

Lake shrugs and smiles at me. "Sorry." She grabs a fry off my plate and puts it in her mouth.

"Your turn, Mr. Cooper," Eddie says. She still calls me that, usually when she's trying to point out that I'm being a "bore."

"My suck was definitely registration, too. I got Monday, Wednesday, Friday."

Lake turns to me, upset. "What? I thought we were both doing Tuesday/Thursday classes."

"I tried, babe. They don't offer my level of courses on those days. I texted you."

She pouts. "Man, that really is a suck," she says. "And I didn't get your text. I can't find my phone again."

She's always losing her phone.

"What's your sweet?" Eddie asks me.

That's easy. "My sweet is right now," I say as I kiss Lake on the forehead.

Kel and Caulder both groan. "Will, that's your sweet *every* night," Caulder says, annoyed.

"My turn," Lake says. "Registration was actually my sweet. I haven't figured out Statistics yet, but my other four classes were exactly what I wanted." She looks at Eddie and continues. "My suck was losing my best friend to an eleven-year-old."

Eddie laughs.

"I wanna go," Kiersten says. No one objects. "My suck was having bread for dinner," she says, eyeing her plate.

She's ballsy. I toss another slice of bread on her plate. "Maybe next time you show up uninvited to a carnivore's house, you should bring your own fake meat."

She ignores my comment. "My sweet was three o'clock."

"What happened at three o'clock?" Gavin asks.

Kiersten shrugs. "School let out. I butterflying *hate* school."

All three kids glance at one another, as if there's

an unspoken agreement. I make a mental note to talk to Caulder about it later. Lake nudges me with her elbow and shoots me a questioning glance, letting me know she's thinking the same thing.

"Your turn, whatever your name is," Kiersten says to Gavin.

"It's Gavin. And my suck would have to be the fact that an eleven-year-old has a larger vocabulary than me," he says, smiling at Kiersten. "My sweet today is sort of a surprise." He looks at Eddie and waits for her response.

"What?" Eddie says.

"Yeah, what?" Lake adds.

I'm curious, too. Gavin just leans back in his seat with a smile, waiting for us to guess.

Eddie gives him a shove. "Tell us!" she says.

He leans forward in his chair and slaps his hands on the table. "I got a job! At Getty's, delivering pizza!" He looks happy, for some reason.

"*That's* your sweet? You're a pizza delivery guy?" Eddie asks. "That's more like a suck."

"You know I've been looking for a job. And it's Getty's. We love Getty's!"

Eddie rolls her eyes. "Well, congratulations," she says unconvincingly.

"Do we get free pizza?" Kel asks.

"No, but we get a discount," Gavin replies.

"That's my sweet, then," Kel says. "Cheap pizza!"

Gavin looks pleased that someone is excited for him. "My suck today was Principal Brill," Kel says.

"Oh Lord, what'd she do?" Lake asks him. "Or better yet, what did *you* do?"

"It wasn't just me," Kel says.

Caulder puts his elbow on the table and tries to hide his face from my line of sight.

"What did you do, Caulder?" I ask him. He brings his hand down and looks up at Gavin. Gavin puts his elbow on the table and shields his face from my line of sight as well. He continues to eat as he ignores my glare. "Gavin? What prank did you tell them about this time?"

Gavin grabs two fries and throws them at Kel and Caulder. "No more! I'm not telling you any more stories. You two get me in trouble every time!" Kel and Caulder laugh and throw the fries back at him.

"I'll tell on them, I don't mind," Kiersten says. "They got in trouble at lunch. Mrs. Brill was on the other side of the cafeteria, and they were thinking of a way to get her to run. Everyone says she waddles like a duck when she runs, and we wanted to see it. So Kel pretended he was choking, and Caulder made a huge spectacle and got behind him and started beating on his back, pretending to give him the Heimlich maneuver. It freaked Mrs. Brill out! When she got to our table, Kel said he was all better. He told Mrs. Brill that Caulder saved his life. It would have been fine, but she had already told someone to call 911. Within minutes, two ambulances and a fire truck showed up at the school. One of the boys at the next table told Mrs. Brill they were faking the whole thing, so Kel got called to the office."

Lake leans forward and glares at Kel. "Please tell me this is a joke."

Kel looks up with an innocent expression. "It was a joke. I really didn't think anyone would call 911. Now I have to spend all next week in detention."

"Why didn't Mrs. Brill call me?" Lake asks him.

"I'm pretty sure she did," he says. "You can't find your phone, remember?"

"Ugh! If she calls me in for another conference, you're grounded!"

I look at Caulder, who's attempting to avoid my gaze. "Caulder, what about you? Why didn't Mrs. Brill try to call me?"

He turns toward me and gives me a mischievous grin. "Kel lied for me. He told her that I really thought he was choking and I was trying to save his life," he says. "Which brings me to my sweet for the day. I was rewarded for my heroic behavior. Mrs. Brill gave me two free study hall passes."

Only Caulder could find a way to avoid detention and get rewarded instead. "You two need to cut that crap out," I say to them. "And Gavin, no more prank stories."

"Yes, Mr. Cooper," Gavin says sarcastically. "But I have to know," he says, looking at the kids, "does she really waddle?"

"Yeah." Kiersten laughs. "She's a waddler, all right." She looks at Caulder. "What was your suck, Caulder?"

Caulder gets serious. "My best friend almost choked to death today. He could have *died*."

We all laugh. As much as Lake and I try to do the responsible thing, sometimes it's hard to draw the line between being the rule enforcer and being the sibling. We choose which battles to pick with the boys, and Lake says it's important that we don't choose very many. I look at her and see she's laughing, so I assume this isn't one she wants to fight.

"Can I finish my food now?" Lake says, pointing to her plate, still on the other side of me, out of her reach. I scoot the plate back in front of her. "Thank you, Mr. Cooper," she says.

I knee her under the table. She knows I hate it when she calls me that. I don't know why it bothers me so much. Probably because when I actually was her teacher, it was absolute torture. Our connection progressed so quickly that first night I took her out. I'd never met anyone I had so much fun just being myself with. I spent the entire weekend thinking about her. The moment I walked around the corner and saw her standing in the hallway in front of my classroom, I felt like my heart had been ripped right out of my chest. I knew immediately what she was doing there, even though it took her a little longer to figure it out. When she realized I was a teacher, the look in her eyes absolutely devastated me. She was hurt. Heartbroken. Just like me. One thing I know for sure, I never want to see that look in her eyes again.

Kiersten stands up and takes her plate to the sink. "I have to go. Thanks for the bread, Will," she says sarcastically. "It was delicious."

"I'm leaving, too. I'll walk you home," Kel says. He jumps out of his seat and follows her to the door. I look at Lake, and she rolls her eyes. It bothers her that Kel has developed his first crush. Lake doesn't like to think that we're about to have to deal with teenage hormones.

Caulder gets up from the table. "I'm gonna watch TV in my room," he says. "See you later, Kel. Bye, Kiersten." They both tell him goodbye as they leave.

"I really like that girl," Eddie says after Kiersten leaves. "I hope Kel asks her to be his girlfriend. I hope they grow up and get married and have lots of weird babies. I hope she's in our family forever."

"Shut up, Eddie," Lake says. "He's only ten. He's too young for a girlfriend."

"Not really, he'll be eleven in eight days," Gavin says. "Eleven is the prime age for first girlfriends."

Lake takes an entire handful of fries and throws them toward Gavin's face.

I just sigh. She's impossible to control. "You're cleaning up tonight," I say to her. "You, too," I say to Eddie. "Gavin, let's go watch some football, like real men, while the women do their job."

Gavin scoots his glass toward Eddie. "Refill this glass, woman. I'm watching some football."

While Eddie and Lake clean the kitchen, I take the opportunity to ask Gavin for a favor. Lake and I haven't had any alone time in weeks due to always having the boys. I really need alone time with her.

"Do you think you and Eddie could take Kel and Caulder to a movie tomorrow night?"

He doesn't answer right away, which makes me feel guilty for even asking. Maybe they had plans already.

"It depends," he finally responds. "Do we have to take Kiersten, too?"

I laugh. "That's up to your girl. She's her new best friend."

Gavin rolls his eyes at the thought. "It's fine; we had plans to watch a movie anyway. What time? How long do you want us to keep them?"

"Doesn't matter. We aren't going anywhere. I just need a couple of hours alone with Lake. There's something I need to give her."

"Oh . . . I see," he says. "Just text me when you're through 'giving it to her,' and we'll bring the boys home."

I shake my head at his assumption and laugh. I like Gavin. What I hate, however, is the fact that everything that happens between me and Lake, and Gavin and Eddie . . . we all seem to *know* about. That's the drawback of dating best friends: there are no secrets.

"Let's go," Eddie says as she pulls Gavin up off the couch. "Thanks for supper, Will. Joel wants you guys to come over next weekend. He said he'd make tamales."

I don't turn down tamales. "We're there," I say.

After Eddie and Gavin leave, Lake comes to the living room and sits on the couch, curling her legs under her as she snuggles against me. I put my arm around her and pull her closer.

"I'm bummed," she says. "I was hoping we'd at least get the same days this semester. We never get any alone time with all these butterflying kids running around."

You would think, with our living across the street from each other, that we would have all the time in the world together. That's not the case. Last semester she went to school Monday, Wednesday, and Friday, and I went all five days. Weekends we spent a lot of time doing homework but mostly stayed busy with Kel's and Caulder's sports. When Julia passed away in September, that put even more on Lake's plate. It's been an adjustment, to say the least. The only place we seem to be lacking is getting quality alone time. It's kind of awkward, if the boys are at one house, to go to the other house to be alone. They almost always seem to follow us whenever we do.

"We'll get through it," I say. "We always do."

She pulls my face toward hers and kisses me. I've been kissing her every day for over a year, and it somehow gets better every time.

"I better go," she says at last. "I have to get up early

and go to the college to finish registration. I also need to make sure Kel's not outside making out with Kiersten."

We laugh about it now, but in a matter of years it'll be our reality. We won't even be twenty-five, and we'll be raising teenagers. It's a scary thought.

"Hold on. Before you leave . . . what are your plans tomorrow night?"

She rolls her eyes. "What kind of question is that? You're my plan. You're always my only plan."

"Good. Eddie and Gavin are taking the boys. Meet me at seven?"

She perks up and smiles. "Are you asking me out on a real, live date?"

I nod.

"Well, you suck at it, you know. You always have. Sometimes girls like to be *asked* and not *told*."

She's trying to play hard to get, which is pointless, since I've already got her. I play her game anyway. I kneel on the floor in front of her and look into her eyes. "Lake, will you do me the honor of accompanying me on a date tomorrow night?"

She leans back into the couch and looks away. "I don't know, I'm sort of busy," she says. "I'll check my schedule and let you know." She tries to look put out, but a smile breaks out on her face. She leans forward and hugs me; I lose my balance, and we end up on the floor. I roll her onto her back, and she stares up at me and laughs. "Fine. Pick me up at seven."

I brush her hair out of her eyes and run my finger along the edge of her cheek. "I love you, Lake."

"Say it again," she says.

I kiss her forehead and repeat, "I love you, Lake."

"One more time."

"I." I kiss her lips. "And love." I kiss them again. "And you."

"I love you, too."

I ease my body on top of hers and interlock my fingers with hers. I bring our hands above her head and press them into the floor, then lean in as if I'm going to kiss her, but I don't. I like to tease her when we're in this position. I barely touch my lips to hers until she closes her eyes, then I slowly pull away. She opens her eyes, and I smile at her, then lean in again. As soon as her eyes are closed, I pull away again.

"Dammit, Will! Butterflying kiss me already!"

She grabs my face and pulls my mouth to hers. We continue kissing until we get to the "point of retreat," as Lake likes to call it. She climbs out from under me and sits up on her knees as I roll onto my back and remain on the floor. We don't like to get carried away when we aren't alone in the house. It's so easy to do. When we catch ourselves taking things too far, one of us always calls retreat.

Before Julia passed away, we made the mistake of taking things too far, too soon—a crucial mistake on my part. It was just two weeks after we started officially dating, and Caulder was spending the night at Kel's house. Lake and I came back to my place after a movie. We started making out on the couch, and one thing led to another, neither of us willing to stop it. We weren't having sex, but we would have eventually if Julia hadn't walked in when she did. She completely flipped out. We were mortified. She grounded Lake and wouldn't let me see her for two weeks. I apologized probably a million times in those two weeks.

Julia sat us down together and made us swear we would wait at least a year. She made Lake get on the pill and made me look her in the eyes and give her my word. She wasn't upset about the fact that her eighteen-year-old daughter almost had sex. Julia was fairly reasonable and knew it would happen at some point. What hurt her was that I was so willing to take that from Lake after only two weeks of dating. It made me feel incredibly guilty, so I agreed to the promise. She also wanted us to set a good example for Kel and Caulder; she asked us not to spend the night at each other's houses during that year, either. After Julia passed away, we've stuck to our word. More out of respect for Julia than anything. Lord knows it's difficult sometimes. A lot of times.

We haven't discussed it, but last week was exactly a year since we made that promise to Julia. I don't want to rush Lake into anything; I want it to be completely up to her, so I haven't brought it up. Neither has she. Then again, we haven't really been alone.

"Point of retreat," she says, and stands up. "I'll see you tomorrow night. Seven o'clock. Don't be late."

"Go find your phone and text me good night," I tell her.

She opens the door and faces me as she backs out of the house, slowly pulling the door shut. "One more time?" she says.

"I love you, Lake."

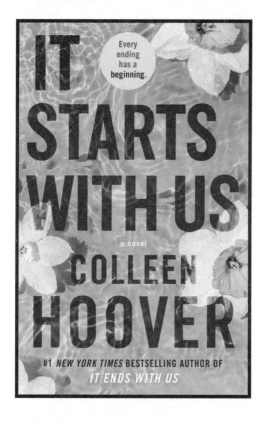